G000320497

Sarah Waters was born in Wales in 1966. She has a Ph.D. in English Literature and has been an associate lecturer with the Open University. She won a Betty Trask Award, the Somerset Maugham Award, was shortlisted twice for the *Mail on Sunday*/John Llewellyn Rhys Award and was the *Sunday Times* Young Writer of the Year in 2000. *Fingersmith*, her third novel, was shortlisted for both the Orange Prize and the Man Booker Prize, and won the CWA Ellis Peters Dagger Award for Historical Crime Fiction and *The South Bank Show* Award for Literature. She won Author of the Year 2002 at the British Book Awards and was chosen as one of *Granta*'s Best of Young British Novelists in 2003.

Her two previous novels, *Tipping the Velvet* and *Affinity*, are also published by Virago. *Tipping the Velvet* was adapted for BBC TV by Andrew Davies. Sarah Waters lives in London.

'Such a brilliant writer . . . her readers would believe anything she told them' A.N. Wilson

'One of the best storytellers alive today' Matt Thorne, *Independent on Sunday*

'Intensely atmospheric, impeccably paced and cunningly structured, this is that rarity in contemporary fiction: a deeply serious novel that is also a thumping great read' Douglas Kennedy, *Mail on Sunday*

'There are always novels that you envy people for not yet having read, for the pleasure they still have to come. Well, this is one. Long, dark, twisted and satisfying, it's a fabulous piece of writing . . . an unforgettable experience' Julie Myerson, *Guardian*

'Immaculately stylish and pleasurable . . . a glittering feat of imagination, complex as a spider's web'   Will Cohu, *Daily Telegraph*

'I actually wanted Fingersmith to win the Booker Prize . . . the story-telling is so gripping'   David Baddiel, *Observer*

'I love *Fingersmith*'   Rowan Pelling, *Daily Telegraph*

'A clever and funny lesbian take on Victorian times'   Jackie Kay, *Sunday Herald*

'Brilliantly crafted, twisting, turning . . .'   Louise Welch, *Herald*

'Sheer inventiveness and energy'   Maggie O'Farrell, *Observer*

'A terrific story'   *Saga Magazine*

'Sparkling performance'   *Sunday Times*

'A wonderful melodrama'   Alexandra Shulman, *Observer*

'Delicious complexities'   Mary Flanagan, *Independent*

'For a lurid pea-souper London gothic, Sarah Waters' daringly plotted *Fingersmith* will give you all the decadent chicanery and literary excess you might expect in a good Wilkie Collins novel   Helen Brown, *Daily Telegraph*

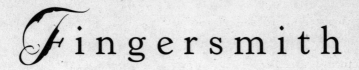

Fingersmith

Sarah Waters

Virago

A *Virago* Book

First published by Virago Press 2002
This edition published by Virago Press 2003
Reprinted 2003 (three times)

Copyright © Sarah Waters 2002

The moral right of the author has been asserted.

A CIP catalogue record for this book
is available from the British Library

ISBN 1 86049 883 3

Typeset in Horley Old Style by M Rules
Printed in Great Britain by
Clays Ltd, St Ives plc

Virago Press
An imprint of
Time Warner Books UK
Brettenham House
Lancaster Place
London WC2E 7EN

www.virago.co.uk

To Sally O-J

Also by Sarah Waters

Tipping the Velvet
Affinity

Acknowledgements

Thanks to Lennie Goodings, Julie Grau, Judith Murray, Markus Hoffmann, Bridget Ibbs, Caroline Halliday, Laura Gowing, Kate Taylor, Joanne Kalogeras, Judith Bennett, Cynthia Herrup, Hirāni Himona and Veronica Rago.

Part One

Chapter One

My name, in those days, was Susan Trinder. People called me Sue. I know the year I was born in, but for many years I did not know the date, and took my birthday at Christmas. I believe I am an orphan. My mother I know is dead. But I never saw her, she was nothing to me. I was Mrs Sucksby's child, if I was anyone's; and for father I had Mr Ibbs, who kept the locksmith's shop, at Lant Street, in the Borough, near to the Thames.

This is the first time I remember thinking about the world and my place in it.

There was a girl named Flora, who paid Mrs Sucksby a penny to take me begging at a play. People used to like to take me begging then, for the sake of my bright hair; and Flora being also very fair, she would pass me off as her sister. The theatre she took me to, on the night I am thinking of now, was the Surrey, St George's Circus. The play was *Oliver Twist*. I remember it as very terrible. I remember the

tilt of the gallery, and the drop to the pit. I remember a drunken
woman catching at the ribbons of my dress. I remember the flares,
that made the stage very lurid; and the roaring of the actors, the
shrieking of the crowd. They had one of the characters in a red wig
and whiskers: I was certain he was a monkey in a coat, he capered so.
Worse still was the snarling, pink-eyed dog; worst of all was that
dog's master—Bill Sykes, the fancy-man. When he struck the poor
girl Nancy with his club, the people all down our row got up. There
was a boot thrown at the stage. A woman beside me cried out,

'Oh, you beast! You villain! And her worth forty of a bully like
you!'

I don't know if it was the people getting up—which made the
gallery seem to heave about; or the shrieking woman; or the sight of
Nancy, lying perfectly pale and still at Bill Sykes's feet; but I became
gripped by an awful terror. I thought we should all be killed. I
began to scream, and Flora could not quiet me. And when the
woman who had called out put her arms to me and smiled, I
screamed out louder. Then Flora began to weep—she was only
twelve or thirteen, I suppose. She took me home, and Mrs Sucksby
slapped her.

'What was you thinking of, taking her to such a thing?' she said.
'You was to sit with her upon the steps. I don't hire my infants out
to have them brought back like this, turned blue with screaming.
What was you playing at?'

She took me upon her lap, and I wept again. 'There now, my
lamb,' she said. Flora stood before her, saying nothing, pulling a
strand of hair across her scarlet cheek. Mrs Sucksby was a devil with
her dander up. She looked at Flora and tapped her slippered foot
upon the rug, all the time rocking in her chair—that was a great
creaking wooden chair, that no-one sat in save her—and beating her
thick, hard hand upon my shaking back. Then,

'I know your little rig,' she said quietly. She knew everybody's rig.
'What you get? A couple of wipers, was it? A couple of wipers, and
a lady's purse?'

Flora pulled the strand of hair to her mouth, and bit it. 'A purse,'
she said, after a second. 'And a bottle of scent.'

'Show,' said Mrs Sucksby, holding out her hand. Flora's face grew darker. But she put her fingers to a tear at the waist of her skirt, and reached inside it; and you might imagine my surprise when the tear turned out to be not a tear at all, but the neck of a little silk pocket that was sewn inside her gown. She brought out a black cloth bag, and a bottle with a stopper on a silver chain. The bag had three-pence in it, and half a nutmeg. Perhaps she got it from the drunken woman who plucked at my dress. The bottle, with its stopper off, smelt of roses. Mrs Sucksby sniffed.

'Pretty poor poke,' she said, 'ain't it?'

Flora tossed her head. 'I should have had more,' she said, with a look at me, 'if she hadn't started up with the sterics.'

Mrs Sucksby leaned and hit her again.

'If I had known what you was about,' she said, 'you shouldn't have had none of it at all. Let me tell you this now: you want an infant for prigging with, you take one of my other babies. You don't take Sue. Do you hear me?'

Flora sulked, but said she did. Mrs Sucksby said, 'Good. Now hook it. And leave that poke behind you, else I shall tell your mother you've been going with gentlemen.'

Then she took me to her bed—first, rubbing at the sheets with her hands, to warm them; then stooping to breathe upon my fingers, to warm me. I was the only one, of all her infants, she would do that for. She said, 'You ain't afraid now, Sue?'

But I was, and said so. I said I was afraid the fancy-man would find me out and hit me with his stick. She said she had heard of that particular fancy-man: he was all bounce. She said,

'It was Bill Sykes, wasn't it? Why, he's a Clerkenwell man. He don't trouble with the Borough. The Borough boys are too hard for him.'

I said, 'But, oh, Mrs Sucksby! You never saw the poor girl Nancy, and how he knocked her down and murdered her!'

'Murdered her?' she said then. 'Nancy? Why, I had her here an hour ago. She was only beat a bit about the face. She has her hair curled different now, you wouldn't know he ever laid his hand upon her.'

I said, 'Won't he beat her again, though?'

She told me then that Nancy had come to her senses at last, and left Bill Sykes entirely; that she had met a nice chap from Wapping, who had set her up in a little shop selling sugar mice and tobacco.

She lifted my hair from about my neck and smoothed it across the pillow. My hair, as I have said, was very fair then—though it grew plain brown, as I got older—and Mrs Sucksby used to wash it with vinegar and comb it till it sparked. Now she smoothed it flat, then lifted a tress of it and touched it to her lips. She said, 'That Flora tries to take you on the prig again, you tell me—will you?'

I said I would. 'Good girl,' she said. Then she went. She took her candle with her, but the door she left half-open, and the cloth at the window was of lace and let the street-lamps show. It was never quite dark there, and never quite still. On the floor above were a couple of rooms where girls and boys would now and then come to stay: they laughed and thumped about, dropped coins, and some-times danced. Beyond the wall lay Mr Ibbs's sister, who was kept to her bed: she often woke with the horrors on her, shrieking. And all about the house—laid top-to-toe in cradles, like sprats in boxes of salt—were Mrs Sucksby's infants. They might start up whimpering or weeping any hour of the night, any little thing might set them off. Then Mrs Sucksby would go among them, dosing them from a bottle of gin, with a little silver spoon you could hear chink against the glass.

On this night, though, I think the rooms upstairs must have been empty, and Mr Ibbs's sister stayed quiet; and perhaps because of the quiet, the babies kept asleep. Being used to the noise, I lay awake. I lay and thought again of cruel Bill Sykes; and of Nancy, dead at his feet. From some house nearby there sounded a man's voice, cursing. Then a church bell struck the hour—the chimes came queerly across the windy streets. I wondered if Flora's slapped cheek still hurt her. I wondered how near to the Borough was Clerkenwell; and how quick the way would seem, to a man with a stick.

I had a warm imagination, even then. When there came footsteps in Lant Street, that stopped outside the window; and when the footsteps were followed by the whining of a dog, the scratching of the dog's claws, the careful turning of the handle of our shop door, I started up off my pillow and might have screamed—except that before I could the dog gave a bark, and the bark had a catch to it, that I thought I knew: it was not the pink-eyed monster from the theatre, but our own dog, Jack. He could fight like a brick. Then there came a whistle. Bill Sykes never whistled so sweet. The lips were Mr Ibbs's. He had been out for a hot meat pudding for his and Mrs Sucksby's supper.

'All right?' I heard him say. 'Smell the gravy on this . . .'

Then his voice became a murmur, and I fell back. I should say I was five or six years old. I remember it clear as anything, though. I remember lying, and hearing the sound of knives and forks and china, Mrs Sucksby's sighs, the creaking of her chair, the beat of her slipper on the floor. And I remember seeing—what I had never seen before—how the world was made up: that it had bad Bill Sykeses in it, and good Mr Ibbses; and Nancys, that might go either way. I thought how glad I was that I was already on the side that Nancy got to at last.—I mean, the good side, with sugar mice in.

It was only many years later, when I saw *Oliver Twist* a second time, that I understood that Nancy of course got murdered after all. By then, Flora was quite the fingersmith: the Surrey was nothing to her, she was working the West End theatres and halls—she could go through the crowds like salts. She never took me with her again, though. She was like everyone, too scared of Mrs Sucksby.

She was caught at last, poor thing, with her hands on a lady's bracelet; and was sent for transportation as a thief.

We were all more or less thieves, at Lant Street. But we were that kind of thief that rather eased the dodgy deed along, than did it. If I had stared to see Flora put her hand to a tear in her skirt and bring out a purse and perfume, I was never so surprised again: for it was a very dull day with us, when no-one came to Mr Ibbs's shop with a bag or a packet in the lining of his coat, in his hat, in his sleeve or stocking.

'All right, Mr Ibbs?' he'd say.

'All right, my son,' Mr Ibbs would answer. He talked rather through his nose, like that. 'What you know?'

'Not much.'

'Got something for me?'

The man would wink. 'Got something, Mr Ibbs, very hot and uncommon . . .'

They always said that, or something like it. Mr Ibbs would nod, then pull the blind upon the shop-door and turn the key—for he was a cautious man, and never saw poke near a window. At the back of his counter was a green baize curtain, and behind that was a passage, leading straight to our kitchen. If the thief was one he knew he would bring him to the table. 'Come on, my son,' he would say. 'I don't do this for everyone. But you are such an old hand that—well, you might be family.' And he would have the man lay out his stuff between the cups and crusts and tea-spoons.

Mrs Sucksby might be there, feeding pap to a baby. The thief would see her and take off his hat.

'All right, Mrs Sucksby?'

'All right, my dear.'

'All right, Sue? Ain't you growed!'

I thought them better than magicians. For out from their coats and sleeves would come pocket-books, silk handkerchiefs and watches; or else jewellery, silver plate, brass candlesticks, petticoats—whole suits of clothes, sometimes. 'This is quality stuff, this is,' they would say, as they set it all out; and Mr Ibbs would rub his hands and look expectant. But then he would study their poke, and his face would fall. He was a very mild-looking man, very honest-seeming—very pale in the cheek, with neat lips and whiskers. His face would fall, it would just about break your heart.

'Rag,' he might say, shaking his head, fingering a piece of paper money. 'Very hard to push along.' Or, 'Candlesticks. I had a dozen top-quality candlesticks come just last week, from a crib at Whitehall. Couldn't do nothing with them. Couldn't give them away.'

He would stand, making a show of reckoning up a price, but looking like he hardly dare name it to the man for fear of insulting him. Then he'd make his offer, and the thief would look disgusted.

'Mr Ibbs,' he would say, 'that won't pay me for the trouble of walking from London Bridge. Be fair, now.'

But by then Mr Ibbs would have gone to his box and be counting out shillings on the table: one, two, three— He might pause, with the fourth in his hand. The thief would see the shine of the silver—Mr Ibbs always kept his coins rubbed very bright, for just that reason—and it was like hares to a greyhound.

'Couldn't you make it five, Mr Ibbs?'

Mr Ibbs would lift his honest face, and shrug.

'I should like to, my son. I should like nothing better. And if you was to bring me something out of the way, I would make my money answer. This, however'—with a wave of his hand above the pile of silks or notes or gleaming brass—'this is so much gingerbread. I should be robbing myself. I should be stealing the food from the mouths of Mrs Sucksby's babies.'

And he would hand the thief his shillings, and the thief would pocket them and button his jacket, and cough or wipe his nose.

And then Mr Ibbs would seem to have a change of heart. He would step to his box again and, 'You eaten anything this morning, my son?' he would say. The thief would always answer, 'Not a crust.' Then Mr Ibbs would give him sixpence, and tell him to be sure and spend it on a breakfast and not on a horse; and the thief would say something like,

'You're a jewel, Mr Ibbs, a regular jewel.'

Mr Ibbs might make ten or twelve shillings' profit with a man like that: all through seeming to be honest, and fair. For, of course, what he had said about the rag or the candlesticks would be so much puff: he knew brass from onions, all right. When the thief had gone, he'd catch my eye and wink. He'd rub his hands again and grow quite lively.

'Now, Sue,' he'd say, 'what would you say to taking a cloth to these, and bringing up the shine? And then you might—if you've a moment, dear, if Mrs Sucksby don't need you—you might have a little go at the fancy work upon these wipers. Only a very little, gentle sort of go, with your little scissors and perhaps a pin: for this is lawn—do you see, my dear?—and will tear, if you tug too hard . . .'

I believe I learned my alphabet, like that: not by putting letters down, but by taking them out. I know I learned the look of my own name, from handkerchiefs that came, marked *Susan*. As for regular reading, we never troubled with it. Mrs Sucksby could do it, if she had to; Mr Ibbs could read, and even write; but, for the rest of us, it was an idea—well, I should say, like speaking Hebrew or throwing somersaults: you could see the use of it, for Jews and tumblers; but while it was their lay, why make it yours?

So I thought then, anyway. I learned to cipher, though. I learned it, from handling coins. Good coins we kept, of course. Bad ones come up too bright, and must be slummed, with blacking and grease, before you pass them on. I learned that, too. Silks and linens there are ways of washing and pressing, to make them seem new. Gems I would shine, with ordinary vinegar. Silver plate we ate our suppers off—but only the once, because of the crests and stampings; and when we had finished, Mr Ibbs would take the cups and bowls and melt them into bars. He did the same with gold and pewter. He never took chances: that's what made him so good. Everything that came into our kitchen looking like one sort of thing, was made to leave it again looking quite another. And though it had come in the front way—the shop way, the Lant Street way—it left by another way, too. It left by the back. There was no street there. What there was, was a little covered passage and a small dark court. You might stand in that and think yourself baffled; there was a path, however, if you knew how to look. It took you to an alley, and that met a winding black lane, which ran to the arches of the railway line; and from one of those arches—I won't say quite which, though I could—led another, darker, lane that would take you, very quick and inconspicuous, to the river. We knew two or three men who kept boats there. All along that crooked way, indeed, lived pals of ours—Mr Ibbs's nephews, say, that I called cousins. We could send poke from our kitchen, through any of them, to all the parts of London. We could pass anything, anything at all, at speeds which would astonish you. We could pass ice, in August, before a quarter of the block should have had a chance to turn to water. We could pass sunshine in summer—Mr Ibbs would find a buyer for it.

In short, there was not much that was brought to our house that was not moved out of it again, rather sharpish. There was only one thing, in fact, that had come and got stuck—one thing that had somehow withstood the tremendous pull of that passage of poke— one thing that Mr Ibbs and Mrs Sucksby seemed never to think to put a price to.

I mean of course, Me.

I had my mother to thank for that. Her story was a tragic one. She had come to Lant Street on a certain night in 1844. She had come, 'very large, dear girl, with you,' Mrs Sucksby said—by which, until I learned better, I took her to mean that my mother had brought me, perhaps tucked in a pocket behind her skirt, or sewn into the lining of her coat. For I knew she was a thief.—'What a thief!' Mrs Sucksby would say. 'So bold! And handsome?'

'Was she, Mrs Sucksby? Was she fair?'

'Fairer than you; but sharp, like you, about the face; and thin as paper. We put her upstairs. No-one knew she was here, save me and Mr Ibbs—for she was wanted, she said, by the police of four divisions, and if they had got her, she'd swing. What was her lay? She said it was only prigging. I think it must have been worse. I know she was hard as a nut, for she had you and, I swear, she never murmured—never called out once. She only looked at you, and put a kiss on your little head; then she gave me six pounds for the keeping of you—all of it in sovereigns, and all of 'em good. She said she had one last job to do, that would make her fortune. She meant to come back for you, when her way was clear . . .'

So Mrs Sucksby told it; and every time, though her voice would start off steady it would end up trembling, and her eyes would fill with tears. For she had waited for my mother, and my mother had not come. What came, instead, was awful news. The job that was meant to make her fortune, had gone badly. A man had been killed trying to save his plate. It was my mother's knife that killed him. Her own pal peached on her. The police caught up with her at last. She was a month in prison. Then they hanged her.

They hanged her, as they did murderesses then, on the roof of the Horsemonger Lane Gaol. Mrs Sucksby stood and watched the drop, from the window of the room that I was born in.

You got a marvellous view of it from there—the best view in South London, everybody said. People were prepared to pay very handsomely for a spot at that window, on hanging days. And though some girls shrieked when the trap went rattling down, I never did. I never once shuddered or winked.

'That's Susan Trinder,' someone might whisper then. 'Her mother was hanged as a murderess. Ain't she brave?'

I liked to hear them say it. Who wouldn't? But the fact is—and I don't care who knows it, now—the fact is, I was not brave at all. For to be brave about a thing like that, you must first be sorry. And how could I be sorry, for someone I never knew? I supposed it was a pity my mother had ended up hanged; but, since she *was* hanged, I was glad it was for something game, like murdering a miser over his plate, and not for something very wicked, like throttling a child. I supposed it was a pity she had made an orphan of me—but then, some girls I knew had mothers who were drunkards, or mothers who were mad: mothers they hated and could never rub along with. I should rather a dead mother, over one like that!

I should rather Mrs Sucksby. She was better by chalks. She had been paid to keep me a month; she kept me seventeen years. What's love, if that ain't? She might have passed me on to the poorhouse. She might have left me crying in a draughty crib. Instead she prized me so, she would not let me on the prig for fear a policeman should have got me. She let me sleep beside her, in her own bed. She shined my hair with vinegar. You treat jewels like that.

And I was not a jewel; nor even a pearl. My hair, after all, turned out quite ordinary. My face was a commonplace face. I could pick a plain lock, I could cut a plain key; I could bounce a coin and say, from the ring, if the coin were good or bad.—But anyone can do those things, who is taught them. All about me other infants came, and stayed a little, then were claimed by their mothers, or found new mothers, or perished; and of course, no-one claimed me, I did not perish, instead I grew up, until at last I was old enough to go among the cradles with the bottle of gin and the silver spoon myself. Mr Ibbs I would seem sometimes to catch gazing at me with a certain light in his eye—as if, I thought, he was seeing me suddenly for the piece of poke I was, and wondering how I had come to stay so long, and who he could pass me on to. But when people talked—as they now and then did—about blood, and its being thicker than water, Mrs Sucksby looked dark.

'Come here, dear girl,' she'd say. 'Let me look at you.' And she'd put her hands upon my head and stroke my cheeks with her thumbs, brooding over my face. 'I see *her* in you,' she'd say. 'She is looking at me, as she looked at me that night. She is thinking that she'll come back and make your fortune. How could she know? Poor girl, she'll never come back! Your fortune's still to be made. Your fortune, Sue, and ours along with it . . .'

So she said, many times. Whenever she grumbled or sighed—whenever she rose from a cradle, rubbing her sore back—her eyes would find me out, and her look would clear, she'd grow contented. *But here is Sue*, she might as well have said. *Things is hard for us, now. But here is Sue. She'll fix 'em . . .*

I let her think it; but thought I knew better. I'd heard once that she'd had a child of her own, many years before, that had been born dead. I thought it was *her* face she supposed she saw, when she gazed so hard at mine. The idea made me shiver, rather; for it was queer to think of being loved, not just for my own sake, but for someone's I never knew . . .

I thought I knew all about love, in those days. I thought I knew all about everything. If you had asked me how I supposed I should go on, I dare say I would have said that I should like to farm infants. I might like to be married, to a thief or a fencing-man. There was a boy, when I was fifteen, that stole a clasp for me, and said he should like to kiss me. There was another a little later, who used to stand at our back door and whistle 'The Locksmith's Daughter', expressly to see me blush. Mrs Sucksby chased them both away. She was as careful of me in that department, as in all others.

'Who's she keeping you for, then?' the boys would say. 'Prince Eddie?'

I think the people who came to Lant Street thought me slow.—
Slow I mean, as opposed to fast. Perhaps I was, by Borough
standards. But it seemed to me that I was sharp enough. You could
not have grown up in such a house, that had such businesses in it,
without having a pretty good idea of what was what—of what could
go into what; and what could come out.

Do you follow?

You are waiting for me to start my story. Perhaps I was waiting,
then. But my story had already started—I was only like you, and
didn't know it.

This is when I thought it really began.

A night in winter, a few weeks after the Christmas that marked
my seventeenth birthday. A dark night—a hard night, full of a fog
that was more or less a rain, and a rain that was more or less snow.
Dark nights are good to thieves and fencing-men; dark nights in
winter are the best nights of all, for then regular people keep close
to their homes, and the swells all keep to the country, and the grand
houses of London are shut up and empty and pleading to be
cracked. We got lots of stuff on nights like those, and Mr Ibbs's
profits were higher than ever. The cold makes thieves come to a bar-
gain very quick.

We did not feel the cold too much at Lant Street, for besides our
ordinary kitchen fire there was Mr Ibbs's locksmith's brazier: he
always kept a flame beneath the coals of it, you could never say
what might not turn up that would need making up or melting
down. On this night there were three or four boys at it, sweating the
gold off sovereigns. Besides them was Mrs Sucksby in her great
chair, a couple of babies in a cradle at her side; and a boy and a girl
who were rooming with us then—John Vroom, and Dainty Warren.

John was a thin, dark, knifish boy of about fourteen. He was
always eating. I believe he had the worm. This night he was cracking peanuts, and throwing their shells on the floor.

Mrs Sucksby saw him do it. 'Will you watch your manners?' she
said. 'You make a mess, and Sue shall have to tidy it.'

John said, 'Poor Sue, ain't my heart bleeding.'

He never cared for me. I think he was jealous. He had come to our house as a baby, like me; and like mine, his mother had died and made an orphan of him. But he was such a queer-looking child, no-one would take him off Mrs Sucksby's hands. She had kept him till he was four or five, then put him on the parish—even then, however, he was a devil to get rid of, always running back from the workhouse: we were forever opening the shop-door and finding him sleeping on the step. She had got the master of a ship to take him at last, and he sailed as far as China; when he came back to the Borough after that, he did it with money, to brag. The money had lasted a month. Now he kept handy at Lant Street by doing jobs for Mr Ibbs; and besides them, ran mean little dodges of his own, with Dainty to help him.

She was a great red-haired girl of three-and-twenty, and more or less a simpleton. She had neat white hands, though, and could sew like anything. John had her at this time stitching dog-skins onto stolen dogs, to make them seem handsomer breeds than what they really were.

He was doing a deal with a dog-thief. This man had a couple of bitches: when the bitches came on heat he would walk the streets with them, tempting dogs away from their owners, then charging a ten pounds' ransom before he'd give them back. That works best with sporting dogs, and dogs with sentimental mistresses; some owners, however, will never pay up—you could cut off their little dog's tail and post it to them and never see a bean, they are that heartless—and the dogs that John's pal was landed with he would throttle, then sell to him at a knocked-down price. I can't say what John did with the meat—passed it off as rabbit, perhaps, or ate it himself. But the skins, as I have said, he had Dainty stitching to plain street-dogs, which he was selling as quality breeds at the Whitechapel Market.

The bits of fur left over she was sewing together to cover him a greatcoat. She was sewing it, this night. She had the collar done and the shoulders and half the sleeves, and there were about forty different sorts of dog in it already. The smell of it was powerful, before a fire, and drove our own dog—which was not the old fighter, Jack, but another, brown dog we called Charley Wag, after the thief in the story—into a perfect fever.

Now and then Dainty would hold the coat up for us all to see how well it looked.

'It's a good job for Dainty that you ain't a deal taller, John,' I said, one time she did this.

'It's a good job for you that you ain't dead,' he answered. He was short, and felt it. 'Though a shame for the rest of us. I should like a bit of your skin upon the sleeves of my coat—perhaps upon the cuffs of it, where I wipes my nose. You should look right at home, beside a bulldog or a boxer.'

He took up his knife, that he always kept by him, and tested the edge with his thumb. 'I ain't quite decided yet,' he said, 'but what I shan't come one night, and take a bit of skin off while you are sleeping. What should you say, Dainty, if I was to make you sew up that?'

Dainty put her hand to her mouth and screamed. She wore a ring, too large for her hand; she had wound a bit of thread about the finger beneath, and the thread was quite black.

'You tickler!' she said.

John smiled, and tapped with the point of his knife against a broken tooth. Mrs Sucksby said,

'That's enough from you, or I'll knock your bloody head off. I won't have Sue made nervous.'

I said at once, that if I thought I should be made nervous by an infant like John Vroom, I should cut my throat. John said he should like to cut it for me. Then Mrs Sucksby leaned from her chair and hit him—just as she had once leaned, on that other night, all that time before, and hit poor Flora; and as she had leaned and hit others, in the years in between—all for my sake.

John looked for a second as if he should like to strike her back; then he looked at me, as if he should like to strike me harder. Then Dainty shifted in her seat, and he turned and struck her.

'Beats me,' he said when he had done it, 'why everyone is so down on me.'

Dainty had started to cry. She reached for his sleeve. 'Never mind their hard words, Johnny,' she said. 'I sticks to you, don't I?'

'You sticks, all right,' he answered. 'Like shit to a shovel.' He pushed her hand away, and she sat rocking in her chair, huddled over the dog-skin coat and weeping into her stitches.

'Hush now, Dainty,' said Mrs Sucksby. 'You are spoiling your nice work.'

She cried for a minute. Then one of the boys at the brazier burned his finger on a hot coin, and started off swearing; and she screamed with laughter. John put another peanut to his mouth and spat the shell upon the floor.

Then we sat quiet, for perhaps a quarter of an hour. Charley Wag lay before the fire and twitched, chasing hansoms in his sleep—his tail was kinked where a cab-wheel had caught it. I got out cards, for a game of Patience. Dainty sewed. Mrs Sucksby dozed. John sat perfectly idle; but would now and then look over at the cards I dealt, to tell me where to place them.

'Jack of Diggers on the Bitch of Hearts,' he would say. Or, 'Lor! Ain't you slow?'

'Ain't you hateful?' I would answer, keeping on with my own game. The pack was an old one, the cards as limp as rags. A man had been killed once, in a fight over a crooked game that was played with those cards. I set them out a final time and turned my chair a little, so that John might not see how they fell.

And then, all at once, one of the babies started out of its slumber and began to cry, and Charley Wag woke up and gave a bark. There was a sudden gust of wind that made the fire leap high in the chimney, and the rain came harder upon the coals and made them hiss. Mrs Sucksby opened her eyes. 'What's that?' she said.

'What's what?' said John.

Then we heard it: a thump, in the passage that led to the back of the house. Then another thump came. Then the thumps became footsteps. The footsteps stopped at the kitchen door—there was a second of silence—and then, slow and heavy, a knock.

Knock—knock—knock. Like that. Like the knocking on a door in a play, when the dead man's ghost comes back. Not a thief's knock, anyway: that is quick and light. You knew what sort of business it was, when you heard that. This business, however, might be anything, anything at all. This business might be bad.

So we all thought. We looked at one another, and Mrs Sucksby reached into the cradle to draw the baby from it and stop its cries against her bosom; and John took hold of Charley Wag and held his jaws shut. The boys at the brazier fell silent as mice. Mr Ibbs said quietly, 'Anyone expected? Boys, put this lot away. Never mind your burning fingers. If it's the blues, we're done for.'

They began picking at the sovereigns and the gold they had sweated from them, wrapping them in handkerchiefs, putting the handkerchiefs beneath their hats or in their trouser pockets. One of them—it was Mr Ibbs's oldest nephew, Phil—went quickly to the door and stood beside it, his back flat to the wall, his hand in his coat. He had passed two terms in prison, and always swore he would not pass a third.

The knock came again. Mr Ibbs said, 'All tidy? Now, be steady, boys, be steady. What do you say, Sue my dear, to opening that door?'

I looked again at Mrs Sucksby, and when she nodded, went and drew back the bolt; the door was flung so quick and hard against me, Phil thought it had been shouldered—I saw him brace himself against the wall, bring out his knife and lift it. But it was only the wind that made the door swing: it came in a rush into the kitchen, blowing half the candles out, making the brazier spark, and sending all my playing-cards flying. In the passage stood a man, dressed dark, wet through and dripping, and with a leather bag at his feet. The dim light showed his pale cheeks, his whiskers, but his eyes were quite hidden in the shadow of his hat. I should not have known him if he had not spoken. He said,

'Sue! Is it Sue? Thank God! I have come forty miles to see you. Will you keep me standing here? I am afraid the cold will kill me!'

Then I knew him, though I had not seen him for more than a year. Not one man in a hundred came to Lant Street speaking like him. His name was Richard Rivers, or Dick Rivers, or sometimes Richard Wells. We called him by another name, however; and it was that name I said now, when Mrs Sucksby saw me staring and called, 'Who is it, then?'

'It's Gentleman,' I said.

That is how we said it, of course: not how a proper gent would say it, using all his teeth on it; but as if the word were a fish and we had filleted it—*Ge'mun*.

'It's Gentleman,' I said; and Phil at once put his knife away, and spat, and went back to the brazier. Mrs Sucksby, however, turned in her chair, the baby twisting its scarlet face from her bosom and opening its mouth.

'Gentleman!' she cried. The baby started shrieking, and Charley Wag, let free by John, dashed barking to Gentleman and put his paws upon his coat. 'What a turn you gave us! Dainty, take a taper to them candles. Put the water on the fire, for a pot.'

'We thought you was the blues,' I said, as Gentleman came into the kitchen.

'I believe I am turned blue,' he answered. He set down his bag, and shivered, and took off his sodden hat and gloves and then his dripping greatcoat, which at once began to steam. He rubbed his hands together, then passed them over his head. He kept his hair and whiskers long and now, the rain having taken the kink from them, they seemed longer than ever, and dark, and sleek. There were rings at his fingers, and a watch, with a jewel on the chain, at his waistcoat. I knew without studying them that the rings and the watch were snide, and the jewel a paste one; but they were damn fine counterfeits.

The room grew brighter as Dainty saw to the lights. Gentleman looked about him, still rubbing his hands together and nodding.

'How do you do, Mr Ibbs?' he called easily. 'How do you do, lads?'

Mr Ibbs said, 'Very well, my tulip.' The boys did not answer. Phil said, to no-one, 'Come in the back way, did he?'—and another boy laughed.

Boys like that always think that men like Gentleman are nancies.

John laughed too, but louder than the others. Gentleman looked at him. 'Hallo, you little tick,' he said. 'Lost your monkey?'

John's cheek being so sallow, everyone always took him for an Italian. Now, hearing Gentleman, he put his finger to his nose. 'You can kiss my arse,' he said.

'Can I?' said Gentleman, smiling. He winked at Dainty, and she ducked her head. 'Hallo, charmer,' he said. Then he stooped to Charley Wag, and pulled his ears. 'Hallo, you Wagster. Where's police? Hey? Where's police? See 'em off!' Charley Wag went wild. 'Good boy,' said Gentleman, rising, brushing off hairs. 'Good boy. That will do.'

Then he went and stood at Mrs Sucksby's chair.

'Hallo, Mrs S,' he said.

The baby, now, had had a dose of gin, and had cried itself quiet. Mrs Sucksby held out her hand. Gentleman caught it up and kissed it—first at the knuckles, and then at the tips. Mrs Sucksby said,

'Get up out of that chair, John, and let Gentleman sit down.'

John looked like thunder for a minute, then rose and took Dainty's stool. Gentleman sat, and spread his legs towards the fire. He was tall, and his legs were long. He was seven- or eight-and-twenty. Beside him, John looked about six.

Mrs Sucksby kept her eyes upon him while he yawned and rubbed his face. Then he met her gaze, and smiled.

'Well, well,' he said. 'How's business?'

'Pretty sweet,' she answered. The baby lay still, and she patted it as she had used to pat me. Gentleman nodded to it.

'And this little bud,' he said: 'is it farm, or is it family?'

'Farm, of course,' she said.

'A he-bud, or a she-bud?'

'A he-bud, bless his gums! Another poor motherless infant what I shall be bringing up by hand.'

Gentleman leaned towards her.

'Lucky boy!' he said, and winked.

Mrs Sucksby cried, 'Oh!' and turned pink as a rose. 'You sauce-box!'

Nancy or not, he could certainly make a lady blush.

We called him Gentleman, because he really was a gent—had been, he said, to a real gent's school, and had a father and a mother and a sister—all swells—whose heart he had just about broke. He had had money once, and lost it all gambling; his pa said he should never have another cent of the family fortune; and so he was obliged to get money the old-fashioned way, by thievery and dodging. He took to the life so well, however, we all said there must have been bad blood way back in that family, that had all come out in him.

He could be quite the painter when he chose, and had done a little work in the forgery line, at Paris; when that fell through, I think he spent a year putting French books into English—or English books into French—anyway, putting them slightly different each time, and pinning different titles on them, and so making one old story pass as twenty brand-new ones. Mostly, however, he worked as a confidence-man, and as a sharper at the grand casinos—for of course, he could mix with Society, and seem honest as the rest. The ladies especially would go quite wild for him. He had three times been nearly married to some rich heiress, but every time the father in the case had grown suspicious and the deal had fallen through. He had ruined many people by selling them stock from counterfeit banks. He was handsome as a plum, and Mrs Sucksby fairly doted on him. He came to Lant Street about once a year, bringing poke to Mr Ibbs, and picking up bad coin, cautions, and tips.

I supposed he had come bringing poke with him, now; and so, it seemed, did Mrs Sucksby, for once he had grown warm again before the fire and Dainty had given him tea, with rum in it, she placed the sleeping baby back in its cradle and smoothed her skirt across her lap and said,

'Well now, Gentleman, this is a pleasure all right. We didn't look for you for another month or two. Have you something with you, as Mr Ibbs will like the look of?'

Gentleman shook his head. 'Nothing for Mr Ibbs, I am afraid.'

'What, nothing? Do you hear that, Mr Ibbs?'

'Very sad,' said Mr Ibbs, from his place at the brazier.

Mrs Sucksby grew confidential. 'Have you something, then, for me?'

But Gentleman shook his head again.

'Not for you, either, Mrs S,' he said. 'Not for you; not for Garibaldi here' (meaning John); 'not for Dainty, nor for Phil and the boys; nor even for Charley Wag.'

He said this, going all about the room with his eyes; and finally looking at me, and then saying nothing. I had taken up the scattered playing-cards, and was sorting them back into their suits. When I saw him gazing—and, besides him, John and Dainty, and Mrs Sucksby, still quite pink in the face, also looking my way—I put the cards down. He at once reached over and picked them up, and started shuffling. He was that kind of man, whose hands must always be busy.

'Well, Sue,' he said, his eyes still upon me. His eyes were a very clear blue.

'Well, what?' I answered.

'What do you say to this? It's you I've come for.'

'Her!' said John, in disgust.

Gentleman nodded. 'I have something for you. A proposal.'

'A proposal!' said Phil. He had overheard it. 'Look out, Sue, he only wants to marry you!'

Dainty screamed, and the boys all sniggered. Gentleman blinked, then took his eyes from me at last, and leaned to Mrs Sucksby to say,

'Get rid of our friends at the brazier, would you? But keep John and Dainty: I shall want their help.'

Mrs Sucksby hesitated, then glanced at Mr Ibbs; and Mr Ibbs said at once, 'Right, lads, these sovs is sweated so hard, the poor queen's quite a shadder. Any more of it, we shall be done for treason.' He took up a pail, and began to drop the hot coins into the water, one by one. 'Listen to them yellow boys cry hush!' he said. 'The gold knows best. Now, what does the gold know?'

'Go on, Uncle Humphry,' said Phil. He drew on his coat and turned up his collar. The other boys did the same. 'So long,' they said, with a nod to me, to John and Dainty and Mrs Sucksby. To Gentleman they said nothing. He watched them go by.

'Watch your back, lads!' he called, as the door was closed behind them. We heard Phil spit again.

Mr Ibbs turned the key in the lock. Then he came and poured himself a cup of tea—splashing rum in it, as Dainty had for Gentleman. The scent of the rum rose on the steam, to mix with the smell of the fire, the sweated gold, the dog-skins, the wet and steaming greatcoat. The rain fell softer upon the grate. John chewed on a peanut, picking shell from his tongue. Mr Ibbs had moved lamps. The table, our faces and hands, showed bright; but the rest of the room was in shadow.

For a minute, no-one spoke. Gentleman still worried the cards, and we sat and watched him. Mr Ibbs watched him hardest of all: his eye grew narrow, and he tilted his head—he might have been lining him up along the barrel of a gun.

'So, my son,' he said. 'What's the story?'

Gentleman looked up.

'The story,' he said. 'The story is this.' He took out a card, and laid it, face-up, on the table. It was the King of Diamonds. 'Imagine a man,' he said, as he did it. 'An old man—a wise man, in his own way—a gentleman scholar, in fact; but with curious habits. He lives in a certain out-of-the-way sort of house, near a certain out-of-the-way kind of village, some miles from London—never mind quite where, just now. He has a great room filled with books and prints, and cares for nothing but for them and for a work he is compiling—let's call it, a dictionary. It is a dictionary of all his books; but he has hopes for the pictures, too—has taken a mind to having them bound in fancy albums. The handling of that, however, is more than he can manage. He places a notice in a newspaper: he needs the services of'—here he put down another card, next to the first: Jack of Spades—'a smart young man, to help him mount the collection; and one particular smart young man—being at that time rather too well known at the London gaming-houses, and highly desirous of a little light out-of-the-way sort of employment, bed and board provided—replies to the advertisement, is examined, and found fit.'

'The smart young man being yourself,' said Mr Ibbs.

'The smart young man being me. How you catch on!'

'And the crib in the country,' said John, taken up in Gentleman's story despite his sulks, 'let's say it's busting with treasure. And you mean to force the locks, on all the cabinets and chests. You have come to Mr Ibbs for a loan of nippers and a jilt; and you want Sue—with her innocent eyes, what looks like they ain't seen butter—for your canary.'

Gentleman tilted his head, drew in his breath and raised a finger, in a teasing sort of way. Then:

'Cold as ice!' he said. 'The crib in the country is a damnable place: two hundred years old, and dark, and draughty, and mort-gaged to the roof—which is leaky, by the by. Not a rug or a vase or piece of plate worth forcing so much as a fart for, I'm afraid. The gent eats his supper off china, just like us.'

'The old hunks!' said John. 'But, tight-wads like that, they stash their money in the bank, don't they? And you have made him write a paper leaving all of it to you; and now you are here for a bottle of poison—'

Gentleman shook his head.

'Not a ounce of poison?' said John, looking hopeful.

'Not an ounce. Not a scruple. And no money in the bank—not in the old man's name, at least. He lives so quietly and so queerly, he scarcely knows what money's for. But there, do you see, he doesn't live alone. Look here, who he keeps for his companion . . .'

The Queen of Hearts.

'Heh, heh,' said John, growing sly. 'A wife, very game.'

But Gentleman shook his head again.

'A daughter, ditto?' said John.

'Not a wife. Not a daughter,' said Gentleman, with his eyes and his fingers on the Queen's unhappy face. 'A niece. In years,' he glanced at me, 'say Sue's years. In looks, say handsome. Of sense, understanding and knowledge,' he smiled, 'why, let's say perfectly shy.'

'A flat!' said John with relish. 'Tell me *she*'s rich, at least.'

'She's rich, oh yes,' said Gentleman, nodding. 'But only as a caterpillar is rich in wings, or clover rich in honey. She's an heiress, Johnny: her fortune is certain, the uncle can't touch it; but it comes with a queer condition attached. She won't see a penny till the day she marries. If she dies a spinster, the money goes to a cousin. If she takes a husband'—he stroked the card with one white finger—'she's rich as a queen.'

'How rich?' said Mr Ibbs. He had not spoken, all this time. Gentleman heard him now, looked up, and held his gaze.

'Ten thousand in ready,' he said quietly. 'Five thousand in the funds.'

A coal in the fire went *pop*. John gave a whistle through his broken tooth, and Charley Wag barked. I glanced at Mrs Sucksby, but her head was bent and her look was dark. Mr Ibbs took a sip from his tea, in a considering way.

'I'll bet the old man keeps her close, don't he?' he said, when the tea was swallowed.

'Close enough,' said Gentleman, nodding, moving back. 'He's made a secretary of her, all these years—has her reading to him for hours at a stretch. I think he hardly knows she has grown up and turned into a lady.' He gave a secret sort of smile. 'I think she knows it, though. No sooner do I start work on the pictures than she discovers in herself a passion for painting. She wants lessons, with me as her master. Now, I know enough in that line to fake my way; and she, in her innocence, can't tell a pastel from a pig. But she takes to her instruction—oh, like anything. We have a week of lessons: I teach her lines, I teach her shadows. The second week goes by: we move from shadows to design. Third week—blushing watercolours. Next, the blending of the oils. Fifth week—'

'Fifth week, you jiggles her!' said John.

Gentleman closed his eyes.

'Fifth week, our lessons are cancelled,' he said. 'Do you think a girl like that may sit in a room, with a gentleman tutor, alone? We have had her Irish maid sit with us, all this time—coughing and turning red in the face, every time my fingers stray too near her lady's, or my breath comes too warm upon her little white cheek. I thought her a marvellous prude; it turns out she had the scarlet fever—is at this moment dying of it, poor bitch. Now my lady has no chaperon but the housekeeper—and the housekeeper is too busy to sit at lessons. The lessons, therefore, must end, the paints are left to dry upon their palette. Now I only see Miss at supper, at her uncle's side; and sometimes, if I pass her chamber door, I hear her sighing.'

'And just,' said Mr Ibbs, 'as you was getting on so nicely.'

'Just so,' said Gentleman. 'Just so.'

'Poor lady!' said Dainty. Her eyes had tears in them. She could cry at anything. 'And her quite a peach, you say? About the figure and the face?'

Gentleman looked careless. 'She can fill a man's eye, I suppose,' he said, with a shrug.

John laughed. 'I should like to fill *her* eye!'

'I should like to fill yours,' said Gentleman, steadily. Then he blinked. 'With my fist, I mean.'

John's cheek grew dark, and he jumped to his feet. 'I should like to see you try it!'

Mr Ibbs lifted his hands. 'Boys! Boys! That's enough! I won't have it, before ladies and kids! John, sit down and stop fucking about. Gentleman, you promised us your story; what we've had so far has been so much pastry. Where's the meat, son? Where's the meat? And, more to our point, how is Susie to help cook it?'

John kicked the leg of his stool, then sat. Gentleman had taken out a packet of cigarettes. We waited, while he found a match and struck it. We watched the flare of the sulphur in his eyes. Then he leaned to the table again and touched the three cards he had laid there, putting straight their edges.

'You want the meat,' he said. 'Very well, here it is.' He tapped the Queen of Hearts. 'I aim to marry this girl and take her fortune. I aim to steal her'—he slid the card to one side—'from under her uncle's nose. I am in a fair way to doing it already, as you have heard; but she's a queer sort of girl, and can't be trusted to herself— and should she take some clever, hard woman for her new servant, why then I'm ruined. I have come to London to collect a set of bindings for the old man's albums. I want to send Sue back before me. I want to set her up there as the lady's maid, so that she might help me woo her.'

He caught my eye. He still played idly with the card, with one pale hand. Now he lowered his voice.

'And there's something else,' he said, 'that I shall need Sue's help with. Once I have married this girl, I shan't want her about me. I know a man who will take her off my hands. He has a house, where he'll keep her. It's a madhouse. He'll keep her close. So close, per- haps . . .' He did not finish, but turned the card face down, and kept his fingers on its back. 'I must only marry her,' he said, 'and—as Johnny would say—I must jiggle her, once, for the sake of the cash. Then I'll take her, unsuspecting, to the madhouse gates. Where's the harm? Haven't I said, she's half-simple already? But I want to be sure. I shall need Sue by her to keep her simple; and to persuade her, in her simpleness, into the plot.'

He drew again upon his cigarette and, as they had before, every- one turned their eyes on me. Everyone that is, save Mrs Sucksby. She had listened, saying nothing, while Gentleman spoke. I had watched her pour a little of her tea out of her cup into her saucer, then swill it about the china and finally raise it to her mouth, while the story went on. She could never bear hot tea, she said it hardened the lips. And certainly, I don't believe I ever knew a grown-up woman with lips as soft as hers.

Now, in the silence, she put her cup and saucer down, then drew out her handkerchief and wiped her mouth. She looked at Gentleman, and finally spoke.

'Why Sue,' she said, 'of all the girls in England? Why my Sue?'

'*Because* she is yours, Mrs S,' he answered. 'Because I trust her; because she's a good girl—which is to say, a bad girl, not too nice about the fine points of the law.'

She nodded. 'And how do you mean,' she asked next, 'to cut the shine?'

Again he looked at me; but he still spoke to her.

'She shall have two thousand pounds,' he said, smoothing his whiskers; 'and shall take any of the little lady's bits and frocks and jewels that she likes.'

That was the deal.

We thought it over.

'What do you say?' he said at last—to me, this time. And then, when I did not answer: 'I am sorry,' he said, 'to spring this upon you; but you can see the little time I have had to act in. I must get a girl soon. I should like it to be you, Sue. I should like it to be you, more than anyone. But if it is not to be, then tell me quickly, will you?—so I might find out another.'

'Dainty will do it,' said John, when he heard that. 'Dainty was a maid once—wasn't you, Daint?—for a lady in a great house at Peckham.'

'As I recall,' said Mr Ibbs, drinking his tea, 'Dainty lost that place through putting a hat-pin to the lady's arm.'

'She was a bitch to me,' said Dainty, 'and got my dander up. This girl don't sound like a bitch. She's a flat, you said so. I could maid for a flat.'

'It was Sue that was asked,' said Mrs Sucksby quietly. 'And she still ain't said.'

Then, again they all looked at me; and their eyes made me nervous. I turned my head. 'I don't know,' I said. 'It seems a rum sort of plot to me. Set me up, as maid to a lady? How shall I know what to do?'

'We can teach you,' said Gentleman. 'Dainty can teach you, since she knows the business. How hard can it be? You must only sit and simper, and hold the lady's salts.'

I said, 'Suppose the lady won't want me for her maid? Why should she want me?'

But he had thought of that. He had thought of everything. He said he meant to pass me off as his old nurse's sister's child—a city girl come on hard times. He said he thought the lady would take me then, for his sake.

He said, 'We'll write you a character—sign it Lady Fanny of Bum Street, something like that—she won't know any better. She never saw Society, doesn't know London from Jerusalem. Who can she ask?'

'I don't know,' I said again. 'Suppose she don't care for *you*, so much as you are hoping?'

He grew modest. 'Well,' he said, 'I think I might be permitted by now, to know when a green girl likes me.'

'Suppose,' said Mrs Sucksby then, 'she don't like you quite

enough? Suppose she turns out another Miss Bamber or Miss Finch?'

Miss Bamber and Miss Finch were two of the other heiresses he had almost netted. But he heard their names, and snorted. 'She won't,' he said, 'turn out like them, I know it. Those girls had fathers—ambitious fathers, with lawyers on every side. This girl's uncle can see no further than the last page of his book. As to her not liking me enough—well, I can only say this: I think she will.'

'Enough to do a flit, from her uncle's house?'

'It's a grim house,' he answered, 'for a girl of her years.'

'But it's the years that will work against you,' said Mr Ibbs. You picked up bits and pieces of Law, of course, in a line like his. 'Till she is one-and-twenty, she shall need her uncle's say. Take her as fast and as quiet as you like: he shall come and take her back again. You being her husband won't count for buttons, then.'

'But her being my wife, will.—If you understand me,' said Gentleman slyly.

Dainty looked blank. John saw her face. 'The jiggling,' he said.

'She shall be ruined,' said Mrs Sucksby. 'No other gent will want her, then.'

Dainty gaped more than ever.

'Never mind it,' said Mr Ibbs, lifting his hand. Then, to Gentleman: 'It's tricky. Uncommonly tricky.'

'I don't say it's not. But we must take our chances. What have we to lose? If nothing else, it will be a holiday for Sue.'

John laughed. 'A holiday,' he said, 'it will be. A fucking long one, if you get caught.'

I bit my lip. He was right. But it wasn't so much the risk that troubled me. You cannot be a thief and always troubling over hazards, you should go mad. It was only that I was not sure I wanted any kind of holiday. I was not sure I cared for it away from the Borough. I had once gone with Mrs Sucksby to visit her cousin in Bromley; I had come home with hives. I remembered the country as quiet and queer, and the people in it either simpletons or gipsies.

How would I like living with a simpleton girl? She would not be like Dainty, who was only slightly touched and only sometimes violent. She might be really mad. She might try and throttle me; and there would be no-one about, for miles and miles, to hear me calling. Gipsies would be no use, they were all for themselves. Everyone knows a gipsy would not cross the street to spit on you, if you were on fire.

I said, 'This girl—what's she like? You said she's queer in her head.'

'Not queer,' said Gentleman. 'Only what I should call fey. She's an innocent, a natural. She has been kept from the world. She's an orphan, like you are; but where you had Mrs Sucksby to sharpen you up, she had—no-one.'

Dainty looked at him then. Her mother had been a drunkard, and got drowned in the river. Her father had used to beat her. He beat her sister till she died. She said, in a whisper:

'Ain't it terribly wicked, Gentleman, what you mean to do?'

I don't believe any of us had thought it, before that moment. Now Dainty said it, and I gazed about me, and nobody would catch my eye.

Then Gentleman laughed.

'Wicked?' he said. 'Why, bless you, Dainty, of course it's wicked! But it's wicked to the tune of fifteen thousand pounds—and oh! but that's a sweet tune, hum it how you will. Then again, do you suppose that when that money was first got, it was got honestly? Don't think it! Money never is. It is got, by families like hers, from the backs of the poor—twenty backs broken for every shilling made. You have heard, have you, of Robin Hood?'

'Have I!' she said.

'Well, Sue and I shall be like him: taking gold from the rich and passing it back to the people it was got from.'

John curled his lip. 'You ponce,' he said. 'Robin Hood was a hero, a man of wax. Pass the money to the people? What people are yours! You want to rob a lady, go and rob your own mother.'

'My mother?' answered Gentleman, colouring up. 'What's my mother to do with anything? Hang my mother!' Then he caught Mrs Sucksby's eye, and turned to me. 'Oh, Sue,' he said. 'I do beg your pardon.'

'It's all right,' I said quickly. And I gazed at the table, and again everyone grew quiet. Perhaps they were all thinking, as they did on hanging days, 'Ain't she brave?' I hoped they were. Then again, I hoped they weren't: for, as I have said, I never was brave, but had got away with people supposing I was, for seventeen years. Now here was Gentleman, needing a bold girl and coming—forty miles, he had said, in all that cold and slippery weather—to me.

I raised my eyes to his.

'Two thousand pounds, Sue,' he said quietly.

'That'll shine very bright, all right,' said Mr Ibbs.

'And all them frocks and jewels!' said Dainty. 'Oh, Sue! Shouldn't you look handsome, in them!'

'You should look like a lady,' said Mrs Sucksby; and I heard her, and caught her gaze, and knew she was looking at me—as she had, so many times before—and was seeing, behind my face, my mother's. *Your fortune's still to be made.*—I could almost hear her saying it. *Your fortune's still to be made; and ours, Sue, along with it . . .*

And after all, she had been right. Here was my fortune, come from nowhere—come, at last. What could I say? I looked again at Gentleman. My heart beat hard, like hammers in my breast. I said:

'All right. I'll do it. But for three thousand pounds, not two. And if the lady don't care for me and sends me home, I shall want a hundred anyway, for the trouble of trying.'

He hesitated, thinking it over. Of course, that was all a show. After a second he smiled, then he held his hand to me and I gave him mine. He pressed my fingers, and laughed.

John scowled. 'I'll give you ten to one she comes back crying in a week,' he said.

'I'll come back dressed in a velvet gown,' I answered. 'With gloves up to here, and a hat with a veil on, and a bag full of silver coin. And you shall have to call me miss. Won't he, Mrs Sucksby?'

He spat. 'I'll tear my own tongue out, before I do that!'

'I'll tear it out first!' I said.

I sound like a child. I was a child! Perhaps Mrs Sucksby was thinking that, too. For she said nothing, only sat, still gazing at me, with her hand at her soft lip. She smiled; but her face seemed troubled. I could almost have said, she was afraid.

Perhaps she was.

Or perhaps I only think that now, when I know what dark and fearful things were to follow.

Chapter Two

$\mathcal{T}$he bookish old man, it turned out, was called Christopher Lilly. The niece's name was Maud. They lived west of London, out Maidenhead-way, near a village named Marlow, and in a house they called Briar. Gentleman's plan was to send me there alone, by train, in two days' time. He himself, he said, must stay in London for another week at least, to do the old man's business over the bindings of his books.

I didn't care much for the detail of my travelling down there, and arriving at the house, all on my own. I had never been much further west before than the Cremorne Gardens, where I sometimes went with Mr Ibbs's nephews, to watch the dancing on a Saturday night. I saw the French girl cross the river on a wire from there, and almost drop—*that* was something. They say she wore stockings; her legs looked bare enough to me, though. But I recall standing on Battersea Bridge as she walked her rope, and looking out, past Hammersmith, to all the countryside beyond it, that was just trees and hills and not a chimney or the spire of a church in sight—and oh! that was a very chilling thing to see. If you had said to me then, that I would one day leave the Borough, with all my pals in it, and Mrs Sucksby and Mr Ibbs, and go quite alone, to a maid's place in a house the other side of those dark hills, I should have laughed in your face.

But Gentleman said I must go soon, in case the lady—Miss Lilly—should spoil our plot, by accidentally taking another girl to be her servant. The day after he came to Lant Street he sat and wrote her out a letter. He said he hoped she would pardon the liberty of his writing, but he had been on a visit to his old nurse—that had been like a mother to him, when he was a boy—and he had found her quite demented with grief, over the fate of her dead sister's daughter. Of course, the dead sister's daughter was meant to be me: the story was, that I had been maiding for a lady who was marrying and heading off for India, and had lost my place; that I was looking out for another mistress, but was meanwhile being tempted on every side to go to the bad; and that if only some soft-hearted lady would give me the chance of a situation far away from the evils of the city—and so on.

I said, 'If she'll believe bouncers like those, Gentleman, she must be even sillier than you first told us.'

But he answered, that there were about a hundred girls between the Strand and Piccadilly, who dined very handsomely off that story, five nights a week; and if the hard swells of London could be separated from their shillings by it, then how much kinder wasn't Miss Maud Lilly likely to be, all alone and unknowing and sad as she was, and with no-one to tell her any better?

'You'll see,' he said. And he sealed the letter and wrote the direction, and had one of our neighbours' boys run with it to the post.

Then, so sure was he of the success of his plan, he said they must begin at once to teach me how a proper lady's maid should be.

First, they washed my hair. I wore my hair then, like lots of the Borough girls wore theirs, divided in three, with a comb at the back and, at the sides, a few fat curls. If you turned the curls with a very hot iron, having first made the hair wet with sugar-and-water, you could make them hard as anything; they would last for a week like that, or longer. Gentleman, however, said he thought the style too fast for a country lady: he made me wash my hair till it was perfectly smooth, then had me divide it once—just the once—then pin it in a plain knot at the back of my head. He had Dainty wash her hair, too, and when I had combed and re-combed mine, and pinned and re-pinned it, until he was satisfied, he made me comb and pin hers in a matching style, as if hers was the lady's, Miss Lilly's. He fussed about us like a regular girl. When we had finished, Dainty and I looked that plain and bacon-faced, we might have been trying for places in a nunnery. John said if they would only put pictures of us in the dairies, it would be a new way of curdling milk.

When Dainty heard that she pulled the pins from her hair and threw them at the fire. Some had hair still clinging to them, and the flames set it hissing.

'Can't you do anything to that girl of yours,' said Mr Ibbs to John, 'but make her cry?'

John laughed. 'I likes to see her cry,' he said. 'It makes her sweat the less.'

He was an evil boy, all right.

But he was quite caught up in Gentleman's plot, despite himself. We all were. For the first time I ever knew, Mr Ibbs kept the blind pulled down on his shop door and let his brazier go cold. When people came knocking with keys to be cut, he sent them away. To the two or three thieves that brought poke, he shook his head.

'Can't do it, my son. Not to-day. Got a little something cooking.'

He only had Phil come, early in the morning. He sat him down and ran him through the points of a list that Gentleman had drawn up the night before; then Phil pulled his cap down over his eyes, and left. When he came back two hours later it was with a bag and a canvas-covered trunk, that he had got from a man he knew, who ran a crooked warehouse at the river.

The trunk was for me to take to the country. In the bag was a brown stuff dress, more or less my size; and a cloak, and shoes, and black silk stockings; and on top of it all, a heap of lady's real white underthings.

Mr Ibbs only undid the string at the neck of the bag, peeped in, and saw the linen; then he went and sat at the far side of the kitchen, where he had a Bramah lock he liked sometimes to take apart, and powder, and put back together. He made John go with him and hold the screws. Gentleman, however, took out the lady's items one by one, and placed them flat upon the table. Beside the table he set a kitchen chair.

'Now, Sue,' he said, 'suppose this chair's Miss Lilly. How shall you dress her? Let's say you start with the stockings and drawers.'

'The drawers?' I said. 'You don't mean, she's naked?'

Dainty put her hand to her mouth and tittered. She was sitting at Mrs Sucksby's feet, having her hair re-curled.

'Naked?' said Gentleman. 'Why, as a nail. What else? She must take off her clothes when they grow foul; she must take them off to bathe. It will be your job to receive them when she does. It will be your job to pass her her fresh ones.'

I had not thought of this. I wondered how it would be to have to stand and hand a pair of drawers to a strange bare girl. A strange bare girl had once run, shrieking, down Lant Street, with a police-man and a nurse behind her. Suppose Miss Lilly took fright like that, and I had to grab her? I blushed, and Gentleman saw. 'Come now,' he said, almost smiling. 'Don't say you're squeamish?'

I tossed my head, to show I wasn't. He nodded, then took up a pair of the stockings, and then a pair of drawers. He placed them, dangling, over the seat of the kitchen chair.

'What next?' he asked me.

I shrugged. 'Her shimmy, I suppose.'

'Her chemise, you must call it,' he said. 'And you must make sure to warm it, before she puts it on.'

He took the shimmy up and held it close to the kitchen fire. Then he put it carefully above the drawers, over the back of the chair, as if the chair was wearing it.

'Now, her corset,' he said next. 'She will want you to tie this for her, tight as you like. Come on, let's see you do it.'

He put the corset about the shimmy, with the laces at the back; and while he leaned upon the chair to hold it fast, he made me pull the laces and knot them in a bow. They left lines of red and white upon my palms, as if I had been whipped.

'Why don't she wear the kind of stays that fasten at the front, like a regular girl?' said Dainty, watching.

'Because then,' said Gentleman, 'she shouldn't need a maid. And if she didn't need a maid, she shouldn't know she was a lady. Hey?' He winked.

After the corset came a camisole, and after that a dicky; then came a nine-hoop crinoline, and then more petticoats, this time of silk. Then Gentleman had Dainty run upstairs for a bottle of Mrs Sucksby's scent, and he had me spray it where the splintered wood of the chair-back showed between the ribbons of the shimmy, that he said would be Miss Lilly's throat.

And all the time I must say:

'Will you raise your arms, miss, for me to straighten this frill?' and,

'Do you care for it, miss, with a ruffle or a flounce?' and,

'Are you ready for it now, miss?'

'Do you like it drawn tight?'

'Should you like it to be tighter?'

'Oh! Forgive me if I pinch.'

At last, with all the bending and the fussing, I grew hot as a pig. Miss Lilly sat before us with her corset tied hard, her petticoats spread out about the floor, smelling fresh as a rose; but rather wanting, of course, about the shoulders and the neck.

John said, 'Don't say much, do she?' He had been sneaking glances at us all this time, while Mr Ibbs put the powder to his Bramah.

'She's a lady,' said Gentleman, stroking his beard, 'and naturally shy. But she'll pick up like anything, with Sue and me to teach her. Won't you, darling?'

He squatted at the side of the chair and smoothed his fingers over the bulging skirts; then he dipped his hand beneath them, reaching high into the layers of silk. He did it so neatly, it looked to me as if he knew his way, all right; and as he reached higher his cheek grew pink, the silk gave a rustle, the crinoline bucked, the chair quivered hard upon the kitchen floor, the joints of its legs faintly shrieking. Then it was still.

'There, you sweet little bitch,' he said softly. He drew out his hand and held up a stocking. He passed it to me, and yawned. 'Now, let's say it's bed-time.'

John still watched us, saying nothing, only blinking and jiggling his leg. Dainty rubbed her eye, her hair half curled, smelling powerfully of toffee.

I began at the ribbons at the waist of the dickies, then let loose the laces of the corset and eased it free.

'Will you just lift your foot, miss, for me to take this from you?'

'Will you breathe a little softer, miss? and then it will come.'

He kept me working like that for an hour or more. Then he warmed up a flat-iron.

'Spit on this, will you, Dainty?' he said, holding it to her. She did; and when the spit gave a sizzle he took out a cigarette, and lit it on the iron's hot base. Then, while he stood by and smoked, Mrs Sucksby—who had once, long ago, in the days before she ever thought of farming infants, been a mangling-woman in a laundry— showed me how a lady's linen should be pressed and folded; and that, I should say, took about another hour.

Then Gentleman sent me upstairs, to put on the dress that Phil had got for me. It was a plain brown dress, more or less the colour of my hair; and the walls of our kitchen being also brown, when I came downstairs again I could hardly be seen. I should have rathered a blue gown, or a violet one; but Gentleman said it was the perfect dress for a sneak or for a servant—and so all the more perfect for me, who was going to Briar to be both.

We laughed at that; and then, when I had walked about the room to grow used to the skirt (which was narrow), and to let Dainty see where the cut was too large and needed stitching, he had me stand and try a curtsey. This was harder than it sounds. Say what you like about the kind of life I was used to, it was a life without masters: I had never curtseyed before to anyone. Now Gentleman had me

dipping up and down until I thought I should be sick. He said curt-
seying came as natural to ladies' maids, as passing wind. He said if
I would only get the trick, I should never forget it—and he was right
about that, at least, for I can still dip a proper curtsey, even now.—
Or could, if I cared to.

Well. When we had finished with the curtseys he had me learn
my story. Then, to test me, he made me stand before him and repeat
my part, like a girl saying a catechism.

'Now then,' he said. 'What is your name?'

'Ain't it Susan?' I said.

'Ain't it Susan, what?'

'Ain't it Susan Trinder?'

'Ain't it Susan, *sir*. You must remember, I shan't be Gentleman to
you at Briar. I shall be Mr Richard Rivers. You must call me sir; and
you must call Mr Lilly sir; and the lady you must call miss or Miss
Lilly or Miss Maud, as she directs you. And we shall all call you
Susan.' He frowned. 'But, not Susan Trinder. That may lead them
back to Lant Street if things go wrong. We must find you a better
second name—'

'Valentine,' I said, straight off. What can I tell you? I was only
seventeen. I had a weakness for hearts. Gentleman heard me, and
curled his lip.

'Perfect,' he said; '—if we were about to put you on the stage.'

'I know real girls named Valentine!' I said.

'That's true,' said Dainty. 'Floy Valentine, and her two sisters.
Lord, I hates those girls, though. You don't want to be named for
them, Sue.'

I bit my finger. 'Maybe not.'

'Certainly not,' said Gentleman. 'A fanciful name might ruin us.
This is a life-and-death business. We need a name that will hide you,
not bring you to everyone's notice. We need a name'—he thought it
over—'an untraceable name, yet one we shall remember . . . Brown?
To match your dress? Or—yes, why not? Let's make it, *Smith*. Susan
Smith.' He smiled. 'You are to be a sort of smith, after all. This sort,
I mean.'

He let his hand drop, and turned it, and crooked his middle

finger; and the sign, and the word he meant—*fingersmith*—being
Borough code for thief, we laughed again.

At last he coughed, and wiped his eyes. 'Dear me, what fun,' he
said. 'Now, where had we got to? Ah, yes. Tell me again. What is
your name?'

I said it, with the *sir* after.

'Very good. And what is your home?'

'My home is at London, sir,' I said. 'My mother being dead, I
live with my old aunty; which is the lady what used to be your
nurse when you was a boy, sir.'

He nodded. 'Very good as to detail. Not so good, however, as to
style. Come now: I know Mrs Sucksby raised you better than that.
You're not selling violets. Say it again.'

I pulled a face; but then said, more carefully,

'The lady that used to be your nurse when you were a boy, sir.'

'Better, better. And what was your situation, before this?'

'With a kind lady, sir, in Mayfair; who, being lately married and
about to go to India, will have a native girl to dress her, and so
won't need me.'

'Dear me. You are to be pitied, Sue.'

'I believe so, sir.'

'And are you grateful to Miss Lilly, for having you at Briar?'

'Oh, sir! Gratitude ain't in it!'

'Violets again!' He waved his hand. 'Never mind, that will do.
But don't hold my gaze so boldly, will you? Look, rather, at my
shoe. That's good. Now, tell me this. This is important. What are
your duties while attending your new mistress?'

'I must wake her in the mornings,' I said, 'and pour out her tea.
I must wash her, and dress her, and brush her hair. I must keep her
jewellery neat, and not steal it. I must walk with her when she has
a fancy to walk, and sit when she fancies sitting. I must carry her fan
for when she grows too hot, her wrap for when she feels nippy, her
eau-de-Cologne for if she gets the head-ache, and her salts for when
she comes over queer. I must be her chaperon for her drawing-
lessons, and not see when she blushes.'

'Splendid! And what is your character?'

'Honest as the day.'

'And what is your object, that no-one but we must know?'

'That she will love you, and leave her uncle for your sake. That she will make your fortune; and that you, Mr Rivers, will make mine.'

I took hold of my skirts and showed him one of those smooth curtseys, my eyes all the time on the toe of his boot.

Dainty clapped me. Mrs Sucksby rubbed her hands together and said,

'Three thousand pounds, Sue. Oh, my crikey! Dainty, pass me an infant, I want something to squeeze.'

Gentleman stepped aside and lit a cigarette. 'Not bad,' he said. 'Not bad, at all. A little fining down, I think, is all that's needed now. We shall try again later.'

'Later?' I said. 'Oh, Gentleman, ain't you finished with me yet? If Miss Lilly will have me as her maid for the sake of pleasing you, why should she care how fined down I am?'

'*She* may not mind,' he answered. 'I think we might put an apron on Charley Wag and send him, for all she will mind or wonder. But it is not only her that you will have to fool. There is the old man, her uncle; and besides him, all his staff.'

I said, 'His staff?' I had not thought of this.

'Of course,' he said. 'Do you think a great house runs itself? First of all there's the steward, Mr Way—'

'Mr Way!' said John with a snort. 'Do they call him Milky?'

'No,' said Gentleman. He turned back to me. 'Mr Way,' he said again. 'I should say he won't trouble you much, though. But there is also Mrs Stiles, the housekeeper—she may study you a little harder, you must be careful with her. And then there is Mr Way's boy Charles, and I suppose one or two girls, for the kitchen work; and one or two parlourmaids; and grooms and stable-boys and gardeners—but you shan't see much of them, don't think of them.'

I looked at him in horror. I said, 'You never said about them before. Mrs Sucksby, did he say about them? Did he say, there will be about a hundred servants, that I shall have to play the maid for?'

Mrs Sucksby had a baby and was rolling it like dough. 'Be fair now, Gentleman,' she said, not looking over. 'You did keep very dark about the servants last night.'

He shrugged. 'A detail,' he said.

A detail? That was like him. Telling you half of a story and making out you had it all.

But it was too late now, for a change of heart. The next day Gentleman worked me hard again; and the day after that he got a letter, from Miss Lilly.

He got it at the post-office in the City. Our neighbours would have wondered what was up, if we'd had a letter come to the house. He got it, and brought it back, and opened it while we looked on; then we sat in silence, to hear it—Mr Ibbs only drumming his fingers a little on the table-top, by which I knew that he was nervous; and so grew more nervous myself.

The letter was a short one. Miss Lilly said, first, what a pleasure it was, to have received Mr Rivers's note; and how thoughtful he was, and how kind to his old nurse. She was sure, she wished more gentlemen were as kind and as thoughtful as him!

Her uncle got on very badly, she said, now his assistant was gone. The house seemed very changed and quiet and dull; perhaps this was the weather, which seemed to have turned. As for her maid— Here Gentleman tilted the letter, the better to catch the light.—As for her maid, poor Agnes: she was pleased to be able to tell him that Agnes looked set not to die after all—

We heard that and drew in our breaths. Mrs Sucksby closed her eyes, and I saw Mr Ibbs give a glance at his cold brazier and reckon up the business he had lost in the past two days. But then Gentleman smiled. The maid was not about to die; but her health was so ruined and her spirits so low, they were sending her back to Cork.

'God bless the Irish!' said Mr Ibbs, taking out his handkerchief and wiping his head.

Gentleman read on.

'I shall be glad to see the girl you speak of,' Miss Lilly wrote. 'I should be glad if you would send her to me, at once. I am grateful to anyone for remembering me. I am not over-used to people thinking of my comforts. If she be only a good and willing girl, then I am sure I shall love her. And she will be the dearer to me, Mr Rivers, because she will have come to me from London, that has *you* in it.'

He smiled again, raised the letter to his mouth, and passed it back and forth across his lips. His snide ring glittered in the light of the lamps.

It had all turned out, of course, just as the clever devil had promised.

That night—that was to be my last night at Lant Street, and the first night of all the nights that were meant to lead to Gentleman's securing of Miss Lilly's fortune—that night Mr Ibbs sent out for a hot roast supper, and put irons to heat in the fire, for making flip, in celebration.

The supper was a pig's head, stuffed at the ears—a favourite of mine, and got in my honour. Mr Ibbs took the carving-knife to the back-door step, put up his sleeves, and stooped to sharpen the blade. He leaned with his hand on the door-post, and I watched him do it with a queer sensation at the roots of my hair: for all up the post were cuts from where, each Christmas Day when I was a girl, he had laid the knife upon my head to see how high I'd grown. Now he drew the blade back and forth across the stone, until it sang; then he handed it to Mrs Sucksby and she dished out the meat. She always carved, in our house. An ear apiece, for Mr Ibbs and Gentleman; the snout for John and Dainty; and the cheeks, that were the tenderest parts, for herself and for me.

It was all got, as I've said, in my honour. But, I don't know—perhaps it was seeing the marks on the door-post; perhaps it was thinking of the soup that Mrs Sucksby would make, when I wouldn't be there to eat it, with the bones of the roast pig's head; perhaps it was the head itself—which seemed to me to be grimacing, rather, the lashes of its eyes and the bristles of its snout gummed brown with treacly tears—but as we sat about the table, I grew sad. John and Dainty wolfed their dinner down, laughing and quarrelling, now and then firing up when Gentleman teased, and now and then sulking. Mr Ibbs went neatly to work on his plate, and

Mrs Sucksby went neatly to work on hers; and I picked over my bit of pork and had no appetite.

I gave half to Dainty. She gave it to John. He snapped his jaws and howled, like a dog.

And then, when the plates were cleared away Mr Ibbs beat the eggs and the sugar and the rum, to make flip. He filled seven glasses, took the irons from the brazier, waved them for a second to take the sting of the heat off, then plunged them in. Heating the flip was like setting fire to the brandy on a plum pudding—everyone liked to see it done and hear the drinks go hiss. John said, 'Can I do one, Mr Ibbs?'—his face red from the supper, and shiny like paint, like the face of a boy in a picture in a toy-shop window.

We sat, and everyone talked and laughed, saying what a fine thing it would be when Gentleman was made rich, and I came home with my cool three thousand; and still I kept rather quiet, and no-one seemed to notice. At last Mrs Sucksby patted her stomach and said,

'Won't you give us a tune, Mr Ibbs, to put the baby to bed by?'

Mr Ibbs could whistle like a kettle, for an hour at a go. He put his glass aside and wiped the flip from his moustache, and started up with 'The Tarpaulin Jacket'. Mrs Sucksby hummed along until her eyes grew damp, and then the hum got broken. Her husband had been a sailor, and been lost at sea.—Lost to her, I mean. He lived in the Bermudas.

'Handsome,' she said, when the song was finished. 'But let's have a lively one next, for heaven's sake!—else I shall be drove quite maudlin. Let's see the youngsters have a bit of a dance.'

Mr Ibbs struck up with a quick tune then, and Mrs Sucksby clapped, and John and Dainty got up and pushed the chairs back. 'Will you hold my earrings for me, Mrs Sucksby?' said Dainty. They danced the polka until the china ornaments upon the mantel-piece jumped and the dust rose inches high about their thumping feet. Gentleman stood and leaned and watched them, smoking a cigarette, calling 'Hup!' and 'Go it, Johnny!', as he might call, laughing, to a terrier in a fight he had no bet on.

When they asked me to join them, I said I would not. The dust made me sneeze and, after all, the iron that had warmed my flip had been heated too hard, and the egg had curdled. Mrs Sucksby had put by a glass and a plate of morsels of meat for Mr Ibbs's sister, and I said I would carry them up.—'All right, dear girl,' she said, still clapping out the beat. I took the plate and the glass and a candle, and slipped upstairs.

It was like stepping out of heaven, I always thought, to leave our kitchen on a winter's night. Even so, when I had left the food beside Mr Ibbs's sleeping sister and seen to one or two of the babies, that had woken with the sounds of the dancing below, I did not go back to join the others. I walked the little way along the landing, to the door of the room I shared with Mrs Sucksby; and then I went up the next pair of stairs, to the little attic I had been born in.

This room was always cold. Tonight there was a breeze up, the window was loose, and it was colder than ever. The floor was plain boards, with strips of drugget on it. The walls were bare, but for a bit of blue oil-cloth that had been tacked to catch the splashes from a wash-stand. The stand, at the moment, was draped with a waist-coat and a shirt, of Gentleman's, and one or two collars. He always slept here, when he came to visit; though he might have made a bed with Mr Ibbs, down in the kitchen. I know which place I would have chosen. On the floor sagged his high leather boots, that he had scraped the mud from and shined. Beside them was his bag, with more white linen spilling from it. On the seat of a chair were some coins from his pocket, a packet of cigarettes, and sealing-wax. The coins were light. The wax was brittle, like toffee.

The bed was roughly made. There was a red velvet curtain upon it, with the rings taken off, for a counterpane: it had been got from a burning house, and still smelt of cinders. I took it up and put it about my shoulders, like a cloak. Then I pinched out the flame of my candle and stood at the window, shivering, looking out at the roofs and chimneys, and at the Horsemonger Lane Gaol where my mother was hanged.

The glass of the window had the first few blooms of a new frost upon it, and I held my finger to it, to make the ice turn to dirty water. I could still catch Mr Ibbs's whistle and the bounce of

Dainty's feet, but before me the streets of the Borough were dark. There was only here and there a feeble light at a window like mine, and then the lantern of a coach, throwing shadows; and then a person, running hard against the cold, quick and dark as the shadows, and as quickly come and gone. I thought of all the thieves that must be there, and all the thieves' children; and then of all the regular men and women who lived their lives—their strange and ordinary lives—in other houses, other streets, in the brighter parts of London. I thought of Maud Lilly, in her great house. She did not know my name—I had not known hers, three days before. She did not know that I was standing, plotting her ruin, while Dainty Warren and John Vroom danced a polka in my kitchen.

What was she like? I knew a girl named Maud once, she had half a lip. She used to like to make out that the other half had been lost in a fight; I knew for a fact, however, she had been born like that, she couldn't fight putty. She died in the end—not from fighting, but through eating bad meat. Just one bit of bad meat killed her, just like that.

But, she was very dark. Gentleman had said that the other Maud, his Maud, was fair and rather handsome. But when I thought of her, I could picture her only as thin and brown and straight, like the kitchen chair that I had tied the corset to.

I tried another curtsey. The velvet curtain made me clumsy. I tried again. I began to sweat, in sudden fear.

Then there came the opening of the kitchen door and the sound of footsteps on the stair, and then Mrs Sucksby's voice, calling for me. I didn't answer. I heard her walk to the bedrooms below, and look for me there; then there was a silence, then her feet again, upon the attic stairs, and then came the light of her candle. The climb made her sigh a little—only a little, for she was very nimble, for all that she was rather stout.

'Are you here then, Sue?' she said quietly. 'And all on your own, in the dark?'

She looked about her, at all that I had looked at—at the coins and the sealing-wax, and Gentleman's boots and leather bag. Then she came to me, and put her warm, dry hand to my cheek, and I said—. just as if she had tickled or pinched me, and the words were a chuckle or a cry I could not stop—I said:

'What if I ain't up to it, Mrs Sucksby? What if I can't do it? Suppose I lose my nerve and let you down? Hadn't we ought to send Dainty, after all?'

She shook her head and smiled. 'Now, then,' she said. She led me to the bed, and we sat and she drew down my head until it rested in her lap, and she put back the curtain from my cheek and stroked my hair. 'Now, then.'

'Ain't it a long way to go?' I said, looking up at her face.

'Not so far,' she answered.

'Shall you think of me, while I am there?'

She drew free a strand of hair that was caught about my ear.

'Every minute,' she said, quietly. 'Ain't you my own girl? And won't I worry? But you shall have Gentleman by you. I should never have let you go, for any ordinary villain.'

That was true, at least. But still my heart beat fast. I thought again of Maud Lilly, sitting sighing in her room, waiting for me to come and unlace her stays and hold her nightgown before the fire. *Poor lady*, Dainty had said.

I chewed at the inside of my lip. Then: 'Ought I to do it, though, Mrs Sucksby?' I said. 'Ain't it a very mean trick, and shabby?'

She held my gaze, then raised her eyes and nodded to the view beyond the window. She said, 'I know *she* would have done it, and not given it a thought. And I know what she would feel in her heart—what dread, but also what pride, and the pride part winning—to see you doing it now.'

That made me thoughtful. For a minute, we sat and said nothing. And what I asked her next was something I had never asked before—something which, in all my years at Lant Street, amongst all those dodgers and thieves, I had never heard anyone ask, not ever. I said, in a whisper,

'Do you think it hurts, Mrs Sucksby, when they drop you?'

Her hand, that was smoothing my hair, grew still. Then it started up stroking, sure as before. She said,

'I should say you don't feel nothing but the rope about your neck. Rather ticklish, I should think it.'

'Ticklish?'

'Say then, pricklish.'

Still her hand kept smoothing.

'But when the drop is opened?' I said. 'Wouldn't you say you felt it then?'

She shifted her leg. 'Perhaps a twitch,' she admitted, 'when the drop is opened.'

I thought of the men I had seen fall at Horsemonger Lane. They twitched, all right. They twitched and kicked about, like monkeys on sticks.

'But it comes that quick at the last,' she went on then, 'that I rather think the quickness must take the pain clean out of it. And when it comes to dropping a lady—well, you know they place the knot in such a way, Sue, that the end comes all the quicker?'

I looked up at her again. She had set her candle on the floor, and the light striking her face all from beneath, it made her cheeks seem swollen and her eyes seem old. I shivered, and she moved her hand to my shoulder and rubbed me, hard, through the velvet.

Then she tilted her head. 'There's Mr Ibbs's sister, quite bewildered again,' she said, 'and calling on her mother. She has been calling on her, poor soul, these fifteen years. I shouldn't like to come to that, Sue. I should say that, of all the ways a body might go, the quick and the neat way might, after all, be best.'

She said it; and then she winked.

She said it, and seemed to mean it.

I do sometimes wonder, however, whether she mightn't only have said it to be kind.

But I didn't think that then. I only rose and kissed her, and made my hair neat where she had stroked it loose; and then came the thud of the kitchen door again, and this time heavier feet upon the stairs, and then Dainty's voice.

'Where are you, Sue? Ain't you coming for a dance? Mr Ibbs has got his wind up, we're having a right old laugh down here.'

Her shout woke half the babies, and that half woke the other. But

Mrs Sucksby said that she would see to them, and I went back down, and this time I did dance, with Gentleman as my partner. He held me in a waltz-step. He was drunk and held me tight. John danced again with Dainty, and we bumped about the kitchen for a half-an-hour—Gentleman all the time still calling, 'Go it, Johnny!' and 'Come up, boy! Come up!', and Mr Ibbs stopping once to rub a bit of butter on his lips, to keep the whistle sweet.

Next day, at midday, was when I left them. I packed all my bits of stuff into the canvas-covered trunk and wore the plain brown dress and the cloak and, over my flat hair, a bonnet. I had learned as much as Gentleman could teach me after three days' work. I knew my story and my new name—Susan Smith. There was only one more thing that needed to be done, and as I sat taking my last meal in that kitchen—which was bread and dried meat, the meat rather too dried, and clinging to my gums—Gentleman did it. He brought from his bag a piece of paper and a pen and some ink, and wrote me out a character.

He wrote it off in a moment. Of course, he was used to faking papers. He held it up for the ink to dry, then read it out. It began:

'*To whom it might concern. Lady Alice Dunraven, of Whelk Street, Mayfair, recommends Miss Susan Smith*'—and it went on like that, I forget the rest of it, but it sounded all right to me. He placed it flat again and signed it in a lady's curling hand. Then he held it to Mrs Sucksby.

'What do you think, Mrs S?' he said, smiling. 'Will that get Sue her situation?'

But Mrs Sucksby said she couldn't hope to judge it.

'You know best, dear boy,' she said, looking away.

Of course, if we ever took help at Lant Street, it wasn't character we looked for so much as lack of it. There was a little dwarfish girl that used to come sometimes, to boil the babies' napkins and to wash the floors; but she was a thief. We couldn't have had honest girls come. They would have seen enough in three minutes of the business of the house to do for us all. We couldn't have had that.

So Mrs Sucksby waved the paper away, and Gentleman read it through a second time, then winked at me, then folded it and sealed it and put it in my trunk. I swallowed the last of my dried meat and bread, and fastened my cloak. There was only Mrs Sucksby to say good-bye to. John Vroom and Dainty never got up before one. Mr Ibbs was gone to crack a safe at Bow: he had kissed my cheek an hour before, and given me a shilling. I put my hat on. It was a dull brown thing, like my dress. Mrs Sucksby set it straight. Then she put her hands to my face and smiled.

'God bless you, Sue!' she said. 'You are making us rich!'

But then her smile grew awful. I had never been parted from her before, for more than a day. She turned away, to hide her falling tears.

'Take her quick,' she said to Gentleman. 'Take her quick, and don't let me see it!'

And so he put his arm about my shoulders and led me from the house. He found a boy to walk behind us, carrying my trunk. He meant to take me to a cab-stand and drive me to the station at Paddington, and see me on my train.

The day was a miserable one. Even so, it was not so often I got to cross the water, and I said I should like to walk as far as Southwark Bridge, to look at the view. I had thought I should see all of London from there; but the fog grew thicker the further we went. At the bridge it seemed worst of all. You could see the black dome of St Paul's, the barges on the water; you could see all the dark things of the city, but not the fair—the fair were lost or made like shadows.

'Queer thing, to think of the river down there,' said Gentleman, peering over the edge. He leaned, and spat.

We had not bargained on the fog. It made the traffic slow to a crawl, and though we found a cab, after twenty minutes we paid the driver off and walked again. I had been meant to catch the one o'clock train; now, stepping fast across some great square, we heard that hour struck out, and then the quarter, and then the half—all maddeningly damp and half-hearted, they sounded, as if the clap-

pers and the bells that rung them had been wound about with flannel.

'Had we not rather turn around,' I said, 'and try again tomorrow?'

But Gentleman said there would be a driver and a trap sent out to
Marlow, to meet my train there; and I had better be late, he thought,
than not arrive at all.

But after all, when we got to Paddington at last we found the
trains all delayed and made slow, just like the traffic: we had to
wait another hour then, until the guard should raise the signal that
the Bristol train—which was to be my train as far as Maidenhead,
where I must get off and join another—was ready to be boarded.
We stood beneath the ticking clock, fidgeting and blowing on our
hands. They had lit the great lamps there, but the fog having come
in and mixed with the steam, it drifted from arch to arch and made
the light very poor. The walls were hung with black, from the death
of Prince Albert; the crape had got streaked by birds. I thought it
very gloomy, for so grand a place. And of course, there was a vast
press of people beside us, all waiting and cursing, or jostling by, or
letting their children and their dogs run into our legs.

'Fuck this,' said Gentleman in a hard peevish voice, when the
wheel of a bath-chair ran over his toe. He stooped to wipe the dust
from his boot, then straightened and lit up a cigarette, then
coughed. He had his collar turned high and wore a black slouch hat.
His eyes were yellow at the whites, as if stained with flip. He did
not, at that moment, look like a man a girl would go silly over.

He coughed again. 'Fuck this cheap tobacco, too,' he said, pulling
free a strand that had come loose on his tongue. Then he caught my
eye and his face changed. 'Fuck this cheap life, in all its forms—eh,
Suky? No more of that for you and me, soon.'

I looked away from him, saying nothing. I had danced a fast
waltz with him the night before; now, away from Lant Street and
Mrs Sucksby and Mr Ibbs, amongst all the men and women that
were gathered grumbling about us, he seemed just another stranger,
and I was shy of him. I thought, *You're nothing to me*. And again I
almost said that we ought to turn round and go home; but I knew

that if I did he would grow more peevish and show his temper; and
so, I did not.

He finished his smoke, then smoked another. He went off for a
piddle, and I went off for a piddle of my own. I heard a whistle
blown as I was tidying my skirts; and when I got back, I found the
guard had sent out the word and half the crowd had started up
and was making in a great sweating rush for the waiting train. We
went with them, Gentleman leading me to a second-class coach,
then handing up my trunk to the man who was fixing the bags and
boxes on the roof. I took a place beside a white-faced woman with
a baby on her arm; across from her were two stout farmer-types. I
think she was glad to see me get on, for of course, me being
dressed so neat and comely, she couldn't tell—ha ha!—that I was
a thieving Borough girl. Behind me came a boy and his old dad,
with a canary in a cage. The boy sat beside the farmers. The old
dad sat by me. The coach tilted and creaked, and we all put back
our heads and stared at the bits of dust and varnish that tumbled
from the ceiling where the luggage thumped and slithered about
above.

The door hung open another minute and then was closed. In all
the fuss of getting aboard I had hardly looked at Gentleman. He
had handed me on, then turned to talk with the guard. Now he
came to the open window and said,

'I'm afraid you may be very late, Sue. But I think the trap will
wait for you at Marlow. I am sure it will wait. You must hope that
it will.'

I knew at once that it would not, and felt a rush of misery and
fear. I said quickly,

'Come with me, can't you? And see me to the house?'

But how could he do that? He shook his head and looked sorry.
The two farmer-types, the woman, the boy and the old dad all
watched us—wondering I suppose what house we meant, and what
a man in a slouch hat, with a voice like that, was doing talking to a
girl like me about it.

Then the porter climbed down from the roof, there came another
whistle, the train gave a horrible lurch and began to move off.

Gentleman lifted up his hat and followed until the engine got up its speed; then he gave it up—I saw him turn, put his hat back on, twist up his collar. Then he was gone. The coach creaked harder and began to sway. The woman and the men put their hands to the leather straps; the boy put his face to the window. The canary put its beak to the bars of its cage. The baby began to cry. It cried for half an hour.

'Ain't you got any gin?' I said to the woman at last.

'Gin?' she said—like I might have said, poison. Then she made a mouth, and showed me her shoulder—not so pleased to have me sitting by her, the uppity bitch, after all.

What with her and the baby, and the fluttering bird; and the old dad—who fell asleep and snorted; and the boy—who made paper pellets; and the farmer-types—who smoked and grew bilious; and the fog—that made the train jerk and halt and arrive at Maidenhead two hours later than its time, so that I missed one Marlow train and must wait for the next one—what with all that, my journey was very wretched. I had not brought any food with me, for we had all supposed I should arrive at Briar in time to take a servant's tea there. I had not had a morsel since that dinner of bread and dried meat, at noon: it had stuck to my gums then, but I should have called it wonderful at Maidenhead, seven hours later. The station there was not like Paddington, where there were coffee-stalls and milk-stalls and a pastry-cook's shop. There was only one place for vittles, and that was shut up and closed. I sat on my trunk. My eyes stung, from the fog. When I blew my nose, I turned a handkerchief black. A man saw me do it. 'Don't cry,' he said, smiling.

'I ain't crying!' I said.

He winked, then asked me my name.

It was one thing to flirt in town, however. But I wasn't in town now. I wouldn't answer. When the train came for Marlow I sat at the back of a coach, and he sat at the front, but with his face my way— he tried for an hour to catch my eye. I remembered Dainty saying that she had sat on a train once, with a gentleman near, and he had opened his trousers and showed her his cock, and asked her to hold it; and she had held it, and he had given her a pound. I wondered

. what I would do, if this man asked me to touch his cock—whether I would scream, or look the other way, or touch it, or what.

But then, I hardly needed the pound, where I was headed!

Anyway, money like that was hard to move on. Dainty had never been able to spend hers for fear her father should see it and know she'd been gay. She hid it behind a loose brick in the wall of the starch works, and put a special mark on the brick, that only she would know. She said she would tell it on her death-bed, and we could use the pound to bury her.

Well, the man on my train watched me very hard, but if he had his trousers open I never saw; and at last he tilted his hat to me and got off. There were more stops after that, and at every one someone else got off, from further down along the train; and no-one got on. The stations grew smaller and darker, until finally there was nothing at them but a tree—there was nothing to see anywhere, but trees, and beyond them bushes, and beyond them fog—grey fog, not brown—with the black night sky above it. And when the trees and the bushes seemed just about at their thickest, and the sky was blacker than I should have thought a sky naturally could be, the train stopped a final time; and that was Marlow.

Here no-one got off save me. I was the last passenger of all. The guard called the stop, and came to lift down my trunk. He said,

'You'll want that carrying. Is there no-one come to meet you?'

I told him there was supposed to be a man with a trap, to take me up to Briar. He said, Did I mean the trap that came to fetch the post? That would have been and gone, three hours before. He looked me over.

'Come down from London, have you?' he said. Then he called to the driver, who was looking from his cab. 'She've come down from London, meant for Briar. I told her, the Briar trap will have come and gone.'

'That'll have come and gone, that will,' called the driver. 'That'll have come and gone, I should say three hours back.'

I stood and shivered. It was colder here than at home. It was colder and darker and the air smelt queer, and the people—didn't I say it?—the people were howling simpletons.

I said, 'Ain't there a cab-man could take me?'

'A cab-man?' said the guard. He shouted it to the driver. 'Wants a cab-man!'

'A cab-man!'

They laughed until they coughed. The guard took out a hand-kerchief and wiped his mouth, saying, 'Dearie me, oh! dearie, dearie me. A cab-man, at Marlow!'

'Oh, fuck off,' I said. 'Fuck off, the pair of you.'

And I caught up my trunk and walked with it to where I could see one or two lights shining, that I thought must be the houses of the village. The guard said, 'Why, you hussy—! I shall let Mr Way know about you. See what he thinks—you bringing your London tongue down here—!'

I can't say what I meant to do next. I did not know how far it was to Briar. I did not even know which road I ought to take. London was forty miles away, and I was afraid of cows and bulls.

But after all, country roads aren't like city ones. There are only about four of them, and they all go to the same place in the end. I started to walk, and had walked a minute when there came, behind me, the sound of hooves and creaking wheels. And then a cart drew alongside me, and the driver pulled up and lifted up a lantern, to look at my face.

'You'll be Susan Smith,' he said, 'come down from London. Miss Maud've been fretting after you all day.'

He was an oldish man and his name was William Inker. He was Mr Lilly's groom. He took my trunk and helped me into the seat beside his own, and geed up the horse; and when—being struck by the breeze as we drove—he felt me shiver, he reached for a tartan blanket for me to put about my legs.

It was six or seven miles to Briar, and he took it at an easy sort of trot, smoking a pipe. I told him about the fog—there was still something of a mist, even now, even there—and the slow trains.

He said, 'That's London. Known for its fogs, ain't it? Been much down to the country before?'

'Not much,' I said.

'Been maiding in the city, have you? Good place, your last one?'

'Pretty good,' I said.

'Rum way of speaking you've got, for a lady's maid,' he said then. 'Been to France ever?'

I took a second, smoothing the blanket out over my lap.

'Once or twice,' I said.

'Short kind of chaps, the French chaps, I expect? In the leg, I mean.'

Now, I only knew one Frenchman—a housebreaker, they called him Jack the German, I don't know why. He was tall enough; but I said, to please William Inker,

'Shortish, I suppose.'

'I expect so,' he said.

The road was perfectly quiet and perfectly dark, and I imagined the sound of the horse, and the wheels, and our voices, carrying far across the fields. Then I heard, from rather near, the slow tolling of a bell—a very mournful sound, it seemed to me at that moment, not like the cheerful bells of London. It tolled nine times.

'That's the Briar bell, sounding the hour,' said William Inker.

We sat in silence after that, and in a little time we reached a high stone wall and took a road that ran beside it. Soon the wall became a great arch, and then I saw behind it the roof and the pointed win-dows of a greyish house, half-covered with ivy. I thought it a grand enough crib, but not so grand nor so grim perhaps as Gentleman had painted it. But when William Inker slowed the horse and I put the blanket from me and reached for my trunk, he said,

'Wait up, sweetheart, we've half a mile yet!' And then, to a man who had appeared with a lantern at the door of the house, he called: 'Good night, Mr Mack. You may shut the gate behind us. Here is Miss Smith, look, safe at last.'

The building I had thought was Briar was only the lodge! I stared, saying nothing, and we drove on past it, between two rows of bare dark trees, that curved as the road curved, then dipped into a kind of hollow, where the air—that had seemed to clear a little, on the open country lanes—grew thick again. So thick it grew, I felt it, damp, upon my face, upon my lashes and lips; and closed my eyes.

Then the dampness passed away. I looked, and stared again. The road had risen, we had broken out from between the lines of trees into a gravel clearing, and here—rising vast and straight and stark out of the woolly fog, with all its windows black or shuttered, and its walls with a dead kind of ivy clinging to them, and a couple of its chimneys sending up threads of a feeble-looking grey smoke—here was Briar, Maud Lilly's great house, that I must now call my home.

We did not cross before the face of it, but kept well to the side, then took up a lane that swung round behind it, where there was a muddle of yards and out-houses and porches, and more dark walls and shuttered windows and the sound of barking dogs. High in one of the buildings was the round white face and great black hands of the clock I had heard striking across the fields. Beneath it, William Inker pulled the horse up, then helped me down. A door was opened in one of the walls and a woman stood gazing at us, her arms folded against the cold.

'There's Mrs Stiles, heard the trap come,' said William. We crossed the yard to join her. Up above us, at a little window, I thought I saw a candle-flame shine, and flutter, and then go out.

The door led to a passage, and this led to a great, bright kitchen, about five times the size of our kitchen at Lant Street, and with pots set in rows upon a whitewashed wall, and a few rabbits hanging on hooks from the beams of the ceiling. At a wide scrubbed table sat a boy, a woman and three or four girls—of course, they looked very hard at me. The girls studied my bonnet and the cut of my cloak. Their frocks and aprons being only servants' wear, I didn't trouble myself to study them.

Mrs Stiles said, 'Well, you're about as late as you could be. Any longer and you should've had to stay at the village. We keep early hours here.'

She was about fifty, with a white cap with frills and a way of not quite looking in your eye as she spoke to you. She carried keys about her, on a chain at her waist. Plain, old-fashioned keys, I could have copied any one of them.

I made her half a curtsey. I did not say—which I might have— that she should be thankful I had not turned back at Paddington;

that I wished I had turned back; and that for anyone to have had the
time that I had had, in trying to get forty miles from London, perhaps went to prove that London wasn't meant to be left—I did not
say that. What I said was:

'I'm sure, I'm very grateful that the trap was sent at all.'

The girls at the table tittered to hear me speak. The woman who
sat with them—the cook, it turned out—got up and set about
making me a supper-tray. William Inker said,

'Miss Smith've come from a pretty fine place in London, Mrs
Stiles. And she've been several times in France.'

'Has she,' said Mrs Stiles.

'Only one or two times,' I said. Now everyone would suppose I
had been boasting.

'She said the chaps there are very short in the leg.'

Mrs Stiles gave a nod. The girls at the table tittered again, and
one of them whispered something that made the boy grow red. But
then my tray was made, and Mrs Stiles said,

'Margaret, you can carry this through to my pantry. Miss Smith,
I suppose I should take you to where you might splash your hands
and face.'

I took this to mean that she would show me to the privy, and I
said I wished she would. She gave me a candle and took me down
another short passage, to another yard, that had an earth closet in it
with paper on a spike.

Then she took me to her own little room. It had a chimney-piece
with white wax flowers on it, and a picture of a sailor in a frame,
that I supposed was Master Stiles, gone off to Sea; and another picture, of an angel, done entirely in black hair, that I presumed was
Mr Stiles, gone off to Glory. She sat and watched me take my
supper. It was mutton, minced, and bread-and-butter; and you may
imagine that, being so hungry as I was, I made very short work of it.
As I ate, there came the slow chiming of the clock that I had heard
before, sounding half-past nine. I said,

'Does the clock chime all night?'

Mrs Stiles nodded. 'All night, and all day, at the hour and the
half. Mr Lilly likes his days run very regular. You'll find that out.'

'And Miss Lilly?' I said, picking crumbs from the corner of my
mouth. 'What does she like?'

She smoothed her apron. 'Miss Maud likes what her uncle likes,'
she answered.

Then she rearranged her lips. She said,

'You'll know, Miss Smith, that Miss Maud is quite a young girl,
for all that she's mistress of this great house. The servants don't
trouble her, for the servants answer to me. I should have said I had
been a housekeeper long enough to know how to secure a maid for
my own mistress—but there, even a housekeeper must do as she is
bid, and Miss Maud've gone quite over my head in this matter.
Quite over my head. I shouldn't have thought that perfectly wise, in
a girl of her years; but we shall see how it turns out.'

I said, 'I am sure whatever Miss Lilly does must turn out well.'

She said, 'I have a great staff of servants, to make sure that it
does. This is a well-kept house, Miss Smith, and I hope you will
take to it. I don't know what you might be used to in your last
place. I don't know what might be considered a lady's maid's duties,
in London. I have never been there'—she had never been to
London!—'so cannot say. But if you mind my other girls, then I am
sure they will mind you. The men and the stable-boys, of course, I
hope I shall never see you talking with more than you can help . . .'

She went on like that for a quarter of an hour—all the time, as I
have mentioned, never quite catching my eye. She told me where I
might walk in the house, and where I must take my meals, and how
much sugar I should be allowed for my own use, and how much
beer, and when I could expect my underclothes laundered. The tea
that was boiled in Miss Maud's teapot, she said, it had been the
habit of the last lady's maid to pass on to the girls in the kitchen.
Likewise the wax-ends from Miss Maud's candle-sticks: they were
to be given to Mr Way. And Mr Way would know how many wax-
ends to expect, since it was him who doled out the candles. Corks
went to Charles, the knife-boy. Bones and skins went to Cook.

'The pieces of soap that Miss Maud leaves in her wash-stand,
however,' she said, 'as being too dry to raise a lather from: those you
may keep.'

Well, that's servants for you—always grubbing over their own little patch. As if I cared, about candle-ends and soap! If I had never quite felt it before, I knew then what it was, to be in expectations of three thousand pounds.

Then she said that if I had finished my supper she would be pleased to show me to my room. But she would have to ask me to be very quiet as we went, for Mr Lilly liked a silent house and couldn't bear upset, and Miss Maud had a set of nerves that were just like his, that wouldn't allow of her being kept from her rest or made fretful.

So she said; and then she took up her lamp, and I took up my candle, and she led me out into the passage and up a dark staircase. 'This is the servants' way,' she said, as we walked, 'that you must always take, unless Miss Maud directs you otherwise.'

Her voice and her tread grew softer the higher we went. At last, when we had climbed three pairs of stairs, she took me to a door, that she said in a whisper was the door to my room. Putting her finger before her lips, she slowly turned the handle.

I had never had a room of my own before. I did not particularly want one, now. But, since I must have one, this one I supposed would do. It was small and plain—would have looked better, perhaps, for a paper garland or two, or a few plaster dogs. But there was a looking-glass upon the mantel and, before the fire, a rug. Beside the bed—William Inker must have brought it up—was my canvas trunk.

Near the head of the bed there was another door, shut quite tight and with no key in it. 'Where does that lead?' I asked Mrs Stiles, thinking it might lead to another passage or a closet.

'That's the door to Miss Maud's room,' she said.

I said, 'Miss Maud is through there, asleep in her bed?'

Perhaps I said it rather loud; but Mrs Stiles gave a shudder, as if I might just have shrieked or sprung a rattle.

'Miss Maud sleeps very poorly,' she answered quietly. 'If she wakes in the night, then she likes her girl to go to her. She won't call out for you, since you are a stranger to her now: we will put Margaret in a chair outside her door, and Margaret shall take her

her breakfast tomorrow, and dress her for the day. After that, you must be ready to be called in and examined.'

She said she hoped Miss Maud would find me pleasing. I said I did, too.

She left me, then. She went very softly, but at the door she paused, to put her hand to the keys at her chain. I saw her do it, and grew quite cold: for she looked all at once like nothing so much as the matron of a gaol. I said, before I could stop myself:

'You're not going to lock me in?'

'Lock you in?' she answered, with a frown. 'Why should I do that?'

I said I didn't know. She looked me over, drew in her chin, then shut the door and left me.

I held up my thumb. *Kiss that!* I thought.

Then I sat upon the bed. It was hard. I wondered if the sheets and blankets had been changed since the last maid left with the scarlatina. It was too dark to see. Mrs Stiles had taken her lamp and I had set my candle down in a draught: the flame of it plunged about and made great black shadows. I unfastened my cloak, but kept it draped about my shoulders. I ached, from the cold and the travelling; and the mince I had eaten had come too late—it sat in my stomach and hurt. It was ten o'clock. We laughed at people who went to bed before midnight, at home.

I might as well have been put in gaol, I thought. A gaol would have been livelier. Here, there was only an awful silence: you listened, and it troubled your ears. And when you got up and went to the window and looked outside, you nearly fainted to see how high you were, and how dark were the yard and the stables, how still and quiet the land beyond.

I remembered the candle I had seen, fluttering at a window as I walked with William Inker. I wondered which room it was that that light had shone from.

I opened my trunk, to look at all the things that I had brought with me from Lant Street—but then, none of them were really mine, they were only the petticoats and shimmies that Gentleman had made me take. I took off my dress, and for a second held it against my face. The dress was not mine, either; but I found the seams that Dainty had made, and smelled them. I thought that her needle had left the scent there, of John Vroom's dog-skin coat.

I thought of the soup that Mrs Sucksby would have made, from the bones of that pig's head; and it was quite as strange as I knew it would be, to imagine them all sitting eating it, perhaps thinking of me, perhaps thinking of something else entirely.

If I had been a crying sort of girl, I should certainly have cried then, imagining that.

But I was never a girl for tears. I changed into my nightgown, put my cloak back on above it, and stood in my stockings and my unbuttoned shoes. I looked at the shut door at the head of the bed, and at the key-hole in it. I wondered if Maud kept a key on her side and had it turned. I wondered what I would see, if I went and bent and looked—and who can think a thing like that, and not go and do it? But when I did go, on tiptoe, and stoop to the lock, I saw a dim light, a shadow—nothing clearer than that, no sign of any kind of sleeping or wakeful or fretful girl, or anything.

I wondered, though, if I might hear her breathing. I straightened up, and held my breath, and put my ear flat to the door. I heard my heart-beat, and the roaring of my blood. I heard a small, tight sound, that must have been the creeping of a worm or a beetle in the wood.

Beyond that, there was nothing—though I listened for a minute, maybe two. Then I gave it up. I took off my shoes and my garters and got into bed: the sheets were cold and felt damp, like sheets of pastry. I put my cloak over the bed-clothes—for extra warmth; and also so that I might quickly seize it, if someone came at me in the night and I wanted to run. You never knew. The candle I left burning. If Mr Way was to complain that that was one stub less, too bad.

Even a thief has her weak points. The shadows still danced about. The pastry sheets stayed cold. The great clock sounded half-past ten—eleven—half-past eleven—twelve. I lay and shivered, and longed with all my heart for Mrs Sucksby, Lant Street, home.

Chapter Three

They woke me at six in the morning. It seemed still the middle of the night to me, for my candle of course had burned to nothing, and the window-curtains were heavy and kept the thin light out. When the maid, Margaret, came knocking at my door, I thought I was in my old room at Lant Street. I was sure she was a thief, broke out from gaol and needing her fetters filed free by Mr Ibbs. That happened, sometimes; and sometimes the thieves were kind men, who knew us, and sometimes they were desperate villains. Once a man put a knife to Mr Ibbs's throat, because he said the file went too slow. So, hearing Margaret's knock now, I started from the bed, crying out, 'Oh! Hold!'—though what I meant to be held, and who ought to have done it, I could not tell you; and neither, I suppose, could Margaret. She put her face about the door, whispering, 'Did you call, miss?' She had a jug of warm water for me, and she came and set my fire; then she reached beneath the bed and took the chamber-pot, and emptied it into her bucket of slops, and wiped it clean with a damp cloth that hung against her apron.

I had used to wash the chamber-pots, at home. Now, seeing Margaret tip my piddle into her bucket, I was not sure I liked it. But I said, 'Thank you, Margaret'—then wished I hadn't; for she heard it and tossed her head, as if to say, Who did I think I was, thanking *her*?

Servants. She said I should take my breakfast in Mrs Stiles's pantry. Then she turned and left me—getting a quick look, I thought, at my frock and my shoes and my open trunk, on the way.

I waited for the fire to take, then rose and dressed. It was too cold to wash. My gown felt clammy. When I drew the window-curtain back and let the daylight in, I saw—what I had not been able to see the night before, by the candle—that the ceiling was streaked brown with damp, and the wood at the walls stained white.

From the next-door room there came the murmur of voices. I heard Margaret saying, 'Yes, miss.' Then there was the shutting of a door.

Then there was silence. I went down to my breakfast—first losing my way among the dark passages at the bottom of the servants' stairs, and finding myself in the yard with the privy in it. The privy, I saw now, was surrounded by nettles, and the bricks in the yard broken up with weeds. The walls of the house had ivy on them, and some of the windows wanted panes. Gentleman was right, after all, about the place being hardly worth cracking. He was right, too, about the servants. When I found Mrs Stiles's pantry at last there was a man there, dressed in breeches and silk stockings, and with a wig on his head with powder on it. That was Mr Way. He had been steward to Mr Lilly for forty-five years, he said; and he looked it. When a girl brought the breakfasts, he was served first. We had gammon and an egg, and a cup of beer. They had beer with all their meals there, there was a whole room where it was brewed. And they say Londoners can lush!

Mr Way said hardly a word to me, but spoke to Mrs Stiles about the running of the house. He asked only after the family I was supposed to have just left; and when I told him, the Dunravens, of

Whelk Street, Mayfair, he nodded and looked clever, saying he thought he knew their man. Which goes to show you what a humbug he was.

He went off at seven. Mrs Stiles would not leave the table before he got up. When she did she said,

'You will be glad to hear, Miss Smith, that Miss Maud slept well.'

I didn't know what to say to that. She went on, anyway:

'Miss Maud rises early. She has asked that you be sent to her. Should you like to wash your hands before you go up? Miss Maud is like her uncle, and particular.'

My hands seemed clean enough to me; but I washed them anyway, in a little stone sink she had there in the corner of her pantry.

I felt the beer I had drunk, and wished I had not drunk it. I wished I had used the privy when I came across it in the yard. I was certain I should never find my way to it again.

I was nervous.

She took me up. We went, as before, by the servants' stairs, but then struck out into a handsomer passage, that led to one or two doors. At one of these she knocked. I didn't catch the answer that came, but suppose she heard it. She straightened her back and turned the iron handle, and led me in.

The room was a dark one, like all the rooms there. Its walls were panelled all over in an old black wood, and its floor—which was bare, but for a couple of trifling Turkey carpets, that were here and there worn to the weave—was also black. There were some great heavy tables about, and one or two hard sofas. There was a painting of a brown hill, and a vase full of dried leaves, and a dead snake in a glass case with a white egg in its mouth. The windows showed the grey sky and bare wet branches. The window-panes were small, and leaded, and rattled in their frames.

There was a little spluttering fire in a vast old grate, and before this—standing gazing into the weak flames and the smoke, but turning as she heard my step, and starting, and blinking—there was Miss Maud Lilly, the mistress of the house, that all our plot was built on.

I had expected her, from all that Gentleman had said, to be quite out of the way handsome. But she was not that—at least, I did not think her so as I studied her then, I thought her looks rather commonplace. She was taller than me by an inch or two—which is to say, of an ordinary height, since I am considered short; and her hair was fairer than mine—but not very fair—and her eyes, which were brown, were lighter. Her lip and her cheek were very plump and smooth—she did lick me there, I will admit, for I liked to bite my own lip, and my cheeks had freckles, and my features as a rule were said to be sharp. I was also thought young-looking; but as to that—well, I should have liked the people who thought it to have studied Maud Lilly as she stood before me now. For if I was young, then she was an infant, she was a chick, she was a pigeon that knew nothing. She saw me come, and started, as I have said; and she took a step or two to meet me, and her pale cheek fired up crimson. Then she stopped, and put her hands before her, neatly, at her skirt. The skirt—I had never seen such a thing before, on a girl her age— the skirt was full and short and showed her ankles; and about her waist—that was astonishingly narrow—there was a sash. Her hair was caught in a net of velvet. On her feet were slippers, of red prunella. Her hands had clean white gloves upon them, buttoned up tight at the wrist. She said,

'Miss Smith. You are Miss Smith, I think? And you have come to be my maid, from London! And may I call you Susan? I hope you shall like it at Briar, Susan; and I hope you shall like me. There is not much to like, in either case. I think you might do it very easily— very easily, indeed.'

She spoke in a soft, sweet, halting voice, tilting her head, hardly looking at me, still quite crimson at the cheek. I said, 'I am sure I shall like you, miss.' Then I remembered all my work at Lant Street, and gripped my skirt and made a curtsey. And when I rose from it she smiled, and came and took my hand in hers.

She looked at Mrs Stiles, who had kept behind me at the door.

'You need not stay, Mrs Stiles,' she said nicely. 'But you will have been kind to Miss Smith, I know.' She caught my eye. 'You've heard, perhaps, that I am an orphan, Susan, like you. I came to

Briar as a child: very young, and with no-one at all to care for me. I cannot tell you all the ways in which Mrs Stiles has made me know what a mother's love is, since that time.'

She smiled and tilted her head. Mrs Stiles would not catch her gaze, but a bit of colour struggled into her cheeks, and her eye-lids fluttered. I should never have put her down as the motherly sort, myself; but servants grow sentimental over the swells they work for, like dogs grow fond of bullies. You take my word for it.

Anyway, she blinked and looked modest another minute; and then she left us. Maud smiled again, and led me to one of the hard-backed sofas, that was close to the fire. She sat beside me. She asked after my journey—'We supposed you lost!' she said—and after my room. Did I like my bed? Did I like my breakfast?

'And have you really,' she said, 'come from London?' That was all that anyone had been asking, since I left Lant Street—as if I might have come from anywhere else! But then again, I thought she asked it in a different sort of way: not in a gaping country way, but in a noticing, hungryish manner—as if London was something to her, and she longed to hear of it.

Of course, I thought I knew why that was.

Next she told me all the duties I should have to do, while I was her maid: the chief of these being, as I also knew, to sit with her and keep her company, and walk with her about the park, and tidy her gowns. She lowered her eyes.

'You'll see we are rather out of the way of fashion, here at Briar,' she said. 'It matters little, I suppose, since we have so few callers. My uncle only likes to see me neat. But you, of course, will be used to the great styles of London.'

I thought of Dainty's hair, John's dog-skin coat. 'Pretty used,' I said.

'And your last mistress,' she went on then, 'she was quite a fine lady? She would laugh to look at me, I expect!'

She coloured still harder as she said that, and again looked from me; and again I thought, 'You pigeon!'

But what I said was, that Lady Alice—who was the mistress that Gentleman had faked up for me—was too kind to laugh at anyone, and would anyway know that grand clothes meant nothing, since it was the person inside the clothes that ought to be judged. All in all, I thought, it was a pretty clever thing to say; and she seemed to think so too, for when I had said it she looked at me in a new way and her colour went down, and she took my hand again, saying,

'You are a good girl, Susan, I think.'

I said, 'Lady Alice always said so, miss.'

Then I remembered the character that Gentleman had written for me, and thought this might be the moment to present it. I took it from my pocket and handed it over. She rose and broke the wax, then walked to the window to hold the paper to the light. She stood a long time looking at the curling hand, and once sneaked a glance at me; and my heart beat a little fast then, to think she might have noticed something queer there. But it was not that: for I saw at last that her hand, which held the paper, trembled; and I guessed that she had no more idea what a proper character was like than I did, and was only figuring out what she should say.

I thought it almost a shame, guessing that, that she had no mother.

'Well,' she said, folding the paper very small and putting it inside her own pocket, 'Lady Alice does indeed speak highly of you. I think you must have been sorry to leave her house.'

'Pretty sorry, miss,' I said. 'But then, you see, Lady Alice has gone to India. I think I should have found the sun there rather fierce.'

She smiled. 'Will you prefer the grey skies of Briar? You know, the sun never shines here. My uncle has forbidden it. Strong light, you see, fades print.'

She laughed and showed her teeth, which were small and very white. I smiled, but kept my lips shut—for my own teeth, that are yellow now, were I am afraid to say quite yellow even then; and seeing hers made me fancy them yellower.

She said, 'You know my uncle is a scholar, Susan?'

I said, 'I heard it, miss.'

'He keeps a great library. The largest library, of its kind, in all of England. I dare say you will see it soon.'

'That will be something, miss, I'm sure.'

She smiled again. 'You like to read, of course?'

I swallowed. 'To read, miss?' She nodded, waiting. 'Pretty much,' I said at last. 'That is, I am sure I should, if I was ever much in the way of books and papers. By which I mean'—I coughed—'if I was to be shown.'

She stared.

'To learn, I mean,' I said.

She stared, even harder; and then she gave a short, disbelieving sort of laugh. 'You are joking,' she said. 'You don't mean, you cannot read? Not really? Not a word, not a letter?' Her smile became a frown. There was, beside her, a little table with a book upon it. Still half smiling, half frowning, she took the book up and handed it to me. 'Go on,' she said kindly. 'I think you are being modest. Read me any part, I shan't mind if you stumble.'

I held the book, saying nothing; but beginning to sweat. I opened it and looked at a page. It was full of a close black print. I tried another. That one was worse. I felt Maud's gaze, like a flame against my hot face. I felt the silence. My face grew hotter. *Take a chance*, I thought.

'*Our Father*,' I tried, '*which art in heaven—*'

But then, I forgot the rest. I closed the book, and bit my lip, and looked at the floor. I thought, very bitterly, 'Well, here will all our scheming end. She won't want a maid that can't read her a book, or write fancy letters in a curling hand!' I lifted my eyes to hers and said,

'I might be taught it, miss. I am that willing. I'm sure I could learn, in half a wink—'

But she was shaking her head, and the look on her face was something.

'Be taught?' she said, coming close and gently taking back the book. 'Oh, no! No, no, I shouldn't allow it. Not read! Ah, Susan, were you to live in this house, as the niece of my uncle, you should know what that meant. You should know, indeed!'

She smiled. And while she still held my gaze, still smiling, there came the slow and heavy tolling of the great house-bell, eight times; and then her smile fell.

'Now,' she said, turning away, 'I must go to Mr Lilly; and when the clock strikes one I shall be free again.'

She said that—sounding, I thought, just like a girl in a story. Aren't there stories, with girls with magic uncles—wizards, beasts, and whatnots? She said,

'Come to me, Susan, at my uncle's chamber, at one.'

'I will, miss,' I said.

She was looking about her, now, in a distracted kind of way. There was a glass above the fire and she went to it, and put her gloved hands to her face, and then to her collar. I watched her lean. Her short gown lifted at the back and showed her calves.

She caught my eye in the glass. I made another curtsey.

'Shall I go, miss?' I said.

She stepped back. 'Stay,' she said, waving her hand, 'and put my rooms in order, will you?'

She went to the door. At the handle, however, she stopped. She said,

'I hope you will be happy here, Susan.' Now *she* was blushing again. My own cheek cooled, when I saw that. 'I hope your aunt, in London, will not miss you too greatly. It was an aunt, I think, that Mr Rivers mentioned?' She lowered her eyes. 'I hope you found Mr Rivers quite well, when you saw him?'

She let the question fall, like it was nothing to her; and I knew confidence men who did the same, dropping one good shilling among a pile of snide, to make all the coins seem honest. As if she gave a fig, for me and my old aunty!

I said, 'He was very well, miss. And sent his compliments.'

She had opened the door now, and half-hid herself behind it. 'Did he truly?' she said.

'Truly, miss.'

She put her brow against the wood. 'I think he is kind,' she said softly.

I remembered him squatting at the side of that kitchen chair, his hand reaching high beneath the layers of petticoat, saying, *You sweet bitch*.

'I'm sure he's very kind, miss,' I said.

Then, from somewhere in the house there came the quick, peevish tinkling of a little hand-bell, and, 'There's Uncle!' she cried,
gazing over her shoulder. She turned and ran, leaving the door half-
closed. I heard the slap of her slippers and the creaking of the stairs
as she went down.

I waited a second, then stepped to the door, put my foot to it, and
kicked it shut. I went to the fire and warmed my hands. I do not
think I had been quite warm since leaving Lant Street. I lifted my
head and, seeing the glass that Maud had looked in, rose and gazed
at my own face—at my freckled cheek and my teeth. I showed
myself my tongue. Then I rubbed my hands and chuckled: for she
was just as Gentleman had promised, and clearly tit over heels in
love with him already; and that three thousand pounds might as
well have been counted and wrapped and had my name put on it,
and the doctor be standing ready with a strait-coat at the madhouse
door.

That's what I thought, after seeing her then.

But I thought it in a discontented sort of way; and the chuckle, I
have to admit, was rather forced. I could not have said quite why,
though. I supposed it was the gloom—for the house seemed darker
and stiller than ever, now that she had gone. There was only the
dropping of ash in the grate, the bumping and rattling of panes of
glass. I went to the window. The draught was awful. There had
been little red sand-bags laid upon the sills to keep it out, but they
didn't work; and they had all got wet, and were mouldy. I put my
hand to one, and my finger came away green. I stood and shivered,
and looked at the view—if you could call it a view, that was just
plain grass and trees. A few black birds pulled worms from the
lawn. I wondered which way London was.

I wished hard to hear an infant cry, or Mr Ibbs's sister. I would
have given five pounds for a parcel of poke or a few bad coins to tarnish.

Then I thought of something else. *Put my rooms in order*, Maud
had said; and here was only one room, that I supposed must be her
parlour; so somewhere else must be another, where she slept in her
bed. Now, the walls in that house were all of dark oak panelling,

very gloomy on the eye and very baffling, for the doors were set so pat in their frames, you could not spot them. But I looked hard and, in the wall across from where I stood, I saw a crack, and then a handle; and then the shape of the door sprung at me, plain as daylight.

It was the door to her bedroom, just as I had supposed; and of course, this room had another door in it, that was the door to my own room, where I had stood the night before and listened for her breaths. That seemed a very foolish thing to have done, now that I saw what was on the other side of it. For it was only an ordinary lady's room—not very grand, but grand enough, with a faint, sweet smell to it, and a high four-posted bed with curtains and a canopy of old moreen. I was not sure that sleeping in a bed like that wouldn't make me sneeze: I thought of all the dust and dead flies and spiders that must be gathered in the canopy, that looked as though it hadn't been taken down in ninety years. The bed had been made, but a night-dress lay upon it—I folded this up and put it beneath the pillow; and there were one or two fair hairs there that I caught up and took to the grate. So much for maiding. Upon the chimney-breast there was a great aged looking-glass, shot through like marble, with silver and grey. Beyond it was a small old-fashioned press, that was carved all over with flowers and grapes, quite black with polish, and here and there split. I should say that ladies wore nothing but leaves in the day it was built, for it had six or seven slight gowns laid carelessly in it now, that made the shelves groan, and a crinoline cage, against which the doors could not be fastened. Seeing that, I thought again what a shame it was that Maud had no mother: for she would certainly have got rid of ancient stuff like this and found her daughter something more up to the minute and dainty.

But one thing a business like ours at Lant Street teaches you is, the proper handling of quality goods. I got hold of the gowns—they were all as odd and short and girlish as each other—and shook them out, then laid them nicely back on their shelf. Then I wedged a shoe against the crinoline to hold it flat; after that, the doors closed as they were meant to. This press was in one alcove. In another was a dressing-table. That was strewn about with brushes and bottles and pins—I tidied those, too—and fitted beneath with a set of fancy drawers. I opened them up. They held—well, here was a thing. They all held *gloves*. More gloves than a milliner's. White ones, in the top drawer; black silk ones in the middle; and buff mittens in the lowest.

They were each of them marked on the inside at the wrist with a crimson thread that I guessed spelled out Maud's name. I should have liked to have a go at that, with scissors and a pin.

I did no such thing, of course, but left the gloves all lying neatly, and I went about the room again until I had touched and studied it all. There was not much more to look at; but there was one more curious thing, and that was a little wooden box, inlaid with ivory, that sat upon a table beside her bed.

The box was locked, and when I took it up it gave a dull sort of rattle. There was no key handy: I guessed she kept it somewhere about her, perhaps on a string. The lock was a simple one, however, and with locks like that, you only have to show them the wire and they open themselves, it's like giving brine to an oyster. I used one of her hairpins.

The wood turned out to be lined with plush. The hinge was of silver, and oiled not to squeak. I am not sure what I thought to find in there—perhaps, something from Gentleman, some keepsake, some letter, some little bill-and-coo. But what there was, was a miniature portrait, in a frame of gold hung on a faded ribbon, of a handsome, fair-haired lady. Her eyes were kind. She was dressed in a style from twenty years before, and the frame was an old one: she did not look much like Maud, but I thought it a pretty safe bet that she was her mother.—Though I also thought that, if she was, then it was queer that Maud kept her picture locked up in a box, and did not wear it.

I puzzled so long over this, turning the picture, looking for marks, that the frame—which had been cold when I took it up, like everything there—grew warm. But then there came a sound, from somewhere in the house, and I thought how it would be, if Maud— or Margaret, or Mrs Stiles—should come to the room and catch me standing by the open box, the portrait in my hand. I quickly laid it back in its place, and made it fast again.

The hairpin I had bent to make a pick-lock with, I kept. I shouldn't have liked Maud to have found it and thought me a thief.

There was nothing to do, after I had done that. I stood some more at the window. At eleven o'clock a maid brought up a tray. 'Miss Maud isn't here,' I said, when I saw the silver tea-pot; but the tea was for me. I drank it in fairy-sips, to make it last the longer. Then I took the tray back down, thinking to save the maid another journey. When they saw me carrying it into the kitchen, however, the girls there stared and the cook said,

'Well, I never! If you think Margaret ain't quick enough coming, you must speak to Mrs Stiles. But I'm sure, Miss Fee never called anyone idle.'

Miss Fee was the Irish maid who had got sick with the scarlatina. It seemed very cruel to be supposed prouder than her, when I was only trying to be kind.

But I said nothing. I thought, 'Miss Maud likes me, if you don't!'

For she was the only one, of all of them, to have spared me a pleasant word; and suddenly I longed for the time to pass, not for its own sake, but as it would take me back to her.

At least at Briar you always knew what hour it was. The twelve struck, and then the half, and I made my way to the back-stairs and hung about there until one of the parlourmaids went by, and she showed me the way to the library. It was a room on the first floor, that you reached from a gallery overlooking a great wood staircase and a hall; but it was all dark and dim and shabby, as it was everywhere in that house—you would never have thought, looking about you there, that you were right in the home of a tremendous scholar. By the door to the library, on a wooden shield, hung some creature's head with one glass eye: I stood and put my fingers to its little white teeth, waiting to hear the clock sound one. Through the door came Maud's voice—very faint, but slow and level, as though she might be reading to her uncle from a book.

Then the hour sounded, and I lifted my hand and knocked. A man's thin voice called out for me to enter.

I saw Maud first: she was sitting at a desk with a book before her, her hands upon the covers. Her hands were bare, she had her little white gloves laid neatly by, but she sat beside a shaded lamp, that threw all its light upon her fingers, and they seemed pale as ashes upon the page of print. Above her was a window. Its glass had yellow paint upon it. All about her, over all the walls of the room, were shelves; and the shelves had books on—you never saw so many. A stunning amount. How many stories does one man need? I looked at them and shuddered. Maud rose, closing the book that was before her. She took up the white gloves and drew them back on.

She looked to her right, to the end of the room that, because of the open door, I could not see. A cross voice said,

'What is it?'

I pushed the door further, and saw another painted window, more shelves, more books, and a second great desk. This one was piled with papers, and had another shaded lamp. Behind it sat Mr Lilly, Maud's old uncle; and to describe him as I saw him then, is to tell everything.

He wore a velvet coat, and a velvet cap, that had a stub of red wool jutting from it where a tassel might once have hung. In his hand there was a pen, that he held clear of the paper; and the hand itself was dark, as Maud's was fair—for it was stained all over with India ink, like a regular man's might be stained with tobacco. His hair, however, was white. His chin was shaved bare. His mouth was small and had no colour, but his tongue—that was hard and pointed—was almost black, from where he must have given a lick to his finger and thumb, when turning pages.

His eyes were damp and feeble. Before them he had a pair of glasses, shaded green. He saw me and said,

'Who the devil are you?'

Maud worked at the buttons at her wrist.

'This is my new maid, Uncle,' she said quietly. 'Miss Smith.'

Behind Mr Lilly's green glasses, I saw his eyes screw themselves up and grow damper.

'Miss Smith,' he said, looking at me but talking to his niece. 'Is she a papist, like the last one?'

'I don't know,' said Maud. 'I have not asked her. Are you a papist, Susan?'

I didn't know what that was. But I said, 'No, miss. I don't think so.'

Mr Lilly at once put his hand across his ear.

'I don't care for her voice,' he said. 'Can't she be silent? Can't she be soft?'

Maud smiled. 'She can, Uncle,' she said.

'Then why is she here, disturbing me now?'

'She has come to fetch me.'

'To fetch you?' he said. 'Did the clock sound?'

He put his hand to the fob of his waistcoat and drew out an ancient great gold repeater, tilting his head to catch the chime, and opening his mouth. I looked at Maud, who stood, still fumbling with the fastening of her glove; and I took a step, meaning to help her. But when he saw me do that, the old man jerked like Mr Punch in the puppet-show, and out came his black tongue.

'The finger, girl!' he cried. 'The finger! The finger!'

He held his own dark finger to me, and shook his pen until the ink flew: I saw later that the piece of carpet underneath his desk was quite black, and so guessed he shook his pen rather often. But at that moment he looked so strange, and spoke so shrilly, my heart quite failed me. I thought he must be prone to fits. I took another step, and that made him shriek still harder—at last Maud came to me and touched my arm.

'Don't be afraid,' she said softly. 'He means only this, look.' And she showed me how, at my feet, there was set into the dark floor-boards, in the space between the doorway and the edge of the carpet, a flat brass hand with a pointing finger.

'Uncle does not care to have servants' eyes upon his books,' she said, 'for fear of spoiling them. Uncle asks that no servant advance further into the room than this mark here.'

She placed the toe of her slipper upon the brass. Her face was smooth as wax, her voice like water.

'Does she see it?' said her uncle.

'Yes,' she answered, drawing back her toe. 'She sees it very well. She will know next time—shan't you, Susan?'

'Yes, miss,' I said—hardly knowing what I should say, or how or who I should look at; for it was certainly news to me, that gazing at a line of print could spoil it. But what did I know, about that? Besides which, the old man was so queer, and had given me such a turn, I thought that anything might have been true. 'Yes, miss,' I said, a second time; and then: 'Yes, sir.'

Then I made a curtsey. Mr Lilly snorted, looking hard at me through his green glasses. Maud fastened her glove, and we turned to leave him.

'Make her soft, Maud,' he said, as she pulled the door behind us.

'I will, Uncle,' she murmured.

Now the passage seemed dimmer than ever. She took me round the gallery and up the staircase to the second floor, where her rooms were. Here there was a bit of lunch laid out, and coffee in another silver pot; but when she saw what Cook had sent up, she made a face.

'Eggs,' she said. 'Done soft, like you must be. What did you think of my uncle, Susan?'

I said, 'I'm sure he's very clever, miss.'

'He is.'

'And writing, I believe, a great big dictionary?'

She blinked, then nodded. 'A dictionary, yes. A great many years' labour. We are presently at F.'

She held my gaze, as if to see what I thought of that.

'Astonishing,' I said.

She blinked again, then put a spoon to the side of the first of the eggs and took its head off. Then she looked at the white and yellow mess inside it and made another face, and put it from her. 'You must eat this for me,' she said. 'You must eat them all. And I shall have the bread-and-butter.'

There were three eggs there. I don't know what she saw in them, to be so choosy over. She passed them to me and, as I ate them, she sat watching me, taking bites of bread and sips of coffee, and once rubbing for a minute at a spot upon her glove, saying, 'Here is a drop of yolk, look, come upon my finger. Oh, how horrid the yellow is, against the white!'

I saw her frowning at that mark, then, until the meal was finished. When Margaret came to take the tray away, she rose and went into her bedroom; and when she came back her gloves were white again—she had been to her drawer and got a new pair. The old ones I found later, as I put coal on her bedroom fire: she had cast them there, at the back of the grate, and the flames had made the kid shrink, they looked like gloves for a doll.

She was certainly, then, what you would call original. But was she mad, or even half-way simple, as Gentleman said at Lant Street? I did not think so, then. I thought her only pretty lonely, and pretty bookish and bored—as who wouldn't be, in a house like that? When we had finished our lunch she went to the window: the sky was grey and threatening rain, but she said she had a fancy to go out walking. She said, 'Now, what shall I wear for it?', and we stood at the door of her little black press, looking over her coats, her bonnets and her boots. That killed nearly an hour. I think that's why she did it. When I was clumsy over the lacing of her shoe, she put her hands upon mine and said,

'Be slower. Why should we hurry? There is no-one to hurry for, is there?'

She smiled, but her eyes were sad. I said,

'No, miss.'

In the end she put on a pale grey cloak, and over her gloves she drew mittens. She had a little leather bag kept ready, that held a handkerchief, a bottle of water, and scissors: she had me carry this, not saying what the scissors were for—I supposed she meant to cut flowers. She took me down the great staircase to the door, and Mr Way heard us and came running to throw back the bolts. 'How do you do, Miss Maud?' he said, making a bow; and then: 'And you, Miss Smith.' The hall was dark. When we went outside we stood blinking, our hands at our eyes against the sky and the watery sun.

The house had seemed grim when I first saw it, at night, in the

fog, and I should like to say it seemed less grim when you saw it by
daylight; but it seemed worse. I suppose it had been grand enough
once, but now its chimneys were leaning like drunks, and its roof
was green with moss and birds' nests. It was covered all over with a
dead kind of creeper, or with the stains where a creeper had long ago
crept; and all about the foot of the walls were the chopped-off
trunks of ivy. It had a great front door, split down the middle; but
rain had made the wood swell, they only ever opened up one half.
Maud had to press her crinoline flat, and walk quite sideways, in
order to leave the house at all.

It was odd to see her stepping out of that gloomy place, like a
pearl coming out of an oyster.

It was odder to watch her going back in, and see the oyster shell
open, then shut at her back.

But there was not much to stay for, out in the park. There was
that avenue of trees, that led up to the house. There was the bare bit
of gravel that the house was set in. There was a place they called a
herb-garden, that grew mostly nettles; and an overgrown wood with
blocked-off paths. At the edge of the wood was a little stone windowless building Maud said was an ice-house. 'Let us just cross to
the door and look inside,' she would say, and she'd stand and gaze at
the cloudy blocks of ice until she shivered. At the back of the ice-
house there started a muddy lane, that led you to a shut-up old red
chapel surrounded by yews. This was the queerest, quietest place I
ever saw. I never heard a bird sing there. I didn't like to go to it, but
Maud took that way often. For at the chapel there were graves, of all
the Lillys that had come before her; and one of these was a plain
stone tomb, that was the grave of her mother.

She could sit and look at that for an hour at a time, hardly blinking. Her scissors she used, not for gathering flowers, but only for
keeping down the grass that grew about it; and where her mother's
name was picked out in letters of lead she would rub with her wet
handkerchief to take off stains.

She would rub until her hand shook and her breath came quick.
She would never let me help her. That first day, when I tried, she
said,

'It is a daughter's duty, to tend to the grave of her mother. Walk off a while, and don't watch me.'

So I left her to it, and wandered among the tombs. The ground was hard as iron and my boots made it ring. I walked and thought of my own mother. She didn't have a grave, they don't give graves to murderesses. They put their bodies in quicklime.

Did you ever pour salt on the back of a slug? John Vroom used to do it, and then laugh to see the slug fizz. He said to me once,

'Your mother fizzed like that. She fizzed, and ten men died that smelt it!'

He never said it again. I took up a pair of kitchen shears and put them to his neck. I said, 'Bad blood carries. Bad blood comes out.' And the look on his face was something!

I wondered how Maud would look, if she knew what bad blood flowed in me.

But she never thought to ask. She only sat, gazing hard at her mother's name, while I wandered and stamped my feet. Then at last she sighed and looked about her, passed her hand across her eyes, and drew up her hood.

'This is a melancholy place,' she said. 'Let's walk a little further.'

She led me away from the circle of yews, back down the lane between the hedges, then away from the wood and the ice-house, to the edge of the park. Here, if you followed a path that ran alongside a wall, you reached a gate. She had a key for it. It took you to the bank of a river. You could not see the river from the house. There was an ancient landing-place there, half rotted away, and a little upturned punt that made a kind of seat. The river was narrow, its water very quiet and muddy and filled with darting fish. All along the bank there grew rushes. They grew thick and high. Maud walked slowly beside them, gazing nervously into the darkness they made where they met the water. I supposed she was frightened of snakes. Then she plucked up a reed and broke it, and sat with the tip of it pressed against her plump mouth.

I sat beside her. The day was windless, but cold, and so quiet it hurt the ears. The air smelled thin.

'Pretty stretch of water,' I said, for politeness' sake.

A barge went by. The men saw us and touched their hats. I waved.

'Bound for London,' said Maud, looking after them.

'London?'

She nodded. I didn't then know—for, who would have guessed it?—that that trifling bit of water was the Thames. I thought she meant the boat would join a bigger river further on. Still, the idea that it would reach the city—maybe sail under London Bridge—made me sigh. I turned to watch it follow a bend in the water; then it passed from sight. The sound of its engine faded, the smoke from its chimney joined the grey of the sky and was lost. The air was thin again. Maud still sat with the tip of the broken reed against her lip, her gaze very vague. I took up stones and began to throw them into the water. She watched me do it, winking at every splash. Then she led me back up to the house.

We went back to her room. She got out a bit of sewing—a colourless, shapeless thing, I don't know if it was meant to be a tablecloth, or what. I never saw her working on anything else. She sewed in her gloves, very badly—making crooked stitches and then ripping half of them out. It made me nervous. We sat together before the spluttering fire, and talked in a weak kind of way—I forget what of—and then it grew dark, and a maid brought lights; and then the wind picked up and the windows began to rattle worse than ever. I said to myself, 'Dear God, let Gentleman come soon! I think a week of this will kill me'; and I yawned. Maud caught my eye. Then she also yawned. That made me yawn harder. At last she put her work aside and tucked up her feet and laid her head upon the arm of the sofa, and seemed to sleep.

That's all there was to do there, until the clock struck seven. When she heard that she gave a bigger yawn than ever, put her fingers to her eyes, and rose. Seven o'clock was when she must change her dress again—and change her gloves, for ones of silk—to have supper with her uncle.

She was two hours with him. I saw nothing of that, of course, but took my dinner in the kitchen, with the servants. They told me that, when he had eaten, Mr Lilly liked his niece to sit and read to him in the drawing-room. That was his idea of fun, I suppose, for they said he hardly ever had guests, and if he did then they were always other bookish gentlemen, from Oxford and London; and it was his pleasure, then, to have Maud read books to them all.

'Does she do nothing, poor girl, but read?' I asked.

'Her uncle won't let her,' said a parlourmaid. 'That's how much he prizes her. Won't hardly let her out—fears she'll break in two. It's him, you know, that keeps her all the time in gloves.'

'That's enough!' said Mrs Stiles. 'What would Miss Maud say?'

Then the parlourmaid fell silent. I sat and thought about Mr Lilly, with his red cap and his gold repeater, his green eye-glasses, his black finger and tongue; and then about Maud, frowning over her eggs, rubbing hard at her mother's grave. It seemed a queer kind of prizing, that would make a girl like her, like that.

I thought I knew all about her. Of course, I knew nothing. I had my dinner, listening to the servants talk, not saying much; and then Mrs Stiles asked me, Should I like to come and take my pudding with her and Mr Way, in her own pantry? I supposed I ought to. I sat gazing at the picture made all of hair. Mr Way read us pieces from the Maidenhead paper, and at every story—that were all about bulls breaking fences, or parsons making interesting sermons in church—Mrs Stiles shook her head, saying, 'Well, did you ever hear the like?' and Mr Way would chuckle and say, 'You'll see, Miss Smith, that we are quite a match for London, news-wise!'

Above his voice came the faint sound of laughter and scraping chairs, that was Cook and the scullery-maids and William Inker and the knife-boy, enjoying themselves in the kitchen.

Then the great house clock struck, and immediately after it the servants' bell sounded; and that meant that Mr Lilly was ready to be seen by Mr Way into his bed, and that Maud was ready to be put by me into hers.

I almost lost my way again, on my way back up; but even so, when she saw me she said,

'Is that you, Susan? You are quicker than Agnes.' She smiled. 'I think you are handsomer, too. I don't think a girl can be handsome—do you?—with red hair. But nor with fair hair, either. I should like to be dark, Susan!'

She had had wine with her supper, and I had had beer. I should say we were both, in our own ways, rather tipsy. She had me stand beside her at the great silvery glass above her fireplace, and drew my head to hers, to compare the colours of our hair. 'Yours is the darker,' she said.

Then she moved away from the fire, for me to put her into her nightgown.

It was not much like undressing the chair in our old kitchen, after all. She stood shivering, saying, 'Quick! I shall freeze! Oh, heavens!'—for her bedroom was as draughty as everywhere else there, and my fingers were cold and made her jump. They grew warm, though, after a minute. Stripping a lady is heavy work. Her corset was long, with a busk of steel; her waist, as I think I have said, was narrow: the kind of waist the doctors speak against, that gives a girl an illness. Her crinoline was made of watchspring. Her hair, inside its net, was fixed with half a pound of pins, and a comb of silver. Her petticoats and shimmy were calico. Underneath it all, however, she was soft and smooth as butter. Too soft, I thought her. I imagined her bruising. She was like a lobster without its shell. She stood in her stockings while I fetched her nightgown, her arms above her head, her eyes shut tight; and for a second I turned, and looked at her. My gaze was nothing to her. I saw her bosom, her bottom, her feather and everything and— apart from the feather, which was brown as a duck's—she was as pale as a statue on a pillar in a park. So pale she was, she seemed to shine.

But again, it was a troubling kind of paleness, and I was glad to cover her up. I tidied her gown back into the press and jammed closed the door. She sat and waited, yawning, for me to come and brush her hair.

Her hair was good, and very long let down. I brushed it, and held it, and thought what it might fetch.

'What are you thinking of?' she said, her eyes on mine in the glass. 'Of your old mistress? Was her hair handsomer?'

'Her hair was very poor,' I said. And then, feeling sorry for Lady Alice: 'But she walked well.'

'Do I walk well?'

'You do, miss.'

She did. Her feet were small, her ankles slender like her waist. She smiled. As she had with our heads, she made me put my foot beside hers, to compare them.

'Yours is almost as neat,' she said kindly.

She got into her bed. She said she didn't care to lie in darkness. She had a rush-light in a tin shade kept beside her pillow, the kind old misers use, and she made me light it from the flame of my candle; and she wouldn't let me tie the curtains of her bed, but had me pull them only a little way shut, so that she might see into the room beyond.

'And you will not, will you, quite close your door?' she said. 'Agnes never used to. I didn't like it, before you came, having Margaret in a chair. I was afraid I would dream and have to call her. When Margaret touches, she pinches. Your hands, Susan, are hard as hers; and yet your touch is gentle.'

She reached and put her fingers quickly upon mine, as she said this; and I rather shuddered to feel the kid-skin on them—for she had changed out of her silk gloves, only to button another white pair back on. Then she took her hands away and tucked her arms beneath the blanket. I pulled the blanket perfectly smooth. I said,

'Shall that be all, miss?'

'Yes, Susan,' she answered. She moved her cheek upon her pillow. She didn't like the prickling of her hair against her neck: she had put it back, and it snaked away into shadow, straight and dark and slender as a rope.

When I took my candle off, the shadow spread across her like a wave. Her room was dimly lit by the lamp, but her bed was in darkness. I half-closed my door, and heard her lift her head. 'A little wider,' she called softly, so I opened it further. Then I stood and rubbed my face. I had been at Briar only a day; but it was the longest day of my life. My hands were sore from pulling laces. When I closed my eyes, I saw hooks. Undressing myself had no fun in it, now I had undressed her.

At last I sat and blew out my candle; and heard her move. There
wasn't a sound in the house: I heard her, very clearly, rise from her
pillow and twist in her bed. I heard her reach and draw out her key,
then put it to the little wooden box. At the click of the lock, I got
up. I thought, 'Well, I can be silent, if you can't. I am softer than
you or your uncle know'; and I made my way to the crack of the
door and peeped through. She had leaned out of the curtained bed,
and had the portrait of the handsome lady—her mother—in her
hand. As I watched, she raised the portrait to her mouth, kissed it,
and spoke soft, sad words to it. Then she put it from her with a sigh.
She kept the key in a book beside her bed. I hadn't thought to look
in there. She locked the box back up, set it neatly on the table—
touched it once, touched it twice—and then moved back behind the
curtain and was still.

I grew too tired to watch her, then. I moved back, too. My room
was dark as ink. I reached with my hands and found the blanket and
sheets, and pulled them down. I got beneath them; and lay cold as
a frog in my own narrow lady's maid's bed.

I cannot say how long I slept for then. I could not say, when I woke
up, what awful sound it was that had woken me. I did not know, for
a minute or two, whether my eyes were open or closed—for the
darkness was so deep, there was no difference—it was only when I
gazed at the open door to Maud's room and saw the faint light
there, that I knew I was awake and not dreaming. What I had heard,
I thought, was some great crash or thud, and then perhaps a cry.
Now, in the instant of my opening my eyes, there was a silence; but
as I lifted my head and felt my heart beat hard, the cry came again.
It was Maud, calling out in a high, frightened voice. She was calling
on her old maid:

'Agnes! Oh! Oh! Agnes!'

I didn't know what I would see when I went in to her—perhaps,
a busted window and a burglar, pulling at her head, cutting the
hair off. But the window, though it still rattled, was quite unbroken;
and there was no-one there with her, she had come to the gap in her
bed-curtains with the blankets all bunched beneath her chin and her

hair flung about, half covering her face. Her face was pale and strange. Her eyes, that I knew were only brown, seemed black. Black, like Polly Perkins's, as the pips in a pear.

She said again, 'Agnes!'

I said, 'It's Sue, miss.'

She said, 'Agnes, did you hear that sound? Is the door shut?'

'The door?' The door was closed. 'Is someone there?'

'A man?' she said.

'A man? A burglar?'

'At the door? Don't go, Agnes! I'm afraid he'll harm you!'

She *was* afraid. She was so frightened, she began to frighten me. I said, 'I don't think there's a man, miss.' I said, 'Let me try and light a candle.'

But have you ever tried to light a candle from a rush-light in a tin shade? I could not get the wick to catch; and she kept on, weeping and calling me Agnes, until my hand shook so much I could not hold the candle steady.

I said, 'You must be quiet, miss. There's no man; and if there is, then I shall call for Mr Way to come and catch him.'

I took up the rush-light. 'Don't take the light!' she cried at once. 'I beg you, don't!'

I said I would only take it to the door, to show her there was no-one there; and while she wept and clutched at the bed-clothes I went with the light to the door to her parlour and—all in a flinching, winking kind of way—I pulled it open.

The room beyond was very dark. The few great bits of furniture sat humped about, like the baskets with the thieves in, in the play of *Ali Baba*. I thought how dismal it would be if I had come all the way to Briar, from the Borough, to be murdered by burglars. And what if the burglar proved to be a man I knew—say, one of Mr Ibbs's nephews? Queer things like that do happen.

So I stood gazing fearfully at the dark room, thinking all this, half-inclined to call out—in case there were burglars there—that they should hold their hands, that I was family; but of course, there was no-one, it was quiet as a church. I saw that, and then went quickly to the parlour door, and looked into the passage; and that was dark and quiet, too—there was only the ticking of some clock, far-off, and more rattling windows. But after all it was not quite pleasant, standing in a night-dress, with a rush-light, in a great dark silent house that, though it didn't have thieves in, might certainly have ghosts. I closed the door quick, and went back to Maud's room and closed that door, and stepped to the side of her bed and put the light down.

She said, 'Did you see him? Oh, Agnes, is he there?'

I was about to answer, but then I stopped. For I had looked towards the corner of the room, where the black press was; and there was something strange there. There was something long and white and gleaming, that was moving against the wood . . . Well, I have said, haven't I, that I've a warm imagination? I was certain that the thing was Maud's dead mother, come back as a ghost to haunt me. My heart leapt so hard into my mouth, I seemed to taste it. I screamed, and Maud screamed, then clutched at me and wept harder. 'Don't look at me!' she cried. And then: 'Don't leave me! Don't leave me!'

And then I saw what the white thing really was, and hopped from foot to foot and almost laughed.

For it was only the cage of her crinoline, sprung out from where I had jammed it on the shelf with one of her shoes. The door of the press had swung open and hit the wall: that was the noise that had woken us. The crinoline was hanging from a hook, and quivering. My footsteps had made the springs bounce.

I saw it, as I say, and almost laughed; but when I looked again at Maud, her eyes were still so black and wild and her face so pale, and she clutched at me so hard, I thought it would be cruel to let her see me smile. I put my hands across my mouth, and the breath came out between my jumping fingers, and my teeth began to chatter. I was colder than ever.

I said, 'It's nothing, miss. After all, it's nothing. You was only dreaming.'

'Dreaming, Agnes?'

She put her head against my bosom, and shook. I smoothed her hair back from her cheek, and held her until she grew calm.

'There,' I said then. 'Shall you sleep again now? Let me put the blanket about you, look.'

But when I made to lay her down, she gripped me harder. 'Don't leave me, Agnes!' she said again.

I said, 'It's Sue, miss. Agnes had the scarlatina, and is gone back to Cork. Remember? You must lie down now, or the cold will make you ill, too.'

She looked at me then, and her gaze, that was still so dark, seemed yet a little clearer.

'Don't leave me, Sue!' she whispered. 'I'm afraid, of my own dreaming!'

Her breath was sweet. Her hands and arms were warm. Her face was smooth as ivory or alabaster. In a few weeks' time, I thought— if our plot worked—she would be lying in the bed of a madhouse. Who would there be to be kind to her, then?

So I put her from me, but only for a moment; and I clambered over her and got beneath the blankets at her side. I put my arm about her, and at once she sank against me. It seemed the least that I could do. I pulled her closer. She was slender as anything. Not like Mrs Sucksby. Not like Mrs Sucksby, at all. She was more like a child. She still shivered a little, and when she blinked I felt the sweep of her lashes against my throat, like feathers. In time, however, the shivering stopped, and her lashes swept again and then were still. She grew heavy, and warm.

'Good girl,' I said, too softly to wake her.

Next morning I woke a minute before she did. She opened her eyes, saw me, looked troubled, and tried to hide it.

'Did my dreams wake me in the night?' she said, not meeting my gaze. 'Did I say foolish things? They say I speak nonsense, in my sleep, as other girls snore.' She blushed, and laughed. 'But how good you were, to come and keep me company!'

I didn't tell her about the crinoline. At eight o'clock she went off to her uncle, and at one I went to fetch her—taking care, this time, to mind the pointing finger on the floor. Then we walked in the park, to the graves and the river; she sewed, and dozed, and was rung to her supper; and I sat with Mrs Stiles until half-past nine, when it was time to go back up and put her to bed. It was all just the first day, over again. She said, 'Good-night,' and laid her head upon her pillow; then I stood in my room and heard her little box unlocked, and peeped through the door to watch her take up the portrait, kiss it, then put it away.

And then, I had not put out my candle two minutes, before her voice came calling softly: 'Sue—!'

She said she could not sleep. She said she was cold. She said she would like to keep me close to her again, in case she woke up frightened.

She said the same thing the next night; and the night after that. 'You don't mind?' she asked me. She said Agnes never minded. 'Did you never,' she said, 'sleep with Lady Alice, at Mayfair?'

What could I tell her? For all I knew, it might have been an ordinary thing, for a mistress and her maid to double up like girls.

It was ordinary at first, with Maud and me. Her dreams never bothered her. We slept, quite like sisters. Quite like sisters, indeed. I always wanted a sister.

Then Gentleman came.

Chapter Four

*H*e came, I suppose, about two weeks after I got there. It was only two weeks and yet, the hours at Briar were such slow ones, and the days—being all quite the same—were so even and quiet and long, it might have been twice that time.

It was long enough, anyway, for me to find out all the peculiar habits of the house; long enough for me to get used to the other servants, and for them to get used to me. For a while, I didn't know why it was they did not care for me. I would go down to the kitchen, saying, 'How do you do?' to whoever I met there: 'How do you do, Margaret? All right, Charles?' (That was the knife-boy.) 'How are you, Mrs Cakebread?' (That was the cook: that really was her name, it wasn't a joke and no-one laughed at it.) And Charles might look at me as if he was too afraid to speak; and Mrs Cakebread would answer, in a nasty kind of way, 'Oh, I'm sure *I'm* very well, thank you.'

I supposed they were peeved to have me about, reminding them of all the flash London things they would never, in that quiet and out-of-the-way place, get a look at. Then one day Mrs Stiles took me aside. She said, 'I hope you don't mind, Miss Smith, if I have a little word? I can't say how the house was run in your last place—' She started everything she said to me with a line like that.—'I can't say how you did things in London, but here at Briar we like to keep very mindful of the footings of the house . . .'

It turned out that Mrs Cakebread had fancied herself insulted, by my saying good-morning to the kitchen-maid and the knife-boy before I said it to her; and Charles thought I meant to tease him, by wishing him good-morning at all. It was all the most trifling sort of nonsense, and enough to make a cat laugh; but it was life and death to them—I suppose, it *would* be life and death to you, if all you had to look forward to for the next forty years was carrying trays and baking pastry. Anyway, I saw that, if I was to get anywhere with them, I must watch my steps. I gave Charles a bit of chocolate, that I had carried down with me from the Borough and never eaten; I gave Margaret a piece of scented soap; and to Mrs Cakebread I gave a pair of those black stockings that Gentleman had had Phil get for me from the crooked warehouse.

I said I hoped there were no hard feelings. If I met Charles on the stairs in the morning, then, I looked the other way. They were all much nicer to me after that.

That's like a servant. A servant says, 'All for my master,' and means, 'All for myself'. It's the two-facedness of it that I can't bear. At Briar, they were all on the dodge in one way or another, but all over sneaking little matters that would have put a real thief to the blush—such as, holding off the fat from Mr Lilly's gravy to sell on the quiet to the butcher's boy; which is what Mrs Cakebread did. Or, pulling the pearl buttons from Maud's chemises, and keeping them, and saying they were lost; which is what Margaret did. I had them all worked out, after three days' watching. I might have been Mrs Sucksby's own daughter after all. Mr Way, now: he had a mark on the side of his nose—in the Borough we should have called it a gin-bud. And how do you think he got that, in a place like his? He had the key to Mr Lilly's cellar, on a chain. You never saw such a

shine as that key had on it! And then, when we had finished our
meals in Mrs Stiles's pantry, he would make a great show of loading
up the tray—and I'd see him, when he thought no-one was looking,
tipping the beer from the bottom of all the glasses into one great
cup, and lushing it away.

I saw it—but, of course, I kept it all to myself. I wasn't there to
make trouble. It was nothing to me, if he drank himself to death.
And I passed most of my time, anyway, with Maud. I got used to
her, too. She had her finicking ways, all right; but they were slight
enough, it didn't hurt me to indulge them. And I was good at working hard, on little things: I began to take a kind of pleasure in the
keeping of her gowns, the tidying of her pins and combs and boxes.
I was used to dressing infants. I grew used to dressing her.

'Lift your arms, miss,' I'd say. 'Lift your foot. Step here. Now,
here.'

'Thank you, Sue,' she would always murmur. Sometimes she
would close her eyes. 'How well you know me,' she might say. 'I
think you know the turning of all my limbs.'

I did, in time. I knew all that she liked and hated. I knew what
food she would eat, and what she'd leave—and when Cook, for
instance, kept sending up eggs, I went and told her to send soup
instead.

'Clear soup,' I said. 'Clear as you can make it. All right?'

She made a face. 'Mrs Stiles,' she said, 'won't like it.'

'Mrs Stiles don't have to eat it,' I answered. 'And Mrs Stiles ain't
Miss Maud's maid. I am.'

So then she did send soup. Maud ate it all up. 'Why are you
smiling?' she said, in her anxious way, when she had finished. I
said I wasn't. She put down her spoon. Then she frowned, like
before, over her gloves. They had got splashed.

'It's only water,' I said, seeing her face. 'It won't hurt you.'

She bit her lip. She sat another minute with her hands in her lap,
stealing glances at her fingers, growing more and more restless.
Finally she said:

'I think the water has a little fat in it . . .'

Then, it was easier to go into her room and get her a fresh pair of

gloves myself, than to sit and watch her fret. 'Let me do it,' I said,
undoing the button at her wrist; and though at first she wouldn't let
me touch her bare hands, in time—since I said I would be gentle—
she began to let me. When her fingernails grew long I cut them,
with a pair of silver scissors she had, that were shaped like a flying
bird. Her nails were soft and perfectly clean, and grew quickly, like
a child's nails. When I cut, she flinched. The skin of her hands was
smooth—but, like the rest of her, too smooth to be right, I never
saw it without thinking of the things—rough things, sharp things—
that would mark or hurt it. I was glad when she put her gloves back
on. The slivers of nail that I had cut away I would gather up out of
my lap and throw on the fire. She would stand and watch them turn
black. She did the same with the hairs I drew from her brushes and
combs—frowning while they wriggled on the coals, like worms,
then flared and turned to ash. Sometimes I'd stand and look with
her.

For there weren't the things to notice, at Briar, that there were at
home. You watched, instead, things like that: the rising of smoke,
the passing of clouds in the sky. Each day we walked to the river, to
see how it had lifted or dropped. 'In the autumn, it floods,' Maud
said, 'and all the rushes are drowned. I don't care for that. And
some nights a white mist comes creeping from the water, almost to
the walls of my uncle's house . . .' She shivered. She always said, *my
uncle's*, she never said *my*. The ground was crisp, and when it gave
beneath our boots she said: 'How brittle the grass is! I think the
river will freeze. I think it is freezing already. Do you see how it
struggles? It wants to flow, but the cold will still it. Do you see, Sue?
Here, among the rushes?'

She gazed, and frowned. I watched the movement of her face.
And I said—as I had said about the soup: 'It's only water, miss.'

'Only water?'

'Brown water.'

She blinked.

'You are cold,' I said then. 'Come back, to the house. We've been
out too long.' I put her arm about mine. I did it, not thinking; and
her arm stayed stiff. But then, the next day—or perhaps, the day

after that—she took my arm again, and was not so stiff; and after that, I suppose we joined arms naturally . . . I don't know. It was only later that I wondered about it and tried to look back. But by then I could only see that there was once a time when we had walked apart; and then a time when we walked together.

She was just a girl, after all; for all that they called her a lady. She was just a girl that had never known fun. One day I was tidying one of her drawers and found a deck of cards in it. She said she thought they must have been her mother's. She knew the suits, but that was all—she called the jacks, cavaliers!—so I taught her one or two soft Borough games—All-fours, and Put. We played for matches and spills, at first; then we found, in another drawer, a box of little counters, made of mother-of-pearl and shaped like fish and diamonds and crescent moons; and after that, we played for them. The mother-of-pearl was very sweet and cool on the hand.—My hand, I mean; for Maud of course still wore her gloves. And when she put down a card she put it down neatly, making the edges and corners match with the ones below. After a while I began to do that, too.

While we played, we talked. She liked to hear me talk of London. 'Is it truly so large?' she'd say. 'And there are theatres? And what they call, fashion-houses?'

'And eating-houses. And every kind of shop. And parks, miss.'

'Parks, like my uncle's?'

'A little like,' I'd say. 'But filled with people, of course.—Are you low, miss, or high?'

'I am high.' She set down a card. '—Quite filled, would you say?'

'I am higher. There. Three fish, to your two.'

'How well you play!—Quite filled, you say, with people?'

'Of course. But dark. Will you cut?'

'Dark? Are you sure? I thought London was said to be bright. With great lamps fired—I believe—with gas?'

'Great lamps, like diamonds!' I said. 'In the theatres and halls. You may dance there, miss, right through the night—'

'Dance, Sue?'

'Dance, miss.' Her face had changed. I put the cards down. 'You like to dance, of course?'

'I—' She coloured, and lowered her gaze. 'I was never taught it. Do you think,' she said, looking up, 'I might be a lady, in London— that is,' she added quickly, 'if I were ever to go there.—Do you think I might be a lady in London, and yet not dance?'

She passed her hand across her lip, rather nervously. I said, 'You might, I suppose. Shouldn't you like to learn, though? You could find a dancing-master.'

'Could I?' She looked doubtful, then shook her head. 'I am not sure . . .'

I guessed what she was thinking. She was thinking of Gentleman, and what he might say when he found out she couldn't dance. She was thinking of all the girls he might be meeting in London, who could.

I watched her fret for a minute or two. Then, 'Look here,' I said, getting up. 'It is easy, look—'

And I showed her a couple of steps, to a couple of dances. Then I made her rise and try them with me. She stood in my arms like wood, and gazed, in a frightened sort of way, at her feet. Her slippers caught on the Turkey carpet. So then I put the carpet back; and then she moved more easily. I showed her a jig, and then a polka. I said, 'There. Now we're flying, ain't we?' She gripped my gown until I thought it should tear. 'This way,' I said. 'Now, this. I am the gentleman, remember. Of course, it will go much better, with a real gent—'

Then she stumbled again, and we flew apart and fell into separate chairs. She put her hands to her side. Her breath came in catches. Her colour was higher than ever. Her cheek was damp. Her skirt stuck out like a little Dutch girl's on a plate.

She caught my eye, and smiled; though she still looked frightened.

'I shall dance,' she said, 'in London. Shan't I, Sue?'

'You shall,' I said. And at that moment, I believed it. I made her rise and dance again. It was only afterwards, when we had stopped and she had grown cool, and stood before the fire to warm up her cold hands—it was only then that I remembered that, of course, she never would.

For, though I knew her fate—though I knew it so well, I was helping to make it!—perhaps I knew it rather in the way you might know the fate of a person in a story or a play. Her world was so queer, so quiet and shut-up, it made the proper world—the ordinary, double-dealing world, where I had sat over a pig's head supper and a glass of flip while Mrs Sucksby and John Vroom laughed to think what I would do with my share of Gentleman's stolen fortune—it made that world seem harder than ever, but so far off, the hardness meant nothing. At first I would say to myself, 'When Gentleman comes I'll do this'; or, 'Once he gets her in the madhouse, I'll do that.' But I'd say it, then look at her; and she was so simple and so good, the thought would vanish, I would end up combing her hair or straightening the sash on her gown. It wasn't that I was sorry—or not much, not then. It was just I suppose that we were put together for so many hours at a time; and it was nicer to be kind to her and not think too hard about what lay before her, than to dwell on it and feel cruel.

Of course, it was different for her. She was looking forwards. She liked to talk; but more often she liked to be silent, and think. I would see her face change, then. I would lie at her side at night, and feel the turning, turning of her thoughts—feel her grow warm, perhaps blush in the dark; and then I knew she was thinking of Gentleman, working out how soon he'd come, wondering if he was thinking of her.—I could have told her, he was. But she never spoke of him, she never said his name. She only asked, once or twice, after my old aunty, that was supposed to be his nurse; and I wished she wouldn't, for when I spoke of her I thought of Mrs Sucksby; and that made me home-sick.

And then there came the morning when we learned he was coming back. It was an ordinary morning, except that Maud had woken and rubbed her face, and winced.—Perhaps that was what they call, a premonition. I only thought that later, though. At the time, I saw her chafing her cheek and said, 'What's the matter?'

She moved her tongue. 'I have a tooth, I think,' she said, 'with a point that cuts me.'

'Let me see,' I said.

I took her to the window and she stood with her face in my hands and let me feel about her gum. I found the pointed tooth almost at once.

'Well, that is sharper—' I began.

'Than a serpent's tooth, Sue?' she said.

'Than a needle, I was going to say, miss,' I answered. I went to her sewing-box and brought out a thimble. A silver thimble, to match the flying scissors.

Maud stroked her jaw. 'Do you know anyone who was bitten by a snake, Sue?' she asked me.

What could you say? Her mind ran to things like that. Perhaps it was the country living. I said I didn't. She looked at me, then opened her mouth again and I put the thimble on my finger and rubbed at the pointed tooth until the point was taken off. I had seen Mrs Sucksby do it many times, with infants.—Of course, infants rather wriggle about. Maud stood very still, her pink lips parted, her face put back, her eyes at first closed then open and gazing at me, her cheek with a flush upon it. Her throat lifted and sank, as she swallowed. My hand grew wet, from the damp of her breaths. I rubbed, then felt with my thumb. She swallowed again. Her eyelids fluttered, and she caught my eye.

And, as she did, there came a knock upon the door; and we both jumped. I stepped away. It was one of the parlourmaids. She had a letter on a tray. 'For Miss Maud,' she said, with a curtsey. I looked at the hand, and knew at once that it must be Gentleman's. My heart gave a dip. So did Maud's, I think.

'Bring it here, will you?' she said. And then: 'Will you pass me my shawl, also?' The flush had gone from her face, though her cheek was still red where I had pressed it. When I put the shawl across her shoulders, I felt her trembling.

I watched her then, seeming not to, as I moved about her rooms, taking up books and cushions, putting away the thimble and closing her box. I saw her turn the letter and fumble with it—of course, she could not tear the paper, with her gloves on. So then she sneaked a look at me, and then she lowered her hands and—still trembling, but making a show of carelessness, that was meant to say it was nothing to her, yet showed that it was everything—she unbuttoned one glove and put her finger to the seal, then drew the letter from the envelope and held it in her naked hand and read it.

Then she let out her breath in a single great sigh. I picked up a cushion and hit the dust from it.

'Good news, miss, is it?' I said; since I thought I ought to.

She hesitated. Then: 'Very good,' she answered, '—for my uncle, I mean. It is from Mr Rivers, in London; and what do you think?' She smiled. 'He is coming back to Briar, tomorrow!'

The smile stayed on her lips all day, like paint; and in the afternoon, when she came from her uncle, she wouldn't sit sewing, or go for a walk, would not even play at cards, but paced about the room, and sometimes stood before the glass, smoothing her brows, touching her plump mouth—hardly speaking to me, hardly seeing me at all.

I got the cards out anyway, and played by myself. I thought of Gentleman, laying out the kings and queens in the Lant Street kitchen while he told us all his plot. Then I thought of Dainty. Her mother—that had ended up drowned—had been able to tell fortunes from a pack of cards. I had seen her do it, many times.

I looked at Maud, standing dreaming at the mirror. I said,

'Should you like to know your future, miss? Did you know that you can read it, from how the cards fall?'

That made her turn from looking at her own face, to look at mine. She said after a moment,

'I thought it was only gipsy women could do that.'

'Well, but don't tell Margaret or Mrs Stiles,' I said. 'My grandmother, you know, was a gipsy-princess.'

And after all, my granny might have been a gipsy-princess, for all I knew of it. I put the cards together again, and held them to her. She hesitated, then came and sat beside me, spreading her great skirt flat, saying, 'What must I do?'

I said she must sit with her eyes closed for a minute, and think of the subjects that were nearest her heart; which she did. Then I said she must take the cards and hold them, then set out the first seven

of them, face down—which is what I thought I remembered
Dainty's mother doing; or it might have been nine cards. Anyway,
Maud set down seven.

I looked her in the eye and said, 'Now, do you really want to
know your fortune?'

She said, 'Sue, you are frightening me!'

I said again, 'Do you really want to know it? What the cards
teach you, you must obey. It is very bad luck to ask the cards to
show you one path, then choose another. Do you promise to be
bound by the fortune you find here?'

'I do,' she answered quietly.

'Good,' I said. 'Here is your life, laid all before us. Let us see the
first part of it. These cards show your Past.'

I turned over the first two cards. They were the Queen of Hearts,
followed by the Three of Spades. I remember them because of
course, while she had been sitting with her eyes tight shut, I had
sprung the pack; as anyone would have I think, being in my place
then.

I studied them and said, 'Hmm. These are sad cards. Here is a
kind and handsome lady, look; and here a parting, and the beginning of strife.'

She stared, then put her hand to her throat. 'Go on,' she said. Her
face was pale now.

'Let us look,' I said, 'at the next three cards. They show your
Present.'

I turned them over with a flourish.

'The King of Diamonds,' I said. 'A stern old gentleman. The
Five of Clubs: a parched mouth. The Cavalier of Spades—'

I took my time. She leaned towards me.

'What's he?' she said. 'The Cavalier?'

I said he was a young man on horseback, with good in his heart;
and she looked at me in such an astonished believing sort of way, I
was almost sorry. She said, in a low voice, 'Now I *am* afraid! Don't
turn over the next cards.'

I said, 'Miss, I must. Or all your luck will leave you. Look here.
These show your Future.'

I turned the first. The Six of Spades.

'A journey!' I said. 'Perhaps, a trip with Mr Lilly? Or perhaps, a journey of the heart . . .'

She didn't answer, only sat gazing at the cards I had turned up. Then: 'Show the last one,' she said in a whisper. I showed it. She saw it first.

'Queen of Diamonds,' she said, with a sudden frown. 'Who's she?'

I did not know. I had meant to turn up the Two of Hearts, for lovers; but after all, must have muddled the deck.

'The Queen of Diamonds,' I said at last. 'Great wealth, I think.'

'Great wealth?' She leaned away from me and looked about her, at the faded carpet and the black oak walls. I took the cards and shuffled them. She brushed at her skirt and rose. 'I don't believe,' she said, 'that your grandmother really was a gipsy. You are too fair in the face. I don't believe it. And I don't like your fortune-telling. It's a game for servants.'

She stepped away from me, and stood again before the glass; and though I thought she would turn and say something kinder, she didn't. But as she went, she moved a chair: and then I saw the Two of Hearts. It had fallen on the floor—she had had her slipper on it, and her heel had creased the pips.

The crease was a deep one. I always knew that card, after that, in the games we played, in the weeks that followed.

That afternoon, however, she made me put the cards away, saying the sight of them made her giddy; and that night she was fretful. She got into bed, but had me pour her out a little cup of water; and as I stood undressing I saw her take up a bottle and slip three drops from it into the cup. It was sleeping-draught. That was the first time I saw her take it. It made her yawn. When I woke next day, though, she was already awake, lying with a strand of her hair pulled to her mouth, and gazing at the figures in the canopy over the bed.

'Brush my hair hard,' she said to me, as she stood for me to dress her. 'Brush it hard and make it shine. Oh, how horrid and white my cheek is! Pinch it, Sue.' She put my fingers to her face, and pressed

them. 'Pinch my cheek, don't mind if you bruise it. I'd rather a blue
cheek than a horrid white one!'

Her eyes were dark, perhaps from the sleeping-drops. Her brow
was creased. It troubled me to hear her talk of bruises. I said,

'Stand still, or I shan't be able to dress you at all.—That's better.
Now, which gown will you have?'

'The grey?'

'The grey's too soft on the eye. Let's say, the blue . . .'

The blue brought out the fairness of her hair. She stood before
the glass and watched as I buttoned it tight. Her face grew
smoother, the higher I went. Then she looked at me. She looked at
my brown stuff dress. She said,

'Your dress is rather plain, Sue—isn't it? I think you ought to
change it.'

I said, 'Change it? This is all I have.'

'All you have? Good gracious. I am weary of it already. What
were you used to wearing for Lady Alice, who was so nice? Did she
never pass any of her own dresses on to you?'

I felt—and I think I was right in feeling it—that Gentleman had
let me down a bit here, sending me off to Briar with just the one
good gown. I said,

'Well, the fact is, miss, Lady Alice was kind as an angel; but she
was also rather near. She kept my frocks back, to take to India for
her girl there.'

Maud blinked her dark eyes and looked sorry. She said,

'Is that how ladies treat their maids, in London?'

'Only the near ones, miss,' I answered.

Then she said, 'Well, I have nothing to be near for, here. You
must and shall have another gown, to spend your mornings in. And
perhaps another besides that, for you to change into when— Well,
say we ever had a visitor?'

She hid her face behind the door of her press. She said,

'Now, I believe we are of a similar size. Here are two or three
dresses, look, that I never wear and shan't miss. You like your skirts
long, I see. My uncle does not care to see me in a long skirt, he
believes long skirts unhealthy. But he shan't mind, of course, about

you. You need only let down this hem a little here. You can do that, of course?'

Well, I was certainly used to taking stitches out; and I could sew a straight seam when I needed to. I said, 'Thank you, miss.' She held a dress before me. It was a queer thing of orange velvet, with fringes and a wide skirt. It looked like it had been blown together by a strong wind in a ladies' tailor's. She studied me, and then said,

'Oh, try it, Susan, do! Look, I shall help you.' She came close, and began to undress me. 'See, I can do it, quite as well as you. Now I am your maid, and you are the mistress!'

She laughed, a little nervously, all the time she worked.

'Why, look here in the glass,' she said at last. 'We might be sisters!'

She had tugged my old brown dress off me and put the queer orange one over my head, and she made me stand before the glass while she saw to the hooks. 'Breathe in,' she said. 'Breathe harder! The gown grips tight, but will give you the figure of a lady.'

Of course, her own waist was narrow, and she was taller by an inch. My hair was the darker. We did not look like sisters, we just both looked like frights. My dress showed all my ankle. If a boy from the Borough had seen me then, I should have fallen down and died.

But there were no Borough boys to see me; and no Borough girls, either. And it was a very good velvet. I stood, plucking at the fringes on the skirt, while Maud ran to her jewel box for a brooch, that she fastened to my bosom, tilting her head to see how it looked. Then there came a knock on the parlour door.

'There's Margaret,' she said, her face quite pink. She called, 'Come here to the dressing-room, Margaret!'

Margaret came and made a curtsey, looking straight at me. She said,

'I have just come for your tray, mi— Oh! Miss Smith! Is it you, there? I should never have known you from the mistress, I'm sure!'

She blushed, and Maud—who was standing in the shadow of the bed-curtain—looked girlish, putting her hand before her mouth. She shivered with laughter, and her dark eyes shone.

'Suppose,' she said, when Margaret had gone, 'suppose Mr . Rivers were to do what Margaret did, and mistake you for me? What would we do, then?'

Again she laughed and shivered. I gazed at the glass, and smiled.

For it was something, wasn't it, to be taken for a lady?

It's what my mother would have wanted.

And anyway, I was to get the pick of all her dresses and her jewels, in the end. I was only starting early. I kept the orange gown and, while she went to her uncle, sat turning the hem down and letting out the bodice. I wasn't about to do myself an injury, for the sake of a sixteen-inch waist.

'Now, do we look handsome?' said Maud, when I fetched her back. She stood and looked me over, then brushed at her own skirts. 'But here is dust,' she cried, 'from my uncle's shelves! Oh! The books, the terrible books!'

She was almost weeping, and wringing her hands.

I took the dust away, and wished I could tell her she was fretting for nothing. She might be dressed in a sack. She might have a face like a coal-heaver's. So long as there was fifteen thousand in the bank marked *Miss Maud Lilly*, then Gentleman would want her.

It was almost awful to see her, knowing what I knew, pretending I knew nothing; and with another kind of girl, it might have been comical. I would say, 'Are you poorly, miss? Shall I fetch you something? Shall I bring you the little glass, to look at your face in?'—and she would answer, 'Poorly? I am only rather cold, and walking to keep my blood warm.' And, 'A glass, Sue? Why should I need a glass?'

'I thought you were looking at your own face, miss, more than was usual.'

'My own face! And why should I be interested in doing that?'

'I can't say, miss, I'm sure.'

I knew his train was due at Marlow at four o'clock, and that William Inker had been sent to meet it, as he had been sent for me. At three, Maud said she would sit at the window and work at her sewing there, where the light was good. Of course, it was nearly

. then; but I said nothing. There was a little padded seat beside the rattling panes and mouldy sand-bags, it was the coldest place in the room; but she kept there for an hour and a half, with a shawl about her, shivering, squinting at her stitches, and sneaking sly little glances at the road to the house.

I thought, if that wasn't love, then I was a Dutchman; and if it *was* love, then lovers were pigeons and geese, and I was glad I was not one of them.

At last she put her fingers to her heart and gave a stifled sort of cry. She had seen the light coming, on William Inker's trap. That made her get up and come away from the window, and stand at the fire and press her hands together. Then came the sound of the horse on the gravel. I said, 'Will that be Mr Rivers, miss?' and she answered, 'Mr Rivers? Is the day so late as that? Well, I suppose it is. How pleased my uncle will be!'

Her uncle saw him first. She said, 'Perhaps he will send for me, to bid Mr Rivers welcome.—How does my skirt sit now? Had I not rather wear the grey?'

But Mr Lilly did not send for her. We heard voices and closing doors in the rooms below, but it was another hour again before a parlourmaid came, to pass on the message that Mr Rivers was arrived.

'And is Mr Rivers made comfortable, in his old room?' said Maud.

'Yes, miss.'

'And Mr Rivers will be rather tired, I suppose, after his journey?'

Mr Rivers sent to say that he was tolerable tired, and looked forward to seeing Miss Lilly with her uncle, at supper. He would not think of disturbing Miss Lilly before then.

'I see,' she said when she heard that. Then she bit her lip. 'Please to tell Mr Rivers that she would not think it any sort of disturbance, to be visited by him, in her parlour, before the supper-hour came . . .'

She went on like this for a minute and a half, falling over her words, and blushing; and finally the parlourmaid got the message and went off. She was gone a quarter of an hour. When she came back, she had Gentleman with her.

He stepped into the room, and did not look at me at first. His
eyes were all for Maud. He said,

'Miss Lilly, you are kind to receive me here, all travel-stained and
tumbled as I am. That is like you!'

His voice was gentle. As for the stains—well, there wasn't a mark
upon him, I guessed he had gone quickly to his room and changed
his coat. His hair was sleek and his whiskers tidy; he wore one
modest little ring on his smallest finger, but apart from that his
hands were bare and very clean.

He looked what he was meant to be—a handsome, nice-minded
gentleman. When he turned to me at last, I found myself making
him a curtsey and was almost shy.

'And here is Susan Smith!' he said, looking me over in my velvet,
his lip twitching towards a smile. 'But I should have supposed her
a lady, I am sure!' He stepped towards me and took my hand, and
Maud also came to me. He said, 'I hope you are liking your place at
Briar, Sue. I hope you are proving a good girl for your new mistress.'

I said, 'I hope I am too, sir.'

'She is a very good girl,' said Maud. 'She is a very good girl,
indeed.'

She said it in a nervous, grateful kind of way—like you would say
it to a stranger, feeling pushed for conversation, about your dog.

Gentleman pressed my hand once, then let it fall. He said, 'Of
course, she could not help but be good—I should say, no girl could
help but be good, Miss Lilly—with you as her example.'

Her colour had gone down. Now it rose again. 'You are too kind,'
she said.

He shook his head and bit at his lip. 'No gentleman could but be,'
he murmured, 'with *you* to be kind to.'

Now his cheeks were pink as hers. I should say he must have had
a way of holding his breath to make the blood come. He kept his
eyes upon her, and at last she gazed at him and smiled; and then she
laughed.

And I thought then, for the first time, that he had been right. She
was handsome, she was very fair and slight—I knew it, seeing her
stand beside him with her eyes on his.

Pigeons and geese. The great clock sounded, and they started and looked away. Gentleman said he had kept her too long. 'I shall see you at supper, I hope, with your uncle?'

'With my uncle, yes,' she said quietly.

He made her a bow, and went to the door; then, when he was almost out of it he seemed to remember me, and went through a kind of pantomime, of patting at his pockets, looking for coins. He came up with a shilling, and beckoned me close to take it.

'Here you are, Sue,' he said. He lifted my hand and pressed the shilling in it. It was a bad one. 'All well?' he added softly, so that Maud should not overhear.

I said, 'Oh, thank you, sir!' And I made another curtsey, and winked.—Two curious things to do together, as it happened, and I would not recommend you try it: for I fear the wink unbalanced the curtsey; and I'm certain the curtsey threw off the wink.

I don't think Gentleman noticed, however. He only smiled in a satisfied way, bowed again, and left us. Maud looked once at me, then went silently to her own room and closed the door—I don't know what she did in there. I sat until she called me, a half-hour later, to help her change into her gown for dinner.

I sat and tossed the shilling. 'Well,' I thought, 'bad coins will gleam as well as good.'

But I thought it in a discontented sort of way; and didn't know why.

That night she stayed an hour or two after supper, reading to her uncle and to Gentleman in the drawing-room. I had not seen the drawing-room then. I only knew what she did when I wasn't with her, through Mr Way or Mrs Stiles happening to remark on it as we took our meals. I still passed my evenings in the kitchen and in Mrs Stiles's pantry; and pretty dull evenings they generally were. This night, however, was different. I went down to find Margaret with two forks in a great piece of roasting ham, and Mrs Cakebread spooning honey on it. Honeyed ham, said Margaret, plumping up her lips, was Mr Rivers's favourite dish. Mr Rivers, said Mrs Cakebread, was a pleasure to cook for.

She had changed her old wool stockings for the black silk pair I had given her. The parlourmaids had changed their caps, for ones with extra ruffles. Charles, the knife-boy, had combed his hair flat, and made the parting straight as a blade: he sat whistling, on a stool beside the fire, rubbing polish into one of Gentleman's boots.

He was the same age as John Vroom; but was fair, where John was swarthy. He said, 'What do you say to this, Mrs Stiles? Mr Rivers says that, in London, you may see elephants. He says they keep elephants in pens in the parks of London, as we keep sheep; and a boy can pay a man sixpence, and ride on an elephant's back.'

'Well, bless my soul!' said Mrs Stiles.

She had fastened a brooch at the neck of her gown. It was a mourning brooch, with more black hair in it.

Elephants! I thought. I could see that Gentleman had come among them, like a cock into a coop of roosting hens, and set them all fluttering. They said he was handsome. They said he was better-bred than many dukes, and knew the proper treating of a servant. They said what a fine thing it was for Miss Maud that a clever young person like him should be about the house again. If I had stood up and told them the truth—that they were a bunch of flats; that Mr Rivers was a fiend in human form, who meant to marry Maud and steal her cash, then lock her up and more or less hope she died—if I had stood and told them that, they should never have believed it. They should have said that I was mad.

They will always believe a gentleman, over someone like me.

And of course, I wasn't about to tell them any such thing. I kept my thoughts to myself; and later, over pudding in her pantry, Mrs Stiles sat, fingering her brooch, and was also rather quiet. Mr Way took his newspaper away to the privy. He had had to serve up two fine wines with Mr Lilly's dinner; and was the only one, out of all of us, not glad that Gentleman had come.

At least, I supposed I was glad. 'You are,' I told myself, 'but just don't know it. You'll feel it, when you've seen him on his own.'—I thought we would find a way to meet, in a day or two. It was almost another two weeks, however, before we did. For of course, I had no reason for wandering, without Maud, into the grand parts of the house. I never saw the room he slept in, and he never came to mine. Besides, the days at Briar were run so very regular, it was quite like some great mechanical show, you could not change it. The house bell woke us up in the mornings, and after that we all went moving on our ways from room to room, on our set courses, until the bell rang us back into our beds at night. There might as well have been grooves laid for us in the floorboards; we might have glided on sticks. There might have been a great handle set into the side of the house, and a great hand winding it.—Sometimes, when the view beyond the windows was dark or grey with mist, I imagined that handle and thought that I could almost hear it turning. I grew afraid of what would happen if the turning was to stop.

That's what living in the country does to you.

When Gentleman came, the show gave a kind of jog. There was a growling of the levers, people quivering for a second upon their sticks, the carving of one or two new grooves; and then it all went on, smooth as before, but with the scenes in a different order. Maud did not go to her uncle, now, to read to him while he took notes. She kept to her rooms. We sat and sewed, or played at cards, or went walking to the river or to the yew trees and the graves.

As for Gentleman: he rose at seven, and took his breakfast in his bed. He was served by Charles. At eight o'clock he began his work on Mr Lilly's pictures. Mr Lilly directed him. He was as mad over his pictures as he was over his books, and had fitted up a little room for Gentleman to work in, darker and closer even than his library. I suppose the pictures were old and pretty precious. I never saw them. Nobody did. Mr Lilly and Gentleman carried keys about with them, and they locked the door to that room whether they were out of it or in it.

They worked until one o'clock, then took their lunch. Maud and I took ours alone. We ate in silence. She might not eat at all, but only sit waiting. Then, at a quarter to two, she would fetch out drawing-things—pencils and paints, papers and cards, a wooden triangle—and she would set them ready, very neatly, in an order that was always the same. She would not let me help. If a brush fell and

I caught it, she would take everything up—papers, pencils, paints,
triangle—and set it out all over again.

I learned not to touch. Only to watch. And then we would both
listen, as the clock struck two. And at a minute after that there
would come Gentleman, to teach her her day's lesson.

At first, they kept to the parlour. He put an apple, a pear and a
water-jug upon a table, and stood and nodded while she tried to
paint them on a card. She was about as handy with a paint-brush as
she would have been with a spade; but Gentleman would hold up
the messes she made and tilt his head or screw up his eye and say,

'I declare, Miss Lilly, you are acquiring quite a method.' Or,

'What an improvement, on your sketches from last month!'

'Do you think so, Mr Rivers?' she would answer, all in a blush.
'Is not the pear a little lean? Had I not ought to practise my perspective?'

'The perspective is, perhaps, a little at fault,' he'd say. 'But you
have a gift, Miss Lilly, which surpasses mere technique. You have an
eye for an essence. I am almost afraid to stand before you! I am
afraid of what might be uncovered, were you to turn that eye upon
me.'

He would say something like that, in a voice that would start off
strong and then grow sweet, and breathless, and hesitating; and she
would look as though she were a girl of wax and had moved too near
to a fire. She would try the fruit again. This time the pear would
come out like a banana. Then Gentleman would say that the light
was poor, or the brush a bad one.

'If I might only take you to London, Miss Lilly, to my own
studio there!'

That was the life he had faked up for himself—an artist's life, in
a house at Chelsea. He said he had many fascinating artist friends.
Maud said, 'Lady artist friends, too?'

'Of course,' he answered then. 'For I think that'—then he shook
his head—'well, my opinions are irregular, and not to everyone's
taste. See here, try this line a little firmer.'

He went to her, and put his hand upon hers. She turned her face
to his and said,

'Won't you tell me what it is you think? You might speak plainly. I am not a child, Mr Rivers!'

'You are not,' he said softly, gazing into her eyes. Then he gave a start. 'After all,' he went on, 'my opinion is mild enough. It concerns your—your sex, and matters of creation. There is something, Miss Lilly, I think your sex must have.'

She swallowed. 'What is that, Mr Rivers?'

'Why, the liberty,' he answered gently, 'of mine.'

She sat still, then gave a wriggle. Her chair creaked, the sound seemed to startle her, and she drew her hand away. She looked up, to the glass, and found my eyes on her, and blushed; then Gentleman looked up too, and watched her—that made her colour still harder and lower her gaze. He looked from her to me, then back to her again. He lifted his hands to his whiskers and gave them a stroke.

Then she put her brush to the picture of the fruit, and—'Oh!' she cried. The paint ran like a tear-drop. Gentleman said she must not mind it, that he had worked her quite enough. He went to the table, took up the pear and rubbed the bloom from it. Maud kept a little pen-knife with her brushes and leads, and he got this out and cut the pear into three wet slices. He gave one to her, kept one for himself, and the last he shook free of its juice and brought to me.

'Almost ripe, I think,' he said, with a wink.

He put his slice of pear to his mouth and ate it in two sharp bites. It left beads of cloudy juice on his beard. He licked his fingers, thoughtfully; and I licked mine; and Maud, for once, let her gloves grow stained, and sat with the fruit against her lip and nibbled at it, her look a dark one.

We were thinking of secrets. Real secrets, and snide. Too many to count. When I try now to sort out who knew what and who knew nothing, who knew everything and who was a fraud, I have to stop and give it up, it makes my head spin.

At last he said she might try painting from nature. I guessed at once what that meant. It meant that he could take her wandering about the park, into all the shady, lonely places, and call it instruction. I think she guessed it, too. 'Will it rain today, do you think?'

she asked in a worried sort of way, her face at the window, her eyes
on the clouds. This was the end of February, and still cold as anything; but just as everyone in that house perked up a bit to see Mr
Rivers come back to it again, so now even the weather seemed to lift
and grow sweet. The wind fell off, and the windows stopped rattling. The sky turned pearly instead of grey. The lawns grew green
as billiard tables.

In the mornings, when I walked with Maud, just the two of us, I
walked at her side. Now, of course, she walked with Gentleman: he
would offer her his arm and, after a show of hesitation, she would
take it; I think she held it more easily, through having grown used to
holding mine. She walked pretty stiffly, though; but then, he would
find little artful ways to pull her closer. He would bend his head
until it was near hers. He would pretend to brush dust from her
collar. There would start off space between them, but steadily the
space would close—at last, there would only be the rub of his sleeve
upon hers, the buckling of her skirt about his trousers. I saw it all;
for I walked behind them. I carried her satchel of paints and
brushes, her wooden triangle, and a stool. Sometimes they would
draw away from me, and seem quite to forget me. Then Maud
would remember, and turn, and say,

'How good you are, Sue! You do not mind the walk? Mr Rivers
thinks another quarter of a mile will do it.'

Mr Rivers always thought that. He kept her slowly walking about
the park, saying he was looking for scenes for her to paint, but
really keeping her close and talking in murmurs; and I had to follow,
with all their gear.

Of course, I was the reason they were able to walk at all. I was
meant to watch and see that Gentleman was proper.

I watched him hard. I also watched her. She would look sometimes at his face; more often at the ground; now and then at some
flower or leaf or fluttering bird that took her fancy. And when she
did that he would half turn, and catch my eye, and give a devilish
kind of smile; but by the time she gazed at him again his face would
be smooth.

You would swear, seeing him then, that he loved her.

You would swear, seeing her, that she loved him.

But you could see that she was fearful, of her own fluttering heart. He could not go too fast. He never touched her, except to let her lean upon his arm, and to guide her hand as she painted. He would bend close to her, to watch her as she dabbled in the colours, and then their breaths would come together and his hair would mix with hers; but if he went a little nearer she would flinch. She kept her gloves on.

At last he found out that spot beside the river, and she began a painting of the scenery there, adding more dark rushes each day. In the evening she sat reading in the drawing-room, for him and Mr Lilly. At night she went fretfully to her bed, and sometimes took more sleeping-drops, and sometimes shivered in her sleep.

I put my hands upon her, when she did that, till she was still again.

I was keeping her calm, for Gentleman's sake. Later on he would want me to make her nervous; but for now I kept her calm, I kept her neat, I kept her dressed very handsome. I washed her hair in vinegar, and brushed it till it shone. Gentleman would come to her parlour and study her, and bow. And when he said, 'Miss Lilly, I believe you grow sweeter in the face with every day that passes!', I knew he meant it. But I knew, too, that he meant it as a compliment not to her—who had done nothing—but to me, who did it all.

I guessed little things like that. He couldn't speak plainly, but made great play with his eyes and with his smiles, as I have said. We waited out our chance for a talk in private; and just as it began to look as though that chance would never come, it did—and it was Maud, in her innocent way, who let us have it.

For she saw him one morning, very early, from the window of her room. She stood at the glass and put her head against it, and said,

'There is Mr Rivers, look, walking on the lawn.'

I went and stood beside her and, sure enough, there he was, strolling about the grass, smoking a cigarette. The sun, being still rather low, made his shadow very long.

'Ain't he tall?' I said, gazing sideways at Maud. She nodded. Her breath made the glass mist, and she wiped it away. Then she said,

'Oh!'—as if he might have fallen over—'Oh! I think his cigarette ·
has gone out. Poor Mr Rivers!'

He was studying the dark tip of his cigarette, and blowing at it;
now he was putting his hand to his trouser pocket, searching for a
match. Maud made another swipe at the window-glass.

'Now,' she said, 'can he light it? Has he a match? Oh, I don't
believe he does! And the clock struck the half, quite twenty minutes
ago. He must go to Uncle soon. No, he does not have a match, in all
those pockets . . .'

She looked at me and wrung her hands, as if her heart was breaking.

I said, 'It won't kill him, miss.'

'But poor Mr Rivers,' she said again. 'Oh, Sue, if you are quick,
you might take a match to him. Look, he is putting his cigarette
away. How sad he looks now!'

We didn't have any matches. Margaret kept them in her apron.
When I told Maud that she said,

'Then take a candle! Take anything! Take a coal from the fire!
Oh, can't you be quicker?—Don't say I sent you, mind!'

Can you believe she had me doing that?—tripping down two
sets of stairs, with a lighted coal in a pair of fire-tongs, just so a man
might have his morning smoke? Can you believe I did it? Well, I
was a servant now, and must. Gentleman saw me stepping across
the grass to him, saw what I carried, and laughed.

I said, 'All right. She has sent me down with it for you to light
your cigarette from. Look glad, she is watching. But make a business of it, if you want.'

He did not move his head, but raised his eyes to her window.

'What a good girl she is,' he said.

'She is too good for you, that I do know.'

He smiled. But only as a gentleman should smile to a servant;
and his face he made kind. I imagined Maud, looking down, breathing quicker upon the glass. He said quietly,

'How do we do, Sue?'

'Pretty well,' I answered.

'You think she loves me?'

'I do. Oh, yes.'

He drew out a silver case and lifted free a cigarette. 'But she hasn't told you so?'

'She don't have to.'

He leaned close to the coal. 'Does she trust you?'

'I think she must. She has nobody else.'

He drew on the cigarette, then breathed out in a sigh. The smoke stained the cold air blue. He said, 'She's ours.'

He stepped back a little way, then gestured with his eyes; I saw what he wanted, let the coal fall to the lawn, and he stooped to help me get it. 'What else?' he said. I told him, in a murmur, about the sleeping-drops, and about her being afraid of her own dreams. He listened, smiling, all the time fumbling with the fire-tongs over the piece of coal, and finally catching it up and rising, and placing my hands upon the handle of the tongs and pressing them tight.

'The drops and the dreams are good,' he said quietly. 'They'll help us, later. But you know, for now, what you must do? Watch her hard. Make her love you. She's our little jewel, Suky. Soon I shall prise her from her setting and turn her into cash.—Keep it like this,' he went on, in an ordinary voice. Mr Way had come to the front door of the house, to see why it was open. 'Like this, so the coal won't fall and scorch Miss Lilly's carpets . . .'

I made him a curtsey, and he moved away from me; and then, while Mr Way stepped out to bend his legs and look at the sun and push back his wig and scratch beneath it, he said in one last murmur:

'They are placing bets on you, at Lant Street. Mrs Sucksby has five pounds on your success. I am charged to kiss you, in her behalf.'

He puckered up his lips in a silent kiss, then put his cigarette into the pucker and made more blue smoke. Then he bowed. His hair fell over his collar. He lifted up his white hand to brush it back behind his ear.

From his place on the step, I saw Mr Way studying him rather as the hard boys of the Borough did—as if not quite sure what he wanted to do most: laugh at him, or punch his lights out. But

Gentleman kept his eyes very innocent. He only lifted his face to the
sun, and stretched, so that Maud might see him better from the
shadows of her room.

She stood and watched him walk and smoke his cigarette, every
morning after that. She would stand at the window with her face
pressed to the glass, and the glass would mark her brow with a
circle of red—a perfect circle of crimson in her pale face. It was like
the spot upon the cheek of a girl with a fever. I thought I saw it
growing darker and fiercer with every day that passed.

Now she watched Gentleman, and I watched them both; and
the three of us waited for the fever to break.

I had thought it might take two weeks, or three. But two weeks had
gone by already, and we had got nowhere. Then another two passed,
and it was all just the same. She was too good at waiting, and the
house was too smooth. She would give a little jump out of her
groove, to be nearer to Gentleman; and he would sneak a little way
out of his, to be closer to her; but that would only make new
grooves for them to glide in. We needed the whole show to go bust.

We needed her to grow confiding, so that I could help her on her
way. But, though I dropped a thousand little hints—such as, what a
kind gentleman Mr Rivers was; and how handsome and how well-
bred; and how her uncle seemed to like him; and how she seemed to
like him, and how he seemed to like her; and if a lady ever thought
of marrying, didn't she think a gent like Mr Rivers might be just the
gent for the job?—though I gave her a thousand little chances like
that, to open up her heart, she never took one. The weather turned
cold again, then grew warmer. It got to March. Then it was almost
April. By May, Mr Lilly's pictures would all be mounted, and
Gentleman would have to leave. But still she said nothing; and he
held back from pressing her, out of fear that a wrong move would
frighten her off.

I grew fretful, waiting. Gentleman grew fretful. We all grew
nervy as narks—Maud would sit fidgeting for hours at a trot, and
when the house clock sounded she would give a little start, that

would make me start; and when it came time for Gentleman to call on her, I would see her flinching, listening for his step—then his knock would come, and she would jump, or scream, or drop her cup and break it. Then at night, she would lie stiff and open-eyed, or turn and murmur in her sleep.

All, I thought, for love! I had never seen anything like it. I thought about how such a business got worked out, in the Borough. I thought of all the things a girl could ordinarily do, when she liked a fellow that she guessed liked her.

I thought of what I would do, if a man like Gentleman liked me.

I thought perhaps I ought to take her aside and tell her, as one girl to another.

Then I thought she might think me rude.—Which is pretty rum, in light of what happened later.

But something else happened first. The fever broke at last. The show went bust, and all our waiting paid off.

She let him kiss her.

Not on her lips, but somewhere altogether better.

I know, because I saw it.

It was down by the river, on the first day of April. The weather was too warm for the time of year. The sun shone bright in a sky of grey, and everyone said there would be thunder.

She had a jacket and a cloak above her gown, and was hot: she called me to her, and had me take away the cloak, and then the jacket. She was sitting at her painting of the rushes, and Gentleman was near her, looking on and smiling. The sun made her squint: every now and then she would raise her hand to her eyes. Her gloves were quite spoiled with paint, and there was paint upon her face.

The air was thick and warm and heavy, but the earth was cold to the touch: it had all the chill of winter in it still, and all the dampness of the river. The rushes smelt rank. There was a sound, as of a locksmith's file, that Gentleman said was bullfrogs. There were long-legged spiders, and beetles. There was a bush, with a show of tight, fat, furry buds.

I sat beside the bush, on the upturned punt: Gentleman had carried it there for me, to the shelter of the wall. It was as far away
from him and Maud as he dared place me. I kept the spiders from
a basket of cakes. That was my job, while Maud painted, and
Gentleman looked on, smiling, and sometimes putting his hand on
hers.

She painted, and the queer hot sun went lower, the grey sky
began to be streaked with red, and the air grew even thicker. And
then I slept. I slept and dreamt of Lant Street—I dreamt of Mr Ibbs
at his brazier, burning his hand and shouting. The shout woke me
up. I started from the punt, not knowing for a second where I was.
Then I looked about me. Maud and Gentleman were nowhere to be
seen.

There was her stool, and there the terrible painting. There were
her brushes—one was dropped upon the ground—and there her
paints. I went over and picked up the fallen brush. I thought it
would be like Gentleman, after all, to have taken her back to the
house and left me to come up, sweating, with everything behind
them. But I could not imagine that she would go with him, alone. I
felt almost afraid for her. I felt almost like a real maid, worried for
her mistress.

And then I heard her voice, murmuring. I walked a little way, and
saw them.

They had not gone far—only just along the river, where it bent
about the wall. They did not hear me come, they did not look
round. They must have walked together along the line of rushes;
and then I suppose he had spoken to her at last. He had spoken, for
the first time, without me to overhear him—and I wondered what
words he had said, that could make her lean against him, like that.
She had her head upon his collar. Her skirt rose at the back, almost
to her knees. And yet, her face she kept turned hard from his. Her
arms hung at her side, like a doll's arms. He moved his mouth
against her hair, and whispered.

Then, while I stood watching, he lifted one of her weak hands
and slowly drew the glove half from it; and then he kissed her
naked palm.

And by that, I knew he had her. I think he sighed. I think she sighed, too—I saw her sag still closer to him, then give a shiver. Her skirt rose even higher, and showed the tops of her stockings, the white of her thigh.

The air was thick as treacle. My gown was damp where it gripped. A limb of iron would have sweated, in a dress on such a day. An eye of marble would have swivelled in its socket to gaze as I did. I could not look away. The stillness of them—her hand, so pale against his beard, the glove still bunched about her knuckles, the lifted skirt—it seemed to hold me like a spell. The purr of the bullfrogs was louder than before. The river lapped like a tongue among the rushes. I watched, and he dipped his head, and softly kissed her again.

I should have been glad to see him do it. I was not. Instead, I imagined the rub of his whiskers upon her palm. I thought of her smooth white fingers, her soft white nails.—I had cut them, that morning. I had dressed her and brushed her hair. I had been keeping her, neat and in her looks—all for the sake of this moment. All for him. Now, against the dark of his jacket and hair, she seemed so neat—so slight, so pale—I thought she might break. I thought he might swallow her up, or bruise her.

I turned away. I felt the heat of the day, the thickness of the air, the rankness of the rushes, too hard. I turned, and stole softly back to where the painting was. After a minute there came thunder, and another minute after that I heard the sound of skirts, and then Maud and Gentleman walked quickly about the curving wall, she with her arm in his, her gloves buttoned up and her eyes on the ground; him with his hand upon her fingers, his head bent. When he saw me he gave me a look. He said,

'Sue! We didn't like to wake you. We have been walking, and lost ourselves in gazing at the river. Now the light is all gone, and we shall have rain, I think. Have you a coat for your mistress?'

I said nothing. Maud, too, was silent, and looked nowhere but at her feet. I put her cloak about her, then took the painting and the paints, the stool and the basket, and followed her and Gentleman back, through the gate in the wall, to the house. Mr Way opened the door to us. As he closed it the thunder came again. Then the rain began to fall, in great, dark, staining drops.

'Just in time!' said Gentleman softly, gazing at Maud and letting her draw her hand from him.

It was the hand he had kissed. She must have felt his lips there still, for I saw her turn from him and hold it to her bosom, and stroke her fingers over her palm.

Chapter Five

The rain fell all that night. It made rivers of water that ran beneath the basement doors, into the kitchen, the still-room and the pantries. We had to cut short our supper so that Mr Way and Charles might lay down sacks. I stood with Mrs Stiles at a back-stairs window, watching the bouncing raindrops and the flashes of lightning. She rubbed her arms and gazed at the sky.

'Pity the sailors at sea,' she said.

I went up early to Maud's rooms, and sat in the darkness, and when she came she did not know, for a minute, that I was there: she stood and put her hands to her face. Then the lightning flashed again, and she saw me, and jumped.

'Are you here?' she said.

Her eyes seemed large. She had been with her uncle, and with Gentleman. I thought, 'She'll tell me now.' But she only stood gazing at me, and when the thunder sounded she turned and moved away. I went with her to her bedroom. She stood as weakly for me to

undress her as she had stood in Gentleman's arms, and the hand he
had kissed she held off a little from her side, as if to guard it. In her
bed she lay very still, but lifted her head, now and then, from her
pillow. There was a steady drip, drip in one of the attics. 'Do you
hear the rain?' she said; and then, in a softer voice: 'The thunder is
moving away . . .'

I thought of the basements, filling with water. I thought of the
sailors at sea. I thought of the Borough. Rain makes London houses
groan. I wondered if Mrs Sucksby was lying in bed, while the damp
house groaned about her, thinking of me.

Three thousand pounds! she had said. *My crikey!*

Maud lifted her head again, and drew in her breath. I closed my
eyes. 'Here it comes,' I thought.

But after all, she said nothing.

When I woke, the rain had stopped and the house was still. Maud
lay, as pale as milk: her breakfast came and she put it aside and
would not eat it. She spoke quietly, about nothing. She did not look
or act like a lover. I thought she would say something lover-like
soon, though. I supposed her feelings had dazed her.

She watched Gentleman walk and smoke his cigarette, as she
always did; and then, when he had gone to Mr Lilly, she said she
would like to walk, herself. The sun had come up weak. The sky
was grey again, and the ground was filled with what seemed puddles
of lead. The air was so washed and pure, it made me bilious. But we
went, as usual, to the wood and the ice-house, and then to the
chapel and the graves. When we reached her mother's grave she sat
a little near it, and gazed at the stone. It was dark with rain. The
grass between the graves was thin and beaten. Two or three great
black birds walked carefully about us, looking for worms. I watched
them peck. Then I think I must have sighed, for Maud looked at me
and her face—that had been hard, through frowning—grew gentle.
She said,

'You are sad, Sue.'

I shook my head.

'I think you are,' she said. 'That's my fault. I have brought you to this lonely place, time after time, thinking only of myself. But *you* have known what it is, to have a mother's love and then to lose it.'

I looked away.

'It's all right,' I said. 'It doesn't matter.'

She said, 'You are brave . . . .'

I thought of my mother, dying game on the scaffold; and I suddenly wished—what I had never wished before—that she had been some ordinary girl, that had died in a regular way. As if she guessed it, Maud said quietly now,

'And what—it doesn't trouble you, my asking?—what did your mother die of?'

I thought for a moment. I said at last that she had swallowed a pin, that had choked her.

I really did know a woman that died that way. Maud stared at me, and put her hand to her throat. Then she gazed down at her own mother's tomb.

'How would you feel,' she said quietly, 'if you had fed her that pin yourself?'

It seemed an odd sort of question; but, of course, I was used by now to her saying odd sorts of things. I told her I should feel very ashamed and sad.

'Would you?' she said. 'You see, I have an interest in knowing. For it was my birth that killed my mother. I am as to blame for her death as if I had stabbed her with my own hand!'

She looked strangely at her fingers, that had red earth at the tips. I said,

'What nonsense. Who has made you think that? They ought to be sorry.'

'No-one made me think it,' she answered. 'I thought it myself.'

'Then that's worse, because you're clever and ought to know better. As if a girl could stop herself from being born!'

'I wish I had been stopped!' she said. She almost cried it. One of the dark birds started up from between the stones, its wings beating the air—it sounded like a carpet being snapped out of a window. We both turned our heads to see it fly; and when I looked at her again, her eyes had tears in them.

I thought, 'What do you have to cry for? You're in love, you're in love.' I tried to remind her.

'Mr Rivers,' I began. But she heard the name and shivered.

'Look at the sky,' she said quickly. The sky had grown darker. 'I think it will thunder again. Here is the new rain, look!'

She closed her eyes and let the rain fall on her face, and after another second I could not have said what were raindrops, and what tears. I went to her and touched her arm.

'Put your cloak about you,' I said. Now the rain fell quick and hard. She let me lift her hood and fasten it, as a child might; and I think, if I had not drawn her from the grave, she would have stayed there and been soaked. But I made her stumble with me to the door of the little chapel. It was shut up fast with a rusting chain and a padlock, but above it was a porch of rotted wood. The rain struck the wood and made it tremble. Our skirts were dark with water at the hems. We stood close to one another, our shoulders tight against the chapel door, and the rain came down—straight down, like arrows. A thousand arrows and one poor heart. She said,

'Mr Rivers has asked me to marry him, Sue.'

She said it in a flat voice, like a girl saying a lesson; and though I had waited so hard to hear her say it, when I answered my words came out heavy as hers. I said,

'Oh, Miss Maud, I am gladder than anything!'

A drop of rain fell between our faces.

'Are you truly?' she said. Her cheeks were damp, her hair clinging to them. 'Then,' she went on miserably, 'I am sorry. For I have not told him yes. How can I? My uncle— My uncle will never give me up. It wants four years until I am twenty-one. How can I ask Mr Rivers to wait so long?'

Of course, we had guessed she'd think that. We had hoped that she would; for in thinking it she'd be all the more ready to run and be married in secret. I said, carefully, 'Are you sure, about your uncle?'

She nodded. 'He will not spare me, so long as there are books still, to be read and noted; and there will always be those! Besides, he is proud. Mr Rivers, I know, is a gentleman's son, but—'

'But your uncle won't think him quite enough a swell?'

She bit her lip. 'I'm afraid that if he knew Mr Rivers had asked for my hand, he would send him from the house. But then, he must go anyway, when his work here is finished! He must go—' Her voice shook. 'And how will I see him, then? How may you keep a heart, for four years, like that?'

She put her hands to her face and wept in earnest. Her shoulders jumped. It was awful to see. I said, 'You mustn't cry.' I touched her cheek, putting the damp hair from it. I said, 'Truly, miss, you mustn't cry. Do you think Mr Rivers will give you up now? How could he? You mean more to him than anything. Your uncle will come round, when he sees that.'

'My happiness is nothing to him,' she said. 'Only his books! He has made me like a book. I am not meant to be taken, and touched, and liked. I am meant to keep here, in a dim light, for ever!'

She spoke more bitterly than I had ever heard her speak before. I said,

'Your uncle loves you, I'm sure. But Mr Rivers—' The words got caught in my throat, and I coughed. 'Mr Rivers loves you, too.'

'You think he does, Sue? He spoke so fiercely yesterday, beside the river, while you slept. He spoke of London—of his house, his studio—he says he longs to take me there, not as his pupil, but as his wife. He says he thinks of nothing but that. He says he thinks that to wait for me will kill him! You think he means it, Sue?'

She waited. I thought, 'It's not a lie, it's not a lie, he loves her for her money. I think he *would* die if he lost it now.' I said,

'I know it, miss.'

She looked at the ground. 'But, what can he do?'

'He must ask your uncle.'

'He cannot!'

'Then'—I drew in my breath—'you must find another way.' She said nothing, but moved her head. 'You must do that.' Still nothing. 'Isn't there,' I said, 'another way you might take . . .?'

She lifted her eyes to mine and blinked back her tears. She looked anxiously to left and to right, then drew a little closer. She said, in a whisper:

'You'll tell no-one, Sue?'

'Tell them what, miss?'

She blinked again, hesitating. 'You must promise not to tell. You must swear it!'

'I swear!' I said. 'I swear!'—all the time thinking, *Come on, say it now!*—for it was dreadful, seeing her so afraid to give up her secret, when I knew what the secret was.

Then she did say it. 'Mr Rivers,' she said, more quietly than ever, 'says we might go away, at night.'

'At night!' I said.

'He says we might be privately married. He says my uncle might try to claim me then; but he does not think he will. Not once I am a—a wife.'

Her face, as she said the word, grew pale, I saw the blood fall out of her cheek. She looked at the stone on her mother's grave. I said,

'You must follow your heart, miss.'

'I am not sure. After all, I am not sure.'

'But to love, and then to lose him!' Her gaze grew strange. I said, 'You love him, don't you?'

She turned a little, and still looked queer, and would not answer. Then she said,

'I don't know.'

'Don't know? How can you not know a thing like that? Doesn't your blood beat hard when you see him coming? Doesn't his voice thrill in your ears, and his touch set you shaking? Don't you dream of him, at night?'

She bit her plump lip. 'And those things mean I love him?'

'Of course! What else could they mean?'

She did not answer. Instead, she closed her eyes and gave a shiver. She put her hands together, and again she stroked the spot upon her palm where he had yesterday touched his lips.

Only now I saw, she was not stroking the flesh so much as rubbing at it. She was not nursing the kiss. She felt his mouth like a burn, like an itch, like a splinter, and was trying to rub the memory of it away.

She didn't love him at all. She was afraid of him.

I drew in my breath. She opened her eyes and held my gaze.

'What will you do?' I said, in a whisper.

'What can I do?' She shivered. 'He wants me. He has asked me. He means to make me his.'

'You might—say no.'

She blinked, as if she could not believe I had said it. I could not believe it, either.

'Say no to him?' she said slowly. 'Say no?' Then her look changed. 'And watch him leave, from my window? Or perhaps when he goes I shall be in my uncle's library, where the windows are all dark; and then I shan't see him leave at all. And then, and then—oh, Sue, don't you think I should wonder, over the life I might have had? Do you suppose another man will come visiting, that will want me half as much as he? What choice have I?'

Her gaze, now, was so steady and so bare, I flinched from it. I did not answer for a moment, but turned and gazed down at the wood of the door we stood against, and the rusting chain that held it closed, and the padlock. The padlock is the simplest kind of lock. The worst are the kind that keep their business parts guarded. They are devils to crack. Mr Ibbs taught me that. I closed my eyes and saw his face; and then, Mrs Sucksby's. *Three thousand pounds*—! I drew in my breath, looked back to Maud, and said,

'Marry him, miss. Don't wait for your uncle's word. Mr Rivers loves you, and love won't harm a flea. You will learn to like him as you ought, in time. Till then go with him in secret, and do everything he says.'

For a second, she looked wretched—as if she might have been hoping I would say anything but that; but it was only for a second. Then her face grew clear. She said,

'I will. I'll do it. But, I can't go alone. You mustn't make me go with him, quite on my own. You must come with me. Say you will. Say you'll come and be my maid, in my new life, in London!'

I said I would. She gave a high, nervous laugh and then, from having wept and been so low, she grew almost giddy. She talked of the house that Gentleman had promised her; and of the fashions of London, that I would help her choose; and of the carriage she would have. She said she would buy me handsome gowns. She said she wouldn't call me her maid then, but her companion. She said she would get me a maid of my own.

'For you know I shall be very rich,' she said simply, 'once I am married?'

She shivered and smiled and clutched at my arm, and then she drew me to her and put her head against mine. Her cheek was cool, and smooth as a pearl. Her hair was bright with beads of rainwater. I think she was weeping. But I did not pull away to try and find out. I did not want her to see my face. I think the look in my eyes must have been awful.

That afternoon she set out her paints and her painting, as usual; but the brushes and the colours stayed dry. Gentleman came to her parlour, walked quickly to her, and stood before her as if he longed to pull her to him but was afraid. He said her name—not *Miss Lilly*, but *Maud*. He said it in a quiet, fierce voice, and she quivered, and hesitated once, then nodded. He gave a great sigh, seized her hand and sank before her—I thought that was pushing it a bit, myself, and even she looked doubtful. She said, 'No, not here!' and gazed quickly at me; and he, seeing her look, said, 'But we may be quite free, before Sue? You've told her? She knows all?' He turned to me with an awkward gesture of his head, as if it hurt his eyes to look at anything but her.

'Ah, Sue,' he said, 'if you were ever a friend to your mistress, be her friend now! If you ever looked kindly on a pair of foolish lovers, look kindly on us!'

He gazed hard at me. I gazed hard back.

'She has promised to help us,' said Maud. 'But, Mr Rivers—'

'Oh, Maud,' he said at that. 'Do you mean to slight me?'

She lowered her head. She said, 'Richard, then.'

'That's better.'

He was still on his knee, with his face tilted upwards. She touched his cheek. He turned his head and kissed her hands, and then she drew them quickly back. She said,

'Sue will help us all she can. But we must be careful, Richard.'

He smiled and shook his head. He said,

'And you think, seeing me now, I shall never be that?' He rose and stepped from her. He said, 'Do you know how careful my love will make me? See here, look at my hands. Say there's a cobweb spun between them. It's my ambition. And at its centre there's a spider, of the colour of a jewel. The spider is you. This is how I shall bear you—so gently, so carefully and without jar, you shall not know you are being taken.'

He said that, with his white hands cupped; and then, as she gazed into the space between them, he spread his fingers and laughed. I turned away. When I looked at her again, he had taken her hands in his and was holding them loosely, before his heart. She seemed a little easier. They sat, and talked in murmurs.

And I remembered all she had said at the graves, and how she had rubbed her palm. I thought, 'That was nothing, she has forgotten it now. Not love him, when he's so handsome and seems so kind?'

I thought, 'Of course she loves him.' I watched as he leaned to her and touched her and made her blush. I thought, 'Who wouldn't?'

Then he raised his head and caught my gaze and, stupidly, I blushed, too. He said,

'You know your duties, Sue. You've a careful eye. We shall be glad of that, in time. But today—well, have you no other little business, that will take you elsewhere?'

He gestured with his eyes to the door of Maud's bedroom.

'There's a shilling in it for you,' he said, 'if you do.'

I almost stood. I almost went. So used had I got, to playing the servant. Then I saw Maud. The colour had quite gone from her face. She said, 'But suppose Margaret or one of the girls should come to the door?'

'Why should they do that?' said Gentleman. 'And if they do, what will they hear? We shall be perfectly silent. Then they will go again.' He smiled at me. 'Be kind, Sue,' he said slyly. 'Be kind, to lovers. Did you never have a sweetheart of your own?'

I might still have gone, before he said that. Now I thought suddenly, Who did he think he was? He might pretend to be a lord; he was only a con-man. He had a snide ring on his finger, and all his coins were bad ones. I knew more than he did about Maud's secrets. I slept beside her in her own bed. I had made her love me like a sister; he had made her afraid. I could turn her heart against him if I wanted to, like that! It was enough that he was going to marry her at last. It was enough that he could kiss her, whenever he liked. I wouldn't leave her now to be tugged about and made nervous. I thought, 'Damn you, I'll get my three thousand just the same!'

So I said, 'I shan't leave Miss Lilly. Her uncle wouldn't like it. And if Mrs Stiles was to hear of it, then I should lose my place.'

He looked at me and frowned. Maud did not look at me at all; but I knew she was grateful. She said gently,

'After all, Richard, we shouldn't ask too much of Sue. We shall have time enough to be together, soon—shan't we?'

He said then that he supposed that that was true. They kept close before the fire, and after a while I went and sat and sewed beside the window and let them gaze at one another's faces undisturbed. I heard the hiss of his whispers, the rush of his breath as he laughed. But Maud was silent. And when he left, and took her hand and pressed it to his mouth, she trembled so hard, I thought back to all the times I had watched her tremble before, and wondered how I had ever mistaken that trembling for love. Once the door was closed she stood at the glass, as she often did, studying her face. She stood there for a minute, then turned. She stepped very slowly and softly, from the glass to the sofa, from the sofa to the chair, from the chair to the window—she moved, in short, across the whole of the room, until she reached my side. She leaned to look at my work and her hair, in its net of velvet, brushed my own.

'You sew neatly,' she said—though I had not, not then. I had sewn hard, and my stitches were crooked.

Then she stood and said nothing. Once or twice she drew in her breath. I thought there was something she longed to ask me, but dared not. In the end she moved away again.

And so our trap—that I had thought so lightly of, and worked so hard to lay—was finally set; and wanted only time to go quickly by and spring it. Gentleman was hired to work as Mr Lilly's secretary until the end of April, and meant to stay out his contract to the last—'So that the old man won't have the breaking of that to charge me with,' he said to me, laughing, 'alongside the breaking of certain other things.' He planned to leave when he was meant to—that is, the evening of the last day of the month; but, instead of taking the train for London, he would hang about, and come back to the house at the dead of night, for me and Maud. He must steal her away and not be caught, and then he must marry her—quick as he could, and before her uncle should hear of it and find her and take her home again. He had it all figured out. He could not fetch her in a pony and cart, for he should never have got it past the gate-house. He meant to bring a boat and take her off along the river, to some small out-of-the-way church where she would not be known as Mr Lilly's niece.

Now, to marry a girl at any church you must have been living in the parish of it for fifteen days; but he fixed that up, as he fixed everything. A few days after Maud had promised him her hand, he found some excuse and took a horse and went riding off to Maidenhead. He got a special licence for the wedding there—that meant they should not have to put out the banns—and then he went about the county, looking out for the right kind of church. He found one, in a place so small and broken-down it had no name—or anyway, that's what he told us. He said the vicar was a drunkard. Hard by the church there was a cottage, owned by a widow who kept black-faced pigs. For two pounds she said she would keep him a room and swear to whoever he liked that he had lived there a month.

Women like that will do anything for gentlemen like him. He got back to Briar that night looking pleased as a weasel, and handsomer than ever; and he came to Maud's parlour and sat us down and spoke to us in murmurs of all he had done.

When he had finished, Maud looked pale. She had begun to leave off eating, and was grown thin about the face. Her eyes were dark at the lids. She put her hands together.

'Three weeks,' she said.

I thought I knew what she meant. She had three weeks left to

make herself want him. I saw her counting the days in her head, and
thinking.

She was thinking of what was coming at the end of them.

For, she never learned to love him. She never grew to like his kisses
or the feel of his hand upon hers. She still shrank from him in a miserable fright—then nerved herself to face him, let him draw her
close, let him touch her hair and face. I supposed at first he thought
her backwards. Then I guessed he liked her to be slow. He would be
kind to her, then pressing, and then, when she grew awkward or
confused he would say,

'Oh! now you are cruel. I think you mean only to practise on my
love.'

'No indeed,' she would answer. 'No, how can you say it?'

'I don't think you love me as you ought.'

'Not love you?'

'You won't show it. Perhaps'—and here he'd give a sly glance, to
catch my eye—'perhaps there's someone else you care for?'

Then she would let him kiss her, as if to prove that there was not.
She would be stiff, or weak as a puppet. Sometimes she would
almost weep. Then he would comfort her. He would call himself a
brute that did not deserve her, that ought to give her up to a better
lover; then she would let him kiss her again. I heard the meeting of
their lips, from my cold place beside the window. I heard the creeping of his hand upon her skirt. Now and then I would look—just to
be sure he had not put her in too much of a fright. But then, I didn't
know what was worse—seeing her face shut up, her cheek made
pale, her mouth against his beard; or meeting her eye as the tears
were pressed from it and came spilling.

'Let her alone, why don't you?' I said to him one day, when she had
been called from the room to find a book for her uncle. 'Can't you
see she don't care for it, having you pestering her like that?'

He looked at me queerly for a second; then raised his brows.
'Not care for it?' he said. 'She is longing for it.'

'She is afraid of you.'

'She is afraid of herself. Girls like her always are. But let them squirm and be dainty as much as they like, they all want the same thing in the end.'

He paused, then laughed. He thought it a filthy kind of joke.

'What she wants from you is to be taken from Briar,' I said. 'For the rest, she knows nothing.'

'They all say they know nothing,' he answered, yawning. 'In their hearts, in their dreams, they know it all. They take it in their milk from the breasts of their mothers. Haven't you heard her, in her bed? Doesn't she wriggle, and sigh? She is sighing for me. You must listen harder. I ought to come and listen with you. Shall I do that? Shall I come to your room, tonight? You could take me to her. We could watch to see how hard her heart beats. You could put back her gown for me to see.'

I knew he was teasing. He would never have risked losing everything, for a lark like that. But I heard his words, and imagined him coming. I imagined putting back her gown. I blushed, and turned away from him. I said,

'You should never find my room.'

'I should find it, all right. I've had the plan of the house, from the little knife-boy. He's a good little boy, with a chattering mouth.' He laughed again, rather harder, and stretched in his chair. 'Only think of the sport! And how would it harm her? I would creep, like a mouse. I am good at creeping. I would only want to look. Or, she might like to wake and find me there—like the girl in the poem.'

I knew many poems. They were all about thieves being plucked by soldiers from their sweethearts' arms; and one was about a cat being tipped down a well. I didn't know the one he mentioned now, however, and not knowing made me peevish.

'You leave her alone,' I said. Perhaps he heard something in my voice. He looked me over, and his voice turned rich.

'Oh, Suky,' he said, 'have you grown squeamish? Have you learned sweet ways, after your spell with the quality? Who would have said you should take so to serving ladies, with pals like yours, and a home like your home! What would Mrs Sucksby say—and Dainty, and Johnny!—if they could see your blushes now?'

'They would say I had a soft heart,' I said, firing up. 'Maybe I do. Where's the crime in that?'

'God damn it,' he answered, firing up in his turn. 'What did a soft heart ever do for a girl like you? What would it do, for a girl like Dainty? Except, perhaps, kill her.' He nodded to the door through which Maud had gone to her uncle. 'Do you suppose,' he said, 'she wants your qualms? She wants your grip, on the laces of her stays— on her comb, on the handle of her chamber-pot. For God's sake, look at you!' I had turned and picked up her shawl, and begun to fold it. He pulled it from my hands. 'When did you become so meek, so tidy? What do you imagine you owe, to her? Listen to me. I know her people. I'm one of them. Don't talk to me as if she keeps you at Briar for kindness' sake—nor as if you came out of sweetness of temper! Your heart—as you call it—and hers are alike, after all: they are like mine, like everyone's. They resemble nothing so much as those meters you will find on gas-pipes: they only perk up and start pumping when you drop coins in. Mrs Sucksby should have taught you that.'

'Mrs Sucksby taught me lots of things,' I said, 'and not what you are saying now.'

'Mrs Sucksby kept you too close,' he answered. 'Too close. The boys of the Borough are right, calling you slow. Too close, too long. Too much like this.' He showed me his fist.

'Go and fuck it,' I said.

At that his cheeks, behind his whiskers, grew crimson, and I thought he might get up and hit me. But he only leaned forward in his seat, and reached to grip the arm of my chair. He said quietly,

'Let me see you in your tantrums again and I will drop you, Sue, like a stone. Do you understand me? I have come far enough now, to do without you if I must. She will do anything I tell her. And say my old nurse, in London, should grow suddenly sick, and need her niece to tend her? What would you do then? Should you like to put on your old stuff gown again, and go back to Lant Street with nothing?'

I said, 'I should tell Mr Lilly!'

'Do you think he would have you in his room, long enough to hear you?'

'Then, I should tell Maud.'

'Go ahead. And why not tell her, while you are about it, that I have a tail with a point, and cloven hooves? So I would have, were I to act my crimes upon the stage. No-one expects to meet a man like me in life, however. She would choose not to believe you. She cannot afford to believe you! For she has come as far as we have, and must marry me now, or be more or less ruined. She must do as I say—or stay here, and do nothing, for the rest of her life. Do you think she'll do that?'

What could I say? She had as good as told me herself that she would not. So I was silent. But from that point on, I think I hated him. He sat with his hand on my chair, his eyes on mine, for another moment or two; then there came the pat of Maud's slippers on the stairs, and after a second her face about the door. And then, of course, he sat back and his look changed. He rose, and I rose, and I made a hopeless sort of curtsey. He went quickly to her and led her to the fire.

'You are cold,' he said.

They stood before the mantel, but I saw their faces in the glass. She looked at the coals in the hearth. He gazed at me. Then he sighed and shook his hateful head.

'Oh, Sue,' he said, 'you are terribly stern today.'

Maud looked up. 'What's this?' she said.

I swallowed, saying nothing. He said,

'Poor Sue is weary of me. I've been teasing her, while you were gone.'

'Teasing her, how?' she asked, half-smiling, half-frowning.

'Why, by keeping her from her sewing, by talking of nothing but you! She claims to have a soft heart. She has no heart at all. I told her my eyes were aching for want of gazing at you; she told me to wrap them in flannel and keep to my room. I said my ears were ringing, for want of your sweet voice; she wanted to call for Margaret to bring castor-oil to put in them. I showed her this blameless white hand, that wants your kisses. She told me to take it and—' He paused.

'And what?' said Maud.

'Well, put it in my pocket.'

He smiled. Maud looked once at me, in a doubtful way. 'Poor hand,' she said at last.

He lifted his arm. 'It still wants your kisses,' he said.

She hesitated, then took his hand and held it in her own two slender ones and touched his fingers, at the knuckles, with her lips.—'Not there,' he said quickly, when she did that. 'Not there, but here.'

He turned his wrist and showed his palm. She hesitated again, then dipped her head to it. It covered her mouth, her nose, and half her face.

He caught my eye, and nodded. I turned away and wouldn't look at him.

For he was right, damn him. Not about Maud—for I knew that, whatever he said about hearts and gas-pipes, she was sweet, she was kind, she was everything that was gentle and handsome and good. But, he was right about me. How could I go back to the Borough, with nothing? I was meant to make Mrs Sucksby's fortune. How could I go back to her, and to Mr Ibbs—and to John—saying, I had thrown off the plot, let slip three thousand pounds, because—

Because what? Because my feelings were finer than I thought? They would say my nerve had failed me. They would laugh in my face! I had a certain standing. I was the daughter of a murderess. I had expectations. Fine feelings weren't in them. How could they be?

And then, say I gave it all up—how would that save Maud? Say I went home: Gentleman would go on and marry her, and lock her up anyway. Or, say I peached him up. He would be sent from Briar, Mr Lilly would keep her all the closer—she might as well be put in a madhouse, then. Either way, I didn't say much to her chances.

But her chances had all been dealt her, years before. She was like a twig on a rushing river. She was like milk—too pale, too pure, too simple. She was made to be spoiled.

Besides, nobody's chances were good, where I came from. And though she was to do badly, did that mean I must?

I didn't think it did. So though, as I have said, I was sorry for her,

I was not quite sorry enough to want to try and save her. I never really thought of telling her the truth, of showing up Gentleman as the villain he was—of doing anything, anything at all, that would spoil our plot and keep us from our fortune. I let her suppose he loved her and was kind. I let her think that he was gentle. I watched her try to make herself like him, knowing all the time that he meant to take her, trick her, fuck her and lock her away. I watched her grow thin. I watched her pale and dwindle. I watched her sit with her head in her hands, passing the points of her fingers across her aching brow, wishing she might be anyone but herself, Briar any house but her uncle's, Gentleman any man but the man she must marry; and I hated it, but turned away. I thought, *It can't be helped.* I thought, *It's their business.*

But, here was a curious thing. The more I tried to give up thinking of her, the more I said to myself, 'She's nothing to you', the harder I tried to pluck the idea of her out of my heart, the more she stayed there. All day I sat or walked with her, so full of the fate I was bringing her to I could hardly touch her or meet her gaze; and all night I lay with my back turned to her, the blanket over my ears to keep out her sighs. But in the hours in between, when she went to her uncle, I felt her—I felt her, through the walls of the house, like some blind crooks are said to be able to feel gold. It was as if there had come between us, without my knowing, a kind of thread. It pulled me to her, wherever she was. It was like—

It's like you love her, I thought.

It made a change in me. It made me nervous and afraid. I thought she would look at me and see it—or Gentleman would, or Margaret, or Mrs Stiles. I imagined word of it getting back to Lant Street, reaching John—I thought of John, more than any of them. I thought of his look, his laugh. 'What have I done?' I imagined I'd say. 'I haven't done anything!' And I hadn't. It was only, as I've said, that I *thought* of her so, that I *felt* her so. Her very clothes seemed changed to me, her shoes and stockings: they seemed to keep her shape, the warmth and scent of her—I didn't like to fold them up and make them flat. Her rooms seemed changed. I took to going about them—just as I had done, on my first day at Briar—

and looking at all the things I knew she had taken up and touched. Her box, and her mother's picture. Her books. Would there be books for her, at the madhouse? Her comb, with hairs snagged in it. Would there be anyone to dress her hair? Her looking-glass. I began to stand where she liked to stand, close to the fire, and I'd study my face as I'd seen her studying hers.

'Ten days to go,' I would say to myself. 'Ten days, and you will be rich!'

But I'd say it, and across the words might come the chiming of the great house bell; and then I would shudder to think of our plot being so much as a single hour nearer its end, the jaws of our trap that little bit closer and tighter about her and harder to prise apart.

Of course, she felt the passing hours, too. It made her cling to her old habits—made her walk, eat, lie in her bed, do everything, more stiffly, more neatly, more like a little clockwork doll, than ever. I think she did it, for safety's sake; or else, to keep the time from running on too fast. I'd watch her take her tea—pick up her cup, sip from it, put it down, pick it up and sip again, like a machine would; or I'd see her sew, with crooked stitches, nervous and quick; and I'd have to turn my gaze. I'd think of the time I had put back the rug and danced a polka with her. I'd think of the day I had smoothed her pointed tooth. I remembered holding her jaw, and the damp of her tongue. It had seemed ordinary, then; but I could not imagine, now, putting a finger to her mouth and it being ordinary . . .

She began to dream again. She began to wake, bewildered, in the night. Once or twice she rose from her bed: I opened my eyes and found her moving queerly about the room. 'Are you there?' she said, when she heard me stirring; and she came back to my side and lay and shook. Sometimes she would reach for me. When her hands came against me, though, she'd draw them away. Sometimes she would weep. Or, she would ask queer questions. 'Am I real? Do you see me? Am I real?'

'Go back to sleep,' I said, one night. It was a night close to the end.

'I'm afraid to,' she said. 'Oh, Sue, I'm afraid . . .'

Her voice, this time, was not at all thick, but soft and clear, and so unhappy it woke me properly and I looked for her face. I could not see it. The little rush-light that she always kept lit must have fallen against its shade, or burned itself out. The curtains were down, as they always were. I think it was three or four o'clock. The bed was dark, like a box. Her breath came out of the darkness. It struck my mouth.

'What is it?' I said.

She said, 'I dreamed— I dreamed I was married . . .'

I turned my head. Then her breath came against my ear. Too loud, it seemed, in the silence. I moved my head again. I said,

'Well, you shall be married, soon, for real.'

'Shall I?'

'You know you shall. Now, go back to sleep.'

But, she would not. I felt her lying, still but very stiff. I felt the beating of her heart. At last she said again, in a whisper: 'Sue—'

'What *is* it, miss?'

She wet her mouth. 'Do you think me good?' she said.

She said it, as a child might. The words unnerved me rather. I turned again, and peered into the darkness, to try and make out her face.

'Good, miss?' I said, as I squinted.

'You do,' she said unhappily.

'Of course!'

'I wish you wouldn't. I wish I wasn't. I wish— I wish I was wise.'

'I wish you were sleeping,' I thought. But I did not say it. What I said was, 'Wise? Aren't you wise? A girl like you, that has read all those books of your uncle's?'

She did not answer. She only lay, stiff as before. But her heart beat harder—I felt it lurch. I felt her draw in her breath. She held it. Then she spoke.

'Sue,' she said, 'I wish you would tell me—'

Tell me the truth, I thought she was about to say; and my own heart beat like hers, I began to sweat. I thought, 'She knows. She has guessed!'—I almost thought, *Thank God!*

But it wasn't that. It wasn't that, at all. She drew in her breath again, and again I felt her, nerving herself to ask some awful thing. I should have known what it was; for she had been nerving herself to ask it, I think, for a month. At last, the words burst from her.

'I wish you would tell me,' she said, 'what it is a wife must do, on her wedding-night!'

I heard her, and blushed. Perhaps she did, too. It was too dark to see.

I said, 'Don't you know?'

'I know there is—something.'

'But you don't know what?'

'How should I?'

'But truly, miss: you mean, you don't know?'

'How *should* I?' she cried, rising up from her pillow. 'Don't you see, don't you see? I am too ignorant even to know what it is I am ignorant of!' She shook. Then I felt her make herself steady. 'I think,' she said, in a flat, unnatural voice, 'I think he will kiss me. Will he do that?'

Again, I felt her breath on my face. I felt the word, *kiss*. Again, I blushed.

'Will he?' she said.

'Yes, miss.'

I felt her nod. 'On my cheek?' she said. 'My mouth?'

'On your mouth, I should say.'

'On my mouth. Of course . . .' She lifted her hands to her face: I saw at last, through the darkness, the whiteness of her gloves, heard the brushing of her fingers across her lips. The sound seemed greater than it ought to have done. The bed seemed closer and blacker than ever. I wished the rush-light had not burned out. I wished—I think it was the only time I ever did—that the clock would chime. There was only the silence, with her breath in it. Only the darkness, and her pale hands. The world might have shrunk, or fallen away.

'What else,' she asked, 'will he want me to do?'

I thought, 'Say it quick. Quick will be best. Quick and plain.' But it was hard to be plain, with her.

'He will want,' I said, after a moment, 'to embrace you.'

Her hand grew still. I think she blinked. I think I heard it. She said,

'You mean, to stand with me in his arms?'

She said it, and I pictured her, all at once, in Gentleman's grip. I saw them standing—as you do see men and girls, sometimes, at night, in the Borough, in doorways or up against walls. You turn your eyes. I tried to turn my eyes, now—but, of course, could not, for there was nothing to turn them to, there was only the darkness. My mind flung figures on it, bright as lantern slides.

I grew aware of her, waiting. I said, in a fretful way,

'He won't want to stand. It's rough, when you stand. You only stand when you haven't a place to lie in or must be quick. A gentleman would embrace his wife on a couch, or a bed. A bed would be best.'

'A bed,' she said, 'like this?'

'Perhaps like this.—Though the feathers, I think, would be devils to shake back into shape, when you've finished!'

I laughed; but the laugh came out too loud. Maud flinched. Then she seemed to frown.

'Finished . . .' she murmured, as if puzzling over the word. Then, 'Finished what?' she said. 'The embrace?'

'Finished *it*,' I said.

'But do you mean, the embrace?'

'Finished *it*.' I turned, then turned again. 'How dark it is! Where is the light?—Finished *it*. Can I be plainer?'

'I think you could be, Sue. You talk instead of beds, of feathers. What are they to me? You talk of *it*. What's *it*?'

'*It* is what follows,' I said, 'from kissing, from embracing on a bed. It is the actual thing. The kissing only starts you off. Then it comes over you, like—like wanting to dance, to a time, to music. Have you never—?'

'Never what?'

'Never mind,' I said. I still moved, restlessly. 'You must not mind. It will be easy. Like dancing is.'

'But dancing is not easy,' she said, pressing on. 'One must be taught to dance. You taught me.'

'This is different.'

'Why is it?'

'There are lots of ways to dance. You can only do this, one way. The way will come to you, when once you have begun.'

I felt her shake her head. 'I don't think,' she said miserably, 'it will come to me. I don't think that kisses *can* start me off. Mr Rivers's kisses never have. Perhaps—perhaps my mouth lacks a certain necessary muscle or nerve—?'

I said, 'For God's sake, miss. Are you a girl, or a surgeon? Of course your mouth will work. Look here.' She had fired me up. She had wound me tight, like a spring. I rose from my pillow. 'Where are your lips?' I said.

'My lips?' she answered, in a tone of surprise. 'They are here.'

I found them, and kissed her.

I knew how to do it all right, for Dainty had shown me, once. Kissing Maud, however, was not like kissing her. It was like kissing the darkness. As if the darkness had life, had a shape, had taste, was warm and glib. Her mouth was still, at first. Then it moved against mine. Then it opened. I felt her tongue. I felt her swallow. I felt—

I had done it, only to show her. But I lay with my mouth on hers and felt, starting up in me, everything I had said would start in her, when Gentleman kissed her. It made me giddy. It made me blush, worse than before. It was like liquor. It made me drunk. I drew away. When her breath came now upon my mouth, it came very cold. My mouth was wet, from hers. I said, in a whisper,

'Do you feel it?'

The words sounded queer; as if the kiss had done something to my tongue. She did not answer. She did not move. She breathed, but lay so still I thought suddenly, 'What if I've put her in a trance? Say she never comes out? What ever will I tell her uncle—?'

Then she shifted a little. And then she spoke.

'I feel it,' she said. Her voice was as strange as mine. 'You have made me feel it. It's such a curious, wanting thing. I never—'

'It wants Mr Rivers,' I said.

'Does it?'

'I think it must.'

'I don't know. I don't know.'

She spoke, unhappily. But she shifted again, and the shift brought
her nearer to me. Her mouth came closer to mine. It was like she
hardly knew what she was doing; or knew, but could not help it. She
said again, 'I'm afraid.'

'Don't be frightened,' I said at once. For I knew that she mustn't
be that. Say she got so frightened she cried off marrying him?

That's what I thought. I thought I must show her how to do it, or
her fear would spoil our plot. So, I kissed her again. Then I touched
her. I touched her face. I began at the meeting of our mouths—at
the soft wet corners of our lips—then found her jaw, her cheek, her
brow— I had touched her before, to wash and dress her; but never
like this. So smooth she was! So warm! It was like I was calling the
heat and shape of her out of the darkness—as if the darkness was
turning solid and growing quick, under my hand.

She began to shake. I supposed she was still afraid. Then I began
to shake, too. I forgot to think of Gentleman, after that. I thought
only of her. When her face grew wet with tears, I kissed them away.

'You pearl,' I said. So white she was! 'You pearl, you pearl, you
pearl.'

It was easy to say, in the darkness. It was easy to do. But next morning I woke, saw the strips of grey light between the curtains of the
bed, remembered what I had done, and thought, *My God*. Maud
lay, still sleeping, her brows drawn together in a frown. Her mouth
was open. Her lip had grown dry. My lip was dry, too, and I brought
up my hand, to touch it. Then I took the hand away. It smelt of her.
The smell made me shiver, inside. The shiver was a ghost of the
shiver that had seized me—seized us both—as I'd moved against
her, in the night. *Being fetched*, the girls of the Borough call it. *Did
he fetch you*—? They will tell you it comes on you like a sneeze; but
a sneeze is nothing to it, nothing at all—

I shivered again, remembering. I put the tip of one finger to my
tongue. It tasted sharp—like vinegar, like blood.

Like money.

I grew afraid. Maud made some movement. I got up, not looking at her. I went to my room. I began to feel ill. Perhaps I *had* been drunk. Perhaps the beer I had had with my supper had been brewed bad. Perhaps I had a fever. I washed my hands and my face. The water was so cold it seemed to sting. I washed between my legs. Then I dressed. Then I waited. I heard Maud wake, and move; and went slowly in to her. I saw her, through the space between her curtains. She had raised herself up from her pillow. She was trying to fasten the strings of her nightdress. I had untied them in the night.

I saw that, and my insides shivered again. But when she lifted her eyes to mine, I looked away.

I looked away! And she didn't call me to her side. She didn't speak. She watched me move about the room, but she said nothing. Margaret came, with coals and water: I stood pulling clothes from the press while she knelt at the hearth, my face blushing scarlet. Maud kept to her bed. Then Margaret left. I put out a gown, and petticoats and shoes. I put out water.

'Will you come,' I said, 'so I may dress you?'

She did. She stood, and slowly raised her arms, and I lifted up her gown. Her thighs had a flush upon them. The curls of hair between her legs were dark. Upon her breast there was a crimson bruise, from where I had kissed too hard.

I covered it up. She might have stopped me. She might have put her hands upon mine. She was the mistress, after all! But, she did nothing. I made her go with me to the silvery looking-glass above her fire, and she stood with her eyes cast down while I combed and pinned her hair. If she felt the trembling of my fingers against her face, she didn't say. Only when I had almost finished did she lift her head and catch my gaze. And then she blinked, and seemed to search for words. She said,

'What a thick sleep I had. Didn't I?'

'You did,' I said. My voice was shaking. 'No dreams.'

'No dreams,' she said, 'save one. But that was a sweet one. I think— I think you were in it, Sue . . .'

She kept her eyes on mine, as if waiting. I saw the blood beat in her throat. Mine beat to match it, my very heart turned in my breast; and I think, that if I had drawn her to me then, she'd have kissed me. If I had said, *I love you*, she would have said it back; and everything would have changed. I might have saved her. I might have found a way—I don't know what—to keep her from her fate. We might have cheated Gentleman. I might have run with her, to Lant Street—

But if I did that, she'd find me out for the villain I was. I thought of telling her the truth; and trembled harder. I couldn't do it. She was too simple. She was too good. If there had only been some stain upon her, some speck of badness in her heart—! But there was nothing. Only that crimson bruise. A single kiss had made it. How would she do, in the Borough?

And then, how would *I* do, back in the Borough with her at my side?

I heard, again, John's laugh. I thought of Mrs Sucksby. Maud watched my face. I put the last pin to her hair, and then her net of velvet. I swallowed, and said,

'In your dream? I don't think so, miss. Not me. I should say— I should say, Mr Rivers.' I stepped to the window. 'Look, there he is! His cigarette almost smoked already. You will miss him, if you wait!'

We were awkward with each other, all that day. We walked, but we walked apart. She reached to take my arm, and I drew away. And when, that night, I had put her into her bed and stood letting down her curtains, I looked at the empty place beside her and said,

'The nights are grown so warm now, miss. Don't you think you will sleep better on your own . . .?'

I went back to my narrow bed, with its sheets like pieces of pastry. I heard her turning, and sighing, all through the night; and I turned, and sighed, myself. I felt that thread that had come between us, tugging, tugging at my heart—so hard, it hurt me. A hundred times I almost rose, almost went in to her; a hundred times I thought, *Go to her! Why are you waiting? Go back to her side!* But every time, I thought of what would happen if I did. I knew that I couldn't lie beside her, without wanting to touch her. I couldn't have felt her breath come upon my mouth, without wanting to kiss her. And I couldn't have kissed her, without wanting to save her.

So, I did nothing. I did nothing the next night, too, and the night after that; and soon, there were no more nights: the time, that had always gone so slow, ran suddenly fast, the end of April came. And by then, it was too late to change anything.

Chapter Six

*G*entleman went first. Mr Lilly and Maud stood at the door to see him leave, and I watched from her window. She shook his hand and he made her a bow. Then the trap took him off, to the station at Marlow. He sat with folded arms, his hat put back, his face our way, his eyes now on hers, now on mine.

There goes the Devil, I thought.

He made no sort of sign. He did not need to. He had gone over his plans with us and we had them by heart. He was to travel three miles by the train, then wait. We were to keep to Maud's parlour till midnight, then go. He was to meet us at the river when the clock struck the half.

That day passed just like all the old ones. Maud went to her uncle, as she had used to do, and I went slowly about her rooms, looking over her things—only this time, of course, I was looking out for what we ought to take. We sat at lunch. We walked in the park, to the ice-house, the graves, and the river. It was the final time we would do it, yet things looked the same as they always had. It was us who had changed. We walked, not speaking. Now and then our skirts came together—and once, our hands—and we started apart, as if stung; but if, like me, she coloured, I don't know, for I didn't look at her. Back in her room she stood still, like a statue. Only now and then I heard her sigh. I sat at her table with her box full of brooches and rings and a saucer of vinegar, shining up the stones. I would rather do that, I thought, than nothing. Once she came to look. Then she moved away, wiping her eyes. She said the vinegar made them sting. It made mine sting, too.

Then came the evening. She went to her dinner, and I went to mine. Downstairs in the kitchen, everyone was gloomy.

'Don't seem the same, now Mr Rivers has gone,' they said.

Mrs Cakebread's face was dark as thunder. When Margaret let a spoon drop, she hit her with a ladle and made her scream. And then, no sooner had we started our dinners than Charles burst out crying at the table, and had to run from the kitchen wiping snot from his chin.

'He've took it very hard,' said one of the parlourmaids. 'Had his heart set on going to London as Mr Rivers's man.'

'You get back here!' called Mr Way, standing up, his powder flying. 'Boy your age, fellow like him, I'd be ashamed!'

But Charles would not come back, not for Mr Way nor anyone. He had been taking Gentleman his breakfasts, polishing his boots, brushing his fancy coats. Now he should be stuck sharpening knives and shining glasses in the quietest house in England.

He sat on the stairs and wept, and hit his head against the banisters. Mr Way went and gave him a beating. We heard the slap of his belt against Charles's backside, and yelps.

That put rather a dampener on the meal. We ate it in silence, and when we had finished and Mr Way had come back, his face quite purple and his wig at a tilt, I did not go with him and Mrs Stiles to the pantry to take my pudding. I said I had a head-ache. I almost did. Mrs Stiles looked me over, then looked away.

'How poorly you keep, Miss Smith,' she said. 'I should say you must have left your health in London.'

But it was nothing to me, what she thought. I should not see her—or Mr Way, or Margaret, or Mrs Cakebread—ever again.

I said Good-night, and went upstairs. Maud, of course, was still with her uncle. Until she came I did what we had planned, and got together all the gowns and shoes and bits and pieces we had agreed ought to be taken. It was all of it hers. My brown stuff dress I left behind me. I hadn't worn it in more than a month. I put it at the bottom of my trunk. I left that, too. We could only take bags. Maud had found out two old things of her mother's. Their leather was damp, with a bloom of white. They were marked, in brass, with letters so bold even I could read them: an *M* and an *L*—for her mother's name, which was like hers.

I lined them with paper, and packed them tight. In one—the heaviest one, which I would carry—I put the jewels I'd shined. I wrapped them in linen, to save them from tumbling about and growing dull. I put in one of her gloves with them—a white kid glove, with buttons of pearl. She had worn it once and supposed it lost. I meant to keep it, to remind me of her.

I thought my heart was breaking in two.

Then she came up from her uncle. She came twisting her hands. 'Oh!' she said. 'How my head aches! I thought he would keep me for ever, tonight!'

I had guessed she would come like this; and had got her some wine from Mr Way, as a nerver. I made her sit and take a little, then I wet a handkerchief with it and rubbed at the hollows of her brow. The wine made the handkerchief pink as a rose, and her head, where I chafed it, grew crimson. Her face was cool under my hand. Her eyelids fluttered. When they lifted, I stepped from her.

'Thank you,' she said quietly, her gaze very soft.

She drank more of the wine. It was quality stuff. What she left, I finished, and it went through me like a flame.

'Now,' I said, 'you must change.' She was dressed for her supper. I had set out her walking-gown. 'But we must leave off the cage.'

For there was no room for a crinoline. Without it, her short dress at last became a long one, and she seemed slenderer than ever. She had grown thin. I gave her stout boots to wear. Then I showed her the bags. She touched them, and shook her head.

'You've done everything,' she said. 'I should never have thought of it all. I should never have done any of it, without you.'

She held my gaze, looking grateful and sad. God knows how my face seemed. I turned away. The house was creaking, settling down as the maids went up. Then came the clock again, chiming half-past nine. She said,

'Three hours, until he comes.'

She said it in the same slow, flinching way that I had heard her say, once, 'Three weeks.'

We put the lamp out in her parlour, and stood at her window. We could not see the river, but we gazed at the wall of the park and thought of the water lying beyond it, cool and ready, waiting like us. We stood for an hour, saying almost nothing. Sometimes she shivered. 'Are you cold?' I'd say then. But she was not cold. At last the waiting began to tell even on me, and I began to fidget. I thought I might not have packed her bags as I should have. I thought I might have left out her linen, or her jewels, or that white glove. I had put the glove in, I knew it; but I was become like her, restless as a flea. I went to her bedroom and opened the bags, leaving her at the window. I took out all the gowns and linen, and packed them again. Then, as I tightened a strap on a buckle, it broke. The leather was so old it was almost perished. I got a needle, and sewed the strap tight, in great, wild stitches. I put my mouth to the thread to bite it, and tasted salt.

Then I heard the opening of Maud's door.

My heart gave a jump. I put the bags out of sight, in the shadow of the bed, and stood and listened. No sound at all. I went to the door to the parlour, and looked inside. The window-curtains were open and let the moonlight in; but the room was empty, Maud was gone.

She had left the door ajar. I tiptoed to it and squinted into the passage. I thought there came another noise then, above the ordinary creakings and tickings of the house—perhaps, the opening

and shutting of another door, far-off. But I couldn't be sure. I called
once, in a whisper, 'Miss Maud!'—but even a whisper sounded
loud, at Briar, and I fell silent, straining my ears, looking hard at the
darkness, then walking a few steps into the passage and listening
again. I put my hands together and pressed them tight, more nervous now than I can say; but I was also, to be honest, rather
peeved—for wasn't it like her, to go wandering off at this late hour,
without a reason or a word?

When the clock struck half-past eleven I called again, and took
another couple of steps along the passage. But then my foot caught
the edge of a rug, and I almost tripped. She could go this way without a candle, she knew it so well; but it was all strange to me. I
didn't dare wander after her. Suppose I took a wrong turning in the
dark? I might never make my way out again.

So I only waited, counting the minutes. I went back to the bedroom and brought out the bags. Then I stood at the window. The
moon was full, the night was bright. The lawn lay stretched before
the house, the wall at the end of it, the river beyond. Somewhere on
the water was Gentleman, coming closer as I watched. How long
would he wait?

At last, when I had sweated myself into a lather, the clock struck
twelve. I stood and trembled at each beating of the bell. The last
one sounded, and left an echo. I thought, 'That's it.'—And, as I
thought it, I heard the soft thud of her boots—she was at the door,
her face pale in the darkness, her breaths coming quick as a cat's.

'Forgive me, Sue!' she said. 'I went to my uncle's library. I wanted
to see it, a final time. But I couldn't go until I knew he was asleep.'

She shivered. I pictured her, pale and slight and silent, alone
among those dark books. 'Never mind,' I said. 'But, we must be
quick. Come here, come on.'

I gave her her cloak, and fastened up mine. She looked about her,
at all she was leaving. Her teeth began to chatter. I gave her the
lightest bag. Then I stood before her and put a finger to her mouth.

'Now, be steady,' I said.

All my nervousness had left me, and I was suddenly calm. I
thought of my mother, and all the dark and sleeping houses she

must have stolen her way through, before they caught her. The bad blood rose in me, just like wine.

We went by the servants' stairs. I had been carefully up and down them the day before, looking for the steps that particularly creaked; now I led her over them, holding her hand, and watching where she placed her feet. At the start of the corridor where there were the doors to the kitchen and to Mrs Stiles's pantry, I made her stop and wait and listen. She kept her hand in mine. A mouse ran, quick, along the wainscot; but there was no other movement, and no sounds from anywhere. The floor had drugget on it, that softened our shoes. Only our skirts went rustle and swish.

The door to the yard was locked with a key, but the key was left in it: I drew it out before I turned it, and put a little beef fat to the bit; and then I put more fat to the bolts that fastened the door closed at the bottom and the top. I had got the fat from Mrs Cakebread's cupboard. That was sixpence less she should have from the butcher's boy! Maud watched me laying it about the locks, with an astounded sort of look. I said softly,

'This is easy. If we was coming the other way, *that* would be hard.'

Then I gave her a wink. It was the satisfaction of the job. I really wished, just then, it had been harder. I licked my fingers clean of the fat, then put my shoulder to the door and pressed it tight into its frame: after that, the key turned smoothly and the bolts slid in their cradles, gentle as babies.

The air, outside, was cold and clear. The moon cast great black shadows. We were grateful for them. We kept to the walls of the house that were darkest, going quickly and softly from one to another and then running fast across a corner of lawn to the hedges and trees beyond. She held my hand again, and I showed her where to run. Only once I felt her hesitate, and then I turned and found her gazing at the house, with a queer expression that seemed half-fearful and yet was almost a smile. There were no lights in the windows. No-one watched. The house looked flat, like a house in a play. I let her stand for almost a minute, then pulled her hand.

'Now you must come,' I said.

She turned her head and did not look again. We walked quickly
to the wall of the park, and then we followed it, along a damp and
tangled path. The bushes caught at the wool of our cloaks, and
creatures leapt in the grass, or slithered before us; and there were
cobwebs, fine and shining like wires of glass, that we must trample
through and break. The noise seemed awful. Our breaths came
harder. We walked so long, I thought we had missed the gate to the
river; but then the path grew clearer, and the arch sprang up, lit
bright by the moon. Maud moved past me and took out her key, and
let us through it, then made the gate fast at our backs.

Now we were out of the park I breathed a little freer. We set
down the bags and stood still in the darkness, in the shadow of the
wall. The moon struck the rushes of the further bank, and made
spears of them, with wicked points. The surface of the river seemed
almost white. The only sound now was the flowing of the water, the
calling of some bird; then came the splash of a fish. There was no
sign of Gentleman. We had come quicker than we planned for. I listened, and heard nothing. I looked at the sky, at all the stars that
were in it. More stars than seemed natural. Then I looked at Maud.
She was holding her cloak about her face, but when she saw me turn
to her she reached and took my hand. She took it, not to be led by
me, not to be comforted; only to hold it, because it was mine.

In the sky, a star moved, and we both turned to watch it.

'That's luck,' I said.

Then the Briar bell struck. Half-past twelve—the chime came
clear across the park, I suppose the bright air made it sharper. For
a second, the echo of it hung about the ear; and then above it rose
another, gentler sound—we heard it, and stepped apart—it was the
careful creak of oars, the slither of water against wood. About the
bend of the silvery river came the dark shape of a boat. I saw the
oars dip and rise, and scatter coins of moonlight; then they were
drawn high, and left a silence. The boat glided towards the rushes,
then rocked and creaked again as Gentleman half-rose from his
seat. He could not see us, where we waited in the shadow of the
wall. He could not see us; but it was not me who stepped forward

first, it was her. She went stiffly to the water's edge, then took the coil of rope he threw and braced herself against the tugging of the boat, until the boat was steady.

I don't remember if Gentleman spoke. I don't believe he looked at me, except, once he had helped Maud across the ancient landing-place, to give me his hand and guide me as he had guided her, over the rotten planks. I think we did it all in silence. I know the boat was narrow, and our skirts bulged as we sat—for, when Gentleman took up the oars to turn us, we rocked again, and I grew suddenly frightened of the boat capsizing, imagining the water filling all those folds and frills and sucking us under. But Maud sat steady. I saw Gentleman looking her over. Still no-one spoke, however. We had done it all in a moment, and the boat moved quick. The stream was with us. For a minute, the river followed the wall of the park; we passed the place where I had seen him kiss her hand; then the wall snaked off. There came a line of dark trees instead. Maud sat with her eyes on her lap, not looking.

We went very carefully. The night was so still. Gentleman kept the boat as close as he could to the shadows of the bank: only now and then, when the trees were thinner, did we move in moonlight. But there was no-one about, to watch us. Where there were houses built near to the river, they were shut up and dark. Once, when the river became broad, and there were islands, with barges moored at them, and grazing horses, he stopped the oars and let us glide in silence; but still no-one heard us pass or came to look. Then the river grew narrow again, and we moved on; and after that, there were no more houses and no more boats. There was only the darkness, the broken moonlight, the creaking of the sculls, the dipping and the rising of Gentleman's hands and the white of his cheek above his whisker.

We did not keep upon the river for long. At a spot upon the bank, two miles from Briar, he pulled up the boat and moored it. This was where he had started from. He had left a horse there, with a lady's saddle on it. He helped us from the water, sat Maud upon the horse's back, and strapped her bags beside her. He said,

'We must go another mile or so. Maud?' She did not answer. 'You must be brave. We are very close now.'

Then he looked at me and nodded. We started off—him leading
the horse by the bridle, Maud hunched and stiff upon it, me walking behind. Still we met no-one. Again I looked at the stars. You
never saw stars so bright at home, the sky was never so dark and so
clear.

The horse was shoeless. Its hooves sounded dull on the dirt of
the road.

We went rather slowly—for Maud's sake, I suppose, so she
should not be shaken about and made sick. She looked sick, anyway;
and when we came at last to the place he had found—it was two or
three leaning cottages, and a great dark church—she looked sicker
than ever. A dog came up and started barking. Gentleman kicked it
and made it yelp. He led us to the cottage that was nearest the
church, and the door was opened, a man came out, and then a
woman, holding a lantern. They had been waiting. The woman
was the one who had kept the rooms for us: she was yawning, but
stretching her neck as she yawned, to get a good look at Maud. She
made Gentleman a curtsey. The man was the parson, the vicar—
whatever you call him. He made a bow. He wore a gown of dirty
white, and wanted shaving. He said,

'Good-night to you. Good-night to you, miss. And what a fair
night, for an escapade!'

Gentleman said only, 'Is everything made ready?' He put his
arms up to Maud, to help her from the horse: she kept her hands
upon the saddle, and slid down awkwardly, and stepped away from
him. She did not come to me, but stood alone. The woman still
studied her. She was studying her pale, set, handsome face, her look
of sickness, and I knew she was thinking—as anyone would think,
I suppose—that she was in the family way, and marrying out of
fear. Perhaps Gentleman had even made her think it, when he
spoke to her before. For it would be all to his advantage, if it came
to a challenge by Mr Lilly, for it to seem that he had had Maud in
her uncle's own house; and we could say the baby got miscarried,
later.

I would say it, I thought, for five hundred more.

I thought that, even as I stood watching the woman looking at

Maud and hating her for doing it; even as I hated myself, for thinking it. The parson came forward and made another bow.

'All's ready indeed, sir,' he said. 'There's only the little matter
of— In light of the special circumstances—'

'Yes, yes,' said Gentleman. He took the parson aside and drew
out his pocket-book. The horse tossed its head, but from one of the
other cottages a boy had come over to lead it away. He also looked
at Maud; but then he looked from her to me, and it was me he
touched his cap to. Of course, he had not seen her in the saddle, and
I was dressed in one of her old gowns and must have seemed quite
a lady; and she stood in such a mean and shrinking kind of way, that
she seemed the maid.

She did not see it. She had her eyes upon the ground. The parson
put his money away in some close pocket under his robe, then he
rubbed his hands together. 'Well and good,' he said. 'And should
the lady like to change her costume? Should she like to visit her
room? Or shall we do the joining at once?'

'We'll do it at once,' said Gentleman, before anyone else could
answer. He took off his hat and smoothed his hair, fussing a little
with the curls about his ears. Maud stood very stiff. I went to her,
and put her hood up nicely, and settled the cloak in neater folds; and
then I passed my hands across her hair and cheeks. She would not
look at me. Her face was cold. The hem of her skirt was dark, as if
dipped in a dye for mourning. Her cloak had mud on it. I said,
'Give me your mittens, miss.'—For I knew that, beneath them, she
had her white kid gloves. I said, 'You had much better go to your
wedding in white gloves, than buff mittens.'

She let me draw them from her, then she stood and crossed her
hands. The woman said to me, 'No flower, for the lady?' I looked at
Gentleman. He shrugged.

'Should you like a flower, Maud?' he said carelessly. She didn't
answer. He said, 'Well, I think we shall not mind the absence of a
flower. Now, sir, if you will—'

I said, 'You might at least get her a flower! Just one flower, for her
to carry into church!'

I had not thought of it until the woman said it; but now—oh! the cruelty of taking her, without a bloom, to be his wife, seemed all at once a frightful thing, I could not bear it. My voice came out sounding almost wild, and Gentleman gazed at me and frowned, and the parson looked curious, the woman sorry; and then Maud turned her eyes to me and said slowly,

'I should like a flower, Richard. I should like a flower. And Sue must have a flower, too.'

With every saying of the one word, *flower*, it seemed to grow a little stranger. Gentleman let out his breath and began to look about him in a peevish sort of way. The parson also looked. It was half-past one or so, and very dark out of the moonlight. We stood in a muddy kind of green, with hedges of brambles. The hedges were black. If there were flowers in there, we should never have found them. I said to the woman,

'Haven't you nothing we might take? Haven't you a flower in a pot?' She thought a minute, then stepped nimbly back into her cottage; and what she came out with at last was, a sprig of dry leaves, round as shillings, white as paper, quivering on a few thin stalks that looked ready to snap.

It was honesty. We stood and gazed at it, and no-one would name it. Then Maud took the stalks and divided them up, giving some to me, but keeping the most for herself. In her hands the leaves quivered harder than ever. Gentleman lit up a cigarette and took two puffs of it, then threw it away. It stayed glowing in the darkness. He nodded to the parson, and the parson took up the lantern, and led us through the church gate and along a path between a line of tilting gravestones that the moon gave deep, sharp shadows. Maud walked with Gentleman, and he held her arm in his. I walked with the woman. We were to be witnesses. Her name was Mrs Cream.

'Come far?' she said.

I did not answer.

The church was of flint and, even with the moon on it, looked quite black. Inside it was whitewashed, but the white had turned to yellow. There were a few candles lit, about the altar and the pews, and a few moths about the candles, some dead in the wax. We did not try to sit, but went straight to the altar, and the parson stood

before us with his Bible. He blinked at the page. He read, and muddled his words. Mrs Cream breathed hard, like a horse. I stood and
held my poor, bent twig of honesty, and watched Maud standing at
Gentleman's side, holding tight on to hers. I had kissed her. I had
lain upon her. I had touched her with a sliding hand. I had called
her a pearl. She had been kinder to me than anyone save Mrs
Sucksby; and she had made me love her, when I meant only to ruin
her.

She was about to be married, and was frightened to death. And
soon no-one would love her, ever again.

I saw Gentleman look at her. The parson coughed over his book.
He had got to the part of the service that asked if anybody there
knew any reason as to why the man and woman before him should
not be married; and he looked up through his eyebrows, and for a
second the church was still.

I held my breath, and said nothing.

So then he went on, looking at Maud and at Gentleman, asking
the same thing of them, saying that, on the Day of Judgement they
should have to give up all the awful secrets of their hearts; and had
much better give them up now, and be done with it.

Again there was a silence.

So then he turned to Gentleman. 'Will you,' he said, and all the
rest of it—'Will you have her and honour her, for as long as you
live?'

'I will,' said Gentleman.

The parson nodded. Then he faced Maud, and asked the same
thing of her; and she hesitated, then spoke.

'I will,' she said.

Then Gentleman stood a little easier. The parson stretched his
throat from his collar and scratched it.

'Who gives this woman to be married?' he said.

I kept quite still, till Gentleman turned to me; and then he
gestured with his head, and I went and stood at Maud's side, and
they showed me how I must take her hand and pass it to the
parson, for him to put it into Gentleman's. I would rather Mrs
Cream had done it, than almost anything. Her fingers, without

her glove, were stiff and cold as fingers made of wax. Gentleman held them, and spoke the words the parson read to him; and then Maud took his hand, and said the same words over. Her voice was so thin, it seemed to rise like smoke into the darkness, and then to vanish.

Then Gentleman brought a ring out, and he took her hand again and put the ring over her finger, all the time repeating the parson's words, that he would worship her, and give her all his goods. The ring looked queer upon her. It seemed gold in the candle-light, but—I saw it later—it was bad.

It was all bad, and couldn't have been worse. The parson read another prayer, then raised his hands and closed his eyes.

'These two that God has joined together,' he said, 'let no man put in sunder.'

And that was it.

They were married.

Gentleman kissed her and she stood and swayed, as if dazed. Mrs Cream said in a murmur,

'She don't know what've hit her, look at her. She'll know it later—plum feller like him. Heh heh.'

I did not turn to her. If I had, I should have punched her. The parson shut his Bible and led us from the altar to the room where they kept the register. Here Gentleman wrote his name and Maud—who was now to be Mrs Rivers—wrote hers; and Mrs Cream and I put ours beneath them. Gentleman had already shown me how to write Smith; but still, I wrote it clumsily and was ashamed.—Ashamed, of that! The room was dark and smelled of damp. In the beams, things fluttered—perhaps birds, perhaps bats. I saw Maud gazing at the shadows, as if afraid the things should swoop.

Gentleman took her arm and held it, and then he led her from the church. There had come clouds before the moon, and the night was darker. The parson shook hands with us, then made Maud a bow; then he went off. He went fast, and as he walked he took his robe off, and his clothes were black beneath it—he seemed to snuff himself out like a light. Mrs Cream took us to her cottage. She carried the lantern, and we walked behind her, stumbling on her path: her doorway was low, and knocked Gentleman's hat off. She took us up a set of tilting stairs too narrow for our skirts, and then to a landing, about as big as a cupboard, where we all jostled about for a moment and the cuff of Maud's cloak got laid upon the chimney of the lantern and was singed.

There were two shut doors there, leading to the two little bedrooms of the house. The first had a narrow straw mattress on a pallet on the floor, and was for me. The second had a bigger bed, an arm-chair and a press, and was for Gentleman and Maud. She went into it, and stood with her eyes on the floor, looking at nothing. There was a single candle lit. Her bags lay beside the bed. I went to them and took her things out, one by one, and put them in the press. Mrs Cream said, 'What handsome linen!'—She was watching from the door. Gentleman stood with her, looking strange. It was him that had taught me the handling of a petticoat but now, seeing me take out Maud's shimmies and stockings, he seemed almost afraid. He said,

'Well, I shall smoke a final cigarette downstairs. Sue, you'll make things comfortable up here?'

I did not answer. He and Mrs Cream went down, their boots sounding loud as thunder and the door and the boards and the crooked staircase trembling. I heard him outside then, striking a match.

I looked at Maud. She was still holding the stalks of honesty. She took a step towards me and said quickly,

'If I should call out to you later, will you come?'

I took the flowers from her, and then the cloak. I said, 'Don't think of it. It will be over in a minute.'

She caught hold of my wrist with her right hand, that still had the glove upon it. She said, 'Listen to me, I mean it. Never mind what he does. If I call out to you, say you'll come. I'll give you money for it.'

Her voice was strange. Her fingers shook, yet gripped me hard. The thought of her giving me so much as a farthing was awful. I said,

'Where are your drops? Look, there's water here, you might take your drops and they will make you sleep.'

'Sleep?' she said. She laughed and caught her breath. 'Do you think I want to sleep, on my wedding-night?'

She pushed my hand away. I stood at her back and began to undress her. When I had taken her gown and her corset I turned and said, quietly,

'You had better use the pot. You had better wash your legs, before he comes.'

I think she shuddered. I did not watch her, but heard the splash of water. Then I combed her hair. There was no glass for her to stand at, and when she got into the bed she looked to her side and there was no table, no box, no portrait, no light—I saw her put out her hand as if blind.

Then the house-door closed, and she fell back and seized the blankets and pulled them high about her breast. Against the white of the pillow her face seemed dark; yet I knew that it was pale. We heard Gentleman and Mrs Cream, talking together in the room below. Their voices came clearly. There were gaps between the boards, and a faint light showed.

I looked at Maud. She met my gaze. Her eyes were black, but gleamed like glass. 'Will you look away, still?' she said, in a whisper, when she saw me turn my head. Then I turned back. I could not help it, though her face was awful, it was terrible to see. Gentleman talked on. Some breeze got into the room and made the candle-flame dip. I shivered. Still she held my gaze with hers. Then she spoke again.

'Come here,' she said.

I shook my head. She said it again. I shook my head again—but then went to her, anyway—went softly to her across the creaking boards, and she lifted her arms and drew my face to hers, and kissed me. She kissed me, with her sweet mouth, made salt with her tears; and I could not help but kiss her back—felt my heart, now like ice in my breast, and now like water, running, from the heat of her lips.

But then she did this. She kept her fingers upon my head and pushed my mouth too hard against hers; and she seized my hand

and took it, first to her bosom, then to where the blankets dipped, between her legs. There she rubbed with my fingers until they burned.

The quick, sweet feeling her kiss had called up in me turned to something like horror, or fear. I pulled from her, and drew my hand away. 'Won't you do it?' she said softly, reaching after me. 'Didn't you do it before, for the sake of this night? Can't you leave me to him now, with your kisses on my mouth, your touch upon me, there, to help me bear his the better?—Don't go!' She seized me again. 'You went, before. You said I dreamed you. I'm not dreaming now. I wish I were! God knows, God knows, I wish I were dreaming, and might wake up and be at Briar again!'

Her fingers slipped from my arm and she fell back and sagged against her pillow; and I stood, clasping and unclasping my hands, afraid of her look, of her words, of her rising voice; afraid she might shriek, or swoon—afraid, God damn me! that she might cry out, loud enough for Gentleman or Mrs Cream to hear, that I had kissed her.

'Hush! Hush!' I said. 'You are married to him now. You must be different. You are a wife. You must—'

I fell silent. She lifted her head. Below, the light had been taken up and moved. Gentleman's boots came loud again upon the narrow stairs. I heard him slow his step, then hesitate at the door. Perhaps he was wondering if he should knock, as he had used to knock at Briar. At last he slowly put his thumb to the latch, and came in.

'Are you ready?' he said.

He brought the chill of the night in with him. I did not say another word, to him or to her. I did not look at her face. I went to my own room and lay upon my bed. I lay, in the darkness, in my cloak and my gown, my head between the pillow and the mattress; and all I heard, each time I woke in the night, was the creeping, creeping of little creatures through the straw beneath my cheek.

In the morning, Gentleman came to my room. He came in his shirt-sleeves.

'She wants you, to dress her,' he said.

He took his breakfast downstairs. Maud had been brought up a tray, with a plate upon it. The plate held eggs and a kidney; she had not touched them. She sat very still, in the arm-chair beside the window; and I saw at once how it would be with her, now. Her face was smooth, but dark about the eyes. Her hands were bare. The yellow ring glittered. She looked at me, as she looked at everything—the plate of eggs, the view beyond the window, the gown I held up to place over her head—with a soft, odd, distant kind of gaze; and when I spoke to her, to ask her some trifling thing, she listened, and waited, then answered and blinked, as if the question, and the answer—even the movement of her own throat making the words—were all perfectly surprising and strange.

I dressed her, and she sat again beside the window. She kept her hands bent at the wrist, the fingers slightly lifted, as if even to let them rest against the soft stuff of her wide skirt might be to hurt them.

She held her head at a tilt. I thought she might be listening for the chiming of the house-bell at Briar. But she never mentioned her uncle, or her old life, at all.

I took her pot and emptied it, in the privy behind the house. At the foot of the stairs Mrs Cream came to me. She had a sheet over her arm. She said,

'Mr Rivers says the linen on the bed needs changing.'

She looked as if she would like to wink. I would not gaze at her long enough to let her. I had forgotten about this part. I went slowly up the stairs and she came behind me, breathing harder than ever. She made Maud a kind of curtsey, then went to the bed and drew back the blankets. There were a few spots of dark blood there, that had been rolled upon and smeared. She stood and looked at them, and then she caught my eye—as much as to say, 'Well, I shouldn't have believed it. Quite a little love-match, after all!' Maud sat gazing out of the window. From the room downstairs came the squeak of Gentleman's knife on his plate. Mrs Cream raised the sheet, to see if the blood had marked the mattress underneath; it hadn't, and that pleased her.

I helped her change it, then saw her to the door. She had made another curtsey, and seen Maud's queer, soft gaze.

'Took it hard, have she?' she whispered. 'Maybe missing her ma?'

I said nothing at first. Then I remembered our plot, and what was to happen. Better, I thought drearily, to make it happen soon. I stood on the little landing with her and closed the door. I said quietly,

'Hard ain't the word for it. There's trouble, up here. Mr Rivers dotes on her and won't bear gossip—he has brought her to this quiet place, hoping the country air will calm her.'

'Calm her?' she said then. 'You mean—? Bless me! She ain't likely to break out—turn the pigs loose—set the place afire?'

'No, no,' I said. 'She is only—only too much in her head.'

'Poor lady,' said Mrs Cream. But I could see her thinking. She hadn't bargained on having a mad girl in the house. And whenever she brought a tray up then, she looked sideways at Maud and set it down very quick, as if afraid she might get bitten.

'She doesn't like me,' said Maud, after she saw her do that two or three times; and I swallowed and said, 'Not like you? What an idea! Why should she not like you?'

'I can't say,' she answered quietly, looking down at her hands.

Later Gentleman heard her say it, too; and then he got me on my own. 'That's good,' he said. 'Keep Mrs Cream in fear of her, and her in fear of Mrs Cream, while seeming not to—very good. That will help us, when it comes time to call in the doctor.'

He gave it a week before he sent for him. I thought it the worst week of my life. He had told Maud they should stay a day; but on the second morning he looked at her and said,

'How pale you are, Maud! I think you aren't quite well. I think we ought to stay a little longer, until your strength comes back to you.'

'Stay longer?' she said. Her voice was dull. 'But can't we go, to your house in London?'

'I really think you are not well enough.'

'Not well? But, I am quite well—you must only ask Sue. Sue, won't you tell Mr Rivers how well I am?'

She sat and shook. I said nothing. 'Just a day or two more,' said Gentleman. 'Until you are rested. Until you are calm. Perhaps, if you were to keep more to the bed—?'

She began to weep. He went to her side, and that made her shudder and weep harder. He said, 'Oh, Maud, it tears at my heart to see you like this! If I thought it would be a comfort to you, of course I should take you to London at once—I should carry you, in my own arms—do you think I would not? But do you look at yourself now, and still tell me you are well?'

'I don't know,' she said then. 'It is so strange here. I'm afraid, Richard—'

'And won't it be stranger, in London? And shouldn't you be frightened there, where it's so loud and crowded and dark? Oh, no, this is the place to keep you. Here you have Mrs Cream, to make you comfortable—'

'Mrs Cream hates me.'

'Hates you? Oh, Maud. Now you are growing foolish; and I should be sorry to think you that; and Sue should also be sorry— shouldn't you, Sue?' I would not answer. 'Of course she would,' he said, with his hard blue eyes on mine. Maud looked at me, too, then looked away. Gentleman took her head in his hands and kissed her brow.

'There now,' he said. 'Let us have no more argument. We'll stay another day—only a day, until that paleness is driven from your cheek, and your eyes are bright again!'

He said the same thing then, the next day. On the fourth day he was stern with her—said she seemed to mean to disappoint him, to make him wait, when he longed only to carry her back to Chelsea as his bride; then on the fifth day, he took her in his arms and almost wept, and said he loved her.

After that, she did not ask how long they were to stay there. Her cheek never grew rosy. Her eye stayed dull. Gentleman told Mrs Cream to make her every kind of nourishing dish, and what she brought were more eggs, more kidneys, livers, greasy bacons and puddings of blood. The meat made the room smell sour. Maud could eat none of it. I ate it instead—since somebody must. I ate it, and she only sat beside the window gazing out, turning the ring upon her finger, stretching her hands, or drawing a strand of hair across her mouth.

Her hair was dull as her eyes. She would not let me wash it—she would hardly let me brush it, she said she couldn't bear the scraping of the comb upon her head. She kept in the gown she had travelled from Briar in, that had mud about the hem. Her best gown—a silk one—she gave to me. She said,

'Why should I wear it, here? I had much rather see you in it. You had much better wear it, than let it lie in the press.'

Our fingers touched beneath the silk, and we flinched and stepped apart. She had never tried to kiss me, after that first night.

I took the dress. It helped to pass the awful hours, sitting letting out the waist; and she seemed to like to watch me sew it. When I had finished it, and put it on and stood before her, her expression was strange. 'How well you look!' she said, her blood rising. 'The colour sets off your eyes and hair. I knew it would. Now you are quite the beauty—aren't you? And I am plain—don't you think?'

I had got her a little looking-glass from Mrs Cream. She caught it up in her trembling hand and came and held it before our faces. I remembered the time she had dressed me up, in her old room, and called us sisters; and how gay she had seemed then, and how plump and careless. She had liked to stand before her glass and make herself look fair, for Gentleman. Now—I saw it! I saw it, in the desperate slyness of her gaze!—now she was glad to see herself grown plain. She thought it meant he would not want her.

I could have told her once that he would want her anyway.

Now, I don't know what he did with her. I never spoke to him more than I had to. I did everything that was needed, but I did it all in a thick, miserable kind of trance, shrinking from thought and feeling—I was as low, almost, as she was. And Gentleman, to do him justice, seemed troubled on his own account. He only came to kiss or bully her, a little while each day; the rest of the time he sat in Mrs Cream's parlour, lighting cigarettes—the smoke came rising through the floor, to mix with the smell of the meat, the chamber-pot, the sheets on the bed. Once or twice he went riding. He went for news of Mr Lilly—but heard only that the word was, there was some queer stir at Briar, no-one knew quite what. In the evenings he would stand at a fence at the back of the house, looking over the black-faced pigs; or he would walk a little, in the lane or about the churchyard. He would walk, however, as if he knew we watched him—not in the old, show-off way he had used to stretch and smoke his cigarettes, but with a twitch to his step, as if he could not bear the feel of our gazes on his back.

Then at night I would undress her, and he would come, and I would leave them, and lie alone, with my head between my pillow and my rustling mattress.

I should have said he needed to do it to her only the once. I should have thought he might have been frightened he should get her with child. But there were other things I thought he might like her to do, now he had learned how smooth her hands were, how soft her bosom was, how warm and glib her mouth.

And every morning, when I went in to her, she seemed paler and thinner and in more of a daze than she had seemed the night before; and he caught my eye less, and plucked at his whiskers, his swagger all gone.

He at least knew what a dreadful business he was about, the bloody villain.

At last he sent for the doctor to come.

I heard him writing the letter in Mrs Cream's parlour. The doctor was one he knew. I believe he had been crooked once, per-haps in the ladies' medicine line, and had taken to the madhouse business as being more safe. But the crookedness, for us, was only a security. He wasn't in on Gentleman's plot. Gentleman wouldn't have cared to cut the cash with him.

Besides, the story was too sound. And there was Mrs Cream to back it. Maud was young, she was fey, and had been kept from the world. She had seemed to love Gentleman, and he loved her; but they hadn't been married an hour before she started to turn queer.

I think any doctor would have done what that one did, hearing Gentleman's story, and seeing Maud, and me, as we were then.

He came with another man—another doctor, his assistant. You need two doctors' words to put a lady away. Their house was near Reading. Their coach was odd-looking, with blinds like louvred shutters and, on its back, spikes. They came not to take Maud, though—not that time; only to study her. The taking came later.

Gentleman told her they were two of his painter friends. She seemed not to care. She let me wash her and make her dull hair a little neater, and tidy her gown; but then she kept to her chair, saying nothing. Only when she saw their coach pull up did she stare, and begin to breathe a little quicker—and I wondered if she had noticed the blinds and the spikes, as I had. The doctors got down. Gentleman went quickly out to talk with them, and they shook hands and put their heads together, and looked slyly up at our window.

Then Gentleman came back, and left them waiting. He came upstairs. He was rubbing his hands together and smiling. He said,

'Well, what do you think! Here are my friends Graves and Christie, come down to visit from London. You remember, Maud, I spoke to you of them? I don't believe they thought me really married! They have come to see the phenomenon for themselves.'

Still he smiled. Maud would not look at him.

'Shall you mind it, dear,' he said, 'if I bring them to you? I have left them now with Mrs Cream.'

I could hear them, then, in the parlour, talking in low, serious voices. I knew what questions they were asking, and what answers Mrs Cream would make. Gentleman waited for Maud to speak and, when she said nothing, looked at me. He said,

'Sue, will you come with me a moment?'

He made a gesture with his eyes. Maud gazed after us, blinking. I went with him to the crooked landing, and he closed the door at my back.

'I think you should leave her with me,' he said quietly, 'when they

go to her. I shall watch her, then; perhaps make her nervous. It
keeps her too calm, having you always about her.'

I said, 'Don't let them hurt her.'

'Hurt her?' He almost laughed. 'These men are scoundrels. They
like to keep their lunatics safe. They'd have them in fire-proof
vaults if they could, like bullion; and so live off the income. They
won't hurt her. But they know their business, too, and a scandal
would ruin them. My word is good, but they shall need to look at
her and talk to her; and they shall also need to talk to you. You'll
know how to answer, of course.'

I made a face. 'Will I?' I said.

He narrowed his eyes. 'Don't make game of me, Sue. Not now
we are so close. You'll know what to say?'

I shrugged, still sulky. 'I think so.'

'Good girl. I shall bring them first to you.'

He made to put his hand upon me. I dodged it and stepped away.
I went to my little room, and waited. The doctors came after a
moment. Gentleman came with them, then closed the door and
stood before it, his eyes on my face.

They were tall men, like him, and one of them was stout. They
were dressed in black jackets and elastic boots. When they moved,
the floor, the walls and the window gave a shudder. Only one of
them—the thinner one—spoke; the other just watched. They made
me a bow, and I curtseyed.

'Ah,' said the speaking doctor quietly, when I did that. His name
was Dr Christie. 'Now, you know who we are, I think? You won't
mind, if we ask you what might seem impertinent questions? We
are friends of Mr Rivers's, and very curious to hear about his marriage, and his new wife.'

'Yes,' I said. 'You mean, my mistress.'

'Ah,' he said again. 'Your mistress. Now, refresh my memory.
Who is she?'

'Mrs Rivers,' I said. 'That was Miss Lilly.'

'Mrs Rivers, that was Miss Lilly. Ah.'

He nodded. The silent doctor—Dr Graves—took out a pencil
and a book. The first one went on:

'Your mistress. And you are—?'

'Her maid, sir.'

'Of course. And what is your name?'

Dr Graves held his pencil, ready to write. Gentleman caught my eye, and nodded. 'Susan Smith, sir,' I said.

Dr Christie looked at me harder. 'You seemed to hesitate,' he said. 'That is your name, you are quite sure?'

'I should say I know my own name!' I said.

'Of course.'

He smiled. My heart still beat hard. Perhaps he saw it. He seemed to grow kind. He said,

'Well, Miss Smith, can you tell us now, how long you have known your mistress . . .?'

It was like the time, at Lant Street, when I had stood before Gentleman and he had put me through my character. I told them about Lady Alice of Mayfair, and Gentleman's old nurse, and my dead mother; and then about Maud. I said she had seemed to like Mr Rivers but now, a week after her wedding-night, she was grown very sad and careless of herself, and made me afraid.

Dr Graves wrote it all down. Dr Christie said,

'Afraid. Do you mean, for your own sake?'

I said, 'Not for mine, sir. For hers. I think she might harm herself, she is so miserable.'

'I see,' he said. Then: 'You are fond of your mistress. You have spoken very kindly of her. Now, will you tell me this. What care do you think your mistress ought to have, that would make her better?'

I said, 'I think—'

'Yes?'

'I wish—'

He nodded. 'Go on.'

'I wish you would keep her, sir, and watch her,' I said in a rush. 'I wish you would keep her some place where no-one could touch her, or hurt her—'

My heart seemed all at once high in my throat, and my voice was spoiled with tears. Gentleman still had his eyes upon me. The

doctor took my hand and held it, close about the wrist, in a familiar way.

'There, there,' he said. 'You must not be so distressed. Your mistress shall have everything you wish for her. She has been lucky,
indeed, to have had so good and faithful a servant, as you!'

He patted and smoothed my hand, then let it go. He looked at his
watch. He caught Gentleman's eye, and nodded. 'Very good,' he
said. 'Very good. Now, if you might just show us—?'

'Of course,' said Gentleman quickly. 'Of course. This way.' He
opened the door, and they turned their black backs to me and all
moved off. I watched them do it, and was gripped suddenly by a
feeling—I could not say if it was misery, or fear. I took a step and
called out after them.

'She don't like eggs, sir!' I called. Dr Christie half turned. I had
lifted my hand. Now I let it fall. 'She don't like eggs,' I said more
feebly, 'in any kind of dish.'

It was all I could think of. He smiled, and bowed; but in a
humouring kind of way. Dr Graves wrote—or pretended to write—
in his book, *Don't care for eggs*. Gentleman led them both across to
Maud's room. Then he came back to me.

'You'll keep here, until they've seen her?' he said.

I did not answer. He shut my door. But those walls were like
paper: I heard them move about, caught the rumble of the doctor's
questions; then, after a minute or so, came the thin rising and falling
of her tears.

They did not stay with her long. I suppose they had all they needed,
from me and Mrs Cream. When they had gone I went to her, and
Gentleman was standing behind her chair, holding her pale head
between his hands. He had been leaning to gaze at her, perhaps to
whisper and tease. When he saw me come he straightened and said,

'Look, Sue, at your mistress. Don't you think her eyes a little
brighter?'

They were bright, with the last of her tears still in them; and they
were red at the rims.

'Are you well, miss?' I said.

'She *is* well,' said Gentleman. 'I think the company of friends has cheered her. I think those dear good fellows, Christie and Graves, were quite delighted with her; and you tell me, Sue, when did a lady ever not begin to flourish, under a gentleman's delight?'

She turned her head and raised her hand, and plucked a little weakly at his pressing fingers. He stood holding her face a moment longer, then stepped away.

'What a fool I've been,' he said to me. 'I've asked Mrs Rivers to grow strong, in this quiet place, thinking the quietness would help her. Now I see that what she needs is the bustle of the city. Graves and Christie saw it, too. They are so eager to have us join them at Chelsea—why, Christie is giving us the use of his own coach and driver! We are to leave tomorrow. Maud, what do you say to that?'

She had turned her gaze to the window. Now she lifted her head to him, and a little blood struggled into her white cheeks.

'Tomorrow?' she said. 'So soon as that?'

He nodded. 'Tomorrow we'll go. To a great house, with fine, quiet rooms, and good servants in it, that waits there just for you.'

Next day she put her breakfast of eggs and meat aside, as usual; but even I could not eat it. I dressed her without looking at her. I knew every part of her. She wore the old gown still, that was stained with mud, and I wore the handsome silk one. She would not let me change out of it, even for travelling, though I knew it would crease.

I thought of wearing it back in the Borough. I could not believe that I would be at home again, with Mrs Sucksby, before it was dark.

I packed her bags. I did it slowly, hardly feeling the things I touched. Into one bag went her linen, her slippers, her sleeping-drops, a bonnet, a brush—that was for her to take to the madhouse. Into the other went everything else. That was for me. Only that white glove I think I have mentioned, did I keep to one side; and when the bags were filled I put it, neatly, inside the bodice of my gown, over my heart.

The coach came, and we were ready. Mrs Cream saw us to the door. Maud wore a veil. I helped her down the tilting staircase, and she gripped my arm. When we stepped out of the cottage she gripped it tighter. She had kept to her room for more than a week. She flinched from the sight of the sky and the black church, and seemed to feel the soft air hard upon her cheek, even through her veil, like a hand that slapped her.

I put my fingers over hers.

'God bless you, ma'am!' cried Mrs Cream, when Gentleman had paid her. She stood and watched us. The boy who had taken our horse, that first night, now appeared again, to see us leaving; and one or two other boys also came to stare, and to stand at the side of the coach, picking at the doors, where an old gold crest had been painted out black. The driver flicked his whip at them. He fastened our bags upon the roof, then let the steps down. Gentleman handed Maud in, drawing her fingers from mine. He caught my eye.

'Now, now,' he said, in a warning sort of way. 'No time for sentiment.'

She sat and leaned her head back, and he sat beside her. I sat opposite. There were no handles to the doors, only a key, like the key to a safe: when the driver closed them Gentleman made them fast, then put the key in his pocket.

'How long will we travel?' asked Maud.

He said, 'An hour.'

It seemed longer than an hour. It seemed like a life. The day was a warm one. Where the sun struck the glass it made the carriage very hot, but the windows had been fixed not to open—I suppose, so a lunatic should not have the chance to leap out. At last Gentleman pulled a cord to make the blinds close, and we sat jolting in the heat and the darkness, not speaking. In time I began to grow sick. I saw Maud's head rolling against the padding of the seat, but could not see if her eyes were open or closed. She kept her hands before her, clasped.

Gentleman fidgeted, however, loosening his collar, looking at his watch, plucking at his cuffs. Two or three times he took out his handkerchief and wiped off his brow. Every time the coach slowed, he leaned close to the window to peer through the louvres. Then it slowed so hard it came almost to a stop, and began to turn: he looked again, sat straight and tightened his neck-tie.

'We are almost there,' he said.

Maud turned her head to him. The coach slowed again. I pulled the cord that moved the blinds. We were at the start of a green lane, with a stone arch across it and, beneath that, iron gates. A man was drawing them back. The coach gave a jerk, and we drove along the lane until we reached the house at the end. It was just like at Briar, though this house was smaller, and neater. Its windows had bars on them. I watched Maud, to see what she would do. She had put back her veil and was gazing from the window in her old dull way; but behind the dullness I thought I saw a rising kind of knowledge or dread.

'Don't be afraid,' said Gentleman.

That was all he said. I don't know if he said it to her, or to me. The coach made another turn, and stopped. Dr Graves and Dr Christie were there, waiting for us, with beside them a great stout woman, her sleeves pushed up to her elbows and her gown covered over with an apron of canvas, like a butcher's. Dr Christie came forward. He had a key like Gentleman's, and let up the lock from his side. Maud flinched at the sound. Gentleman put his hand upon her. Dr Christie made a bow.

'Good day,' he said. 'Mr Rivers. Miss Smith. Mrs Rivers, you remember me of course?'

He held out his hand.

He held it to me.

There was a second, I think, of perfect stillness. I looked at him, and he nodded. 'Mrs Rivers?' he said again. Then Gentleman leaned and caught hold of my arm. I thought at first he meant to keep me in my seat; then I understood that he was trying to press me from it. The doctor took my other arm. They got me to my feet. My shoes caught upon the steps. I said,

'Wait! What are you doing? What—?'

'Don't struggle, Mrs Rivers,' said the doctor. 'We are here to care for you.'

He waved his hand, and Dr Graves and the woman came forward. I said,

'It's not me you want! What are you doing? Mrs Rivers? I'm Susan Smith! Gentleman! Gentleman, tell them!'

Dr Christie shook his head.

'Still keeping up the old, sad fiction?' he said to Gentleman.

Gentleman nodded and said nothing, as if he were too unhappy to speak. I hope he was! He turned and took down one of the bags—one of Maud's mother's bags. Dr Christie held me tighter. 'Now,' he said, 'how can you be Susan Smith, late of Whelk Street, Mayfair? Don't you know there's no such place? Come, you do know it. And we shall have you admitting it, though it take us a year. Now, don't twist so, Mrs Rivers! You are spoiling your handsome dress.'

I had struggled against his grip. At his words, I grew slack. I gazed at my sleeve of silk, and at my own arm, that had got plump and smooth with careful feeding; and then at the bag at my feet, with its letters of brass—the *M*, and the *L*.

It was in that second that I guessed, at last, the filthy trick that Gentleman had played on me.

I howled.

'You bloody swine!' I cried, twisting again, and pulling towards him. 'You fuckster! Oh!'

He stood in the doorway of the coach, making it tilt. The doctor gripped me harder and his face grew stern.

'There's no place for words like those in my house, Mrs Rivers,' he said.

'You sod,' I said to him. 'Can't you see what he's done? Can't you see the dodge of it? It ain't me you want, it's—'

I still pulled, and he still held me; but now I looked past him, to the swaying coach. Gentleman had moved back, his hand before his face. Beyond him, the light in bars upon her from the louvred blinds, sat Maud. Her face was thin, her hair was dull. Her dress was worn with use, like a servant's dress. Her eyes were wild, with tears starting in them; but beyond the tears, her gaze was hard. Hard as marble, hard as brass.

Hard as a pearl, and the grit that lies inside it.

Dr Christie saw me looking.

'Now, why do you stare?' he said. 'You know your own maid, I think?'

I could not speak. She could, however. She said, in a trembling voice, not her own:

'My own poor mistress. Oh! My heart is breaking!'

You thought her a pigeon. Pigeon, my arse. That bitch knew everything. She had been in on it from the start.

Part Two

Chapter Seven

*T*he start, I think I know too well. It is the first of my
mistakes.

I imagine a table, slick with blood. The blood is my mother's. There
is too much of it. There is so much of it, I think it runs, like ink. I
think, to save the boards beneath, the women have set down china
bowls; and so the silences between my mother's cries are filled—*drip
drop! drip drop!*—with what might be the staggered beating of
clocks. Beyond the beat come other, fainter cries: the shrieks of
lunatics, the shouts and scolds of nurses. For this is a madhouse.
My mother is mad. The table has straps upon it to keep her from
plunging to the floor; another strap separates her jaws, to prevent
the biting of her tongue; another keeps apart her legs, so that I
might emerge from between them. When I am born, the straps
remain: the women fear she will tear me in two! They put me upon
her bosom and my mouth finds out her breast. I suck, and the

house falls silent about me. There is only, still, that falling blood—
drip drop! drip, drop!—the beat telling off the first few minutes of
my life, the last of hers. For soon, the clocks run slow. My mother's
bosom rises, falls, rises again; then sinks for ever.

I feel it, and suck harder. Then the women pluck me from her.
And when I weep, they hit me.

I pass my first ten years a daughter to the nurses of the house. I
believe they love me. There is a tabby cat upon the wards, and I
think they keep me, rather as they keep that cat, a thing to pet and
dress with ribbons. I wear a slate-grey gown cut like their own, an
apron and a cap; they give me a belt with a ring of miniature keys
upon it, and call me 'little nurse'. I sleep with each of them in turn,
in their own beds, and follow them in their duties upon the madhouse wards. The house is a large one—seems larger to me, I
suppose—and divided in two: one side for female lunatics, one side
for male. I see only the female. I never mind them. Some of them
kiss and pet me, as the nurses do. Some of them touch my hair and
weep. I remind them of their daughters. Others are troublesome,
and these I am encouraged to stand before and strike with a wooden
wand, cut to my hand, until the nurses laugh and say they never saw
anything so droll.

Thus I learn the rudiments of discipline and order; and incidentally
apprehend the attitudes of insanity. This will all prove useful, later.

When I am old enough to reason I am given a gold ring said to be
my father's, the portrait of a lady called my mother, and understand
I am an orphan; but, never having known a parent's love—or rather,
having known the favours of a score of mothers—I am not greatly
troubled by the news. I think the nurses clothe and feed me, for my
own sake. I am a plain-faced child but, in that childless world, pass
for a beauty. I have a sweet singing voice and an eye for letters. I
suppose I shall live out all my days a nurse, contentedly teasing
lunatics until I die.

So we believe, at nine and ten. Some time in my eleventh year, I
am summoned to the nurses' parlour by the matron of the house. I
imagine she means to make me some treat. I am wrong. Instead, she

greets me strangely, and will not meet my eye. There is a person with her—a gentleman, she says—but then, the word means little to me. It will mean more, in time. 'Step closer,' the matron says. The gentleman watches. He wears a suit of black, and a pair of black silk gloves. He holds a cane with an ivory knob, upon which he leans, the better to study me. His hair is black tending to white, his cheek cadaverous, his eyes imperfectly hidden by a pair of coloured glasses. An ordinary child might shrink from gazing at him; but I know nothing of ordinary children, and am afraid of no-one. I walk until I stand before him. He parts his lips, to pass his tongue across them. His tongue is dark at the tip.

'She's undersize,' he says; 'but makes enough noise with her feet, for all that. How's her voice?'

His own voice is low, tremulous, complaining, like the shadow of a shivering man.

'Say a word to the gentleman,' says the matron quietly. 'Say how you are.'

'I am very well,' I say. Perhaps I speak stoutly. The gentleman winces.

'That will do,' he says, raising his hand. Then: 'I hope you can whisper? I hope you can nod?'

I nod. 'Oh yes.'

'I hope you can be silent?'

'I can.'

'Be silent, then.—That's better.' He turns to the matron. 'I see she wears her mother's likeness. Very good. It will remind her of her mother's fate, and may serve to keep her from sharing it. I don't care at all for her lip, however. It is too plump. It has a bad promise. Likewise her back, which is soft, and slouches. And what of her leg? I shan't want a thick-legged girl. Why do you hide her leg behind so long a skirt? Did I ask for that?'

The matron colours. 'It has been a harmless sport of the women, sir, to keep her dressed in the costume of the house.'

'Have I paid you, to provide sport for nurses?'

He moves his stick upon the rug, and works his jaws. He turns again to me, but speaks to her. He says, 'How well does she read?

How fair is her hand? Come, give her a piece of text and let her demonstrate.'

The matron hands me an open Bible. I read a passage from it, and again the gentleman winces. 'Softly!' he says, until I speak it in a murmur. Then he has me write the passage out while he looks on.

'A girl's hand,' he says, when I have finished, 'and burdened with serifs.' But he sounds pleased, nonetheless.

I am also pleased. I understand from his words that I have marked the paper with the marks of angels. Later I will wish that I had scrawled and blotted the page. The fair characters are my undoing. The gentleman leans harder upon his stick and tilts his head so low I can see, above the wire of his spectacles, the bloodless rims of his eyes.

'Well, miss,' he says, 'how should you like to come and live in my house? Don't push your pert lip at me, mind! How should you like to come to me, and learn neat ways and plain letters?'

He might have struck me. 'I should like it not at all,' I say at once.

The matron says, 'For shame, Maud!'

The gentleman snorts. 'Perhaps,' he says, 'she has her mother's unlucky temper after all. She has her dainty foot, at least. So you like to stamp, miss? Well, my house is a large one. We shall find a room for you to stamp in, far away from my fine ears; and you may work yourself into fits there, no-one shall mind you; and perhaps we shall mind you so little we shall forget to feed you, and then you shall die. How should you like that—hmm?'

He rises and dusts down his coat, that has no dust upon it. He gives some instruction to the matron and does not look at me again. When he has gone, I take up the Bible I have read from and throw it to the floor.

'I *will* not go!' I cry. 'He *shall* not make me!'

The matron draws me to her. I have seen her take a whip to fractious lunatics, but now she clutches me to her apron and weeps like a girl, and tells me gravely what my future is to be, in the house of my uncle.

Some men have farmers raise them veal-calves. My mother's brother has had the house of nurses raise him me. Now he means to take me home and make me ready for the roast. All at once, I must give up my little madhouse gown, my ring of keys, my wand: he sends his housekeeper with a suit of clothes, to dress me to his fancy. She brings me boots, wool gloves, a gown of buff—a hateful, girlish gown, cut to the calf, and stiffened from the shoulder to the waist with ribs of bone. She pulls the laces tight and, at my complaints, pulls them tighter. The nurses watch her, sighing. When it comes time for her to take me, they kiss me and hide their eyes. Then one of them quickly puts a pair of scissors to my head, to take a curl of hair to keep inside a locket; and, the others seeing her do that, they seize the shears from her, or take up knives and scissors of their own, and pluck and grasp at me until my hair tears at the root. They reach and squabble over the falling tresses like gulls—their voices rousing the lunatics in their own close rooms, making them shriek. My uncle's servant hurries me from them. She has a carriage with a driver. The madhouse gate shuts hard behind us.

'What a place to raise a girl in!' she says, passing a handkerchief across her lip.

I will not speak to her. My strait gown cuts me and makes my breath come quick, and my boots chafe at my ankles. My wool gloves prickle—at last I tear them from my hands. She watches me do it, complacently. 'Got a temper, have you?' she says. She has a basket of knitting and a parcel of food. There are bread rolls, a packet of salt and three white eggs, boiled hard. She rolls two of the eggs across her skirt, to break their shells. The flesh inside is grey, the yolk as dry as powder. I will remember the scent of it. The third egg she places on my lap. I will not eat it, but let it jerk there until it falls upon the carriage floor and is spoiled. 'Tut tut,' she says at that. She takes out her knitting, then her head droops and she sleeps. I sit beside her, stiff, in a miserable rage. The horse goes slowly, the journey seems long. Sometimes we pass through trees. Then my face shows in the window-glass, dark as blood.

I have seen no house but the madhouse I was born in. I am used to grimness and solitude, high walls and shuttered windows. It is the stillness of my uncle's house that bewilders and frightens me, that first day. The carriage stops at a door, split down the middle into two high, bulging leaves: as we watch, they are tugged from within and seem to tremble. The man who opens them is dressed in dark silk breeches and what I take to be a powdered hat. 'That's Mr Way, your uncle's steward,' says the woman, her face beside mine. Mr Way observes me, then looks at her; I think she must make some gesture with her eyes. The driver puts the steps down for us, but I will not let him take my hand; and when Mr Way makes me a bow, I think he does it to tease—for I have many times seen nurses curtsey, laughing, to lady lunatics. He shows me past him, into a darkness that seems to lap at my buff gown. When he closes the door, the dark at once grows deeper. My ears feel full, as if with water or with wax. That is the silence, that my uncle cultivates in his house, as other men grow vines and flowering creepers.

The woman takes me up a staircase while Mr Way looks on. The stairs are not quite even, and the rug is sometimes torn: my new boots make me clumsy, and once I fall. 'Come up, child,' says the woman when I do that; and now when she puts her hand upon me, I let it stay there. We climb two flights. I grow more frightened, the higher we go. For the house seems awful to me—the ceilings high, the walls not like the smooth undecorated walls of the madhouse, but filled with portraits, shields and rusting blades, creatures in frames and cases. The staircase turns upon itself, to make a gallery about the hall; at every turning there are passages. In the shadows of these, pale and half-hidden—like expectant grubs, in the cells of a hive—there stand servants, come to see me make my progress through the house.

I do not know them for servants, however. I see their aprons and suppose them nurses. I think the shadowy passages must hold rooms, with quiet lunatics.

'Why do they watch?' I say to the woman.

'Why, to see your face,' she answers. 'To see if you turned out handsome as your mother.'

'I have twenty mothers,' I say at that; 'and am handsomer than any of them.'

The woman has stopped before a door. 'Handsome is as handsome does,' she says. 'I mean your proper mother, that died. These were her rooms, and are now to be yours.'

She takes me into the chamber beyond, and then into the dressing-room that joins it. The windows rattle as if battered by fists. They are chill rooms even in summer, and it is winter now. I go to the little fire—I am too small to see my face in the glass above—and stand and shiver.

'Should have kept your mittens,' says the woman, seeing me breathe upon my hands. 'Mr Inker's daughter shall have those.' She takes my cloak from me, then draws the ribbons from my hair and brushes it with a broken comb. 'Tug all you like,' she says as I pull away. 'It shall only hurt you, it shan't harm me. Why, what a business those women made of your head! Anyone would have supposed them savages. How I'm to see you neat, after their work, I can't say. Now, look here.' She reaches beneath the bed. 'Let's see you use your chamber-pot. Come along, no foolish modesty. Do you think I never saw a little girl lift up her skirts and piddle?'

She folds her arms and watches me, and then she wets a cloth with water and washes my face and hands.

'I saw them do this for your mother, when I was parlourmaid here,' she says, pulling me about. 'She was a deal gratefuller than you are. Didn't they teach you manners, in that house of yours?'

I long for my little wooden wand: I would show her all I'd learned of manners, then! But I have observed lunatics, too, and know how to struggle while only seeming to stand limp. At length she steps from me and wipes her hands.

'Lord, what a child! I hope your uncle knows his business, bringing you here. He seems to think he'll make a lady of you.'

'I don't want to be a lady!' I say. 'My uncle cannot make me.'

'I should say he can do what he likes, in his own house,' she answers. 'There now! How late you've made us.'

There has come the stifled ringing of a bell, three times. It is a clock; I understand it, however, as a signal to the house, for I have been raised to the sound of similar bells, that told the lunatics to rise, to dress, to say their prayers, to take their dinners. I think,

Now I shall see them!, but when we go from the room the house is still and quiet as before. Even the watchful servants have retired. Again my boots catch on the carpets. 'Walk softly!' says the woman in a whisper, pinching my arm. 'Here's your uncle's room, look.'

She knocks, then takes me in. He has had paint put on the windows years before, and the winter sun striking the glass, the room is lit strangely. The walls are dark with the spines of books. I think them a kind of frieze or carving. I know only two books, and one is black and creased about the spine—that is the Bible. The other is a book of hymns thought suitable for the demented; and that is pink. I suppose all printed words to be true ones.

The woman sets me very near the door and stands at my back, her hands like claws upon my shoulders. The man they have called my uncle rises from behind his desk; its surface is hidden by a mess of papers. Upon his head is a velvet cap with a swinging tassel on a fraying thread. Before his eyes is another, paler, pair of coloured glasses.

'So, miss,' he says, stepping towards me, moving his jaw. The woman makes a curtsey. 'How is her temper, Mrs Stiles?' he asks her.

'Rather ill, sir.'

'I can see it, in her eye. Where are her gloves?'

'Threw them aside, sir. Wouldn't have them.'

My uncle comes close. 'An unhappy beginning. Give me your hand, Maud.'

I will not give it. The woman catches my arm about the wrist and lifts it. My hand is small, and plump at the knuckles. I am used to washing with madhouse soap, which is not kind. My nails are dark, with madhouse dirt. My uncle holds my finger-ends. His own hand has a smear or two of ink upon it. He shakes his head.

'Now, did I want a set of coarse fingers upon my books,' he says, 'I should have had Mrs Stiles bring me a nurse. I should not have given her a pair of gloves, to make those coarse hands softer. *Your* hands I shall have soft, however. See here, how we make children's hands soft, that are kept out of their gloves.' He puts his own hand to the pocket of his coat, and uncoils from it—one of those things, that bookmen use—a line of metal beads, bound tight with silk, for keeping down springing pages. He makes a loop of it, seeming to weigh it; then he brings it smartly down upon my dimpling knuckles. Then, with Mrs Stiles's assistance, he takes my other hand and does the same to that.

The beads sting like a whip; but the silk keeps the flesh from breaking. At the first blow I yelp, like a dog—in pain, in rage and sheer astonishment. Then, Mrs Stiles releasing my wrists, I put my fingers to my mouth and begin to weep.

My uncle winces at the sound. He returns the beads to his pocket and his hands flutter towards his ears.

'Keep silence, girl!' he says. I shake and cannot. Mrs Stiles pinches the flesh of my shoulder, and that makes me cry harder. Then my uncle draws forth the beads again; and at last I grow still.

'Well,' he says quietly. 'You shan't forget the gloves in future, hmm?'

I shake my head. He almost smiles. He looks at Mrs Stiles. 'You'll keep my niece mindful of her new duties? I want her made quite tame. I can't have storms and tantrums, here. Very well.' He waves his hand. 'Now, leave her with me. Don't stray too far, mind! You must be in reach of her, should she grow wild.'

Mrs Stiles makes a curtsey and—under cover of plucking my trembling shoulder as if to keep it from falling into a slouch—gives me another pinch. The yellow window grows bright, then dim, then bright again, as the wind sends clouds across the sun.

'Now,' says my uncle, when the housekeeper has gone. 'You know, do you not, why I have brought you here.'

I put my crimson fingers to my face, to wipe my nose.

'To make a lady of me.'

He gives a quick, dry laugh.

'To make a secretary of you. What do you see here, all about these walls?'

'Wood, sir.'

'Books, girl,' he says. He goes and draws one from its place and turns it. The cover is black, by which I recognise it as a Bible. The others, I deduce, hold hymns. I suppose that hymn-books, after all,

might be bound in different hues, perhaps as suiting different qual-
ities of madness. I feel this, as a great advance in thought.

My uncle keeps the book in his hand, close to his breast, and taps
its spine.

'Do you see this title, girl?—Don't take a step! I asked you to
read, not to prance.'

But the book is too far from me. I shake my head, and feel my
tears return.

'Ha!' cries my uncle, seeing my distress. 'I should say you can't!
Look down, miss, at the floor. Down! Further! Do you see that
hand, beside your shoe? That hand was set there at my word, after
consultation with an oculist—an eye-doctor. These are uncommon
books, Miss Maud, and not for ordinary gazes. Let me see you step
once past that pointing finger, and I shall use you as I would a servant of the house, caught doing the same—I shall whip your eyes
until they bleed. That hand marks the bounds of innocence here.
Cross it you shall, in time; but at my word, and when you are ready.
You understand me, hmm?'

I do not. How could I? But I am already grown cautious, and nod
as if I do. He puts the book back in its place, lingering a moment
over the aligning of the spine upon the shelf.

The spine is a fine one, and—I will know it well, in time—a
favourite of his. The title is—

But now I run ahead of my own innocence; which is vouchsafed
to me a little while yet.

After my uncle has spoken he seems to forget me. I stand for
another quarter-hour before he lifts his head and catches sight of
me, and waves me from the room. I struggle a moment with the iron
handle of his door, making him wince against the grinding of the
lever; and when I close it, Mrs Stiles darts from the gloom to lead
me back upstairs. 'I suppose you're hungry,' she says, as we walk.
'Little girls always are. I should say you'd be grateful for a white egg
now.'

I am hungry, but will not admit to it. But she rings for a girl to
come, and the girl brings a biscuit and a glass of sweet red wine. She
sets them down before me, and smiles; and the smile is harder to

bear, somehow, than a slap would have been. I am afraid I will weep again. But I swallow my tears with my dry biscuit, and the girl and Mrs Stiles stand together, whispering and watching. Then they leave me quite alone. The room grows dark. I lie upon the sofa with my head upon a cushion, and pull my own little cloak over myself, with my own little whipped, red hands. The wine makes me sleep. When I wake again, I wake to shifting shadows, and to Mrs Stiles at the door, bringing a lamp. I wake with a terrible fear, and a sense of many hours having passed. I think the bell has recently tolled. I believe it is seven or eight o'clock.

I say, 'I should like, if you please, to be taken home now.'

Mrs Stiles laughs. 'Do you mean to that house, with those rough women? What a place to call your home!'

'I should think they miss me.'

'I should say they are glad to be rid of you—the nasty, pale-faced little thing that you are. Come here. It's your bed-time.' She has pulled me from the sofa, and begins to unlace my gown. I tug away from her, and strike her. She catches my arm and gives it a twist.

I say, 'You've no right to hurt me! You're nothing to me! I want my mothers, that love me!'

'Here's your mother,' she says, plucking at the portrait at my throat. 'That's all the mother you'll have here. Be grateful you have that, to know her face by. Now, stand and be steady. You must wear this, to give you the figure of a lady.'

She has taken the stiff buff dress from me, and all the linen beneath. Now she laces me tight in a girlish corset that grips me harder than the gown. Over this she puts a nightdress. On to my hands she pulls a pair of white skin gloves, which she stitches at the wrists. Only my feet remain bare. I fall upon the sofa and kick them. She catches me up and shakes me, then holds me still.

'See here,' she says, her face crimson and white, her breath coming hard upon my cheek. 'I had a little daughter once, that died. She had a fine black head of curling hair and a temper like a lamb's. Why dark-haired, gentle-tempered children should be made to die, and peevish pale girls like you to thrive, I cannot say. Why your mother, with all her fortune, should have turned out trash and perished, while I must live to keep your fingers smooth and see you grow into a lady, is a puzzle. Weep all the artful tears you like. You shall never make my hard heart the softer.'

She catches me up and takes me to the dressing-room, makes me climb into the great, high, dusty bed, then lets down the curtains. There is a door beside the chimney-breast: she tells me it leads to another chamber, and a bad-tempered girl sleeps there. The girl will listen in the night, and if I am anything but still and good and quiet, she will hear; and her hand is very hard.

'Say your prayers,' she says, 'and ask Our Father to forgive you.'

Then she takes up the lamp and leaves, and I am plunged in an awful darkness.

I think it a terrible thing to do to a child; I think it terrible, even now. I lie, in an agony of misery and fear, straining my ears against the silence—wide awake, sick, hungry, cold, alone, in a dark so deep the shifting black of my own eye-lids seems the brighter. My corset holds me like a fist. My knuckles, tugged into their stiff skin gloves, are starting out in bruises. Now and then the great clock shifts its gears, and chimes; and I draw what comfort I can from my idea that somewhere in the house walk lunatics, and with them watchful nurses. Then I begin to wonder over the habits of the place. Perhaps here they give their lunatics licence to wander; perhaps a mad-woman will come to my room, mistaking it for another? Perhaps the wicked-tempered girl that sleeps next door is herself demented, and will come and throttle me with her hard hand! Indeed, no sooner has this idea risen in me, than I begin to hear the smothered sounds of movement, close by—unnaturally close, they seem to me to be: I imagine a thousand skulking figures with their faces at the curtain, a thousand searching hands. I begin to cry. The corset I wear makes the tears come strangely. I long to lie still, so the lurk-ing women shall not guess that I am there; but the stiller I try to be, the more wretched I grow. Presently, a spider or a moth brushing my cheek, I imagine the throttling hand has come at last, and jerk in a convulsion and, I suppose, shriek.

There comes the sound of an opening door, a light between the seams of the curtain. A face appears, close to my own—a kind face, not the face of a lunatic, but that of the girl who earlier brought my little tea of biscuits and sweet wine. She is dressed in her nightgown, and her hair is let down.

'Now, then,' she says softly. Her hand is not hard. She puts it to my head and strokes my face, and I grow calmer. My tears flow naturally. I say I have been afraid of lunatics, and she laughs.

'There are no lunatics here,' she says. 'You are thinking of that other place. Now, aren't you glad, to have left there?' I shake my head. She says, 'Well, it is only strange for you here. You will soon grow used to it.'

She takes up her light. I see her do it, and begin at once again to cry.—'Why, you shall be asleep in a moment!' she says.

I say I do not like the darkness. I say I am frightened to lie alone. She hesitates, thinking perhaps of Mrs Stiles. But I dare say my bed is softer than hers; and besides, it is winter, and fearfully cold. She says at last that she will lie with me until I sleep. She snuffs her candle, I smell the smoke upon the darkness.

She tells me her name is Barbara. She lets me rest my head against her. She says, 'Now, isn't this nice as your old home? And shan't you like it here?'

I say I think I shall like it a little, if she will lie with me every night; and at that she laughs again, then settles herself more comfortably upon the feather mattress.

She sleeps at once, and heavily, as housemaids do. She smells of a violet face-cream. Her gown has ribbons upon it, at the breast, and I find them out with my gloved hands and hold them while I wait for sleep to come—as if I am tumbling into the perfect darkness and they are the ropes that will save me.

I am telling you this so that you might appreciate the forces that work upon me, making me what I am.

Next day, I am kept to my two bleak rooms and made to sew. I forget my terrors of the darkness of the night, then. My gloves make me clumsy, the needle pricks my fingers. 'I shan't do it!' I cry,

tearing the cloth. Then Mrs Stiles beats me. My gown and corset
being so stiff, she hurts her palm in the striking of my back. I take
what little consolation I might, from that.

I am beaten often, I believe, in my first days there. How could it
be otherwise? I have known lively habits, the clamour of the wards,
the dotings of twenty women; now the hush and regularity of my
uncle's house drives me to fits and foaming tempers. I am an amiable
child, I think, made wilful by restraint. I dash cups and saucers from
the table to the floor. I lie and kick my legs until the boots fly from
my heels. I scream until my throat bleeds. My passions are met with
punishments, each fiercer than the last. I am bound about the wrists
and mouth. I am shut into lonely rooms, or into cupboards. One
time—having overturned a candle and let the flame lap at the fringes
of a chair until they smoke—I am taken by Mr Way into the park
and carried, along a lonely path, to the ice-house. I don't remember,
now, the chill of the place; I remember the blocks of grey ice—I
should have supposed them clear, like crystal—that tick in the wintry
silence, like so many clocks. They tick for three hours. When Mrs
Stiles comes to release me I have made myself a kind of nest and
cannot be uncurled, and am as weak as if they had drugged me.

I think that frightens her. She carries me back quietly, by the servants' stairs, and she and Barbara bathe me, then rub my arms with
spirits.

'If she loses the use of her hands, my God, he'll have our characters for ever!'

It is something, to see her made afraid. I complain of pains in my
fingers, and weakness, for a day or two after that, and watch her
flutter; then I forget myself, and pinch her—and by that, she knows
my grip is a strong one, and soon punishes me again.

This makes a period of, perhaps a month; though to my childish
mind it seems longer. My uncle waits, all that time, as he might wait
for the breaking of a horse. Now and then he has Mrs Stiles conduct
me to his library, and questions her as to my progress.

'How do we do, Mrs Stiles?'

'Still badly, sir.'

'Still fierce?'

'Fierce, and snappish.'

'You've tried your hand?'

She nods. He sends us away. Then come more shows of temper, more rages and tears. At night, Barbara shakes her head.

'What a dot of a girl, to be so naughty! Mrs Stiles says she never saw such a little Tartar as you. Why can't you be good?'

I was good, in my last home—and see how I was rewarded! Next morning I upturn my chamber-pot and tread the mess into the carpet. Mrs Stiles throws up her hands and screams; then strikes my face. Then, half-clad and dazed as I am, she drags me from my dressing-room to my uncle's door.

He flinches from the sight of us. 'Good God, what is it?'

'Oh, a frightful thing, sir!'

'Not more of her violence? And do you bring her here, where she might break out, among the books?'

But he lets her speak, looking all the time at me. I stand very stiff, with a hand at my hot face, my pale hair loose about my shoulders.

At length he takes off his spectacles and closes his eyes. His eyes appear naked to me, and very soft at the lids. He raises his thumb and smudged forefinger to the bridge of his nose, and pinches.

'Well, Maud,' he says as he does it, 'this is sorry news. Here is Mrs Stiles, and here am I, and here are all my staff, all waiting on your good manners. I had hoped the nurses had raised you better than this. I had hoped to find you biddable.' He comes towards me, blinking, and puts his hand upon my face. 'Don't shrink so, girl! I want only to examine your cheek. It is hot, I think. Well, Mrs Stiles's hand is a large one.' He looks about him. 'Come, what have we that is cool, hmm?'

He has a slim brass knife, blunt-edged, for cutting pages. He stoops and puts the blade of it against my face. His manner is mild, and frightens me. His voice is soft as a girl's. He says, 'I am sorry to see you hurt, Maud. Indeed I am. Do you suppose I want you harmed? Why should I want that? It is you who must want it, since you provoke it so. I think you must like to be struck.—That is cooler, is it not?' He has turned the blade. I shiver. My bare arms

creep with cold. He moves his mouth. 'All waiting,' he repeats, 'on
your good manners. Well, we are good at that, at Briar. We can wait,
and wait, and wait again. Mrs Stiles and my staff are paid to do it;
I am a scholar, and inclined to it by nature. Look about you here, at
my collection. Do you suppose this the work of an impatient man?
My books come to me slowly, from obscure sources. I have contentedly passed many tedious weeks in expectation of poorer
volumes than you!' He laughs, a dry laugh that might once have
been moist; moves the point of the knife to a spot beneath my chin;
tilts up my face and looks it over. Then he lets the knife fall, and
moves away. He tucks the wires of his spectacles behind his ears.

'I advise you to whip her, Mrs Stiles,' he says, 'if she prove troublesome again.'

Perhaps children are like horses after all, and may be broken. My
uncle returns to his mess of papers, dismissing us; and I go docilely
back to my sewing. It is not the prospect of a whipping that makes me
meek. It is what I know of the cruelty of patience. There is no
patience so terrible as that of the deranged. I have seen lunatics labour
at endless tasks—conveying sand from one leaking cup into another;
counting the stitches in a fraying gown, or the motes in a sunbeam;
filling invisible ledgers with the resulting sums. Had they been gentlemen, and rich—instead of women—then perhaps they would have
passed as scholars and commanded staffs.—I cannot say. And of
course, these are thoughts that come to me later, when I know the full
measure of my uncle's particular mania. That day, in my childish
way, I glimpse only its surface. But I see that it is dark, and know that
it is silent—indeed, its substance is the substance of the darkness and
the silence which fills my uncle's house like water or like wax.

Should I struggle, it will draw me deep into itself, and I will
drown.

I do not wish, then, to do that.

I cease struggling at all, and surrender myself to its viscid, cir-
cular currents.

That is the first day, perhaps, of my education. But next day, at eight, begin my lessons proper. I never have a governess: my uncle tutors me himself, having Mr Way set a desk and a stool for me close to the pointing finger on his library floor. The stool is high: my legs swing from it and the weight of my shoes makes them tingle and finally grow numb. Should I fidget, however—should I cough, or sneeze—then my uncle will come and snap at my fingers with the rope of silk-covered beads. His patience has curious lapses, after all; and though he claims to be free of a desire to harm me, he harms me pretty often.

Still, the library is kept warmer than my own room, to ward off mould from the books; and I find I prefer to write, than to sew. He gives me a pencil with a soft lead that moves silently upon paper, and a green-shaded reading-lamp, to save my eyes.

The lamp smells, as it heats, of smouldering dust: a curious smell—I shall grow to hate it!—the smell of the parching of my own youth.

My work itself is of the most tedious kind, and consists chiefly of copying pages of text, from antique volumes, into a leather-bound book. The book is a slim one, and when it is filled my job is to render it blank again with a piece of india-rubber. I remember this task, more than I remember the pieces of matter I am made to copy: for the pages, from endless friction, grow smudged and fragile and liable to tear; and the sight of a smudge on a leaf of text, or the sound of tearing paper, is more than my uncle, in his delicacy, can bear. They say children, as a rule, fear the ghosts of the dead; what I fear most as a child are the spectres of past lessons, imperfectly erased.

I call them lessons; but I am not taught as other girls are. I learn to recite, softly and clearly; I am never taught to sing. I never learn the names of flowers and birds, but am schooled instead in the hides with which books are bound—as say, morocco, russia, calf, chagrin; and their papers—Dutch, China, motley, silk. I learn inks; the cutting of pens; the uses of pounce; the styles and sizes of founts: sans-serif, antique, Egyptian, pica, brevier, emerald, ruby, pearl . . . They are named for jewels. It is a cheat. For they are hard and dull as cinders in a grate.

But I learn quickly. The season turns. I am made small rewards: new gloves, soft-soled slippers, a gown—stiff as the first, but of velvet. I am allowed to take my supper in the dining-room, at one end of a great oak table, set with silver. My uncle sits at the other end. He keeps a reading-easel beside his place, and speaks very seldom; but if I should be so unlucky as to let fall a fork, or to jar my knife against my plate, then he will raise his face and fix me with a damp and terrible eye. 'Have you some weakness about the hands, Maud, that obliges you to grind your silver in that way?'

'The knife is too large and too heavy, Uncle,' I answer him fretfully once.

Then he has my knife taken away, and I must eat with my fingers. The dishes he prefers being all bloody meats, and hearts, and calves' feet, my kid-skin gloves grow crimson—as if reverting to the substance they were made from. My appetite leaves me. I care most for the wine. I am served it in a crystal glass engraved with an M. The ring of silver that holds my napkin is marked a tarnished black with the same initial. They are to keep me mindful, not of my name, but of that of my mother; which was Marianne.

She is buried in the loneliest spot of all that lonely park—hers a solitary grey stone among so many white. I am taken to see it, and made to keep the tomb neat.

'Be grateful that you may,' says Mrs Stiles, watching me trim the springing cemetery grass, her arms folded across her bosom. 'Who shall tend my grave? I shall be all but forgotten.'

Her husband is dead. Her son is a sailor. She has taken all her little daughter's curling black hair to make ornaments with. She brushes my own hair as if the locks are thorns and might cut her; I wish they were. I think she is sorry not to whip me. She still bruises my arms with pinches. My obedience enrages her more than ever my passions did; and seeing that, I grow meeker, with a hard, artful meekness that, receiving the edge of her sorrow, keeps it sharp. That provokes her to the pinches—they are profitless enough— and to scolds, which pay more, as being revealing of her griefs. I take her often to the graves, and make certain to sigh, to the full strength of my lungs, over my mother's stone. In time—so cunning am I!—I find out the name of her dead daughter; then, the kitchen cat giving birth to a litter of kittens, I take one for a pet, and name it for her. I make sure to call it loudest when Mrs Stiles is near: 'Come, Polly! Oh, Polly! What a pretty child you are! How fine your black fur is! Come, kiss your mama.'

Do you see, what circumstances make of me?

Mrs Stiles trembles and winks at the words.

'Take the filthy creature and have Mr Inker drown it!' she says to Barbara, when she can bear it no more.

I run and hide my face. I think of my lost home, and the nurses that loved me, and the thought brings the hot tears coolly to my eyes.

'Oh, Barbara!' I cry. 'Say you shan't! Say you wouldn't!'

Barbara says she never could. Mrs Stiles sends her away.

'You're a sly, hateful child,' she says. 'Don't think Barbara don't know it. Don't think she can't see through you and your designing ways.'

But it is she who cries then, in great hard sobs; and my own eyes soon dry in the studying of hers. For what is she, to me? What is anyone now? I had thought my mothers, the nurses, might send to save me; six months go by—another six, another—and they send nothing. I am assured they have forgotten me. 'Think of you?' says Mrs Stiles, with a laugh. 'Why, I dare say your place at the mad-house has been filled by a new little girl with a happier temper. I am sure, they were glad to be rid of you.' In time, I believe her. I begin to forget. My old life grows shadowy in proportion to the new—or, sometimes emerges to darken or trouble it, in dreams and half-memories, just as those smudged strokes of forgotten lessons now and then start out upon the pages of my copy-book.

My proper mother I hate. Didn't she forsake me, before anyone? I keep her portrait in a little wooden box beside my bed; but her sweet white face has nothing of me in it, and I grow to loathe it. 'Let me kiss mama good-night,' I say one time, unlocking my box. But I do it only to torment Mrs Stiles. I raise the picture to my lips and, while she looks on, thinking me sorry—'I hate you,' I whisper, my breath tarnishing the gold. I do it that night, and the night which follows, and the night which follows that; at last, as a clock must tick to a regular beat, I find I must do it or lie fretful in my bed. And then, the portrait must be set down gently, with its ribbon quite uncreased. If the frame strikes the velvet lining of the wooden box too hard, I will take it out and set it down carefully again.

Mrs Stiles watches me do it, with a curious expression. I never lie quite still until Barbara comes.

Meanwhile my uncle observes my work and finds my letters, my hand, my voice, greatly improved. He is used occasionally to entertaining gentlemen at Briar: now he has me stand for them and read. I read from foreign texts, not understanding the matter I am made to recite; and the gentlemen—like Mrs Stiles—watch me strangely. I grow used to that. When I have finished, at my uncle's instruction I curtsey. I curtsey well. The gentlemen clap, then come to shake or stroke my hand. They tell me, often, how rare I am. I believe myself a kind of prodigy, and pink under their gazes.

So white blooms blush, before they curl and tumble. One day I arrive at my uncle's room to find my little desk removed, and a place made ready for me among his books. He sees my look, and beckons me to him.

'Take off your gloves,' he says. I do, and shudder to touch the surfaces of common things. It is a cold, still, sunless day. I have been at Briar, then, two years. My cheek is round as a child's, and my voice is high. I have not yet begun to bleed as women do.

'Well, Maud,' says my uncle. 'At last you cross the finger of brass, and come to my books. You are about to learn the proper quality of your vocation. Are you afraid?'

'A little, sir.'

'You do well to be. For here is fearful matter. You think me a scholar, hmm?'

'Yes, sir.'

'Well, I am more than that. I am a curator of poisons. These books—look, mark them! mark them well!—they are the poisons I mean. And this—' Here he reverently puts his hand upon the great pile of ink-stained papers that litter his desk—'this is their Index.

This will guide others in their collection and proper study. There is
no work on the subject so perfect as this will be, when it is complete.
I have devoted many years to its construction and revision; and
shall devote many more, as the work requires it. I have laboured so
long among poisons I am immune to them, and my aim has been to
make you immune, that you might assist me. My eyes—do you
look at my eyes, Maud.' He takes off his spectacles and brings his
face to mine; and I flinch, as once before, from the sight of his soft
and naked face—yet see now, too, what the coloured lenses hide: a
certain film, or milkiness, upon the surface of his eye. 'My eyes
grow weak,' he says, replacing his glasses. 'Your sight shall save my
own. Your hand shall be my hand. For you come here with naked
fingers, while in the ordinary world—the commonplace world, outside this chamber—the men who handle vitriol and arsenic must do
so with their flesh guarded. You are not like them. This is your
proper sphere. I have made it so. I have fed you poison, by scruple
and grain. Now comes the larger dose.'

He turns and takes a book from his shelves, then hands it to me,
pressing my fingers hard about it.

'Keep this from others. Remember the rareness of our work. It
will seem queer, to the eyes and ears of the untutored. They will
think you tainted, should you tell. You understand me? I have
touched your lip with poison, Maud. Remember.'

The book is called *The Curtain Drawn Up, or the Education of
Laura*. I sit alone, and turn the cover; and understand at last the
matter I have read, that has provoked applause from gentlemen.

The world calls it pleasure. My uncle collects it—keeps it neat,
keeps it ordered, on guarded shelves; but keeps it strangely—not for
its own sake, no, never for that; rather, as it provides fuel for the satisfying of a curious lust.

I mean, the lust of the bookman.

'See here, Maud,' he will say to me softly, drawing back the glass
doors of his presses, passing his fingers across the covers of the texts
he has exposed. 'Do you note the marbling upon these papers, the
morocco of this spine, the gilt edge? Observe this tooling, look.' He

tilts the book to me but, jealously, will not let me take it. 'Not yet, not yet! Ah, see this one, also. Black-letter; the titles, look, picked out in red. The capitals flowered, the margin as broad as the text. What extravagance! And this! Plain board; but see here, the frontispiece'— the picture is of a lady reclined on a couch, a gentleman beside her, his member bare and crimson at the tip—'done after Borel, most rare. I had this as a young man from a stall at Liverpool, for a shilling. I should not part with it now, for fifty pounds.—Come, come!' He has seen me blush. 'No schoolgirl modesty here! Did I bring you to my house, and teach you the ways of my collection, to see you colour? Well, no more of that. Here is work, not leisure. You will soon forget the substance, in the scrutiny of the form.'

So he says to me, many times. I do not believe him. I am thirteen. The books fill me, at first, with a kind of horror: for it seems a frightful thing, that children, in becoming women and men, should do as they describe—get lusts, grow secret limbs and cavities, be prone to fevers, to crises, seek nothing but the endless joining together of smarting flesh. I imagine my mouth, stopped up with kisses. I imagine the parting of my legs. I imagine myself fingered and pierced . . . I am thirteen, as I have said. The fear gives way to restlessness: I begin to lie each night at Barbara's side, wakeful while she sleeps on; one time I put back the blanket to study the curve of her breast. Then I take to watching her as she bathes and dresses. Her legs—that I know from my uncle's books should be smooth—are dark with hair; the place between them—which I know should be neat, and fair—darkest of all. That troubles me. Then at last, one day, she catches me gazing.

'What are you looking at?' she says.

'Your cunt,' I answer. 'Why is it so black?'

She starts away from me as if in horror, lets her skirt fall, puts her hands before her breast. Her cheek flares crimson. 'Oh!' she cries. 'I never did! Where did you learn such words?'

'From my uncle,' I say.

'Oh, you liar! Your uncle's a gentleman. I'll tell Mrs Stiles!'

She does. I think Mrs Stiles will hit me; instead, like Barbara, she starts back. But then, she takes up a block of soap and, while

Barbara holds me, she presses the soap into my mouth—presses it hard, then passes it back and forth across my lips and tongue.

'Speak like a devil, will you?' she says as she does it. 'Like a slut and a filthy beast? Like your own trash mother? Will you? Will you?'

Then she lets me fall, and stands and wipes her hands convulsively upon her apron. She has Barbara keep to her own bed, from that night on; and she makes her keep the door between our rooms ajar, and put out a light.

'Thank God she wears gloves, at least,' I hear her say. 'That may keep her from further mischief . . .'

I wash my mouth, until my tongue grows cracked, and bleeds; I weep and weep; but still taste lavender. I think my lip must have poison in it, after all.

But soon, I do not care. My cunt grows dark as Barbara's, I understand my uncle's books to be filled with falsehoods, and I despise myself for having supposed them truths. My hot cheek cools, my colour dies, the heat quite fades from my limbs. The restlessness turns all to scorn. I become what I was bred to be. I become a librarian.

'*The Lustful Turk,*' my uncle might say, looking up from his papers. 'Where do we have it?'

'We have it here, Uncle,' I will answer.—For within a year I know the place of every book upon his shelves. I know the plan of his great index—his *Universal Bibliography of Priapus and Venus*. For to Priapus and Venus he has devoted me, as other girls are apprenticed to the needle or the loom.

I know his friends—those gentlemen who visit, and still hear me recite. I know them now for publishers, collectors, auctioneers—enthusiasts of his work. They send him books—more books each week—and letters:

'"Mr Lilly: on the Cleland. Grivet of Paris claims no knowledge of the lost, sodomitical matter. Shall I pursue?"'

My uncle hears me read, his eyes creased hard behind their lenses.

'What think you, Maud?' he says. '—Well, never mind it now. We must leave the Cleland to languish, and hope for more in the spring. So, so. Let me see . . .' He divides the slips of paper upon his desk. 'Now, *The Festival of the Passions*. Have we still the second volume, on loan from Hawtrey? You must copy it, Maud . . .'

'I will,' I say.

You think me meek. How else should I answer? Once, early on, I forget myself, and yawn. My uncle studies me. He has taken his pen from his page, and slowly rolls its nib.

'It appears you find your occupation dull,' he says at last. 'Perhaps you would like to return to your room.' I say nothing. 'Should you like it?'

'Perhaps, sir,' I say, after a moment.

'Perhaps. Very good. Put back your book then, and go. But, Maud—' This last, as I cross to the door. 'Do you instruct Mrs Stiles to keep the fuel from your fire. You don't suppose I shall pay, to keep you warm in idleness, hmm?'

I hesitate, then go. This is, again, in winter—it seems always winter there! I sit wrapped in my coat until made to dress for dinner. But at the table, when Mr Way brings the food to my plate, my uncle stops him. 'No meat,' he says, laying a napkin across his lap, 'for idle girls. Not in this house.'

Then Mr Way takes the platter away. Charles, his boy, looks sorry. I should like to strike him. Instead I must sit, twisting my hands into the fabric of my skirt, biting down my rage as I once swallowed tears, hearing the sliding of the meat upon my uncle's ink-stained tongue, until I am dismissed.

Next day at eight o'clock, I return to my work; and am careful never to yawn again.

I grow taller, in the months that follow. I become slender and more pale. I become handsome. I outgrow my skirts and gloves and slippers.—My uncle notes it, vaguely, and instructs Mrs Stiles to cut me new gowns to the pattern of the old. She does, and makes me sew them. I believe she must take a sort of malicious pleasure from the dressing of me to suit his fancy; then again, perhaps in her grief for her daughter she has forgotten that little girls are meant to turn out women. Anyway, I have been too long at Briar, and draw a comfort, now, from regularity. I have grown used to my gloves and my hard-boned gowns, and flinch at the first unloosening of the strings. Undressed, I seem to feel myself as naked and unsafe as one of my uncle's lenseless eyes.

Asleep, I am sometimes oppressed by dreams. Once I fall into a fever, and a surgeon sees me. He is a friend of my uncle's and has heard me read. He fingers the soft flesh beneath my jaw, puts his thumbs to my cheeks, draws down my eye-lids. 'Are you troubled,' he says, 'with uncommon thoughts? Well, we must expect that. You are an uncommon girl.' He strokes my hand and prescribes me a medicine—a single drop to be taken in a cup of water—'for restlessness'. Barbara puts out the mixture, while Mrs Stiles looks on.

Then Barbara leaves me, to be married, and I am given another maid. Her name is Agnes. She is small, and slight as a bird—one of those little, little birds that men bring down with nets. She has red hair and white skin marked with freckles, like paper foxed with damp. She is fifteen, innocent as butter. She thinks my uncle kind. She thinks me kind, at first. She reminds me of myself, as I once was. She reminds me of myself as I once was and ought still to be, and will never be again. I hate her for it. When she is clumsy, when she is slow, I hit her. That makes her clumsier. Then I hit her again. That makes her weep. Her face, behind her tears, keeps still its look of mine. I beat her the harder, the more I fancy the resemblance.

So my life passes. You might suppose I would not know enough of ordinary things, to know it queer. But I read other books besides my uncle's; and overhear the talk of servants, and catch their looks, and so, by that—by the curious and pitying glances of parlour-maids and grooms!—I see well enough the oddity I have become.

I am as worldly as the grossest rakes of fiction; but have never, since I first came to my uncle's house, been further than the walls of its park. I know everything. I know nothing. You must remember this, in what follows. You must remember what I cannot do, what I have not seen. I cannot, for example, sit a horse, or dance. I have never held a coin in order to spend it. I have never seen a play, a railway, a mountain, or a sea.

I have never seen London; and yet, I think I know it, too. I know it, from my uncle's books. I know it lies upon a river—which is the same river, grown very much broader, that runs beyond his park. I like to walk beside the water, thinking of this. There is an ancient, overturned punt there, half rotted away—the holes in its hull a perpetual mockery, it seems to me, of my confinement; but I like to sit upon it, gazing at the rushes at the water's edge. I remember the Bible story, of the child that was placed in a basket and was found by the daughter of a king. I should like to find a child. I should like it, not to keep it!—but to take its place in the basket and leave it at Briar to grow up to be me. I think often of the life I would have, in London; and of who might claim me.

That is when I am still young, and given to fancies. When I am older I do not walk by the river so much as stand at the windows of the house and gaze at where I know the water flows. I stand at my own casement, for many hours at a time. And in the yellow paint that covers the glass of the windows of my uncle's library I one day, with my finger-nail, make a small and perfect crescent, to which I afterwards occasionally lean and place my eye—like a curious wife at the keyhole of a cabinet of secrets.

But I am inside the cabinet, and long to get out . . .

I am seventeen when Richard Rivers comes to Briar with a plot and a promise and the story of a gullible girl who can be fooled into helping me do it.

Chapter Eight

I have said it was my uncle's custom, occasionally to invite interested gentlemen to the house, to take a supper with us and, later, hear me read. He does so now.

'Make yourself neat tonight, Maud,' he says to me, as I stand in his library buttoning up my gloves. 'We shall have guests. Hawtrey, Huss, and another fellow, a stranger. I hope to employ him with the mounting of our pictures.'

Our pictures. There are cabinets, in a separate study, filled with drawers of lewd engravings, that my uncle has collected in a desultory sort of manner, along with his books. He has often spoken of taking on some man to trim and mount them, but has never found a man to match the task. One needs a quite particular character, for work of that sort.

He catches my eye, thrusts out his lips. 'Hawtrey claims to have a gift for us, besides. An edition of a text we have not catalogued.'

'That is great news, sir.'

Perhaps I speak drily; but my uncle, though a dry man himself, does not mark it. He only puts his hand to the slips of paper before him and divides the heap into two uneven piles. 'So, so. Let me see . . .'

'May I leave you, Uncle?'

He looks up. 'Has the hour struck?'

'It has, I believe.'

He draws out from his pocket his chiming watch and holds it to his ear. The key to his library door—sewn about, at the stem, with faded velvet—swings noiselessly beside it. He says, 'Go on then, go on. Leave an old man to his books. Go and play, but—gently, Maud.'

'Yes, Uncle.'

Now and then I wonder how he supposes I spend my hours, when not engaged by him. I think he is too used to the particular world of his books, where time passes strangely, or not at all, and imagines me an ageless child. Sometimes that is how I imagine myself—as if my short, tight gowns and velvet sashes keep me bound, like a Chinese slipper, to a form I should otherwise outleap. My uncle himself—who is at this time, I suppose, not quite above fifty—I have always considered to have been perfectly and permanently aged; as flies remain aged, yet fixed and unchanging, in cloudy chips of amber.

I leave him squinting at a page of text. I walk very quietly, in soft-soled shoes. I go to my rooms, where Agnes is.

I find her at work at a piece of sewing. She sees me come, and flinches. Do you know how provoking such a flinch will seem, to a temperament like mine? I stand and watch her sew. She feels my gaze, and begins to shake. Her stitches grow long and crooked. At last I take the needle from her hand and gently put the point of it against her flesh; then draw it off; then put it back; then do this, six or seven times more, until her knuckles are marked between the freckles with a rash of needle-pricks.

'There are to be gentlemen here tonight,' I say, as I do it. 'One a stranger. Do you suppose he will be young, and handsome?'

I say it—idly enough—as a way of teasing. It is nothing to me. But she hears me, and colours.

'I can't say, miss,' she answers, blinking and turning her head; not drawing her hand away, however. 'Perhaps.'

'You think so?'

'Who knows? He might be.'

I study her harder, struck with a new idea.

'Should you like it if he was?'

'Like it, miss?'

'Like it, Agnes. It seems to me now, that you would. Shall I tell him the way to your room? I shan't listen at the door. I shall turn the key, you will be quite private.'

'Oh, miss, what nonsense!'

'Is it? Here, turn your hand.' She does, and I jab the needle harder. 'Now, say you don't like it, having a prick upon your palm!'

She takes her hand away and sucks it, and begins to cry. The sight of her tears—and of her mouth, working on the bit of tender flesh that I have stabbed—first stirs, then troubles me; then makes me weary. I leave her weeping, and stand at my rattling window, my eyes upon the lawn that dips to the wall, the rushes, the Thames.

'Will you be quiet?' I say, when her breath still catches. 'Look at you! Tears, for a gentleman! Don't you know that he won't be handsome, or even young? Don't you know, they never are?'

But of course, he is both.

'Mr Richard Rivers,' my uncle says. The name seems auspicious to me. Later I will discover it to be false—as false as his rings, his smile, his manner; but now, as I stand in the drawing-room and he rises to make me his bow, why should I think to doubt him? He has fine features, even teeth, and is taller than my uncle by almost a foot. His hair is brushed and has oil upon it, but is long: a curl springs from its place and tumbles across his brow. He puts a hand to it, repeatedly. His hands are slender, smooth and—but for a single finger, stained yellow by smoke—quite white.

'Miss Lilly,' he says, as he bends towards me. The lock of hair falls forward, the stained hand lifts to brush it back. His voice is very low, I suppose for my uncle's sake. He must have been cautioned in advance, by Mr Hawtrey.

Mr Hawtrey is a London bookseller and publisher, and has been many times to Briar. He takes my hand and kisses it. Behind him comes Mr Huss. He is a gentleman collector, a friend from my uncle's youth. He also takes my hand, but takes it to draw me closer to him, then kisses my cheek. 'Dear child,' he says.

I have been several times surprised by Mr Huss upon the stairs. He likes to stand and watch me climb them.

'How do you do, Mr Huss?' I say now, making him a curtsey.

But it is Mr Rivers I watch. And once or twice, when I turn my face his way, I find his own eyes fixed on me, his gaze a thoughtful one. He is weighing me up. Perhaps he has not supposed I would be so handsome. Perhaps I am not so handsome as rumour has had him think. I cannot tell. But, when the dinner-bell sounds and I move to my uncle's side to be walked to the table, I see him hesitate; then he chooses the place next to mine. I wish he had not. I think he will continue to watch me, and I don't like to be watched, while eating. Mr Way and Charles move softly about us, filling our glasses—mine, that crystal cup, cut with an M. The food is set upon our plates, then the servants leave: they never stay when we have company, but return between courses. At Briar we eat, as we do everything, by the chiming of the clock. A supper of gentlemen lasts one hour and a half.

We are served hare soup, this night; then goose, crisp at the skin, pink at the bones, and with its innards devilled and passed about the table. Mr Hawtrey takes a dainty kidney, Mr Rivers has the heart. I shake my head at the plate he offers.

'I'm afraid you're not hungry,' he says quietly, watching my face.

'Don't you care for goose, Miss Lilly?' asks Mr Hawtrey. 'Nor does my eldest daughter. She thinks of goslings, and grows tearful.'

'I hope you catch her tears and keep them,' says Mr Huss. 'I often think I should like to see the tears of a girl made into an ink.'

'An ink? Don't mention it to my daughters, I beg you. That I must hear their complaints, is one thing. Should they once catch the idea of impressing them also upon paper, and making me read them, I assure you, my life would not be worth the living.'

'Tears, for ink?' says my uncle, a beat behind the others. 'What rubbish is this?'

'Girls' tears,' says Mr Huss.

'Quite colourless.'

'I think not. Truly, sir, I think not. I fancy them delicately tinged—perhaps pink, perhaps violet.'

'Perhaps,' says Mr Hawtrey, 'as depending on the emotion that has provoked them?'

'Exactly. You have hit it, Hawtrey, there. Violet tears, for a melancholy book; pink, for a gay. It might be sewn up, too, with hair from a girl's head . . .' He glances at me and his look changes. He puts his napkin to his mouth.

'Now,' says Mr Hawtrey, 'I really wonder that that has never been attempted. Mr Lilly? One hears barbarous stories of course, of hides and bindings . . .'

They discuss this for a time. Mr Rivers listens but says nothing. Of course, his attention is all with me. Perhaps he will speak, I think, under cover of their talk. I hope he will. I hope he won't. I sip my wine and am suddenly weary. I have sat at suppers like this, hearing my uncle's friends chase tedious points in small, tight circles, too many times. Unexpectedly, I think of Agnes. I think of Agnes's mouth teasing a bead of blood from her pricked palm. My uncle clears his throat, and I blink.

'So, Rivers,' he says, 'Hawtrey tells me he has you translating, French matter into English. Poor stuff, I suppose, if his press is involved in it.'

'Poor stuff indeed,' answers Mr Rivers; 'or I should not attempt it. It is hardly my line. One learns, in Paris, the necessary terms; but it was as a student of the fine arts that I was lately there. I hope to find a better application for my talents, sir, than the conjuring of bad English from worse French.'

'Well, well. We shall see.' My uncle smiles. 'You would like to view my pictures.'

'Very much indeed.'

'Well, another day will do for that. They are handsome enough, I think you'll find. I care less for them than for my books, however. You've heard, perhaps'—he pauses—'of my Index?'

Mr Rivers inclines his head. 'It sounds a marvellous thing.'

'Pretty marvellous—eh, Maud? But, are we modest? Do we blush?'

I know my own cheek is cool; and his is pale as candle-wax. Mr Rivers turns, searches my face with his thoughtful gaze.

'How goes the great work?' asks Mr Hawtrey lightly.

'We are close,' answers my uncle. 'We are very close. I am in consultation with finishers.'

'And the length?'

'A thousand pages.'

Mr Hawtrey raises his brow. If my uncle's temper would permit it, he might whistle. He reaches for another slice of goose.

'Two hundred more then,' he says, as he does it, 'since I spoke to you last.'

'For the first volume, of course. The second shall be greater. What think you of that, Rivers?'

'Astonishing, sir.'

'Has there ever been its like? An universal bibliography, and on such a theme? They say the science is a dead one amongst Englishmen.'

'Then you have raised it to life. A fantastic achievement.'

'Fantastic, indeed—more so, when one knows the degrees of obscurity in which my subject is shrouded. Consider this: that the authors of the texts I collect must cloak their identity in deception and anonymity. That the texts themselves are stamped with every kind of false and misleading detail as to place and date of publication and impress. Hmm? That they are burdened with obscure titles. That they must pass darkly, via secret channels, or on the wings of rumour and supposition. Consider those checks to the bibliographer's progress. Then speak to me, sir, of fantastic labour!' He trembles in a mirthless laughter.

'I cannot conceive it,' says Mr Rivers. 'And the Index is organised . . .?'

'By title, by name, by date when we have it; and, mark this, sir: by species of pleasure. We have them tabled, most precisely.'

'The books?'

'The pleasures! Where are we presently, Maud?'

The gentlemen turn to me. I sip my wine. 'At the Lust,' I say, 'of Men for Beasts.'

My uncle nods. 'So, so,' he says. 'Do you see, Rivers, the assistance our bibliography will provide, to the student of the field? It will be a veritable Bible.'

'The flesh made word,' says Mr Hawtrey, smiling, enjoying the phrase. He catches my eye, and winks. Mr Rivers, however, is still looking earnestly at my uncle.

'A great ambition,' he says now.

'A great labour,' says Mr Huss.

'Indeed,' says Mr Hawtrey, turning again to me. 'I am afraid, Miss Lilly, your uncle continues to work you very mercilessly.'

I shrug. 'I was bred to the task,' I say, 'as servants are.'

'Servants and young ladies,' says Mr Huss, 'are different sorts of creatures. Have I not said so, many times? Girls' eyes should not be worn out with reading, nor their small hands made hard through the gripping of pens.'

'So my uncle believes,' I say, showing my gloves; though it is his books he is anxious to save, of course, not my fingers.

'And what,' he says now, 'if she labour five hours a day? I labour ten! What should we work for, if not books? Hmm? Think of Smart, and de Bury. Or think of Tinius, so dedicated a collector he killed two men for the sake of his library.'

'Think of Frère Vincente, who, for the sake of his, killed twelve!' Mr Hawtrey shakes his head. 'No, no, Mr Lilly. Work your niece if you must. But drive her to violence for literature's sake, and we shall never forgive you.'

The gentlemen laugh.

'Well, well,' says my uncle.

I study my hand, saying nothing. My fingers show red as ruby through the glass of dark wine, my mother's initial quite invisible until I turn the crystal; then the cuts leap out.

There are two more courses before I might be excused, and then two more soundings of the clock to be sat through, alone, before the gentlemen join me in the drawing-room. I hear the murmur of their

voices and wonder what, in my absence, they discuss. When they
come at last they are all a little pinker in the face, and their breaths
are soured with smoke. Mr Hawtrey produces a package, bound in
paper and string. He hands it to my uncle, who fumbles with the
wrappings.

'So, so,' he says; and then, with the book uncovered and held
close to his eyes: 'Aha!' He works his lips. 'Look here, Maud, look,
at what the little grubbian has brought us.' He shows me the
volume. 'Now, what do you say?'

It is a common novel in a tawdry binding, but with an unfamiliar frontispiece that renders it rare. I look and, despite myself, feel
the stirrings of a dry excitement. The sensation makes me queasy.
I say, 'A very fine thing for us, Uncle, without a doubt.'

'See here, the fleuron? You see it?'

'I see it.'

'I don't believe we have considered the possibility of such a thing.
I am sure we have not. We must go back. And we thought that
entry complete? We shall return to it, tomorrow.' He stretches his
neck. He likes the anticipation of pleasure. 'For now—well, take
your gloves off, girl. Do you suppose Hawtrey brings us books to
have you press gravy into the binding? That's better. Let's hear a
little of it. Do you sit, and read to us. Huss, you must sit also.
Rivers, mark my niece's voice, how soft and clear she reads. I
coached her myself. Well, well.—You crease the spine, Maud!'

'Indeed, Mr Lilly, she does not,' says Mr Huss, gazing at my
uncovered hands.

I place the book upon a stand and carefully weight its pages. I
turn a lamp so that its light falls bright upon the print.

'How long shall I read for, Uncle?'

He puts his watch against his ear. He says, 'Until the next
o'clock. Now, note this, Rivers, and tell me if you suppose its like
may be encountered in any other English drawing-room!'

The book is filled, as I have said, with common enough obsceni-
ties; but my uncle is right, I have been trained too well, my voice
is clear and true and makes the words seem almost sweet. When I

have finished, Mr Hawtrey claps, and Mr Huss's pink face is pinker, his look rather troubled. My uncle sits with his spectacles removed, his head at an angle, his eyes screwed tight.

'Poor words enough,' he says. 'But I have a home for you, upon my shelves. A home, and brothers, too. Tomorrow we shall see you placed there. The fleuron: I am certain we have not thought of that.—Maud, the covers are closed, and quite unbent?'

'Yes, sir.'

He draws on his eye-glasses, working the wires about his ears. Mr Huss pours brandy. I button up my gloves, smooth creases from my skirt. I turn the lamp, and dim it. But I am conscious of myself. I am conscious of Mr Rivers. He has heard me read, apparently without excitement, his eyes upon the floor; but his hands are clasped and one thumb beats a little nervously upon the other. Presently he rises. He says the fire is hot and scorches him. He walks a minute about the room, leaning rigidly to gaze into my uncle's book-presses—now his hands are behind his back; his thumb still twitches, however. I think he knows I watch. In time he comes close, catches my eye, makes a careful bow. He says, 'It is rather chill, so far from the fire. Shouldn't you like, Miss Lilly, to sit closer to the flames?'

I answer: 'Thank you, Mr Rivers, I prefer this spot.'

'You like to be cool,' he says.

'I like the shadows.'

When I smile again he takes it as a kind of invitation, lifts his coat, twitches at his trousers and sits beside me, not too close, still with his eyes upon my uncle's shelves, as if distracted by the books. But when he speaks, he speaks in a murmur. He says, 'You see, I also like the shadows.'

Mr Huss glances once our way. Mr Hawtrey stands at the fire and lifts a glass. My uncle has settled into his chair and its wings obscure his eyes; I see only his dry mouth, puckered at the lip. 'The greatest phase of eros?' he is saying. 'We have missed it, sir, by seventy years! The cynical, improbable fictions which pass for voluptuous literature nowadays I should be ashamed to show to the man that shoes my horse . . .'

I stifle a yawn, and Mr Rivers turns to me. I say, 'Forgive me, Mr Rivers.'

He bows his head. 'Perhaps, you don't care for your uncle's subject.'

He still speaks in a murmur; and I am obliged to make my own voice rather low, by way of answer. 'I am my uncle's secretary,' I say. 'The appeal of the subject is nothing to me.'

Again he bows. 'Well, perhaps,' he says, while my uncle talks on. 'It is only curious, to see a lady left cool and unmoved, by that which is designed to provoke heat, and motion.'

'But there are many ladies, I think, unmoved by that you speak of; and aren't those who know the matter best, moved least?' I catch his eye. 'I speak not from experience of the world, of course, but from my reading merely. But I should have said that—oh, even a priest would note a palling in his passion for the mysteries of his church, if put too often to the scrutiny of wafer and wine.'

He does not blink. At last he almost laughs.

'You are very uncommon, Miss Lilly.'

I look away. 'So I understand.'

'Ah. Now your tone is a bitter one. Perhaps you think your education a sort of misfortune.'

'On the contrary. How could it be a misfortune, to be wise? I can never be deceived, for instance, in the matter of a gentleman's attentions. I am a connoisseur of all the varieties of methods by which a gentleman might seek to compliment a lady.'

He puts his white hand to his breast. 'Then I should be daunted indeed,' he says, 'did I want only to compliment you.'

'I was not aware that gentlemen had any other wants, than that one.'

'Perhaps not in the books that you are used to. But in life—a great many; and one that is chief.'

'I supposed,' I say, 'that that was the one the books were written for.'

'Oh, no.' He smiles. His voice dips even lower. 'They are read for that, but written for something keener. I mean, of course, the want of—money. Every gentleman minds that. And those of us who are not quite so gentlemanly as we would like, mind it most of all.—I am sorry to embarrass you.'

I have coloured, or flinched. Now, recovering, I say, 'You forget, I have been bred to be quite beyond embarrassment. I am only surprised.'

'Then I must take a satisfaction from the knowledge that I have surprised you.' He lifts his hand to his beard. 'It is something to me,' he goes on, 'to have made a small impression upon the evenness and regularity of your days.'

He speaks so insinuatingly, my cheek grows warmer still.

'What do you know,' I say, 'of those?'

'Why, only what I surmise, from my observation of the house . . .'

Now his voice and his face are grown bland again. I see Mr Huss tilt his head and observe him. Then he calls, pointedly: 'What do you think, Rivers, of this?'

'Of what, sir?'

'Of Hawtrey's championing, now, of photography.'

'Photography?'

'Rivers,' says Mr Hawtrey. 'You are a young man. I appeal to you. Can there be any more perfect record of the amatory act—'

'Record!' says my uncle, peevishly. 'Documentary! The curses of the age!'

'—of the amatory act, than a photograph? Mr Lilly will have it that the science of photography runs counter to the spirit of the Paphian life. I say it is an image of life, and has this advantage over it: that it endures, where life—the Paphian life, the Paphian moment, in especial—must finish and fade.'

'Doth not a book endure?' asks my uncle, plucking at the arm of his chair.

'It endureth, so long as words do. But, in a photograph you have a thing beyond words, and beyond the mouths that speak them. A photograph will provoke heat in an Englishman, a Frenchman, a savage. It will outlast us all, and provoke heat in our grandsons. It is a thing apart from history.'

'It is gripped by history!' answers my uncle. 'It is corrupted by it! Its history hangs about it like so much smoke!—you may see it, in the fitting of a slipper, a gown, the dressing of a head. Give photographs to your grandson: he will study them and think them quaint. He will laugh at the wax tips of your moustaches! But words, Hawtrey, words—hmm? They seduce us in darkness, and the mind clothes and fleshes them to fashions of its own. Don't you think so, Rivers?'

'I do, sir.'

'You know I won't allow daguerreotypes and nonsense like that into my collection?'

'I think you are right not to, sir.'

Mr Hawtrey shakes his head. He says, to my uncle: 'You still believe photography a fashion, that will pass? You must come to Holywell Street, and spend an hour in my shop. We have albums made up, now, for men to choose from. It is all our buyers come for.'

'Your buyers are brutes. What business have I with them? Rivers, you have seen them. What is your opinion as to the quality of Hawtrey's trade . . .?'

The debate will go on, he cannot escape. He answers, then catches my eye as if in apology, rises, goes to my uncle's side. They talk until the striking of ten o'clock—which is when I leave them.

That is the Thursday night. Mr Rivers is due to remain at Briar until Sunday. Next day I am kept from the library while the men look over the books; at supper he watches me, and afterwards hears me read, but then is obliged to sit again with my uncle and cannot come to my side. Saturday I walk in the park with Agnes, and do not see him; Saturday night, however, my uncle has me read from an antique book, one of his finest—and then, when I have finished, Mr Rivers comes and sits beside me, to study its singular covers.

'You like it, Rivers?' asks my uncle as he does so. 'You know it is very rare?'

'I should say it must be, sir.'

'And you think I mean by that, that there are few other copies?'

'I had supposed that, yes.'

'So you might. But we collectors, we gauge rarity by other means. You think a unique item rare, if no-one wants it? We call that a dead book. But, say a score of identical copies are sought by a thousand men: each of those single books is rarer than the unique one. You understand me?'

Mr Rivers nods. 'I do. The rareness of the article is relative to the desire of the heart which seeks it.' He glances at me. 'That is very quaint. And how many men seek this book, that we have just heard?'

My uncle grows coy. 'How many indeed, sir? I'll answer you like this: put it up for auction, and see! Ha?'

Mr Rivers laughs. 'To be sure, yes . . .'

But beyond the film of his politeness, he looks thoughtful. He bites his lip—his teeth showing yellow, wolfish, against the dark of his beard, but his mouth a soft and surprising pink. He says nothing while my uncle sips at his drink and Mr Hawtrey fusses with the fire. Then he speaks again.

'And what of a pair of books, Mr Lilly,' he says, 'sought by a single buyer? How are they to be valued?'

'A pair?' My uncle puts down his glass. 'A set, of two volumes?'

'A pair of complementary titles. A man has one, and seeks to secure the other. The second will greatly add to the value of the first?'

'Of course, sir!'

'I thought it.'

'Men pay absurdly for such things,' says Mr Huss.

'They do,' says my uncle. 'They do. You will find a reference to such matters, of course, in my Index . . .'

'The Index,' says Mr Rivers softly; and the others talk on. We sit and listen—or pretend to—and soon he turns and studies my face. 'May I ask you something, Miss Lilly?' he says. And then, when I nod: 'What do you see, for yourself, after the completion of your uncle's work?—Now, why do you do that?'

I have given him what I suppose must be a bitter sort of smile. I say, 'Your question means nothing, I can hardly answer it. My uncle's work will never be finished. There are too many new books written that must be added to the old; too many lost books to be rediscovered; too much uncertainty. He and Mr Hawtrey will debate it for ever. Look at them now. Should he publish the Index as he intends, he will only at once begin its supplements.'

'You mean to keep beside him, then, for all that time?'—I will not answer.—'You are as dedicated as he?'

'I have no choice,' I say at last. 'My skills are few and, as you have already noted, quite uncommon.'

'You are a lady,' he says softly, 'and young, and handsome.—I don't speak from gallantry now, you know that. I say only what is true. You might do anything.'

'You are a man,' I answer. 'Men's truths are different from ladies'. I may do nothing, I assure you.'

He hesitates—perhaps, catches his breath. Then: 'You might— marry,' he says. 'That is something.'

He says it, with his eyes upon the book that I have read from; and I hear him, and laugh aloud. My uncle, supposing I have laughed at some parched joke of his, looks over and nods. 'You think so, Maud? You see, Huss, even my niece believes it so . . .'

I wait until his face is turned from me again, his attention captured. Then I reach for the book on its stand and gently lift its cover. 'Look here, Mr Rivers,' I say. 'This is my uncle's plate, that is attached to all his books. Do you see the device of it?'

The plate bears his emblem, a clever thing of his own design—a lily, drawn strangely, to resemble a phallus; and wound about with a stem of briar at the root. Mr Rivers tilts his head to study it, and nods. I let the cover close.

'Sometimes,' I say, not looking up, 'I suppose such a plate must be pasted upon my own flesh—that I have been ticketed, and noted and shelved—so nearly do I resemble one of my uncle's books.' I raise my eyes to his. My face is warm, but I am speaking coolly, still. 'You said, two nights ago, that you have studied the ways of this house. Surely, then, you have understood. We are not meant for common usage, my fellow books and I. My uncle keeps us separate from the world. He will call us poisons; he says we will hurt unguarded eyes. Then again, he names us his children, his foundlings, that have come to him, from every corner of the world—some rich and handsomely provided for, some shabby, some injured, some broken about the spine, some gaudy, some gross. For all that he speaks against them, I believe he likes the gross ones best; for they are the ones that other parents—other bookmen and collectors, I mean—cast out. I was like them, and had a home, and lost it—'

Now I do not speak coolly. I have been overtaken by my own words. Mr Rivers watches, then leans to take my uncle's book very gently from its stand.

'Your home,' he murmurs, as his face comes close to mine. 'The madhouse. Do you think very often of your time there? Do you think of your mother, and feel her madness in you?—Mr Lilly, your book.' My uncle has looked over. 'Do you mind my handling it? Won't you show me, sir, the features that mark it as rare . . .?'

He has spoken very swiftly; and has startled me, horribly. I don't like to be startled. I don't like to lose my place. But now, as he rises and returns, with the book, to the fire, a second or two passes that I cannot account for. I discover at last that I have put my hand to my breast. That I am breathing quickly. That the shadows in which I sit are all at once denser than before—so dense, my skirt seems bleeding into the fabric of the sofa and my hand, rising and falling above my heart, is pale as a leaf upon a swelling pool of darkness.

I will not swoon. Only girls in books do that, for the convenience of gentlemen. But I suppose I whiten and look strange, for when Mr Hawtrey gazes my way, smiling, his smile quite falls. 'Miss Lilly!' he says. He comes and takes my hand.

Mr Huss comes also. 'Dear child, what is it?' He holds me close, about the armpit.

Mr Rivers hangs back. My uncle looks peevish. 'Well, well,' he says. 'What now?' He shuts his book, but keeps his finger, carefully, between the pages.

They ring for Agnes. She comes, blinking at the gentlemen, curt-seying at my uncle, a look of terror on her face. It is not yet ten o'clock. 'I am perfectly well,' I say. 'You must not trouble. I am only tired, suddenly. I am sorry.'

'Sorry? Pooh!' says Mr Hawtrey. 'It is we who should be sorry. Mr Lilly, you are a tyrant, and overtask your niece most miserably.

I always said it, and here is the proof. Agnes, take your mistress's
arm. Go steadily, now.'

'Shall you manage the stairs?' Mr Huss asks anxiously. He stands
in the hall as we prepare to mount them. Behind him I see Mr
Rivers; but I do not catch his eye.

When the drawing-room door is closed I push Agnes away, and
in my own room I look about me for some cool thing to put upon
my face. I finally go to the mantel, and lean my cheek against the
looking-glass.

'Your skirts, miss!' says Agnes. She draws them from the fire.

I feel queer, dislocated. The house clock has not chimed. When
it sounds, I will feel better. I will not think of Mr Rivers—of what
he must know of me, how he might know it, what he means by
seeking me out. Agnes stands awkwardly, half-crouched, my skirts
still gathered in her hands.

The clock strikes. I step back, then let her undress me. My heart
beats a little smoother. She puts me in my bed, unlooses the curtains—now the night might be any night, any at all. I hear her in
her own room, unfastening her gown: if I lift my head and look
through the gap in my curtains I will see her upon her knees with
her eyes hard shut, her hands pressed together like a child's, her
lips moving. She prays every night to be taken home; and for safety
as she slumbers.

While she does it, I unlock my little wooden box and whisper
cruel words to my mother's portrait. I close my eyes. I think, *I shall
not study your face!*—but, once having thought it, I know I must do
it or lie sleepless and grow ill. I look hard into her pale eyes. *Do you
think of your mother*, he said, *and feel her madness in you?*

Do I?

I put the portrait away, and call for Agnes to bring me a tumbler of water. I take a drop of my old medicine—then, unsure that
that will calm me, I take another. Then I lie still, my hair put back.
My hands, inside their gloves, begin to tingle. Agnes stands and
waits. Her own hair is let down—coarse hair, red hair, coarser and
redder than ever against the fine white stuff of her nightdress.
One slender collar-bone is marked a delicate blue with what is

perhaps only a shadow, but might—I cannot remember—be a
bruise.

I feel the drops at last, sour in my stomach.

'That's all,' I say. 'Go on.'

I hear her climb into her bed, draw up her blankets. There is a
silence. After a little time there comes a creak, a whisper, the faint
groan of machinery: my uncle's clock, shifting its gears. I lie and
wait for sleep. It does not come. Instead, my limbs grow restless
and begin to twitch. I feel, too hard, my blood—I feel the bafflement of it, at the dead points of my fingers and my toes. I raise my
head, call softly: 'Agnes!' She does not hear; or hears, but fears to
answer. 'Agnes!'—At last, the sound of my own voice unnerves
me. I give it up, lie still. The clock groans again, then strikes.
Then come other sounds, far-off. My uncle keeps early hours.
Closing doors, lowered voices, shoes upon the stairs: the gentlemen
are leaving the drawing-room and going each to their separate
chambers.

Perhaps I sleep, then—but if I do, it is only for a moment. For suddenly I give a start, and am wide awake; and I know that what has
roused me is not sound, but movement. Movement, and light.
Beyond the bed-curtain the rush-lamp's wick has flared suddenly
bright, and the doors and the window-glasses are straining against
their frames.

The house has opened its mouth, and is breathing.

Then I know that, after all, this night is not like any other. As if
summoned to it by a calling voice, I rise. I stand at the doorway to
Agnes's room until I am sure, from the evenness of her breaths, that
she is sleeping; then I take up my lamp and go, on naked feet, to my
drawing-room. I go to the window and stand at the glass, cup my
hands against their own feeble reflection, peer through the darkness
at the sweep of gravel, the edge of lawn, that I know lie below. For
a time I see nothing. Then I hear the soft fall of a shoe, and then
another, still softer. Then comes the single noiseless flaring of a
match between slender fingers; and a face, made hollow-eyed and
garish as it tilts towards the flame.

Richard Rivers keeps restless as I; and walks upon the lawns of Briar, perhaps hoping for sleep.

Cold weather for walking. About the tip of his cigarette, his breath shows whiter than the smoke of his tobacco. He gathers his collar about his throat. Then he looks up. He seems to know what he will see. He does not nod, or make any gesture; only holds my gaze. The cigarette fades, glows bright, fades again. His stance grows more deliberate.

He moves his head; and all at once I understand what he is doing. He is surveying the face of the house. He is counting the windows.

He is calculating his way to my room!—and when he is certain of his route he lets his cigarette fall and crushes the glowing point of it beneath his heel. He comes back across the gravel-walk and some-one—Mr Way, I suppose—admits him. I cannot see that. I only hear the front door open, feel the movement of the air. Again my lamp flares, and the window-glass bulges. This time, however, the house seems holding its breath.

I step back with my hands before my mouth, my eyes on my own soft face: it has started back into the darkness beyond the glass, and seems to swim, or hang, in space. I think, *He won't do it! He dare not do it!* Then I think: *He will.* I go to the door and put my ear against the wood. I hear a voice, and then a tread. The tread grows soft, another door closes—of course, he will wait for Mr Way to go to his bed. He will wait for that.

I take up my lamp and go quickly, quickly: the shade throws crescents of light upon the walls. I have not time to dress—cannot dress, without Agnes to help me—but know I must not see him in my nightgown. I find stockings, garters, slippers, a cloak. My hair, that is loose, I try to fasten; but I am clumsy with the pins, and my gloves—and the medicine I have swallowed—make me clumsier. I grow afraid. My heart beats quick again, but now it beats against the drops, it is like a vessel beating hard against the pull of a slug-gish river. I put my hand to it, and feel the yielding of my breast—unlaced, it feels; unguarded, unsafe.

But the tug of the drops is greater than the resistance of my fear.

That is the point of them, after all. *For restlessness.* When at length he comes, tapping at my door with his fingernail, I think I seem calm to him. I say at once, 'You know my maid is very close—asleep, but close. One cry will wake her.' He bows and says nothing.

Do I suppose he will try to kiss me? He does not do that. He only comes very stealthily into the room and gazes about him in the same cool, thoughtful way in which I saw him take his measure of the house. He says, 'Let us keep from the window, the light shows plainly from the lawn.' Then, nodding to the inner door: 'Is that where she lies? She won't hear us? You are sure?'

Do I think he will embrace me? He never once steps close. But I feel the cool of the night, still clinging to his coat. I smell the tobacco on his hair, his whiskers, his mouth. I do not remember him so tall. I move to one side of the sofa and stand tensely, gripping the back of it. He keeps at the other, leans into the space between us, and speaks in whispers.

He says, 'Forgive me, Miss Lilly. This is not how I would have met you. But I have come to Briar, after so much careful labour; and tomorrow I may be obliged to leave without seeing you. You understand me. I make no judgement on your receiving me like this. If your girl stirs, you are to say that you were wakeful; that I found out your room and came, without invitation. I've been guilty of as much, in other men's houses.—It's as well you know at once, what manner of fellow I am. But here, Miss Lilly, tonight, I mean you no sort of harm. I think you *do* understand me? I think you *did* wish me to come?'

I say, 'I understand that you have found out something you think perhaps a secret: that my mother was a lunatic; that my uncle had me from a ward of the place she died in. But that is no secret, anyone might know it; the very servants here know it. I am forbidden to forget it. I am sorry for you, if you meant to profit by it.'

'I am sorry,' he says, 'to have been obliged to remind you of it again. It means nothing to me, except as it has led to your coming to Briar and being kept by your uncle in such a curious way. It is he, I think, who has profited from your mother's misfortune.—You'll forgive my speaking plainly. I am a sort of villain, and know other villains best. Your uncle is the worst kind, for he keeps to his own house, where his villainy passes as an old man's quirk. Don't tell me you love him,' he adds quickly, seeing my face, 'for manners' sake. I know you are above them. That is why I have come like this. We make our own manners, you and I; or take the ones that suit us. But for now, will you sit and let me speak with you, as a gentleman to a lady?'

He gestures and, after a second—as if we might be awaiting the maid and the tea-tray—we take our places on the sofa. My dark cloak gapes and shows my nightgown. He turns his eyes while I draw close the folds.

'Now, to tell you what I know,' he says.

'I know you gain nothing unless you marry. I first had it from Hawtrey. They speak about you—perhaps you know—in the shady bookshops and publishers' houses of London and Paris. They speak about you, as of some fabulous creature: the handsome girl at Briar, whom Lilly has trained, like a chattering monkey, to recite voluptuous texts for gentlemen—perhaps to do worse. I needn't tell you all they say, I suppose you can guess it. That's nothing to me.' He holds my gaze, then looks away. 'Hawtrey, at least, is a little kinder; and thinks me honest, which is more to our point. He told me, in a pitying sort of way, a little of your life—your unfortunate mother— your expectations, the conditions attached. Well, one hears of such girls, when one is a bachelor; perhaps not one in a hundred is worth the pursuit . . . But Hawtrey was right. I have made enquiries into your mother's fortune, and you are worth—well, do you know what you are worth, Miss Lilly?'

I hesitate, then shake my head. He names the figure. It is several hundred times the value of the costliest book upon my uncle's shelves; and many thousand times the price of the cheapest. This is the only measure of value I know.

'It is a great sum,' says Mr Rivers, watching my face.

I nod.

'It shall be ours,' he says, 'if we marry.'

I say nothing.

'Let me be honest,' he goes on. 'I came to Briar, meaning to get you in the ordinary way—I mean, seduce you from your uncle's house, secure your fortune, perhaps dispose of you after. I saw in ten minutes what your life has made of you, and knew I should never achieve it. More, I understood that to seduce you would be to insult you—to make you only a different kind of captive. I don't wish to do that. I wish rather to free you.'

'You are very gallant,' I say. 'Suppose I don't care to be freed?'

He answers simply: 'I think you long for it.'

Then I turn my face—afraid that the beating of blood, across my cheek, will betray me to him. My voice I make steady. I say, 'You forget, my longings count for nothing here. As well might my uncle's books long to leap from their presses. He has made me like them—'

'Yes, yes,' he says, in impatience. 'You have said as much to me already. I think perhaps you say it often. But, what can such a phrase mean? You are seventeen. I am twenty-eight, and believed for many years I should be rich now, and idle. Instead I am what you see me: a scoundrel, not too poor in pocket, but nor too easy in it that I shan't be scrambling to line it for a little time to come. Do you think yourself weary? Think how weary am I! I have done many gross deeds, and thought each one the last. Believe me: I have some knowledge of the time that may be misspent, clinging to fictions and supposing them truths.'

He has lifted his hand to his head, and now puts back his hair from his brow; and his pallor, and the dark about his eye, seem suddenly to age him. His collar is soft, and creased from the grip of his neck-tie. His beard has a single strand of grey. His throat bulges queerly, as men's throats do: as if inviting the blow that will crush it.

I say, 'This is madness. I think you are mad—to come here, to confess yourself a villain, to suppose me willing to receive you.'

'And yet you have received me. You receive me still. You have not called for your maid.'

'You intrigue me. You have seen for yourself, the evenness of my days here.'

'You seek a distraction from those? Why not give them up, for ever? So you shall—like that, in a moment! gone!—when you marry me.'

I shake my head. 'I think you cannot be serious.'

'I am, however.'

'You know my age. You know my uncle would never permit you to take me.'

He shrugs, speaks lightly. 'We shall resort, of course, to devious methods.'

'You wish to make a villain of me, too?'

He nods. 'I do. But then, I think you are half a villain already.— Don't look like that. Don't suppose I am joking. You don't know all.' He has grown serious. 'I am offering you something very great and strange. Not the commonplace subjection of a wife to a husband— that servitude, to lawful ravishment and theft, that the world terms *wedlock*. I shan't ask you for that, that is not what I mean. I am speaking, rather, of liberty. A liberty of a kind not often granted to the members of your sex.'

'Yet to be achieved'—I almost laugh—'by a marriage?'

'To be achieved by a ceremony of marriage, performed under certain unusual conditions.' Again he smooths his hair, and swallows; and I see at last that he is nervous—more nervous than I. He leans closer. He says, 'I suppose you're not squeamish, or soft about the heart, as another girl might be? I suppose your maid is really sleeping, and not listening at the door?'

I think of Agnes, of Agnes's bruises; but say nothing, only watch him. He passes his hand across his mouth.

'God help me, Miss Lilly, if I have misjudged you!' he says. 'Now, listen.'

This is his plan. He means to bring a girl to Briar, from London, and install her as my maid. He means to use her, then cheat her. He says he has a girl in mind, a girl of my years and colouring. A sort of thief—not over-scrupulous, not too clever in her ways, he says; he thinks he will secure her with the promise of some slight share in the fortune—'Say, two or three thousand. I don't believe she'll have the ambition to ask for more. Her set are a small set, as crooks go; though, like crooks everywhere, think themselves grander.' He shrugs. The sum means nothing, after all: for he will agree to whatever she asks for; and she will not see a shilling of it. She will

suppose me an innocent, and believe herself assisting in my seduc-
tion. She will persuade me, first, into marriage with him, then into
a—he hesitates, before admitting the word—a madhouse. But, there
she will take my place. She will protest—he hopes she will!—for the
more she does, the more the madhouse keepers will read it as a
form of lunacy; and so keep her the closer.

'And with her, Miss Lilly,' he says finally, 'they keep close your
name, your history as your mother's daughter, your uncle's niece—
in short, all that marks you as yourself. Think of it! They will pluck
from your shoulders the weight of your life, as a servant would lift
free your cloak; and you shall make your naked, invisible way to any
part of the world you choose—to any new life—and there re-clothe
yourself to suit your fancy.'

This is the liberty—the rare and sinister liberty—he has come to
Briar to offer. For payment he wants my trust, my promise, my
future silence; and one half of my fortune.

When he has finished I sit not speaking, my face turned from his,
for almost a minute. What I say at last is:
    'We should never achieve it.'
    He answers at once: 'I think we will.'
    'The girl would suspect us.'
    'She will be distracted by the plot into which I shall draw her. She
will be like everyone, putting on the things she sees the constructions
she expects to find there. She will look at you, here, knowing nothing
of your uncle—who wouldn't, in her place, believe you innocent?'
    'And her people, the thieves: shan't they look for her?'
    'They shall look—as a thousand thieves look every day for the
friends who have cheated and robbed them; and, finding nothing,
they'll suppose her flown, and curse her for a while, and then forget
her.'
    'Forget her? Are you sure? Has she no—no mother?'
    He shrugs. 'A sort of mother. A guardian, an aunt. She loses
children all the time. I don't think she will trouble very hard over
one child more. Especially if she supposes—as I mean that she

will—that the child has turned out swindler. Do you see? Her own
reputation will help to bury her. Crooked girls can't expect to be
cared for, like honest ones.' He pauses. 'They will watch her more
closely, however, in the place we'll put her.'

I gaze away from him. 'A madhouse . . .'

'I am sorry for that,' he says quickly. 'But your own reputation—
your own mother's reputation—will work for us there, just as our
crooked girl's will. You must see how it will. You have been held in
thrall to it, all these years. Here is your chance to profit by it, once;
then be free of it, for ever.'

I still look away. Again, I am afraid he will see how deeply his
words have stirred me. I am almost afraid of how deeply they stir
me, myself. I say, 'You speak as though my freedom were something
to you. It's the money you care for.'

'I've admitted as much, have I not? But then, your freedom and
my money are the same. That will be your safeguard, your insurance,
until our fortune is secure. You may trust yourself, till then, not to my
honour—for I have none—but, say, to my cupidity; which is anyway
a greater thing than honour, in the world outside these walls. You will
find that out. I might teach you how to profit from it. We can take
some house, in London, as man and wife.—Live separately, of
course,' he adds, with a smile, 'when the door of the house is
closed . . . Once our money is got, however, your future will be your
own; you must only be silent, then, as to the manner in which you got
it. You understand me? Being once committed to this thing, we must
be true to each other, or founder. I don't speak lightly. I don't wish to
mislead you as to the nature of the business I'm proposing. Perhaps
your uncle's care has kept you from a knowledge of the law . . .'

'My uncle's care,' I say, 'has made me ready to consider any strat-
egy that will relieve me of the burden of it. But—'

He waits and, when I add nothing, says, 'Well, I don't expect to
hear you give me your decision now. It's my aim that your uncle will
keep me here, to work on his pictures—I am to view them tomorrow. If he does not, then we shall anyway be obliged to reconsider.
But there are ways about that, as about everything.'

He passes his hand again before his eyes, and again looks older.

The clock has struck the twelve, the fire has died an hour before, and the room is terribly chill. I feel it, all at once. He sees me shiver. I think he reads it as fear, or doubt. He leans, and at last takes my hand in his. He says, 'Miss Lilly, you say your freedom is nothing to me; but how could I see the life that is yours—how could any honest man see you kept down, made a slave to lewdness, leered at and insulted by fellows like Huss—and not wish to free you of it? Think of what I have proposed. Then think of your choices. You may wait for another suitor: shall you find one, among the gentlemen your uncle's work brings here? And, if you do, shall he be as scrupulous as I, in the handling of your fortune?—of your person? Or, say you wait for your uncle to die, and find a liberty that way; meantime, his eyes have faded, his limbs have a tremor, he has worked you the harder as he has felt his powers fail. By then you are—what age? Say thirty-five, or forty. You have given your youth to the curating of books, of a kind that Hawtrey sells, for a shilling, to drapers' boys and clerks. Your fortune sits untouched in the vault of a bank. Your consolation is to be mistress of Briar—where the clock strikes off the hollow half-hours of all the life that is left to you, one by one.'

As he speaks, I look not at his face; but at my own foot in its slipper. I think again of the vision I have sometimes had—of myself, as a limb bound tight to a form it longs to outgrow. With the drops in me the vision is fiercer, I see the limb made crooked, the flesh sour and grow dense. I sit quite still, then raise my eyes to his. He is watching me, waiting to know if he has won me. He has. Not by what he has told me, about my future at Briar—for he has said nothing that I have not, long ago, already concluded for myself; but by the fact that he is here, telling it at all—that he has plotted, and travelled, forty miles—that he has stolen his way to the heart of the sleeping house, to my dark room, *to me.*

Of the girl in London—who, in less than a month, he will persuade to her doom by a similar method; and to whom, a little later, with tears on my cheek, I will repeat his own arguments—I think nothing, nothing at all.

*

I say, 'Tomorrow, when you are shown my uncle's pictures: praise the Romano, though the Caracci is more rare. Praise Morland over Rowlandson. He thinks Rowlandson a hack.'

That is all I say. It is enough, I suppose. He holds my gaze, nods, does not smile—I think he knows I should not like to see him smile, at such a moment. He looses his grip about my fingers and then he stands, straightening his coat. That breaks the spell of our conspiracy: now he is large, dark, out of place. I hope he will leave. Again I shiver and, seeing that, he says, 'I'm afraid I've kept you very late. You must be cold, and tired.'

He watches. Perhaps he is gauging my strength and beginning to grow doubtful. I shiver harder. He says, 'You won't be troubled— too troubled—by all I've said?'

I shake my head. But I am afraid to rise from the sofa, in case I tremble upon my legs and seem to him weak. I say, 'Will you go?'

'You are sure?'

'Quite sure. I shall do better if you leave me.'

'Of course.'

He would like to say more. I turn my face and will not let him, and in time hear his careful tread upon the carpet, the gentle opening and closing of the door. I sit a moment, then lift my feet, tuck the skirts of my cloak about my legs, raise my hood, lie with my head upon the hard and dusty sofa cushion.

This is not my bed, and the hour for bed has sounded and passed, and there are none of the things—my mother's portrait, my box, my maid—about me, that I like to have close while I lie sleeping. But tonight, all things are out of their order, all my patterns have been disturbed. My liberty beckons: gaugeless, fearful, inevitable as death.

I sleep, and dream I am moving, swiftly, in a high-prowed boat, upon a dark and silent water.

Chapter Nine

I suppose that even then—or rather, especially then, when our
compact is so new, so unproved, its threads still slender and
weak—I suppose that even then I might draw back, unloose myself
from the tugging of his ambition. I believe I wake thinking I will;
for the room—the room in which, in whispers, at the hush of midnight, he took my hand, unfolded his dangerous plan, like a man
putting back the rustling wrappers about a poison—the room
reassembles itself in the chill half-hour of dawn into all its rigid
familiar lines. I lie and watch it. I know every curve and angle. I
know them, too well. I remember weeping, as a girl of eleven, at the
strangeness of Briar—at the silence, the stillness, the turning passages and cluttered walls. I supposed then that those things would
be strange to me for ever, I felt their strangeness make me strange—
make me a thing of points and hooks, a burr, a splinter in the gullet
of the house. But Briar crept on me. Briar absorbed me. Now I feel
the simple weight of the woollen cloak with which I have covered

myself and think, *I shall never escape! I am not meant to escape! Briar will never let me!*

But, I am wrong. Richard Rivers has come into Briar like a spore of yeast into dough, changing it utterly. When I go, at eight o'clock, to the library, I am sent away: he is there with my uncle, looking over the prints. They pass three hours together. And when, in the afternoon, I am summoned downstairs to make my farewells to the gentlemen, it is only Mr Hawtrey and Mr Huss that I must give my hand to. I find them in the hall, fastening their greatcoats, drawing on their gloves, while my uncle leans upon his cane and Richard stands, a little way off, his hands in his pockets, looking on. He sees me first. He meets my gaze, but makes no gesture. Then the others hear my step and lift their heads to watch me. Mr Hawtrey smiles.

'Here comes fair Galatea,' he says.

Mr Huss has put on his hat. Now he takes it off. 'The nymph,' he asks, his eyes on my face, 'or the statue?'

'Well, both,' Mr Hawtrey says; 'but I meant the statue. Miss Lilly shows as pale, don't you think?' He takes my hand. 'How my daughters would envy you! They eat clay, you know, to whiten their complexions? Pure clay.' He shakes his head. 'I do think the fashion for pallor a most unhealthy one. As for you, Miss Lilly, I am struck again—as I always am, when I must leave you!—by the unfairness of your uncle keeping you here in such a miserable, mushroom-like way.'

'I am quite used to it,' I say quietly. 'Besides, I think the gloom makes me show paler than I am. Does Mr Rivers not go with you?'

'The gloom is the culprit. Really, Mr Lilly, I can barely make out the buttons on my coat. Do you mean never to join civilised society, and bring gas to Briar?'

'Not while I keep books,' says my uncle.

'Say never, then. Rivers, gas poisons books. Did you know?'

'I did not,' says Richard. Then he turns to me, and adds, in a lower voice: 'No, Miss Lilly, I am not to go up to London just yet. Your uncle has been kind enough to offer me a little work among his prints. We share a passion, it seems, for Morland.'

His eye is dark—if a blue eye can be dark. Mr Hawtrey says,

'Now Mr Lilly, how's this for an idea: What say, while the mounting of the prints is in progress, you let your niece make a visit to Holywell Street? Shouldn't you like a holiday, Miss Lilly, in London? There, I see by your look that you should.'

'She should not,' says my uncle.

Mr Huss draws close. His coat is thick and he is sweating. He takes the tips of my fingers. 'Miss Lilly,' he says. 'If I might ever—'

'Come come,' says my uncle. 'Now you grow tedious. Here's my coachman, look. Maud, do you step back from the door . . .'

'Fools,' he says, when the gentlemen have gone. 'Eh, Rivers? But come, I'm impatient to begin. You have your tools?'

'I can fetch them, sir, in a moment.'

He bows, and goes. My uncle makes to follow. Then he turns, to look at me. He looks, in a considering sort of way, then beckons me closer. 'Give me your hand, Maud,' he says. I think he means to have me support him on the stairs. But when I offer him my arm he takes it, holds it, raises my wrist to his face, draws back the sleeve and squints at the strip of skin exposed. He peers at my cheek. 'Pale, do they say? Pale as mushroom? Hmm?' He works his mouth. 'You know what kind of matter mushrooms spring from?—Ho!' He laughs. 'Not pale, now!'

I have coloured and drawn away. Still laughing, he lets fall my hand, turns from me, begins to mount the stairs alone. He wears a pair of soft list slippers, that show his stockinged heels; and I watch him climb, imagining my spite a whip, a stick, with which I could lash at his feet and make him stumble.

I am standing, thinking this, hearing his step fade, when Richard returns to the gallery from the floors above. He does not look for me, does not know that I am there, still there, in the shadow of the fastened front door. He only walks; but he walks briskly, his fingers drumming the gallery rail. I think perhaps he even whistles, or hums. We are not used to such sounds at Briar, and with my passion raised and set smarting by my uncle's words they strike me now as thrilling, perilous, like a shifting of timbers and beams. I think the dust must be rising in a cloud from the antique carpets beneath his

shoes; and when I raise my eyes to follow his tread I am sure I can
see fine crumbs of paint flake and tumble from the ceiling. The
sight makes me giddy. I imagine the house walls cracking—
gaping—collapsing in the concussion of his presence. I am only
afraid they will do so before I have had my chance to escape.

But I am afraid, too, of escaping. I think he knows it. He cannot
speak privately with me, once Mr Huss and Mr Hawtrey have gone;
and he does not dare to steal his way, a second time, to my own
rooms. But he knows he must secure me to his plan. He waits, and
watches. He takes his supper with us, still; but sits at my uncle's
side, not mine. One night, however, he breaks their conversation to
say this:

'It troubles me, Miss Lilly, to think of how bored you must be,
now I have come and taken your uncle's attention from his Index. I
imagine you are longing to return to your work among the books.'

'The books?' I say. Then, letting my gaze fall to my plate of
broken meat: 'Very much, of course.'

'Then I wish I might do something, to make the burden of your
days a little lighter. Have you no work—no painting or sketching,
material of that sort—that I might mount for you, in my own time?
I think you must. For I see you have many handsome prospects,
from the windows of the house.'

He raises a brow, as a conductor of music might raise a baton. Of
course, I am nothing if not obedient. I say, 'I cannot paint, or draw.
I have never been taught it.'

'What, never?—Forgive me, Mr Lilly. Your niece strikes one as
being so competent a mistress of the general run of the female arts,
I should have said— But, you know, we might remedy this, with
very little trouble. Miss Lilly could take lessons from me, sir. Might
I not teach her, in my afternoons? I have a little experience in the
field: I taught drawing for all of one season at Paris, to the daughters of a Comte.'

My uncle screws up his eyes. 'Drawing?' he says. 'What would
my niece want with that? Do you mean to assist us, Maud, in the
making up of the albums?'

'I mean drawing for its own sake, sir,' says Richard gently, before I can reply.

'For its own sake?' My uncle blinks at me. 'Maud, what do you say?'

'I'm afraid I have no skill.'

'No skill? Well, that may be true. Certainly your hand, when I first had you here, was ungainly enough; and tends to slope, even now. Tell me, Rivers: should a course of instruction in drawing help the firmness of my niece's hand?'

'I should say it would, sir, most definitely.'

'Then, Maud, do you let Mr Rivers teach you. I don't care, anyhow, to imagine you idle. Hmm?'

'Yes, sir,' I say.

Richard looks on, a sheen of blandness across his gaze like the filmy lid that guards a cat's eye as it slumbers. My uncle bending to his plate, however, he quickly meets my look: then the film draws back, the eye is bared; and the sudden intimacy of his expression makes me shudder.

Don't misunderstand me. Don't think me more scrupulous than I am. It's true I shudder in fear—fear of his plot—fear of its success, as well as of its failure. But I tremble, too, at the boldness of him— or rather, his boldness sets me quivering, as they say a vibrating string will find out unsuspected sympathies in the fibres of idle bodies. *I saw in ten minutes what your life has made of you*, he said to me, that first night. And then: *I think you are half a villain already*. He was right. If I never knew that villainy before—or if, knowing it, I never named it—I know it, name it, now.

I know it, when he comes each day to my room, raises my hand to his mouth, touches his lips to my knuckles, rolls his cold, blue, devilish eyes. If Agnes sees, she does not understand. She thinks it gallantry. It is gallantry!—The gallantry of rogues. She will watch while we put out paper, leads and paints. She will see him take his place at my side, guide my fingers in the making of curves and crooked lines. He will drop his voice. Men's voices do badly in mur-murs, as a rule—they break, they jar, they long to rise—but his can fall, insinuate, and yet, like a musical note, stay clear; and while she sits and sews, half the length of a room away, he will take me, in secret, point by point across his scheme, until the scheme is perfect.

'Very good,' he'll say—like a proper drawing-master with an able girl. 'Very good. You learn quickly.'

He will smile. He will straighten and put back his hair. He will look at Agnes and find her eyes on his. Her gaze will flutter away.

'Well, Agnes,' he'll say, marking her nervousness like a hunter marks his bird, 'what do you say to your mistress's gifts as an artist?'

'Oh, sir! I couldn't hope to judge.'

He might take up a pencil, go closer to her. 'You see how I have Miss Lilly hold the lead? Her grip is a lady's grip, however, and needs firming. I think your hand, Agnes, would bear a pencil better. Here, won't you try?'

Once he takes her fingers. She colours scarlet at his touch.

'Do you blush?' he says then, in amazement. 'You don't suppose I mean to insult you?'

'No, sir!'

'Well, why do you blush?'

'I am only a little warm, sir.'

'Warm, in December—?'

And so on. He has a talent for torment, quite as polished as my own; and I ought, in observing this, to grow cautious. I do not. The more he teases, the more bewildered Agnes becomes, the more—like a top, revolving faster at the goading of a whip!—the more I taunt her myself.

'Agnes,' I say, while she undresses me or brushes out my hair, 'what are you thinking of? Of Mr Rivers?' I stop her wrist, feel the grinding of the bones inside it. 'Do you think him handsome, Agnes? You do, I see it in your eye! And don't young girls want handsome men?'

'Indeed, miss, I don't know!'

'Do you say that? Then you're a liar.' I pinch her, in some soft part of her flesh—for of course, by now I know them all. 'You're a liar and a flirt. Will you put those crimes upon your list, when you kneel beside your bed and ask your Father to forgive you? Do you think He *will* forgive you, Agnes? I think He must forgive a red-headed girl, for she can't help it that she's wicked, it's in her nature to be so. He would be cruel indeed, to put a passion in her, and then to punish her for feeling it. Don't you think? Don't you feel your passion, when Mr Rivers gazes at you? Don't you listen for the sound of his quick step?'

She says she doesn't. She swears it, against her own mother's life! God knows what she really thinks. She must only say it, or the play will founder. She must say it and be bruised, and keep the habit of her innocence complete; and I must bruise her. I must bruise her, for all the commonplace wanting of him that—were I an ordinary girl, with an ordinary heart—I would surely feel myself.

I never do feel it. Don't imagine I do. Does de Merteuil feel it, for Valmont? I don't want to feel it. I should hate myself, if I did! For I know it, from my uncle's books, for too squalid a thing—an itch, like the itch of inflamed flesh, to be satisfied hecticly, wetly, in closets and behind screens. What he has called up in me, set stirring in my breast—that dark propinquity—is something altogether rarer. I might say, it rises like a shadow in the house, or creeps like a bloom across its walls. But the house is full of shadows and stains, already; and so no-one marks it.

No-one, perhaps, save Mrs Stiles. For I think only she, of anyone there, ever gazes at Richard and wonders if he is all the gentleman he claims to be. I catch her look, sometimes. I believe she sees through him. I believe she thinks he has come to cheat me and do me harm. But, thinking it—and hating me—she keeps the thought to herself; and nurses her hope of my ruin, smiling, as she once nursed her dying child.

These, then, are the metals with which our trap is made, the forces that prime it and sharpen its teeth. And when it is all complete— 'Now,' says Richard, 'our work begins.

'We must get rid of Agnes.'

He says it in a whisper, with his eyes upon her, as she sits at the window bent over her work. He says it so coolly, with so steady a gaze, I am almost afraid of him. I think I draw back. Then he looks at me.

'You know that we must,' he says.

'Of course.'

'And you understand how?'

I have not, until this moment. Now I see his face.

'It's quite the only way,' he goes on, 'with virtuous girls like that. Will stop up a mouth, better even than menaces, or coins . . .' He has picked up a paintbrush, puts the hairs to his lip and begins to run them, idly, back and forth. 'Don't trouble with the details,' he says smoothly. 'There's not much to it. Not much, at all—' He smiles. She has looked up from her work, and he has caught her eye. 'How is the day, Agnes?' he calls. 'Still fair?'

'Quite fair, sir.'

'Good. Very good . . .' Then she must I suppose lower her head, for the kindness sinks from his face. He puts the paintbrush to his tongue and sucks the hairs into a point. 'I'll do it tonight,' he says, thoughtfully. 'Shall I? I will. I'll make my way to her room, as I made my way to yours. All you must do is, give me fifteen minutes alone with her'—again he looks at me—'and not come, if she cries out.'

It has seemed, until this point, a sort of game. Don't gentlemen and young ladies, in country houses, play games—flirt and intrigue? Now comes the first failing, or shrinking back, of my heart. When Agnes undresses me that night, I cannot look at her. I turn my head. 'You may close the door to your room, this once,' I say; and I feel her hesitate—perhaps catch the weakness in my voice, grow puzzled. I do not watch her leave me. I hear the clicking of the latch, the murmur of her prayers; I hear the murmur broken off, when he comes to her door. She does not cry out, after all. Should I really be able to keep from going to her, if she did? I do not know. But, she does not, her voice only lifts high, in surprise, in indignation and then—I suppose—a kind of panic; but then it drops, is stifled or soothed, gives way in a moment to whispers, to the rub of linen or limbs . . . Then the rub becomes silence. And the silence is worst of all: not an absence of sound, but teeming—as they say clear water teems, when viewed through a lens—with kicks and squirming movements. I imagine her shuddering, weeping, her clothes put back—but her freckled arms closing, despite herself, about his plunging back, her white mouth seeking out his—

I put my hands to my own mouth; and feel the dry chafe of my gloves. Then I stop up my ears. I don't hear it when he leaves her. I don't know what she does when he is gone. I let the door stay closed; take drops, at last, to help me sleep; and then, next day, wake late. I hear her calling, weakly, from her bed. She says she is ill. She parts her lips, to show me the lining of her mouth. It is red and raised and swollen.

'Scarlet fever,' she whispers, not meeting my gaze.

There are fears, then, of infection. Fears, of that! She is moved to an attic, and plates of vinegar burned in her room—the smell makes me sick. I see her again, but only once, the day she comes to make me her good-bye. She seems thin, and dark about the eye; and her hair is cut. I reach for her hand, and she flinches, perhaps expecting a blow; I only kiss her, lightly, on her wrist.

Then she looks at me in scorn.

'You are soft on me now,' she says, drawing back her arm, pulling down her sleeve, 'now you've another to be hard to. Good luck to you trying. I'd like to see you bruise him, before he bruises you.'

Her words shake me a little—but only a little; and when she is gone, it seems to me that I forget her. For Richard is also gone—gone three days before, on my uncle's business, and on ours—and my thoughts are all with him, with him and with London. London! where I have never been, but which I have imagined so fiercely, so often, I am sure I know. London, where I will find my liberty, cast off my self, live to another pattern—live without patterns, without hides and bindings—without books! I will ban paper from my house!

I lie upon my bed and try to imagine the house that I will take, in London. I cannot do it. I see only a series of voluptuous rooms—dim rooms, close rooms, rooms-within-rooms—dungeons and cells—the rooms of Priapus and Venus.—The thought unnerves me. I give it up. The house will come clearer in time, I am sure of it.

I rise and walk and think again of Richard, making his passage across the city, picking his way through the night to the dark thieves' den, close to the river. I think of him roughly greeted by crooks, I think of him casting off his coat and hat, warming his hands at a fire, looking about him. I think of him, Macheath-like, counting off a set of vicious faces—*Mrs Vixen, Betty Doxy, Jenny Diver, Molly Brazen*—until he finds the face he seeks . . .

Suky Tawdry.

Her. I think of her. I think so hard of her I think I know her colour—fair—her figure—plump—her walk, the shade of her eye.—I am sure it is blue. I begin to dream of her. In the dreams she speaks and I hear her voice. She says my name, and laughs.

I think I am dreaming of her when Margaret comes to my room with a letter, from him.

She's ours, he writes.

I read it, then fall back upon my pillow and hold the letter to my mouth. I put my lips to the paper. He might be my lover, after all—or, she might. For I could not want her now, more than I could a lover.

But I could not want a lover, more than I want freedom.

I put his letter upon the fire, then draw up my reply: *Send her at once. I am sure I shall love her. She shall be the dearer to me for coming from London, where you are!*—we settled on the wording before he left.

That done, I need only wait, one day and then another. The day after that is the day she comes.

She is due at Marlow at three o'clock. I send William Inker for her, in good time. But though I sit and seem to feel her drawing close, the trap comes back without her: the trains are late, there are fogs. I pace, and cannot settle. At five o'clock I send William again—again he comes back. Then I must take supper with my uncle. While Charles pours out my wine I ask him, 'Any news yet, of Miss Smith?'—My uncle hearing me whisper, however, he sends Charles away.

'Do you prefer to talk with servants, Maud, than with me?' he says. He is peevish, since Richard left us.

He chooses a book of little punishments for me to read from, after the meal: the steady recitation of cruelty makes me calmer. But when I go up to my chill and silent rooms, I grow fretful again; and after Margaret has undressed me and put me into my bed, I rise, and walk—stand now at the fire, now at the door, now at the window, looking out for the light of the trap. Then I see it. It shows feebly in the fog—seems to glow, rather than to shine—and to flash, with the motion of the horse and the passage of the trap behind the trees, like a thing of warning. I watch it come, my hand at my heart. It draws close—slows, narrows, fades—I see beyond it, then, the horse, the cart, William, a vaguer figure. They drive to the rear of the house, and I run to Agnes's room—Susan's room, it will be now—and stand at the window there; and finally see her.

She is lifting her head, gazing up at the stables, the clock. William jumps from his seat and helps her to the ground. She holds a hood about her face. She is dressed darkly, and seems small.

But, she is real. The plot is real.—I feel the force of it all at once, and tremble.

It is too late to receive her, now. Instead I must wait further, while she is given a supper and brought to her room; and then I must lie, hearing her step and murmur, my eyes upon the door—an inch or two of desiccated wood!—that lies between her chamber and mine.

Once I rise and go stealthily to it, and put my ear to the panels; but hear nothing.

Next morning I have Margaret carefully dress me, and while she pulls at my laces I say, 'I believe Miss Smith has come. Did you see her, Margaret?'

'Yes, miss.'

'Do you think she will do?'

'Do, miss?'

'As girl to me.'

She tosses her head. 'Seemed rather low in her manners,' she says. 'Been half a dozen times to France and I don't know where, though. Made sure Mr Inker knew that.'

'Well, we must be kind to her. It will seem dull to her here, per-haps, after London.' She says nothing. 'Will you have Mrs Stiles bring her to me, so soon as she has taken her breakfast?'

I have lain all night, sometimes sleeping, sometimes waking, oppressed with the nearness and obscurity of her. I must see her now, before I go to my uncle, or I fear I will grow ill. At last, at half-past seven or so, I hear an unfamiliar tread in the passage that leads from the servants' staircase; and then Mrs Stiles's murmur: 'Here we are.' There comes a knock upon my door. How should I stand? I stand at the fire. Does my voice sound queer, when I call out? Does she mark it? Does she hold her breath? I know I hold mine; then I feel myself colour, and will the blood from my face. The door is opened. Mrs Stiles comes first and, after a moment's hesitation, she is before me: Susan—Susan Smith—Suky Tawdry—the gullible girl, who is to take my life from me and give me freedom.

Sharper than expectation, comes dismay. I have supposed she will resemble me, I have supposed she will be handsome: but she is a small, slight, spotted thing, with hair the colour of dust. Her chin comes almost to a point. Her eyes are brown, darker than mine. Her gaze is now too frank, now sly: she gives me a single, searching look that takes in my gown, my gloves, my slippers, the very clocks upon my stockings. Then she blinks—remembers her training, I suppose—makes a hasty curtsey. She is pleased with the curtsey, I can tell. She is pleased with me. She thinks me a fool. The idea upsets me, more than it should. I think, *You have come to Briar to ruin me.* I step to take her hand. *Won't you colour, or tremble, or hide your eyes?* But she returns my gaze and her fingers—which are bitten, about the nails—are cold and hard and perfectly steady in mine.

We are watched by Mrs Stiles. Her look says plainly: 'Here is the girl you sent for, to London. She is about good enough for you, I think.'

'You need not stay, Mrs Stiles,' I say. And then, as she turns to go: 'But you will have been kind to Miss Smith, I know.' I look again at Susan. 'You've heard, perhaps, that I am an orphan, Susan; like you. I came to Briar as a child—very young, and with no-one at all to care for me. I cannot tell you all the ways in which Mrs Stiles has made me know what a mother's love is, since that time . . .'

I say this, smiling. The tormenting of my uncle's housekeeper is too routine an occupation, however, to hold me. It is Susan I want; and when Mrs Stiles has twitched and coloured and left us, I draw her to me, to lead her to the fire. She walks. She sits. She is warm and quick. I touch her arm. It is as slender as Agnes's, but hard. I can smell beer upon her breath. She speaks. Her voice is not at all how I have dreamed it, but light and pert; though she tries to make it sweeter. She tells me of her journey, of the train from London—when she says the word, *London*, she seems conscious of the sound; I suppose she is not in the habit of naming it, of considering it a place of destination or desire. It is a wonder and a torment to me that a girl so slight, so trifling as she, should have lived her life in London, while mine has been all at Briar; but a consolation, also—for if she can thrive there, then might not I, with all my talents, thrive better?

So I tell myself, while describing her duties. Again I see her eye my gown and slippers and now, recognising the pity in her gaze as well as the scorn, I think I blush. I say, 'Your last mistress, of course, was quite a fine lady? She would laugh, I suppose, to look at me!'

My voice is not quite steady. But if there is a bitterness to my tone, she does not catch it. Instead, 'Oh, no, miss,' she says. 'She was far too kind a lady. And besides, she always said that grand clothes weren't worth buttons; but that it was the heart inside them that counts.'

She looks so taken with this—so *taken in*, by her own fiction—so innocent, not sly—I sit a moment and regard her in silence. Then I take her hand again. 'You are a good girl, Susan, I think,' I say. She smiles and looks modest. Her fingers move in mine.

'Lady Alice always said so, miss,' she says.

'Did she?'

'Yes, miss.'

Then she remembers something. She pulls from me, reaches into her pocket, and brings out a letter. It is folded, sealed, directed in an

affected feminine hand; and of course comes from Richard. I hesitate, then take it—rise and walk, unfold it, far from her gaze.

No names! it says;—*but I think you know me. Here is the girl
who will make us rich—that fresh little fingersmith, I've had
cause in the past to employ her skills, and can commend her. She
is watching as I write this, and oh! her ignorance is perfect. I
imagine her now, gazing at you. She is luckier than I, who must
pass two filthy weeks before enjoying that pleasure.—Burn this,
will you?*

I have thought myself as cool as he. I am not, I am not, I feel her
watching—just as he describes!—and grow fearful. I stand with the
letter in my hand, then am aware all at once that I have stood too long.
If she should have seen—! I fold the paper, once, twice, thrice—
finally it will not fold at all. I do not yet know that she cannot read or
write so much as her own name; when I learn it I laugh, in an awful
relief. But I don't quite believe her. 'Not read?' I say. 'Not a letter, not
a word?'—and I hand her a book. She does not want to take it; and
when she does, she opens its covers, turns a page, gazes hard at a piece
of text—but all in a way that is wrong, indefinably anxious and
wrong, and too subtle to counterfeit.—At last, she blushes.

Then I take the book back. 'I am sorry,' I say. But I am not sorry,
I am only amazed. Not to read! It seems to me a kind of fabulous
insufficiency—like the absence, in a martyr or a saint, of the capac-
ity for pain.

The eight o'clock sounds, to call me to my uncle. At the door I
pause. I must, after all, make some blushing reference to Richard;
and I say what I ought and her look, as it should, becomes suddenly
crafty and then grows clear. She tells me how kind he is. She says
it—again—as if she believes it. Perhaps she does. Perhaps kindness
is measured to a different standard, where she comes from. I feel the
points and edges of the folded note he has sent by her hand, in the
pocket of my skirt.

What she does while alone in my chambers I cannot say, but I imagine her fingering the silks of my gowns, trying out my boots, my gloves, my sashes. Does she take an eye-glass to my jewels? Perhaps she is planning already what she will do, when they are hers: this brooch she will keep, from this she will prise the stones to sell them, the ring of gold that was my father's she will pass to her young man . . .

'You are distracted, Maud,' my uncle says. 'Have you another occupation to which you would rather attend?'

'No, sir,' I say.

'Perhaps you begrudge me your little labour. Perhaps you wish that I had left you at the madhouse, all those years ago. Forgive me: I had supposed myself performing you some service, by taking you from there. But perhaps you would rather dwell among lunatics, than among books? Hmm?'

'No, Uncle.'

He pauses. I think he will return to his notes. But he goes on.

'It would be a simple matter enough, to summon Mrs Stiles and have her take you back. You are sure you don't desire me to do that?—send for William Inker and the dog-cart?' As he speaks, he leans to study me, his weak gaze fierce behind the spectacles that guard it. Then he pauses again, and almost smiles. 'What would they make of you upon the wards, I wonder,' he says, in a different voice, 'with all that you know now?'

He says it slowly, then mumbles the question over; as if it is a biscuit that has left crumbs beneath his tongue. I do not answer, but lower my gaze until he has worked his humour out. Presently he twists his neck and looks again at the pages upon his desk.

'So, so. *The Whipping Milliners*. Read me the second volume, with the punctuation all complete; and mark—the paging is irregular. I'll note the sequence here.'

It is from this that I am reading when she comes to take me back to my drawing-room. She stands at the door, looking over the walls of books, the painted windows. She hovers at the pointing finger that my uncle keeps to mark the bounds of innocence at Briar, just as I once did; and—again, like me—in her innocence she does not see it,

and tries to cross it. I must keep her from that, more even than my
uncle must!—and while he jerks and screams I go softly to her, and
touch her. She flinches at the feel of my fingers.

I say, 'Don't be frightened, Susan.' I show her the brass hand in
the floor.

I have forgotten that, of course, she might look at anything there,
anything at all, it would be so much ink upon paper. Remembering,
I am filled again with wonder—and then with a spiteful kind of
envy. I have to draw back my hand from her arm, for fear I will
pinch her.

I ask her, as we walk to my room, What does she think of my
uncle?

She believes him composing a dictionary.

We sit at lunch. I have no appetite, and pass my plate to her. I
lean back in my chair, and watch as she runs her thumb along the
edge of china, admires the weave of the napkin she spreads on her
knee. She might be an auctioneer, a house-agent: she holds each
item of cutlery as if gauging the worth of the metal from which it
is cast. She eats three eggs, spooning them quickly, neatly into her
mouth—not shuddering at the yielding of the yolk, not thinking, as
she swallows, of the closing of her own throat about the meat. She
wipes her lips with her fingers, touches her tongue to some spot
upon her knuckle; then swallows again.

You have come to Briar, I think, *to swallow up me.*

But of course, I want her to do it. I need her to do it. And already I
seem to feel myself beginning to give up my life. I give it up easily, as
burning wicks give up smoke, to tarnish the glass that guards them;
as spiders spin threads of silver, to bind up quivering moths. I imagine it settling, tight, about her. She does not know it. She will not
know it until, too late, she will look and see how it has clothed and
changed her, made her like me. For now, she is only tired, restless,
bored: I take her walking about the park, and she follows, leadenly;
we sit and sew, and she yawns and rubs her eyes, gazing at nothing.
She chews her fingernails—stops, when she sees me looking; then
after a minute draws down a length of hair and bites the tip of that.

'You are thinking of London,' I say.

She lifts her head. 'London, miss?'

I nod. 'What do ladies do there, at this hour in the day?'

'Ladies, miss?'

'Ladies, like me.'

She looks about her. Then, after a second: 'Make visits, miss?'

'Visits?'

'To other ladies?'

'Ah.'

She does not know. She is making it up. I am sure she is making it up! Even so, I think over her words and my heart beats suddenly hard. *Ladies*, I said, *like me*. There are no ladies like me, however; and for a second I have a clear and frightening picture of myself in London, alone, unvisited—

But I am alone and unvisited, now. And I shall have Richard there, Richard will guide and advise me. Richard means to take us a house, with rooms, with doors that will fasten—

'Are you cold, miss?' she says. Perhaps I have shivered. She rises, to fetch me a shawl. I watch her walk. Diagonally she goes, over the carpet—heedless of the design, the lines and diamonds and squares, beneath her feet.

I watch and watch her. I cannot look too long, too narrowly at her, in her easy doing of commonplace things. At seven o'clock she makes me ready for supper with my uncle. At ten she puts me into my bed. After that, she stands in her room and I hear her sighing, and I lift my head and see her stretch and droop. Her candle lights her, very plainly; though I lie hidden in the dark. Quietly she passes, back and forth across the doorway—now stooping to pick up a fallen lace; now taking up her cloak and brushing mud from its hem. She does not kneel and pray, as Agnes did. She sits on her bed, out of my sight, but lifts her feet: I see the toe of one shoe put to the heel of the other and work it down. Now she stands, to undo the buttons of her gown; now she lets it fall, steps awkwardly out of her skirt; unlaces her stays, rubs her waist, sighs again. Now she steps away. I lift my head, to follow. She comes back, in her nightgown— shivering. I shiver, in sympathy. She yawns. I also yawn. She

stretches—enjoying the stretch—liking the approach of slumber!
Now she moves off—puts out her light, climbs into her bed—grows
warm I suppose, and sleeps . . .

She sleeps, in a sort of innocence. So did I, once. I wait a
moment, then take out my mother's picture and hold it close to my
mouth.

That's her, I whisper. *That's her. She's your daughter now!*

How effortless it seems! But when I have locked my mother's face
away I lie, uneasily. My uncle's clock shudders and strikes. Some
animal shrieks, like a child, in the park. I close my eyes and think—
what I have not thought so vividly of, in years—of the madhouse,
my first home; of the wild-eyed women, the lunatics; and of the
nurses. I remember all at once the nurses' rooms, the mattings of
coir, a piece of text on the limewashed wall: *My meat is to do the will
of Him that sent me.* I remember an attic stair, a walk upon the roof,
the softness of lead beneath my fingernail, the frightful drop to the
ground—

I must fall into sleep, thinking this. I must plunge to the deepest
layers of the night. But then, I am woken—or, not quite woken, not
quite drawn free from the tugging of the dark. For I open my eyes
and am bewildered—perfectly bewildered—and filled with dread. I
look at my form in the bed and it seems shifting and queer—now
large, now small, now broken up with spaces; and I cannot say what
age I am. I begin to shake. I call out. I call for Agnes. I have quite
forgotten that she has gone. I have forgotten Richard Rivers, and all
our plot. I call for Agnes, and it seems to me she comes; but she
comes, to take away my lamp. I think she must do it to punish me.
'Don't take the light!' I say; but she takes it, she leaves me in the terrible darkness and I hear the sighing of doors, the passage of feet,
beyond the curtain. It seems to me then that much time passes
before the light comes back. But when Agnes lifts it and sees my
face, she screams.

'Don't look at me!' I cry. And then: 'Don't leave me!' For I have
a sense that, if she will only stay, some calamity, some dreadful
thing—I do not know it, cannot name it—will be averted; and I—

or she—will be saved. I hide my face against her and seize her hand.
But her hand is pale where it used to be freckled. I gaze at her, and
do not know her.

She says, in a voice that is strange to me: 'It's Sue, miss. Only Sue.
You see me? You are dreaming.'

'Dreaming?'

She touches my cheek. She smooths my hair—not like Agnes,
after all, but like— Like no-one. She says again, 'It's Sue. That
Agnes had the scarlatina, and is gone back home. You must lie
down now, or the cold will make you ill. You mustn't be ill.'

I swim in black confusion for another moment; then the dream
slips from me all at once and I know her, and know myself—my
past, my present, my ungaugeable future. She is a stranger to me,
but part of it all.

'Don't leave me, Sue!' I say.

I feel her hesitate. When she draws away, I grip her tighter. But
she moves only to climb across me, and she comes beneath the
sheet and lies with her arm about me, her mouth against my hair.

She is cold, and makes me cold. I shiver, but soon lie still.
'There,' she says then. She murmurs it. I feel the movement of her
breath and, deep in the bone of my cheek, the gentle rumble of her
voice. 'There. Now you'll sleep—won't you? Good girl.'

Good girl, she says. How long has it been since anyone at Briar
believed me good? But she believes it. She must believe it, for the
working of our plot. I must be good, and kind, and simple. Isn't
gold said to be good? I am like gold to her, after all. She has come to
ruin me; but, not yet. For now she must guard me, keep me sound
and safe as a hoard of coins she means, at last, to squander—

I know it; but cannot feel it as I should. I sleep in her arms,
dreamless and still, and wake to the warmth and closeness of her.
She moves away as she feels me stir. She rubs her eye. Her hair is
loose and touches my own. Her face, in sleep, has lost a little of its
sharpness. Her brow is smooth, her lashes powdery, her gaze, when
it meets mine, quite clear, untinged with mockery or malice . . .
She smiles. She yawns. She rises. The blanket lifts and falls, and

sour heat comes gusting. I lie and remember the night. Some feeling—shame, or panic—flutters about my heart. I put my hand to
the place where she has lain, and feel it cool.

She is changed with me. She is surer, kinder. Margaret brings
water, and she fills me a bowl. 'Ready, miss?' she says. 'Better use it
quick.' She wets a cloth and wrings it and, when I stand and
undress, passes it, unasked, across my face and beneath my arms. I
have become a child to her. She makes me sit, so she may brush my
hair. She tuts: 'What tangles! The trick with tangles is, to start at the
bottom . . .'

Agnes had used to wash and dress me with quick and nervous fingers, wincing with every catching of the comb. One time I struck her
with a slipper—so hard, she bled. Now I sit for Susan—*Sue*, she
called herself, in the night—now I sit patiently while Sue draws out
the knots from my hair, my eyes upon my own face in the glass . . .

Good girl.

Then: 'Thank you, Sue,' I say.

I say it often, in the days and nights that follow. I never said it to
Agnes. 'Thank you, Sue.' 'Yes, Sue,' when she bids me sit or stand,
lift an arm or foot. 'No, Sue,' when she is afraid my gown must
pinch me.

No, I am not cold.—But she likes to look me over as we walk, to
be quite sure; will gather my cloak a little higher about my throat,
to keep off draughts. No, my boots are not taking in the dew.—But
she'll slide a finger between my stockinged ankle and the leather of
my shoe, for certainty's sake. I must not catch cold, at any cost. I
must not tire. 'Wouldn't you say you had walked enough, miss?' I
mustn't grow ill. 'Here is all your breakfast, look, untouched. Won't
you take a little more?' I mustn't grow thin. I am a goose that must
be plump, to be worth its slaughter.

Of course, though she does not know it, it is she who must be
plump—she who will learn, in time, to sleep, to wake, to dress, to
walk, to a pattern, to signals and bells. She thinks she humours me.
She thinks she pities me! She learns the ways of the house, not
understanding that the habits and the fabrics that bind me will,
soon, bind her. Bind her, like morocco or like calf . . . I have grown

used to thinking of myself as a sort of book. Now I feel myself a book, as books must seem to her: she looks at me with her unreading eyes, sees the shape, but not the meaning of the text. She marks the white flesh—'Ain't you pale!' she says—but not the quick, corrupted blood beneath.

I oughtn't to do it. I cannot help it. I am too compelled by her idea—her idea of me as a simple girl, abused by circumstance, prone to nightmare. No nightmares come, while she sleeps at my side; and so, I find ways to bring her to my bed, a second night and a third.—At last she comes, routinely. I think her wary, at first; but it is only the canopy and drapes that trouble her: she stands each time with a lifted candle, peering into the folds of cloth. 'Don't you think,' she says, 'of the moths and spiders that might be up there, miss, and waiting to drop?' She seizes a post, and shakes it; a single beetle falls, in a shower of dust.

Once grown used to that, however, she lies easily enough; and from the neat and comfortable way she holds her limbs, I think that she must be used to sleeping with someone; and wonder who.

'Do you have sisters, Sue?' I ask her once, perhaps a week after she has come. We are walking by the river.

'No, miss.'

'Brothers?'

'Not as I know of,' she says.

'And so you grew up—like me—quite alone?'

'Well, miss, not what you would call, alone . . . Say, with cousins all about.'

'Cousins. You mean, your aunt's children?'

'My aunt?' She looks blank.

'Your aunt, Mr Rivers's nurse.'

'Oh!' She blinks. 'Yes, miss. To be sure . . .'

She turns away, and her look grows vague. She is thinking of her home. I try to imagine it; and cannot. I try to imagine her cousins: rough boys and girls, sharp-faced like her, sharp-tongued, sharp-fingered— Her fingers are blunt, however; though her tongue—for sometimes, when putting the pins to my hair, or frowning over slithering laces, she shows it—her tongue has a point. I watch her sigh.

'Never mind,' I say—like any kindly mistress with an unhappy maid. 'Look, here is a barge. You may send your wishes with it. We shall both send wishes, to London.' *To London*, I think again, more darkly. Richard is there. I will be there, a month from now. I say, 'The Thames will take them, even if the boat does not.'

She looks, however, not at the barge, but at me.

'The Thames?' she says.

'The river,' I answer. 'This river, here.'

'This trifling bit of water, the Thames? Oh, no, miss.' She laughs, uncertainly. 'How can that be? The Thames is very wide'— she holds her hands far apart—'and this is narrow. Do you see?'

I say, after a moment, that I have always supposed that rivers grow wider as they flow. She shakes her head.

'This trifling bit of water?' she says again. 'Why, the water we have from our taps, at home, has more life to it than this.—There, miss! Look, there.' The barge has passed us. Its stern is marked in six-inch letters, ROTHERHITHE; but she is pointing, not to them, but to the wake of grease spreading out from the spluttering engine. 'See that?' she says excitedly. 'That's how the Thames looks. That's how the Thames looks, every day of the year. Look at all those colours. A thousand colours . . .'

She smiles. Smiling, she is almost handsome. Then the wake of grease grows thin, the water browns, her smile quite falls; and she looks like a thief again.

You must understand, I have determined to despise her. For how, otherwise, will I be able to do what I must do?—how else deceive and harm her? It is only that we are put so long together, in such seclusion. We are obliged to be intimate. And her notion of intimacy is not like Agnes's—not like Barbara's—not like any lady's maid's. She is too frank, too loose, too free. She yawns, she leans. She rubs at spots and grazes. She will sit picking over some old dry cut upon her knuckle, while I sew. Then, 'Got a pin, miss?' she will ask me; and when I give her a needle from my case she will spend ten minutes probing the skin of her hand with that. Then she will give the needle back to me.

But she will give it, taking care to keep the point from my soft fingers. 'Don't hurt yourself,' she will say—so simply, so kindly, I quite forget that she is only keeping me safe for Richard's sake. I think that she forgets it, too.

One day she takes my arm as we are walking. It is nothing to her; but I feel the shock of it, like a slap. Another time, after sitting, I complain that my feet are chilled: she kneels before me, unlaces my slippers, takes my feet in her hands and hold and chafes them— finally dips her head and carelessly breathes upon my toes. She begins to dress me as she pleases; makes little changes to my gowns, my hair, my rooms. She brings flowers: throws away the vases of curling leaves that have always stood on my drawing-room tables, and finds primroses in the hedges of my uncle's park to put in their place. 'Of course, you don't get the flowers that you get in London, in the country,' she says, as she sets them in the glass; 'but these are pretty enough, ain't they?'

She has Margaret bring extra coals for my fires, from Mr Way. Such a simple thing to do!—and yet no-one has thought to do it before, for my sake; even I have not thought to do it; and so I have gone cold, through seven winters. The heat makes the windows cloud. She likes to stand, then, and draw loops and hearts and spirals upon the glass.

One time she brings me back from my uncle's room and I find the luncheon-table spread with playing-cards. My mother's cards, I suppose; for these are my mother's rooms, and filled with her things; and yet for a second it quite disconcerts me, to imagine my mother here—actually here—walking *here*, sitting *here*, setting out the coloured cards upon the cloth. My mother, unmarried, still sane—perhaps, idly leaning her cheek upon her knuckles—perhaps, sighing—and waiting, waiting . . .

I take up a card. It slides against my glove. But in Sue's hands, the deck is changed: she gathers and sorts it, shuffles and deals it, neatly and nimbly; and the golds and reds are vivid between her fingers, like so many jewels. She is astonished, of course, to learn I cannot play; and at once makes me sit, so she may teach me. The games are things of chance and simple speculation, but she plays earnestly, almost greedily—tilting her head, narrowing her eye as she surveys her fan of cards. When I grow tired, she plays alone— or else, will stand the cards upon their ends and tilt their tips together, and from doing this many times will build a rising structure, a kind of pyramid of cards—always keeping back, for the top-most point, a king and a queen.

'Look here,' she says, when she has finished. 'Look here, miss. Do you see?' Then she will ease a card from the pyramid's foundation; and as the structure topples, she will laugh.

She will laugh. The sound is as strange, at Briar, as I imagine it must be in a prison or a church. Sometimes, she will sing. Once we talk of dancing. She rises and lifts her skirt, to show me a step. Then she pulls me to my feet, and turns and turns me; and I feel, where she presses against me, the quickening beat of her heart—I feel it pass from her to me and become mine.

Finally I let her smooth a pointed tooth with a silver thimble.

'Let me look,' she says. She has seen me rubbing my cheek. 'Come to the light.'

I stand at the window, put back my head. Her hand is warm, her breath—with the yeast of beer upon it—warm also. She reaches, and feels about my gum.

'Well, that is sharper,' she says, drawing back her hand, 'than—'

'Than a serpent's tooth, Sue?'

'Than a needle, I was going to say.' She looks about her. 'Do snakes have teeth, miss?'

'I think they must, since they are said to bite.'

'That's true,' she says distractedly. 'Only, I had imagined them gummier . . .'

She has gone to my dressing-room. I can see, through the open door, the bed and, pushed well beneath it, the chamber-pot: she has warned me, more than once, of how china pots may break beneath the toes of careless risers and make them lame. She has cautioned me, in a similar spirit, against the stepping on, in naked feet, of

hairs (since hairs—*like worms*, she says—may work their way into
the flesh, and fester); the darkening of eye-lashes with impure
castor-oil; and the reckless climbing—for purposes of concealment,
or flight—of chimneys. Now, looking through the items on my
dressing-table, she says no more. I wait, then call.

'Don't you know anyone who died from a snake-bite, Sue?'

'A snake-bite, miss?' She reappears, still frowning. 'In London?
Do you mean, at the Zoo?'

'Well, perhaps at the Zoo.'

'I can't say as I do.'

'Curious. I was certain, you know, that you would.'

I smile, though she does not. Then she shows me her hand, with
the thimble on it; I see for the first time what she means to do, and
perhaps look strange. 'It won't hurt you,' she says, watching my
changing face.

'Are you sure?'

'Yes, miss. If I hurt, you may scream; and then I will stop.'

It does not hurt, I do not scream. But it makes for a queer mix of
sensations: the grinding of the metal, the pressure of her hand
holding my jaw, the softness of her breath. As she studies the tooth
she files, I can look nowhere but at her face; and so I look at her
eyes: one is marked, I see now, with a fleck of darker brown, almost
black. I look at the line of her cheek—which is smooth; and her
ear—which is neat, its lobe pierced through for the wearing of
hoops and pendants. 'Pierced, how?' I asked her once, going close to
her, putting my finger-tips to the little dimples in the curving flesh.
'Why, miss, with a needle,' she said, 'and a bit of ice . . .' The thimble rubs on. She smiles. 'My aunty does this,' she says as she works,
'for babies. I dare say she done it for me.—Almost got it! Ha!' She
grinds more slowly, then pauses, to test the tooth. Then she rubs
again. 'Tricky thing to do to an infant, of course. For if you happen
to let slip the thimble—well, I know several as were lost like that.'

I do not know if she means thimbles, or infants. Her fingers, and
my lips, are becoming wet. I swallow, then swallow again. My
tongue rises and moves against her hand. Her hand seems, all at
once, too big, too strange; and I think of the tarnish on the silver—

I think my breath must have made it wet and set it running, I think
I can taste it. Perhaps, if she were to work a little longer at the
tooth, I should fall into a sort of panic; but now the thimble rubs
slower again, and soon, she stops. She tests again with her thumb,
keeps her hand another second at my jaw, and then draws back.

I emerge from her grip a little unsteadily. She has held me so
tight, so long, when she moves away the cold air leaps to my face. I
swallow, then run my tongue across my blunted tooth. I wipe my
lips. I see her hand: her knuckles marked red and white from the
pressure of my mouth; her finger also marked, and with the thimble still upon it. The silver is bright—not tarnished, not tarnished
at all. What I have tasted, or imagine I have tasted, is the taste of
her; only that.

May a lady taste the fingers of her maid? She may, in my uncle's
books.—The thought makes me colour.

And it is as I am standing, feeling the blood rush awkwardly
into my cheek, that a girl comes to my door with a letter, from
Richard. I have forgotten to expect it. I have forgotten to think of
our plan, our flight, our marriage, the looming asylum gate. I have
forgotten to think of him. I must think of him now, however. I
take the letter and, trembling, break its seal.

> *Are you as impatient as I?* he writes. *I know that you are. Do*
> *you have her with you, now? Can she see your face? Look glad.*
> *Smile, simper, all of that. Our waiting is over. My business in*
> *London is done, and I am coming!*

Chapter Ten

*T*he letter works upon me like the snap of a mesmerist's fingers: I blink, look giddily about me, as if emerging from a trance. I look at Sue: at her hand, at the mark of my mouth upon it. I look at the pillows upon my bed, with the dints of our two heads. I look at the flowers in their vase on the table-top, at the fire in my grate. The room is too warm. The room is too warm and yet I am still trembling, as if cold. She sees it. She catches my eye, and nods to the paper in my hand. 'Good news, miss?' she asks; and it is as if the letter has worked some trick upon her, too: for her voice seems light to me—dreadfully light—and her face seems sharp. She puts away the thimble; but watches, watches. I cannot meet her gaze.

Richard is coming. Does she feel it, as I do? She gives no sign. She walks, she sits, as easily as before. She eats her lunch. She takes out my mother's playing-cards, begins the patient dealing-out of solitary games. I stand at the glass and, in reflection, see her reach to take a card and place it, turn it, set it upon another, raise up the

kings, pull out the aces . . . I look at my face and think what makes
it mine: the certain curve of cheek, the lip too full, too plump, too
pink.

At last she gathers the pack together and says that if I will shuf-
fle and hold it, and wish, she will study the fall of the cards and tell
me my future. She says it, apparently quite without irony; and
despite myself I am drawn to her side, and sit, and clumsily mix the
cards, and she takes them and lays them down. 'These show your
past,' she says, 'and these your present.' Her eyes grow wide. She
seems suddenly young to me: for a moment we bend our heads and
whisper as I think other, ordinary girls, in ordinary parlours or
schools or sculleries, might whisper: *Here is a young man, look, on
horseback. Here is a journey. Here is the Queen of Diamonds, for
wealth—*

I have a brooch that is set with brilliants. I think of it now. I
think—as I have, before, though not in many days—of Sue, breathing proprietorially over the stones, gauging their worth . . .

After all, we are not ordinary girls, in an ordinary parlour; and
she is interested in my fortune only as she supposes it hers. Her eye
grows narrow again. Her voice lifts out of its whisper and is only
pert. I move away from her while she sits gathering the deck, turning the cards in her hands and frowning. She has let one fall, and has
not seen it: the two of hearts. I place my heel upon it, imagining one
of the painted red hearts my own; and I grind it into the carpet.

She finds it, when I have risen, and tries to smooth the crease
from it; then plays on at Patience, as doggedly as before.

I look, again, at her hands. They have grown whiter, and are healed
about the nails. They are small, and in gloves will seem smaller; and
then will resemble my own.

This must be done. This should have been done, before. Richard
is coming, and I am overtaken by a sense of duties unmet: a pan-
icking sense that hours, days—dark, devious fish of time—have
slithered by, uncaptured. I pass a fretful night. Then, when we rise
and she comes to dress me, I pluck at the frill on the sleeve of her
gown.

'Have you no other gown,' I say, 'than this plain brown thing you always wear?'

She says she has not. I take, from my press, a velvet gown, and have her try it. She bares her arms unwillingly, steps out of her skirt and turns, in a kind of modesty, away from my eyes. The gown is narrow. I tug at the hooks. I settle the folds of cloth about her hips, then go to my box for a brooch—that brooch of brilliants—and pin it carefully over her heart.

Then I stand her before the glass.

Margaret comes, and takes her for me.

I have grown used to her, to the life, the warmth, the particularity of her; she has become, not the gullible girl of a villainous plot—not Suky Tawdry—but a girl with a history, with hates and likings. Now all at once I see how near to me in face and figure she'll come, and I understand, as if for the first time, what it is that Richard and I mean to do. I place my face against the post of my bed and watch her, gazing at herself in a rising satisfaction, turning a little to the left, a little to the right, brushing the creases from her skirt, settling her flesh more comfortably into the seams of the gown. 'If my aunty could see me!' she says, growing pink; and I think, then, of who might be waiting for her, in that dark thieves' den in London: the aunt, the mother or grandmother. I think how restless she must be, as she counts off the lengthening days that keep her little fingersmith on perilous business, far from home. I imagine her, as she waits, taking out some small thing of Sue's—some sash, some necklace, some bracelet of gaudy charms—and turning it, over and over, in her hands . . .

She will turn it for ever, though she does not know it yet. Nor does Sue suppose that the last time she kissed her aunt's hard cheek was the last of all her life.

I think of that; and I am gripped with what I take to be pity. It is hard, painful, surprising: I feel it, and am afraid. Afraid of what my future may cost me. Afraid of that future itself, and of the unfamiliar, ungovernable emotions with which it might be filled.

She does not know it. He must not know it, either. He comes that

afternoon—comes, as he used to come, in the days of Agnes: takes my
hand, holds my gaze with his, bends to kiss my knuckles. 'Miss Lilly,'
he says, in a tone of caress. He is dressed darkly, neatly; yet carries his
daring, his confidence, close and gaudy about him, like swirls of
colour or perfume. I feel the heat of his mouth, even through my
gloves. Then he turns to Sue, and she makes a curtsey. The stiff-
bodiced dress is not made for curtseying in, however: the dip is a
jagged one, the fringes upon her skirt tumble together and seem to
shake. Her colour rises. I see him smile as he notes it. But I see, too,
that he marks the gown, and perhaps also the whiteness of her fingers.

'I should have supposed her a lady, I'm sure,' he says, to me. He
moves to her side. There, he seems tall, and darker than ever, like a
bear; and she seems slight. He takes her hand, his fingers moving
about hers: they seem large, also—his thumb extends almost to the
bone of her wrist. He says, 'I hope you are proving a good girl for
your mistress, Sue.'

She gazes at the floor. 'I hope I am, too, sir.'

I take a step. 'She is a very good girl,' I say. 'A very good girl,
indeed.'

But the words are hasty, imperfect. He catches my eye, draws
back his thumb. 'Of course,' he says smoothly, 'she could not help
but be good. No girl could help it, Miss Lilly, with you for her
example.'

'You are too kind,' I say.

'No gentleman could but be, I think, with *you* to be kind to.'

He keeps his gaze on mine. He has picked me out, found sympathies in me, means to pluck me from the heart of Briar,
unscratched; and I would not be myself, niece to my uncle, if I
could meet the look he shows me now without feeling the stir of
some excitement, dark and awful, in my own breast. But I feel it too
hard, and grow almost queasy. I smile; but the smile stretches tight.

Sue tilts her head. Does she suppose me smiling at my own love?
The thought makes the smile tighter still, I begin to feel it as an
ache about my throat. I avoid her eye, and his. He goes, but makes
her step to him and they stand a moment, murmuring at the door.
He gives her a coin—I see the yellow gleam of it—he puts it into

her hand, closes her fingers about it with his own. His nail shows brown against the fresh pink of her palm. She falls in another awkward curtsey.

Now my smile is fixed like the grimace on the face of a corpse. When she turns back, I cannot look at her. I go to my dressing-room and close the door, lie face down upon my bed, and am seized and shaken by laughter—a terrible laughter, it courses silently through me, like filthy water—I shudder, and shudder, and finally am still.

'How do you find your new girl, Miss Lilly?' he asks me at dinner, his eyes upon his plate. He is carefully parting meat from the spine of a fish—the bone so pale and so fine it is almost translucent, the meat in a thickening coating of butter and sauce. Our food comes cold to the table in winter. In summer it comes too warm.

I say, 'Very—biddable, Mr Rivers.'

'You think she will suit?'

'I think so, yes.'

'You won't have cause to complain, of my recommendation?'

'No.'

'Well, I am relieved to hear it.'

He will always say too much, for the sport of the thing. My uncle is watching. 'What's this?' he says now.

I wipe my mouth. 'My new maid, Uncle,' I answer. 'Miss Smith, who replaces Miss Fee. You've seen her, often.'

'Heard her, more like, kicking the soles of her boots against my library door. What of her?'

'She came to me on Mr Rivers's word. He found her in London, in need of a place; and was so kind as to remember me.'

My uncle moves his tongue. 'Was he?' he says slowly. He looks from me to Richard, from Richard back to me, his chin a little raised, as if sensing dark currents. 'Miss Smith, you say?'

'Miss Smith,' I repeat steadily, 'who replaces Miss Fee.' I neaten my knife and fork. 'Miss Fee, the papist.'

'The papist! Ha!' He returns excitedly to his own meat. 'Now, Rivers,' he says as he does it.

'Sir?'

'I defy you—positively defy you, sir!—to name me any institution so nurturing of the atrocious acts of lechery as the Catholic Church of Rome . . .'

He does not look at me again until supper is ended. Then has me read for an hour from an antique text, *The Nunns' Complaint Against the Fryars.*

Richard sits and hears me, perfectly still. But when I have finished and rise to leave, he rises also: 'Let me,' he says. We walk together the little way to the door. My uncle does not lift his head, but keeps his gaze on his own smudged hands. He has a little pearl-handled knife, its ancient blade sharpened almost to a crescent, with which he is paring the skin from an apple—one of the small, dry, bitter apples that grow in the Briar orchard.

Richard checks to see that his gaze is turned, then looks at me frankly. His tone he keeps polite, however. 'I must ask you,' he says, 'if you wish to continue with your drawing-lessons, now that I'm returned? I hope you do.' He waits. I do not answer. 'Shall I come, as usual, tomorrow?' He waits again. He has his hand upon the door and has drawn it back—not far enough, though, to let me step about it; nor does he pull it further when he sees me wishing to pass. Instead, his look grows puzzled. 'You mustn't be modest,' he says. He means, *You mustn't be weak.* 'You are not, are you?'

I shake my head.

'Good, then. I shall come, at the usual time. You must show me the work you've done while I've been away. I should say a little more labour and—well, who knows? We might be ready to surprise your uncle with the fruits of your instruction. What do you think? Shall we give it another two weeks? Two weeks or, at the most, three?'

Again, I feel the nerve and daring of him, feel my own blood rise to meet it. But there comes, beneath or beyond it, a sinking, a fluttering—a vague and nameless movement—a sort of panic. He waits for my reply, and the fluttering grows wilder. We have plotted so carefully. We have committed, already, one dreadful deed, and set in train another. I know all that must be done now. I know I must seem to love him, let him appear to win me, then confess his winning to Sue. How easy it should be! How I have longed for it! How hard I have gazed at the walls of my uncle's estate, wishing they might part and release me! But now that the day of our escape is close, I hesitate; and am afraid to say why. I gaze again at my uncle's hands, the pearl, the apple giving up its skin to the knife.

'Let us say, three weeks—perhaps longer,' I say finally. 'Perhaps longer, should I feel I need it.'

A look of irritation or anger disturbs the surface of his face; but when he speaks, he makes his voice soft. 'You *are* modest. Your talent is better than that. Three weeks will do it, I assure you.'

He draws back the door at last and bows me out. And though I do not turn, I know he lingers to watch me mount the stairs—as solicitous for my safety, as any of my uncle's gentlemen friends.

He will grow more solicitous, soon; but for now, at least, the days fall back into something like a familiar pattern. He passes his mornings at work on the prints, then comes to my rooms, to teach me drawing—to keep close to me, that is to say; to look and to murmur, while I daub paint on card; to be grave and ostentatiously gallant.

The days fall back in their pattern—except that, where before they had Agnes in them, now they have Sue.

And Sue is not like Agnes. She knows more. She knows her own worth and purpose. She knows she must listen and watch, to see that Mr Rivers does not come too close, or speak too confidentially, to her mistress; but she also knows that when he does come near she is to turn her head aside and be deaf to his whispers. She does turn her head, I see her do it; but I see her, too, steal glances at us from the edge of her eye—study our reflections in the chimney-glass and windows—watch our very shadows! The room, in which I have passed so many captive hours I know it as a prisoner knows his cell—the room seems changed to me now. It seems filled with shining surfaces, each one an eye of hers.

When those eyes meet mine, they are veiled and blameless. But when they meet Richard's, I see the leap of knowledge or understanding that passes between them; and I cannot look at her.

For of course, though she knows much, what she has is a counterfeit knowledge, and worthless; and her satisfaction in the keeping of it—in the nursing of what she supposes her secret—is awful to me. She does not know she is the hinge of all our scheme, the point about which our plot turns; she thinks I am that point. She does not suspect that, in seeming to mock me, Richard mocks her: that after he has turned to her in private, perhaps to smile, perhaps to grimace, he turns to me, and smiles and grimaces in earnest.

And where his torturing of Agnes pricked me on to little cruelties of my own, now I am only unnerved. My consciousness of Sue makes me too conscious of myself—makes me, now reckless, as Richard is sometimes reckless, in the gross performance of our sham passion; now guarded and watchful, hesitating. I will be bold for an hour—or meek, or coy—and then, in the final minute of his stay, I will tremble. I will be betrayed by the movement of my own limbs, my blood, my breath.—I suppose she reads that as love.

Richard, at least, knows it for weakness. The days creep by: the first week passes, and we begin the second. I sense his bafflement, feel the weight of his expectation: feel it gather, turn, grow sour. He looks at my work, and begins to shake his head.

'I am afraid, Miss Lilly,' he says, more than once, 'that you want discipline, yet. I thought your touch firmer than this. I am sure it was firmer, a month ago. Don't say you've forgotten your lessons, in my short absence. After all our labour! There is one thing an artist must always avoid, in the execution of his work: that is, hesitation. For that leads to weakness; and through weakness, greater designs than this one have foundered. You understand? You do understand me?'

I will not answer. He leaves, and I keep at my place. Sue comes to my side.

'Never mind it, miss,' she says gently, 'if Mr Rivers seems to say hard things about your picture. Why, you got those pears, quite to the life.'

'You think so, Sue?'

She nods. I look into her face—into her eye, with its single fleck of darker brown. Then I look at the shapeless daubs of colour I have put upon the card.

'It's a wretched painting, Sue,' I say.

She puts her hand upon mine. 'Well,' she says, 'but ain't you learning?'

I am, but not quickly enough. He suggests, in time, that we go walking in the park.

'We must work from nature now,' he says.

'I should rather not,' I tell him. I have my paths, that I like to walk with Sue beside me. I think that to walk them with him will spoil them. 'I should rather not,' I say again.

He frowns, then smiles. 'As your instructor,' he says, 'I must insist.'

I hope it will rain. But though the sky above Briar has been grey all that winter long—has been grey, it seems to me, for seven years!—it lightens now, for him. There is only a quick, soft wind, that comes gusting about my unskirted ankles as Mr Way tugs open the door.—'Thank you, Mr Way,' says Richard, bending his arm for me to take. He wears a low black hat, a dark wool coat, and lavender gloves. Mr Way observes the gloves, then looks at me in a kind of satisfaction, a kind of scorn.

Fancy yourself a lady, do you? he said to me, the day he carried me, kicking, to the ice-house. *Well, we'll see.*

I will not walk to the ice-house today, with Richard, but choose another path—a longer, blander path, that circles my uncle's estate, rises and overlooks the rear of the house, the stables, woods, and chapel. I know the view too well to want to gaze at it, and walk with my eyes upon the ground. He keeps my arm in his, and Sue follows behind us—first close, then falling back when he makes our pace grow brisk. We do not speak, but as we walk he slowly draws me to him. My skirt rises, awkwardly.

When I try to pull away, however, he will not let me. I say at last: 'You need not hold me so close.'

He smiles. 'We must seem convincing.'

'You needn't grip me so. Have you anything to whisper, that I don't already know?'

He gazes quickly over his shoulder. 'She would think it queer,' he says, 'were I to let slip these chances to be near you. Anyone would think that queer.'

'She knows you do not love me. You have no need to dote.'

'Shouldn't a gentleman dote, in the springtime, when he has the chance?' He puts back his head. 'Look at this sky, Maud. See how sickeningly blue it shows. So blue'—he has lifted his hand—'it jars with my gloves. That's nature for you. No sense of fashion. London skies, at least, are better-mannered: they're like tailors' walls, an eternal drab.' He smiles again, and draws me closer. 'But of course, you will know this, soon.'

I try to imagine myself in a tailor's shop. I recall scenes from *The Whipping Milliners*. I turn and, like him, quickly glance at Sue. She is watching, with a frown of what I take to be satisfaction, the bulging of my skirt about his leg. Again I attempt to pull from him, and again he keeps me close. I say, 'Will you let me go?' And, when he does nothing: 'I must suppose, then, since you know I don't care to be smothered, that you take a delight in tormenting me.'

He catches my eye. 'I am like any man,' he says, 'preoccupied with what I may not have. Hasten the day of our union. I think you'll find my attention will cool pretty rapidly, after that.'

Then I say nothing. We walk on, and in time he lets me go, in order to cup his hands about a cigarette and light it. I look again at Sue. The ground has risen, the breeze is stronger, and two or three lengths of brown hair have come loose from beneath her bonnet and whip about her face. She carries our bags and baskets, and has no hand free to secure them. Behind her, her cloak billows like a sail.

'Is she all right?' asks Richard, drawing on his cigarette.

I turn and look ahead. 'Quite all right.'

'She is stouter than Agnes, anyway. Poor Agnes! I wonder how *she* does, hey?' He takes my arm again, and laughs. I do not answer, and his laughter fades. 'Come, Maud,' he says, in a cooler tone, 'don't be so spinsterish. What has happened to you?'

'Nothing has happened to me.'

He studies my profile. 'Then, why do you make us wait? Everything is in place. Everything is ready. I have taken a house for us, in London. London houses do not come cheaply, Maud . . .'

I walk on, in silence, aware of his gaze. He pulls me close again. 'You have not, I suppose,' he says, 'had a change of heart? Have you?'

'No.'

'You are sure?'

'Quite sure.'

'And yet, you still delay. Why is that?' I do not answer. 'Maud, I ask you again. Something has happened, since I saw you last. What is it?'

'Nothing has happened,' I say.

'Nothing?'

'Nothing, but what we planned for.'

'And you know what must be done now?'

'Of course.'

'Do it then, will you? Act like a lover. Smile, blush, grow foolish.'

'Do I not do those things?'

'You do—then spoil them, with a grimace or a flinch. Look at you now. Lean into my arm, damn you. Will it kill you, to feel my hand upon yours?—I am sorry.' I have grown stiff at his words. 'I am sorry, Maud.'

'Let go of my arm,' I say.

We go further, side by side but in silence. Sue plods behind—I hear her breaths, like sighs. Richard throws down the butt of his cigarette, tears up a switch of grass and begins to lash at his boots. 'How filthy red this earth is!' he says. 'But, what a treat for little Charles . . .' He smiles to himself. Then his foot turns up a flint and he almost stumbles. That makes him curse. He rights himself, and looks me over. 'I see *you* walk more nimbly. You like it, hmm? You may walk in London like this, you know. On the parks and heaths. Did you know? Or else, you may choose not to walk, ever again— you may rent carriages, chairs, men to drive and carry you about—'

'I know what I may do.'

'Do you? Truly?' He puts the stem of grass to his mouth and grows thoughtful. 'I wonder. You are afraid, I think. Of what? Being alone? Is it that? You need never fear solitude, Maud, while you are rich.'

'You think I fear solitude?' I say. We are close to the wall of my
uncle's park. It is high, grey, dry as powder. 'You think I fear that?
I fear nothing, nothing.'

He casts the grass aside, takes up my arm. 'Why, then,' he says,
'do you keep us here, in such dreadful suspense?'

I do not answer. We have slowed our step. Now we hear Sue, still
breathing hard behind us, and walk on more quickly. When he
speaks again, his tone has changed.

'You spoke, a moment ago, of torment. The truth is, I think you
like to torment yourself, by prolonging this time.'

I shrug, as if in carelessness; though I do not feel careless. 'My
uncle said something similar to me once,' I say. 'That was before I
became like him. It is hardly a torment to me now, to wait. I am
used to it.'

'I am not, however,' he replies. 'Nor do I wish to take instruction
in the art, from you or anyone. I have lost too much, in the past,
through *waiting*. I am cleverer now, at manipulating events to match
my needs. That is what I have learned, while you have learned
patience. Do you understand me, Maud?'

I turn my head, half-close my eyes. 'I don't want to understand
you,' I say tiredly. 'I wish you would not speak at all.'

'I will speak, until you hear.'

'Hear what?'

'Hear this.' He brings his mouth close to my face. His beard, his
lips, his breath, are tainted with smoke, like a devil's. He says:
'*Remember our contract*. Remember how we made it. Remember
that when I came to you first I came, not quite as a gentleman, and
with little to lose—unlike you, Miss Lilly, who saw me alone, at
midnight, in your own room . . .' He draws back. 'I suppose your
reputation must count for something, even here; I'm afraid that
ladies' always do.—But naturally you knew that, when you received
me.'

His tone has some new edge to it, some quality I have not heard
before. But we have changed our course: when I gaze at his face the
light is all behind him, making his expression hard to read.

I say carefully, 'You call me a lady; but I am hardly that.'

'And yet, I think your uncle must consider you one. Will he like to think you corrupted?'

'He has corrupted me himself!'

'Then, will he like to think the work taken over by another man's hand?—I am speaking only, of course, of what he will suppose to be the case.'

I move away. 'You misunderstand him, entirely. He considers me a sort of engine, for the reading and copying of texts.'

'All the worse. He shan't like it, when the engine bucks. What say he disposes of it and makes himself another?'

Now I can feel the beat of the blood in my brow. I put my fingers to my eyes. 'Don't be tiresome, Richard. Disposes of it, how?'

'Why, by sending it home . . .'

The beat seems to stumble, then quickens. I draw back my fingers, but again the light is behind him and I cannot quite make out his face. I say, very quietly, 'I shall be no use to you, in a madhouse.'

'You are no use to me now, while you delay! Be careful I don't grow tired of this scheme. I shan't be kind to you, then.'

'And is *this* kindness?' I say.

We have moved, at last, into shadow, and I see his look: it is honest, amused, amazed. He says: 'This is dreadful villainy, Maud. When did I ever call it anything else?'

We stop, close as sweethearts. His tone has grown light again, but his eye is hard—quite hard. I feel, for the first time, what it would be to be afraid of him.

He turns and calls to Sue. 'Not far now, Suky! We are almost there, I think.' To me he murmurs: 'I shall need some minutes with her, alone.'

'To secure her,' I say. 'As you have me.'

'That work is done,' he says complacently; 'and she, at least, sticks better.—What?' I have shuddered, or my look has changed. 'You don't suspect her of qualms? Maud? You don't suppose her weakening, or playing us false? Is that why you hesitate?' I shake my head. 'Well,' he goes on, 'all the more reason for me to see her, to find out how she thinks we do. Have her come to me, today or tomorrow. Find out some way, will you? Be sly.'

He puts his smoke-stained finger to his mouth. Presently Sue comes, and rests at my side. She is flushed from the weight of the bags. Her cloak still billows, her hair still whips, and I want more than anything to draw her to me, to touch and tidy her. I think I begin to, I think I half-reach for her; then I become conscious of Richard and his shrewd, considering gaze. I cross my arms before me and turn away.

Next morning I have her take him a coal from the fire, to light his cigarette from; and I stand with my brow against my dressing-room window and watch them whisper. She keeps her head turned from me, but when she leaves him he raises his eyes to me and holds my gaze, as he held it once before, in darkness. *Remember our contract*, he seems again to say. Then he drops his cigarette and stands heavily upon it; then shakes free the clinging red soil from his shoes.

After that, I feel the mounting pressure of our plot as I think men must feel the straining of checked machinery, tethered beasts, the gathering of tropical storms. I wake each day and think: Today I will do it! Today I will draw free the bolt and let the engine race, unleash the beast, puncture the lowering clouds! Today, I will let him claim me—!

But, I do not. I look at Sue, and there comes, always, that shadow, that darkness—a panic, I suppose it, a simple fear—a quaking, a caving—a dropping, as into the sour mouth of madness—

Madness, my mother's malady, perhaps beginning its slow ascent in me! That thought makes me more frightened yet. I take, for a day or two, more of my drops: they calm me, but change me. My uncle marks it.

'You grow clumsy,' he says, one morning. I have mishandled a book. 'You think I have you come, day after day, to my library, to abuse it?'

'No, Uncle.'

'What? Do you mumble?'

'No, sir.'

He wets and purses his mouth, and studies me harder. When he speaks again, his tone is strange to me.

'What age are you?' he says. I am surprised, and hesitate. He sees it. 'Don't strike coy attitudes with me, miss! What age are you? Sixteen? Seventeen?—You may show astonishment. You think me insensible to the passage of years, because I am a scholar? Hmm?'

'I am seventeen, Uncle.'

'Seventeen. A troublesome age, if we are to believe our own books.'

'Yes, sir.'

'Yes, Maud. Only remember: your business is not with belief, but with study. Remember this, also: you are not too great a girl— nor am I too aged a scholar—for me to have Mrs Stiles come and hold you still while I take a whip to you. Hmm? You'll remember these things? Will you?'

'Yes, sir,' I say.

It seems to me now, however, that I must remember too much. My face, my joints, are set aching with the effort of striking looks and poses. I can no longer say with certainty which of my actions— which of my feelings, even—are true ones, which are sham. Richard still keeps his gaze close upon me. I will not meet it. He is reckless, teasing, threatening: I choose not to understand. Perhaps I am weak, after all. Perhaps, as he and my uncle believe, I draw a pleasure from torment. It is certainly a torment to me now, to sit at a lesson with him, to sit at a dinner-table with him, to read to him, at night, from my uncle's books. It begins to be a torment, too, to pass time with Sue. Our routines are spoiled. I am too conscious that she waits, as he does: I feel her watching, gauging, willing me on. Worse, she begins to speak in his behalf—to tell me, bluntly, how clever he is, how kind and interesting.

'You think so, Sue?' I ask her, my eyes upon her face; and her gaze might flutter uneasily away, but she will always answer: 'Yes, miss. Oh, yes, miss. Anyone would say it, wouldn't they?'

Then she will make me neat—always neat, handsome and neat— she will take down my hair and dress it, straighten seams, lift lint from the fabric of my gowns. I think she does it as much to calm

herself, as to calm me. 'There,' she will say, when she has finished.
'Now you are better.'—Now *she* is better, she means. 'Now your brow
is smooth. How creased it was, before! It mustn't be creased—'

It mustn't be creased, for Mr Rivers's sake: I hear the unspoken
words, my blood surges again; I take her arm in mine and pinch it.

'Oh!'

I do not know who cries it, she or I: I reel away, unnerved. But in
the second I have her skin between my fingers, my own flesh leaps
in a kind of relief. I shake, horribly, for almost an hour.

'Oh, God!' I say, hiding my face. 'I'm afraid, for my own mind!
Do you think me mad? Do you think me wicked, Sue?'

'Wicked?' she answers, wringing her hands. And I can see her
thinking: *A simple girl like you?*

She puts me into my bed and lies with her arm against mine; but
soon she sleeps, and then draws away. I think of the house in which
I lie. I think of the room beyond the bed—its edges, its surfaces. I
think I shall not sleep, unless I touch them. I rise, it is cold, but I go
quietly from thing to thing—chimney-piece, dressing-table, carpet,
press. Then I come to Sue. I would like to touch her, to be sure that
she is there. I dare not. But I cannot leave her. I lift my hands and
move and hold them an inch, just an inch, above her—her hip, her
breast, her curling hand, her hair on the pillow, her face, as she
sleeps.

I do that, perhaps three nights in a row. Then this happens.

Richard begins to make us go to the river. He has Sue sit far
from me, against the upturned boat; and he, as always, keeps close
at my side, pretending to watch as I paint. I paint the same spot so
many times, the card starts to rise and crumble beneath my brush;
but I paint on, stubbornly, and he will now and then lean close to
whisper, idly but fiercely:

'God damn you, Maud, how can you sit so calm and steady?
Hey? Do you hear that bell?' The Briar clock sounds clearly there,
beside the water. 'There's another hour gone, that we might have
passed in freedom. Instead, you keep us here—'

'Will you move?' I say. 'You are standing in my light.'

'You are standing in mine, Maud. See how easy it is, to remove that shadow? One little step is all that must be made. Do you see? Will you look? She won't. She prefers her painting. That piece of— Oh! Let me find a match, I shall burn it!'

I glance at Sue. 'Be quiet, Richard.'

But the days grow warm, and at last comes a day, so close and air-less, the heat overpowers him. He spreads his coat upon the ground and sprawls upon it, tilts his hat to shadow his eyes. For a time, then, the afternoon is still and almost pleasant: there is only the call-ing of frogs in the rushes, the slapping of water, the cries of birds, the occasional passing of boats. I draw the paint across the card in ever finer, ever slower strokes, and almost fall into slumber.

Then Richard laughs, and my hand gives a jump. I turn to look at him. He puts his finger to his lip. 'See there,' he says softly. And he gestures to Sue.

She still sits before the upturned boat, but her head has fallen back against the rotten wood and her limbs are spread and loose. A blade of hair, dark at the tip where she has been biting at it, curves to the corner of her mouth. Her eyes are closed, her breaths come evenly. She is quite asleep. The sun slants against her face and shows the point of her chin, her lashes, her darkening freckles. Between the edges of her gloves and the cuffs of her coat are two narrow strips of pinking flesh.

I look again at Richard—meet his eye—then turn back to my painting. I say quietly, 'Her cheek will burn. Won't you wake her?'

'Shall I?' He sniffs. 'They are not much used to sunlight, where she comes from.' He speaks almost fondly, but laughs against the words; then adds in a murmur: 'Nor where she's going, I think. Poor bitch—she might sleep. She has been asleep since I first got her and brought her here, and has not known it.'

He says it, not with relish, but as if with interest at the idea. Then he stretches and yawns and gets to his feet, and sneezes. The fine weather troubles him. He puts his knuckles to his nose and vio-lently sniffs. 'I beg your pardon,' he says, drawing out his handkerchief.

Sue does not wake, but frowns and turns her head. Her lower lip slightly falls. The blade of hair swings from her cheek, but keeps its curve and point. I have lifted my brush and touched it once to my crumbling painting; now I hold it, an inch from the card; and I watch, as she sleeps. Only that. Richard sniffs again, softly curses the heat, the season. Then, as before, I suppose he grows still. I suppose he studies me. I suppose the brush in my fingers drops paint—for I find it later, black paint upon my blue gown. I do not mark it as it falls, however; and perhaps it is my not marking it, that betrays me. That, or my look. Sue frowns again. I watch, a little longer. Then I turn, and find Richard's eyes upon me.

'Oh, Maud,' he says.

That is all he says. But in his face I see, at last, how much I want her.

For a moment we do nothing. Then he steps to me and takes my wrist. The paintbrush falls.

'Come quickly,' he says. 'Come quickly, before she wakes.'

He takes me, stumbling, along the line of rushes. We walk as the water flows, about the bend of the river and the wall. When we stop, he puts his hands to my shoulders and holds me fast.

'Oh, Maud,' he says again. 'Here I have been, supposing you gripped by a conscience, or some other weakness like that. But this—!'

I have turned my face from him, but feel him laugh. 'Don't smile,' I say, shuddering. 'Don't laugh.'

'Laugh? You might be glad I don't do worse. You'll know—you'll know, if anyone will!—the sports to which gentlemen's appetites are said to be pricked, by matters like this. Thank heavens I'm not a gentleman so much as a rogue: we go by different codes. You may love and be damned, for all I care.—Don't wriggle, Maud!' I have tried to twist from his hands. He holds me tighter, then lets me lean from him a little, but grips my waist. 'You may love and be damned,' he says again. 'But keep me from my money—keep us languishing here: put back our plot, our hopes, your own bright future—you shall not, no. Not now I know what trifling thing you have made us stay for. Now, let her wake up.—I promise you, it is as tiresome to me as to you, when you twist so!—Let her wake up and seek us out. Let her see us like this. You won't come to me? Very good. I shall hold you here, and let her suppose us lovers at last; and so have done with it. Stand steady, now.'

He leans from me and gives a wordless shout. The sound beats against the thick air and makes it billow, then fades to a silence.

'That will bring her,' he says.

I move my arms. 'You are hurting me.'

'Stand like a lover then, and I shall grow gentle as anything.' He smiles again. 'Suppose me her.—Ah!' Now I have tried to strike him. 'Do you mean to make me bruise you?'

He holds me harder, keeping his hands upon me but pinning down my arms with his own. He is tall, he is strong. His fingers meet about my waist—as young men's fingers are meant to do, I believe, on the waists of their sweethearts. For a time I strain against the pressure: we stand braced and sweating as a pair of wrestlers in a ring. But I suppose that, from a distance, we might seem swaying in a kind of love.

But I think this dully; and soon I feel myself begin to tire. The sun is still hot upon us. The frogs still chant, the water still laps among the reeds. But the day has been punctured or ripped: I can feel it begin to droop and settle, close about me, in suffocating folds.

'I am sorry,' I say weakly.

'You needn't be sorry, now.'

'It is only—'

'You must be strong. I have seen you be strong, before.'

'It is only—'

But, only what? How might I say it? Only that she held my head against her breast, when I woke bewildered. That she warmed my foot with her breath, once. That she ground my pointed tooth with a silver thimble. That she brought me soup—clear soup—instead of an egg, and smiled to see me drink it. That her eye has a darker fleck of brown. That she thinks me good . . .

Richard is watching my face. 'Listen to me, Maud,' he says now. He pulls me tight. I am sagging in his arms. 'Listen! If it were any girl but her. If it were Agnes! Hey? But this is the girl that must be cheated, and robbed of her liberty, for us to be free. This is the girl

the doctors will take, while we look on without a murmur. You
remember our plan?'

I nod. 'But—'

'What?'

'I begin to fear that, after all, I haven't the heart for it . . .'

'You've a heart, instead, for little fingersmiths? Oh, Maud.' Now
his voice is rich with scorn. 'Have you forgotten what she has come
to you for? Do you think *she* has forgotten? Do you suppose yourself anything to her, but that? You have been too long among your
uncle's books. Girls love easily, there. That is the point of them. If
they loved so in life, the books would not have to be written.'

He looks me over. 'She would laugh in your face, if she knew.'
His tone grows sly. 'She would laugh in mine, were I to tell her . . .'

'You shall not tell her!' I say, lifting my head and stiffening. The
thought is awful to me. 'Tell her once, and I keep at Briar for good.
My uncle shall know how you've used me—I shan't care how he
treats me for it.'

'I shall not tell her,' he answers slowly, 'if you will only do as you
must, with no further delay. I shall not tell her, if you will let her
think you love me and have agreed to be my wife; and so make
good our escape, as you promised.'

I turn my face from his. Again there is a silence. Then I
murmur—what else should I murmur?—'I will.' He nods, and
sighs. He still holds me tightly, and after another moment he puts
his mouth against my ear.

'Here she comes!' he whispers. 'She is creeping about the wall.
She means to watch and not disturb us. Now, let her know I have
you . . .'

He kisses my head. The bulk and heat and pressure of him, the
warmth and thickness of the day, my own confusion, make me
stand and let him, limply. He takes one hand from about my waist
and lifts my arm. He kisses the cloth of my sleeve. When I feel his
mouth upon my wrist, I flinch. 'Now, now,' he says. 'Be good, for a
moment. Excuse my whiskers. Imagine my mouth hers.' The words
come wetly upon my flesh. He pushes my glove a little way along
my hand, he parts his lips, he touches my palm with the point of his

tongue; and I shudder, with weakness, with fear and distaste—with dismay, to know Sue stands and watches, in satisfaction, thinking me his.

For, he has shown me to myself. He leads me to her, we walk to the house, she takes my cloak, takes my shoes; her cheek is pink, after all: she stands frowning at the glass, moves a hand, lightly, across her face . . . That is all she does; but I see it, and my heart gives a plunge—that caving, or dropping, that has so much panic in it, so much darkness, I supposed it fear, or madness. I watch her turn and stretch, walk her random way about the room—see her make all the careless unstudied gestures I have marked so covetously, so long. Is this desire? How queer that I, of all people, should not know! But I thought desire smaller, neater; I supposed it bound to its own organs as taste is bound to the mouth, vision to the eye. This feeling haunts and inhabits me, like a sickness. It covers me, like skin.

I think she must see it. Now he has named it, I think it must colour or mark me—I think it must mark me crimson, like paint marks the hot red points, the lips and gashes and bare whipped limbs, of my uncle's pictures. I am afraid, that night, to undress before her. I am afraid to lie at her side. I am afraid to sleep. I am afraid I will dream of her. I am afraid that, in dreaming, I will turn and touch her . . .

But after all, if she senses the change in me, she thinks I am changed because of Richard. If she feels me tremble, if she feels my heart beat hard, she thinks I tremble for him. She is waiting, still waiting. Next day I take her walking to my mother's grave. I sit and gaze at the stone, that I have kept so neat and free from blemish. I should like to smash it with a hammer. I wish—as I have wished many times—that my mother were alive, so that I might kill her again. I say to Sue: 'Do you know, how it was she died? It was my birth that did it!'—and it is an effort, to keep the note of triumph from my voice.

She does not catch it. She watches me, and I begin to weep; and where she might say anything to comfort me—anything at all—what she says is: 'Mr Rivers.'

I look from her in contempt, then. She comes and leads me to the chapel door—perhaps, to turn my thoughts to marriage. The door is locked and can't be passed. She waits for me to speak. At last I tell her, dutifully: 'Mr Rivers has asked me to marry him, Sue.'

She says she is glad. And, when I weep again—false tears, this time, that wash away the true ones—and when I choke and wring my hands and cry out, 'Oh! What shall I do?', she touches me and holds my gaze, and says: 'He loves you.'

'You think he does?'

She says she knows it. She does not flinch. She says, 'You must follow your heart.'

'I am not sure,' I say. 'If I might only be sure!'

'But to love,' she says, 'and then to lose him!'

I grow too conscious of the closeness of her gaze, and look away. She talks to me of beating blood, of thrilling voices, of dreams. I feel his kiss, like a burn upon my palm; and all at once she sees, not that I love him, but how much I have come to fear and hate him.

She grows white. 'What will you do?' she says, in a whisper.

'What can I do?' I say. 'What choice have I?'

She does not answer. She only turns from me, to gaze for a moment at the barred chapel door. I look at the pale of her cheek, at her jaw, at the mark of the needle in the lobe of her ear. When she turns back, her face has changed.

'Marry him,' she tells me. 'He loves you. Marry him, and do everything he says.'

She has come to Briar to ruin me, to cheat me and do me harm. *Look at her*, I tell myself. *See how slight she is, how brown and trifling! A thief, a little fingersmith—!* I think I will swallow down my desire, as I have swallowed down grief, and rage. *Shall I be thwarted, shall I be checked—held to my past, kept from my future—by* her? I think, *I shan't.* The day of our flight draws near. *I shan't.* The month grows warmer, the nights grow close. *I shan't, I shan't—*

'You are cruel,' Richard says. 'I don't think you love me as you ought. I think—' and he glances, slyly, at Sue—'I think there must be someone else you care for . . .'

Sometimes I see him look at her, and think he has told her. Sometimes she looks at me, so strangely—or else her hands, in touching me, seem so stiff, so nervous and unpractised—I think she knows. Now and then I am obliged to leave them alone together, in my own room; he might tell her, then.

What do you say, Suky, to this? She loves you!

Loves me? Like a lady loves her maid?

Like certain ladies love their maids, perhaps. Hasn't she found little ways to keep you close about her?—*Have I done that? Hasn't she feigned troublesome dreams?*—*Is that what I have done? Has she had you kiss her? Careful, Suky, she doesn't try to kiss you back . . .*

Would she laugh, as he said she would? Would she shiver? It seems to me she lies more cautiously beside me now, her legs and arms tucked close. It seems to me she is often wary, watchful. But the more I think it, the more I want her, the more my desire rises and swells. I have come to terrible life—or else, the things about me have come to life, their colours grown too vivid, their surfaces too harsh. I flinch, from falling shadows. I seem to see figures start out from the fading patterns in the dusty carpets and drapes, or creep, with the milky blooms of damp, across the ceilings and walls.

Even my uncle's books are changed to me; and this is worse, this is worst of all. I have supposed them dead. Now the words— like the figures in the walls—start up, are filled with meaning. I grow muddled, stammer. I lose my place. My uncle shrieks— seizes, from his desk, a paperweight of brass, and throws it at me. That steadies me, for a time. But then he has me read, one night, from a certain work . . . Richard watches, his hand across his mouth, a look of amusement dawning on his face. For the work tells of all the means a woman may employ to pleasure another, when in want of a man.

'*And she pressed her lips and tongue to it, and into it—*'

'You like this, Rivers?' asks my uncle.

'I confess, sir, I do.'

'Well, so do many men; though I fear it is hardly to my taste. Still, I am glad to note your interest. I address the subject fully, of course, in my Index. Read on, Maud. Read on.'

I do. And despite myself—and in spite of Richard's dark, tormenting gaze—I feel the stale words rouse me. I colour, and am
ashamed. I am ashamed to think that what I have supposed the
secret book of my heart may be stamped, after all, with no more
miserable matter than this—have its place in my uncle's collection.
I leave the drawing-room each night and go upstairs—go slowly,
tapping the toes of my slippered feet against each step. If I strike
them equally, I shall be safe. Then I stand in darkness. When Sue
comes to undress me I will myself to suffer her touch, coolly, as I
think a mannequin of wax might suffer the quick, indifferent
touches of a tailor.

And yet, even wax limbs must yield at last, to the heat of the
hands that lift and place them. There comes a night when, finally, I
yield to hers.

I have begun, in sleeping, to dream unspeakable dreams; and to
wake, each time, in a confusion of longing and fear. Sometimes she
stirs. Sometimes she does not. 'Go back to sleep,' she will say, if she
does. Sometimes I do. Sometimes I don't. Sometimes I rise and go
about the room; sometimes, take drops. I take drops, this night;
then return to her side; but sink, not into lethargy, but only into
more confusion. I think of the books I have lately read, to Richard
and to my uncle: they come back to me, now, in phrases, frag-
ments—*pressed her lips and tongue*—*takes hold of my hand*—*hip, lip
and tongue*—*forced it half-strivingly*—*took hold of my breasts*—*opened
wide the lips of my little*—*the lips of her little cunt*—

I cannot silence them. I can almost see them, rising darkly from
their own pale pages, to gather, to swarm and combine. I put my
hands before my face. I do not know how long I lie for, then. But I
must make some sound, or movement; for when I draw my hands
away, she is awake, and watching. I know that she is watching,
though the bed is so dark.

'Go to sleep,' she says. Her voice is thick.

I feel my legs, very bare inside my gown. I feel the point at which
they join. I feel the words, still swarming. The warmth of her limbs
comes inching, inching through the fibres of the bed.

I say, 'I'm afraid . . .'

Then her breathing changes. Her voice grows clearer, kinder. She yawns. 'What is it?' she says. She rubs her eye. She pushes the hair back from her brow. If she were any girl but Sue! If she were Agnes! If she were a girl in a book—!

Girls love easily, there. That is their point.

Hip, lip and tongue—

'Do you think me good?' I say.

'Good, miss?'

She does. It felt like safety, once. Now it feels like a trap. I say, 'I wish— I wish you would tell me—'

'Tell you what, miss?'

Tell me. Tell me a way to save you. A way to save myself. The room is perfectly black. *Hip, lip—*

Girls love easily, there.

'I wish,' I say, 'I wish you would tell me what it is a wife must do, on her wedding-night . . .'

And at first, it is easy. After all, this is how it is dóne, in my uncle's books: two girls, one wise and one unknowing . . . 'He will want,' she says, 'to kiss you. He will want to embrace you.' It is easy. I say my part, and she—with a little prompting—says hers. The words sink back upon their pages. It is easy, it is easy . . .

Then she rises above me and puts her mouth to mine.

I have felt, before, the pressure of a gentleman's still, dry lips against my gloved hand, my cheek. I have suffered Richard's wet, insinuating kisses upon my palm. Her lips are cool, smooth, damp: they fit themselves imperfectly to mine, but then grow warmer, damper. Her hair falls against my face. I cannot see her, I can only feel her, and taste her. She tastes of sleep, slightly sour. Too sour. I part my lips—to breathe, or to swallow, or perhaps to move away; but in breathing or swallowing or moving I only seem to draw her into my mouth. Her lips part, also. Her tongue comes between them and touches mine.

And at that, I shudder, or quiver. For it is like the finding out of something raw, the troubling of a wound, a nerve. She feels me jolt, and draws away—but slowly, slowly and unwillingly, so that

our damp mouths seem to cling together and, as they part, to tear.
She holds herself above me. I feel the rapid beating of a heart, and
suppose it my own. But it is hers. Her breath comes, fast. She has
begun, very lightly, to tremble.

Then I catch the excitement of her, the amazement of her.

'Do you feel it?' she says. Her voice sounds strangely in the
absolute darkness. 'Do you feel it?'

I do. I feel it as a falling, a dropping, a trickling, like sand from a
bulb of glass. Then I move; and I am not dry, like sand. I am wet.
I am running, like water, like ink.

I begin, like her, to shake.

'Don't be frightened,' she says. Her voice has a catch. I move
again, but she moves, too, she comes nearer to me, and my flesh
gives a leap, to hers. She is trembling, worse than before. She is
trembling, from the closeness of me! She says, 'Think more of Mr
Rivers.'—I think of Richard, watching. She says again, 'Don't be
frightened.'—But it is she who seems frightened. Her voice still
has its catch. She kisses me again. Then she raises her hand and I
feel the tips of her fingers flutter against my face.

'Do you see?' she says. 'It is easy, it is easy. Think more of him.
He will want— He will want to touch you.'

'To touch me?'

'Only touch you,' she says. The fluttering hand moves lower.
'Only touch you. Like this. Like this.'

When she puts up my nightgown and reaches between my legs, we
both grow still. When her hand moves again, her fingers no longer
flutter: they have grown wet, and slide, and in sliding seem, like her
lips as they rub upon mine, to quicken and draw me, to gather me,
out of the darkness, out of my natural shape. I thought I longed for
her, before. Now I begin to feel a longing so great, so sharp, I fear it
will never be assuaged. I think it will mount, and mount, and make
me mad, or kill me. Yet her hand moves slowly, still. She whispers.
'How soft you are! How warm! I want—' The hand moves even
slower. She begins to press. I catch my breath. That makes her hesitate, and then press harder. At last she presses so hard I feel the

giving of my flesh, I feel her inside me. I think I cry out. She does not hesitate now, however, but comes nearer to me and puts her hips about my thigh; then presses again. So slight she is!—but her hip is sharp, her hand is blunt, she leans, she pushes, she moves her hips and hand as if to a rhythm, a time, a quickening beat. She *reaches*. She reaches so far, she catches the life, the shuddering heart of me: soon I seem to be nowhere but at the points at which my flesh is gripped by hers. And then, 'Oh, there!' she says. 'Just there! Oh, there!'—I am breaking, shattering, bursting out of her hand. She begins to weep. Her tears come upon my face. She puts her mouth to them. *You pearl*, she says, as she does it. Her voice is broken. *You pearl*.

I don't know how long we lie, then. She sinks beside me, with her face against my hair. She slowly draws back her fingers. My thigh is wet from where she has leaned and moved upon me. The feathers of the mattress have yielded beneath us, the bed is close and high and hot. She puts back the blanket. The night is still deep, the room still black. Our breaths still come fast, our hearts beat loud—faster, and louder, they seem to me, in the thickening silence; and the bed, the room—the house!—seem filled with echoes of our voices, our whispers and cries.

I cannot see her. But after a moment she finds my hand and presses it, hard, then takes it to her mouth, kisses my fingers, lies with my palm beneath her cheek. I feel the weight and shape of the bones of her face. I feel her blink. She does not speak. She closes her eyes. Her face grows heavy. She shivers, once. The heat is rising from her, like a scent. I reach and draw the blanket up again, and lay it gently about her.

Everything, I say to myself, *is changed*. I think I was dead, before. Now she has touched the life of me, the quick of me; she has put back my flesh and opened me up. *Everything is changed*. I still feel her, inside me. I still feel her, moving upon my thigh. I imagine her waking, meeting my gaze. I think, 'I will tell her, then. I will say, "I meant to cheat you. I cannot cheat you now. This was Richard's plot. We can make it ours."'—We can make it ours, I think; or else, we can give it up entirely. I need only escape from Briar: she can

help me do that—she's a thief, and clever. We can make our own
secret way to London, find money for ourselves . . .

So I calculate and plan, while she lies slumbering with her face
upon my hand. My heart beats hard again. I am filled, as with
colour or light, with a sense of the life we will have, together. Then
I also sleep. And in sleeping I suppose I must move away from
her—or she must move, from me—and then she must wake, with
the day, and rise: for when I open my eyes she has gone, the bed is
cool. I hear her in her own room, splashing water. I rise up from my
pillow, and my nightgown gapes at my breast: she has undone the
ribbons, in the dark. I move my legs. I am wet, still wet, from the
sliding and the pressing of her hand.

You pearl, she said.

Then she comes, and meets my gaze. My heart leaps within me.
She looks away.

I think her only awkward, at first. I think her shy and self-con-
scious. She goes silently about the room, taking out my petticoats
and gown. I stand, so she may wash and dress me. *Now she will
speak*, I think. But, she does not. And when she sees the blush upon
my breast, the marks left by her mouth, the dampness between my
legs, it seems to me that she shudders. Only then do I begin to
grow afraid. She calls me to the glass. I watch her face. It seems
queer in reflection, crooked and wrong. She puts the pins to my
hair, but keeps her eyes all the time on her own uncertain hands. I
think, *She is ashamed.*

So then, I speak.

'What a thick sleep I had,' I say, very softly. 'Didn't I?'

Her eyelids flutter. 'You did,' she answers. 'No dreams.'

'No dreams, save one,' I say. 'But that was a—a sweet one. I
think you were in it, Sue . . .'

She colours; and I watch her rising blush and feel, again, the
pressure of her mouth against mine, the drawing of our fierce,
imperfect kisses, the pushing of her hand. I meant to cheat her. I
cannot cheat her, now. 'I am not what you think,' I will say. 'You
think me good. I am not good. But I might, with you, begin to try
to be. This was his plot. We can make it ours—'

'In your dream?' she says at last, moving from me. 'I don't think so, miss. Not me. I should say, Mr Rivers. Look! There he is. His cigarette almost smoked. You will miss him—' She falters once; but then goes on, 'You will miss him, if you wait.'

I sit dazed for a moment, as if struck by her hand; then I rise, go lifelessly to the window, watch Richard walk, smoke his cigarette, put back the tumbling hair from his brow. But I keep at the glass, long after he has left the lawn and gone in to my uncle. I would see my face, if the day were dark enough; I see it anyway, though: my hollowing cheek, my lips, too plump, too pink—plumper and pinker than ever now, from the pressing of Sue's mouth. I remember my uncle—'*I have touched your lip with poison, Maud*'—and Barbara, starting away. I remember Mrs Stiles, grinding lavender soap against my tongue, then wiping and wiping her hands upon her apron.

Everything has changed. Nothing has changed, at all. She has put back my flesh; but flesh will close, will seal, will scar and harden. I hear her go to my drawing-room; I watch her sit, cover up her face. I wait, but she does not look—I think she will never look honestly at me, again. I meant to save her. Now I see very clearly what will happen, if I do—if I draw back from Richard's plot. He will go from Briar, with her at his side. Why should she stay? She will go, and I shall be left—to my uncle, to the books, to Mrs Stiles, to some new meek and bruisable girl . . . I think of my life—of the hours, the minutes, the days that have made it up; of the hours, the minutes and days that stretch before me, still to be lived. I think of how they will be—without Richard, without money, without London, without liberty. Without Sue.

And so you see it is love—not scorn, not malice; only love—that makes me harm her, in the end.

Chapter Eleven

We leave, just as we have planned, on the last day of April. Richard's stay is complete. My uncle's prints are mounted and bound: he takes me to view them, as a sort of treat.

'Fine work,' he says. 'You think, Maud? Hmm?'

'Yes, sir.'

'Do you look?'

'Yes, Uncle.'

'Yes. Fine work. I believe I shall send for Hawtrey and Huss. I shall have them come—next week? What do you say? Shall we make an occasion of it?'

I do not answer. I am thinking of the dining-room, the drawing-room—and me, in some other shadowy place, far off. He turns to Richard.

'Rivers,' he says, 'should you like to come back, as a guest, with Hawtrey?'

Richard bows, looks sorry. 'I fear, sir, I shall be occupied elsewhere.'

'Unfortunate. You hear that, Maud? Most unfortunate . . .'

He unlocks his door. Mr Way and Charles are going about the gallery with Richard's bags. Charles is rubbing his eyes with his sleeve.—'Get on with you!' says Mr Way savagely, kicking out with his foot. Charles lifts his head, sees us emerging from my uncle's room—sees my uncle, I suppose—and shakes in a sort of convulsion, and runs. My uncle also shakes, then.

'Do you see, Rivers, the torments to which I am exposed? Mr Way, I hope you will catch that boy and whip him!'

'I will, sir,' says Mr Way.

Richard looks at me, and smiles. I do not smile back. And when, at the steps, he takes my hand, my fingers sit quite nervelessly against his own. 'Good-bye,' he says. I say nothing. He turns to my uncle: 'Mr Lilly. Farewell to you, sir!'

'A handsome man,' my uncle says, as the trap is drawn from sight. 'Hmm, Maud? What, are you silent? Shan't you like it, to have to return to our solitary ways?'

We go back into the house. Mr Way pulls closed the swollen door, and the hall grows dark. I climb the stairs at my uncle's side, as I once, as a girl, climbed them with Mrs Stiles. How many times, I think, have I mounted them, since then? How many times has my heel struck *this* spot, *that* spot? How many slippers, how many strait gowns, how many gloves, have I outgrown or outworn? How many voluptuous words have I silently read?—how many mouthed, for gentlemen?

The stairs, the slippers and gloves, the words, the gentlemen, will all remain, though I escape. Will they? I think again of the rooms of my uncle's house: the dining- and drawing-room, the library. I think of the little crescent I once picked out in the paint that covers the library windows: I try to imagine it, eyeless. I remember how once I woke and watched my room seem to gather itself together out of the dark, and thought, *I shall never escape!* Now I know that I shall. But I think that Briar will haunt me, too.— Or else, I will haunt it, while living out some dim and partial life beyond its walls.

I think of the ghost I shall make: a neat, monotonous ghost,

walking for ever on soft-soled feet, through a broken house, to the
pattern of ancient carpets.

But perhaps, after all, I am a ghost already. For I go to Sue and
she shows me the gowns and linens she means for us to take, the
jewels she means to shine, the bags she will fill; but she does it all
without meeting my gaze; and I watch, and say nothing. I am more
aware of her hands than of the objects she takes up; feel the stir of
her breath, see the movement of her lip, but her words slip from my
memory the moment she has said them. At last she has nothing
more to show. We must only wait. We take our lunch. We walk to
my mother's grave. I stare at the stone, feeling nothing. The day is
mild, and damp: our shoes, as we walk, press dew from the springing green earth and mark our gowns with streaks of mud.

I have surrendered myself to Richard's plan, as I once gave
myself to my uncle. The plot, the flight—they seem fired, now, not
so much by my wants as by his. I am empty of want. I sit at my
supper, I eat, I read; I return to Sue and let her dress me as she likes,
take wine when she offers it, stand at the window at her side. She
moves fretfully, from foot to foot. 'Look at the moon,' she says
softly, 'how bright it is! Look at the shadows on the grass.—What
time is it? Not eleven, yet?—To think of Mr Rivers, somewhere
upon the water, now . . .'

There is only one thing I mean to do, before I go: one deed—one
terrible deed—the vision of which has risen, to goad and console me,
through all the bitten-down rages, the dark and uneasy sleeps, of my
life at Briar; and now, as the hour of our flight nears, as the house
falls silent, still, unsuspecting, I do it. Sue leaves me, to look over our
bags. I hear her, unfastening buckles.—That is all I wait for.

I go stealthily from the room. I know my way, I do not need a
lamp, and my dark dress hides me. I go to the head of the stairs,
cross quickly the broken carpets of moonlight that the windows
there throw upon the floor. Then I pause, and listen. Silence. So
then I go on, into the corridor which faces mine, along a path which
is the mirror of the path that has led from my own rooms. At the
first door I pause again, and listen again, to be sure that all is still
within.

This is the door to my uncle's rooms. I have never entered here, before. But, as I guess, the handle and hinges are kept greased, and turn without a sound. The rug is a thick one, and makes a whisper of my step.

His drawing-room is even darker, and seems smaller, than mine: he has hangings upon the walls, and more book-presses. I don't look at them. I go to his dressing-room door, put my ear to the wood; take the handle and turn it. One inch, two inches, three.—I hold my breath, my hand upon my heart. No sound. I push the door further, stand and listen again. If he stirs, I will turn and go. Does he move? For a second there is nothing. Still I wait, uncertain. Then comes the soft, even rasp of his breathing.

He has his bed-curtains pulled close but keeps a light, as I do, upon a table: this seems curious to me, I should never have supposed him to be nervous of the dark. But the dim light helps me. Without moving from my place beside the door, I look about me; and at last see the two things I have come to take. On his dressing-stand, beside his jug of water: his watch-chain with, upon it, the key to his library, bound in faded velvet; and his razor.

I go quickly and take them up—the chain uncurling softly, I feel it slither against my glove. If it should fall—! It does not fall. The door-key swings like a pendulum. The razor is heavier than I expect, the blade is free of its clasp, at an angle, showing its edge. I pull it a little freer, and turn it to the light: it must be sharp, for what I want it for. I think it is sharp enough. I lift my head. In the glass above the mantel, picked out against the shadows of the room, I see myself—my hands: in one a key, in the other a blade. I might pass for a girl in an allegory. *Confidence Abused.*

Behind me, the drapes to my uncle's bed do not quite meet. In the space between them a shaft of light—so weak it is hardly light, but rather a lessening of darkness—leads to his face. I have never seen him sleep before. In form he seems slight, like a child. The blanket is drawn to his chin, uncreased, pulled tight. His lips let out his breath in a puff. He is dreaming—black-letter dreams, perhaps, or pica, morocco, calf. He is counting spines. His spectacles sit neatly, as if with folded arms, on the table beside his head. Beneath

the lashes of one of his soft eyes there is a gleaming line of mois-
ture. The razor is warming in my hand . . .

But this is not that kind of story. Not yet. I stand and watch him
sleep for almost a minute; and then I leave him. I go as I have
come—carefully, silently. I go to the stairs, and from there to the
library, and once inside that room I lock the door at my back and
light a lamp. My heart is beating hardest, now. I am queasy with
fear and anticipation. But time is racing, and I cannot wait. I cross
to my uncle's shelves and unfasten the glass before the presses. I
begin with *The Curtain Drawn Up*, the book he gave me first: I
take it, and open it, and set it upon his desk. Then I lift the razor,
grip it tight, and fully unclasp it. The blade is stiff, but springs the
last inch. It is its nature to cut, after all.

Still, it is hard—it is terribly hard, I almost cannot do it—to put
the metal for the first time to the neat and naked paper. I am almost
afraid the book will shriek, and so discover me. But it does not
shriek. Rather, it *sighs*, as if in longing for its own laceration; and
when I hear that, my cuts become swifter and more true.

When I return to Sue she is at the window, wringing her hands.
Midnight has sounded. She supposed me lost. But she is too
relieved to scold me. 'Here's your cloak,' she says. 'Fasten it up
now, quick. Take your bag.—Not that one, that one's too heavy for
you. Now, we must go.' She thinks me nervous. She puts her finger
to my mouth. She says, 'Be steady.' Then she takes my hand and
leads me through the house.

Soft as a thief, she goes. She tells me where I may walk. She does
not know that I have recently stood, light as a shadow, and watched
my uncle sleep. But then, we go by the servants' way, and the naked
passages and stairs are strange to me, all this part of the house is
strange to me. She keeps her hand in mine until we reach the basement door. Then she sets down her bag, so she may smear the key
and the bolts with grease, to make them turn. She catches my eye
and winks, like a boy. My heart aches in my breast.

Then the door is opened and she takes me into the night; and the
park is changed, the house seems queer—for of course, I have never

before seen it at such an hour as this, I have only stood at my window and gazed out. If I stood there now, would I see myself running, Sue tugging my hand? Would I seem so bleached of depth and colour, like the lawn, the trees, the stones and stumps of ivy? For a second I hesitate, turn and watch the glass, quite sure that, if I only wait, I will see my face. Then I look at the other windows. Will no-one wake, and come, and call me back?

No-one wakes, no-one calls. Sue pulls at my hand again, and I turn and follow. I have the key to the gate in the wall: when we are through and the lock is fast again I let it fall among the rushes. The sky is clear. We stand in shadow, saying nothing—two Thisbes, awaiting a Pyramus. The moon makes the river half silver, half deepest black.

He keeps to the black part. The boat sits low upon the water—a dark-hulled boat, slender, rising at the prow. The dark boat of my dreams. I watch it come, feel Sue's hand turn in mine; then step from her, take the rope he casts, let him guide me to my seat, unresisting. She comes beside me, staggering, her balance all gone. He braces the boat against the bank with a single oar, and as she sits, we turn, and the current takes us.

No-one speaks. No-one moves, save Richard as he rows. We glide, softly, in silence, into our dark and separate hells.

What follows? I know that the journey upon the river is a smooth one: that I should like to keep upon the boat, but am made to leave it and mount a horse. I should be afraid of the horse, at any other time; but I sit lifelessly upon it now, letting it bear me—as, I think, I would let it throw me, if it chose to. I remember the church of flint, the stalks of honesty, my own white gloves—my hand, that is bared then passed from one set of fingers to another, then bruised by the thrusting of a ring. I am made to say certain words, that I have now forgotten. I remember the minister, in a surplice smudged with grey. I do not recall his face. I know that Richard kisses me. I remember a book, the handling of a pen, the writing of my name. I do not remember the walk from the church: what I recall next is a room, Sue loosening my gown; and then a pillow, coarse against my cheek; a blanket, coarser; and weeping. My hand is bare and has that ring upon it, still. Sue's fingers slip from mine.

'You must be different now,' she says, and I turn my face.

When I look again, she has left me. In her place stands Richard. He keeps for a second before the door, his eyes on mine; then he lets out his breath, puts the back of his hand to his mouth to stifle laughter.

'Oh, Maud,' he says quietly, shaking his head. He wipes his beard and lips. 'Our wedding-night,' he says; and laughs again.

I watch him and do not speak, the blankets pulled high before my breast. I am sober, now. I am quite awake. When he falls quiet, I hear the house beyond him: the stairs expand, throw off the pressure of his step. A mouse, or bird, moves in the space above the rafters. The sounds are wrong. The thought must show in my face.

'It's queer for you, here,' he says, coming closer to me. 'Don't mind it. You shall be at London soon. There's more life there. Think of that.' I say nothing. 'Will you speak? Hmm, Maud? Come, you needn't be fey; not now, with me. Our wedding-night, Maud!' He has come to my side. He raises his hand and grips the head-board above my pillow and shakes it, hard, until the legs of the bed lurch and grind against the floor.

I close my eyes. The shuddering continues another moment, then the bed grows still. But he keeps his arm above me, and I feel him watching. I feel the bulk of him—seem to see the darkness of him, even through my eyelids. I sense him change. The mouse or bird still moves in the ceiling of the room, and I think he puts back his head, to follow its path. Then the house falls quiet, and he studies me again.

And then his breath comes, quick, against my cheek. He has blown in my face. I open my eyes. 'Hey,' he says softly. His look is strange. 'Don't say you're afraid.' He swallows. Then he brings back his arm from the head-board, slowly. I flinch, thinking he might strike me. But he does not do that. His gaze moves over my face, then settles at the hollow of my throat. He looks, as if fascinated. 'How fast your heart beats,' he whispers. He lowers his hand, as if he means to test, with his finger, the racing of my blood.

'Touch it,' I say. 'Touch it, and die. I have poison in me.'

His hand stops, an inch from my throat. I hold his gaze, not blinking. He straightens. His mouth gives a twitch, then curls in scorn.

'Did you think I wanted you?' he says. 'Did you?' He almost hisses the words—for of course, he cannot speak too loudly, in case Sue should hear. He moves away, agitatedly smoothing his hair behind his ears. A bag lies in his path, and he kicks it. 'God damn it,' he says. He takes off his coat, then tugs at the link in a cuff, begins to work savagely at one of his sleeves. 'Must you stare so?' he says, as he bares his arm. 'Haven't I already told you, you are safe? If you think I am any gladder than you, to be married—' He comes back to the bed. 'I must act glad, however,' he says moodily. 'And this is a part of what passes for gladness, in marriage. Had you forgotten?'

He has drawn back the blanket, exposing the sheet that covers the mattress, at the level of my hips. 'Move over,' he says. I do. He sits, and awkwardly turns. He reaches into the pocket of his trousers and draws something out. A pen-knife.

I see it, and think at once of my uncle's razor. It was in a different life, however, that I went stealthily through that sleeping house, cut the pages of books. Now I watch as Richard puts his nail to the groove of the knife and eases free the blade. It is spotted black. He looks distastefully at it, then lays it against his arm. But he does it uncertainly, flinching when the metal touches. Then he lowers the knife.

'God damn it,' he says again. He smooths his whiskers, his hair. He catches my eye. 'Don't look, so uselessly. Have you no blood about you, to save me the pain? None of those—*courses*, that women suffer?' I say nothing. His mouth twists again. 'Well, that is like you. I should have thought that, being obliged to bleed, you might as well bleed to some advantage; but, no . . .'

'Do you mean,' I say, 'to insult me, in every possible way?'

'Be quiet,' he answers. We are still speaking in whispers. 'This is for both our good. I don't see you offering up your arm to the knife.' At once, I offer it. He waves it away. 'No, no,' he says. 'I shall do it, in a moment.' He draws in his breath, moves the blade further down his arm, rests it in one of the creases at the base of his palm, where the flesh is hairless. He pauses again, takes another breath; slices, quickly. 'Good Christ!' he says, wincing. A little blood springs to the cut—it seems dark, in the candle-light, upon the white heel of his hand. He lets it fall to the bed. There is not much of it. He presses with his thumb at the skin of his wrist and palm, and then it falls faster. He does not catch my eye.

After a moment, however, he says quietly: 'Do you suppose that enough?'

I study his face. 'Don't you know?'

'No, I do not know.'

'But—'

'But what?' He blinks. 'You mean Agnes, I suppose. Don't flatter her. There are more ways of shaming a virtuous girl, than that one. You ought to know.'

The blood still feebly runs. He curses. I think of Agnes, showing me her red and swollen mouth. I turn away from him, in a sort of sickness. 'Come, Maud,' he says then, 'tell me before I fall in a swoon. You must have read of such things. I am sure your uncle must have some entry on it in his damn Index—doesn't he? Maud?'

I look again, reluctantly, at the spreading drops of blood; and I nod. As a final gesture he puts his wrist to them, and smears them. Then he frowns at his cut. His cheek is quite white. He makes a face.

'How ill a man may grow,' he says, 'from the sight of the spilling of a little of his own blood. What monsters you females must be, to endure this, month upon month. No wonder you are prone to madness. See how the flesh parts?' He shows me his hand. 'I think after all I cut too deep. That was your fault, provoking me. Have you brandy? I think a little brandy would restore me.'

He has drawn out his handkerchief, and now presses it to his arm. I say, 'I have no brandy.'

'No brandy. What have you, then? Some draught or other? Come, I see by your face that you do.' He looks about him. 'Where is it kept?'

I hesitate; but now he has named it, the desire for drops begins to make its creeping way about my heart and limbs. 'In my leather bag,' I say. He brings the bottle to me, draws out its stopper, puts his nose to it, grimaces. 'Bring me a glass, also,' I say. He finds a cup, adds a little dusty water.

'Not like that, for me,' he says, as I let the medicine slip. 'That will serve for you. I want it quicker.' He takes the bottle from me, uncovers his cut, lets a single drop fall into the parted flesh. It stings. He winces. Where it runs, he licks it. Then he sighs, half closing his eyes, watching me as I drink then shiver then lean back upon my pillow, the cup at my breast.

At length, he smiles. He laughs. '"The Fashionable Couple on their Wedding-Night,"' he says. 'They would write a column on us, in the London papers.'

I shiver again, draw the blankets higher; the sheet falls, covering the smears of blood. I reach for the bottle. He reaches it first, however, and puts it out of my grasp.

'No, no,' he says. 'Not while you keep so contrary. I shall have it, tonight.' He puts it in his pocket, and I am too weary to try to take it from him. He stands and yawns, wipes his face, rubs hard at his eyes. 'How tired I am!' he says. 'It is past three o'clock, do you know?' I say nothing, and he shrugs. But he lingers at the foot of the bed, looking down, in a hesitating manner, at the place at my side; then he sees my face, and pretends to shudder.

'I should not be astonished, after all,' he says, 'to wake to the grip of your fingers at my throat. No, I shall not risk it.'

He steps to the fire, wets his thumb and finger upon his tongue, puts out the candle; then he sits in a huddle in the arm-chair and makes a blanket of his coat. He swears against the cold, the pose, the angles of the chair, for perhaps a minute. But he sleeps, sooner than I do.

And when he does, I rise, go quickly to the window, put the curtain back. The moon is still bright, and I don't want to lie in darkness. But after all, every surface that takes up the silver light is strange to me; and when once I reach, to put my fingers to some mark upon the wall, the mark and the wall in taking my touch seem only to grow stranger. My cloak and gown and linen are closed in the press. My bags are shut. I look, and look, for something of mine; and see only at last, in the shadow of the wash-hand stand, my shoes. I go to them, and stoop, and place my hands upon them. Then I draw back and almost straighten; then touch them again.

Then I lie in the bed, and listen hard for the sounds I am used to—for bells and growling levers. There are only those meaningless noises—the yawning boards, the creeping bird or mouse. I put back my head and gaze at the wall behind me. Beyond it lies Sue. If she turned in her bed, if she said my name, I think I would hear it. She might make any sound, any at all—I would catch it, I am certain I would.

She makes no sound. Richard shifts in his chair. The moonlight creeps across the floor. In time, I sleep. I sleep and dream of Briar. But the passages of the house are not as I recall them. I am late for my uncle, and lost.

She comes each morning, after that, to wash me, to dress me, to set food before me, to take away my untouched plate; but, as in the last of our days at Briar, she never meets my gaze. The room is small. She sits near me, but rarely do we speak. She sews. I play at cards— the two of hearts with the crease of my heel upon it, rough beneath my naked finger. Richard keeps all day from the room. At night, he curses. He curses the filthy lanes of the country, that muddy his boots. He curses my silence, my strangeness. He curses the wait. Above all, he curses the angular arm-chair.

'See here,' he says, 'my shoulder. You see it? It is rising from its socket—it is quite thrown out. I shall be deformed, in a week. As for these creases—' He angrily smooths his trousers. 'I should have brought Charles, after all. At this rate I shall arrive at London only to be laughed off its streets.'

London, I think. The word means nothing to me now.

He rides out, every other day, for news of my uncle. He smokes so many cigarettes the stain on his scorched forefinger spreads to the finger beside it. Now and then he lets me take a dose of my draught; but he always keeps hold of the bottle.

'Very good,' he says, watching me drink. 'Not much longer, now.

Why, how thin and pale you've grown!—and Sue grows sleeker by the hour, like one of Mother Cream's black-faced sows. Get her into your best gown tomorrow, will you?'

I do. I will do anything, now, to bring an end to our long wait. I will pretend fear, and nervousness, and weeping, while he leans to caress or chide me. I will do it, not looking at Sue—or else, looking at her slyly, desperately, to see if she colours or seems ashamed. She never does. Her hands, that I remember sliding upon me, pressing, turning, opening me up—her hands, when they touch me now, are perfectly lifeless and white. Her face is closed. She only waits, as we do, for the coming of the doctors.

We wait—I cannot say how long. Two weeks, or three. At last: 'They come tomorrow,' Richard tells me one night; and then, next morning: 'They come today. You remember?'

I have woken from terrible dreams.

'I cannot see them,' I say. 'You must send them back. They must come another time.'

'Don't be tiresome, Maud.'

He stands and dresses, fastening his collar, his neck-tie. His coat lies neatly on the bed.

'I won't see them!' I say.

'You will,' he answers; 'for in seeing them you bring this thing to completion. You hate it here. Now is our time to leave.'

'I am too nervous.'

He does not answer. He turns, to raise a brush to his head. I lean and seize his coat—find the pocket, the bottle of drops—but he sees, comes quickly to me and plucks it from my hand.

'Oh, no,' he says, as he does it. 'I won't have you half in a dream—or risk you muddling the dose, and so spoiling everything! Oh, no. You must be quite clear in your mind.'

He returns the bottle to the pocket. When I reach again, he dodges.

'Let me have it,' I say. 'Richard, let me have it. One drop only, I swear.' My lips jump about the words. He shakes his head, wipes at the nap of the coat to remove the impression of my fingers.

'Not yet,' he says. 'Be good. Work for it.'

'I cannot! I shan't be calm, without a dose of it.'

'You shall try, for my sake. For our sake, Maud.'

'Damn you!'

'Yes, yes, damn us all, damn us all.' He sighs; then returns to the brushing of his hair. When after a moment I sink back, he catches my eye.

'Why throw such a tantrum, hey?' he says, almost kindly. And then: 'You are calmer, now? Very good. You know what to do, when they see you? Have Sue make you neat, no more than that. Be modest. Weep if you must, a little. You are sure what to say?'

I am, despite myself; for we have planned this, many times. I wait, then nod. 'Of course,' he says. He pats at his pocket, at the bottle of drops. 'Think of London,' he says. 'There are druggists on every street corner, there.'

My mouth trembles in scorn. 'You think,' I say, 'I shall still want my medicine, in London?'

The words sound weak, even to my ears. He turns his head, saying nothing, perhaps suppressing a smile. Then he takes up his pen-knife and stands at the fire and cleans his nails—now and then giving a flick of the blade, to cast slivers of dirt, fastidiously, into the flames.

He takes them first to talk with Sue. Of course, they suppose her his wife, turned mad, thinking herself a servant, speaking in the manner of a maid, keeping to a maid's room. I hear the creaking of the stairs and floorboards beneath their boots. I hear their voices— low, monotonous—but not their words. Sue's voice I do not hear at all. I sit upon the bed until they come, and then I stand and curtsey.

'Susan,' says Richard quietly. 'My wife's maid.'

They nod. I say nothing, yet. But I think my look must be strange. I see them studying me. Richard also watches. Then he comes close.

'A faithful girl,' he says to the doctors. 'Her strength has been sadly over-taxed, these past two weeks.' He makes me walk from the bed to the arm-chair, puts me in the light of the window. 'Sit here,'

he says gently, 'in your mistress's chair. Be calm, now. These gentlemen only wish to ask you a number of trifling questions. You
must answer them honestly.'

He presses my hand. I think he does it to reassure or to warn me;
then I feel his fingers close about one of mine. I still wear my wedding-ring. He draws it free and holds it, hidden, against his palm.

'Very good,' says one of the doctors, more satisfied now. The
other makes notes in a book. I watch him turn a page and, suddenly,
long for paper. 'Very good. We have seen your mistress. You do well
to think of her comfort and health for—I am sorry to tell you this—
we fear she is ill. Very ill indeed. You know she believes her name to
be your name, her history one that resembles yours? You know
that?'

Richard watches.

'Yes, sir,' I say, in a whisper.

'And your name is Susan Smith?'

'Yes, sir.'

'And you were maid to Mrs Rivers—Miss Lilly, as was—in her
uncle's house, of Briar, before her marriage?'

I nod.

'And before that—where was your place? Not with a family
named Dunraven, at the supposed address of Whelk Street,
Mayfair?'

'No, sir. I never heard of them. They are all Mrs Rivers's fancy.'

I speak, as a servant might. And I name, reluctantly, some other
house and family—some family of Richard's acquaintance, who
might be relied on to provide the history we need, if the doctors
think to seek them out. We do not think they will, however.

The doctor nods again. 'And Mrs Rivers,' he says. 'You speak of
her "fancy". When did such fancies begin?'

I swallow. 'Mrs Rivers has often seemed strange,' I say quietly.
'The servants at Briar would speak of her as of a lady not quite
right, in the brain. I believe her mother was mad, sir.'

'Now, now,' says Richard smoothly, interrupting. 'The doctors
don't want to hear the gossip of servants. Go on with your obser-
vations, only.'

'Yes, sir,' I say. I gaze at the floor. The boards are scuffed, there are splinters rising from the wood, thick as needles.

'And Mrs Rivers's marriage,' says the doctor. 'How did that affect her?'

'It was that, sir,' I say, 'which made the change in her. Before that time, she had seemed to love Mr Rivers; and we had all at Briar supposed his care, which was'—I catch Richard's eye—'so good, sir!—we had all supposed it would lift her out of herself. Then, since her wedding-night, she has started up very queer . . .'

The doctor looks at his colleague. 'You hear,' he says, 'how well the account matches Mrs Rivers's own? It is quite remarkable!—as if, in making a burden of her life, she seeks to hand that burden to another, better able to bear it. She has made a fiction of herself!' He returns to me. 'A fiction, indeed,' he says thoughtfully. 'Tell me this, Miss Smith: does your mistress care for books? for reading?'

I meet his gaze, but my throat seems to close, or be splintered, like the boards on the floor. I cannot answer. Richard speaks in my behalf. 'My wife,' he says, 'was born to a literary life. Her uncle, who raised her, is a man dedicated to the pursuit of learning, and saw to her education as he might have seen to a son's. Mrs Rivers's first passion was books.'

'There you have it!' says the doctor. 'Her uncle, an admirable gentleman I don't doubt. But the over-exposure of girls to litera-ture— The founding of women's colleges—' His brow is sleek with sweat. 'We are raising a nation of brain-cultured women. Your wife's distress, I'm afraid to say, is part of a wider *malaise*. I fear for the future of our race, Mr Rivers, I may tell you now. And her wedding-night, you say, the start of this most recent bout of insanity? Could that'—he drops his voice meaningfully, and exchanges a glance with the doctor who writes—'be plainer?' He taps at his lip. 'I saw how she shrank from my touch, when I felt for the pulse at her wrist. I noted, too, that she wears no marriage ring.'

Richard starts into life at the words, and pretends to draw some-thing from his pocket. They say fortune favours villains.

'Here it is,' he says gravely, holding out the yellow band. 'She put

it from her, with a curse.—For she speaks like a servant now, and
thinks nothing of mouthing filthy words. God knows where she
learned them!' He bites at his lip. 'You might imagine the sensations
that produced, sir, in my breast.' He puts his hand to his eyes, and
sits heavily upon the bed; then rises, as if in horror. 'This bed!' he
says hoarsely. 'Our marriage-bed, I thought it. To think my wife
would rather the room of a servant, a pallet of straw—!' He shudders. *That's enough*, I think. *No more.* But he is a man in love with
his own roguery.

'A wretched case,' says the doctor. 'But we will work on your
wife, you may be sure, to shake her of her unnatural fancy—'

'Unnatural?' says Richard. He shudders again. His look grows
strange. 'Ah, sir,' he says, 'you don't know all. There is something
else. I had hoped to keep it from you. I feel now, I cannot.'

'Indeed?' says the doctor. The other pauses, his pencil raised.

Richard wets his mouth; and all at once I know what he means to
say, and quickly turn my face to his. He marks it. He speaks, before
I can.

'Susan,' he says, 'you do well to feel shame in behalf of your mistress. You need feel none, however, in behalf of yourself. No guilt
attaches to you. You did nothing to invite or encourage the gross
attentions my wife, in her madness, attempted to force on you—'

He bites at his hand. The doctors stare, then turn to gaze at me.

'Miss Smith,' says the first, leaning closer, 'is this true?'

I think of Sue. I think of her, not as she must be now, in the room
beyond the wall—satisfied to have betrayed me, glad to suppose
herself about to return at last to her home, the dark thieves' den, in
London. I think of her holding herself above me, her hair let down,
You pearl . . .

'Miss Smith?'

I have begun to weep.

'Surely,' says Richard, coming to me, putting his hand heavily
upon my shoulder, 'surely these tears speak for themselves? Do we
need to name the unhappy passion? Must we oblige Miss Smith to
rehearse the words, the artful poses—the caresses—to which my
distracted wife has made her subject? Aren't we gentlemen?'

'Of course,' says the doctor quickly, moving back. 'Of course. Miss Smith, your grief does you credit. You need not fear for your safety, now. You need not fear for the safety of your mistress. Her care will soon be our concern, not yours. Then we shall keep her, and cure her of all her ills. Mr Rivers, you understand—a case such as this—the treatment may well be a lengthy one . . .?'

They rise. They have brought papers, and look for a surface on which to put them out. Richard clears the dressing-table of brushes and pins and they lay them there, then sign: a paper each. I don't watch them do it, but hear the grinding of the pen. I hear them moving together, to shake each other's hands. The staircase thunders as they go down. I keep in my seat beside the window. Richard stands in the path to the house while they drive off.

Then he comes back. He closes the door. He steps to me and tosses the wedding-ring into my lap. He rubs his hands together and almost capers.

'You devil,' I say, without passion, wiping the tears from my cheek.

He snorts. He moves to the back of my chair and puts his hands to my head, one hand to either side of my face; then tilts it back until our gazes meet. 'Look at me,' he says, 'and tell me, honestly, that you don't admire me.'

'I hate you.'

'Hate yourself, then. We're alike, you and I. More alike than you know. You think the world ought to love us, for the kinks in the fibres of our hearts? The world scorns us. Thank God it does! There was never a profit to be got from love; from scorn, however, you may twist riches, as filthy water may be wrung from a cloth. You know it is true. You are like me. I say it again: hate me, hate yourself.'

His hands are warm upon my face, at least. I close my eyes.

I say, 'I do.'

Then Sue comes from her room, to knock upon our door. He keeps his pose, but calls for her to enter.

'Look here,' he says when she does, his voice quite changed, 'at your mistress. Don't you think her eyes a little brighter . . .?'

We leave next day, for the madhouse.

She comes to dress me, for the final time.

'Thank you, Sue,' I say, in the old soft way, each time she hooks a button or draws a lace. I wear, still, the gown in which I left Briar, that is spotted with mud and river-water. She wears my gown of silk—blue silk, against which the white of her wrists and throat is turned to the colour of cream, and the browns of her hair and eyes are made rich. She has grown handsome. She moves about the room, taking up my linen, my shoes, my brushes and pins, and putting them carefully in bags. Two bags, there are: one destined for London, the other for the madhouse—the first, as she supposes, for herself; the second for me. It is hard to watch her make her choices—to see her frown over a petticoat, a pair of stockings or shoes, to know she is thinking, *These* will surely be good enough for mad people and doctors. *This* she ought to take, in case the nights are cool. Now, *that* and *those* (the bottle of drops, my gloves) she must have.—I move them, when she leaves me, and place them deep in the other bag.

And one other thing I put with them, that she does not know I keep: the silver thimble, from the sewing-box at Briar, with which she smoothed my pointed tooth.

The coach comes, sooner than I think it will. 'Thank God,' says Richard. He carries his hat. He is too tall for this low and tilting house: when we step outside, he stretches. I have kept to my room so long, however, the day feels vast to me. I walk with Sue's arm gripped in mine, and at the door of the coach, when I must give it up—give it up, for ever!—I think I hesitate.

'Now, now,' says Richard, taking my hand from her. 'No time for sentiment.'

Then we drive. I feel it, as more than a matter of galloping horses and turning wheels. It is like an undoing of my first journey, with Mrs Stiles, from the madhouse to Briar: I put my face to the window

as the carriage slows, and almost expect to see the house and the
mothers I was snatched from. I should remember them still, I know
it. But, that house was large. This one is smaller, and lighter. It has
rooms for female lunatics, only. That house was set in bare earth.
This one has a bed of flowers beside its door—tall flowers, with tips
like spikes.

I fall back in my seat. Richard catches my eye.

'Don't be afraid,' he says.

Then they take her. He helps her into their hands, and stands
before me at the door, looking out.

'Wait,' I hear her say. 'What are you doing?' Then: 'Gentlemen!
Gentlemen!'—an odd and formal phrase.

The doctors speak in soothing tones, until she begins to curse;
then their voices grow hard. Richard draws back. The floor of the
carriage tilts, the doorway rises, and I see her—the two men's hands
upon her arms, a nurse gripping her waist. Her cloak is falling from
her shoulders, her hat is tilted, her hair is tearing from its pins. Her
face is red and white. Her look is wild, already.

Her eyes are fixed on mine. I sit like a stone, until Richard takes
my arm and presses, hard, upon my wrist.

'Speak,' he whispers, 'damn you.' Then I sing out, clear, mechan-
ically:

'Oh! My own poor mistress!' Her brown eyes—wide—with that
darker fleck. Her tumbling hair. 'Oh! Oh! My heart is breaking!'

The cry seems to ring about the coach, even after Richard has
swung closed the door and the driver whipped the horse into life
and turned us. We do not speak. Beside Richard's head is a lozenge-
shaped window of milky glass, and for a moment I see her again:
still struggling, lifting her arm to point or reach— Then the road
makes a dip. There come trees. I take off my wedding-ring and
throw it to the floor. I find, in my bag, a pair of gloves, and draw
them on. Richard watches my trembling hands.

'Well—' he says.

'Don't speak to me,' I say, almost spitting the words. 'If you
speak to me, I shall kill you.'

He blinks, and attempts to smile. But his mouth moves strangely and his face, behind his beard, is perfectly white. He folds his arms. He sits, first one way and then another. He crosses and uncrosses his legs. At length he takes a cigarette from his pocket, and a match, and tries to draw down the carriage window. It will not come. His hands are damp, grow damper, and finally slide upon the glass. 'Damn this!' he cries then. He rises, staggers, beats upon the ceiling for the driver to stop the horse, then fumbles with the key. We have gone no more than a mile or two, but he jumps to the ground and paces, coughs. He puts his hand to the lock of springing hair at his brow, many times. I watch him.

'How like a villain,' I say, when he takes his seat again, 'you are now.'

'And how like a lady, you!' he answers, with a sneer.

Then he turns his face from me, rests his head against the jolting cushion; and pretends, with twitching eye-lids, to sleep.

My own eyes stay open. I gaze through the lozenge of glass at the road we have travelled—a winding red road, made cloudy by dust, like a thread of blood escaping from my heart.

We make part of our journey like this, but then must give up the asylum carriage and take a train. I have never ridden a train before. We wait at a country station. We wait at an inn, since Richard is still afraid that my uncle will have sent out men to watch for us. He has the landlord put us in a private room and bring me tea and bread-and-butter. I will not look at the tray. The tea grows brown and cool, the bread curls. He stands at the fire and rattles the coins in his pocket, then bursts out: 'God damn you, do you think I take food for you, for free?' He eats the bread-and-butter himself. 'I hope I see my money soon,' he says. 'God knows I need it, after three months with you and your uncle, doing what he calls a gentleman's labour, receiving wages that would barely keep a proper gentleman in cuffs. Where's that damn porter? How much do they mean to swindle me of for our tickets, I wonder?'

At last a boy appears to fetch us and take our bags. We stand on the station platform and study the rails. They shine, as if polished.

In time they begin to purr, and then—unpleasantly, like nerves in failing teeth—to hum. The hum becomes a shriek. Then the train comes hurtling about the track, a plume of smoke at its head, its many doors unfolding. I keep my veil about my face. Richard hands a coin to the guard, saying easily: 'You'll see to it, perhaps, that my wife and I are kept quite private, till London?' The guard says he will; and when Richard comes and takes his place in the coach across from me he is more peevish than ever.

'That I must pay a man to think me lewd, so I may sit chastely, with my own little virgin of a wife! Let me tell you now, I am keeping a separate account of the costs of this journey, to charge against your share.'

I say nothing. The train has shuddered, as if beaten with hammers, and now begins to roll upon its tracks. I feel the growing speed of it, and grip the hanging strap of leather until my hand cramps and blisters in its glove.

So the journey proceeds. It seems to me that we must cross vast distances of space.—For you will understand that my sense of distance and space is rather strange. We stop at a village of red-bricked houses, and then at another, very similar; and then at a third, rather larger. At every station there is what seems to me a press of people clamouring to board, the thud and shake of slamming doors. I am afraid the crowds will overburden the train—perhaps overturn it.

I think, I deserve to be crushed in the wreck of a train; and almost hope they do.

They do not. The engine speeds us onward, then slows, and again there are streets and the spires of churches—more streets and spires than I have yet seen; more houses, and between them a steady traffic of cattle and vehicles and people. *London!* I think, with a lurch of my heart. But Richard studies me as I gaze, and smiles unpleasantly. 'Your natural home,' he says. We stop at the station and I see the name of it: MAIDENHEAD.

Though we have come so swiftly we have travelled no more than twenty miles, and have another thirty to go. I sit, still gripping the strap, leaning close to the glass; but the station is filled with men and women—the women in groups, the men idly walking; and from them I shrink. Soon the train gives a hiss, and gathers its bulk, and shudders back into terrible life. We leave the streets of Maidenhead. We pass through trees. Beyond the trees there are open parklands, and houses—some as great as my uncle's, some greater. Here and there are cottages with pens of pigs, with gardens set with broken sticks for climbing beans, and hung with lines of laundry. Where the lines are full there is laundry hung from windows, from trees, on bushes, on chairs, between the shafts of broken carts—laundry everywhere, drooping and yellow.

I keep my pose and watch it all. *Look, Maud*, I think. *Here is your future. Here's all your liberty, unfolding like a bolt of cloth* . . .

I wonder if Sue is very much injured. I wonder what kind of place they have her in, now.

Richard tries to see beyond my veil. 'You're not weeping, are you?' he says. 'Come on, don't trouble over it still.'

I say, 'Don't look at me.'

'Should you rather be back at Briar, with the books? You know you should not. You know you have wanted this. You'll forget, soon, the manner in which you got it. Believe me, I know these things. You must only be patient. We must both be patient now. We have many weeks to pass together, before the fortune becomes ours. I am sorry I spoke harshly, before. Come, Maud. We shall be at London, soon. Things will seem different to you there, I assure you . . .'

I do not answer. At last, with a curse, he gives it up. The day is darkening now—or rather, the sky is darkening, as we draw close to the city. There come streaks of soot upon the glass. The landscape is slowly growing meaner. The cottages have begun to be replaced by wooden dwellings, some with broken windows and boards. The gardens are giving way to patches of weed; soon the weed gives way to ditches, the ditches to dark canals, to dreary wastes of road, to mounds of stones or soil or ashes. Still, *Even ashes*, I think, *are a part of your freedom*—and I feel, despite myself, the kindling in me of a sort of excitement. But then, the excitement becomes unease. I have always supposed London a place, like a house in a park, with walls: I've imagined it rising, straight and clean and solid. I have not supposed it would sprawl so brokenly, through villages and suburbs. I've believed it complete: but now, as I watch, there come stretches of wet red land, and gaping trenches; now come half-built houses, and half-built churches, with glassless windows and slateless roofs and jutting spars of wood, naked as bones.

Now there are so many smuts upon the glass they show like faults in the fabric of my veil. The train begins to rise. I don't like the sensation. We begin to cross streets—grey streets, black streets—so many monotonous streets, I think I shall never be able to tell them apart! Such a chaos of doors and windows, of roofs and chimneys, of horses and coaches and men and women! Such a muddle of hoardings and garish signs: SPANISH BLINDS.—LEAD COFFINS.—OIL TALLOW & COTTON WASTE. Words, everywhere. Words, six-feet high. Words, shrieking and bellowing: LEATHER AND GRINDERY.—SHOP TO LET.—BROUGHAMS & NEAT CARRIAGES.—PAPER-STAINERS.—SUPPORTED ENTIRELY.—TO LET!— TO LET!—BY VOLUNTARY SUBSCRIPTION.—

There are words, all over the face of London. I see them, and cover my eyes. When I look again we have sunk: brick walls, thick with soot, have risen about the train and cast the coach in gloom. Then comes a great, vast, vaulting roof of tarnished glass, hung about with threads of smoke and steam and fluttering birds. We shudder to a frightful halt. There is the shrieking of other engines, a thudding of doors, the pressing passage—it seems to me—of a thousand, thousand people.

'Paddington terminus,' says Richard. 'Come on.'

He moves and speaks more quickly here. He is changed. He does not look at me—I wish he would, now. He finds a man to take our bags. We stand in a line of people—a *queue*, I know the word—and wait for a carriage—a *hackney*, I know that word also, from my uncle's books. One may kiss in a hackney; one may take any kind of liberty with one's lover; one tells one's driver to go about the Regent's Park. I know London. London is a city of opportunities fulfilled. This place, of jostling and clamour, I do not know. It is thick with purposes I do not understand. It is marked with words, but I cannot read it. The regularity, the numberless repetition, of brick, of house, of street, of person—of dress, and feature, and expression—stuns and exhausts me. I stand at Richard's side and keep my arm in his. If he should leave me—! A whistle is blown and men, in dark suits—ordinary men, gentlemen—pass by us, *running*.

We take our place in the hackney at last, and are jerked out of the terminus into choked and filthy roads. Richard feels me tense. 'Are you startled, by the streets?' he says. 'We must pass through worse, I'm afraid. What did you expect? This is the city, where respectable men live side by side with squalor. Don't mind it. Don't mind it at all. We are going to your new home.'

'To our house,' I say. I think: There, with the doors and windows shut, I will grow calm. I will bathe, I will rest, I will sleep.

'To our house,' he answers. And he studies me a moment longer, then reaches across me. 'Here, if the sight troubles you—' He pulls down the blind.

And so once again we sit, and sway to the motion of a coach, in a kind of twilight; but we are pressed about, this time, by all the roar of London. I do not see it when we go about the park. I do not see what route the driver takes, at all: perhaps I should not know it, if I did, though I have studied maps of the city, and know the placing of the Thames. I cannot say, when we stop, how long we have driven for—so preoccupied am I with the desperate stir of my senses and heart. *Be bold*, I am thinking. *God damn you, Maud! You have longed for this. You have given up Sue, you have given up everything, for this. Be bold!*

Richard pays the man, then returns for our bags. 'From here we must walk,' he says. I climb out, unassisted, and blink at the light— though the light here is dim enough: we have lost the sun, and the sky is anyway thick with cloud—brown cloud, like the dirty fleece of a sheep. I have expected to find myself at the door to his house, but there are no houses here: we have entered streets that appear to me unspeakably shabby and mean—are hedged on one side by a great, dead wall, on the other by the lime-stained arches of a bridge. Richard moves off. I catch at his arm.

'Is this right?' I say.

'Quite right,' he answers. 'Come, don't be alarmed. We cannot live grandly, yet. And we must make our entrance the quiet way, that's all.'

'You are still afraid that my uncle may have sent men, to watch us?'

He again moves off. 'Come. We can talk soon, indoors. Not here. Come on, this way. Pick up your skirts.'

He walks quicker than ever now, and I am slow to follow. When he sees me hanging back he holds our bags in one hand and, with the other, takes my wrist. 'Not far, now,' he says, kindly enough; his grip is tight, however. We leave that road and turn into another: here I can see the stained and broken face of what I take to be a single great house, but which is in fact the rear of a terrace of narrow dwellings. The air smells riverish, rank. People watch us, curiously. That makes me walk faster. Soon we turn again, into a lane of crunching cinders. Here there are children, in a group: they are standing idly about a bird, which lurches and hops. They have tied its wings with twine. When they see us, they come and press close. They want money, or to tug at my sleeve, my cloak, my veil. Richard kicks them away. They swear for a minute, then return to the bird. We take another, dirtier, path—Richard all the time gripping me harder, walking faster, faster, certain of his way. 'We are very close now,' he says. 'Don't mind this filth, this is nothing. All London is filthy like this. Just a little further, I promise. And then you may rest.'

And at last, he slows. We have reached a court, with a thick mud floor and nettles. The walls are high, and running with damp. There is no open route from here, only two or three narrow covered passages, filled with darkness. Into one of these he makes to draw me, now; but, so black and foul is it, I suddenly hesitate, and pull against his grip.

'Come on,' he says, turning round, not smiling.

'Come to where?' I ask him.

'To your new life, that has waited for you to start it, too long. To our house. Our housekeeper expects us. Come, now.—Or shall I leave you here?'

His voice is tired, hard. I look behind me. I see the other passages, but the muddy path he has led me down is hidden—as if the glistening walls have parted to let us come, then closed to trap me.

What can I do? I cannot go back, alone, to the children, the labyrinth of lanes, the street, the city. I cannot go back to Sue. I am not meant to. Everything has been impelling me here, to this dark point. I must go forward, or cease to exist. I think again of the room that is waiting for me: of the door, with its key that will turn; of the bed, on which I shall lie and sleep, and sleep—

I hesitate, one second more; then let him draw me into the passage. It is short, and ends with a flight of shallow stairs, leading downwards; and these, in turn, end at a door, on which he knocks. From beyond the door there comes at once the barking of a dog, then soft, quick footsteps, a grinding bolt. The dog falls silent. The door is opened, by a fair-haired boy—I suppose, the housekeeper's boy. He looks at Richard and nods.

'All right?' he says.

'All right,' answers Richard. 'Is Aunty home? Here's a lady, look, come to stay.'

The boy surveys me, I see him squinting to make out the features behind my veil. Then he smiles, nods again, draws back the door to let us pass him; closes it tightly at our backs.

The room beyond is a kind of kitchen—I suppose, a servants' kitchen, for it is small, and windowless, dark and unwholesome, and chokingly hot: there is a good fire lit, and one or two smoking lamps upon a table and—perhaps, after all, these are the grooms' quarters—a brazier in a cage, with tools about it. Beside the brazier is a pale man in an apron who, on seeing us come, sets down some fork or file and wipes his hands and looks me over, frankly. Before the fire sit a young woman and a boy: the girl fat-faced, red-haired, also watching me freely; the boy sallow and scowling, chewing with broken teeth on a strip of dry meat, and dressed—I notice this, even in my confusion—in an extraordinary coat, that seems pieced together from many varieties of fur. He holds, between his knees, a squirming dog, his hand about its jaws to keep it from barking. He looks at Richard and then at me. He surveys my coat and gloves and bonnet. He whistles.

'What price them togs,' he says.

Then he flinches as, from another chair—a rocking chair, that creaks as it tilts—a white-haired woman leans to strike him. I suppose her the housekeeper. She has watched me, more closely and more eagerly than any of the others. She holds a bundle: now she puts it down and struggles from her seat, and the bundle gives a shudder. This is more astonishing than the lighted brazier, the coat of fur—it is a sleeping, swollen-headed baby in a blanket.

I look at Richard. I think he will speak, or lead me on. But he has taken his hand from me and stands with folded arms, very leisurely. He is smiling, but smiling oddly. Everyone is silent. No-one moves save the white-haired woman. She has left her chair and comes about the table. She is dressed in taffeta, that rustles. Her face has a blush, and shines. She comes to me, she stands before me, her head weaves as she tries to catch the line of my features. She moves her mouth, wets her lips. Her gaze is still close and terribly eager. When she raises her blunt red hands to me, I flinch.—'Richard,' I say. But he still does nothing, and the woman's look, that is so awful and so strange, compels me. I stand and let her fumble for my veil. She puts it back. And then her gaze changes, grows stranger still, when she sees my face. She touches my cheek, as if uncertain it will remain beneath her fingers.

She keeps her eyes on mine, but speaks to Richard. Her voice is thick with the tears of age, or of emotion.

'Good boy,' she says.

Chapter Twelve

*T*hen there comes a kind of chaos.

The dog barks and leaps, the baby in its blanket gives a cry; another baby, that I have not noticed—it lies in a tin box, beneath the table—begins to cry also. Richard takes off his hat and his coat, sets down our bags, and stretches. The scowling boy drops open his mouth and shows the meat within.

'It ain't Sue,' he says.

'Miss Lilly,' says the woman before me, quietly. 'Ain't you just the darling. Are you very tired, dear? You have come quite a journey.'

'It ain't Sue,' says the boy again, a little louder.

'Change of plan,' says Richard, not catching my eye. 'Sue stays on behind, to take care of a few last points.—Mr Ibbs, how are you, sir?'

'Sweet, son,' the pale man answers. He has taken off his apron and is quieting the dog. The boy who opened the door to us has

gone. The little brazier is cooling and ticking and growing grey.
The red-haired girl bends over the screaming babies with a bottle
and a spoon, but is still stealing looks at me.

The scowling boy says, 'Change of plan? I don't get it.'

'You will,' answers Richard. 'Unless—' He puts his finger against
his mouth, and winks.

The woman, meanwhile, is still before me, still describing my
face with her hands, telling off my features as if they were beads
upon a string. 'Brown eyes,' she says, beneath her breath; her breath
is sweet as sugar. 'Pink lips, two pouters. Nice and dainty at the
chin. Teeth, white as china. Cheeks—rather soft, I dare say? Oh!'

I have stood, as if in a trance, and let her murmur; now, feeling
her fingers flutter against my face, I start away from her.

'How dare you?' I say. 'How dare you speak to me? How dare
you look at me, any of you? And you—' I go to Richard and seize
his waistcoat. 'What is this? Where have you brought me to? What
do they know of Sue, here?'

'Hey, hey,' calls the pale man mildly. The boy laughs. The
woman looks rueful.

'Got a voice, don't she?' says the girl.

'Like the blade on a knife,' says the man. 'That clean.'

Richard meets my gaze, then looks away. 'What can I say?' He
shrugs. 'I am a villain.'

'Damn your attitudes now!' I say. 'Tell me what this means.
Whose house is this? Is it yours?'

'Is it his!' The boy laughs harder, and chokes on his meat.

'John, be quiet, or I'll thrash you,' says the woman. 'Don't mind
him, Miss Lilly, I implore you now, don't!'

I can feel her wringing her hands, but do not look at her. I keep
my eyes upon Richard. 'Tell me,' I say.

'Not mine,' he answers at last.

'Not ours?' He shakes his head. 'Whose, then? Where, then?'

He rubs at his eye. He is tired. 'It is theirs,' he says, nodding to
the woman, the man. 'Their house, in the Borough.'

The Borough . . . I have heard him say the name, once or twice
before. I stand for a moment in silence, thinking back across his

words; then my heart drops. 'Sue's house,' I say. 'Sue's house, of thieves.'

'Honest thieves,' says the woman, creeping closer, 'to those that know us!'

I think: *Sue's aunt!* I was sorry for her, once. Now I turn and almost spit at her. 'Will you keep from me, you witch?' The kitchen grows silent. It seems darker, too, and close. I still have Richard gripped by the waistcoat. When he tries to pull away, I hold him tighter. My thoughts are leaping, fast as hares. I think, *He has married me, and has brought me here, as a place to be rid of me. He means to keep my money for himself. He means to give them some trifling share for the killing of me, and Sue*—even in the midst of my shock and confusion, my heart drops again, as I think it—*Sue they will free. Sue knows it all.*

'You shan't do it!' I say, my voice rising. 'You think I don't know what you mean to do? All of you? What trick?'

'You don't know anything, Maud,' he answers. He tries to draw my hands from his coat. I will not let him. I think, if he does that, they will certainly kill me. For a second we struggle. Then: 'The stitching, Maud!' he says. He plucks my fingers free. I catch at his arm instead.

'Take me back,' I say. I say it, thinking: *Don't let them see you are afraid!* But my voice has risen higher and I cannot make it firm. 'Take me back, at once, to the streets and hackneys.'

He shakes his head, looks away. 'I can't do it.'

'Take me now. Or I go, alone. I shall make my way—I saw the route! I studied it, hard!—and I shall find out a—a policeman!'

The boy, the pale man, the woman and girl, all flinch or wince. The dog barks.

'Now now,' says the man, stroking his moustache. 'You must be careful how you talk, dear, in a house like this.'

'It is you who must be careful!' I say. I look from one face to another. 'What is it you think you shall have from this? Money? Oh, no. It is you who must be careful. It is all of you! And you, Richard—you—who must be most careful of all, should I once find a policeman and begin to talk.'

But Richard looks and says nothing.

'Do you hear me?' I cry.

The man winces again, and puts his finger to his ear as if to clear it of wax. 'Like a blade,' he says, to no-one, to everyone. 'Ain't it?'

'Damn you!' I say. I look wildly about me for a moment, then make a sudden grab at my bag. Richard reaches it first, however, he hooks it with his long leg and kicks it across the floor, almost playfully. The boy takes it up, and holds it in his lap. He produces a knife and begins to pick at the lock. The blade flashes.

Richard folds his arms. 'You see you cannot leave, Maud,' he says simply. 'You cannot go, with nothing.'

He has moved to the door, to stand before it. There are other doors, that lead, perhaps to a street, perhaps only into other dark rooms. I shall never choose the right one.

'I am sorry,' he says.

The boy's knife flashes again. *Now*, I think, *they will kill me.* The thought itself is like a blade, and astonishingly sharp. For haven't I willed my life away, at Briar? Haven't I felt it rising from me, and been glad? Now I suppose they mean to kill me; and I am more afraid than I have imagined it possible to be, of anything, anything at all.

You fool, I say to myself. But to them I say: 'You shan't. You shan't!' I run one way, and then another; finally I dart, not for the door at Richard's back, but for the slumbering, swollen-headed baby. I seize it, and shake it, and put my hand to its neck. 'You shan't!' I say again. 'Damn you, do you think I have come so far, for this?' I look at the woman. 'I shall kill your baby first!'—I think I would do it.—'See, here! I shall stifle it!'

The man, the girl, the boy, look interested. The woman looks sorry. 'My dear,' she says, 'I have seven babies about the place, just now. Make it six, if you want. Make it'—with a gesture to the tin box beneath the table—'make it five. It is all the same to me. I fancy I am about to give the business up, anyway.'

The creature in my arms slumbers on, but gives a kick. I feel the rapid palpitation of its heart beneath my fingers, and there is a fluttering at the top of its swollen head. The woman still watches. The girl puts her hand to her neck, and rubs. Richard searches in his pocket for a cigarette. He says, as he does it, 'Put the damn child down, Maud, won't you?'

He says it mildly; and I become aware of myself, my hands at a baby's throat. I set the child carefully down upon the table, among the plates and china cups. At once, the boy takes his knife from the lock of my bag and waves it over its head.

'Ha-ha!' he cries. 'The lady wouldn't do it. John Vroom shall have him—lips, nose and ears!'

The girl squeals, as if tickled. The woman says sharply, 'That's enough. Or are all my infants to be worried out of their cradles, into their graves? Fine farm I should be left with then. Dainty, see to little Sidney before he scalds himself, do. Miss Lilly will suppose herself come among savages. Miss Lilly, I can see you're a spirited girl. I expected nothing less. But you don't imagine we mean to hurt you?' She comes to me again. She cannot stand without touching me—now she puts her hand upon me and strokes my sleeve. 'You don't imagine you ain't more welcome here, than anyone?'

I still shake, a little. 'I can't imagine,' I say, pulling myself away from her hands, 'that you mean me any kind of good, since you persist in keeping me here, when I so clearly wish to leave.'

She tilts her head. 'Hear the grammar in that, Mr Ibbs?' she says. The man says he does. She strokes me again. 'Sit down, my darling. Look at this chair: got from a very grand place, it might be waiting for you. Won't you take off your cloak, and your bonnet? You shall swelter, we keep a very warm kitchen. Won't you slip off your gloves?—Well, you know best.'

I have drawn in my hands. Richard catches the woman's eye. 'Miss Lilly,' he says quietly, 'is rather particular about the fingers. Was made to wear gloves, from an early age'—he lets his voice drop still further, and mouths the last few words in an exaggerated way—'by her uncle.'

The woman looks sage.

'Your uncle,' she says. 'Now, I know all about him. Made you look at a lot of filthy French books. And did he touch you, dear,

where he oughtn't to have? Never mind it now. Never mind it, here.
Better your own uncle than a stranger, I always say.—Oh, now ain't
that a shame?'

I have sat, to disguise the trembling of my legs; but have pushed
her from me. My chair is close to the fire and she is right, it is hot,
it is terribly hot, my cheek is burning; but I must not move, I must
think. The boy still picks at the lock. 'French books,' he says, with
a snigger. The red-haired girl has the fingers of the baby's hands in
her mouth and is sucking on them, idly. The man has come nearer.
The woman is still at my side. The light of the fire picks out her
chin, her cheek, an eye, a lip. The lip is smooth. She wets it.

I turn my head, but not my gaze. 'Richard,' I say. He doesn't
answer. 'Richard!' The woman reaches to me and unfastens the
string of my bonnet and draws it from my head. She pats my hair,
then takes up a lock of it and rubs it between her fingers.

'Quite fair,' she says, in a sort of wonder. 'Quite fair, like gold
almost.'

'Do you mean to sell it?' I say then. 'Here, take it!' I snatch at the
lock she has caught up and rip it from its pins. 'You see,' I say,
when she winces, 'you cannot hurt me as much as I can hurt myself.
Now, let me go.'

She shakes her head. 'You are growing wild, my dear, and spoiling your pretty hair. Haven't I said? We don't mean to harm you.
Here is John Vroom, look; and Delia Warren, that we call Dainty:
you shall think them cousins, I hope, in time. And Mr Humphry
Ibbs: he has been waiting for you—haven't you, Mr Ibbs? And
here am I. I've been waiting for you, hardest of all. Dear me, how
hard it has been.'

She sighs. The boy looks up at her and scowls.

'Jigger me,' he says, 'if I know which way the wind is blowing
now.' He nods to me. 'Ain't she meant to be'—he hugs his arms
about himself, shows his tongue, lets his eyes roll—'on a violent
ward?'

The woman lifts her arm, and he winks and draws back.

'You watch your face,' she says savagely. And then, gazing gently
at me: 'Miss Lilly is throwing in her fortunes with ours. Miss Lilly

don't know her own mind just yet—as who would, in her place?
Miss Lilly, I daresay you ain't had a morsel of food in hours. What
we got, that will tempt you?' She rubs her hands together. 'Should
you care for a mutton chop? A piece of Dutch cheese? A supper of
fish? We got a stall on the corner, sells any kind of fish—you name
me the breed, Dainty shall slip out, bring it back, fry it up, quick as
winking. What shall it be? We got china plates, look, fit for royalty.
We got silver forks— Mr Ibbs, pass me one of them forks. See
here, dear. A little rough about the handle, ain't it? Don't mind it,
darling. That's where we takes the crest off. Feel the weight of it,
though. Ain't them prongs very shapely? There's a Member of
Parliament had his mouth about those. Shall it be fish, dear? Or the
chop?'

She stands, bending to me, with the fork close to my face. I push
it aside.

'Do you suppose,' I say, 'I mean to sit and eat a supper with you?
With any of you? Why, I should be ashamed to call you servants!
Throw in my fortunes with yours? I should rather be beggared. I
should rather die!'

There is a second of silence; then: 'Got a dander,' says the boy.
'Don't she?'

But the woman shakes her head, looks almost admiring. 'Dainty's
got a dander,' she answers. 'Why, I've got one myself. Any ordinary
girl can have one of them. What a lady has, they call something else.
What do they call it, Gentleman?' She says this to Richard, who is
leaning tiredly to tug upon the ears of the slavering dog.

'*Hauteur*,' he answers, not looking up.

'*Hauteur*,' she repeats.

'*Mersee*,' says the boy, giving me a leer. 'I should hate, after all, to
have mistook it for common bad manners, and punched her.'

He returns to the clasp of my bag. The man watches, and winces.
'Ain't you learned yet,' he says, 'the handling of a lock? Don't prise
it, boy, and mash the levers. That's sweet little work. You are just
about to bust it.'

The boy makes a final stab with his knife, his face darkening.
'Fuck!' he says.—The first time I have ever heard the word used as

a curse. He takes the point of the blade from the lock and puts it to the leather beneath, and before I can cry out and stop him he slices it, swiftly, in one long gash.

'Well, that's like you,' says the man complacently.

He has taken out a pipe, and lights it. The boy puts his hands to the slit in the leather. I watch him do it and, though my cheek is still burning from the heat of the fire, I grow cold. The cutting of the bag has shocked me, more than I can say. I begin to tremble.

'Please,' I say. 'Please give me back my things. I shall not trouble about the policeman, if you will only give back what is mine, and let me go.'

I suppose my voice has some new, piteous note to it; for now they all turn their heads and study me, and the woman comes close again and again strokes my hair.

'Not frightened, still?' she says amazedly. 'Not frightened, of John Vroom? Why, he is just being playful.—John, how dare you? Put your knife away and pass me Miss Lilly's bag.—There. Are you sorry for it, dear? Why, it's a creased old thing, that looks like it ain't been used in fifty years. We shall get you a proper one. Shan't we, though!'

The boy makes a show of grumbling but gives up the bag; and when the woman hands it to me I take it and hug it. There are tears, rising in my throat.

'Boo-hoo,' says the boy in disgust, when he sees me swallow. He leans and leers at me again. 'I liked you better,' he says, 'when you was a chair.'

I am sure he says that. The words bewilder me, and I shrink away. I twist to look at Richard. 'Please, Richard,' I say. 'For God's sake, isn't it enough to have tricked me? How can you stand so coolly while they torment me?'

He holds my gaze, stroking his beard. Then he says to the woman: 'Haven't you a quieter place, for her to sit in?'

'A quieter place?' she answers. 'Why, I have a room made ready. I only supposed Miss Lilly should like to warm her face first down here. Should you like to come up, dear, now? Make your hair neat? Wash your hands?'

'I should like to be shown to the street, and a hackney,' I answer. 'Only that, only that.'

'Well, we shall put you at the window; and you shall see the street from there. Come up, my darling. Let me take that old bag.— Want to keep it? All right. Ain't your grip a strong one! Gentleman, you come along, too, why don't you? You'll take your old room, at the top?'

'I will,' he answers, 'if you'll have me. For the wait.'

They exchange a glance. She has put her hands upon me and, in drawing from her grasp, I have risen. Richard comes and stands close. I shrink from him, too, and between them—as a pair of dogs might menace a sheep into a pen—they guide me from the kitchen, through one of the doors, towards a staircase. Here it is darker and cooler, and I feel the draught perhaps of a street-door, and slow my steps; but I think, too, of what the woman has said, about the window: I imagine I might call from it, or drop from it—or fling myself from it—should they try to hurt me. The staircase is narrow, and bare of carpet; here and there, on the steps, are chipped china cups half-filled with water, holding floating wicks, casting shadows.

'Lift your skirts, dear, above the flames,' says the woman, going up before me. Richard comes, very close, behind.

At the top there are doors, all shut: the woman opens the first, and shows me through it to a small square room. A bed, a wash-hand stand, a box, a chest of drawers, a horse-hair screen—and a window, to which I instantly cross. It is narrow, and has a bleached net scarf hung before it. The hasp has been broken long ago: the sashes are fixed together with nails. The view is of a slip of muddy street, a house with ointment-coloured shutters with heart-shaped holes, a wall of brick, with loops and spirals marked upon it in yellow chalks.

I stand and study it all, my bag still clutched to me, but my arms growing heavy. I hear Richard pause, then climb a second set of stairs; then he walks about the room above my head. The woman crosses to the wash-hand stand and pours a little water from the jug into the bowl. Now I see my mistake, in coming so quickly to the window: for she stands between me and the door. She is stout, and her arms are thick. I think I might push her aside, however, if I was to surprise her.

Perhaps she is thinking the same thing. Her hands are hovering about the wash-hand stand, her head is tilted, but she is watching me, in the same close, eager, half-awed, half-admiring way as before.

'Here's scented soap,' she says. 'And here's a comb. Here's a hair-brush.' I say nothing. 'Here's a towel for your face. Here's eau-de-Cologne.' She draws the stopper from the bottle and the liquid slops. She comes to me, her wrist bared and made wet with a sickening perfume. 'Don't you care,' she says, 'for lavender?'

I have stepped away from her, and look at the door. From the kitchen, the boy's voice comes very clearly: *'You tart!'*

'I don't care,' I say, taking another step, 'to be tricked.'

She steps, too. 'What trickery, darling?'

'Do you think I meant to come here? Do you think I mean to stay?'

'I think you are only startled. I think you ain't quite yourself.'

'Not quite myself? What's myself to you? Who are you, to say how I might or might not be?'

At that, her gaze falls. She draws her sleeve over her wrist, returns to the wash-hand stand, touches again the soap, the comb, the brush and towel. Downstairs, a chair is drawn across the floor, something is thrown or falls, the dog barks. Upstairs, Richard walks, coughs, mutters. If I am to run, I must do it now. Which way shall I go? Down, down, the way I have come. Which was the door, at the bottom, that they led me through?—the second, or the first? I am not sure. *Never mind*, I think. *Go now!* But I do not. The woman lifts her face, catches my eye, I hesitate; and in the moment of that hesitation Richard crosses his floor and steps heavily down the stairs. He comes into the room. He has a cigarette behind his ear. He has rolled his sleeves up to his elbows, and his beard is dark with water.

He closes the door, and locks it.

'Take your cloak off, Maud,' he says.

I think: *He is going to strangle me.*

I keep my cloak quite fastened, and move backwards, slowly, away from him and from the woman, back to the window. I will smash it with my elbow if I must. I will shriek into the street. Richard watches me and sighs. He makes his eyes wide. 'You need not,' he says, 'look so like a rabbit. Do you think I would bring you all this way, to hurt you?'

'And do you think,' I answer, 'I will trust you not to? You told me yourself, at Briar, what lengths you will go to, for money's sake. I wish I had listened harder, then! Tell me now you don't mean to cheat me of all my fortune. Tell me you shan't get it, through Sue. I suppose you will fetch her, after some slight delay. She will be *cured*, I suppose.' My heart contracts. 'Clever Sue. Good girl.'

'Shut up, Maud.'

'Why? So you may kill me in silence? Go on and do it. Then live with the deed upon your conscience. I suppose you have one?'

'Not one,' he says, quickly and lightly, 'that would be troubled by the murder of you, I assure you.' He presses his fingers to his eyes. 'Mrs Sucksby, however, would not like it.'

'*Her*,' I say, with a glance at the woman. She is still gazing at the soap, the brush, not speaking. 'You do everything, at *her* word?'

'Everything in this case.' He says it meaningfully; and when I hesitate, not understanding, he goes on: 'Listen to me, Maud. The scheme was hers, all of it. From start to finish, hers. And, villain that I am, I am not so great a swindler that I would swindle her of that.'

His face seems honest—but then, it has seemed honest to me before. 'You are lying,' I say.

'No. This is the truth.'

'Her scheme.' I cannot believe it. 'She that sent you to Briar, to my uncle? And before that, to Paris? To Mr Hawtrey?'

'She that sent me to you. No matter all the twisting paths I took to reach you. I might have taken them anyway, and not known what lay at the end of them. I might have passed you by! Perhaps many men have. They have not had Mrs Sucksby, guiding their steps.'

I glance between them. 'She knew of my fortune, then,' I say after a moment. 'So anyone might, I suppose. She knew—who? My uncle? Some servant of the house?'

'She knew you, Maud, you; before almost anyone.'

The woman lifts her eyes to mine again at last, and nods.

'I knew your mother,' she says.

My mother! My hand goes to my throat—a curious thing, for my mother's portrait lies with my jewels, its ribbon fraying, I have not worn it in years. *My mother!* I came to London to escape her. Now, all at once, I think of her grave in the park at Briar—untended, untrimmed, its white stone creeping with grey.

The woman still watches. I let my hand drop.

'I don't believe you,' I say. 'My mother? What was her name?— tell me that.'

She begins to look sly. 'I know it,' she says, 'but won't say it just yet. I'll tell you the letter that started it, though. That was a *M*, like what starts your name. I'll tell you the second letter. That was a *A*.—Why, that's like your name, too! The next letter, though, is where they runs off different. That was a *R* . . .'

She knows it, I know she knows it. How can she? I study her face—her eye, her lip. They seem familiar to me. What is it? Who is she?

'A nurse,' I say. 'You were a nurse—'

But she shakes her head, almost smiles. 'Now, why should I have been that?'

'You don't know everything, then!' I say. 'You don't know that I was born in a madhouse!'

'Was you?' she answers quickly. 'Why do you say so?'

'You think I don't remember my own home?'

'I should say you remember the place you lived in when you was little. Why, so do we all. Don't mean we was born there.'

'I was, I know it,' I say.

'You was told it, I expect.'

'Every one of my uncle's servants knows it!'

'They was told it, too, perhaps. Does that make it true? Maybe. Maybe not.'

As she speaks, she moves from the wash-hand stand to the bed, and sits upon it, slowly and heavily. She looks at Richard. She puts her hand to her ear, and strokes the lobe. With a show of lightness she says, 'Find your room all right, Gentleman?'—I have guessed at last that this is some name he goes by here, among the thieves. 'Find your room all right?' He nods. She gazes at me again. 'We keeps that room,' she goes on, in the same light, friendly, dangerous tone, 'for Gentleman to kip in when he comes. A very high, out-of-the-way sort of room it is, I can tell you. Seen all manner of business up there; all sorts of tricks. People been known to come here, rather quiet'—she pretends surprise—'why, just as you have come!—to spend a day, two days, two weeks, who knows how long? tucked away up there. Chaps, maybe, that the police would like a word with. Can't be found—do you see?—when they come here. Chaps, girls, kids, ladies . . .'

After this last word she pauses. She pats the space at her side. 'Won't you sit, dear girl? Don't care to? Hmm? Perhaps in a minute, then.' The bed has a blanket upon it—a quilt of coloured squares, roughly knitted, and roughly sewn together. She begins to pluck at one of its seams, as if in distraction. 'Now, what was I speaking of?' she says, her eyes on mine.

'Of ladies,' says Richard.

She moves her hand, lifts her finger. 'Of ladies,' she says. 'That's right. Of course, there come so few true ladies, you find they rather sticks in the mind. I remember one, particular, that came—oh, how long ago? Sixteen years? Seventeen? Eighteen . . .?' She watches my face. 'Seems a long time to you, sweetheart, I dare say. Seems a life-time, don't it? Only wait, dear girl, till you are my age. The years all run together, then. All run together, like so many tears . . .' She gives a jerk of her head, draws in her breath in a backwards sigh, quick and rueful. She waits. But I have grown still, and cold, and cautious, and say nothing. So then she goes on.

'Well, this particular lady,' she says, 'she wasn't much older than you are now. But wasn't she in a fix? She had got my name from a woman in the Borough, that did girls and their complaints. You know what I am saying, dear? Made girls be poorly, in the regular way, when their poorliness had stopped?' She moves her hand, makes a face. 'I never bothered with that. That was out of my line. My idea was, if it wasn't going to kill you on its way out, then have

it, and sell it; or what's better, give it to me and let me sell it for
you!—I mean, to people that want infants, for servants or appren-
tices, or for regular sons and daughters. Did you know, dear girl,
that there were people in the world, like that?—and people like me,
providing the infants? No?' Again, I make no answer. Again she
moves her hand. 'Well, perhaps this lady I am speaking of now
didn't know it either, till she came to me. Poor thing. The Borough
woman had tried to help her, but she was too far on, she had only
got sick. "Where's your husband?" I said, before I took her in.
"Where's your ma? Where's all your people? Won't follow you
here, will they?" She said they wouldn't. She had no husband—that
was her trouble, of course. Her mother was dead. She had run away
from a great, grand house, forty miles from London—up-river, she
said . . .' She nods, still keeping her eyes on mine. I have grown
colder than ever. 'Her father and her brother were looking for her,
and seemed likely to just about kill her; but would never find their
way to the Borough, she swore it. As for the gentleman that had
started her troubles all off, by saying he loved her—well, he had a
wife and a kiddie of his own, and had given her up as ruined, and
washed his hands.—As gentlemen, of course, will do.

'Which, in a line like mine, you say thank heavens for!' She
smiles, almost winks. 'This lady had money. I took her, and put her
upstairs. Perhaps I oughtn't to have done it. Mr Ibbs did say I
oughtn't to. For I had five or six babies in the house already, and was
worn out and fretful—more fretful, through having just borne a
little infant of my own, that had died—' Here her look changes, and
she waves a hand before her eyes. 'I won't talk of that, however. I
won't talk of that.'

She swallows and looks about her for a moment, as if in search of
the fallen threads of her story. Then she seems to find them. The
confusion passes from her face, she catches my eye again, then gestures upwards. I glance, with her, at the ceiling. It is a dirty yellow,
marked grey with the smoke of lamps.

'Up there we put her,' she says, 'in Gentleman's room. And all
day long I would sit beside her and hold her hand, and every night
I would hear her turning in her bed, and crying. Nearly broke your

heart. She had no more harm in her than milk does. I supposed she might die. Mr Ibbs supposed it. I think even she supposed it, for she was meant to go another two months, and anyone could see that she wouldn't have the strength to go half that time. But maybe the baby knew it, too—they do know, sometimes. For we only have her here a week, before her water busts and it starts coming. Takes a day and a night. Means to come, all right! Even so, it's a shrimp of a thing, but the lady—being so poorly already—is quite made rags of. Then she hears her baby cry, and picks up her head from her pillow. "What's that, Mrs Sucksby?" she says. "That's your baby, my dear!" I tell her. "My baby?" says she. "Is my baby a boy, or a girl?" "It's a girl," I say. And when she hears that she cries out with all her lungs: "Then God help her! For the world is cruel to girls. I wish she had died, and me with her!"'

She shakes her head, lifts her hands, lets them fall upon her knees. Richard leans against the door. The door has a hook, with a silk dressing-gown hanging from it: he has taken up the belt of the gown and is idly passing it across his mouth. His eyes are on mine, their lids a little lowered; his look is unreadable. From the kitchen below us there comes laughter and a ragged shrieking. The woman listens, gives another of those backwards, rueful sighs.

'There's Dainty, crying again . . .' She rolls her eyes. 'But how I have run on!—haven't I, Miss Lilly? Not finding me tiresome, dear? Ain't much to hold the interest, perhaps, in these old tales . . .'

'Go on,' I say. My mouth is dry, and sticks. 'Go on, about the woman.'

'The lady, what had the little girl? Such a slight little scrap of a girl, she was: fair-haired, blue-eyed—well, they all come out blue, of course; and brown up, later . . .'

She looks, meaningfully, into my own brown eyes. I blink, and colour. But my voice I make flat. 'Go on,' I say again. 'I know you mean to tell me. Tell me now. The woman wished her daughter dead. What then?'

'Wished her dead?' She moves her head. 'So she said. So women do say, sometimes. And sometimes they mean it. Not her, though. That child was everything to her, and when I said she had much better give her up to me, than keep her, she grew quite wild. "What, you don't mean to raise her yourself?" I said. "You, a lady, without a husband?" She said she would pass herself off as a widow—meant to go abroad, where no-one knew her, and make her living as a seamstress. "I'll see my daughter married to a poor man before she knows my shame," she said. "I'm through with the quality life." That was her one thought, poor thing, that no amount of sensible talking from me could shake her of: that she would sooner see her girl live low but honest, than give her back to the world of money she come from. She meant to start for France so soon as her strength was all back—and I'll tell you this now, I thought she was a fool; but I would have cut my own arm to help her, she was that simple and good.'

She sighs. 'But it's the simple and the good that are meant to suffer in this world—ain't it, though! She kept very weak, and her baby hardly grew. Still she talked, all the time, of France, it was all she thought of; until one night, I was putting her into her bed when there comes a knocking on our kitchen door. It's the woman, from the Borough, what first put her on to me: I see her face, and know there's trouble. There is. What do you think? The lady's pa and brother have tracked her down after all. "They're coming," says the woman. "Lord help me, I never meant to tell them where you was; but the brother had a cane, and whipped me." She shows me her back, and it's black. "They've gone for a coach," she says, "and a bully to help them. I should say you've an hour. Get your lady out now, if she means to go. Try to hide her and they'll pull your house apart!"

'Well! The poor lady had followed me down and heard it all, and started shrieking. "Oh, I'm done for!" she said. "Oh, if I might only have got to France!"—but the trip downstairs had half-killed her, she was so weak. "They'll take my baby!" she said. "They'll take her and make her theirs! They'll put her in their great house, they might as well lock her into a tomb! They'll take her, and turn her heart against me—oh! and I haven't even named her! I haven't even named her!" That's all she would say. "I haven't even named her!"—"Name her now, then!" I said, just to make her be quiet. "Name her quick, while you still got the chance." "I will!" she said.

"But, what name shall I give her?" "Well," I said, "think on: she's to be a lady after all, there's no helping it now. Give her a name that'll fit her. What's your own name? Give her that." Then she looked dark. She said, "My name's a hateful one, I'd sooner curse her before I let anyone call her Marianne—'"

She stops, seeing my face. It has jumped, or twisted—though I have known that the story must reach this point, and have stood, feeling my breath come shorter, my stomach grow sourer, as the tale proceeds. I draw in my breath. 'It's not true,' I say. 'My mother, coming here, without a husband? My mother was mad. My father was a soldier. I have his ring. Look here, look here!'

I have gone to my bag, and I stoop to it, and pull at the torn leather and find the little square of linen that holds my jewels. There is the ring that they gave me in the madhouse: I hold it up. My hand is shaking. Mrs Sucksby studies it and shrugs.

'Rings may be got,' she says, 'from just about anywhere.'

'From him,' I say.

'From anywhere. I could get you ten like that, have them stamped *V.R.*—Would that make them the Queen's?'

I cannot answer. For what do I know about where rings come from and how they may be stamped? I say again, more weakly, 'My mother coming here, without a husband. Ill, and coming here. My father— My uncle—' I look up. 'My uncle. Why should my uncle lie?'

'Why should he tell the truth?' says Richard, coming forward, speaking at last. 'I dare swear his sister was honest enough, before her ruin, and only unlucky; but that's the sort of unluckiness— well, that a man doesn't care to talk about too freely . . .'

I gaze again at the ring. There is a cut upon it I liked, as a girl, to suppose made by a bayonet. Now the gold feels light, as if pierced and made hollow.

'My mother,' I say, doggedly, 'was mad. She bore me, strapped to a table.—No.' I put my hands to my eyes. 'That part, perhaps, was my own fancy. But not the rest. My mother was mad—was kept in the cell of a madhouse; and I was made to be mindful of her example, lest I should follow it.'

'She was certainly, once they had got her, put in a cell,' says Richard; 'as we know girls are, from time to time, for the satisfaction of gentlemen.—Well, no more of that, just yet.' He has caught Mrs Sucksby's eye. 'And you were certainly kept in fear of following her, Maud. And what did that do to you?—save make you anxious, obedient, careless of your own comforts—in other words, exactly fit you to your uncle's fancy? Didn't I tell you once, what a scoundrel he was?'

'You are wrong,' I say. 'You are wrong, or mistaken.'

'No mistake,' answers Mrs Sucksby.

'You may be lying, even now. Both of you!'

'We may be.' She taps her mouth. 'But you see, dear girl, we ain't.'

'My uncle,' I say again. 'My uncle's servants. Mr Way, Mrs Stiles . . .'

But I say it, and I feel—the ghost of a pressure—Mr Way's shoulder against my ribs, his finger in the crook of my knee: *Fancy yourself a lady, do you?*—And then, and then, Mrs Stiles's hard hands on my pimpling arms and her breath against my cheek:

Why your mother, with all her fortune, should have turned out trash—!

I know it, I know it. I still hold the ring. Now, with a cry, I throw it to the floor—as I once, as a furious child, threw cups and saucers.

'Damn him!' I say. I think of myself at the foot of my uncle's bed, the razor in my hand, his unguarded eye. *Confidence Abused.* 'Damn him!' Richard nods. I turn upon him, then. 'And damn you, with him! You knew this, all along? Why not tell me, at Briar? Don't you think it would have made me the likelier to go with you? Why wait, and bring me here—to this foul place!—to trick and surprise me?'

'Surprise you?' he says, with a curious laugh. 'Oh, Maud, sweet Maud, we haven't begun to do that.'

I don't understand him. I hardly try to. I am thinking still of my uncle, my mother—my mother, ill, ruined, coming here . . . Richard puts his hand to his chin, works his lips. 'Mrs Sucksby,' he says, 'do you keep any drink up here? I find myself rather dry about the mouth. It's the anticipation, I think, of sensation. I am the same at the casino, at the spinning of the wheel; and at the pantomime, when they're about to let fly the fairies.'

Mrs Sucksby hesitates, then goes to a shelf, opens a box, lifts out a bottle. She produces three short tumblers with gold about the rim. She wipes them, on a fold of her skirt.

'I hope, Miss Lilly, you won't suppose this sherry,' she says, as she pours. The scent of the liquid comes sharp and sickly upon the close air of the room. 'Sherry in a lady's chamber I could never agree to; but a bit of honest brandy, meant for use now and then as a bracer—well, you tell me, where's the harm in that?'

'No harm at all,' says Richard. He holds a glass to me and, so confused am I—so dazed and enraged—I take it at once, and sip it as if it were wine. Mrs Sucksby watches me swallow.

'Got a good mouth for spirits,' she says approvingly.

'Got a mouth for them,' says Richard, 'when they're marked up, *Medicine*. Hey, Maud?'

I will not answer. The brandy is hot. I sit, at last, upon the edge of the bed and unfasten the cord of my cloak. The room is darker than before: the day is turning into night. The horse-hair screen looms black, and casts shadows. The walls—that are papered here in a pattern of flowers, there in muddy diamonds—are gloomy and close. The scarf stands out against the window: a fly is caught behind it, and buzzes in hopeless fury against the glass.

I sit with my head in my hands. My brain, like the room, seems hedged about with darkness; my thoughts run, but run uselessly. I do not ask—as I would, I think, if this were some other girl's story and I was only reading it or hearing it told—I do not ask why they have got me here; what they mean to do with me now; how they plan to profit from the cheating and stunning of me. I only rage, still, against my uncle. I only think, over and over: *My mother, ruined, shamed, coming here, lying bleeding in a house of thieves. Not mad, not mad* . . .

I suppose my expression is a strange one. Richard says, 'Maud, look at me. Don't think, now, of your uncle and your uncle's house. Don't think of that woman, Marianne.'

'I shall think of her,' I answer, 'I shall think of her as I always have: as a fool! But, my father— You said, a gentleman? They have made me out an orphan, all these years. Does my father still live? Did he never—?'

'Maud, Maud,' he says, sighing, moving back to his place at the door. 'Look about you. Think how you came here. Do you suppose I snatched you from Briar, did the deed I did this morning—ran the risks I have run—so that you might learn family secrets, no more than that?'

'I don't know!' I say. 'What do I know, now? If you will only give me a little time, to think in. If you will only tell me—'

But Mrs Sucksby has come to me, and lightly touches my arm.

'Wait up, dear girl,' she says, very gently. She puts a finger to her lip, half closes one eye. 'Wait up, and listen. You ain't heard all my story. The better part's to come. For there's the lady, you remember, that's been made rags of. There's the father and the brother and the bully, due in one hour's time. There's the baby, and me saying, "What'll we name her? What about your own name, Marianne?", and the lady saying as how she'd sooner curse her, than call her that. You remember, my dear? "As for being the daughter of a lady," says the poor girl next, "you tell me this: what does being a lady do for you, except let you be ruined? I want her named plain," she says, "like a girl of the people. I want her named plain." "You name her plain, then," I say—still meaning, as it were, to humour her. "I will," she says. "I will. There was a servant that was kind to me once—kinder than ever my father or my brother was. I want her named for her. I shall call her for her. I shall call her—"'

'*Maud*,' I say, wretchedly. I have lowered my face again. But when Mrs Sucksby is silent, I lift it. Her look is strange. Her silence is strange. She slowly shakes her head. She draws in her breath—hesitates, for another second—and then says:

'*Susan.*'

Richard watches, his hand before his mouth. The room, the house, is still. My thoughts, that have seemed to turn like grinding wheels, now seem to stop. Susan. Susan. I will not let them see how the word confounds me. *Susan.* I will not speak. I will not move, for

fear I should stumble or shake. I only keep my eyes upon Mrs
Sucksby's face. She takes another, longer sip from her glass of
brandy, then wipes her mouth. She comes and sits again, beside
me, upon the bed.

'*Susan*,' she says again. 'That's what the lady named her. Seems
a shame to have named that baby for a servant, don't it? So I
thought, anyway. But what could I say? Poor girl, she was quite off
her head—still crying, still shrieking, still saying as how her father
would come, would take the child, would make her hate her own
mother's name. "Oh, how can I save her?" she said. "I would rather
anyone got her, than him and my brother! Oh, what can I do? How
can I save her? Oh, Mrs Sucksby, I swear to you now, I would rather
they took any other poor woman's baby, than mine!"'

Her voice has risen. Her cheek is flushed. A pulse beats,
briefly—very fast—in the lid of her eye. She puts her hand to it,
then drinks again, and again wipes her mouth.

'That's what she said,' she says, more quietly. 'That's what she
said. And as she says it, all the infants that are lying about the
house seem to hear her, and all start up crying at once. They all
sound the same, when you ain't their mother. They all sounded the
same to her, anyway. I had got her to the stairs, just outside that
door'—she tilts her head, Richard shifts his pose and the door gives
a creak—'and now, she stops. She looks at me, and I see what she's
thinking, and my heart goes cold. "We can't!" I say. "Why can't
we?" she answers. "You have said yourself, my daughter shall be
brought up a lady. Why not let some other little motherless girl have
that, in her place—poor thing, she shall have the grief of it, too! But
I swear, I'll settle a half my fortune on her; and Susan shall have the
rest. She shall have it, if you'll only take her for me now, and bring
her up honest, and keep her from knowing about her inheritance till
she has grown up poor and can feel the worth of it! Don't you
have," she says, "some motherless baby we can give to my father in
Susan's place? Don't you? Don't you? For God's sake, say you do!
There's fifty pounds in the pocket of my gown. You shall have it!—
I shall send you more!—if you'll only do this thing for me, and not
tell a living soul you've done it."'

Perhaps there is movement in the room below, in the street—I do not know, I do not hear it if there is. I keep my gaze on Mrs Sucksby's flushed face, on her eyes, her lips.—'Now, here was a thing,' she is saying, 'to be asked to do. Wouldn't you say, dear girl? Here was a thing, all right. I think I never thought harder or quicker before in all my life. And what I said at last was: "Keep your money. Keep your fifty pounds. I don't want it. What I want, is this: Your pa is a gentleman, and gents are tricky. I'll keep your baby, but I want for you to write me out a paper, saying all you mean to do, and signing it, and sealing it; and that makes it binding." "I'll do it!" she says, straight off. "I'll do it!" And we come in here, and I fetch her a bit of paper and ink, and she sets it all down—just as I have told you, that Susan Lilly is her own child, though left with me, and that the fortunes are to be cut, and so on—and she folds it and seals it with the ring off her finger, and puts on the front that it ain't to be opened till the day her daughter turns eighteen. Twenty-one, she wanted to make it: but my mind was running ahead, even as she was writing, and I said it must be eighteen—for we oughtn't to risk the girls taking husbands, before they knew what was what.' She smiles. 'She liked that. She thanked me for it.

'And then, no sooner had she sealed it than Mr Ibbs sends up a cry: there's a coach, pulled up at his shop door, with two gents—an old one, and a younger—getting out, and with them, a bully with a club. Well! The lady runs shrieking to her room and I stand, tearing the hair out of my head. Then I go to the cribs, and I fetch up this one particular baby that is there—a girl, same size as the other, looks to turn out fair, like her—and I carry her upstairs. I said, "Here! Take her quick, and be kind to her! Her name's Maud; and that's a name for a lady after all. Remember your word." "Remember yours!" the poor girl cries; and she kisses her own baby, and I take it, and bring it down and lay it in the empty cot . . .'

She shakes her head. 'Such a trifling little thing it was to do!' she says. '—And done in a minute. Done, while the gentlemen are still hammering at the door. "Where is she?" they're crying. "We know you've got her!" No stopping them, then. Mr Ibbs lets them in, they fly through the house like furies—see me and knock me down, next thing I know, there's the poor lady being dragged downstairs by her pa—her gown all flapping, her shoes undone, the mark of her brother's stick on her face—and there's you, dear girl—there's you in her arms, and nobody thinking you was anyone's but hers.— Why should they? Too late to change it, then. She gave me one quick look as her father took her down, and that was all; I fancy she watched me, though, from the window of the coach. But if she was ever sorry she done it, I can't tell you. I dare say she thought often of Sue; but no more than— Well, no more than she ought.'

She blinks and turns her head. She has placed her glass of brandy upon the bed between us; the seams in the quilt keep it from spilling. Her hands she has clasped: she is stroking the knuckles of one with the blunt red thumb of the other. Her foot in its slipper goes tap upon the floor. She has not taken her eyes from my face, all the time she has spoken, until now.

My own eyes I close. My hands I place before them, and I gaze into the darkness that is made by my palms. There is a silence. It lengthens. Mrs Sucksby leans closer.

'Dear girl,' she murmurs. 'Won't you say a word to us?' She touches my hair. Still I will not speak or move. Her hand falls. 'I can see this news've dashed your spirits, rather,' she says. Perhaps she gestures then to Richard, for he comes and squats before me.

'You understand, Maud,' he says, trying to see about my fingers, 'what Mrs Sucksby has told you? One baby becomes another. Your mother was not your mother, your uncle not your uncle. Your life was not the life that you were meant to live, but Sue's; and Sue lived yours . . .'

They say that dying men see, played before their eyes with impossible swiftness, the show of their lives. As Richard speaks, I see mine: the madhouse, my baton of wood, the gripping gowns of Briar, the string of beads, my uncle's naked eyes, the books, the books . . . The show flickers and is gone, is lost and useless, like the gleam of a coin in murky water. I shudder, and Richard sighs. Mrs Sucksby shakes her head and tuts. But, when I show them my face they both start back. I am not weeping, as they suppose. I am laughing—I am gripped with a terrible laughter—and my look must be ghastly.

'Oh, but this,' I think I say, 'is perfect! This is all I have longed for! Why do you stare? What are you gazing at? Do you suppose a girl is sitting here? That girl is lost! She has been drowned! She is lying, fathoms deep. Do you think she has arms and legs, with flesh and cloth upon them? Do you think she has hair? She has only bones, stripped white! She is as white as a page of paper! She is a book, from which the words have peeled and drifted—'

I try to take a breath; and might as well have water in my mouth: I draw at the air, and it does not come. I gasp, and shake and gasp again. Richard stands and watches.

'No madness, Maud,' he says, with a look of distaste. 'Remember. You have no excuse for it now.'

'I have excuse,' I say, 'for anything! Anything!'

'Dear girl—' says Mrs Sucksby. She has caught up her tumbler of liquor and is waving it close to my face. 'Dear girl—' But I shudder with laughter still—a hideous laughter—and I jerk, as a fish might jerk on the end of a line. I hear Richard curse; then I see him go to my bag and grope inside it, bring out my bottle of medicine: he lets the liquid drop, three times, into the glass of brandy, then seizes my head and presses the glass to my lips. I taste it, then swallow and cough. I put my hands to my mouth. My mouth grows numb. I close my eyes again. I do not know how long I sit, but at length I feel the blanket that covers the bed come against my shoulder and cheek. I have sunk upon it. I lie—still twitching, from time to time, in what feels like laughter; and again Richard and Mrs Sucksby stand, in silence, and watch me.

Presently, however, they come a little nearer. 'Now,' says Mrs Sucksby softly, 'are you better, darling?' I do not answer. She looks at Richard. 'Oughtn't we to go, and let her sleep?'

'Sleep be damned,' he answers. 'I still believe she thinks we have brought her here for her own convenience.' He comes, and taps my face. 'Open your eyes,' he says.

I say, 'I have no eyes. How could I? You have taken them from me.'

He catches hold of one of my lids and pinches it hard. 'Open your damn eyes!' he says. 'That's better. Now, there is a little more

for you to know—just a little more, and then you may sleep. Listen
to me. Listen! Don't ask me, how you are meant to, I shall cut the
fucking ears off the sides of your head if you do. Yes, I see you hear
that. Do you feel this, also?' He strikes me. 'Very good.'

The blow is not so hard as it might have been: Mrs Sucksby has
seen him lift his arm and tried to check it.

'Gentleman!' she says, her cheek growing dark. 'No call for that.
No call at all. Hold your temper, can't you? I believe you've bruised
her. Oh, dear girl.'

She reaches towards my face. Richard scowls. 'She ought to be
grateful,' he says, straightening, putting back his hair, 'that I have
not done worse, any time in the past three months. She ought to
know I will do it again, and count it nothing. Do you hear me,
Maud? You have seen me at Briar, a sort of gentleman. I make a
holiday from gallantry, however, when I come here. Understand?'

I lie, nursing my cheek, my eyes on his, saying nothing. Mrs
Sucksby wrings her hands. He takes the cigarette from behind his
ear, puts it to his mouth, looks for a match.

'Go on, Mrs Sucksby,' he says as he does it. 'Tell the rest. As for
you, Maud: listen hard, and know at last what your life was lived
for.'

'My life was not lived,' I say in a whisper. 'You have told me, it
was a fiction.'

'Well'—he finds a match, and strikes it—'fictions must end.
Hear now how yours is to.'

'It has ended already,' I answer. But his words have made me cautious. My head is thick with liquor, with medicine, with shock; but
not so thick that I cannot, now, begin to be fearful of what they will
tell me next, how they plan to keep me, what they mean to keep me
for . . .

Mrs Sucksby sees me grow thoughtful, and nods. 'Now you start
to get it,' she says. 'You are starting to see. I got the lady's baby and,
what's better, I got the lady's word.—The word's the thing, of
course. The word's the thing with the money in—ain't it?' She
smiles, touches her nose. Then she leans a little closer. 'Like to see
it?' she says, in a different sort of voice. 'Like to see the lady's word?'

She waits. I do not answer, but she smiles again, moves from me, glances at Richard, then turns her back to him and fumbles for a second with the buttons of her gown. The taffeta rustles. When the bodice is part-way open she reaches inside—reaches, it seems to me, into her very bosom, her very heart—and then draws out a folded paper. 'Kept this close,' she says, as she brings it to me, 'all these years. Kept this closer than gold! Look, here.'

The paper is folded like a letter, and bears a tilting instruction: *To Be Opened on the Eighteenth Birthday of My Daughter, Susan Lilly.*—I see that name, and shudder, and reach, but she holds it jealously and, like my uncle—not my uncle, now!—with an antique book, won't let me take it; she lets me touch it, however. The paper is warm, from the heat of her breast. The ink is brown, the folds furred and discoloured. The seal is quite unbroken. The stamp is my mother's—Sue's mother's, I mean; not mine, not mine—

M.L.

'You see it, dear girl?' Mrs Sucksby says. The paper trembles. She draws it back to herself, with a miser's gesture and look—lifts it to her face and puts her lips to it, then turns her back and restores it to its place inside her gown. As she buttons her dress, she glances again at Richard. He has been watching, closely, curiously; but says nothing.

I speak, instead. 'She wrote it,' I say. My voice is thick, I am giddy. 'She wrote it. They took her. What then?'

Mrs Sucksby turns. Her gown is closed and perfectly smooth again, but she has her hand upon the bodice, as if nursing the words beneath. 'The lady?' she says, distractedly. 'The lady died, dear girl.' She sniffs, and her tone changes. 'Bust me, however, if she didn't linger on another month before she done it! Who would have thought? That month was against us. For now her pa and her brother, having got her home, made her change her will.—You can guess what to. No penny to go to the daughter—meaning you, dear girl, so far as they knew—till the daughter marries. There's gentlemen for you—ain't it? She sent me a note to tell me, by a nurse. They'd got her into the madhouse by then, and you alongside her—well, that soon finished her off. It was a puzzle to her, she said, how things might turn out now; but she took her consolation from the thought of my honesty. Poor girl!' She seems almost sorry. '—That was her slip.'

Richard laughs. Mrs Sucksby smooths her mouth, and begins to look crafty. 'As for me,' she says, '—well, I had seen from the first that the only puzzle was, how to get the whole of the fortune when I was only due to have half. My comfort must be, that I had eighteen years for figuring it out in. I thought many times of you.'

I turn my face. 'I never asked for your thoughts,' I say. 'I don't want them now.'

'Ungrateful, Maud!' says Richard. 'Here has Mrs Sucksby been, plotting so hard in your behalf, so long. Another girl—don't girls seek only to be the heroines of romance?—another girl might fancy herself distinguished.'

I look from him back to Mrs Sucksby, saying nothing. She nods. 'I thought often of you,' she says again, 'and wondered how you got on. I supposed you handsome. Dear girl, you are!' She swallows. 'I had two fears, only. The first was, that you might die. The second was, that your grand-dad and uncle should take you away from England and have you married before the lady's secret come out. Then I read in a paper that your grand-dad died. Then I heard how your uncle lived quietly, in the country; and had you with him, and kept you in a quiet way, too. There's my two fears both gone!' She smiles. 'Meanwhile,' she says—and now her eyelids flutter—'Meanwhile, here's Sue. You have seen, dear girl, how close and quiet I have kept the lady's word.' She pats her gown. 'Well, what was the word to me, without Sue to pin it to? Think how close and quiet I have kept her. Think how safe. Think how sharp such a girl might have grown, in a house like this one, in a street like ours; then think how hard Mr Ibbs and me have worked to keep her blunt. Think how deep I puzzled it over— knowing I must use her at the last, but never quite knowing how. Think how it begins to come clear, when I meets Gentleman— think how quick my fear that you might be secretly married, turns into my knowing that he is the chap that must secretly marry you . . . It's the work of another minute, then, to look at Sue and know what ought to be done with her.' She shrugs. 'Well, and

now we've done it. Sue's you, dear girl. And what we brought you
here for is—'

'Listen, Maud!' says Richard. I have closed my eyes and turned
my head. Mrs Sucksby comes to me, lifts her hand, begins to stroke
my hair.

'What we brought you here for,' she goes on, more gently, 'is for
you to start being Sue. Only that, dear girl! Only that.'

I open my eyes, and suppose look stupid.

'Do you see?' says Richard. 'We keep Sue as my wife in the madhouse, and with the opening of her mother's statement, her share of
the fortune—*Maud*'s share, I mean—comes to me. I should like to
say I will keep every cent of it; but the scheme was Mrs Sucksby's
after all, and half goes to her.' He makes a bow.

'That's fair, ain't it?' says Mrs Sucksby, still stroking my hair.

'But the other share,' Richard goes on, '—which is to say, Sue's
real share—Mrs Sucksby stands also to get. The statement names
her Sue's guardian; and guardians, I am afraid, are often less than
scrupulous in the handling of their wards' fortunes . . . That all
means nothing, of course, if Sue herself has vanished. But then, it's
Maud Lilly—the true Maud Lilly'—he blinks—'by which I mean
of course, the false Maud Lilly—who has vanished. Isn't that what
you wanted? To vanish? You said, a minute ago, that you have
excuse for anything now. What will it hurt you, then, to be passed
off as Sue, and so make Mrs Sucksby rich?'

'Make us both rich, darling,' Mrs Sucksby says quickly. 'I ain't so
heartless, dear, as to rob you quite of everything! You're a lady,
ain't you, and handsome? Why, I shall need a handsome lady, to
show me what's what when I comes into my fortune. I got plans for
us both, sweetheart, that grand!'—She taps her nose.

I push myself up, away from her; but am too giddy, still, to
stand. 'You are mad,' I say to them both. 'You are mad! I— Pass me
off as Sue?'

'Why not?' says Richard. 'We need only convince a lawyer. I
think we shall.'

'Convince him, how?'

'How? Why, here are Mrs Sucksby and Mr Ibbs—that have been

like parents to you, and so might be supposed, I think, to know you, if anyone might. And here are John and Dainty, too—they'll swear to any kind of mischief with money in, you may be sure. And here am I—that met you at Briar, when you were maid to Miss Maud Lilly, later my wife. You've seen, haven't you, what gentlemen's words are worth?' He pretends to be struck with the thought. 'But of course you have! For in a madhouse in the country are a pair of doctors—they'll remember you, I think. For didn't you, only yesterday, give them your hand and make them a curtsey, and stand in a good light before them, for quite twenty minutes, answering questions to the name of Susan?'

He lets me consider that. Then he says, 'All we ask is that, when the moment arrives, you give the performance over again, before a lawyer. What have you to lose? Dear Maud, you have nothing: no friends in London, no money to your name—why, not so much *as* a name!'

I have put my fingers to my mouth. 'Suppose,' I say, 'I won't do it? Suppose, when your lawyer comes, I tell him—'

'Tell him what? Tell him how you plotted to swindle an innocent girl?—looked on, while the doctors dosed her and carried her off? Hmm? What do you think he will make of that?'

I sit and watch him speak. At last I say, in a whisper: 'Are you truly so wicked as this?' He shrugs. I turn to Mrs Sucksby. 'And you,' I say. 'Are you so wicked? To think, of Sue— Are you so vile?'

She waves her hand before her face, says nothing. Richard snorts. '*Wickedness*,' he says. '*Vileness*. What terms! The terms of fiction. Do you think, that when women swap children, they do it, as nurses do it in the operettas—for comedy's sake? Look about you, Maud. Step to the window, look into the street. There is life, not fiction. It is hard, it is wretched. It would have been yours, but for Mrs Sucksby's kindness in keeping you from it.—Christ!' He moves from the door, puts his arms above his head and stretches. 'How tired I am! What a day's work I have done today—haven't I? One girl pressed into a madhouse; another— Well.' He looks me over, nudges my foot with his. 'No arguments?' he says. 'No bluster? That may come later, I suppose. No matter if it does. Sue's birthday falls at the start of August. We have more than three months, to persuade you into our plot. I think three days—of Borough living, I mean—will do that.'

I am gazing at him, but cannot speak. I am thinking, still, of Sue. He tilts his head. 'Don't say we have broken your spirit, Maud,' he says, 'so quickly? I should be sorry to think it.' He pauses. Then: 'Your mother,' he adds, 'would have been sorry, also.'

'My mother,' I start to say.—I think of Marianne, with lunacy in her eye. Then I catch my breath. Through all of it, I have not thought of this. Richard watches, looks sly. He puts his hand to his collar and stretches his throat, and coughs, in a feeble, girlish and yet deliberate kind of way.

'Now, Gentleman,' says Mrs Sucksby anxiously as he does it, 'don't tease her.'

'Tease her?' he says. He still pulls at his collar as if it chafes him. 'I am only dry about the throat, from talking.'

'You have said too much, that's why,' she answers. 'Miss Lilly—I'll call you that, shall I, my dear? Seems natural, don't it?—Miss Lilly, don't mind him. We've plenty of time for talking of that.'

'Of my mother, you mean,' I say. 'My true mother, that you made out to be Sue's. That choked—you see, I know something!—that choked, on a pin.'

'On a pin!' says Richard, laughing. 'Did Sue say that?' Mrs Sucksby bites her mouth. I look from one to the other of them.

'What was she?' I ask wearily. 'For God's sake, tell me. Do you think I have it in me, now, to be astonished? Do you imagine I care? What was she? A thief, like you? Well, if I must lose the mad-woman, a thief I suppose will do . . .'

Richard coughs again. Mrs Sucksby looks away from me, and joins and works her hands. When she speaks, her voice is quiet, grave. 'Gentleman,' she says, 'you ain't got nothing more to tell Miss Lilly, now. I have some words, however. The sort of words a lady likes to say to a girl in private.'

He nods. 'I know,' he says. He folds his arms. 'I am dying to hear them.'

She waits, but he will not leave. She comes and, again, sits beside me; again, I flinch away.

'Dear girl,' she says. 'The fact of it is, there ain't a pleasant way to tell it; and I ought to know, if anyone ought!—for I told it once already, to Sue. Your mother—' She wets her lips, then looks at Richard.

'Tell her,' he says. 'Or I will.'

So then she speaks again, more quickly. 'Your mother,' she says, 'was took before the courts, not just for thieving, but for killing a man; and—oh, my dear, they hanged her for it!'

'Hanged?'

'A murderess, Maud,' says Richard, with relish. 'You may see the place they hanged her, from the window of my room—'

'Gentleman, I mean it!'

He falls silent. I say again, '*Hanged!*'

'Hanged game,' says Mrs Sucksby—as if this, whatever it means, will make me bear it better. Then she studies my face. 'Dear girl, don't think of it,' she says. 'What does it matter now? You're a lady, ain't you? Who'll trouble with where you come from? Why, look about you here.'

She has risen, and lights a lamp: a score of gaudy surfaces—the silk dressing-gown, the cloudy brass of the bedstead, china ornaments upon the mantel-shelf—start out of the darkness. She goes again to the wash-hand stand, and again she says: 'Here's soap. What soap! Got from a shop up West. Come in a year ago—I saw it come and thought, "Now, shan't Miss Lilly like that!" Kept it wrapped in paper, all this time. And here's a towel, look—got a nap like a peach. And scent! Don't care for lavender, we'll get you one of rose. Are you looking, dear?' She moves to the chest of drawers, pulls the deepest drawer open. 'Why, what have we here!' Richard leans to see. I also look, in a kind of horrified wonder. 'Petticoats, and stockings, and stays! Bless me, here's pins for a lady's hair. Here's rouge for a lady's cheek. Here's crystal drops—one pair of blue, one red. That comes of my not knowing, darling, the shade of the eyes they was to match! Well, Dainty shall have the blue pair . . .'

She holds the gaudy beads up by their wires, and I watch the crystals turn. The colour seems to blur. I have begun, in hopelessness, to weep.

As if weeping could save me.

Mrs Sucksby sees me, and tuts. 'Oh, now,' she says, 'ain't that a shame! Crying? And all these handsome things? Gentleman, you see her? Crying, and for what?'

'Crying,' I say bitterly, unsteadily, 'to find myself here, like this! Crying to think of the dream I lived in, when I supposed my mother only a fool! Crying in horror at the closeness and foulness of you!'

She has stepped back. 'Dear girl,' she says, dropping her voice, gazing quickly at Richard, 'do you despise me so, for letting them take you?'

'I despise you,' I say, 'for bringing me back!'

She stares, then almost smiles. She gestures about the room. 'Don't think,' she says, with a look of amazement, 'I mean for you to keep at Lant Street! Dear girl, dear girl, you was taken from here so they might make a lady of you. And a lady they've made you— a perfect jewel! Don't think I shall have you wasting your shine in this low place. Haven't I said? I want you by me, dear, when I am rich. Don't ladies take companions? Only wait till I have got my hands on your fortune; then see if we don't take the grandest house in London! See what carriages and footmen we'll have then!—what pearls, what dresses!'

She puts her hands on me again. She means to kiss me, to eat me. I rise and shake her off. 'You don't think,' I say, 'I shall stay with you, when your wretched scheme is done?'

'What else?' she says. 'Who ought to have you, if not me? It was fortune took you; it is me that has got you back. I been working it over for seventeen years. I been plotting and thinking on this, every minute since I first laid you in the poor lady's arms. I been looking at Sue—'

She swallows. I cry still harder. 'Sue,' I say. 'Oh, Sue . . .'

'Now, why look like that? Didn't I do everything for her, just as her mother wanted?—kept her safe, kept her tidy, made a commonplace girl of her? What have I done, but give her back the life you had from her?'

'You have killed her!' I say.

'Killed her? When there's all those doctors about her, all supposing her a lady?—And that don't come cheap, I can tell you.'

'It certainly doesn't,' says Richard. 'You're paying for that, don't forget. I should have had her in the county asylum, were it down to me.'

'You see, dear girl? Killed her! Why, she might have been killed any day of her life, but for me! Who was it nursed her, when she took sick? Who kept the boys off her? I should have given my hands, my legs, my lungs, for the saving of hers. But do you think, that when I did those things I was doing them for her? What use will a commonplace girl be to me, when I am rich? I was doing them for you! Don't think of her. She was water, she was coal, she was dust, in comparison with what's been made of you.'

I stare at her. 'My God!' I say. 'How could you? How could you?'

Again, she looks amazed. 'How could I not?'

'But, to cheat her! To leave her, there—!'

She reaches, and pats my sleeve. 'You let them take her,' she says. Then her look changes. She almost winks. 'And oh, dear girl, don't you think you was your mother's daughter, then?'

From the rooms below there come again shrieks, and blows, and laughter. Richard stands watching, with folded arms. The fly at the window still buzzes, still beats against the glass. Then the buzzing stops. As if it is a signal, I turn, and sink out of Mrs Sucksby's grasp. I sink to my knees at the side of the bed, and hide my face in the seams of the quilt. I have been bold and determined. I have bitten down rage, insanity, desire, love, for the sake of freedom. Now, that freedom being taken from me utterly, is it to be wondered at if I fancy myself defeated?

I give myself up to darkness; and wish I may never again be required to lift my head to the light.

Chapter Thirteen

The night which follows I remember brokenly. I remember that I keep at the side of the bed with my eyes quite hidden, and will not rise and go down to the kitchen, as Mrs Sucksby wishes. I remember that Richard comes to me, and again puts his shoe to my skirts, to nudge me, then stands and laughs when I will not stir, then leaves me. I remember that someone brings me soup, which I will not eat. That the lamp is taken away and the room made dark. That I must rise at last, to visit the privy; and that the red-haired, fat-faced girl—Dainty—is made to show me to it, then stands at the door to keep me from running from it into the night. I remember that I weep again, and am given more of my drops in brandy. That I am undressed and put in a night-gown not my own. That I sleep, perhaps for an hour—that I am woken by the rustling of taffeta—that I look in horror to see Mrs Sucksby with her hair let down, shrugging off her gown, uncovering flesh and dirty linen, snuffing out her candle, then climbing into the bed beside me. I remember that she lies, thinking me sleeping—puts her hands to me, then draws them back—finally, like a miser with a piece of gold, catches up a lock of my hair and presses it to her mouth.

I know that I am conscious of the heat of her, the unfamiliar bulk and sour scents of her. I know that she falls swiftly into an even sleep, and snores, while I start in and out of slumber. The fitful sleeping makes the hours pass slowly: it seems to me the night has many nights in it—has years of nights!—through which, as if through drifts of smoke, I am compelled to stumble. I wake now, believing I am in my dressing-room at Briar; now, in my room at Mrs Cream's; now, in a madhouse bed, with a nurse vast and comfortable beside me. I wake, a hundred times. I wake to moan and long for slumber—for always, at the last, comes the remembrance, sharp and fearful, of where I truly lie, how I arrived there, who and what I am.

At last I wake and do not sleep again. The dark has eased a little. There has been a street-lamp burning, that has lit the threads of the bleached net scarf hung at the window; now it is put out. The light turns filthy pink. The pink gives way, in time, to a sickly yellow. It creeps, and with it creeps sound—softly at first, then rising in a staggering crescendo: crowing cocks, whistles and bells, dogs, shrieking babies, violent calling, coughing, spitting, the tramp of feet, the endless hollow beating of hooves and the grinding of wheels. Up, up it comes, out of the throat of London. It is six or seven o'clock. Mrs Sucksby sleeps on at my side, but I am wide awake now, and wretched, and sick at my stomach. I rise, and— though it is May, and milder here than at Briar—I shiver. I still wear my gloves, but my clothes and shoes and leather bag Mrs Sucksby has locked in a box—'In case you should wake bewildered, darling, and, thinking you was at home, get dressed, walk off and be lost.'— I remember her saying it, now, as I stood dosed and dazed before her. Where did she put the key?—and the key to the door of the room? I shiver again, more violently, and grow sicker than ever; but my thoughts are horribly clear. I must get out. I must get out! I must get out of London—go anywhere—back to Briar. I must get money. *I must,* I think—this is the clearest thought of all—*I must get*

Sue! Mrs Sucksby breathes heavily, evenly. Where might she have put the keys? Her taffeta gown is hanging from the horse-hair screen: I go silently to it and pat the pockets of its skirt. Empty. I stand and study the shelves, the chest of drawers, the mantelpiece—no keys; but many places, I suppose, where they might be concealed.

Then she stirs—does not wake, but moves her head; and I think I know—think I begin to remember . . . She has the keys beneath her pillow: I recall the crafty movement of her hand, the muffled ringing of the metal. I take a step. Her lips are parted, her white hair loose upon her cheek. I step again, and the floorboards creak. I stand at her side—wait a moment, uncertain; then put my fingers beneath the edge of pillow and slowly, slowly, reach.

She opens her eyes. She takes my wrist, and smiles. She coughs.

'My dear, I loves you for trying,' she says, wiping her mouth. 'But the girl ain't been born that's got the touch that will get past me, when I've a mind to something.' Her grip is strong about my arm; though turns to a caress. I shudder. 'Lord, ain't you cold!' she says then. 'Here, sweetheart, let us cover you up.' She pulls the knitted quilt from the bed and puts it about me. 'Better, dear girl?'

My hair is tangled, and has fallen before my face. I regard her through it.

'I wish I were dead,' I say.

'Oh, now,' she answers, rising. 'What kind of talk is that?'

'I wish you were dead, then.'

She shakes her head, still smiles. 'Wild words, dear girl!' She sniffs. There has come, from the kitchen, a terrible odour. 'Smell that? That's Mr Ibbs, a-cooking up our breakfasts. Let's see who wishes she was dead, now, that's got a plate of bloaters before her!'

She rubs her hands again. Her hands are red, but the sagging flesh upon her arms has the hue and polish of ivory. She has slept in her chemise and petticoat; now she hooks on a pair of stays, climbs into her taffeta gown, then comes to dip her comb in water and brush her hair. 'Tra la, hee hee,' she sings brokenly, as she does it. I keep my own tangled hair before my eyes, and watch her. Her naked feet are cracked, and bulge at the toe. Her legs are almost hairless. When she bends to her stockings, she groans. Her thighs are fat and permanently marked by the pinch of her garters.

'There, now,' she says, when she is dressed. A baby has started crying. 'That will set my others all off. Come down, dear girl—will you?—while I give 'em their pap.'

'Come down?' I say. I must go down, if I am to escape. But I look at myself. 'Like this? Won't you give me back my gown, my shoes?'

Perhaps I say it too keenly, however; or else my look has something of cunning, or desperation, in it. She hesitates, then says, 'That dusty old frock? Them boots? Why, that's walking-gear. Look here, at this silken wrapper.' She takes up the dressing-gown from the hook on the back of the door. 'Here's what ladies wear, for their mornings at home. Here's silken slippers, too. Shan't you look well, in these? Slip 'em on, dear girl, and come down for your breakfast. No need to be shy. John Vroom don't rise before twelve, there's only me, and Gentleman—he's seen you in a state of dishabilly, I suppose!—and Mr Ibbs. And him, dear girl, you might consider now in the light of—well, let's say an uncle. Eh?'

I turn away. The room is hateful to me; but I will not go with her, undressed, down to that dark kitchen. She pleads and coaxes a little longer; then gives me up, and goes. The key turns in the lock.

I step at once to the box that holds my clothes, to try the lid. It is shut up tight, and is stout.

So then I go to the window, to push at the sashes. They will lift, by an inch or two, and the rusting nails that keep them shut I think might give, if I pushed harder. But then, the window frame is narrow, the drop is great; and I am still undressed. Worse than that, the street has people in it; and though at first I think to call to them—to break the glass, to signal and shriek—after a second I begin to look more closely at them, and I see their faces, their dusty clothes, the packets they carry, the children and dogs that run and tumble at their sides. *There is life*, said Richard, twelve hours ago. *It*

is hard, it is wretched. It would have been yours, but for Mrs Sucksby's
kindness in keeping you from it . . .

At the door to the house with the shutters with the heart-shaped
holes, a girl in a dirty bandage sits and feeds her baby. She lifts her
head, catches my gaze; and shakes her fist at me.

I start back from the glass, and cover my face up with my hands.

When Mrs Sucksby comes again, however, I am ready.

'Listen to me,' I say, going to her. 'You know that Richard took
me away from my uncle's house? You know my uncle is rich, and
will seek me out?'

'Your uncle?' she says. She has brought me a tray, but stands in
the door-place until I move back.

'Mr Lilly,' I say, as I do it. 'You know who I mean. He still thinks
me his niece, at least. Don't you suppose he will send a man, and
find me? Do you think he will thank you, for keeping me like this?'

'I should say he will—if he cares so much about it. Ain't we
made you cosy, dear?'

'You know you have not. You know you are keeping me here
against my will. For God's sake, give me my gown, won't you?'

'All right, Mrs Sucksby?'—It is Mr Ibbs. My voice has risen, and
has brought him out of the kitchen to the foot of the stairs. Richard,
too, has stirred in his bed: I hear him cross his floor, draw open his
door, and listen.

'All right!' calls Mrs Sucksby lightly. 'There, now,' she says to me.
'And here's your breakfast, look, growing chilly.'

She sets the tray upon the bed. The door is open; but I know that
Mr Ibbs still stands at the foot of the stairs, that Richard waits and
listens at the top. 'There, now,' she says again. The tray has a plate
and a fork upon it, and a linen napkin. Upon the plate there are two
or three amber-coloured fish in a juice of butter and water. They
have fins, and faces. About the napkin there is a ring of polished
silver, a little like the one that was kept for my especial use at Briar;
but without the initial.

'Please let me go,' I say.

Mrs Sucksby shakes her head. 'Dear girl,' she says, 'go where?'

She waits and, when I do not answer, leaves me. Richard closes his door and goes back to his bed. I hear him humming.

I think of taking up the plate, hurling it against the ceiling, the window, the wall. Then I think: *You must be strong. You must be strong and ready to run.* And so I sit and eat—slowly, wretchedly, carefully picking out the bones from the amber flesh. My gloves grow damp and stained; and I have none with which to replace them.

After an hour, Mrs Sucksby comes back, to take the empty plate. Another hour, and she brings me coffee. While she is gone I stand, again, at the window, or press my ear to the door. I pace, and sit, and pace again. I pass from fury to maudlin grief, to stupor. But then Richard comes. 'Well, Maud—' is all he says. I see him, and am filled with a blistering rage. I make a run at him, meaning to strike his face: he wards off the blows and knocks me down, and I lie upon the floor and kick, and kick—

Then they dose me again with medicine and brandy; and a day or two passes in darkness.

When I wake next, it is again unnaturally early. There has appeared in the room a little basket chair, painted gold, with a scarlet cushion on it. I take it to the window and sit with the dressing-gown about me, until Mrs Sucksby yawns and opens her eyes.

'Dear girl, all right?' she says, as she will say every day, every day; and the idiocy or perversity of the question—when all is so far from being right, as to be so wrong I would almost rather die than endure it—prompts me to grind my teeth or pull at my hair, and gaze at her in loathing. 'Good girl,' she says then, and, 'Like your chair, do you, dear? I supposed you would.' She yawns again, and looks about her. 'Got the po?' she says. I am used in my modesty to taking the chamber-pot behind the horse-hair screen. 'Pass it over, will you, sweetheart? I'm ready to bust.'

I do not move. After a second she rises and fetches it herself. It is a thing of white china, dark inside with what, when I saw it first, in the half-light of morning, I queasily took to be clumps of hair; but which proved to be decoration merely—a great eye with lashes, and about it, in a plain black fount, a motto:

USE ME WELL AND KEEP ME CLEAN
AND I'LL NOT TELL OF WHAT I'VE SEEN!

A PRESENT FROM WALES

The eye gives me, always, a moment or two of uneasiness; but Mrs Sucksby sets the pot down and carelessly lifts her skirt, and stoops. When I shudder, she makes a face.

'Not nice, is it, dear? Never mind. We shall have you a closet, in our grand house.'

She straightens, pushes her petticoat between her legs. Then she rubs her hands.

'Now, then,' she says. She is looking me over, and her eyes are gleaming. 'What do you say to this? How about we dress you up today, make you look handsome? There's your own gown in the box. But, it's a dull old thing, ain't it? And queer and old-fashioned? How about we try you in something nicer. I got dresses saved for you—got 'em wrapped in silver-paper—that fine, you won't believe it. What say we bring Dainty in and get 'em fitted up? Dainty's clever with a needle, though she seems so rough—don't she? That's just her way. She was what you would say, not brought up, but dragged up. But she is kind at her heart.'

She has my attention, now. *Dresses*, I think. Once I am dressed, I might escape.

She sees the change in me, and is pleased. She brings me another breakfast of fish, and again I eat it. She brings me coffee, sweet as syrup: it makes my heart beat hard. Then she brings me a can of hot water. She wets a towel and tries to wash me. I will not let her, but take the towel from her, press it against my face, under my arms, between my legs.—The first time, in all my life, that I washed myself.

Then she goes off—locks the door, of course, behind her—comes back with Dainty. They are carrying paper boxes. They set them down upon the bed, untie their strings and draw out gowns. Dainty sees them, and screams. The gowns are all of silk: one of violet, with yellow ribbon trimming it, another of green with a silver stripe, and a third of crimson. Dainty takes up an edge of cloth and strokes it.

'Pongee?' she says, as if in wonder.

'Pongee, with a foulard rouche,' says Mrs Sucksby—the words coming awkwardly, fleshily out of her mouth, like cherry stones. She lifts the crimson skirt, her chin and cheeks as red in the reflected light of the silk as if stained with cochineal.

She catches my eye. 'What do you say, my dear, to these?'

I have not known such colours, such fabrics, such gowns, exist. I imagine myself in them, upon the streets of London. My heart has sunk. I say, 'They are hideous, hideous.'

She blinks, then recovers. 'You say that now. But you been kept too long in that dreary great house of your uncle's. Is it to be wondered at if you've no more idea of fashion, than a bat? When you makes your début, dear girl, upon the town, you shall have a set of dresses so gay, you shall look back on these and laugh your head off to think you ever supposed 'em bright.' She rubs her hands. 'Now, which best takes your fancy? The arsenic green and the silver?'

'Haven't you a grey,' I say, 'or a brown, or a black?'

Dainty looks at me in disgust.

'Grey, brown or black?' says Mrs Sucksby. 'When there's silver here, and violet?'

'Make it the violet, then,' I say at last. I think the stripe will blind me, the crimson make me sick; though I am sick, anyway. Mrs Sucksby goes to the chest of drawers and opens it up. She brings out stockings, and stays, and coloured petticoats. The petticoats astonish me: for I have always supposed that linen must be white—just as, when I was a child, I thought that all black books must turn out Bibles.

But I must be coloured now, or go naked. They dress me, like two girls dressing a doll.

'Now, where must we nip it?' says Mrs Sucksby, studying the gown. 'Hold still, my dear, while Dainty takes her measure. Lord,

look at your waist.—Hold steady! A person don't want to wriggle
while Dainty's by with a pin in her hand, I can tell you.—That's
better. Too loose, is it? Well, we can't be particular about the size—
ha, ha!—the way we gets 'em.'

They take away my gloves; but bring me new ones. On my feet
they put white silk slippers. 'May I not wear shoes?' I say, and Mrs
Sucksby answers: 'Shoes? Dear girl, shoes are for walking in.
Where've you got to walk to . . .?'

She says it distractedly. She has opened up the great wooden
box and brought out my leather bag. Now, as I look on, and while
Dainty stitches, she goes with it to the light of the window, makes
herself comfortable in the creaking basket chair, and begins to
sort through the items inside. I watch as she fingers slippers, playing-cards, combs. It's my jewels she wants, however. She finds in
time the little linen packet, unwraps it and tips the contents into
her lap.

'Now, what's here? A ring. A bangle. A lady's picture.' She gazes
at this in an assessing way; then all at once her expression changes.
I know whose features she is seeing there, upon the face where once
I looked for mine. She puts it quickly aside. 'A bracelet of emeralds,'
she says next, 'in fashion at the time of King George; but with
handsome stones. We shall find you a nice price for those. A pearl
on a chain. A ruby necklace—that's too heavy, that is, for a girl
with your looks. I got you a nice set of beads—glass beads, but with
such a shine, you'd swear they was sapphires!—suit you much
better. And— Oh! What's this? Ain't that a beauty? Look Dainty,
look at the stunning great stones in that!'

Dainty looks. 'What a spanker!' she says.

It is the brooch of brilliants I once imagined Sue breathing upon,
and polishing, and gazing at with a squinting eye. Now Mrs
Sucksby holds it up and studies it with her own eye narrowed. It
sparkles. It sparkles, even here.

'I know the place for this,' she says. 'Dear girl, you won't mind?'
She opens its clasp and pins it to the bosom of her gown. Dainty lets
fall her needle and thread, to watch her.

'Oh, Mrs S!' she says. 'You looks like a regular queen.'

My heart beats hard again. 'The Queen of Diamonds,' I say.

She eyes me uncertainly—not knowing if I mean to compliment or mock. I do not know, myself.

For a time, then, we say nothing. Dainty finishes her work, then combs my hair and twists and pins it into a knot. Then they make me stand, so they might survey me. They look expectant, tilt their heads; but their faces fall. Dainty rubs her nose. Mrs Sucksby drums her fingers across her lips, and frowns.

There is a square of glass upon the chimney-piece, with plaster hearts about it: I turn, and see what I can of my face and figure, in that. I barely recognise myself. My mouth is white. My eyes are swollen and red, my cheeks the texture and colour of yellowing flannel. My unwashed hair is dark with grease at the scalp. The neck of the gown is low, and shows the lines and points of the bones about my throat.

'Perhaps violet, after all,' says Mrs Sucksby, 'ain't the colour for you, dear girl. Brings out the shadows under your eyes and makes 'em seem rather too like bruises. And as for your cheek—what say you give it a bit of a pinch, put the roses back in it? No? Let Dainty try for you then. She's got a grip like thunder, she has.'

Dainty comes and seizes my cheek, and I cry out and twist from her grasp.

'All right, you cat!' she says, tossing her head and stamping. 'I'm sure, you can keep your yellow face!'

'Hi! Hi!' says Mrs Sucksby. 'Miss Lilly is a lady! I want her spoke to like one. You put that lip in.' Dainty has begun to pout. 'That's better. Miss Lilly, how about we take the gown off and try the green and silver? Only a touch of arsenic in that green—won't harm you at all, so long as you keep from sweating too hard in the bodice.'

But I cannot bear to be handled again, and will not let her unfasten the violet dress. 'You like it, dear girl?' she says then, her face and voice grown softer. 'There! I knew the silks would bring you round at last. Now, what say we go down and stun the gents? Miss Lilly?—Dainty, you go on first. Them stairs are tricky, I should hate for Miss Lilly to take a tumble.'

She has unlocked the door. Dainty passes before me and, after a second, I follow. I still wish I had shoes, a hat, a cloak; but I will run, bare-headed, in silken slippers, if I must. I will run, all the way to Briar. Which was the door, at the foot of the stairs, that I ought to take? I am not sure. I cannot see. Dainty walks ahead of me, and Mrs Sucksby follows anxiously behind. 'Find your step, dear girl?' she says. I do not answer. For there has come, from some room close by, an extraordinary sound—a sound, like the cry of a pea-hen, rising, then trembling, then fading to silence. I start, and turn. Mrs Sucksby has also turned. 'Go on, you old bird!' she cries, shaking her fist. And then, to me, more sweetly: 'Not frightened, dear? Why, that's only Mr Ibbs's aged sister, that is kept to her bed, poor thing, and prone to the horrors.'

She smiles. The cry comes again, I hear it and hasten down the shadowy stairs—my limbs aching and cracking as I do it, and my breath coming quick. Dainty waits at the bottom. The hall is small, she seems to fill it. 'In here,' she says. She has opened the door to the kitchen. There is a street-door behind her, I think, with bolts across it. I slow my step. But then Mrs Sucksby comes and touches my shoulder. 'That's right, dear girl. This way.' I step again, and almost stumble.

The kitchen is warmer than I recall, and darker. Richard and the boy, John Vroom, are sitting at the table playing at dice. They both look up when I appear, and both laugh. John says, 'Look at the face on that! Who bruised the eyes, then? Dainty, say it was you and I'll kiss you.'

'I'll bruise your eyes, get my hands on you,' says Mrs Sucksby. 'Miss Lilly is only tired. Get out of that chair, you little waster, and let her sit down.'

She says this, locking the door at her back, pocketing the key, then crossing the kitchen and trying the other two doors, making sure they are fast.—'Keep the draughts out,' she says, when she sees me watching her.

John throws the dice again, and reckons up his score, before he rises. Richard pats the empty seat. 'Come, Maud,' he says. 'Come, sit beside me. And if you will only promise not to fly at my eyes—

as you did, you know, on Wednesday—then I shall swear, on Johnny's life! not to knock you down again.'

John scowls. 'Don't you make so free with my life,' he says; 'else, I might make free with yours—you hear me?'

Richard does not answer. He holds my gaze, and smiles. 'Come, let us be friends again, hmm?'

He puts his hand to me, and I dodge it, drawing my skirts away. The fastening of the doors, the closeness of the kitchen, has filled me with a kind of bleak bravado. 'I don't care,' I say, 'to be thought a friend of yours. I don't care to be thought a friend to any of you. I come among you because I must; because Mrs Sucksby wills it, and I haven't life left in me to thwart her. For the rest, remember this: I loathe you all.'

And I sit, not in the empty place beside him, but in the great rocking-chair, at the head of the table. I sit in it and it creaks. John and Dainty gaze quickly at Mrs Sucksby, who blinks at me, two or three times.

'And why not?' she says at last, forcing a laugh. 'You make yourself comfy, my dear. I'll take this hard old chair here, do me good.' She sits and wipes her mouth. 'Mr Ibbs not about?'

'Gone off on a job,' says John. 'Took Charley Wag.'

She nods. 'And all my infants sleeping?'

'Gentleman give 'em a dose, half an hour ago.'

'Good boy, good boy. Keep it nice and quiet.' She gazes at me. 'All right, Miss Lilly? Like a spot of tea, perhaps?' I do not answer, but rock in my chair, very slowly. 'Or, coffee?' She wets her lips. 'Make it coffee, then. Dainty, hot up some water.—Like a cake, dear girl, to chase it down with? Shall John slip out and fetch one? Don't care for cakes?'

'There's nothing,' I say slowly, 'that could be served to me here, that wouldn't be to me as ashes.'

She shakes her head. 'Why, what a mouth you've got, for poetry! As for the cake, now—?' I look away.

Dainty sets about making the coffee. A gaudy clock ticks, and strikes the hour. Richard rolls a cigarette. Tobacco smoke, and smoke from the lamps and spitting candles, already drifts from wall to wall. The walls are brown, and faintly gleam, as if painted with gravy; they are pinned, here and there, with coloured pictures—of cherubs, of roses, of girls on swings—and with curling paper clippings, engravings of sportsmen, horses, dogs and thieves. Beside Mr Ibbs's brazier three portraits—of MR CHUBB, MR YALE and MR BRAMAH—have been pasted to a board of cork; and are much marked by dart-holes.

If I had a dart, I think, I might threaten them with it, make Mrs Sucksby give up her keys. If I had a broken bottle. If I had a knife.

Richard lights his cigarette, narrows his eyes against the smoke and looks me over. 'Pretty dress,' he says. 'Just the colour for you.' He reaches for one of the yellow ribbon trimmings, and I hit his hand away. 'Tut, tut,' he says then. 'Temper not much improved, I fear. We were in hopes that you would sweeten up in confinement. As apples do. And veal-calves.'

'Go to hell, will you?' I say.

He smiles. Mrs Sucksby colours, then laughs. 'Hark at that,' she says. 'Common girl says that, sounds awfully vulgar. Lady says it, sounds almost sweet. Still, dear'—here she leans across the table, drops her voice—'I wish you mightn't speak so nasty.'

I hold her gaze. 'And you think,' I answer levelly, 'your wishes are something to me, do you?'

She flinches, and colours harder; her eyelids flutter and she looks away.

I drink my coffee, then, and don't speak again. Mrs Sucksby sits, softly beating her hands upon the table-top, her brows drawn together into a frown. John and Richard play again at dice, and quarrel over the game. Dainty washes napkins in a bowl of brown water, then sets them before the fire to steam and stink. I close my eyes. My stomach aches and aches. If I had a knife, I think again. Or an axe . . .

But the room is so stiflingly hot, and I am so weary and sick, my head falls back and I sleep. When I wake, it is five o'clock. The dice are put away. Mr Ibbs is returned. Mrs Sucksby is feeding babies, and Dainty is cooking a supper. Bacon, cabbage, crumbling potatoes and bread: they give me a plate and, miserably picking free the strips of fat from the bacon, the crusts from the bread, as I pick bones from my breakfasts of fish, I eat it. Then they put out glasses. 'Care for some tipple, Miss Lilly?' Mrs Sucksby says. 'A stout, or a sherry?'

'A gin?' says Richard, some look of mischief in his eye.

I take a gin. The taste of it is bitter to me, but the sound of the silver spoon, striking the glass as it stirs, brings a vague and nameless comfort.

So that day passes. So pass the days that follow. I go early to bed—am undressed, every time, by Mrs Sucksby, who takes my gown and petticoats and locks them up, then locks up me. I sleep poorly, and wake, each morning, sick and clear-headed and afraid; and I sit in the little gold chair, running over the details of my confinement, working out my plan of escape. For I must escape. I will escape. I'll escape, and go to Sue. What are the names of the men who took her? I cannot remember. Where is their house? I do not know. Never mind, never mind, I shall find it out. First, though, I will go to Briar, beg money from my uncle—he'll still believe himself my uncle, of course—and if he'll give me none, I'll beg from the servants! I'll beg from Mrs Stiles! Or, I'll steal! I'll steal a book from the library, the rarest book, and sell it—!

Or, no, I won't do that.—For the thought of returning to Briar makes me shudder, even now; and it occurs to me in time that I have friends in London, after all. I have Mr Huss and Mr Hawtrey. Mr Huss—who liked to see me climb a staircase. Could I go to him, put myself in his power? I think I could, I am desperate enough . . . Mr Hawtrey, however, was kinder; and invited me to his house, to his shop on Holywell Street.—I think he'll help me. I am sure he will. And I think Holywell Street cannot be far—can it? I do not know, and there are no maps here. But I shall find out the way. Mr Hawtrey will help me, then. Mr Hawtrey will help me find Sue . . .

So my thoughts run, while the dawns of London break grubbily about me; while Mr Ibbs cooks bloaters, while his sister screams, while Gentleman coughs in his bed, while Mrs Sucksby turns in hers, and snores, and sighs.

If only they would not keep me so close! *One day*, I think, each time a door is made fast at my back, *one day they'll forget to lock it. Then I'll run. They'll grow tired of always watching.*—But, they do not. I complain of the thick, exhausted air. I complain of the mounting heat. I ask to go, oftener than I need, to the privy: for the privy lies at the other end of that dark and dusty passage at the back of the house, and shows me daylight. I know I could run from there to freedom, if I had the chance; but the chance does not come: Dainty walks there with me every time, and waits until I come out.—Once I do try to run, and she easily catches me and brings me back; and Mrs Sucksby hits her, for letting me go.

Richard takes me upstairs, and hits me.

'I'm sorry,' he says, as he does it. 'But you know how hard we have worked for this. All you must do is wait, for the bringing of the lawyer. You are good at waiting, you told me once. Why won't you oblige us?'

The blow makes a bruise. Every day I see how it has lightened, thinking, *Before that bruise quite fades, I will escape!*

I pass many hours in silence, brooding on this. I sit, in the kitchen, in the shadows at the edge of lamp-light—*Perhaps they'll forget me*, I think. Sometimes it almost seems that they do: the stir of the house goes on, Dainty and John will kiss and quarrel, the babies will shriek, the men will play at cards and dice. Now and then, other men will come—or boys, or else, more rarely, women and girls—with plunder, to be sold to Mr Ibbs and then sold on. They come, any hour of the day, with astonishing things—gross things, gaudy things—poor stuff, it seems to me, all of it: hats, handkerchiefs, cheap jewels, lengths of lace—once a hank of yellow hair still bound with a ribbon. A tumbling stream of things—not like the books that came to Briar, that came as if sinking to rest on the bed of a viscid sea, through dim and silent fathoms; nor like the things the books described, the things of convenience and pur- pose—the chairs, the pillows, the beds, the curtains, the ropes, the rods . . .

There are no books, here. There is only life in all its awful chaos. And the only purpose the things are made to serve, is the making of money.

And the greatest money-making thing of all, is me.

'Not chilly, dear girl?' Mrs Sucksby will say. 'Not peckish? Why, how warm your brow is! Not taking a fever, I hope? We can't have you sick.' I do not answer. I have heard it all before. I let her tuck rugs about me, I let her sit and chafe my fingers and cheek. 'Are you rather low?' she'll say. 'Just look at them lips. They'd look handsome in a smile, they would. Not going to smile? Not even'—she swallows—'for me? Only glance, dear girl, at the almanack.' She has scored through the days with crosses of black. 'There's a month nearly gone by already, and only two more to come. Then we know what follows! That ain't so long, is it?'

She says it, almost pleadingly; but I gaze steadily into her face— as if to say that a day, an hour, a second, is too long, when passed with her.

'Oh, now!' Her fingers clench about my hand; then slacken, then pat. 'Still seems rather queer to you, does it, sweetheart?' she says. 'Never mind. What can we get you, that will lift your spirits? Hey? A posy of flowers? A bow, for your pretty hair? A trinket box? A singing bird, in a cage?' Perhaps I make some movement. 'Aha! Where's John? John, here's a shilling—it's a bad one, so hand it over fast—nip out and get Miss Lilly a bird in a cage.—Yellow bird, my dear, or blue?—No matter, John, so long as it's pretty . . .'

She winks. John goes, and returns in half an hour with a finch in a wicker basket. They fuss about that, then. They hang it from a beam, they shake it to make it flutter; Charley Wag, the dog, leaps and whines beneath it. It will not sing, however—the room is too dark—it will only beat and pluck at its wings and bite the bars of its cage. At last they forget it. John takes to feeding it the blue heads of matches—he says he plans, in time, to make it swallow a long wick, and then to ignite it.

Of Sue, no-one speaks at all. Once, Dainty looks at me as she puts out our suppers, and scratches her ear.

'Funny thing,' she says, 'how Sue ain't come back from the country, yet. Ain't it?'

Mrs Sucksby glances at Richard, at Mr Ibbs, and then at me. She wets her mouth. 'Look here,' she says to Dainty, 'I haven't wanted to talk about it, but you might as well know it, now. The truth is, Sue ain't coming back, not ever. That last little bit of business that Gentleman left her to see to had money in. More money than was meant for her share. She's up and cut, Dainty, with the cash.'

Dainty's mouth falls open. 'No! Sue Trinder? What was like your own daughter?—Johnny!' John chooses that moment to come down, for his supper. 'Johnny, you ain't going to guess what! Sue's took all of Mrs Sucksby's money, and that's why she ain't come back. Done a flit. Just about broke Mrs Sucksby's heart. If we see her, we got to kill her.'

'Done a flit? Sue Trinder?' He snorts. 'She ain't got the nerve.'

'Well, she done it.'

'She done it,' says Mrs Sucksby, with another glance at me, 'and I don't want to hear her name said in this house. That's all.'

'Sue Trinder, turned out a sharper!' says John.

'That's bad blood for you,' says Richard. He also looks at me. 'Shows up in queer ways.'

'What did I just say?' says Mrs Sucksby hoarsely. 'I won't have her name said.' She lifts her arm, and John falls silent. But he shakes his head and gives a whistle. Then after a moment, he laughs.

'More meat for us, though, ain't it?' he says, as he fills his plate. '—Or would be, if it wasn't for the lady there.'

Mrs Sucksby sees him scowling at me; and leans and hits him.

After that, if the men and women who come to the house ask after Sue, they are taken aside and told, like John and Dainty, that she has turned out wicked, double-crossed Mrs Sucksby and broken her heart. They all say the same: 'Sue Trinder? Who'd have thought her so fly? That's the mother, that is, coming out in the child . . .' They shake their heads, look sorry. But it seems to me, too, that they forget her quickly enough. It seems to me that even John and Dainty forget her. It is a short-memoried house, after all. It is a

short-memoried district. Many times I wake in the night to the
sound of footsteps, the creak of wheels—a man is running, a family
taking flight, quietly, in darkness. The woman with the bandaged
face, who nurses her baby on the step of the house with the shutters
with the heart-shaped holes, disappears; her place is taken by
another—who, in her turn, moves on, to be replaced by another,
who drinks. What's Sue, to them?

What's Sue, to me? I'm afraid, here, to remember the pressing
of her mouth, the sliding of her hand. But I'm afraid, too, of forgetting. I wish I could dream of her. I never do. Sometimes I
take out the picture of the woman I supposed my mother, and
look for her features there—her eyes, her pointed chin. Mrs
Sucksby sees me do it. She watches, fretfully. Finally she takes the
picture away.

'Don't you be thinking,' she says, 'on things that are done and
can't be changed. All right, dear girl? You think of the time to
come.'

She imagines I brood upon my past. But I am still brooding on my
future. I am still watching keys as they are turned—soon one will be
left in a lock, I know it. I am watching Dainty and John, Mr Ibbs—
they are growing too used to me. They'll turn careless, they'll
forget. *Soon*, I think. *Soon, Maud.*

So I think; until this happens.

Richard takes to leaving the house each day, not saying where he
is going. He has no money, and will have none until the bringing of
the lawyer: I think he goes only to walk the dusty streets, or to sit in
the parks; I think the heat and the closeness of the Borough kitchen
stifles him as much as it stifles me. One day, however, he goes, but
returns in an hour. The house is quiet, for once: Mr Ibbs and John
are out, and Dainty is sleeping in a chair. Mrs Sucksby lets him into
the kitchen, and he throws off his hat and kisses her cheek. His face
is flushed and his eyes are gleaming.

'Well, what do you think?' he says.

'Dear boy, I can't imagine! Have all your horses come up at
once?'

'Better than that,' he says. He reaches for me. 'Maud? What do you think? Come, out of the shadows. Don't look so fierce! Save that, till you've heard my news. It concerns you, rather.'

He has seized my chair and begun to haul me closer to the table. I shake him off. 'Concerns me, how?' I say, moodily. I have been sitting, thinking over the shape of my life.

'You'll see. Look here.' He puts his hand to his waistcoat pocket and draws something out. A paper. He waves it.

'A bond, dear boy?' says Mrs Sucksby, stepping to his side.

'A letter,' he says, 'from—well, guess who? Will you guess, Maud?' I say nothing. He pulls a face. 'Won't you play? Shall I give you a clue? It is someone you know. A friend, very dear.'

My heart gives a lurch. 'Sue!' I say at once. But he jerks his head, and snorts.

'Not *her*. You think they give them paper, where she is?' He glances at Dainty; who opens and closes her eyes, and then sleeps on. 'Not *her*,' he says again, more quietly. 'I mean, another friend of yours. You won't guess?'

I turn my face. 'Why should I? You mean to tell me, don't you?'

He waits another moment; then: 'Mr Lilly,' he says. 'Your uncle, that was.—Aha!' I have started. 'You *are* interested!'

'Let me see,' I say. Perhaps my uncle is searching for me, after all.

'Now, now.' He holds the letter high. 'It has my name upon it, not yours.'

'Let me see!'

I rise, pull down his arm, see a line of ink; then push him away.

'That's not my uncle's hand,' I say—so disappointed, I could strike him.

'I never said it was,' says Richard. 'The letter's from him, but sent by another: his steward, Mr Way.'

'Mr Way?'

'More curious still, hmm? Well, you shall understand that, when you read it. Here.' He unfolds the paper and hands it to me. 'Read this side, first. It's a postscript; and explains, at least—what I've always thought so queer—why we've heard nothing from Briar, till now . . .'

The hand is cramped. The ink is smeared. I tilt the paper to catch what light I can; then read.

Dear Sir.—I found today among my master's private papers, this letter, & do suppose he meant it to be sent; only, he fell into a grave indisposition shortly after having wrote it, sir, which indisposition he continues in to this day.—Mrs Stiles & me did think at first, that this was through his niece having run off in such a scandalous manner; though we beg leave to notice, sir, that his words herein suggest him not to have been overly astonished by that deed; as, begging leave again sir, no more were we.—We send this respectfully, sir, and presume to hope it finds you cheerful.—Mr Martin Way, Steward of Briar.

I look up, but say nothing. Richard sees my expression and smiles. 'Read the rest,' he says. I turn the paper over. The letter is short, and dated 3rd of May—seven weeks ago, now. It says this.

To Mr Richard Rivers, from Christopher Lilly, Esq.—Sir. I suppose you have taken my niece, Maud Lilly. I wish you joy of her! Her mother was a strumpet, and she has all her mother's instincts, if not her face. The check to the progress of my work will be severe; but I take comfort in my loss, from this: that I fancy you, sir, a man who knows the proper treating of a whore.—C.L.

I read it, two or three times; then read it again; then let it fall. Mrs Sucksby instantly takes it up, to read herself. As she labours over the words, she grows flushed. When she has finished, she gives a cry:

'That blackguard! Oh!'

Her cry wakes Dainty. 'Who, Mrs Sucksby? Who?' she says.

'A wicked man, that's all. A wicked man, who is ill, as he ought to be. No-one you know. Go back to sleep.' She reaches for me. 'Oh, my dear—'

'Leave me alone,' I say.

The letter has upset me, more than I should have believed. I

don't know if it is the words that have wounded me most; or the
final proof they seem to give, to Mrs Sucksby's story. But I cannot
bear to be watched by her, and by Richard, with my feelings in such
a stir. I walk as far from them as I may—some two or three steps—
to the brown kitchen wall; then I walk from there to another wall,
and from there to a door; and I seize and vainly turn the handle.

'Let me out,' I say.

Mrs Sucksby comes to me. She makes to reach, not for the door,
but for my face. I push her off—go quickly, to the second door, and
then the third.—'Let me out! Let me out!' She follows.

'Dear girl,' she says, 'don't let yourself be upset by that old villain. Why, he ain't worth your tears!'

'Will you let me out?'

'Let you out, to where? Ain't everything here, that you need
now? Ain't everything here, or coming? Think of them jewels, them
gowns—'

She has come close again. Again, I push her away. I step back to
the gravy-coloured wall, and put my hand to it—a fist—and beat
and beat it. Then I look up. Before my eyes is the almanack, its
pages swarming with crosses of black. I catch hold of it, and pluck
it from its pin. 'Dear girl—' Mrs Sucksby says again. I turn and
throw it at her.

But afterwards, I fall weeping; and when the fit of tears has passed,
I think I am changed. My spirit has gone. The letter has taken it
from me. The almanack goes back upon the wall, and I let it stay
there. It grows steadily blacker, as we all inch nearer to our fates.
The season advances. June grows warm, then even warmer. The
house begins to be filled with flies. They drive Richard to a fury: he
pursues them with a slipper, red-faced and sweating.—'You know I
am a gentleman's son?' he will say. 'Would you think it, to look at
me now? Would you?'

I do not answer. I have begun, like him, to long for the coming of
Sue's birthday in August. I will say anything they wish, I think, to
any kind of solicitor or lawyer. But I pass my days in a sort of restless lethargy; and at night—for it is too hot to sleep—at night I

stand at the narrow window in Mrs Sucksby's room, gazing blankly at the street.

'Come away from there, sweetheart,' Mrs Sucksby will murmur if she wakes. They say there is cholera in the Borough. 'Who knows but you won't take a fever, from the draught?'

May one take a fever, from a draught of fœtid air? I lie down at her side until she sleeps; then go back to the window, press my face to the gap between the sashes, breathe deeper.

I almost forget that I mean to escape. Perhaps they sense it. For at last they leave me, one afternoon—at the start of July, I think— with only Dainty to guard me.

'You watch her close,' Mrs Sucksby tells her, drawing on gloves. 'Anything happen to her, I'll kill you.' Me, she kisses. 'All right, my dear? I shan't be gone an hour. Bring you back a present, shall I?'

I do not answer. Dainty lets her out, then pockets the key. She sits, draws a lamp across the table-top, and takes up work. Not washing napkins—for there are fewer babies, now: Mrs Sucksby has begun to find homes for them, and the house is daily growing stiller—but the pulling of silk stitches from stolen handkerchiefs. She does it listlessly, however. 'Dull work,' she says, seeing me look. 'Sue used to do this. Care to try?'

I shake my head, let my eyelids fall; and presently, she yawns. I hear that; and am suddenly wide awake. If she will sleep, I think, I might try the doors—steal the key from her pocket! She yawns again. I begin to sweat. The clock ticks off the minutes—fifteen, twenty, twenty-five. Half an hour. I am dressed in the violet gown and white silk slippers. I have no hat, no money—never mind, never mind. Mr Hawtrey will give you that.

Sleep, Dainty. Dainty, sleep. Sleep, sleep . . . *Sleep, damn you!*

But she only yawns, and nods. The hour is almost up.

'Dainty,' I say.

She jumps. 'What is it?'

'I'm afraid— I'm afraid I must visit the privy.'

She puts down her work, pulls a face. 'Must you? Right now, this minute?'

'Yes.' I place my hand on my stomach. 'I think I am sick.'

She rolls her eyes. 'Never knew a girl for sickness, like you. Is that what they call a lady's constitution?'

'I think it must be. I'm sorry, Dainty. Will you open the door?'

'I'll go with you, though.'

'You needn't. You might stay at your sewing, if you like . . .'

'Mrs Sucksby says I must go with you, every time; else I'll catch it. Here.'

She sighs, and stretches. The silk of her gown is stained beneath the arms, the stain edged white. She takes out the key, unlocks the door, leads me into the passage. I go slowly, watching the lurching of her back. I remember having run from her before, and how she caught me: I know that, even if I might hit her aside now, she would only rise again at once and chase me. I might knock her head against the bricks . . . But I imagine doing it, and my wrists grow weak, I don't think I could.

'Go on,' she says, when I hesitate. 'Why, what's up?'

'Nothing.' I catch hold of the privy door and draw it to me, slowly. 'You needn't wait,' I say.

'No, I'll wait.' She leans against the wall. 'Do me good, take the air.'

The air is warm and foul. In the privy it is warmer, and fouler. But I step inside and close the door and bolt it; then look about me. There is a little window, no bigger than my head, its broken pane stopped up with rag. There are spiders, and flies. The privy seat is cracked and smeared. I stand and think, perhaps for a minute. 'All right?' calls Dainty. I do not answer. The floor is earth, stamped hard. The walls are powdery white. From a wire hang strips of news-print. LADIES' AND GENTLEMEN'S CAST-OFF CLOTHING, IN GOOD OR INFERIOR CONDITION, WANTED FOR— WELSH MUTTON & NEW-LAID EGGS—

Think, Maud.

I turn to face the door, put my mouth to a gap in the wood.

'Dainty,' I say quietly.

'What is it?'

'Dainty, I am not well. You must fetch me something.'

'What?' She tries the door. 'Come out, miss.'

'I can't. I daren't. Dainty, you must go to the drawer, in the chest in my room upstairs. Will you? There is something there. Will you? Oh, I wish you would hurry! Oh, how it rushes! I am afraid of the men coming back—'

'Oh,' she says, understanding me at last. She drops her voice. 'Caught you out, has it?'

'Will you go for me, Dainty?'

'But I'm not to leave you, miss!'

'I must keep here, then, until Mrs Sucksby comes! But say that John, or Mr Ibbs, should come first! Or say I swoon? And the door is bolted! What will Mrs Sucksby think of us, then?'

'Oh, Lord,' she mutters. And then: 'In the chest of drawers, you say?'

'The top-most drawer, on the right. Will you hurry? If I might just make myself neat, and then lie down. I always take it so badly—'

'All right.'

'Be quick!'

'All right!'

Her voice is fading. I press my ear to the wood, hear her feet, the opening and swinging back of the kitchen door.—I slide the bolt and run. I run out of the passage and into the court—I remember this, I remember the nettles, the bricks. Which way from here? There are high walls all about me. But I run further, and the walls give way. There's a dusty path—it was slick with mud, when I came down it before; but I see it, and know it—I know it!—it leads to an alley and this, in turn, leads to another path, which crosses a street and leads me—where? To a road I do not recognise, that runs under the arches of a bridge. I recall the bridge, but remember it nearer, lower. I recall a high, dead wall. There is no wall here.

No matter. Keep going. Keep the house at your back, and run. Take wider roads now: the lanes and alleys twist, and are dark, you must not get caught in them. Run, run. No matter that the sky seems vast and awful to you. No matter that London is loud. No matter that there are people here—no matter that they stare—no matter that their clothes are worn and faded, and your gown bright;

that their heads are covered, yours bare. No matter that your slippers are silk, that your feet are cut by every stone and cinder—

So I whip myself along. Only the traffic checks me, the rushing horses and wheels: at every crossing I pause, then cast myself into the mass of cabs and waggons; and I think it is only my haste, my distraction—that, and perhaps the vividness of my dress—that makes the drivers pull at their reins and keep from running me down. On, on, I go. I think once a dog barks at me, and snaps at my skirt. I think boys run beside me, for a time—two boys, or three—shrieking to see me stagger. 'You,' I say, holding my hand against my side, 'will you tell me, where is Holywell Street? Which way, to Holywell Street?'—but at the sound of my voice, they fall back.

I go more slowly then. I cross a busier road. The buildings are grander here—and yet, two streets beyond them the houses are shabby. Which way must I go? I will ask again, I will ask in a moment; for now, I will only walk, put streets and streets between myself and Mrs Sucksby, Richard, Mr Ibbs. What matter if I grow lost? I am lost already . . .

Then I cross the mouth of a rising passage of yellow brick and see at the end of it, dark and humped above the tips of broken roofs, its gold cross gleaming, the church of St Paul's. I know it, from illustrations; and I think Holywell Street is near it. I turn, pick up my skirts, make for it. The passage smells badly; but the church seems close. So close, it seems! The brick turns green, the smell grows worse. I climb, then suddenly sink, emerge in open air and almost stumble. I have expected a street, a square. Instead, I am at the top of a set of crooked stairs, leading down to filthy water. I have reached the shore of the river. St Paul's is close, after all; but the whole of the width of the Thames is flowing between us.

I stand and gaze at it, in a sort of horror, a sort of awe. I remember walking beside the Thames, at Briar. I remember seeing it seem to fret and worry at its banks: I thought it longed—as I did—to quicken, to spread. I did not know it would spread to this. It flows, like poison. Its surface is littered with broken matter—with hay, with wood, with weed, with paper, with tearings of cloth, with cork and tilting bottles. It moves, not as a river moves, but as a sea: it heaves. And where it breaks, against the hulls of boats, and where it is thrown, upon the shore, and about the stairs and the walls and wooden piers that rise from it, it froths like sour milk.

It is an agony of water and of waste; but there are men upon it, confident as rats—pulling the oars of rowing-boats, tugging at sails. And here and there, at the river's edge—bare-legged, bent-backed—are women, girls and boys, picking their way through the churning litter like gleaners in a field.

They don't look up, and do not see me, though I stand for a minute and watch them wade. All along the shore I have come to, however, are warehouses, with working men about them; and presently, as I become aware of them, they also spot me—spot my gown, I suppose—first stare, then signal and call. That jerks me out of my daze. I turn—go back along the yellow passage, take up the road again. I have seen the bridge that I must cross to reach St Paul's, but it seems to me that I am lower than I ought to be, and I cannot find the road that will lead me up: the streets I am walking now are narrow, unpaved, still reeking of dirty water. There are men upon them, too—men of the boats and warehouses, who, like the others, try to catch my eye, whistle and sometimes call; though they do not touch me. I put my hand before my face, and go on faster. At last I find a boy, dressed like a servant. 'Which way is the bridge,' I say, 'to the other shore?' He points me out a flight of steps, and stares as I climb them.

Everybody stares—men, women, children—even here, where the road is busy again, they stare. I think of tearing off a fold of skirt to cover my naked head. I think of begging a coin. If I knew what coin to beg for, how much a hat would cost me, where it might be bought, I would do it. But I know nothing, nothing; and so simply walk on. The soles of my slippers I think are beginning to tear. *Don't mind it, Maud. If you start to mind it, you will weep.* Then the road ahead of me begins to rise, and I see again the gleam of water. The bridge, at last!—that makes me walk quicker. But walking quicker makes the slippers tear more; and after a moment, I am obliged to stop. There is a break in the wall at the start of the bridge

with, set into it, a shallow stone bench. Hung up beside it is a belt
of cork—meant for throwing, it says upon a sign, to those in diffi-
culties upon the river.

I sit. The bridge is higher than I imagined it. I have never been so
high! The thought makes me dizzy. I touch my broken shoe. May a
woman nurse her foot on a public bridge? I do not know. The traffic passes, swift and unbroken, like roaring water. Suppose Richard
should come? Again, I cover my face. A moment, and I'll go on.
The sun is hot. A moment, to find my breath. I close my eyes.
Now, when people stare, I cannot see them.

Then someone comes and stands before me, and speaks.

'I'm afraid you're unwell.'

I open my eyes. A man, rather aged. A stranger to me. I let my
hand fall.

'Don't be afraid,' he says. Perhaps I look bewildered. 'I didn't
mean to surprise you.'

He touches his hat, makes a sort of bow. He might be a friend of
my uncle's. His voice is a gentleman's voice, and his collar is white.
He smiles, then studies me closer. His face is kind. '*Are* you unwell?'

'Will you help me?' I say. He hears my voice and his look
changes.

'Of course,' he says. 'What is it? Are you hurt?'

'Not hurt,' I say. 'But I have been made to suffer dreadfully. I—'
I cast a look at the coaches and waggons upon the bridge. 'I'm
afraid,' I say, 'of certain people. Will you help me? Oh, I wish you
would say you will!'

'I have said it, already. But, this is extraordinary! And you, a
lady— Will you come with me? You must tell me all your story; I
shall hear it all. Don't try to speak, just yet. Can you rise? I'm afraid
you're injured about the feet. Dear, dear! Let me look for a cab.
That's right.'

He gives me his arm, and I take it and stand. Relief has made me
weak. 'Thank God!' I say. 'Oh, thank God! But, listen to me.' I grip
him harder. 'I have nothing—no money to pay you with—'

'Money?' He puts his hand over mine. 'I should not take it. Don't
think of it!'

'—But I have a friend, who I think will help me. If you'll take me to him?'

'Of course, of course. What else? Come, look, here's what we need.' He leans into the road, raises his arm: a cab pulls out of the stream of traffic and halts before us. The gentleman seizes the door and draws it back. The cab is covered, and dark. 'Take care,' he says. 'Can you manage? Take care. The step is rather high.'

'Thank God!' I say again, lifting my foot. He comes behind me as I do it.

'That's right,' he says. And then: 'Why look, how prettily you climb!'

I stop, with my foot upon the step. He puts his hand upon my waist. 'Go on,' he says, urging me into the coach.

I step back.

'After all,' I say quickly, 'I think I should walk. Will you tell me the way?'

'The day is too hot to walk. You are too weary. Go on.'

His hand is upon me still. He presses harder. I twist away and we almost struggle.

'Now, then!' he says, smiling.

'I have changed my mind.'

'Come, now.'

'Let go of me.'

'Do you wish to cause a fuss? Come, now. I know a house—'

'A house? Haven't I told you that I want only to see my friend?'

'Well, he'll like you better, I think, when you have washed your hands and changed your stockings and taken a tea. Or else—who knows?—when you have done those things you may find you like *me* better.—Hmm?'

His face is still kind, he still smiles; but he takes my wrist and moves his thumb across it, and tries, again, to hand me into the coach. We struggle properly, now. No-one tries to intervene. From the other vehicles in the road I suppose we are quite hidden. The men and women passing upon the bridge look once, then turn their heads.

There is the driver, however. I call to him. 'Can't you see?' I call.

'There's been a mistake here. This man is insulting me.'—The man lets me go, then. I move further about the coach, still calling up. 'Will you take me? Will you take me, alone? I shall find someone to pay you, I give you my word, when we arrive.'

The driver looks me over blankly as I speak. When he learns I have no money, he turns his head and spits.

'No fare, no passage,' he says.

The man has come close again. 'Come on,' he says—not smiling, now. 'There's no need for this. What are you playing at? It's clear you're in some sort of fix. Shouldn't you like the stockings, the tea?'

But I still call up to the driver. 'Will you tell me, then,' I say, 'which way I must walk? I must reach Holywell Street. Will you tell me, which way I must take, for there?'

He hears the name and snorts—in scorn, or laughter, I cannot tell. But he raises his whip. 'That way,' he says, gesturing over the bridge; 'then westwards, by Fleet Street.'

'Thank you.' I begin to walk. The man reaches for me. 'Let go of me,' I say.

'You don't mean it.'

'Let go!'

I almost shriek it. He falls back. 'Go on, then!' he says. 'You damn little teaser.'

I walk, as quickly as I can. I almost run. But then, after a moment, the cab comes beside me and slows to match my pace. The gentleman looks out. His face has changed again.

'I'm sorry,' he says, coaxingly. 'Come up. I'm sorry. Will you come? I'll take you to your friend, I swear it. Look here. Look here.' He shows me a coin. 'I'll give you this. Come up. You mustn't go to Holywell Street, they are bad men there—not at all like me. Come now, I know you're a lady. Come, I'll be kind . . .'

So he calls and murmurs, half the length of the bridge; until finally a line of waggons forms behind the crawling cab, and the driver shouts that he must go on. Then the man draws back, puts up his window with a bang; the cab pulls away. I let out my breath. I have begun to shake. I should like to stop, to rest; I dare not, now.

I leave the bridge: here the road meets another, more busy than those on the southern shore; but more anonymous too, I think. I am grateful for that, though the crowds—the crowds are terrible. Never mind, never mind, push through them. Go on. Westwards, as the driver directed.

Now the street changes again. It is lined with houses with bulging windows—*shops*, I understand them to be, at last: for there are goods on show, marked up with prices on cards. There are breads, there are medicines. There are gloves. There are shoes and hats.—Oh, for a little money! I think of the coin the gentleman offered, from the window of the coach: should I have seized it, and run? Too late to wonder it now. No matter. Go on. Here is a church, parting the road like the column of a bridge parts water. Which side ought I to take? A woman passes, bare-headed like me: I catch her arm, ask her the way. She points it out and then, like everyone else, stands staring as I take it.

But here is Holywell Street at last!—Only, now I hesitate. How have I imagined it? Not like this, perhaps—not so narrow, so crooked, so dark. The London day is still hot, still bright; in turning into Holywell Street, however, I seem to step into twilight. But the twilight is good, after all: it hides my face, and robs my gown of its colours. I walk further. The way grows narrower. The ground is dusty, broken, unpaved. There are shops, lit up, on either side of me: some with lines of tattered clothes hung before them, some with broken chairs and empty picture-frames and coloured glasses spilling from them, in heaps; the most, however, selling books. I hesitate again, when I see that. I have not handled a book since I left Briar; and now, to come so suddenly upon them, in such numbers; to see them laid, face-up, like loaves in trays, or piled, haphazardly, in baskets; to see them torn, and foxed, and bleached—marked up *2d.*, *3d.*, THIS BOX *1s.*—quite unnerves me. I stop, and watch as a man picks idly through a box of coverless volumes and takes one up. *The Mousetrap of Love.*—I know it, I have read that title so many times to my uncle I know it almost by heart!

Then the man lifts his head and finds me watching; and I walk on. More shops, more books, more men; and finally a window, a little brighter than the rest. The display is of prints, hung up on strings. The glass has Mr Hawtrey's name upon it, in letters of flaking gold. I see it, and shake so hard I almost stumble.

Inside, the shop is small and cramped. I have not expected that. The walls are all given over to books and prints, and there are cabinets, besides. Three or four men stand at them, each leafing rapidly and intently through some album or book: they don't look up when the door is opened; but when I take a step and my skirts give a rustle, they all turn their heads, see me, and openly stare. But I am used to stares, by now. At the rear of the shop is a little writing-table, with a youth sitting at it, dressed in a waistcoat and sleeves. He stares, as they do—then, when he sees me advancing, gets up.

'What are you looking for?' he says.

I swallow. My mouth is dry.

I say, quietly, 'I'm looking for Mr Hawtrey. I wish to speak with Mr Hawtrey.'

He hears my voice, and blinks; the customers shift a little, and look me over again. 'Mr Hawtrey,' he says, his tone a little changed. 'Mr Hawtrey doesn't work in the shop. You oughtn't to have come to the shop. Have you got an appointment?'

'Mr Hawtrey knows me,' I say. 'I don't need an appointment.'

He glances at the customers. He says, 'What's your business with him?'

'It's private,' I say. 'Will you take me to him? Will you bring him to me?'

There must be something to my look, however, or my voice. He grows more guarded, steps back.

'I'm not sure, after all, if he's in,' he says. 'Really, you oughtn't to have come to the shop. The shop is for selling books and prints—do you know what kind? Mr Hawtrey's rooms are upstairs.'

There's a door, at his back. 'Will you let me go to him?' I say.

He shakes his head. 'You may send up a card, something like that.'

'I don't have a card,' I say. 'But give me a paper, and I'll write him out my name. He'll come, when he reads it. Will you give me a paper?'

He does not move. He says again, 'I don't believe he's in the house.'

'Then I'll wait, if I must,' I say.

'You cannot wait here!'

'Then I think,' I answer, 'you must have an office, some room like that; and I will wait there.'

He looks again at the customers; picks up a pencil and puts it down.

'If you will?' I say.

He makes a face. Then he finds me a slip of paper and a pen. 'But you shan't,' he says, 'be able to wait, if it turns out he's not in.' I nod. 'Put your name on there,' he says, pointing.

I begin to write. Then I remember what Richard told me once— how the booksellers speak of me, in the shops of London. I am afraid to write, *Maud Lilly*. I am afraid the youth will see. At last— remembering something else—I put this: *Galatea*.

I fold it, and hand it to him. He opens the door, whistles into the passage beyond. He listens, then whistles again. There come footsteps. He leans and murmurs, gestures to me. I wait.

And, as I do, one of the customers closes his album and catches my eye. 'Don't mind him,' he says softly, meaning the youth. 'He supposes you gay, that's all. Anyone can see, though, that you're a lady . . .' He looks me over, then nods to the shelves of books. 'You like them, hmm?' he says, in a different tone. 'Of course you do. Why shouldn't you?'

I say nothing, do nothing. The youth steps back.

'We're seeing,' he says, 'if he's in.'

There are pictures behind his head, pinned to the wall in wax-paper wrappers: a girl on a swing, showing her legs; a girl in a boat, about to slip; a girl falling, falling from the breaking branch of a tree . . . I close my eyes. He calls to one of the men: 'Do you wish to buy that book, sir—?'

Presently, however, there come more footsteps, and the door is opened again.

It is Mr Hawtrey.

He looks shorter, and slighter, than I remember him. His coat and trousers are creased. He stands in the passage in some agitation, does not come into the shop—meets my gaze, but does not smile— looks about me, as if to be sure I am alone; then beckons me to him. The youth steps back to let me pass. 'Mr Hawtrey—' I say. He shakes his head, however; waits until the door is closed behind me before he will speak. What he says then—in a whisper so fierce it is almost a hiss—is:

'Good God! Is it you? Have you really come here, to me?'

I say nothing, only stand with my eyes on his. He puts his hand, in distraction, to his head. Then he takes my arm. 'This way,' he says, leading me to a set of stairs. The steps have boxes upon them. 'Be careful. Be careful,' he says, as we climb them. And then, at the top: 'In here.'

There are three rooms, set up for the printing and binding of books. In one, two men work, loading type; another, I think, is Mr Hawtrey's own office. The third is small, and smells strongly of glue. It's in there that he shows me. The tables are piled with papers—loose papers, ragged at the edges: the leaves of unfinished books. The floor is bare and dusty. One wall—the wall to the type-setters' room—has frosted glass panels in it. The men are just visible, bending over their work.

There is a single chair, but he does not ask me to sit. He closes the door and stands before it. He takes out a handkerchief and wipes his face. His face is yellowish-white.

'Good God,' he says again. And then: 'Forgive me. Forgive me. It's only the surprise of the thing.'

He says it, more kindly; and I hear him and half turn away.

'I'm sorry,' I say. My voice is not steady. 'I'm afraid I will weep. I have not come to you to weep.'

'You may weep, if you like!' he says, with a glance at the frosted glass.

But I will not weep. He watches me struggling against my tears for a moment, then shakes his head.

'My dear,' he says gently at last. 'What have you done?'

'Don't ask me.'

'You have run away.'

'From my uncle, yes.'

'From your husband, I think.'

'My husband?' I swallow. 'Do you know, then, of that?'

He shrugs, colours, looks away.

I say, 'You think me wrong. You do not know what I have been made to suffer! Don't worry'—for he has lifted his eyes to glance, again, at the panels of glass—'don't worry, I shan't grow wild. You may think what you like of me, I don't care. But you must help me. Will you?'

'My dear—'

'You will. You must. I have nothing. I need money, a house to stay in. You used to like to say you would make me welcome—'

Despite myself, my voice is rising.

'Be calmer,' he says—lifting his hands as if to soothe me; but not moving from his place at the door. 'Be calmer. You know how queer this will look? Do you? What are my staff to think? A girl comes asking for me urgently, sending up a riddling name . . .' He laughs, not happily. 'What would my daughters say, my wife?'

'I am sorry.'

Again he wipes his face. He lets out his breath. 'I wish you would tell me,' he says, 'why you have come, to me. You mustn't think I will take your part against your uncle. I never liked to see him keep you so meanly, but he mustn't know you've come here. Nor must you think—is it what you are hoping?—that I'll help you back into his favours. He has quite cast you off, you know. Besides that, he is ill—seriously ill—over this business. Did you know that?'

I shake my head. 'My uncle is nothing to me, now.'

'But he is something to me, you understand. If he should hear of your coming—'

'He will not.'

'Well.' He sighs. Then his face grows troubled again. 'But to come to me! To come here!' And he looks me over, takes in my gaudy dress and gloves—which are filthy; my hair—which I think is tangled; my face—which must be dusty, lustreless, white. 'I should hardly have known you,' he says, still frowning, 'you seem so changed. Where is your coat, and your hat?'

'There was not time—'

He looks appalled. 'Did you come, like this?' He squints at the hem of my skirt; then he sees my feet, and starts. 'Why, look at your slippers! Your feet are bleeding! Did you leave, without shoes?'

'I must. I have nothing!'

'Not shoes?'

'No. Not so much as that.'

'Rivers keeps you without shoes?'

He does not believe it. 'If I might only,' I say, 'make you know—' But he is not listening. He is looking about him, as if seeing for the first time the tables, the piles of paper. He takes up a few blank sheets, begins hurriedly to cover up the naked print.

'You oughtn't to have come here,' he says, as he does it. 'Look at this! Look at this!'

I catch sight of a line of print. '—*you shall have enough, I warrant you, and I shall whip, whip*—' 'Do you try and hide it,' I say, 'from me? I have seen worse at Briar. Have you forgotten?'

'This is not Briar. You don't understand. How could you? You were among gentlemen, there. It is Rivers I blame for this. He ought—having taken you—at least to have kept you closer. He saw what you were.'

'You don't know,' I say. 'You don't know how he's used me!'

'I don't want to know! It is not my place to know! Don't tell me.—Oh, only look at yourself! Do you know how you will have seemed, upon the streets? You can't have come unnoticed, surely?'

I gaze down at my skirt, my slippers. 'There was a man,' I say, 'upon the bridge. I thought he meant to help me. But he meant only—' My voice begins to shake.

'You see?' he says then. 'You see? Suppose a policeman should have seen you, and followed you here? Do you know what would happen to me—to my staff, to my stock—if the police were to come down heavily upon us? They might, for such a matter as this.—Oh, God, only look at your feet! Are they bleeding, truly?'

He helps me into the chair, then gazes about him. 'There's a sink,' he says, 'next door. Wait here, will you?' He goes off, to the room with the typesetters in it. I see them lift their heads, hear his voice.—I don't know what he must tell them. I don't care. In sitting, I have grown tired; and the soles of my feet, which until now have been almost numb, have begun to smart. The room has no window of its own, and no chimney, and the smell of glue seems stronger. I have come close to one of the tables: I lean upon it, and gaze across it—at the piles of pages, untrimmed, unsewn, some of them disturbed or concealed by Mr Hawtrey. '—*and I shall whip, whip, whip, your backside till the blood runs down your heels*—' The print is new, and black; but the paper is poor, the ink has feathered. What is the fount? I know it, but—it troubles me—I cannot name it.

'—*so, so, so, so, so, you like the birch, do you?*'

Mr Hawtrey returns. He has a cloth, and a bowl, half-filled with water; also a glass, with water for me to drink.

'Here you are,' he says, putting the bowl before me, wetting the cloth and handing it to me; then glancing nervously away. 'Can you do it? Just enough to take the blood away, for now . . .'

The water is cold. When I have wiped my feet I wet the cloth again and, for a second, sit and hold it to my face. Mr Hawtrey looks round and sees me do it. 'You're not feverish?' he says. 'You're not ill?'—'I am only warm,' I say. He nods, and comes and takes the bowl. Then he gives me the glass, and I drink a little of it. 'Very good,' he says.

I look again at the leaves of print upon the table; but the name of the fount escapes me, still. Mr Hawtrey checks his watch. Then he puts his hand to his mouth and bites at the skin of his thumb, and frowns.

I say, 'You are good, to help me. I think other men would blame me.'

'No, no. Haven't I said? It is Rivers I blame. Never mind. Tell me, now. Be honest with me. What money have you, upon you now?'

'I have none.'

'No money at all?'

'I have only this gown. But we might sell it, I think? I should sooner take a plainer one, anyway.'

'Sell your gown?' His frown grows deeper. 'Don't speak so oddly, will you? When you go back—'

'Go back? To Briar?'

'To Briar? I mean, to your husband.'

'To him?' I look at him in amazement. 'I cannot go back to him! It has taken me two months to escape him!'

He shakes his head. 'Mrs Rivers—' he says. I shudder.

'Don't call me that,' I say, 'I beg you.'

'Again, so odd! What ought I to call you, if not that?'

'Call me Maud. You asked me, just now, what I have that is mine. I have that name; that, and nothing else.'

He makes some movement with his hand. 'Don't be foolish,' he says. 'Listen to me, now. I am sorry for you. You have had some quarrel, haven't you—?'

I laugh—so sharply, he starts; and the two typesetters look up. He sees them do it, then turns back to me.

'Will you be reasonable?' he says quietly, warningly.

But how can I be that?

'A quarrel,' I say. 'You think it a quarrel. You think I have run on bleeding feet, half-way across London, for that? You know nothing. You cannot guess what danger I am in, what coils—! But, I can't tell you. It's too great a thing.'

'What is?'

'A secret thing. A scheme. I cannot say. I cannot— Oh!' I have lowered my gaze, and it has fallen again upon the pages of print. *you like the birch, do you?* 'What is this type?' I say. 'Will you tell me?'

He swallows. 'This type?' he says, his voice quite changed.

'This fount.'

For a second he does not answer. Then: 'Clarendon,' he says, quietly.

Clarendon. Clarendon. I knew it, after all. I continue to gaze at the paper—I think I put my fingers to the print—until Mr Hawtrey comes and places a blank sheet upon it, as he did with the others.

'Don't look there,' he says. 'Don't stare so! What is the matter with you? I think you must be ill.'

'I am not ill,' I answer. 'I am only tired.' I close my eyes. 'I wish I might stay here, and sleep.'

'Stay here?' he says. 'Stay here, in my shop? Are you *mad*?'

At sound of that word I open my eyes, and meet his gaze; he colours, looks quickly away. I say again, more steadily, 'I am only tired.' But he does not answer. He puts his hand to his mouth and begins to bite, again, at the skin of his thumb; and he watches me, carefully, cautiously, from the side of his eye. 'Mr Hawtrey—' I say.

'I wish,' he says suddenly then, 'I just wish you would tell me what it is you mean to do. How am I even to get you from the shop? I must bring a cab, I suppose, to the back of the building.'

'Will you do that?'

'You have somewhere to go, to sleep? To eat?'

'I have nowhere!'

'You must go home, then.'

'I cannot do that. I have no home! I need only a little money, a little time. There is a person I mean to find, to save—'

'To *save*?'

'To find. To find. And, having found her, then I may need help again. Only a little help. I have been cheated, Mr Hawtrey. I have been wronged. I think, with a lawyer—if we might find an honest man— You know I am rich?—or, ought to be.' Again, he watches but does not speak. I say, 'You know I am rich. If you'll only help me, now. If you'll only keep me—'

'*Keep* you! Do you know what you are saying? Keep you, where?'

'Not in your own house?'

'My house?'

'I thought—'

'My house? With my wife and daughters? No, no.' He has begun to pace.

'But at Briar you said, many times—'

'Haven't I told you? This is not Briar. The world is not like Briar. You must find that out. How old are you? You are a child. You cannot leave a husband, as you may leave an uncle. You cannot live, in London, on nothing. How do you think you will live?'

'I do not know. I supposed—' *I supposed you would give me money,*

I want to say. I look about me. Then I am struck with an idea. 'Might I not,' I say, 'work for you?'

He stands still. 'For me?'

'Might I not work here? In the putting together of books?—the writing, even? I know that work. You know how well I know it! You may pay me a wage. I shall take a room—I need only one room, one quiet room!—I shall take it secretly, Richard shall never know, you shall keep my secret for me. I shall work, and earn a little money— enough to find out my friend, to find out an honest lawyer; and then— What is it?'

He has kept still, all this time; but his look has changed, is odd.

'Nothing,' he says, moving. 'I— Nothing. Drink your water.'

I suppose I am flushed. I have spoken rapidly, and grown warm: I swallow, and feel the chill descent of the water inside my breast, like a sword. He moves to the table and leans upon it, not looking at me, but thinking, thinking. When I set down the glass he turns back. He does not catch my eye.

'Listen to me,' he says. He speaks quietly. 'You cannot stay here, you know that. I must send for a cab, to take you. I— I must send for some woman, also. I will pay for a woman to go with you.'

'Go with me, where?'

'To some—hotel.' Now he has turned again, has taken up a pen—looks in a book, begins to set down a direction upon a slip of paper. 'Some house,' he says, as he does it, 'where you may rest and take a supper.'

'Where I may rest?' I say. 'I don't think I shall rest, ever again! But a room! A room!—And will you come to me there? Tonight?' He does not answer. 'Mr Hawtrey?'

'Not tonight,' he says, still writing. 'Tonight I cannot.'

'Tomorrow, then.'

He waves the paper, to dry it; then folds it. 'Tomorrow,' he says. 'If I can.'

'You must!'

'Yes, yes.'

'And the work—my working for you. You'll consider that? Say you will!'

'Hush. Yes, I'll consider it. Yes.'

'Thank God!'

I put my hand before my eyes. 'Stay here,' he says. 'Will you? Don't go from here.'

I hear him step, then, to the room next door; and when I look, I see him speaking quietly to one of the typesetters—see the man draw on his jacket, then go. Mr Hawtrey comes back. He nods to my feet.

'Put your shoes on, now,' he says, turning away. 'We must be ready.'

'You are kind, Mr Hawtrey,' I say, as I lean to tug on my broken slippers. 'God knows, no-one has been so kind to me, since—' My voice is lost.

'There, there,' he says, distractedly. 'Don't think of it, now . . .'

Then I sit in silence. He waits, takes out his watch, goes now and then to the top of the stairs, to stand and listen. At last he goes and comes quickly back.

'They are here,' he says. 'Now, have you everything? Come this way, carefully.'

He takes me down. He takes me through a set of rooms, piled high with crates and boxes, and then through a sort of scullery, to a door. The door leads to a little grey area: there are steps from this, to an alley. A cab waits there with, beside it, a woman. She sees us and nods.

'You know what to do?' Mr Hawtrey says to her. She nods again. He gives her money, wrapped in the paper on which he has written. 'Here is the lady, look. Her name is Mrs Rivers. You are to be kind to her. Have you some shawl?'

She has a plaid wool wrap, which she puts about me, to cover up my head. The wool is hot against my cheek. The day is still warm, though it is almost twilight. The sun has gone from the sky. I have been three hours from Lant Street.

At the door to the cab, I turn. I take Mr Hawtrey's hand.

'You will come,' I say, 'tomorrow?'

'Of course.'

'You won't talk of this, to anyone? You'll remember the danger I spoke of?'

He nods. 'Go on,' he says quietly. 'This woman will care for you now, better than I.'

'Thank you, Mr Hawtrey!'

He hands me into the cab—hesitates, before lifting my fingers to his mouth. The woman comes next. He closes the door at her back, then moves off, out of the path of the turning wheel. I lean to the glass and see him take out his handkerchief, wipe his face and neck; then we turn, pull out of the alley, and he is gone. We drive away from Holywell Street—northwards, so far as I can tell; for I know— I am almost certain—that we do not cross the river.

We go very fitfully, however. The traffic is thick. I keep with my face at the window at first, watching the crowds upon the streets, the shops. Then I think, Suppose I see Richard?—and I fall back against the leather seat and study the streets from there.

Only after some time of this do I look again at the woman. She has her hands in her lap: they are gloveless, and coarse. She catches my eye.

'All right, dearie?' she says, not smiling. Her voice is rough as her fingers.

Do I begin, then, to feel wary? I am not sure. I think, After all, Mr Hawtrey had not the time to be careful, in his finding of a woman. What matter if she's not kind, so long as she's honest? I look more closely at her. Her skirt is a rusty black. Her shoes are the colour and texture of roasted meat. She sits placidly, not speaking, while the cab shudders and jolts.

'Must we go far?' I ask her at last.

'Not too far, dearie.'

Her voice is still rough, her face without expression. I say, fretfully, 'Do you call me that? I wish you wouldn't.'

She shrugs. The gesture is so bold and yet so careless, I think I do then grow uneasy. I put my face again to the window, to try to draw in air. The air will not come. Where is Holywell Street, I think, from here?

'I don't like this,' I say, turning back to the woman. 'May we not walk?'

'Walk, in them slippers?' She snorts. She looks out. 'Here's

Camden Town,' she says. 'We've a fair way, yet. Sit back and be good.'

'Will you talk to me, so?' I say again. 'I am not a child.'

And again, she shrugs. We drive on, more smoothly. We drive for, perhaps, half an hour, up a rising road. The day is darker now. I am tenser. We have left the lights and shops, and are in some street—some street of plain buildings. We turn a corner, and the buildings grow plainer still. Presently we draw up before a great, grey house. There is a lamp, at the foot of its steps. A girl in a ragged apron is reaching with a taper to light it. The glass of its shade is cracked. The street is perfectly silent.

'What's this?' I say to the woman, when the coach has stopped and I understand it will not go on.

'Here's your house,' she says.

'The hotel?'

'Hotel?' She smiles. 'You may call it that.' She reaches for the latch on the door. I put my hand on her wrist.

'Wait,' I say—feeling real fear now, at last. 'What do you mean? Where has Mr Hawtrey directed you to?'

'Why, to here!'

'And what is here?'

'It's a house, ain't it? What is it to you, what sort? You shall get your supper all the same.—You might leave off gripping me, mind!'

'Not until you tell me where I am.'

She tries to pull her hand away, but I will not let her. Finally, she sucks her teeth.

'House for ladies,' she says, 'like you.'

'Like me?'

'Like you. Poor ladies, widow ladies—wicked ladies, I shouldn't wonder.—There!'

I have thrust her wrist aside.

'I don't believe you,' I say. 'I am meant to come to an hotel. Mr Hawtrey paid you for that—'

'Paid me to bring you here, and then to leave you. Most particular. If you don't like it—' She reaches into her pocket. 'Why, here's his very hand.'

She has brought out a piece of paper. It is the paper that Mr Hawtrey put about the coin. It has the name of the house upon it—

A home, he calls it, *for destitute gentlewomen*.

For a moment I gaze at the words in a sort of disbelief: as if my gazing at them will change them, change their meaning or shape. Then I look at the woman. 'This is a mistake,' I say. 'He didn't mean this. He has misunderstood, or you have. You must take me back—'

'I'm to bring you, and leave you, most particular,' she says stubbornly again. '"Poor lady, weak in her head, needs taking to a charity place." There's charity, ain't it?'

She nods again to the house. I do not answer. I am remembering Mr Hawtrey's look—his words, the odd tone of his voice. I think, *I must go back! I must go back to Holywell Street!*—and yet, even as I think it, I know, with a dreadful chill contraction of my heart, what I will find there if I do: the shop, the men, the youth; and Mr Hawtrey gone, to his own home—his home, which might be anywhere in the city, anywhere at all . . . And after that, the street—the street in darkness.—How shall I manage it? How shall I live a night, in London, on my own?

I begin to shake. 'What am I to do?' I say.

'What, but go over,' says the woman, nodding again to the house. The girl with the taper is gone, and the lamp burns feebly. The windows are shuttered, the glass above them black, as if the rooms are filled with darkness. The door is high—divided in two, like the great front door at Briar. I see it, and am gripped by panic.

'I cannot,' I say. 'I cannot!'

Again the woman sucks her teeth. 'Better that than the road— ain't it? It's one or the other. I am paid to bring you here and leave you, that's all. Go on out, now, and let me get home.'

'I cannot,' I say again. I grab at her sleeve. 'You must take me, somewhere else.'

'Must I?' She laughs—does not shake me off, however. Instead, her look changes. 'Well, I will,' she says; 'if you'll pay me.'

'Pay you? I have nothing to pay you with!'

She laughs again. 'No money?' she says. 'And a dress like that?'

She looks at my skirt.

'Oh, God,' I say, plucking at it in desperation. 'I would give you the gown, if I might!'

'Would you?'

'Take the shawl!'

'The shawl's my own!' She snorts. She still looks at my skirt. Then she tilts her head. 'What you got,' she says more quietly, 'underneath?'

I shudder. Then slowly, shrinkingly, I draw up my hem, show her my petticoats—two petticoats there are, one white and one crimson. She sees them, and nods.

'They'll do. Silk, are they? They'll do.'

'What, both?' I say. 'Will you take both?'

'There's the driver needs his fare, ain't there?' she answers. 'You must pay me, once for myself; and once for him.'

I hesitate—but what can I do? I lift my skirt higher, find out the strings at my waist and pull them loose; then, modestly as I can, draw the petticoats down. She does not look away. She takes them from me and tucks them swiftly under her coat.

'What the gentleman don't know, eh?' she says, with a chuckle; as if we are close conspirators now. She rubs her hands. 'Where to, then? Eh? Where must I tell the driver?'

She has opened the window, to call. I sit with my arms about myself, feeling the prickle of the fabric of my gown against my bare thighs. I think I would colour, I think I would weep, if I had life enough.

'Where to?' she asks again. Beyond her head, the street is filled with shadow. A moon has risen—a crescent, slender, filthy-brown.

I bow my head. With this last, awful bafflement of my hopes, I have only one place to go. I tell her, she calls it, and the coach starts up. She settles herself more comfortably in her seat, rearranges her coat. She looks at me.

'All right, dearie?' she says. I do not answer, and she laughs. She turns away. 'Don't mind it now, does she?' she says, as if to herself. 'Don't mind it, now.'

Lant Street is dark when we reach it. I know the house to stop at, from the house which faces it—the one with the ointment-coloured shutters, that I have gazed at so hard from Mrs Sucksby's window. John answers my knock. His face is white. He sees me, and stares. '*Fuck*,' he says. I go past him. The door leads into what I suppose is Mr Ibbs's shop, and a passage from that takes me directly into the kitchen. They are all there, apart from Richard. He is out in search of me. Dainty is weeping: her cheek is bruised, worse than before, her lip split and bleeding. Mr Ibbs paces in his shirt-sleeves, making the floorboards jump and creak. Mrs Sucksby stands, her eyes on nothing, her face white as powder, like John's. She stands still. But when she sees me come she folds and winces—puts her hand to her heart as if struck.

'Oh, my girl,' she says.

I don't know what they do after that. Dainty screams, I think. I go by them, not looking. I go up the stairs to Mrs Sucksby's room—*my* room, *our* room, I suppose I must call it now—and I sit upon the bed, my face to the window. I sit with my hands in my lap, my head bowed. My fingers are marked with dirt. My feet have begun, again, to bleed.

She gives me a minute, before she comes. She comes quietly. She closes the door and locks it at her back—turning the key gently in the lock, as if she thinks me sleeping and fears to wake me. Then she stands at my side. She does not try to touch me. I know, however, that she is trembling.

'Dear girl,' she says. 'We supposed you lost. We supposed you drowned, or murdered—'

Her voice catches, but does not break. She waits and, when I do nothing, 'Stand up, sweetheart,' she says.

I do. She takes the gown from me, and the stays. She does not ask what has become of my petticoats. She does not exclaim over my slippers and feet—though she shudders, as she draws off my stockings. She puts me, naked, into the bed; draws up the blanket to my jaw; then sits beside me. She strokes my hair—teases out the pins and tangles with her hands. My head is loose, and jerks as she tugs. 'There, now,' she says.

The house is silent. I think Mr Ibbs and John are talking, but talking in whispers. Her fingers move more slowly. 'There, now,' she says again; and I shiver, for her voice is Sue's.

Her voice is Sue's, but her face— The room is dark, however, she has not brought a candle. She sits with her back to the window. But I feel her gaze, and her breath. I close my eyes.

'We thought you lost,' she murmurs again. 'But you came back. Dear girl, I knew you should!'

'I have nowhere else,' I answer, slowly and hopelessly. 'I have nowhere and no-one. I thought I knew it; I never knew it till now. I have nothing. No home—'

'*Here* is your home!' she says.

'No friends—'

'*Here* are your friends!'

'No love—'

She draws in her breath; then speaks, in a whisper.

'Dear girl, don't you know? Ain't I said, a hundred times—?'

I begin to weep—in frustration, exhaustion. 'Why *will* you say it?' I cry, through my tears. 'Why *will* you? Isn't it enough, to have got me here? Why must you also love me? Why must you smother and torment me, with your grasping after my heart?'

I have raised myself up; but the cry takes the last of my strength and soon, I fall back. She does not speak. She watches. She waits, until I have grown still. Then she turns her head and tilts it. I think, from the curve of her cheek, that she is smiling.

'How quiet the house is,' she says, 'now so many infants are gone! Ain't it?' She turns back to me. I hear her swallow. 'Did I tell you, dear girl,' she says softly, 'that I once bore an infant of my own, that died? Round about the time that that lady, Sue's mother, came?' She nods. 'So I said. So you'll hear it told, round here, if you ask. Babies do die. Who'd think that queer . . .?'

There is something to her voice. I begin to shake. She feels it, and reaches again to stroke my tangled head. 'There, now. Hush, now. You are quite safe, now . . .' Then the stroking stops. She has caught up a lock of hair. She smiles again. 'Funny thing,' she says, in a different tone, 'about your hair. Your eye I did suppose brown, and your colour white, and your waist and hands I knew would be

slender. Only your hair come out rather fairer than I had it pictured . . .'

The words drop away. In reaching, she has moved her head: the
light from the street-lamp, and from the sliver of tarnished moon,
falls full upon her, and all at once I see her face—the brown of her
own eye, and her own pale cheek—and her lip, that is plump and
must, I understand suddenly, must once have been plumper . . .
She wets her mouth. 'Dear girl,' she says. 'My own, my own dear
girl—'

She hesitates another moment; then speaks, at last.

Part Three

Chapter Fourteen

I shrieked. I shrieked and shrieked. I struggled like a fiend. But the more I twisted, the tighter I was held. I saw Gentleman fall back in his seat and the coach start up and begin to turn. I saw Maud put her face to the window of cloudy glass. At sight of her eyes, I shrieked again.

'There she is!' I cried, lifting my hand and pointing. 'There she is! Don't let her go! Don't you fucking let her go—!'

But the coach drove on, the wheels throwing up dust and gravel as the horse got up its speed; and the faster it went, the harder I think I fought. Now the other doctor came forward, to help Dr Christie. The woman in the apron came, too. They were trying to pull me closer to the house. I wouldn't let them. The coach was speeding, growing smaller. 'They're getting away!' I cried. Then the woman got behind me and seized my waist. She had a grip on her like a man's. She lifted me up the two or three steps that led to the house's front door, as if I might be so many feathers in a bag.

'Now then,' she said as she hauled me. 'What's this? Kick your legs, will you, and trouble the doctors?'

Her mouth was close to my ear, her face behind me. I hardly knew what I was doing. All I knew was, she had me there, and Gentleman and Maud were escaping. I felt her speak, bent my head forward, then took it sharply back.

'Oh!' she cried. Her grip grew slack. 'Oh! Oh!'

'She's becoming demented,' said Dr Christie. I thought he was talking about her. Then I saw he meant me. He took a whistle from his pocket and gave it a blow.

'For God's sake,' I cried, 'won't you hear me? They have tricked me, they have tricked me—!'

The woman grabbed me again—about the throat, this time; and as I turned in her arms she hit me hard, with the points of her fingers, in my stomach. I think she did it in such a way, the doctors did not see. I gave a jerk, and swallowed my breath. Then she did it again. 'Here's fits!' she said.

'Watch your hands!' called Dr Graves. 'She may snap.'

Meanwhile, they had got me into the hall of the house and the sound of the whistle had brought another two men. They were pulling on brown paper cuffs over their coat-sleeves. They did not look like doctors. They came and caught hold of my ankles.

'Keep her steady,' said Dr Graves. 'She's in a convulsion. She may put out her joints.'

I could not tell them that I was not in a fit, but only winded; that the woman had hurt me; that I was anyway not a lunatic, but sane as them. I could not say anything, for trying to find my breath. I could only croak. The men drew my legs straight, and my skirts rose to my knees. I began to be afraid of the skirts rising higher. That made me twist about, I suppose.

'Hold her tight,' said Dr Christie. He had brought out a thing like a great flat spoon, made of horn. He came to my side and held my head, and put the spoon to my mouth, between my teeth. It was smooth, but he pushed it hard and it hurt me. I thought I should be choked: I bit it, to keep it from going down my throat. It tasted bad.

I still think of all the other people's mouths it must have gone in, before mine.

He saw my jaws close. 'Now she takes it!' he said. 'That's right. Hold her steady.' He looked at Dr Graves. 'To the soft room? I think so. Nurse Spiller?'

That was the woman that held me by the throat. I saw her nod to him, and then to the men in the cuffs, and they turned so that they might walk with me, further into the house. I felt them do it and began to struggle again. I was not thinking, now, of Gentleman and Maud. I was thinking of myself. I was growing horribly afraid. My stomach ached from the nurse's fingers. My mouth was cut by the spoon. I had an idea that, once they got me into a room, they would kill me.

'A thrasher, ain't she?' said one of the men, as he worked for a better grip on my ankle.

'A very bad case,' said Dr Christie. He looked into my face. 'The convulsion is passing, at least.' He raised his voice. 'Don't be afraid, Mrs Rivers! We know all about you. We are your friends. We have brought you here to make you well.'

I tried to speak. 'Help! Help!' I tried to say. But the spoon made me gobble like a bird. It also made me dribble; and a bit of dribble flew out of my mouth and struck Dr Christie's cheek. Perhaps he thought I had spat it. Anyway, he moved quickly back, and his face grew grim. He took out his handkerchief.

'Very good,' he said to the men and the nurse, as he wiped his cheek. 'That will do. Now you may take her.'

They carried me along a passage, through a set of doors and a room; then to a landing, another passage, another room—I tried to study the way, but they had me on my back: I could make out only so many drab-coloured ceilings and walls. After about a minute I knew they had got me deep into the house, and that I was lost. I could not cry out. The nurse kept her arm about my throat, and I still had the spoon of horn in my mouth. When we reached a staircase they took me down it, saying, 'To you, Mr Bates,' and, 'Watch this turn, it's a tight one!'—as if I might be, not a sack of feathers

now, but a trunk or a piano. Not once did they look me in the face.
Finally, one of the men began to whistle a tune, and to beat out the
time of it, with his finger-ends, on my leg.

Then we reached another room, with a ceiling of a paler shade of
drab; and here they stopped.

'Careful, now,' they said.

The men put down my legs. The woman took her arm from my
neck and gave me a push. It was only a little push and yet, they had
so pulled and shaken me about, I found I staggered and fell. I fell
upon my hands. I opened my mouth and the spoon fell out. One of
the men reached, quick, to take it. He shook the spit from it.

'Please,' I said.

'You may say please, now,' said the woman. Then she spoke to
the men. 'Gave me a crack with her head, upon the steps. Look
here. Am I bruised?'

'I believe you shall be.'

'Little devil!'

She put her foot to me. 'Now, does Dr Christie have you here to
give us all bruises? Eh, my lady? Mrs What-is-your-name? Mrs
Waters, or Rivers? Does he?'

'Please,' I said again. 'I ain't Mrs Rivers.'

'She ain't Mrs Rivers? Hear that, Mr Bates? And I ain't Nurse
Spiller, I dare say. And Mr Hedges ain't himself. Very likely.'

She came closer to me, and she picked me up about my waist;
and she dropped me. You could not say she threw me, but she lifted
me high and let me fall; and me being just then so dazed and so
weak, I fell badly.

'That's for cracking my face,' she said. 'Be glad we ain't on stairs,
or a roof. Crack me again—who knows?—we might be.' She pulled
her canvas apron straight, and leaned and caught hold of my collar.
'Right, let's have this gown off. You may look like thunder, too.
That's nothing to me. Why, what small little hooks! And my hand's
hard, is it? Used to better, are you? I should say you are, from what
I've heard.' She laughed. 'Well, we don't keep ladies' maids, here.
We has Mr Hedges and Mr Bates.' They still stood, watching, at the
door. 'Shall I call them over?'

I supposed she meant to strip me bare; which I would rather die first, than endure. I got on to my knees and twisted from her.

'You may call who you like, you great bitch,' I said, in a pant. 'You ain't having my dress.'

Her face grew dark. 'Bitch, am I?' she answered. 'Well!'

And she drew back her hand and curled her fingers into a fist, and she hit me.

I had grown up in the Borough, surrounded by every kind of desperate dodger and thief; but I had had Mrs Sucksby for a mother, and had never been hit. The blow knocked me almost out of my head. I put my hands to my face, and lay down in a crouch; but she got the gown off me anyway—I suppose she was used to getting gowns off lunatics, and had a trick for it; and next she got hold of my corset and took that. Then she took my garters, and then my shoes and stockings, and finally my hair-pins.

Then she stood, darker-faced than ever, and sweating.

'There!' she said, looking me over in my petticoat and shimmy. 'There's all your ribbons and laces gone. If you chokes yourself now, it'll be no business of ours. You hear me? Mrs Ain't-Mrs-Rivers? You sit in the pads for a night, and stew. See how you care for that. Convulsions? I think I know a temper from a fit. Kick all you like in here. Put out your joints, chew your tongue off. Keep you quiet. We prefers them quiet, makes our job nicer.'

She said all that, and she made a bundle of my clothes and swung them over her shoulder; and then she left me. The men went with her. They had seen her hit me, and done nothing. They had watched her take my stockings and stays. I heard them pull off their paper cuffs. One began to whistle again. Nurse Spiller closed the door and locked it, and the whistling grew very much fainter.

When it had grown so faint I could no longer hear it, I got to my feet. Then I fell down again. My legs had been pulled so hard they shook like things of rubber, and my head was ringing, from the punch. My hands were trembling. I was, not to put too fine a point on it, properly funked. I went, on my knees, to the door, to look at the key-hole. There was no handle. The door itself was covered in a dirty canvas, padded with straw; the walls were covered in padded canvas, too. The floor had oil-cloth on it. There was a single blanket, very much torn and stained. There was a little tin pot I was meant to piddle in. There was a window, high up, with bars on. Beyond the bars were curling leaves of ivy. The light came in green and dark, like the water in a pond.

I stood and looked at it all, in a sort of daze—hardly believing, I think, that those were my cold feet on the oil-cloth floor; that it was my sore face, my arms, that the green light struck. Then I turned back to the door and put my fingers to it—to the key-hole, to the canvas, to the edge, anywhere—to try and pull it. But it was tight as a clam—and, what was worse, as I stood plucking at it I began to make out little dints and tears in the dirty canvas—little crescents, where the weave was worn—that I understood all at once must be the marks left by the finger-nails of all the other lunatics—all the real lunatics, I mean—who had been put in that room before me. The thought that I was standing, doing just what they had done, was horrible. I stepped away from the door, the daze slipped from me, and I grew wild with fright. I flung myself back, and began to beat at the padded canvas with my hands. Each blow made a cloud of dust.

'Help! Help!' I cried. My voice sounded strange. 'Oh, help! They have put me in here, thinking I'm mad! Call Richard Rivers!' I coughed. 'Help! Doctor! Help! Can you hear me?' I coughed again. 'Help! Can you hear me—?'

And so on. I stood and called, and coughed, and beat upon the door—only stopping, now and then, to put my ear to it, to try to tell if there might be anyone near—for I can't say how long; and no-one came. I think the padding was too thick; or else, the people that heard me were used to lunatics calling, and had learned not to mind. So then I tried the walls. They were also thick. And when I had given up banging and shouting, I put the blanket and the little tin pot together in a heap beneath the window, and climbed on them, trying to reach the glass; but the tin pot buckled, and the blanket slithered and I fell.

At last I sat on the oil-cloth floor and cried. I cried, and my own tears stung me. I put my finger-tips to my cheek and felt about my swelling face. I felt my hair. The woman had pulled it to take the pins out, and it lay all about my shoulders; and when I took up a length of it, meaning to comb it, some of it came away in my hands. That made me cry worse than ever. I don't say I was much of a beauty; but I thought of a girl I knew, who had lost her hair to a wheel in a workshop—that hair had never grown back. Suppose I should be bald? I went over my head, taking out the hair that was loose, wondering if I ought to keep it, perhaps for making a wig with later; but there was not much of it, after all. In the end I rolled it up and put it in a corner.

And as I did that, I saw something, pale upon the floor. It looked like a crumpled white hand, and it gave me a start, at first; then I saw what it was. It had fallen out of my bosom when the nurse had got the gown off me, and been kicked out of sight. There was the mark of a shoe upon it, and one of its buttons was crushed.

It was that glove of Maud's, that I had taken that morning from her things and meant to hold on to, as a keepsake of her.

I picked it up and turned it over and over in my hands. If I had thought myself funked, a minute before—well, that funking was nothing to what I felt now, looking at that glove, thinking of Maud, and of the awful trick that she and Gentleman had played me. I hid my face in my arms, for very shame. I walked, from one wall to another, and from that to another: if I once tried to be still, it was as if I was resting on needles and pins—I started up, crying out and sweating. I thought of all my time at Briar, when I had supposed myself such a sharper, and been such a simpleton. I thought of the days I had spent, with those two villains—the looks the one must have given the other, the smiles. *Leave her alone, why don't you?* I had said to him, feeling sorry for her. And then, to her: *Don't mind him, miss. He loves you, miss. Marry him. He loves you.*

He will do it like this . . .

Oh! Oh! I feel the sting of it, even now. Then, I might really have been demented. I walked, and my bare feet went slap, slap, slap on the oil-cloth; and I put the glove to my mouth and I bit it. *Him* I suppose I expected no better of. It was *her* I thought of most—that bitch, that snake, that— Oh! To think I had ever looked at her and taken her for a flat. To think I had laughed at her. To think I had loved her! To think I had thought she loved me! To think I had kissed her, in Gentleman's name. To think I had touched her! To think, to think—!

To think I lay on the night of her wedding with a pillow over my head, so I should not hear the sound of her tears. To think that, if I had listened, I might have heard—might I? might I?—the sound of her sighs.

I could not bear it. I forgot, for the moment, the little detail of how, in swindling me, she had only turned my own trick back on myself. I walked, and moaned, and swore, and cursed her; I gripped and bit and twisted that glove, until the light beyond the window faded, and the room grew dark. No-one came to look at me. No-one brought me food, or a gown, or stockings. And though I was warm at first, from all the walking, when at last I grew so tired I found I must lie upon the blanket or drop, I became cold; and then I could not get warm again.

I did not sleep. From the rest of the house there came, every so often, queer noises—shouts, and running feet and, once, the blowing of the doctor's whistle. At some hour of the night it began to rain, and the water went drip against the window. In the garden, a dog barked: I heard that and began to think, not of Maud, but of Charley Wag, of Mr Ibbs and Mrs Sucksby—of Mrs Sucksby in her bed, the empty place beside her, waiting for me. How long would she wait?

How soon would Gentleman go to her? What would he say? He might say I was dead. But then, if he said that, she would ask for my body, to bury.—I thought of my funeral, and who would cry most. He might say I was drowned or lost in marshes. She would ask for the papers to prove it. Could those papers be faked? He might say I had taken my share of the money, and cut.

He would say that, I knew it. But Mrs Sucksby wouldn't believe him. She would see through him like he was glass. She would hunt me out. She had not kept me seventeen years to lose me now, like this! She would look in every house in England, until she found me!

That's what I thought, as I grew calmer. I thought I must only speak with the doctors and they would see their mistake and let me go; but that anyway, Mrs Sucksby would come, and I should get out like that.

And when I was free, I would go to wherever Maud Lilly was, and—wasn't I my mother's own daughter, after all?—I would kill her.

You can see what little idea I had of the awfulness of the fix I was really in.

Next morning, the woman who had thrown me about came back for me. She came, not with the two men, Mr Bates and Mr Hedges, but with another woman—*nurses*, they called them there; but they were no more nurses than I was, they only got that work through being stout and having great big hands like mangles. They came into the room and stood and looked me over. Nurse Spiller said,

'Here she is.'

The other, who was dark, said,

'Young, to be mad.'

'Listen here,' I said, very carefully. I had worked this out. I had heard them coming, and had got to my feet and put my petticoat straight, and tidied my hair. 'Listen here. You think I am mad. I am not. I am not the lady you and the doctors suppose me to be, at all. That lady, and her husband—Richard Rivers—are a pair of swindlers; and they have swindled you, and me, and just about everybody; and it is very important that the doctors know it, so I may be let out and those swindlers caught. I—'

'Right in the face,' said Nurse Spiller, speaking across my words. 'Right here, with her head.'

She put her hand to her cheek, close to her nose, where there was the smallest, faintest mark of crimson. My own face, of course, was swollen like a pudding; and I dare say my eye was almost black. But I said, still carefully,

'I am sorry I hurt your face. I was only so thrown, to be brought in here, as a lunatic; when all the time it was the other lady, Miss Lilly—Mrs Rivers—that was meant to come.'

Again they stood and looked me over.

'You must call us *nurse* when you speak to us,' the dark one said at last. 'But between you and me, dear, we would rather you didn't speak to us at all. We hear that much nonsense—well. Come along. You must be bathed, so that Doctor Christie may look at you. You must be put in a gown. Why, what a little girl! You must be no more than sixteen.'

She had come close, and made to catch at my arm. I drew away from her.

'Will you listen to me?' I said.

'Listen to you? La, if I listened to all the rubbish I heard in this house, I should go mad myself. Come on, now.'

Her voice, that had started off mild, grew sharper. She took hold of my arm. I flinched from the feel of her fingers. 'Watch her,' said Nurse Spiller, seeing me twitch.

I said, 'If you'll only not touch me, I'll go with you, wherever you want.'

'Ho!' said the dark nurse then. 'There's manners. Come with us, will you? Very grateful, I'm sure.'

She pulled me and, when I tugged against her grip, Nurse Spiller came to help her. They got their hands beneath my arms and more or less lifted me, more or less dragged me, out of the room. When I kicked and complained—which I did, from the shock of it—Nurse Spiller got those great hard fingers of hers into my arm-pit, and jabbed. You can't see bruises in an arm-pit. I think she knew it. 'She's off!' she said, when I cried out.

'That's my head ringing for the rest of the day,' said the other. And she gripped me tighter and shook me.

Then I grew quiet. I was afraid I should be punched again. But I was also looking hard at the way we were taking—at the windows and the doors. Some doors had locks. All the windows had bars on. They looked over a yard. This was the back part of the house— what should have been, in a house like Briar, the servants' part. Here it was given over to nurses. We met two or three of them as we walked. They wore aprons and caps, and carried baskets, or bottles, or sheets.

'Good morning,' they all sang out.

'Good morning,' my nurses answered.

'New 'un?' one asked at last, with a nod at me. 'Come up from the pads? Is she bad?'

'Cracked Nancy on the cheek.'

She whistled. 'They should bring 'em in bound. Young, though, ain't she?'

'Sixteen, if she's a day.'

'I'm seventeen,' I said.

The new nurse looked at me, in a considering sort of way.

'Sharp-faced,' she said, after a minute.

'Ain't she, though?'

'What's her trouble? Delusions?'

'And the rest,' said the dark nurse. She dropped her voice. 'She's the one—you know?'

The new nurse looked more interested. 'This one?' she said. 'Looks too slight for that.'

'Well, they come in all sizes . . .'

I didn't know what they meant. But being held up for strangers to study, and talk and smile over, made me ashamed, and I kept silent. The woman went off on her way and my two nurses gripped me tight again and took me, down another passage, to a little room. It might have once been a pantry—it was very like Mrs Stiles's pantry, at Briar—for there were cupboards, with locks upon them, and an arm-chair and a sink. Nurse Spiller sat down in the chair, giving a great sigh as she did so. The other nurse put water in the sink. She showed me a slip of yellow soap and a dirty flannel.

'Here you are,' she said. And then, when I did nothing: 'Come on. You've hands, haven't you? Let's see you wash.'

The water was cold. I wet my face and arms, then made to wash my feet.

'That will do,' she said, when she saw me do that. 'Do you think Dr Christie cares how dusty your toes are? Here, now. Let's see your linen.' She caught hold of the hem of my shimmy, then turned her head to Nurse Spiller, who nodded. 'Good, ain't it? Too good for this house. That'll boil up to nothing, that will.' She gave it a tug. 'You take that off, dear. We shall keep it, quite safe, against the day you leave us.—What, are you shy?'

'Shy?' said Nurse Spiller, yawning. 'Don't waste our time. And you, a married lady.'

'I ain't married,' I said. 'And I'll thank you both to keep your hands off my linen. I want my own gown back, and my stockings and shoes. I need only speak with Dr Christie, and then you'll be sorry.'

They looked at me and laughed.

'Hoity-toity!' cried the dark nurse. She wiped her eyes. 'Dear me. Come, now. It's no use growing sulky. We must have your linen—it's nothing to me and Nurse Spiller, it's the rules of the house. Here's a new set, look, and a gown and—look here—slippers.'

She had gone to one of the cupboards and brought out a set of greyish underthings, and a wool gown, and boots. She came back to me, holding them, and Nurse Spiller joined her; and it was no good then how hard I argued and cursed, they got hold of me and stripped me bare. When they took off my petticoat, that glove of Maud's fell out. I had had it under the waistband. I bent and caught it up. 'What's that?' they said at once. Then they saw it was only a glove. They looked at the stitching inside the wrist.

'Here's your own name, *Maud*,' they said. 'That's pretty work, that is.'

'You shan't have it!' I cried, snatching it back. They had taken my clothes and my shoes; but I had walked and torn and bitten that glove all night, it was all I had to keep my nerve up. I had the idea that, if they were to take it, I should be like a Samson shorn.

Perhaps they noticed a look in my eye.

'One glove's no use, after all,' said the dark nurse to Nurse Spiller, quietly. 'And remember Miss Taylor, who had the buttons on a thread that she called her babies? Why, she'd take the hand off, that tried to get a hold of one of those!'

So they let me keep it; and then I stood limp and let them dress me, through fear they would change their minds. The clothes were all madhouse things. The corset had hooks instead of laces, and was too big for me.—'Never mind,' they said, laughing. They had chests like boats. 'Plenty of room for growing in.' The gown was meant to be a tartan, but the colours had run. The stockings were short, like a boy's. The shoes were of india-rubber.

'Here you are, Cinderella,' said the dark nurse, putting them on me. And then, looking me over: 'Well! You shall bounce like a ball all right, in those!'

They laughed again then, for quite a minute. Then they did this. They sat me in the chair and combed my hair and made it into plaits; and they took out a needle and cotton, and sewed the plaits to my head.

'It's this, or cut it,' the dark nurse said when I struggled; 'and no skin off my nose either way.'

'Let me see to it,' said Nurse Spiller. She finished it off—two or three times, as if by accident, putting the point of the needle to my scalp. That is another place that don't show cuts and bruises.

And so, between the two of them, they got me ready; and then they took me to the room that was to be mine.

'Mind, now, you remember your manners,' they said as we walked. 'Start going off your head again, we shall have you back in the pads, or plunge you.'

'This ain't fair!' I said. 'This ain't fair, at all!'

They shook me, and did not answer. So then I fell silent and, again, tried hard to study the way they took me. I was also growing afraid. I had had an idea in my head—that I think I had got from a picture, or a play—of how a madhouse should be; and so far, this house was not like it. I thought, 'They have got me in the place where the doctors and nurses live. Now they'll take me to the mad bit.'—I think I supposed it would be something like a dungeon or a gaol. But we walked only down more drab-coloured corridors, past door after drab-coloured door, and I began to look about me and see little things—such as, the lamps being ordinary brass ones, but with strong wire guards about the flames; and the doors having fancy latches, but ugly locks; and the walls having, here and there, handles, that looked as though they might, if you turned them, ring bells. And finally it broke upon me that this was the mad-house after all; that it had once been an ordinary gentleman's house; that the walls had used to have pictures and looking-glasses on them, and the floors had used to have rugs; but that now, it had all been made over to madwomen—that it was, in its way, like a smart and handsome person gone mad itself.

And I can't say why, but somehow the idea was worse and put me in more of a creep than if the place had looked like a dungeon after all.

I shuddered and slowed my step, then almost stumbled. The india-rubber boots were hard to walk in.

'Come on,' said Nurse Spiller, giving me a prod.

'Which do we want?' asked the other nurse, looking at the doors.

'Fourteen. Here we are.'

All the doors had little plates screwed to them. We stopped at one of them, and Nurse Spiller gave a knock, then put a key to the lock and turned it. The key was a plain one, shined from use. She kept it on a chain inside her pocket.

The room she took us into was not a proper room, but had been made, by the building of a wooden wall, inside another.—For, as I said, that house had been all chopped up and made crazy. The wooden wall had glass at the top, that let in light from a window beyond it, but the room had no window of its own. The air was close. There were four beds in it, along with a cot where a nurse slept. Three of the beds had women beside them, getting dressed. One bed was bare.

'This is to be yours,' said Nurse Spiller, taking me to it. It was placed very near the nurse's cot. 'This is where we puts our ques-tionable ladies. Try a queer trick here, Nurse Bacon shall know all about it. Shan't you, Nurse Bacon?'

This was the nurse of that room. 'Oh, yes,' she said. She nodded and rubbed her hands. She had some ailment that made her fingers very fat and pink, like sausages—an unlucky ailment, I suppose, for someone with a name like hers—and she liked to rub them often. She looked me over in the same cool way that all the other nurses had, and she said, as they had,

'Young, ain't you?'

'Sixteen,' said the dark nurse.

'Seventeen,' I said.

'Sixteen? We should call you the child of the house, if it weren't for Betty. Look here, Betty! Here's a fresh young lady, look, almost your age. I should say she can run very quick up and down a set of stairs. I should say she's got neat ways. Eh, Betty?'

She had called to a woman who stood at the bed across from mine, pulling a gown on over a great fat stomach. I thought her a girl at first; but when she turned and showed her face, I saw that she was quite grown-up, but a simpleton. She looked at me in a troubled sort of way, and the nurses laughed. I found out later that they used her more or less as they would a servant, and had her running every sort of chore; though she was—if you could believe it—the daughter of a very grand family.

She ducked her head while the nurses laughed, and cast a few sly looks at my feet—as if to see for herself how quick they might be, really. At last one of the other two women said quietly,

'Don't mind them, Betty. They seek only to provoke you.'

'Who spoke to you?' said Nurse Spiller at once.

The woman worked her lips. She was old, and slight, and very pale in the cheek. She caught my eye, then glanced away as if ashamed.

She seemed harmless enough; but I looked at her, and at Betty, and at the other woman there—a woman who stood, gazing at nothing, pulling her hair before her face—and I thought that, for all I knew, they might be so many maniacs; and here was I, being obliged to make a bed among them. I went to the nurses. I said,

'I won't stay here. You can't make me.'

'Can't we?' said Nurse Spiller. 'I think we know the law. Your order's been signed, ain't it?'

'But this is all a mistake!'

Nurse Bacon yawned and rolled her eyes. The dark nurse sighed. 'Come, Maud,' she said. 'That's enough.'

'My name ain't Maud,' I answered. 'How many times do I have to tell you? It ain't Maud Rivers!'

She caught Nurse Bacon's eye. 'Hear that? She will speak like that, by the hour.'

Nurse Bacon put her knuckles to her hips and rubbed them.

'Don't care to speak nicely?' she said. 'Ain't that a shame! Perhaps she'd like a situation as a nurse. See how she'd like that. Spoil her white little hands, though.'

Still rubbing her own hands against her skirt, she gazed at mine. I gazed with her. My fingers looked like Maud's. I put them behind my back. I said,

'I only got hands so white through being maid to a lady. It was that lady that tricked me. I—'

'Maid to a lady!' The nurses laughed again. 'Well, don't that take the cake! We got plenty girls suppose themselves duchesses. I never met one that thought herself a duchess's maid! Dear me, that's novel, that is. We shall have to put you in the kitchen, give you polish and a cloth.'

I stamped my foot.

'For fuck's sake!' I cried.

That stopped them laughing. They caught hold of me, and shook me; and Nurse Spiller hit me again about the face—upon the same spot as before—though not so hard. I suppose she thought the old bruise would cover up the new. The pale old woman saw her do it and gave a cry. Betty, the idiot girl, began to moan.

'There, now you've set them off!' said Nurse Spiller. 'And here's the doctors due, any minute.'

She shook me again, then let me stagger away so she might put straight her apron. The doctors were like kings to them. Nurse Bacon went to Betty, to bully her out of her tears. The dark nurse ran to the old woman.

'You finish fastening your buttons, you creature!' she said, waving her arms. 'And you, Mrs Price, you take your hair from out your mouth this instant. Haven't I told you a hundred times, you shall swallow a ball of it, and choke? I'm sure I don't know why I warn you, we should all be glad if you did . . .'

I looked at the door. Nurse Spiller had left it open, and I wondered if I might reach it if I ran. But from the room next to

ours—and then, from all down the corridor, from all the other
rooms we had passed—there came, as I wondered, the sound of
doors being unlocked and opened; and then the grumbling voices of
nurses, the odd shriek. Somewhere, a bell was rung. That was the
signal that meant the doctors were coming.

And I thought, after all, that I should make a far better case for
myself in standing and talking quietly with Dr Christie, than in
running at him in a pair of rubber boots. I moved close to my
bed, putting my knee to it to keep my leg from trembling; and I
felt for my hair, meaning to tidy it—forgetting, for the moment,
that they had stitched it to my head. The dark nurse went off,
running. The rest of us stood in silence, listening out for the
sound of the doctors' footsteps. Nurse Spiller shook her finger at
me.

'You watch your filthy tongue, you trollop,' she said.

We waited for about ten minutes, then there was a stir in the passage and Dr Christie and Dr Graves came walking very quickly
into the room, their heads bent over Dr Graves's note-book.

'Dear ladies, good morning,' said Dr Christie, looking up. He
went first to Betty. 'How are you, Betty? Good girl. You want your
medicine, of course.'

He put his hand to his pocket and brought out a piece of sugar.
She took it, and curtseyed.

'Good girl,' he said again. Then, moving past her: 'Mrs Price.
The nurses tell me you have been giving in to tears. That is not
good. What will your husband say? Shall he be pleased to think
you melancholy? Hmm? And all your children? What shall they
think?'

She answered in a whisper: 'I don't know, sir.'

'Hmm?'

He took her wrist, all the time murmuring to Dr Graves, who
finally made some note in his book. Then they walked to the pale
old lady.

'Miss Wilson, what complaints have you for us today?' asked Dr
Christie.

'None but the usual ones,' she answered.

'Well, we have heard them many times. You need not repeat them.'

'The want of pure air,' she said quickly.

'Yes, yes.' He looked at Dr Graves's book.

'And of wholesome food.'

'You will find the food wholesome enough, Miss Wilson, if you will only sample it.'

'The frigid water.'

'A tonic, for shattered nerves. You know this, Miss Wilson.'

She moved her lips, and swayed on her feet. Then all at once she cried out: 'Thieves!'

I jumped at the sound. Dr Christie looked up at her. 'That's enough,' he said. 'Remember your tongue. What have you upon it?'

'Thieves! Devils!'

'Your tongue, Miss Wilson! What do we keep upon it? Hmm?'

She worked her mouth; then said, after a minute:

'A curb.'

'That is right. A curb. Very good. Draw it tight. Nurse Spiller—' He turned and called the nurse to him, and spoke to her quietly. Miss Wilson put her hands to her mouth, as if to feel for a chain; and again, she caught my eye, and her fingers fluttered, and she seemed ashamed.

I should have been sorry for her, at any other time; but for now, if they had laid her and ten more ladies like her down upon the floor and told me my way out was across their backs, I'd have run it with clogs on. I waited only until Dr Christie had finished giving his instructions to the nurse, and then I licked my mouth and leaned and said,

'Dr Christie, sir!'

He turned and came towards me.

'Mrs Rivers.' He took my hand about the wrist, not smiling. 'How are you?'

'Sir,' I said. 'Sir, I—'

'Pulse rather rapid,' he said quietly, to Dr Graves. Dr Graves made a note of it. He turned back to me. 'You have hurt your face, I am sorry to see.'

Nurse Spiller spoke before I could.

'Cast herself to the floor, Dr Christie,' she said, 'while in the grip of her fit.'

'Ah, yes. You see, Mrs Rivers, the violence of the condition in which you arrived here. I hope you slept?'

'Slept? No, I—'

'Dear, dear. We cannot have that. I shall have the nurses give you a draught. You shall never grow well, without slumber.'

He nodded to Nurse Bacon. She nodded back.

'Dr Christie,' I said, more loudly.

'Pulse quickening, now,' he murmured.

I pulled my hand away. 'Will you listen to me? You have got me here, by mistake.'

'Is that so?' He had narrowed his eyes and was looking into my mouth. 'Teeth sound enough, I think. Gums may be putrid, how-ever.—You must tell us, if they start troubling you.'

'I'm not staying here,' I said.

'Not staying, Mrs Rivers?'

'Mrs Rivers? For God's sake, how can I be her? I stood and saw her married. You came to me, and heard me speak. I—'

'So I did,' he said slowly. 'And you told me how you feared for your mistress's health; how you wished she might be kept quiet and free from harm. For sometimes it is easier—is it not?—to ask for assistance in behalf of another, than for ourselves? We under-stand you, Mrs Rivers, very well.'

'I am not Maud Rivers!'

He raised a finger, and almost smiled.

'You are not ready to admit that you are Maud Rivers. Hmm? That is quite a different thing. And when you are ready to admit to it, our work shall be done. Until then—'

'You shan't keep me here. You shan't! You keep me, while those swindling villains—'

He folded his arms. 'Which swindling villains, Mrs Rivers?'

'I am not Maud Rivers! My name is Susan—'

'Yes?'

But here, for the first time, I faltered.

'Susan Smith,' I said finally.

'Susan Smith. Of—where was it, Dr Graves? Of Whelk Street, Mayfair?'

I did not answer.

'Come, come,' he went on. 'That is all your fancy, is it not?'

'It was Gentleman's fancy,' I said, thrown off. 'That devil—!'

'Which gentleman, Mrs Rivers?'

'Richard Rivers,' I answered.

'Your husband.'

'*Her* husband.'

'Ah.'

'*Her* husband, I tell you! I saw them married. You may find out the vicar that did it. You may bring Mrs Cream!'

'Mrs Cream, the lady you lodged with? We spoke at length with her. She told us, very sadly, of the melancholy temper that stole upon you, in her house.'

'She was speaking of Maud.'

'Of course.'

'She was speaking of Maud, not me. You bring her here. You show her my face, see what she says then. Bring anyone here that has known Maud Lilly and me. Bring Mrs Stiles, the housekeeper at Briar. Bring old Mr Lilly!'

He shook his head. 'And don't you think,' he said, 'your own husband might be supposed to know you, as well as your uncle? And your maid? She stood before us, and spoke of you, and wept.' He lowered his voice. 'What had you done to her, hmm, to make her do that?'

'Oh!' I said, twisting my hands together. ('See her colour change now, Dr Graves,' he said softly.) 'She wept, to trick you! She's nothing but an actress!'

'An actress? Your maid?'

'Maud Lilly! Don't you hear me? Maud Lilly and Richard Rivers. They have put me here—they have cheated and tricked me—they have made you think me her, and her me!'

He shook his head again, and drew close his brows; and again, he almost smiled. Then he said, slowly and very easily:

'But, my dear Mrs Rivers, why should they go to the trouble of doing that?'

I opened my mouth. Then I closed it. For, what could I say? I still supposed that if I only told him the truth, he would believe it. But the truth was I had plotted to steal a lady's fortune; that I had made myself out a servant, when I was really a thief. If I had not been so afraid, and so tired, and so bruised from my night in the pads, I might have thought up a clever story. Now I could not think, at all. Nurse Bacon rubbed her hands and yawned. Dr Christie still watched me, with a humouring expression on his face.

'Mrs Rivers?' he said.

'I don't know,' I answered at last.

'Ah.'

He nodded to Dr Graves, and they began to move off.

'Wait! Wait!' I cried.

Nurse Spiller came forward. 'That's enough from you,' she said. 'You are wasting the doctors' time.'

I did not look at her. I watched Dr Christie turn from me, and saw beyond him the pale old lady, her fingers still chafing at her mouth; and the sad-faced woman with her hair pulled all before her eyes; and Betty, the idiot girl, her lip gleaming with sugar; and I grew wild again. I thought, 'I don't care if they put me in a prison for it! Better a prison, with thieves and murderesses, than a madhouse!' I said,

'Dr Christie, sir! Dr Graves! Listen to me!'

'That's enough,' said Nurse Spiller again. 'Don't you know what busy men the doctors are? Don't you think they got better things to do than hear all your nonsense? Get back!'

I had stepped after Dr Christie and was reaching for his coat.

'Please, sir,' I said. 'Listen to me. I haven't been perfectly straight with you. My name ain't Susan Smith, after all.'

He had made to shake me off. Now he turned a little to me.

'Mrs Rivers,' he began.

'Susan Trinder, sir. Sue Trinder, of—' I was about to say, Lant Street; then knew that of course I must not say it, for fear it should lead the police to Mr Ibbs's shop. I closed my eyes and shook my head. My brain felt hot. Dr Christie drew himself from my hand.

'You must not touch my coat,' he said, his voice grown sterner.

I clutched it again. 'Only hear me out, I beg you! Only let me tell you of the terrible plot I was made to be part of, by Richard Rivers. That devil! He is laughing at you, sir! He is laughing at all of us! He has stolen a fortune. He has fifteen thousand pounds!'

I would not let go of his coat. My voice was high, like the yelp of a dog. Nurse Spiller got her arm about my neck, and Dr Christie put his hands over mine and worked free my fingers. Dr Graves came to help him. At the feel of their hands, I shrieked. I suppose I really seemed mad, then; but it was only through the awfulness of having said nothing but the truth, and being thought to be deluded. I shrieked, and Dr Christie got out his whistle, just like before. There was a bell rung. Mr Bates and Mr Hedges came running, in their brown-paper cuffs. Betty bellowed.

They put me back in the pads. They let me wear the gown and boots, however; and they gave me a basin of tea.

'When I get out, you'll be sorry!' I said, as they closed the door on me. 'I got a mother in London. She is looking for me, in every house in the land!'

Nurse Spiller nodded. 'Is she?' she said. 'That's yours, and all our other ladies', then'; and she laughed.

I think the tea—which tasted bitter—must have had a draught in it. I slept through a day—or it might have been two days; and when I finally came to myself, I came to stupid. I let them take me, stumbling, back to the room with the beds. Dr Christie made his tour, and held my wrist.

'You are calmer today, Mrs Rivers,' he said; and my mouth being dry, from the draught and from sleeping, it was as much as I could do to unstick my tongue from my gums, to answer,

'I ain't Mrs Rivers!'

And he had gone, before I said it.

My head grew clearer as the day wore on, though. I lay on my bed and tried to think. They made us keep to our rooms in the morning, and we were meant to sit and be silent—or to read, if we liked—while Nurse Bacon watched. But I think what books there were in the house, the ladies had already read; for they only, like me, lay upon their beds, doing nothing, and it was Nurse Bacon who sat, with her feet put up on a stool, looking over the pages of a little magazine—now and then licking one of her fat red fingers, to turn a page; and now and then chuckling.

And then, at twelve, she put the magazine away and gave a great yawn, and took us downstairs for our dinners. Another nurse came to help her. 'Come on, come on,' they said. 'No dawdling.'

We walked in a line. The pale old lady—Miss Wilson—pressed close at my back.

'Don't be frightened,' she said, 'of— Don't turn your head! Hush! Hush!' I felt her breath on my neck. 'Don't be frightened,' she said, 'of your soup.'

Then I walked faster, to be nearer Nurse Bacon.

She led us to the dining-room. They were ringing a bell there, and as we went our line was joined by other nurses, with ladies from the rooms they watched in. I should say there were sixty or so ladies kept in that house; and they seemed to me now, after my spell in the pads, a vast and horrible crowd. They were dressed as I was—I mean badly, in all sorts of fashions; and this—and the fact that some had had their hair cut to their heads; and some had lost teeth, or had their teeth taken from them; and some had cuts and bruises, and others wore canvas bracelets or muffs—this made them look queerer than perhaps they really were. I'm not saying they weren't all mad, in their own fashions; and to me, just then, they looked mad as horse-flies. But there are as many different ways of being mad, after all, as there are of being crooked. Some were perfect maniacs. Two or three, like Betty, were only simpletons. One liked to shout bad words. Another threw fits. The rest were only miserable: they walked, with their eyes on the floor, and sat and turned their hands in their laps, and mumbled, and sighed.

I sat among them, and ate the dinner I was served. It was soup, as Miss Wilson had said, and I saw her looking at me, nodding her head, as I supped it; but I would not catch her eye. I would not catch anyone's eye. I had been drugged and stupid, before; now I was back in a sort of fright—a sort of fever of fright—sweating, and twitching, and wild. I looked at the doors and windows—I think, if I had seen a window of plain glass, I should have run through it. But the windows all had bars on. I don't know what we should have done in a fire. The doors had ordinary locks, and with the right sort of tools I suppose I might have picked them. But I hadn't any kind of tool—not so much as a hair-pin—and nothing to make one with. The spoons we ate our soup with were made of tin, and so soft, they might have been rubber. You could not have picked your nose with them.

Dinner lasted half an hour. We were watched by the nurses and a few stout men—Mr Bates and Mr Hedges, and one or two others. They stood at the side of the room, and now and then walked between the tables. When one drew close I twitched and lifted up my hand and said,

'Please, sir, where are the doctors? Sir? May I see Dr Christie, sir?'

'Dr Christie is busy,' he said. 'Be quiet.' He walked on.

A lady said, 'You shan't see the doctors now. They come only in the mornings. Don't you know?'

'She is new here,' said another.

'Where are you from?' asked the first.

'From London,' I said, still looking after the man. 'Though here they think I come from somewhere else.'

'From London!' she cried. Some of the other ladies said it, too: 'London!' 'Ah! London! How I miss it!'

'And the season just beginning. That is very hard for you. And so young! Are you out?'

I said, 'Out?'

'Who are your people?'

'What?' The stout man had turned and was walking back towards us. I lifted my hand again, and waved it. 'Will you tell me,' I said to him, 'where I can find Dr Christie? Sir? Please, sir?'

'Be quiet!' he said again, moving past.

The lady beside me put her hand upon my arm. 'You must be familiar,' she said, 'with the squares of Kensington.'

'What?' I said. 'No.'

'I should say the trees are all in leaf.'

'I don't know. I don't know. I never saw them.'

'Who *are* your people?'

The stout man walked as far as the window, then turned and folded his arms. I had raised my hand again, but now let it droop.

'My people are thieves,' I said miserably.

'Oh!' The ladies made faces. 'Queer girl . . .'

The woman beside me, however, beckoned me close.

'Your property gone?' she said, in a whisper. 'Mine, too. But see here.' She showed me a ring that she wore, on a string, around her neck. It was gilt, and wanted stones. 'Here's my capital,' she said. 'Here's my security.' She tucked the ring beneath her collar, and touched her nose, and nodded. 'My sisters have taken the rest. They shan't have this, however! Oh, no!'

I spoke to no-one, after that. When dinner was ended the nurses took us to a garden and made us walk about it for an hour. The garden had walls on every side, and a gate: the gate was locked, but you could see through its bars to the rest of the park that the house was set in. There were many trees there, some of them close to the great park wall. I made a note of that. I had never climbed a tree in my life, but how hard could it be? If I might get to a high enough branch I would risk breaking both my legs in a jump, if the jump meant freedom.

If Mrs Sucksby didn't come first.

But then, I still supposed, too, that I should make my case with Dr Christie. I meant to show him how sane I was. At the end of our hour in the garden a bell was rung, and we were taken back to the house and made to sit, until tea-time, in a great grey room that smelt of leaking gas, that they called the drawing-room; and then we were locked back in our bedrooms. I went—still twitching, still sweating—and said nothing. I did all that the other ladies—sad Mrs Price, and pale Miss Wilson, and Betty—did: I washed my face and hands, at the wash-stand, when they were finished with the water; and cleaned my teeth, when they had all used the brush; and put my hateful tartan gown in a tidy heap, and pulled on a night-gown; and said Amen, when Nurse Bacon mumbled out a prayer. But then, when Nurse Spiller came to the door with a can of tea and gave me a basin of it, I took it, but did not drink it. I tipped it on the floor, when I thought no-one was looking. It steamed for a second, then seeped between the boards. I put my foot on the place I had tipped it. I looked up, and saw Betty watching.

'Made a mess,' she said loudly. She had a voice like a man's. 'Bad girl.'

'Bad girl?' said Nurse Bacon, turning round. 'I know who's one of them, all right. Into your bed. Quick! quick! all of you. God bless me, what a life!'

She could grumble like an engine. All the nurses there could. We had to be quiet, however. We had to lie still. If we didn't, they came and pinched or smacked us.—'You, Maud,' said Nurse Bacon, that first night, when I turned and trembled. 'Stop moving!'

She sat up, reading, and the light of her lamp shone in my eyes. Even when, after hours and hours, she put down her magazine and took off her apron and gown and got into her bed, she left a light still burning, so she could see us if we stirred in the night; and then she went straight to sleep and started snoring. Her snores were like the sound of a file on iron; and made me more homesick than ever.

She took her chain of keys to bed with her, and slept with it about her neck.

I lay with Maud's white glove in my fist, and now and then put the tip of one of its fingers to my mouth, imagining Maud's soft hand inside it; and I bit and bit.

But I slept, at last; and when next morning the doctors came back on their round with Nurse Spiller, I was ready.

'Mrs Rivers, how are you?' said Dr Christie, after he had given Betty her sugar and spent a minute looking over Mrs Price and Miss Wilson.

'I am perfectly clear in my head,' I said.

He looked at his watch. 'Splendid!'

'Dr Christie, I beg you—!'

I dipped my head and caught his eye, and I told him my story, all over again—how I was not Maud Rivers, but had only been put in his house through a terrible trick; how Richard Rivers had had me at Briar as Maud Lilly's servant, so I might help him marry her and, afterwards, make her out to be mad. How they had swindled me and taken her fortune, all for themselves.

'They have played me false,' I said. 'They have played *you* false! They are laughing at you! You don't believe me? Bring anyone from Briar! Bring the vicar of the church they were married in! Bring the great church book—you'll see their names put there, and next to them, my own!'

He rubbed his eye. 'Your name,' he said. 'Susan—what are you calling it, now?—Trinder?'

'Susan— No!' I said. 'Not in that book. It is Susan Smith, in there.'

'Susan Smith, again!'

'Only in there. They made me put it. He showed me how! Don't you see?'

But now I was almost weeping. Dr Christie began to look grim. 'I have let you say too much,' he said. 'You are growing excited. We cannot have that. We must have calm, at all times. These fancies of yours—'

'Fancies? God help me, it's the plainest truth!'

'*Fancies*, Mrs Rivers. If you might only hear yourself! Terrible plots? Laughing villains? Stolen fortunes and girls made out to be mad? The stuff of lurid fiction! We have a name for your disease. We call it a hyper-aesthetic one. You have been encouraged to over-indulge yourself in literature; and have inflamed your organs of fancy.'

'Inflamed?' I said. 'Over-indulge? Literature?'

'You have read too much.'

I looked at him and could not speak.

'God help me,' I said at last, as he turned away, 'if I can read two words in a row! As for writing—give me a pencil, and I'll put you down my name; and that's as much as I should ever be able to put, though you sit me down and make me try it for a year!'

He had begun to walk to the door of the room, with Dr Graves close behind him. My voice was broken, for Nurse Spiller had caught hold of me to keep me from following after. 'How dare you speak,' she said, 'to the doctors' backs! Don't pull from me! I should say you're wild enough to be put back in the pads. Dr Christie?'

But Dr Christie had heard my words and had turned at the door and was looking at me in a new sort of way, his hand at his beard. He glanced at Dr Graves. He said quietly,

'It would show us, after all, the extent of the delusion; and may even serve to startle her out of it. What do you say? Yes, give me a page from your note-book. Nurse Spiller, let Mrs Rivers go. Mrs Rivers—' He came back to me and gave me the little piece of paper that Dr Graves had torn from his book. Then he put his hand to his pocket and brought out a pencil, and made to give me that.

'Watch her, sir!' said Nurse Spiller, when she saw the pencil's point. 'She's a sly one, this one!'

'Very good, I see her,' he answered. 'But I do not think she means us any harm. Do you, Mrs Rivers?'

'No, sir,' I said. I took the pencil in my hand. It trembled. He watched me.

'You may hold it better than that, I think,' he said.

I moved it in my fingers, and it fell. I picked it up. 'Watch her! Watch her!' said Nurse Spiller again, ready to make another grab at me.

'I am not used to holding pencils,' I said.

Dr Christie nodded. 'I think you are. Come, write me a line upon this paper.'

'I can't,' I said.

'Of course you can. Sit neatly on the bed and rest the paper on your knee. That is how we sit to write, is it not? You know it is. Now, write me your name. You can do that, at least. You have told us so. Go on.'

I hesitated, then wrote it. The paper tore beneath the lead. Dr

Christie watched and, when I had finished, took the sheet from me and showed it to Dr Graves. They frowned.

'You have written *Susan*,' said Dr Christie. 'Why is that?'

'It is my name.'

'You have written badly. Did you do so on purpose? Here.' He gave me the paper back. 'Write me out a line, as I requested first.'

'I can't. I can't!'

'Yes, you can. Write a single word, then. Write me this. Write: *speckle*.'

I shook my head.

'Come, come,' he said, 'this word is not difficult. And you know the first letter of it, we have seen you write that already.'

Again, I hesitated. And then, because he watched so closely— and because, beyond him, Dr Graves and Nurse Spiller and Nurse Bacon, and even Mrs Price and Miss Wilson, also tilted their heads to see me do it—I wrote an S. Then I made a hazard at the other letters. The word went on and on, and grew larger as I wrote.

'You still press hard,' Dr Christie said.

'Do I?'

'You know you do. And your letters are muddled, and very ill-formed. What letter is this? It is one of your own imagining, I think. Now, am I to understand that your uncle—a scholar, I believe?—would countenance work like this, from his assistant?'

Here was my moment. I quivered right through. Then I held Dr Christie's gaze and said, as steadily as I could:

'I haven't an uncle to my name. You mean old Mr Lilly. I dare say his niece Maud writes neatly enough; but you see, I ain't her.'

He tapped at his chin.

'For you,' he said, 'are Susan Smith, or Trinder.'

I quivered again. 'Sir, I am!'

He was silent. I thought, *That's it!* and almost swooned, with relief. Then he turned to Dr Graves and shook his head.

'Quite complete,' he said. 'Isn't it? I don't believe I ever saw a case so pure. The delusion extending even to the exercise of the motor faculties. It's there we will break her. We must study on this, until our course of treatment is decided. Mrs Rivers, my pencil if you please. Ladies, good-day.'

He plucked the pencil from between my fingers, and turned, and left us. Dr Graves and Nurse Spiller went with him, and Nurse Bacon locked the door at their backs. I saw her turn the key, and it was just as if she had struck me or knocked me down: I fell upon my bed and broke out crying. She gave a tut—but they were too used to tears in that house, it was nothing to see a woman sitting at dinner, weeping into her soup, or walking about the garden crying her head off. Her tut turned into a yawn. She looked me over, then looked away. She sat in her chair and rubbed her hands, and winced.

'You think you've torments,' she said, to me or to all of us. 'Have these knuckles for an hour—have these thumbs. Here's torments, with mustard on. Here's torments, with whips. Oh! Oh! God bless me, I think I shall die! Come, Betty, be a good girl to your poor old nurse. Fetch out my ointment, will you?'

She still held her chain of keys. The sight of them made me cry worse. She shook one free, and Betty took it to the nurse's cupboard, unlocked the door, and brought out a jar of grease. The grease was white and hard, like lard. Betty sat, took a handful of it, and began to work it into Nurse Bacon's swollen fingers. Nurse Bacon winced again. Then she sighed, and her face grew smooth.

'That finds the mark!' she said; and Betty chuckled.

I turned my head into my pillow and closed my eyes. If the house had been hell, and Nurse Bacon the Devil, and Betty a demon at her side, I could not have been more wretched. I cried until I could cry no more.

And then there came a movement beside my bed, and then a voice, very gentle.

'Come, my dear. You must not give in to tears.'

It was the pale old lady, Miss Wilson. She had put out her hand to me. I saw it, and flinched.

'Ah,' she said then. 'You shrink from me. I don't wonder at it. I am not quite in my right mind. You will grow used to that, here. Hush! Not a word. Nurse Bacon watches. Hush!'

She had taken a handkerchief from her sleeve, and made signs that I should dry my face. The handkerchief was yellow with age, but soft; and the softness of it, and the kindness of her look—which, for all that she was mad, was the first piece of kindness that anyone had shown me since I came to the house—made me begin to cry again. Nurse Bacon looked over. 'I've got my eye on you,' she said to me. 'Don't think I haven't.' Then she settled back in her chair. Betty still worked grease into her fingers.

I said quietly,

'You mustn't think I cry so easily as this, at home.'

'I am sure you do not,' answered Miss Wilson.

'I'm only so frightened they will keep me here. I have been done very wrong. They say I am mad.'

'You must keep your spirit. This house is not so hard as some others. But nor is it perfectly kind. The air of this room, for example, that we must breathe, like oxen in a stall. The suppers. They call us ladies, yet the food—the merest pap!—I should blush to see it served to a gardener's boy.'

Her voice had risen. Nurse Bacon looked over again, and curled her lip.

'I should like to see you blush, you phantom!' she said.

Miss Wilson worked her mouth and looked embarrassed.

'A reference,' she said to me, 'to my pallor. Will you believe me if I tell you, there is a substance in the water here, related to chalk—? But, hush! No more of that!'

She waved her hand, and looked for a moment so mad, my heart quite sank.

'Have you been here very long?' I asked, when her fluttering hand had fallen.

'I believe—let me see—we know so little of the passing seasons . . . I should say, many years.'

'Two-and-twenty,' said Nurse Bacon, still listening. 'For you were quite an old hand—were you not?—when I first come in as a young one. And that was fourteen years, this autumn.—Ah, press harder, Betty, there! Good girl.'

She pulled a face, let out her breath, and her eyes closed. I thought in horror, *Two-and-twenty years!*—and the thought must have shown on my face, for Miss Wilson said,

'You must not think you shall stay so long as that. Mrs Price comes, every year; but her husband has her home again, when the worst of her spells are past. It was a husband, I think, who signed your order? It is my brother who keeps me here. But men want wives, when they may do without their sisters.' Her hand rose. 'I would speak plainer, if I could. My tongue— You understand.'

'The man,' I said, 'that has put me here, is a dreadful villain; and only pretends to be my husband.'

'That is hard for you,' said Miss Wilson, shaking her head and sighing. 'That is the worst of all.'

I touched her arm. My heart, that had sunk, now rose like a float—so hard, it hurt me.

'You believe it,' I said. I looked at Nurse Bacon; but she had heard me and opened her eyes.

'Don't make anything of that,' she said, in a comfortable voice. 'Miss Wilson believes all sorts of nonsense. Only ask her, now, what creatures live in the moon.'

'Curse you!' said Miss Wilson. 'I told you that as a confidence!— You may see, Mrs Rivers, how they work to diminish my standing.—Does my brother pay a guinea a week for you to abuse me? Thieves! Devils!'

Nurse Bacon made a show of rising from her chair and making her hands into fists; and Miss Wilson grew quiet again. I said, after a moment,

'You may think what you like about the moon, Miss Wilson. Why shouldn't you? But when I tell you I have been put in here by swindlers and am perfectly right in my head, I say no more than the truth. Dr Christie shall find it out, in time.'

'I hope he will,' she answered. 'I am sure he will. But you know, it is your husband who must sign you out.'

I stared at her. Then I looked at Nurse Bacon. 'Is that true?' I asked. Nurse Bacon nodded. I began to weep again. 'Then, God help me, I'm done for!' I cried. 'For that shyster never, never will!'

Miss Wilson shook her head. 'So hard! So hard! But perhaps he will visit, and take a change of heart? They must let us see our visitors, you know; that is the law.'

I wiped my face. 'He won't come,' I said. 'He knows that, if he did, I would kill him!'

She looked about her, in a sort of fear. 'You must not say such things, in here. You must be good. Don't you know, that they have ways of taking you, of binding you— That they have water—'

'*Water*,' murmured Mrs Price, in a shuddering way.

'That's enough!' Nurse Bacon said. 'And you, Miss Muffet'—she meant me—'stop stirring up the ladies.'

And again, she showed her fist.

So then we all fell silent. Betty worked the grease in for another minute or two, then put the jar away and went back to her bed. Miss Wilson bent her head and her gaze grew dark. Mrs Price now and then let out a murmur or a moan from behind her veil of hair. From the room next door there came a burst of ragged shrieking. I thought of Mr Ibbs's sister. I thought of all my home, and all the people in it. I began, again, to sweat. I felt suddenly I think as a fly must feel, when wrapped in the thread of a spider. I got to my feet and walked from one wall of the room to the other, and back.

'If only there was a window!' I said. 'If only we might see out.' And then: 'If only I had never left the Borough!'

'Will you sit down?' said Nurse Bacon.

Then she cursed. There had come a knocking at the door, and she must get up from her chair to answer it. It was another nurse, with a paper. I waited until their heads were close together, then stole back to Miss Wilson. Desperation was beginning to make me sly.

'Listen to me,' I said quietly. 'I must get out of here, quick as I can. I have people in London, with money. I've a mother. You've been here so long, you must know of a way. What is it? I'll pay you for it, I swear.'

She looked at me, and then drew back. 'I hope,' she said, in an ordinary tone, 'I hope you don't suppose that I was the kind of girl brought up to speak in whispers?'

Nurse Bacon looked round and stared.

'You, Maud,' she said. 'What are you doing now?'

'Whispering,' said Betty, in her gruff voice.

'Whispering? I'll whisper her, all right! Get back to your bed and leave Miss Wilson alone. Can't I turn my back a minute without you start up trying to tamper with the ladies?'

I supposed she guessed I had been trying to escape. I went back to my bed. She stood at the door with the other nurse, and said something to her in a murmur. The other nurse wrinkled her nose. Then they looked me over in the same cool, nasty way that I had seen other nurses look at me, before.

I was still too ignorant then, of course, to know what the nasty look meant. God help me, though!—for I was to find out, soon enough.

Chapter Fifteen

*U*ntil then, however, I didn't trouble myself to wonder; for I still supposed I should get out. Even when a week went by, and then another, I supposed it. I only understood at last that I must give up my idea that Dr Christie would be the man to release me— for if he believed that I was mad when I went in, then everything I said as time went on only seemed to serve to make him think me madder. Worse than that, he still held firm to his idea that I should be cured, and know myself again, if I might only be made to write.

'You have been put too much to literary work,' he said on one of his visits, 'and that is the cause of your complaint. But sometimes we doctors must work by paradoxical methods. I mean to put you to literary work again, to restore you. Look here.' He had brought me something, wrapped in paper. It was a slate and chalk. 'You shall sit with this blank slate before you,' he said, 'and before this day is done, you shall have written me out—neatly, mind!—your name. Your true name, I mean. Tomorrow you shall write me the start of an account of your life; and you shall add to it, on each day that follows. You shall recover the use of your faculty of reason, as you recover your facility with the pen . . .'

And so he made Nurse Bacon keep me sitting with the chalk in my hand, for hours at a stretch; and of course, I could write nothing, the chalk would crumble to a powder—or else, grow damp and slippery from the sweating of my palm. Then he'd come back and see the empty slate, and frown and shake his head. He might have Nurse Spiller with him. 'Ain't you wrote a word?' she'd say. 'And here's the doctors spending all their time to make you well. Ungrateful, I call that.'

When he'd gone, she'd shake me. And when I'd cry and swear, she'd shake me harder. She could shake you so, you thought your teeth were being rattled out of your head. She could shake you until you were sick.—'Got the grips,' she'd tell the other nurses then, with a wink; and the nurses would laugh. They hated the ladies. They hated me. They thought that when I spoke in the way that was natural to me, I did it to tease them. I know they put it out that I got special attentions from Dr Christie, through pretending to be low. That made the ladies hate me, too. Only mad Miss Wilson was now and then kind to me. Once she saw me weeping over my slate and, when Nurse Bacon's back was turned, came over and wrote me out my name—Maud's name, I mean. But, though she meant it well, I wished she hadn't done it; for when Dr Christie came and saw it, he smiled and cried, 'Well done, Mrs Rivers! Now we are half-way there!' And when, next day, I again could make nothing but scribbles, of course he thought me shamming.

'Keep her from her dinner, Nurse Bacon,' he said sternly, 'until she writes again.'

So then, I wrote out: *Susan, Susan*—I wrote it, fifty times. Nurse Bacon hit me. Nurse Spiller hit me, too. Dr Christie shook his head. He said my case was worse than he had thought, and needed another method. He gave me drinks of creosote—had the nurses hold me, while he poured it into my mouth. He talked of bringing a leech-man in, to bleed my head. Then a new lady came to the house, who would speak nothing but a made-up language she said was the language of snakes; and after that he passed all his time with her, pricking her with needles, bursting paper bags behind her ear, scalding her with boiling water—looking for ways to startle her into speaking English.

I wished he would go on pricking and scalding her for ever. The creosote had almost choked me. I was frightened of leeches. And his leaving me alone, it seemed to me, would give me more time for sitting and planning my escape in. For I still thought of nothing but of that. It got to June. I had gone in there some time in May. But I still had spirit enough to learn the lie of the house, to study the windows and doors, looking out for weak ones; and every time Nurse Bacon took out her chain of keys, I watched, and saw which did what. I saw that, as far as the locks on the bedroom and passage doors went, one key worked them all. If I could slip that key from a nurse's chain, I could make my escape, I was certain of it. But those chains were stout; and each nurse kept her keys very close; and Nurse Bacon—who was warned I might be crafty—kept hers closest of all. She gave them up only to Betty when she wanted something got out from her cupboard; and then she took them back at once, and dropped them into her pocket.

I never saw her do it, without trembling in a hopeless rage. It seemed too hard that I—of all people in the world!—should be kept so low, so long, from everything that was mine, by a single key—a single, simple key! not even a fancy key, but a plain one, with four straight cuts upon it that, given the right kind of blank and file, I knew I should have been able, in half a moment, to fake up. I thought it, a hundred times a day. I thought it as I washed my face, and as I took my dinner. I thought it as I walked the little garden; as I sat in the drawing-room, hearing ladies mumble and weep; as I lay in my bed, with the nurse's lamp blazing in my eyes. If thoughts were hammers or picks I should have been free, ten thousand times over. But my thoughts were more like poisons. I had so many, they made me sick.

It was a dull sort of sickness, not like the sharp panic that had gripped me and made me sweat, in my first days there. It was a kind

of creeping misery, that crept so slow, and was so much a part of the
habits of the house—like the colour of the walls, the smell of the dinners, the sound of weeping and shrieks—I did not know it had gained
upon me, until too late. I still said, to everyone who spoke to me, that
I was quite in my right mind—that I was there, through a mistake—
that I was not Maud Rivers, and must be let out at once. But I said it
so often, the words grew soft—like coins losing their faces through
being too much spent. One day at last, I walked with a lady in the
garden and said it again; and the lady looked at me in pity.

'I thought the same thing, once,' she said kindly. 'But you see,
I'm afraid you must be mad, since you are here. There is something
queer about us all. You need only look about you. You need only
look at yourself.'

She smiled—but, as before, she smiled in a kind of pity; then she
walked on. I stopped, however. I had not thought, I could not say in
how long, of how I must look, to others. Dr Christie kept no looking-glasses, for fear they should get smashed, and it seemed to me
now that the last time I had gazed at my own face was at Mrs
Cream's—was it at Mrs Cream's?—when Maud had made me put
on her blue silk gown—was it blue? or had it been grey?—and held
up the little mirror. I put my hands to my eyes. The gown was
blue, I was certain of it. Why, I had been wearing it when they got
me into the madhouse! They had taken it from me—and they had
taken, too, Maud's mother's bag, and all the things that were in
it—the brushes and combs, the linen, the red prunella slippers—I
never saw those again. Instead— I looked down at myself, at the
tartan dress and rubber boots. I had grown almost used to them.
Now I saw them again for what they were; and wished I might see
them better. The nurse who had been set to watch us was sitting
with her eyes closed, dozing in the sun, but a little to the left of her
was the window that looked into the drawing-room. It was dark,
and showed the line of circling ladies, clear as a mirror. One of
them had stopped, and had her hand at her face.—I blinked. She
blinked. She was me.

I went slowly towards her, and looked myself over, in horror.

I looked, as the lady had said, like a lunatic. My hair was still sewn to my head, but had grown or worked loose from its stitches, and stood out in tufts. My face was white but marked, here and there, with spots and scratches and fading bruises. My eyes were swollen—from want of sleep, I suppose—and red at the rims. My face was sharper than ever, my neck like a stick. The tartan gown hung on me like a laundry bag. From beneath its collar there showed the dirty white tips of the fingers of Maud's old glove, that I still wore next to my heart. You could just make out, on the kid-skin, the marks of my teeth.

I looked, for perhaps a minute. I looked, and thought of all the times that Mrs Sucksby had washed and combed and shined my hair, when I was a girl. I thought of her warming her bed before she put me in it, so I should not take chills. I thought of her putting aside, for me, the tenderest morsels of meat; and smoothing my teeth, when they cut; and passing her hands across my arms and legs, to be sure that they grew straight. I remembered how close and safe she had kept me, all the years of my life. I had gone to Briar, to make my fortune, so I might share it with her. Now my fortune was gone. Maud Lilly had stolen it and given me hers. She was supposed to be here. She had made me be her, while she was loose in the world, and every glass she gazed at—as say, in milliners' shops, while she was fitted with gowns; or in theatres; or in halls, as she went dancing—every glass showed her to be everything I was not—to be handsome, and cheerful, and proud, and free—

I might have raged. I think I began to. Then I saw the look in my eye, and my face frightened me. I stood, not knowing what I should do, until the nurse on duty woke up, and came and jabbed me.

'All right, Miss Vanity,' she said with a yawn. 'I dare say your heels are worth looking at, too. So let's see 'em.' She pushed me back into the middle of the turning line; and I bowed my head and walked, watching the hem of my skirt, my boots, the boots of the lady in front—anything, anything at all, to save me from lifting my gaze to the drawing-room window and seeing again the look in my own mad eye.

That, I suppose, was at the end of June. It might have been sooner,

though. It was hard to know what dates were what. It was hard to
tell so much as the day—you only knew another week had gone by
when, instead of spending all morning on your bed, you were made
to stand in the drawing-room and listen while Dr Christie read
prayers; then you knew it was a Sunday. Perhaps I ought to have
made a mark, like convicts do, for every Sunday that came round;
but of course, for many weeks there seemed no point—each time
one came I thought that, by the next, I should have got out. Then I
began to grow muddled. It seemed to me that some weeks had two
or three Sundays in them. Others seemed to have none. All we
could tell for certain was, that spring had turned to summer: for the
days grew long, the sun grew fiercer; and the house grew hot, like an
oven.

I remember the heat, almost more than anything. It was enough
to make you mad all by itself. The air in our rooms, for instance,
became like soup. I think one or two ladies actually died, through
breathing that air—though of course, being medical men, Dr
Graves and Dr Christie were able to pass off their deaths as strokes.
I heard the nurses say that. They grew bad-tempered as the days
grew warm. They complained of headaches and sweats. They complained of their gowns. 'Why I stay here, looking after you, in
wool,' they'd say, pulling us about, 'when I might be at Tunbridge
Asylum, where the nurses all wear poplin—!'

But the fact of it was, as we all knew, no other madhouse would
have had them; and they wouldn't have gone, anyway. They had it
too easy. They talked all the time of how troublesome and sly their
ladies were, and showed off bruises; but of course, the ladies were
far too dazed and miserable to be sly, the trouble came all from the
nurses when they fancied some sport. The rest of the time their job
was the slightest one you can imagine, for they got us in bed at
seven o'clock—gave us those draughts, to make us sleep—then they
sat till midnight reading papers and books, making toast and cocoa,
doing fancy-work, whistling, farting, standing at the door and calling down the hall to each other, even slipping in and out of each
other's rooms when they were especially bored, leaving their ladies
locked up and unguarded.

And in the mornings, when Dr Christie had made his round, they would take off their caps, unpin their hair, roll down their stockings and lift their skirts; and they gave us newspapers and made us stand beside them and fan their great white legs.

Nurse Bacon did, anyway. She complained of the heat more than anyone, because of the itch in her hands. She had Betty rubbing grease into her fingers ten times a day. Sometimes she would scream. And when the weather was at its warmest she put two china basins beside her bed and slept with her hands in water. That gave her dreams.

'He's too slippy!' she cried one night. And then, in a mumble: 'There, I've lost him . . .'

I also dreamed. I seemed to dream every time I closed my eyes. I dreamed, as you might suppose I would, of Lant Street, of the Borough, of home. I dreamed of Mr Ibbs and Mrs Sucksby.— Those were troubling dreams, however; often I woke weeping from dreams like that. Now and then I dreamed only of the madhouse: I would dream I had woken and had my day. Then I really would wake, and have the day still to do—and yet, the day was so like the day I had dreamed, I might as well have dreamed them both.— Those dreams bewildered me.

The worst dreams of all, however, were the dreams I began to have as the weeks slipped by and the nights grew hotter and I began to get more and more muddled in my mind. They were dreams of Briar, and of Maud.

For I never dreamed of her as I knew she really was—as a viper or a thief. I never dreamed of Gentleman. I only ever used to dream that we were back in her uncle's house, and I was her maid. I dreamed we walked to her mother's grave, or sat by the river. I dreamed I dressed her and brushed her hair. I dreamed—you can't be blamed, can you, for what you dream?—I dreamed I loved her. I knew I hated her. I knew I wanted to kill her. But sometimes I would wake, in the night, not knowing. I would open my eyes and look about me, and the room would be so warm everyone would have turned and fretted in their beds—I would see Betty's great bare leg, Nurse Bacon's sweating face, Miss Wilson's arm. Mrs

Price put back her hair as she slept, rather in the way that Maud had
used to do: I would gaze at her in my half-sleep and quite forget the
weeks that had passed, since the end of April. I would forget the
flight from Briar, forget the wedding in the black flint church, forget
the days at Mrs Cream's, the drive to the madhouse, the awful trick;
forget I meant to escape, and what I planned to do when I had done
it. I would only think, in a kind of panic, *Where is she? Where is
she?*—and then, with a rush of relief: *There she is . . .* I would close
my eyes again and, in an instant, be not in my bed at all but in hers.
The curtains would be let down, and she would be beside me. I
would feel her breath. 'How close the night is, tonight!' she would
say, in her soft voice; and then: 'I'm afraid! I'm afraid—!'

'Don't be frightened,' I would always answer. 'Oh, don't be
frightened.'—And at that moment, the dream would slip from me
and I would wake. I would wake in a kind of dread, to think that,
like Nurse Bacon, I might have said the words aloud—or sighed, or
quivered. And then I would lie and be filled with a terrible shame.
For I hated her! I hated her!—and yet I knew that, every time, I
secretly wished that the dream had gone on to its end.

I began to be afraid I would rise in my sleep. Say I tried to kiss
Mrs Price, or Betty? But if I tried to stay awake, then I grew bewildered. I imagined fearful things. Those nights were queer nights.
For though the heat made us all grow stupid, it also now and then
sent ladies—even quiet, obedient ladies—into fits. You caught the
commotion of it from your bed: the shrieking, the ringing of bells,
the pounding of running feet. It broke into the hot and silent night,
like a clap of thunder; and though you knew, each time, what it was,
still the sounds came so strangely—and sometimes one lady would
set off another; and then you would lie and wonder whether that
mightn't set off *you*, and you would seem to feel the fit gathering
inside you, you would start to sweat, perhaps to twitch—oh, those
were dreadful nights! Betty might moan. Mrs Price would start to
weep. Nurse Bacon would rise: 'Hush! Hush!' she'd say. She would
open the door, lean out and listen. Then the shrieking would stop,
the footsteps begin to fade. 'That's got her,' she'd say. 'Now, will
they pad her, I wonder, or plunge her?'—and at that word, *plunge*,

Betty would moan again, and Mrs Price and even old Miss Wilson would shudder and hide their heads. I didn't know why. The word was a peculiar one and no-one would explain it: I could only suppose it must involve being pumped, like a drain, with a black rubber sucker. That thought was so horrible that soon whenever Nurse Bacon said it I began to shudder, too.

'I don't know what you're quaking at,' she would say to all of us, nastily, as she went back to her bed. 'Wasn't one of you that went off, was it?'

But then, one time, it was. We woke to the sound of choking and found sad Mrs Price on the floor beside her bed, biting her fingers so hard she was making them bleed. Nurse Bacon went for the bell, and the men and Dr Christie came running: they bound Mrs Price and carried her off downstairs, and when they brought her back, an hour later, her gown and her hair were streaming water and she looked half-drowned.—I learned then that being plunged meant being dropped in a bath. That gave me some comfort, at least; for it seemed to me that being bathed could not be nearly so bad as being suckered and pumped . . .

I still knew nothing, nothing, nothing at all.

Then something happened. There came a day—I think it was the hottest day of all that stifling summer—that turned out to be Nurse Bacon's birthday; and on the night of it, she had some other nurses come secretly to our room, to give them a party. They did this, sometimes, as I think I have said. They weren't allowed to, and their talking made it harder than ever for the rest of us to sleep; but we should never have dared tell a doctor—for then the nurses would have put it down to delusions and, after, hit us. They made us lie very still, while they sat about playing cards or dominoes, drinking lemonade and, sometimes, beer.

They had beer on this night, on account of it being Nurse Bacon's birthday night; and because it was hot they took too much of it and got drunk. I lay with the sheet across my face, but kept my eyes half open. I dared not try to sleep while they were there, in case I dreamed of Maud again; for it had got with me what you might call—or what Dr Christie, I suppose, might call—a morbid fear, of giving myself away. And then again, I thought I ought to keep awake, in case they drank so much they drank themselves into a stupor; for then I could rise and steal their keys . . .

They did not, however. Instead, they grew livelier and more noisy and red in the face, and the room grew hotter. I think that now and then I did fall into a doze: I began to hear their voices like the far-off, hollow voices you hear in dreams. Then, every so often one of them would give a shout, or snort with laughter; the others would shush her, then snort with laughter themselves—that would bring me back to myself, with a horrible jolt. At last I looked at their fat red sweating faces and their great wet open mouths, and wished I had a gun and could shoot them. They sat boasting of which ladies they had recently hurt, and how they had done it. They fell to comparing grips. They put their hands to one another's, palm to palm, to see who had the biggest. Then one of them showed her arm.

'Let us see yours, Belinda,' another cried then. Belinda was Nurse Bacon. They all had dainty names like that. You could imagine their mothers looking at them when they were babies, thinking they would grow up ballerinas. 'Go on, let us see it.'

Nurse Bacon pretended to look modest; then she put back her cuff. Her arm was thick as a coal-whipper's, but white. When she bent it, it bulged. 'That's Irish muscle,' she said, 'come down on my grandmother's side.' The other nurses felt it, and whistled. Then one of them said,

'I should say, with an arm like that, you're almost a match for Nurse Flew.'

Nurse Flew was a swivel-eyed woman with a room on the floor below. She was said to have once been a matron in a gaol. Now Nurse Bacon coloured up. 'A match?' she said. 'I should like to see her arm beside mine, that's all. Then we'd see whose was the greater. A match? I'll match her, all right!'

Her voice woke Betty and Mrs Price. She looked, and saw them stirring. 'Get back to sleep,' she said. She did not see me, watching her and wishing her dead through half-closed eyes. She showed her arm again, and again made the muscle bulge. 'A match, indeed,' she grumbled. She nodded to one of the nurses. 'You fetch Nurse Flew up here. Then we'll see. Margaretta, you get a string.'

The nurses rose, and swayed, and tittered, and then went off. The first came back after a minute with Nurse Flew, Nurse Spiller, and the dark-headed nurse that had helped to undress me on my first day. They had all been drinking together, downstairs. Nurse Spiller looked about her with her hands on her hips and said,

'Well, if Dr Christie could see you!' She belched. 'What's this about arms?'

She bared her own. Nurse Flew and the dark nurse bared theirs. The other nurse came back with a length of ribbon and a ruler, and they took it in turns to measure their muscles. I watched them do it, as a man in a darkened wood might, disbelieving his own eyes, watch goblins; for they stood in a ring and moved the lamp from arm to arm, and it threw strange lights and cast queer shadows; and the beer, and the heat, and the excitement of the measuring made them seem to lurch and hop.

'Fifteen!' they cried, their voices rising. Then: 'Sixteen!—Seventeen!—Eighteen-and-a-half!—Nineteen! Nurse Flew has it!'

They broke their circle then, and put down the light, and fell about quarrelling—not so much like goblins, suddenly, as like sailors. You half expected them to have tattoos. Nurse Bacon's face was darker than ever. She said sulkily,

'As to arms, well, I'll let Nurse Flew take it this time; though I'm sure fat oughtn't to count the same as muscle.' She rubbed her hands across her waist. 'Now, what about weight?' She put up her chin. 'Who here says they're heavier than me?'

At once, two or three of them got up beside her and said they were. The others tried to pick them up, in order to prove it. One of them fell down.

'It's no good,' they said. 'You wriggle about so, we can't tell. We need another way. What say you stand upon a chair and jump? We'll see who makes the floor creak most.'

'What say,' said the dark-haired nurse with a laugh, 'you jump on Betty? See who makes *her* creak.'

'See who makes her squeak!'

They looked at Betty's bed. Betty had opened her eyes at the sound of her name—now she shut them and began to shake.

Nurse Spiller snorted. 'She'd squeak for Belinda,' she said, 'every time. Don't make it her, that ain't fair. Make it old Miss Wilson.'

'She'd squeak all right!'

'Or, Mrs Price.'

'She'd cry! Crying's no—'

'Make it *Maud*!'

One of them said it—I don't know who—and, though they had all been laughing, now their laughter died. I think they looked at each other. Then Nurse Spiller spoke.

'Pass a chair,' I heard her say, 'for standing on—'

'Wait! Wait!' cried another nurse. 'What are you thinking of? You can't jump on her, it'll kill her.' She paused, as if to wipe her mouth. 'Lie on her, instead.'

And at that, I put back the sheet from my face and opened my eyes up wide. Perhaps I shouldn't have done it, just then. Perhaps, after all, they had only been larking. But I put back the sheet, and they saw me looking; and then they all started laughing again and came towards me in a rush. They plucked the blankets off me and took the pillow from under my head. Two of them leaned on my feet, and another two caught my arms. They did it in a moment. They were like one great hot sweating beast with fifty heads, with fifty panting mouths and a hundred hands. When I struggled, they pinched me. I said,

'You leave me alone!'

'Shut up,' they said. 'We aren't going to hurt you. We only want to see who's heaviest out of Nurse Bacon, Nurse Spiller and Nurse Flew. We only want to see which of them will make you squeak most. Are you ready?'

'Get off me! Get off me! I'll tell Dr Christie!'

Someone hit me in the face. Someone else jerked my leg. 'Spoilsport,' they said. 'Now, who's to go on her first?'

'I will,' I heard Nurse Flew say, and the others moved back a little for her to come forward. She was smoothing down her gown. 'Have you got her?' she said.

'We've got her.'

'Right. Hold her still.'

Then they pulled me tight, as if I were a wet sheet and they meant to wring me. My thoughts, at that moment, aren't fit to be described. I was sure they would tear the arms and legs off me. I was sure they would snap my bones. I started to shout and, again, I was struck in the face and jerked about; so then I fell silent. Then Nurse Flew got on to the bed and, lifting up her skirt, knelt astride of me. The bed gave a creak. She rubbed her hands and fixed me with her swivel-eye. 'Here I come!' she said, making to fall upon me. But the fall never came, though I screwed up my face and drew in my breath, to take it. Nurse Bacon had stopped her.

'No dropping,' she said. 'Dropping won't be fair. Go down slowly, or not at all.'

So Nurse Flew moved back, then came slowly forward, and lowered herself down by her hands and knees until her weight was all upon me. The breath I had drawn in was all squeezed out. I think, if I had had a floor underneath me instead of a bed, she would have killed me. My eyes, my nose and mouth, began to run. 'Please—!' I said.

'She cries Please!' said the dark-haired nurse. 'That means five points to Nurse Flew!'

They eased off tugging me, then. Nurse Flew kissed my cheek and got off me, and I saw her stand with her hands above her head, like the winner of a boxing match. I sucked in my breath, I spluttered and coughed. Then they drew me tight again, for Nurse Spiller's turn. She was worse than Nurse Flew—not heavier, but more awkward, for she lay with the points of her limbs, her knees and her elbows and her hips, pressing hard into mine; and her corset was a stiff one, with edges that seemed to cut me like a saw. Her hair had an oil upon it and smelt sour, and her breath was loud, like thunder, in my ear. 'Come on, you little bitch,' she said to me, 'sing out!'—but I had some pride, even then. I closed my jaws and wouldn't, though she pressed and pressed; at last the nurses cried, 'Oh, shame! No points for Nurse Spiller at all!'—and she gave a final grind to her knees, and swore, and got off. I lifted my head from the mattress. My eyes were streaming water, but beyond the circle of nurses I could see Betty and Miss Wilson and Mrs Price, looking on and shaking but pretending to sleep. They were afraid of what might be done to them. I don't blame them. I let my head fall back, and again shut tight my jaws. Now came Nurse Bacon. Her cheeks were still flushed, and her swollen hands so red against the white of her arms, she might have had gloves on.

She sat astride of me as Nurse Flew had, and flexed her fingers.

'Now, Maud,' she said. She caught hold of the hem of my night-gown, and pulled it and made it tidy. She patted my leg. 'Now then, Miss Muffet. Who's my own good girl?'

Then she came upon me. She came faster than the others, and the shock and the weight of her was awful. I cried out, and the nurses clapped. 'Ten points!' they said. Nurse Bacon laughed. I felt the shudder of it, like rolling-pins; and that made me screw up my eyes and cry out louder. Then she shuddered again, on purpose. The nurses cheered. Then she did this. She pushed herself up on her hands, so that her face was above me but her bosom and stomach and legs still hard on my own; and she moved her hips. She moved them in a certain way. My eyes flew open. She gave me a leer.

'Like it, do you?' she said, still moving. 'No? We heard you did.'

And at that, the nurses roared. They roared, and I saw on their faces as they gazed at me that nasty look I had seen before but never understood. I understood it now, of course; and all at once I guessed what Maud must have said to Dr Christie, that time at Mrs Cream's. The thought that she had said it—that she had said it, before Gentleman, as a way of making me out to be mad—struck me like a blow to the heart. I had had many such blows, since I left Briar; but this, just then, seemed like the worst. It was as if I were filled with gunpowder, and had just been touched with a match. I began to struggle, and to shriek.

'Get off me!' I shrieked. 'Get off me! Get off me! Get off!'

Nurse Bacon felt me wriggle, and her laughter died. She pushed again upon me, harder, with her hips. I saw her hot red face above my own and butted it with my head. Her nose went crack. She gave a cry. There came blood on my cheek.

Then, I can't quite say what happened. I think the nurses that were holding me let go; but I think I kept on struggling and shrieking, as if they had me still. Nurse Bacon rolled from me; I think that someone—probably, Nurse Spiller—hit me; yet still my fit kept on. I have an idea that Betty started up bellowing—that other ladies, in rooms close by, took up the screams and shouts from ours. I think the nurses ran. 'Catch up these bottles and cups!' I heard one of them say, as she flew off with the others. Then someone must have taken fright and caught hold of one of the handles in the hall: there came a bell. The bell brought men and then, after another minute, Dr Christie. He was pulling on his coat. He saw me, still kicking and thrashing on the bed, with the blood from Nurse Bacon's nose upon me.

'She's in a paroxysm,' he cried. 'A bad one. Good Lord, what was it set her off?'

Nurse Bacon said nothing. She had her hand at her face, but her eyes were on mine. 'What was it?' Dr Christie said again. 'A dream?'

'A dream,' she answered. Then she looked at him, and started into life. 'Oh, Dr Christie,' she said, 'she was saying a lady's name, and moving, as she slept!'

That made me shriek all over again. Dr Christie said, 'Right. We know our treatment for paroxysms. You men, and Nurse Spiller. Cold water plunge. Thirty minutes.'

The men caught hold of me by the arms and picked me up. I had been pressed so hard by the nurses that it seemed to me now, as they set me upright, that I was beginning to float. In fact, they dragged me: I found the grazes upon my toes, next day. But I don't remember, now, being taken down from that floor, to the basement of the house. I don't remember passing the door to the pads—going on, down that dark corridor, to the room where they kept the bath. I remember the roaring of the faucets, the chill of the tiles beneath my feet—but, only dimly. What I recall most is the wooden frame they fixed me to, at the arms and legs; and then, the creaking of it, as they winched it up and swung it over the water; the swaying of it, as I pulled against the straps.

Then I remember the drop, as they let fly the wheel—the shock, as they caught it—the closing of the icy water over my face, the rushing of it into my mouth and nose, as I tried to gasp—the suck-ing of it, when I spluttered and coughed.

I thought they had hanged me.

I thought I had died. Then they winched me up, and dropped me again. A minute to winch me, and a minute to plunge. Fifteen plunges in all. Fifteen shocks. Fifteen tugs on the rope of my life.

After that, I don't remember anything.

They might have killed me, after all. I lay in darkness. I did not dream. I did not think. You could not say I was myself, for I was no-one. Perhaps I never was to be quite myself, again. For when I woke, everything was changed. They put me back in my old gown and my old boots and took me back to my old room, and I went with them just like a lamb. I was covered in bruises and burns, yet hardly felt them. I did not weep. I sat and, like the other ladies, looked at nothing. There was talk of putting canvas bracelets on me, in case I should break out in another fit; but I lay so quietly, they gave the idea up. Nurse Bacon spoke with Dr Christie, in my behalf. Her eye was black where I had butted it, and I supposed that, get-ting me alone, she would knock me about—I think that, if she had, I would have taken the blows, unflinching. But it seemed to me that she was changed, like everything else. She looked at me oddly; and when that night I lay in bed and the other ladies had closed their eyes, she caught my gaze. 'All right?' she said softly. She glanced at the other beds, then looked back at me. 'No harm—eh, Maud? All fun, ain't it? We must have our bit of fun, mustn't we? or we should go mad . . .'

I turned my face away. I think she still watched me, though. I did not care. I cared for nothing, now. I had kept up my nerve and my spirit, all that time. I had waited for my chance of escaping and got nowhere. Suddenly, my memories of Mrs Sucksby and Mr Ibbs, of Gentleman, even of Maud, seemed to grow dim. It was as if my head were filled with smoke, or had a fluttering curtain across it. When I tried to go over the streets of the Borough in my mind, I found I lost my way. No-one else in that house knew those streets. If the ladies spoke of London ever, they spoke of a place they remembered from when they were girls, in Society—a place so different from the city I knew, it might as well have been Bombay. No-one called me by my own name. I began to answer to *Maud* and *Mrs Rivers*; sometimes it seemed to me I *must* be Maud, since so many people said I was. And sometimes I even seemed to dream, not my own dreams, but hers; and sometimes to remember things, from Briar, that she had said and done, as if I had said and done them.

The nurses—all except Nurse Bacon—grew cooler than ever with me, after the night I was plunged. But I got used to being shaken and bullied and slapped. I got used to seeing other ladies bullied in their turn. I got used to it all. I got used to my bed, to the blazing lamp, to Miss Wilson and Mrs Price, to Betty, to Dr Christie. I should not, now, have minded a leech. But he never brought one. He said my calling myself Maud showed, not that I was better, but only that my malady had taken a different turn, and would turn back. Until it did, there was no point in trying to cure me; so he stopped trying. I heard, however, that the truth was he had gone off cures altogether: for he had cured the lady who had spoken like a snake, and done it so well her mother had taken her home; and what with that, and the ladies who had died, the house had lost money. Now, each morning, he felt my heart-beat and looked into my mouth, and then moved on. He did not stay long in the bedrooms at all, once the air grew so close and so foul. We, of course, spent most of our time there; and I even got used to that.

God knows what else I might have got used to. God knows how long they would have kept me in that place—maybe, years. Maybe as long as poor Miss Wilson: for perhaps she—who knows?—was as sane as I had been, when her brother first put her in. I might be there, today. I still think of that and shudder. I might never have got out; and Mrs Sucksby and Mr Ibbs, and Gentleman, and Maud—where would they be, now?

I think of that, too.

But then, I did get out. Blame Fortune. Fortune's blind, and works in peculiar ways. Fortune sent Helen of Troy to the Greeks—didn't

it?—and a prince, to the Sleeping Beauty. Fortune kept me at Dr
Christie's nearly all that summer long; then listen to who it sent me.

This was five or six weeks, I suppose, after they had plunged
me—some time in July. Think how stupid I had got by then. The
season was still a warm one, and we had all begun to sleep, all the
hours of the day. We slept in the mornings, while we waited for the
dinner-bell to be rung; and, in the afternoons, you would see ladies
all over the drawing-room, dozing, nodding their heads, dribbling
into their collars. There was nothing else to do. There was nothing
to stay awake for. And sleeping made time pass. I slept as much as
anyone. I slept so much that when Nurse Spiller came to our room
one morning and said, 'Maud Rivers, you're to come with me,
you've a visitor', they had to wake me up and tell me again; and
when they had, I didn't know what they meant.

'A visitor?' I said.

Nurse Spiller folded her arms. 'Don't want him, then? Shall I
send him home?' She looked at Nurse Bacon, who was still rubbing
her knuckles and wincing. 'Bad?' she said.

'Like scorpions' stings, Nurse Spiller.'

Nurse Spiller tutted. I said again,

'A visitor? For me?'

She yawned. 'For Mrs Rivers, anyway. Are you her today, or
not?'

I did not know. But I rose, on shaking legs, feeling the blood
rush from my heart—for if the visitor was a man then I could only
think that, whether I was Maud, or Sue, or whoever I was, he must
be Gentleman. My world had shrunk to that point, that I only
knew that I had been harmed, and that he had done it. I looked at
Miss Wilson. I had an idea that I had said to her, three months
before, that if Gentleman came I would kill him. I had meant it,
then. Now the thought of seeing his face was so unexpected, it
made me sick.

Nurse Spiller saw me hesitate. 'Come on,' she said, 'if you are
coming! Don't mind your hair.'—I had put my hand to my head.
'I'm sure, the madder he knows you to be, the better. Saves disappointment, don't it?' She glanced at Nurse Bacon. Then: 'Come on!'

she said again; and I gave a twitch, then stumbled after her into the passage and down the stairs.

It was a Wednesday—that was luck, though I did not know it yet, for on Wednesdays Dr Christie and Dr Graves went off in their coach to drum up new lady lunatics, and the house was quiet. Some nurses, and one or two men, were standing about in the hall, taking breaths from the open door; one of the men held a cigarette and, when he saw Nurse Spiller, he hid it. They did not look at me, however, and I hardly looked at them. I was thinking of what was to come, and feeling sicker and stranger by the second.

'In here,' said Nurse Spiller, jerking her head towards the door of the drawing-room. Then she caught my arm and pulled me to her. 'And you remember: none of your fibs. The pads are nice and cool, on a day like this. Ain't been used in a while. My word's as good as a man's, while the doctors are away. You hear me?'

She shook me. Then she pushed me into the room. 'Here she is,' she said, in a different voice, to the person waiting there.

I had expected Gentleman. It wasn't him. It was a fair-haired, blue-eyed boy in a blue pea-jacket, and in the first second of my seeing him I felt a rush of mixed relief and disappointment so sharp, I almost swooned away; for I thought him a stranger, and supposed that there had been a mistake, he must have come for someone else. Then I saw him looking over my features in a bewildered sort of way; and then at last, at last—as if his face and name were slowly rising to the surface of my brain, through mists or cloudy water—at last I knew him, even out of his servant's suit. He was Charles, the knife-boy from Briar. He looked me over, as I have said; then he tilted his head and looked past me, and past Nurse Spiller, as if he thought that Maud must be coming along behind. Then he looked at me again, and his eyes grew wide.

And it was that, that saved me. His were the first two eyes, in all the time that had passed since I left Mrs Cream's, that had looked at me and seen, not Maud, but Sue. They gave me back my past. They gave me my future, too—for in the second of standing in the doorway, meeting his gaze, seeing it slip from me and then come back baffled, my own confusion began to leave me and I formed a plan. I formed it whole, complete in every part.

It was desperate.

'Charles!' I said. I was not used to speaking, and it came out like a croak. 'Charles, you hardly know me. I think— I think I must be very changed. But oh, how good of you to come and make a visit to your old mistress!'

And I went to him and caught hold of his hand, not taking my eyes away from his; and then I pulled him to me and I whispered, almost weeping, in his ear:

'Say I'm her, or I'm done for! I'll give you anything at all! Say I'm her! Oh, please say I'm her!'

I kept hold of his hand, and wrung it. He stepped back. He had been wearing a cap, that had left a scarlet line across his brow. Now his face grew scarlet all over. He opened his mouth. He said,

'Miss, I— Miss—'

Of course, he called me that, at Briar. Thank God he did! Nurse Spiller heard him and said, in a sort of nasty satisfaction, 'Well, ain't it marvellous how quick a lady's head will clear, when she sees a dear face from home? Shan't Dr Christie be pleased?'

I turned and caught her eye. She looked sour. She said, 'Will you keep your young man standing? That have come all this way? That's right, you sit. Not too close, though, young sir, if I was you. We can't say when they won't fly off and start clawing; even the meek ones. That's better. Now, I'll keep over here, by the door, and if she starts kicking up, you sing out—all right?'

We had sat, in two hard chairs, close to the window. Charles still looked bewildered; now he also began to wink and look afraid. Nurse Spiller stood in the open doorway. It was cooler there. She folded her arms and watched us; but she also, now and then, turned her head into the hall, to nod and murmur to the nurses beyond.

I still held Charles's hand in both of mine. I could not give it up. I leaned towards him, trembling, and spoke in a whisper. I said,

'Charles, I— Charles, I never was so glad to see anyone, anyone in all my life! You have— You have to help me.'

He swallowed. He said, in the same low voice,

'You *are* Miss Smith?'

'Hush! Hush! I am. Oh, I am!' My eyes began to water. 'But you mustn't say it here. You must say—' I glanced at Nurse Spiller, then spoke more quietly still. 'You must say I'm Miss Lilly. Don't ask me why.'

What was I thinking of? Well, the fact was I was thinking of the lady who had spoken like a snake, and the two old ladies that had died. I was thinking of what Dr Christie had said, about my malady having taken a different turn, but being sure, in time, to turn back. I was thinking that if he heard Charles say that I was Sue not Maud, he might find a way to keep me closer—perhaps bind me, pad me, plunge me, plunge Charles too.—In other words, terror had turned my brain. But I also had that plan. It was growing clearer by the second.

'Don't ask me why,' I said again. 'But, oh, what a trick has been played on me! They have made out I'm mad, Charles.'

He looked about him. 'This house is a house for mad people?' he said. 'I supposed it a great hotel. I supposed I should find Miss Lilly here. And—and Mr Rivers.'

'Mr Rivers,' I said. 'Oh! Oh! That devil! He has swindled me, Charles, and gone to London with money that was to be mine. Him and Maud Lilly! Oh! What a pair! They have left me here, to die—!'

My voice had risen, I could not help it: someone else—someone really mad—might have been speaking out of my mouth. I squeezed Charles's fingers, to keep from talking louder. I squeezed them, almost out of their joints. And I glanced fearfully towards Nurse Spiller at the door. Her head was turned. She had her back to the doorpost and was laughing with the nurses and the men. I looked back at Charles, meaning to speak again. But his face had changed, and stopped me. His cheek had turned from flaming scarlet, to white. He said, in a whisper,

'Mr Rivers, gone to London?'

'To London,' I said, 'or to heaven knows where. To hell, I shouldn't wonder!'

He swallowed. He twitched. Then he tore his fingers from mine and covered his face with his hands.

'Oh! Oh!' he said, in a shaking voice—just as I had. 'Oh, then I'm ruined!'

And to my very great astonishment, he began to cry.

His story came leaking out, then, along with his tears. It turned out that—just as I had guessed, months before—a life spent sharpening knives at Briar seemed a life not worth having, once Gentleman had gone. Charles had felt it so hard, he had begun to mope. He had moped so long, Mr Way the steward had taken a whip to him.

'He said he would whip me raw,' he said; 'and he did. Lord, how he made me shriek! But that whipping was nothing—I should say, a hundred whippings would be nothing!—compared to the smarting, miss, of my disappointed heart.'

He said that, in a way that made me think he had practised it; then he held himself stiff, as if he imagined I would hit him, or laugh, and was ready to suffer any blow. But what I said—bitterly— was, 'I believe you. Mr Rivers makes hearts do that.'

I was thinking of Maud's. Charles seemed not to notice. 'He does!' he said. 'What a gentleman! Oh, but ain't he?'

His face grew shiny. He wiped his nose. Then he started crying again. Nurse Spiller looked over and curled her lip. But that was all she did. Perhaps people cried a lot, when they came to see their lady relatives, at Dr Christie's.

When she had looked into the hall again, I turned back to Charles. Seeing him so miserable made me calmer in my own head. I let him shake a little longer and, as he did it, studied him closer. I saw, what I had not seen at first—that his neck was dirty, and his hair was strange—here pale and fluffy as feathers, here dark and stiff where he had wet it to make it lie smooth. There was a twig caught up in the wool of the sleeve of his jacket. His trousers were marked with dust.

He wiped his eyes and saw me looking, and blushed harder than ever. I said quietly,

'Be a good boy now, and tell me the truth. You've run off, haven't you, from Briar?'

He bit his lip, then nodded. I said, 'And all for Mr Rivers's sake?' He nodded again. Then he drew in a shuddering breath.

'Mr Rivers used to say to me, miss,' he said, 'that he would take me on to man for him, if only he'd the money for a proper man's wages. I thought, I would rather work for him for no wages at all, than stay at Briar. But how was I to find him out, in London? Then came all that stir, with Miss Lilly taking off. The house've been on its head since then. We did suppose her flown after him, but no-one was quite sure. They are calling it a scandal. Half the girls have gone. Mrs Cakebread've gone, to another man's kitchen! Now Margaret cooks. Mr Lilly ain't in his right mind. Mr Way has to feed him his dinners off a spoon!'

'Mrs Cakebread,' I said, frowning. 'Mr Way.' The names were like so many lights: each time one was lit, another part of my brain grew brighter. 'Margaret. Mr Lilly.' And then: 'Off a spoon! And all— And all from Maud's running off with Mr Rivers?'

'I don't know, miss.' He shook his head. 'They say it took him a week to feel it. For he was calm at first; then he found some harm had been done to some of his books—or, something like that. Then he fell in a fit on his library floor. Now he can't hold a pen or anything, and forgets his words. Mr Way made me push him about, in a great wheeled chair; but, I could hardly go ten yards—I could hardly do anything!—for breaking out crying. In the end I got sent to my aunty's, to look at her black-faced pigs. They do say'—he wiped his nose again—'they do say that watching pigs cures melancholy. It never cured mine, though . . .'

I had stopped listening. There had come on a light in my head, that was brighter than all the rest. I took his hand again. 'Black-faced pigs?' I said, screwing up my eyes. He nodded.

His aunty was Mrs Cream.

I suppose it's like that in the country. I had never thought to ask him his last name. He had slept in the very same room as me, on the same straw mattress, that was filled with bugs. When his aunty had begun to talk of the gentleman and lady that had come and been secretly married, he had guessed at once who they were but, hardly believing his own luck, had said nothing. He found out they'd gone off together in a coach; and from his cousin—Mrs Cream's eldest son, who had talked with the coachman—he had got the name of Dr Christie's house, and where it was.

'I supposed it a great hotel,' he said again—again looking fearfully about him, at the wire on the lamps, the bare grey walls, the bars on the windows. He had run off from Mrs Cream's three nights before, and had slept in ditches and hedges since then.—'Too late,' he said, 'to turn back, when I got here. I asked at the gate for Mr Rivers. They looked in a book, and said I must mean his wife. Then I remembered what a kind lady Miss Maud always was; and that if anyone should talk Mr Rivers round to taking me on, she should. And now—!'

His lip began again to tremble. Really, Mr Way was right: he was far too big a boy to be so tearful, and at any other time, in any other, ordinary place, I should have hit him myself. But for now, I looked at his tears, and to my bruised and desperate eyes they were like so many pick-locks and keys.

'Charles,' I said, leaning closer to him and nerving myself to seem calm. 'You can't go back to Briar.'

'I can't, miss,' he said. 'Oh, I can't! Mr Way would skin me alive!'

'And I dare say your aunty don't want you.'

He shook his head. 'She would call me a fool, for running off.'

'It's Mr Rivers you're after.'

He bit his lip, and nodded, still crying.

'Then listen to me,' I said—barely speaking at all, barely whispering now, only breathing the words, for fear Nurse Spiller would catch them. 'Listen to me. I can take you to him. I know where he is. I know the very house! I can take you to him. But first, you must help me out of here.'

If it wasn't quite true that I knew where Gentleman was, then it wasn't quite a lie, either; for I was pretty certain that, once I reached London and got help from Mrs Sucksby, I should find him. But I would have lied anyway, just then. I dare say you would have, too. Charles stared at me, and wiped his face with the heel of his hand.

'Help you out of here, how?' he said. 'Why mayn't you walk out, miss, just whenever you please?'

I swallowed. 'They think I'm mad, Charles. There's an order been signed—well, never mind by who—that keeps me here. It's the law. See that nurse? See her arm? They've got twenty nurses with arms like that; and they know how to use 'em. Now, look at my face. Am I mad?'

He looked, and blinked. 'Well—'

'Of course I ain't. But here, there are some lunatics so crafty, they pass as sane; and the doctors and nurses can't see the difference between me, and one of them.'

Again he looked about him. Then he looked at me—just as, a moment before, I had looked at him—as if seeing me for the first time. He looked at my hair, my dress, my india-rubber boots. I drew my feet under my skirt.

'I— I'm not sure,' he said.

'Not sure? Not sure of what? Of whether you want to go back to your aunty's and live with the pigs? Or whether you want to go and be man to Mr Rivers, in London—London, mind! Remember them elephants a boy can ride on for a shilling? Tricky choice, I call that.'

He lowered his gaze. I looked at Nurse Spiller. She had glanced our way, was yawning, and had taken out a watch.

'Pigs?' I said quickly. 'Or elephants? Which is it to be? For God's sake, which?'

He worked his lips.

'Elephants,' he said, after a terrible silence.

'Good boy. Good boy. Thank God. Now, listen. How much money have you got?'

He swallowed. 'Five shillings and sixpence,' he said.

'All right. Here's what you must do. You must go to any town, and find a locksmith's shop; and when you find it you must ask them for—' I pressed my hand to my eyes. I thought I felt that cloudy water rising again, that flapping curtain. I nearly screamed in fright. Then the curtain drew back—'for a ward key,' I said, 'a ward key, with a one-inch blank. Say your master wants it. If the man won't sell it, you must steal one. Now, don't look like that! We shall send the man another when we reach London. When you've got the blank, keep it safe. Go next to a blacksmith's. Get a file—see my fingers?—same width as this. Show me the width I mean. Good boy, you got it. Keep the file safe as the blank. Bring them back here, next week—next Wednesday, only Wednesday will do! do you hear me?—and slip them to me. Understand me? Charles?'

He stared. I had begun to grow wild again. But then he nodded. Then his gaze moved past me and he twitched. Nurse Spiller had left the door-place and was headed our way.

'Time's up,' she said.

We stood. I kept hold of the back of my chair, to keep from sinking. I looked at Charles, as if my eyes could burn into his. I had let his hand fall, but now reached for it again.

'You'll remember, won't you, what I've said?'

He nodded, in a frightened way. He dropped his gaze. He made to draw free his hand and step away. Then a queer thing happened. I felt his fingers move across my palm and found I could not let them go.

'Don't leave me!' I said. The words came from nowhere. 'Don't leave me, please!'

He jumped.

'Now then,' said Nurse Spiller. 'We've no time for this. Come on.'

She began to ungrip my fingers. It took her a moment or two. When his hand was free, Charles drew it quickly back and put his knuckles to his mouth.

'Sad, ain't it?' Nurse Spiller said to him, her arms about my own. My shoulders jumped. 'Don't you mind it, though. It takes them all like this. Better not to come at all, we say. Better not to remind 'em of home. Whips 'em up.' She drew me tighter. Charles shrank away. 'You be sure now, to tell your people that, when you say what a sad way you found her in—won't you?'

He looked from her to me, and nodded. I said,

'Charles, I'm sorry.' My teeth were chattering about the words. 'Don't mind it. It's nothing. Nothing at all.'

But I could see him looking at me now and thinking that I must be mad, after all; and if he thought that, then I was done for, I should be at Dr Christie's house for ever, I should never see Mrs

Sucksby and never have my revenge on Maud.—That thought was sharper than my fear. I willed myself calm, and Nurse Spiller at last let me go. Another nurse came forward, to see Charles to the door: they let me watch him leave, and oh! it was all I could do to keep from running after. As he went, he turned, and stumbled, and met my gaze. Then he looked shocked again. I had tried to smile, and suppose the smile was dreadful.

'You'll remember!' I called, my voice high and strange. 'You'll remember the elephants!'

The nurses shrieked with laughter then. One gave me a push. My strength was all gone, and the push knocked me over. I lay in a heap. 'Elephants!' they said. They stood and laughed at me, until they wept.

That week was a terrible one. I had got my own mind back, the house seemed crueller than ever, and I saw how far I had sunk before in growing used to it. Say I grew used to it again, in seven days? Say I grew stupid? Say Charles came back, and I was too funked to know him? The thought nearly killed me. I did everything I could to keep myself from slipping into a dream again. I pinched my own arms, until they were black with bruises. I bit my own tongue. Each morning I woke with a horrible sense that days had slipped away and I had not noticed. 'What day is today?' I'd ask Miss Wilson and Mrs Price. Of course, they never knew. Miss Wilson always thought, Good Friday. Then I'd ask Nurse Bacon.

'What day is today, Nurse Bacon?'

'Punishment Day,' she'd answer, wincing and rubbing her hands.

Then there was the fear that, after all, Charles wouldn't come—that I had been too mad—that he would lose his nerve, or be overtaken by disaster. I thought of all the likely and unlikely things that might keep him from me—such as, his being seized by gipsies or thieves; run down by bulls; falling in with honest people, who would persuade him to go back home. One night it rained, and I thought of the ditch he was sleeping in filling up with water and him being drowned. Then there came thunder and lightning; and I imagined him sheltering under a tree, with a file in his hand . . .

The whole week passed like that. Then Wednesday came. Dr Graves and Dr Christie went off in their coach and, late in the morning, Nurse Spiller arrived at the door to our room, looked at me and said, 'Well, ain't we charming? There's a certain young shaver downstairs, come back for another visit. We shall be putting out the banns, at this rate . . .' She led me down. In the hall, she gave me a poke. 'No monkeying about,' she said.

This time, Charles looked more afraid than ever. We sat in the same two seats as before and, again, Nurse Spiller stood in the door-place and larked with the nurses in the hall. We sat for a minute in silence. His cheek was white as chalk. I said, in a whisper,

'Charles, did you do it?'

He nodded.

'The blank?'

He nodded again.

'The file?'

Another nod. I put my hand before my eyes.

'But the blank,' he said, in a complaining tone, 'cost nearly all my money. The locksmith said that some blanks are blanker than others. You never told me that. I got the blankest he had.'

I parted my fingers, and met his gaze.

'How much did you give him?' I asked.

'Three shillings, miss.'

Three shillings for a sixpenny blank! I covered my eyes again. Then, 'Never mind,' I said. 'Never mind. Good boy . . .'

Then I told him what he must do next. I said he must wait for me, that night, on the other side of Dr Christie's park wall. I said he must find the spot where the highest tree grew, and wait for me there. He must wait all night, if he had to—for I could not say, for sure, how long my escape would take me. He must only wait, and be ready to run. And if I did not come at all, he must know that some-thing had happened to stop me; and then he must come back the next night and wait again—he must do that, three nights over.

'And if you don't come, then?' he asked, his eyes wide.

'If I don't come then,' I said, 'you do this: you go to London, and you find out a street named Lant Street, and a lady that lives there, named Mrs Sucksby; and you tell her where I am. God help me, Charles, that lady loves me!—and she'll love you, for being my friend. She'll know what to do.'

I turned my head. My eyes had filled with water. 'You got it?' I said at last. 'You swear?'

He said he did. 'Show me your hand,' I said then; and when I saw how it shook, I dared not let him try and slip me the blank and file, for fear he would drop them. He kept them in his pocket, and I hooked them out just before I left him—while Nurse Spiller looked on, laughing to see him kiss my cheek and blush. The file went up my sleeve. The blank I held on to—then, as I went upstairs, I stooped as if to tug up a stocking, and let it fall into one of my boots.

Then I lay on my bed. I thought of all the burglars I had ever heard of, and all the burglars' boasts. I was like them, now. I had my file, I had my blank. I had my pal on the other side of the madhouse wall. Now all I must do was get hold of a key, long enough to make my copy.

I did it like this.

That night, when Nurse Bacon sat in her chair and flexed her fingers, I said,

'Let me rub your hands for you tonight, Nurse Bacon, instead of Betty. Betty doesn't like it. She says the grease makes her smell like a chop.'

Betty's mouth fell open. 'Oh! Oh!' she cried.

'God help us,' said Nurse Bacon. 'As if this heat weren't enough. Be quiet, Betty!—Like a chop, did you say? And after all my kindness?'

'I never!' said Betty. 'I never!'

'She did,' I said. 'Like a chop, done up for the pan. You let me do it instead. Look how neat and soft my hands are.'

Nurse Bacon looked, not at my fingers, but at my face. Then she screwed up her eyes. 'Betty, shut up!' she said. 'What a row, and my flesh blazing. I'm sure I don't care who does it; but I'd rather a quiet girl than a noisy one. Here.' She put the tip of her thumb to the

edge of the pocket in her skirt and pulled it back. 'Fetch 'em out,'
she said to me.

She meant her keys. I hesitated, then put in my hand and drew
them up. They were warm from the heat of her leg. She watched me
do it. 'That littlest one,' she said. I held it and let the others swing,
then went to the cupboard and got out the jar of grease. Betty lay on
her stomach and kicked up her heels, weeping into her pillow. Nurse
Bacon sat back and put up her cuffs. I sat beside her and worked the
ointment in, all about her swollen hands, just as I had seen it done
a hundred times. I rubbed for half an hour. Now and then she
winced. Then her eyes half closed and she gazed at me from
beneath the lids. She gazed in a warm and thoughtful way, and
almost smiled.

'Not so bad, is it?' she murmured. 'Eh?'

I didn't answer. I was thinking, not of her, but of the night and
the work to come. If my colour was up, she must have taken it for a
blush. If I seemed strange, and conscious of myself, what was that to
her? We were all strange, there. When at last she yawned and drew
her hands away, and stretched, my heart gave a thump; but she did
not see it. I moved from her side, to take the ointment back to its
cupboard. My heart thumped again. I had only a second to do what
I needed to do. The loop of keys was hanging from the lock, the one
I wanted—the one to the doors—hanging lowest. I did not plan to
steal it, she would have noticed if I had. But men came all the time
to Lant Street, with bits of soap, and putty, and wax . . . I caught the
key up and quickly but very carefully pressed it into the jar.

The grease took the shape of the bitting, good as anything. I
looked at it once, then screwed on the lid and set the jar back on its
shelf. The cupboard door I closed, but only pretended to lock. The
key I wiped on my sleeve. I took it back to Nurse Bacon, and she
opened up her pocket with the tip of her thumb, like before.

'Right in,' she said, as I made to put in the keys. 'All the way to
the bottom. That's right.'

I would not meet her eye. I went to my bed, and she yawned, and
sat in her chair and dozed, as she always did, until Nurse Spiller
brought round our draughts. I had got used to taking mine, along

with the other ladies, but tonight I tipped it away—into the mattress, this time—then gave back my empty bowl. Then I watched, in a sort of fever, to see what Nurse Bacon would do next. If she had gone to the cupboard—say, for a paper, or a cake, or a piece of knitting, or any small thing; if she had gone to the cupboard and found it open, and locked it, and spoiled my plan, I can't say what I would have done. I really think I might have killed her. But anyway, she did not go. She only sat sleeping in her chair. She slept so long, I began to despair of her ever waking up again: I coughed; picked up my boot and dropped it; ground the legs of my bed against the floor—and still she slept on. Then some dream woke her. She got up, and put her nightgown on. I had my fingers across my face, and saw her do it, through the cracks: I saw her stand, rubbing her stomach through the cotton of her gown; and I saw her looking at all the ladies and then at me, seeming to turn some idea over in her mind . . .

But then, she gave the idea up. Perhaps it was the heat. She yawned again, put the chain of keys around her neck, got into her bed; and started snoring.

I counted her snores. When I had counted twenty I rose, like a ghost, crept back to the cupboard, and got out the jar of grease.

Then I cut my copy. I can't say how long it took. I only know, it took hours—for of course, though the file was a fine one, and though I worked with the sheets and blankets bunched about my hands to muffle the sound, still the rasp of the iron seemed loud, and I dared only cut in time to Nurse Bacon's snores. And I could not file too quickly even then, for I had always to be matching up the blank with the impression, making sure the cuts were right; then again, my fingers would ache, I would have to stop and flex them; or they'd grow wet, the blank would slip and swivel in my hands. It was terrible work to be doing in a desperate mood. I seemed to feel the night slipping away, like so much sand—or else, Nurse Bacon would fall silent, I would pause and look about me and be brought back to myself—to the beds, and the sleeping ladies—and the room would seem so still I feared that time had stopped and I should be caught in it for ever. No-one called out that night, no-one had awful dreams, no bells were rung, everyone lay heavy in their beds. I was the only wakeful soul in the house—the only wakeful soul, I might as well have been, in all the world; except, that I knew that Charles was also wakeful—was waiting, on the other side of Dr Christie's walls—was waiting for me; and that, beyond him, Mrs Sucksby was also waiting—perhaps, was sighing in her bed—or walking, wringing her hands and calling out my name . . . It must have been the thought of that, that gave me courage and made the file run true.

For at last there came a time when I put the blank to the jar, and saw that the cuts all matched. The key was finished. I held it, in a sort of daze. My fingers were stained from the iron, and grazed from the slipping of the file, and almost numb from gripping. I dared not stay to bind them up, though. Very carefully I rose, pulled on my tartan gown, and took up my rubber boots. I also took Nurse Bacon's comb.—That was all, just that. I lifted it from off her table, and, as I did, she moved her head: I held my breath, but she did not wake. I stood quite still, looking into her face. And I was filled, suddenly, with guilt. I thought, 'How disappointed she'll be, when she finds how I've tricked her!'—I thought of how pleased she had got, when I'd said I would rub her hands.

Queer, the things you think at such times. I watched her another minute, then went to the door. Slowly, slowly, I put the key in the lock. Slowly, slowly, I turned it. 'Please, God,' I whispered, as it moved. 'Dear God, I swear, I'll be good, I'll be honest the rest of my days, I swear—' It caught, and stuck. 'Fuck! Fuck!' I said. The wards had jammed, I had not cut true after all: now it would not turn, either forwards or backwards. '*Fuck!* You fuckster! Oh!' I gripped it harder, and tried again—still nothing—at last I let it go. I went silently back to my bed, got Nurse Bacon's ointment jar, stole back with it to the door, put grease across the key-hole and blew it into the lock. Then, almost fainting with fear, I gripped the key again; and this time—this time, it worked.

There were three more doors to be got through, after that. The key did the same in all of them—got stuck, and must be greased—and every time, I shuddered to hear the grinding of the iron in the lock, and went on faster. But no-one woke. The passages were hot and quiet, the stairs and hall quite still. The front door was bolted and latched, I didn't need a key for that. I left it open behind me. It was as easy as the time that I had gone from Briar with Maud: only on the walk before the house did I get a fright, for as I made to cross the bit of gravel there, I heard a step, and then a voice. The voice called, softly, 'Hey!'—I heard it, and almost died. I thought it was calling me. Then there came a woman's laugh, and I saw figures: two men—Mr Bates, I think, and another; and a nurse—Nurse Flew, with the swivel-eye. 'You'll get your—' one of them said; but that was all I heard. They went through bushes, at the side of the house. Nurse Flew laughed again. Then the laugh got stifled, and there came silence.

I did not wait to see what the silence would become. I ran— lightly, at first, across the strip of gravel—then fast and hard, across the lawn. I didn't look back at the house. I didn't think about the ladies, still inside it. I should like to say I went and threw my key into the little walled garden, for one of them to find; but I did not. I didn't save anyone but myself. I was too afraid. I found the tallest tree: it took me another half-hour, then, to get myself up the knots in its trunk—to fall, to try again—to fall a second time, a third, a fourth—to heave myself finally on to its lowest branch—to climb from there to the branch above—to work my way across a creaking bough until I reached the wall . . . God knows how I did it. I can only say, I did. 'Charles! Charles!' I called, from the top of the bricks. There was no answer. But I did not wait. I jumped. I hit the ground and heard a yelp. It was him. He had waited so long, he had fallen asleep; and I almost struck him.

The yelp made a dog bark, back at the house. That dog set off another. Charles put his hand before his mouth.

'Come on!' I said.

I caught his arm. We turned our backs to the wall, and ran and ran.

We ran through grass and hedges. The night was still dark, the paths all hidden, and I was too afraid, at first, to take the time to find them out. Every now and then Charles would stumble, or slow his step to press his hand to his side and find his breath, and then I'd tilt my head and listen; but there was nothing to hear but birds, and breezes, and mice. Soon the sky grew lighter, and we made out the pale strip of a road. 'Which way?' said Charles. I did not know. It had been months and months since I had stood on any kind of path and had to choose the way to take. I looked about me, and the land and the lightening sky seemed suddenly vast and fearful. Then I saw Charles looking, and waiting. I thought of London. 'This way,' I said, beginning to walk; and the fear passed from me.

It was like that, then, all the way: every time we met the crossing of two or three roads, I would stand for a minute and think hard of London; and just as if I were Dick Whittington, the idea would come to me which road we ought to take. When the sky grew even paler, we began to hear horses and wheels. We should have been glad of a lift, but I was afraid, each time, that the cart or coach might have been sent out after us, from the madhouse. Only when we saw an old farmer driving out of a gate in a donkey-cart, did I think we could be sure he was not one of Dr Christie's men: we put ourselves in his way, and he slowed the donkey and let us ride beside him for an hour. I had combed out the plaits and stitches from my hair and it stood up like coir, and I had no hat, so put a handkerchief of Charles's about my head. I said that we were brother and sister, and going back to London after a stay with our aunty.

'London, eh?' said the farmer. 'They say a man can live forty years there and never meet his neighbour. Is that right?'

He put us down at the side of the road at the edge of a town, and showed us the way we must take from there. I guessed we had gone about nine or ten miles. We had forty more to do. This was still early morning. We found a baker's shop, and bought bread; but the woman in the shop looked so queerly at my hair and my gown, and my rubber boots, I wished we had given up the bread and gone hungry. We sat in a church-yard, upon the grass, against two leaning stones. The church bell rang, and we both started.

'Seven o'clock,' I said. I felt suddenly gloomy. I looked at Nurse

Bacon's comb. 'They'll be waking up now, and finding my empty bed; if they haven't found it already.'

'Mr Way will be polishing shoes,' said Charles. His lip began to jump.

'Think of Mr Rivers's boots,' I said quickly. 'I bet they want a polish. London is awfully hard on a gentleman's shoes.'

'Is it?'

That made him feel better. We finished our bread, and then rose and brushed the grass off. A man went by with a shovel. He looked at us rather as the woman in the baker's shop had.

'They think we're tinkers,' said Charles, as we watched him pass.

But I imagined men coming from the madhouse, asking about after a girl in a tartan dress and rubber boots. 'Let's go,' I said, and we left the road again and took a quiet path that went off across fields. We kept as much as we could to the hedges, though the grass was higher there, and harder and slower to walk on.

The sun made the air grow warm. There came butterflies, and bees. Now and then I stopped and untied the handkerchief from about my head, and wiped my face. I had never walked so far, so hard, in my life; and for three months I had not been further than round and round the little walled garden at the madhouse. There were blisters on my heels, the size of shillings. I thought, 'We shall never get to London!'

But each time I thought it, I thought of Mrs Sucksby, and imagined the look upon her face when I turned up at the Lant Street door. Then I thought of Maud, wherever she was; and imagined *her* face.

Her face seemed dim to me, however. The dimness bothered me. I said,

'Tell me, Charles, what colour are Miss Lilly's eyes? Are they brown, or blue?'

He looked at me strangely.

'I think they are brown, miss.'

'Are you sure?'

'I think so, miss.'

'I think so, too.'

But I was not sure. I walked a little faster. Charles ran beside me, panting.

Near noon that day we came across a row of little cottages, on the side of the path to a village. I made Charles stop, and we stood behind a hedge, and I watched the doors and windows. At one, a girl stood shaking cloths—though after a minute she went inside, and then the window was closed. At another, a woman with a bucket passed back and forth, not looking out. The windows of the next cottage down were all shut and dark; but I guessed there must be something behind them, worth stealing: I thought of going to the door and knocking and, if no-one came, trying the latch. But as I stood, working up my nerve, there came voices, from the very last house: we looked, and there at the garden gate was a woman and two little children. The woman was tying on a bonnet and kissing the children good-bye.

'Now, Janet,' she was saying to the biggest one, 'mind you watch Baby nicely. I shall be back to give you your egg. You may hem your hankie if you like, if you'll only be careful with the needle.'

'Yes, Ma,' said the girl. She put her face up to be kissed, then stood on the gate and swung it. Her mother walked quickly away from the cottage—past me and Charles, though she didn't know it; for we were still hidden behind our hedge.

I watched her go. Then I looked from her to the little girl—who had left the gate now, and was walking back up the path, leading her brother towards the open cottage door. Then I looked at Charles. I said,

'Charles, here's Fate turned our way at last. Give me a sixpence, will you?' He felt about in his pocket. 'Not that one. Haven't you got a brighter?'

I took the brightest he had, and gave it an extra shine on the sleeve of my gown.

'What are you going to do, miss?' he asked.

'Never mind. Stay here. And if anyone comes, give a whistle.'

I stood and straightened my skirt; then I went out from behind the hedge and walked smartly over to the gate of the cottage, as if I had come along the path. The little girl turned her head and saw me.

'All right?' I said. 'You'll be Janet. I just met your ma. Look here, what she gave me. A sixpence. Ain't it a nice one? She said, "Please give this sixpence to my little girl Janet, and tell her to please go quick to the shop and buy flour." Said she forgot, just now. Know what flour is, don't you? Good girl. Know what else your ma said? She said, "My girl Janet is such a good little girl, tell her she's to have the half-penny left over, for sweets." Ah. Like sweets, do you? So do I. Nice, ain't they? But hard on your teeth. Never mind. I dare say you ain't got all your teeth yet. Oh! Look at them dazzlers! Like pearls on a string! Better nip down the shop, before the rest come up. I'll stay here and mind the house, shall I? Don't that sixpence shine! And here's your little brother, look. Don't you want to take him with you? Good girl . . .'

It was the shabbiest trick there was, and I hated doing it; but what can I say? I had had a shabby trick played on me. All the time I spoke, I was glancing quickly about me, at the windows of the other cottages, and along the path; but no-one came. The little girl put the coin in the pocket of her apron and picked up her baby brother, and staggered away; and I watched her do it, then darted into the house. It was a pretty poor place, but in a trunk upstairs I found a pair of black shoes, more or less my size, and a print dress, put in paper. I thought the dress might have been the one that the woman was married in, and I swear to God! I almost didn't take it; but in the end, I did.

And I also took a black straw bonnet, a shawl, a pair of woollen stockings, a pie from the pantry; and a knife.

Then I ran back to the hedge where Charles was hiding.

'Turn round,' I said, as I changed. 'Turn round! Don't look so frightened, you bloody big girl. Damn her! Damn her!'

I meant Maud. I was thinking of the little girl, Janet, coming back to the cottage with the flour and her bag of sweets. I was thinking of her mother, coming home in time for tea, and finding her wedding-gown gone.

'Damn her!'

I got hold of Maud's glove, and ripped it till the stitches gave. Then I threw it to the ground and jumped on it. Charles watched, with a look of terror on his face.

'Don't look at me, you infant!' I said. 'Oh! Oh!'

But then I grew frightened of someone coming. I took the glove up again and put it back next to my bosom, and tied up the strings of the bonnet. I threw my madhouse gown and my rubber boots into a ditch. The blisters on my feet had opened, and were weeping like eyes; but the stockings were thick ones, and the black shoes were worn and soft. The dress had a pattern of roses on it, and the bonnet had daisies at the brim. I imagined how I must look—like a picture, I thought, of a milkmaid on a dairy wall.

But that was just the thing, I supposed, for the country. We left the fields and the shady paths and went back to the road; and after a time another old farmer came by, and he drove us another few miles; and then we walked again.

We still walked hard. Charles was silent all the way. Finally he broke out with:

'You took them shoes and that gown, without asking.'

'I took this pie as well,' I said. 'Bet you'll eat it, though.'

I said we would send the woman her clothes back, and buy her a brand-new pie, in London. Charles looked doubtful. We spent the night in the hay of an open barn, and he lay with his back to me, his shoulder-blades shaking. I wondered if he might run off to Briar while I slept; and I waited until he grew quiet, then tied the laces of one his boots to the laces of one of mine, so I should wake up if he tried to. He was an aggravating boy; but I knew I should do better with him than without him, just now—for Dr Christie's men would be looking for a girl on her own, not a girl and her brother. I thought that if I had to, I would give him the slip once we reached London.

But London still seemed far off. The air still smelled too pure. Some time in the night I woke, and the barn was full of cows: they stood in a circle and looked us over, and one of them coughed like a man. Don't tell me that's natural. I woke up Charles, and he was as frightened as I was. He got up and tried to run—of course, he fell down, and nearly took my foot off. I undid our laces. We went backwards out of the barn, then ran, then walked. We saw the sun rise over a hill.

'That means east,' said Charles. The night had been cold as winter, but the hill was a steep one and we grew warm as we climbed. When we got to the top, the sun was higher in the sky and the day was lightening up. I thought, *The morning has broken.*—I thought of the morning like an egg, that had split with a crack and was spreading. Before us lay all the green country of England, with its rivers and its roads and its hedges, its churches, its chimneys, its rising threads of smoke. The chimneys grew taller, the roads and rivers wider, the threads of smoke more thick, the farther off the country spread; until at last, at the farthest point of all, they made a smudge, a stain, a darkness—a darkness, like the darkness of the coal in a fire—a darkness that was broken, here and there, where the sun caught panes of glass and the golden tips of domes and steeples, with glittering points of light.

'London,' I said. 'Oh, London!'

Chapter Sixteen

*S*till, it took all that day to reach it. We might have found out the railway station and taken a train: but I thought we ought to keep the little money we had left, for food. We walked for a while with a boy who had a great big basket on his back, that he had filled with onions: he showed us to a place where waggons came, to pick up vegetables for the city markets. We had missed the best of the traffic, but we got a ride, in the end, with a man with a slow horse, taking scarlet beans to Hammersmith. He said Charles made him think of his son—Charles had that sort of face—so I let them ride up front together, and sat in the back of the cart, with the beans. I sat with my cheek against a crate, my eyes on the road ahead, and now and then the road would rise and show us London again, grown a little nearer. I might have slept; but I couldn't keep from watching. I watched as the roads began to be busier and the coun-try hedges began to give way to palings and walls; I watched the leaf become brick, the grass become cinders and dust, the ditches kerb-stones. When once the cart drew close to the side of a house that was pasted, two inches thick, with fluttering bills, I reached and tore free a strip of poster—held it for a second, then let it fly. It had a picture of a hand upon it, holding a pistol. It left soot on my fingers. Then I knew I was home.

From Hammersmith, we walked. That part of London was strange to me, but I found I knew my way all right—just as I had known, in the country, which road to take at a fork. Charles walked beside me, blinking, and sometimes catching hold of the cuff of my sleeve; in the end I took his hand to lead him across a street, and he let his fingers stay there. I saw us reflected in the glass of a great shop window—me in my bonnet, him in his plain pea-jacket—we looked like the Babes in the bloody Wood.

Then we reached Westminster, and got our first proper view of the river; and I had to stop.

'Wait, Charles,' I said, putting my hand to my heart and turning away from him. I did not want him to see me so stirred up. But then, the sharpest part of my feelings being over, I began to think.

'We ought not to cross the water just yet,' I said, as we walked on. I was thinking of who we might bump into. Suppose we chanced upon Gentleman? Or, suppose he chanced upon us? I did not think he would put a hand upon me, himself; but fifteen thousand pounds is a deal of money, and I knew he was up to hiring bullies to do his bad work for him. I had not thought of this, until now. I had thought only of reaching London. I began to look about me, in a new way. Charles saw me do it.

'What is it, miss?' he said.

'Nothing,' I answered. 'Only, I'm afraid there may still be men, sent out by Dr Christie. Let's cut down here.'

I took him down a dark and narrow street. But then I thought, a dark and narrow street would be the worst kind of street to be caught in. I turned instead—we were somewhere near Charing Cross now—into the Strand; and after a time we came to the end of a road that had one or two little stalls, selling second-hand clothes. I went to the first we came to, and bought Charles a woollen scarf. For myself, I got a veil. The man who sold it to me teased me.

'Don't care for a hat, instead?' he said. 'Your face is too pretty to hide.'

I held out my hand for my half-penny change. 'All right,' I said, impatient. 'So's my arse.'

Charles flinched. I did not care. I put on the veil and felt better. It looked badly above my bonnet and pale print gown, but I thought I might pass for a girl with scars, or with some kind of ailment of the face. I made Charles draw the woollen scarf about his mouth and pull down his cap. When he complained that the day was hot I said,

'If I get taken by Dr Christie's spies before I bring you to Mr Rivers, how hot do you think you'll find it, then?'

He looked ahead, to the crush of coaches and horses at Ludgate Hill. It was six o'clock, and the traffic was at its worst.

'Then when *will* you bring me to him?' he said. 'And how much further does he live?'

'Not much at all. But, we must be careful. I have to think. Let us find somewhere quiet . . .'

We ended up at St Paul's. We went in, and I sat in one of the pews while Charles walked about and looked at the statues. I thought, 'I must only get to Lant Street, and then I shall be saved'; but what was worrying me was the thought of the story that Gentleman might have put about the Borough. Say all of Mr Ibbs's nephews had had their hearts turned against me? Say I met John Vroom before I reached Mrs Sucksby? His heart did not need turning; and he would know me, even behind my veil. I must be careful. I should have to study the house—make my move only when I knew how the land lay. It was hard, to be cautious and slow; but I thought of my mother, who had not been cautious enough. Look what happened to her.

I shivered. St Paul's was cold, even in July. The glass at the windows was losing its colours, as the afternoon turned to night. At Dr Christie's, now, they would be waking us up to take us down to our suppers. We would have bread-and-butter, and a pint of tea . . . Charles came and sat beside me. I heard him sigh. He had his cap in his hands, and his fair hair shone. His lip was perfectly pink.

Three boys in white gowns went about with flames on sticks of brass, lighting more lamps and candles; and I looked at him and thought how well he would fit in among them, in a gown of his own.

Then I looked at his coat. It was a good one, though rather marked by dust.

'How much money have we now, Charles?' I said.

We had a penny and a half. I took him to a pawn-shop on Watling Street, and we pledged his coat for two shillings.

He cried as he handed it over.

'Oh, how,' he said, 'shall I ever see Mr Rivers now? He'll never want a boy in shirt-sleeves!'

I said we would get the coat back in a day or two. I bought him some shrimps and a piece of bread-and-butter, and a cup of tea.

'London shrimps,' I said. 'Yum, ain't they lovely?'

He did not answer. When we walked on, he walked a step behind me with his arms about himself, his eyes on the ground. His eyes were red—from tears, and also from grit.

We crossed the river at Blackfriars, and from there, though I had been going so carefully, I went more carefully still. We kept away from the back lanes and alleys, and stuck to the open roads; and the twilight—which is a false light, and always a good light for doing any kind of shady business in, better even than darkness—helped to hide us. Every step we took, however, was taking me closer to home: I began to see certain familiar things—even, certain familiar people—and felt, again, a stir in my head and heart, that I thought would quite undo me. Then we reached Gravel Lane and the Southwark Bridge Road, turned up to the west end of Lant Street and stood looking along it; and my blood rushed so fast and my heart rose so high, I thought I should swoon. I gripped the brick wall we rested against and let my head drop, until the blood went slower. When I spoke, my voice was thick. I said,

'See that black door, Charles, with the window in it? That's the door to my own house. The lady lives there, that's been like my mother. I should like more than anything now, to run to that door; but I shan't. It ain't safe.'

'Not safe?' he said. He gazed about him, fearfully. I suppose those streets—that looked so dear to my eyes I could have lain down and kissed them—might have looked rather low to his.

'Not safe,' I said again, 'while Dr Christie's men are still behind us.'

But I looked along the street, at Mr Ibbs's door, and then at the window above it. It was the window to the room I shared with Mrs Sucksby, and the temptation to go closer to it was too great. I caught hold of Charles and pushed him before me, and we walked, then stood at a wall where there was a bit of shadow between two bulging bow-windows. Some kids went by, and laughed at my veil. I knew their mothers, they were neighbours of ours; and I began to be afraid again, of being seen, and recognised. I thought I was a fool, after all, to have come so far down the street; then I thought, 'Why don't I just make a run at the door, calling out for Mrs Sucksby?' Maybe I'd have done it. I can't say. For I had turned, as if to rearrange my bonnet; and while I was still making up my mind Charles put his hand to his mouth, and cried out, 'Oh!'

The kids that had laughed at my veil had run far down the street, and then had parted, to let someone walk between them. It was Gentleman. He was wearing that old slouch hat, and had a scarlet cloth at his throat. His hair and whiskers were longer than ever. We watched him saunter. I think he was whistling. Then, at Mr Ibbs's shop-door, he came to a stop. He put his hand to the pocket of his coat and drew out a key. He kicked his feet against the step—first the right, then the left—to knock the dust from them; then he fitted the key in the lock, glanced idly about, and went inside. He did it all, in the easiest and most familiar way you can imagine.

I saw him, and quivered right through. But my feelings were queer. 'The devil!' I said. I should like to have killed him, to have shot him, to have run at him and struck his face. But the sight of him had also made me afraid—more afraid than I ought to have been—as afraid as if I were still at Dr Christie's and might at any moment be taken, shaken, bound and plunged in water. My breath came strangely, in little catches. I don't think Charles noticed. He was thinking of his shirt-sleeves.—'Oh!' he still said. 'Oh! Oh!'

He was looking at his finger-nails, and at the smudges of dirt on his cuffs.

I caught hold of his arm. I wanted to run—back, the way we had come. I wanted to run, more than anything. I almost did. 'Come on,' I said. 'Come, quick.' Then I looked again at Mr Ibbs's door— thought of Mrs Sucksby behind it—thought of Gentleman, cool and easy at her side. Damn him, for making me afraid of my own home! 'I *won't* be chased away!' I said. 'We'll stay, but we'll hide. Come, here.' And I gripped Charles tighter and began to push him, not away from Lant Street, but further along it. There were room- ing-houses, all along that side. We reached one, now. 'Got beds?' I said, to the girl at the door.—'Got half a one,' she said. Half was not enough. We went to the next house, and then the next. They were both full. At last we reached the house right across from Mr Ibbs's. There was a woman on the step with a baby. I did not know her. That was good.

'Got a room?' I said quickly.

'Might have,' she answered, trying to see beyond my veil.

'At the front?' I looked up and pointed. 'That one?'

'That one costs more.'

'We'll have it for the week. I'll give you a shilling now, and pay you the rest tomorrow.'

She made a face; but she wanted gin, I knew it. 'All right,' she said. She got to her feet, put the baby on the step, and took us up a slippery staircase. There was a man dead drunk on the landing. The door to the room she led us into had no lock to it, only a stone for propping it shut. The room was small and dark, with two low beds and a chair. The window had shutters closed before it, on the street-side, and there was a stick with a hook hung next to the glass, meant for opening them.

'You do it like this,' said the woman, beginning to show us. I stopped her. I said I had a weakness of the eye and didn't care for sunlight.

For I had seen straight away that the shutters had little holes cut in them, that were more or less perfect for what I wanted; and when the woman had got our shilling off us and gone, I shut the door behind her, took off my veil and bonnet, then put myself at the glass and looked out.

There was nothing to see, however. Mr Ibbs's shop door was still shut, and Mrs Sucksby's window dark. I watched for quite a minute before I remembered Charles. He was standing, gazing at me, squeezing his cap between his hands. In some other room a man gave a shout, and he jumped.

'Sit down,' I said. I put my face back to the window.

'I want my jacket,' he said.

'You can't have it. The shop is closed. We shall get it tomorrow.'

'I don't believe you. You told a lie to that lady, about having a poor eye. You took that gown and those shoes, and that pie. That pie made me sick. You have brought me to a horrible house.'

'I have brought you to London. Ain't that what you wanted?'

'I thought London would be different.'

'You haven't seen the best parts yet. Go to sleep. We'll get your jacket back in the morning. You shall feel like a new man then.'

'How shall we get it? You just gave our shilling to that lady.'

'I shall get us another shilling tomorrow.'

'How?'

'You mustn't ask. Go to sleep. Ain't you tired?'

'This bed've got black hairs in it.'

'Then take the other.'

'That one has red hairs.'

'Red hairs won't hurt you.'

I heard him sit and rub his face. I thought he might be about to cry again. But then, after a minute he spoke, and his voice had changed.

'Weren't Mr Rivers's whiskers long, though?' he said.

'Weren't they,' I answered, my eye at the shutter still. 'I'd say he needs a boy to trim them.'

'Don't he just!'

He sighed then, and lay back upon the bed, putting his cap over his eyes; and I kept watch at the glass. I kept watch, like cats keep watch at mouse-holes—not minding the hours as they passed, not thinking of anything but what I gazed at. The night grew dark, and the street—that was a busy street, in summer—grew empty and still, the kids all gone to their beds, the men and women come back from the public houses, the dogs asleep. In the other rooms in the house, people walked, pulled chairs across the floor; a baby cried. A girl—she was drunk, I suppose—laughed, on and on. Still I watched. Some clock struck off the hours. I could not hear bells without wincing, now, and felt every one of them: at last came the twelve, and then the half, and I was listening out for the three-quarters—still watching, still waiting; but beginning to wonder, perhaps, what it was I thought I would see—when this happened:

There came a light and a shadow, in Mrs Sucksby's room; and then a figure—Mrs Sucksby herself! My heart nearly flew into bits. Her hair showed white, and she had her old black taffeta gown on. She stood with a lamp in her hand, her face turned from me, her jaw moving—she was talking to someone else farther back in the room, someone who now came forward, as she moved back. A girl. A girl, very slim at the waist . . . I saw her, and began to shake. She came on, while Mrs Sucksby moved about the room behind her, taking off her brooches and rings. She came right to the glass. She lifted her arm to rest it upon the bar of the window-sash, and then she stood with her brow upon her wrist, and grew still. Only her fingers moved, as they plucked idly at the lace across the window. Her hand was bare. Her hair was curled. I thought, *It can't be her*.

Then Mrs Sucksby spoke again, the girl lifted her face, the light of the street-lamp fell full upon it; and I cried out loud.

She might have heard me—though I don't think she can have—for she turned her head and seemed to look at me, to hold my gaze across the dusty street and the darkness, for quite a minute. I don't think I blinked, in all that time. I don't think she did, her eyes stayed open— I saw them, and remembered their colour at last. Then she turned back into the room, took a step away, caught up the lamp; and as she lowered the flame Mrs Sucksby went close to her, lifted her hands, and begin to unfasten the hooks at the back of her collar.

Then came darkness.

I moved back from the window. My own white face was reflected there, the streetlight striking it—on the cheek, beneath my eye—in the shape of a heart. I turned from the glass. My cry had woken Charles, and I suppose my look was peculiar.

'Miss, what is it?' he said in a whisper.

I put my hand before my mouth.

'Oh, Charles!' I said. I took a couple of staggering steps towards him. 'Charles, look at me! Tell me who I am!'

'Who, miss?'

'Not *miss*, don't call me *miss*! I never was a miss, though they made me out one.—Oh! She has taken everything from me, Charles. She has taken everything and made it hers, in spite. She has made Mrs Sucksby love her, as she made— Oh! I'll kill her, tonight!'

I ran in a kind of fever, back to the shutter, to look at the face of the house. I said, 'Now, might I climb to the window? I could force the bolt, creep in, and stab her as she lies sleeping. Where is that knife?'

I ran again, and caught it up and tried its edge. 'Not sharp enough,' I said. I looked about me, then picked up the stone that was used as a door-stop, and drew the blade across it. 'Like this?' I said to Charles. 'Or like this? Which makes the best edge? Come on, come on. You're the bloody knife-boy, aren't you?'

He watched me in terror; then came and, with trembling fingers, showed me how. I ground the blade. 'That's good,' I said. 'That will feel good, with its point against her breast.' Then I stopped. 'But, don't you think that, after all, a death by stabbing comes rather quick? Had I not ought to find a slower way?'—I thought of stifling, strangling, beating with a club.—'Have we a club, Charles? That will take longer; and oh! I should like to have her know me, as she dies. You shall come with me, Charles. You shall help.—What's the matter?'

He had walked to the wall and stood with his back against it, and begun to quiver.

He said, 'You ain't— You ain't the lady you seemed to be at Briar!'

I said, 'Look at you. You ain't the boy. That boy had nerve.'

'I want Mr Rivers!'

I laughed, a mad laugh. 'I've got news for you. Mr Rivers ain't quite the gent you thought him, either. Mr Rivers is a devil and a rogue.'

He stepped forward. 'He ain't!'

'He is, though. He ran off with Miss Maud, told everyone I was her and put me in a madhouse. Who else do you think it was, signed my order?'

'If he signed it, it must have been true!'

'He's a villain.'

'He's a gem of a man! Everyone at Briar said so.'

'They never knew him like I did. He's bad, he's rotten.'

He made his hands into fists. 'I don't care!' he cried.

'You want to man for a devil?'

'Better that, than— Oh!' He sat upon the floor and hid his face. 'Oh! Oh! I was never more miserable, in all of my life. I hate you!'

'And I hate you,' I said, 'you fucking nancy.'

I still had the stone in my hand. I threw it at him.

It missed him by about a foot; but the sound of it striking the wall and floor was awful. I was shaking, now, almost as badly as he was. I looked at the knife I held, then put it from me. I touched my face. My cheek and brow were wet with a horrible sweat. I went to Charles and knelt beside him. He tried to push me away.

'Get off me!' he cried. 'Or, kill me now! I don't care!'

'Charles, listen to me,' I said, in a steadier voice. 'I don't hate you, truly. And you mustn't hate me. I am all you've got. You have lost your place at Briar, and your aunty don't want you. You can't go back to the country now. Besides, you should never find your way out of Southwark, without my help. You should wander and grow bewildered; and London is full of cruel hard men who do unspeakable things to bewildered fair-haired boys. You might be taken by the master of a ship, and finish up in Jamaica. How should you like that? Don't cry, for God's sake!'—He had begun to sob.—'You think I shouldn't like to cry? I have been dreadfully cheated, and the person that cheated me worst is lying at this moment in my own bed, with my own mother's arms about her. This is a greater thing than you can understand. This is a matter of life and death. I was foolish to say I would kill her tonight. But give me a day or two more, and let me think. There's money over there and—I swear it, Charles!—there are people there too who, once they know how I've been wronged, will give any kind of sum to the boy that has helped me back to them . . .'

He shook his head, still crying; and now, at last, I began to cry, too. I put my arm about him and he leaned into my shoulder, and we shuddered and wailed until, finally, someone in the room next door began to bang on the wall and call out for us to stop.

'There, now,' I said, wiping my nose. 'You're not afraid, now? You'll sleep, like a good boy?'

He said he thought he would, if I would keep beside him; and so we lay together on the bed with the red hairs in it, and he slept, with his pink lips parted, and his breaths coming even and smooth.

But I kept wakeful, all through that night. I thought of Maud, across the street, lying breathing in Mrs Sucksby's arms, her mouth open like his, like a flower, her throat perfectly slender, and perfectly white and bare.

By the time the morning came, I had the beginnings of a plan worked out. I stood at the window and watched Mr Ibbs's door for a time but then, seeing no-one stirring, gave it up. That could wait. What I needed now was money. I knew how to get it. I made Charles brush his hair and put a parting in it, then took him quietly from the house, by the back way. I took him to Whitechapel—a place, I thought, far enough from the Borough for me to risk going about without my veil. I found a spot on the High Street.

'Stand here,' I said. He did. 'Now, remember how you cried so hard last night? Let's see you do it again.'

'Let's what?'

I caught hold of his arm and pinched it. He gave a squeal, then began to snivel. I put my hand on his shoulder and looked up and down the street, in an anxious way. A few people gazed curiously at us. I beckoned them over.

'Please, sir, please, lady,' I said. 'I just come upon this poor boy, he's come in from the country this morning and has lost his master.

Can you spare a couple of farthings, set him back upon his way? Can you? He's all alone and don't know no-one, don't know Chancery Lane from Woolwich. He has left his coat in his master's cart.—God bless you, sir! Don't cry, mate! Look, this gentleman is giving you twopence. Here comes some more! And they say Londoners' hearts is hard, in the country—don't they . . .?'

Of course, the idea of a gentleman giving him money made Charles cry worse than ever. His tears were like so many magnets. We made three shillings, that first day—which paid for our room; and when we tried the same dodge the day after, on a different street, we made four. That got us our suppers. The money that was left over after that I kept, along with the ticket to Charles's coat, in my shoe. I wore my shoes, even in bed. 'I want my jacket,' Charles would say, a hundred times an hour; and every time I'd answer, 'Tomorrow. I swear. I promise. Just one more day . . .'

And then, all day, I would stand at the shutters, my eye at the heart-shaped hole. I was watching the house, figuring out its habits. I was marking it, patient as a cracksman. I saw thieves come, bringing pieces of poke to Mr Ibbs: I saw him turn the lock on his door, pull down his blind. The sight of his hands, of his honest face, made me want to weep. I'd think, 'Why *can't* I go to him?' Then, a little later, I'd see Gentleman, and be filled again with fear. Then I'd see Maud. I'd see her at the window. She liked to stand there, with her face against the sash—as if she knew I was watching, and mocked me! I saw Dainty, helping her dress in the mornings, fastening up her hair. And I saw Mrs Sucksby, at night, letting it down.—Once I saw her lift a tress of it to her mouth, and kiss it.

With each new thing, I would press my face so hard against the glass I stood at, it would groan in its frame. And at night, when the house was dark, I would take up my candle and walk, back and forth, back and forth, from one wall to another.

'They have got them all in their power,' I'd say. 'Dainty, and Mr Ibbs, and Mrs Sucksby; and I dare say John and even Phil. Like two great spiders, they have spun their web. We've got to be careful, Charles. Oh, haven't we! For say they know, through Dr Christie, that I've escaped? They *must* know by now! They are waiting,

Charles. They are waiting for me. *She* never leaves the house—
that's clever!—for, in keeping there, she keeps near Mrs Sucksby. *He*
goes, however. I've seen him. I've been waiting, too. They don't
know that. *He* goes. We'll make our move, next time he does. I'm
the fly they want. They shan't get me. We'll send them *you*. They
won't have thought of that! Hey, Charles?'

Charles never answered. I had kept him so long in that dark
room, doing nothing, his face had got pale, and his eyes had begun
to grow glassy, like a doll's. 'I want my jacket,' he still said, now and
then, in a feeble sort of bleat; but I think he had almost forgotten
what it was he wanted it for. For at last there came a time when he
said it, and I answered: 'All right. Today you'll get it. We've waited
long enough. Today's our day'; and instead of looking pleased, he
stared and looked frightened.

Perhaps he thought he saw a certain feverish something in my
eye. I don't know. It seemed to me I was thinking like a sharper, for
the first time in my life. I took him back to Watling Street and got
his jacket out of pawn. But I kept hold of it. Then I took him on a
'bus.—'For a treat,' I said. 'Look out the window, at the shops.'

I found us places next to a woman holding a baby. I sat with the
coat across my lap. Then I looked at the baby. The woman caught
my eye, and I smiled.

'Pretty boy,' she said. 'Isn't he? Won't sleep for his mother,
though. I bring him on the 'buses and the bumping sends him off.
We've been from Fulham to Bow; now we're on our way back.'

'He's a peach,' I said. I leaned in and stroked his cheek. 'Look at
them lashes! He'll break hearts, he will.'

'Won't he!'

Then I leaned back. When the next stop came, I made Charles
get off. The woman said good-bye, and from the window, as the
'bus moved away; she waved. But I didn't wave back. For, under
cover of Charles's coat, I had had a feel about her waistband; and
had prigged her watch. It was a nice little ladies' watch, and just
what I needed. I showed it to Charles. He looked at it as though it
were a snake that might bite him.

'Where did you get that?' he said.

'Someone gave it to me.'

'I don't believe you. Give me my jacket.'

'In a minute.'

'Give me my coat!'

We were walking on London Bridge. 'Shut up,' I said, 'or I'll throw it over the side.—That's better. Now, tell me this: can you write?'

He would not answer until I had gone to the wall of the bridge and dangled his jacket over; then he began to cry again, but said that he could. 'Good boy,' I said. I made him walk a little further, until we found a man hawking papers and inks. I bought a plain white sheet, and a pencil; and I took Charles back to our room and had him sit and write out a letter. I stood with my hand on the back of his neck, and watched.

'Write, *Mrs Sucksby*,' I said.

He said, 'How do you spell it?'

'Don't you know?'

He frowned, then wrote. It looked all right to me. I said,

'Now you write this. Write: *I was put in the madhouse by that villain your friend—so called!—Gentleman—*'

'You are going too fast,' he said, as he wrote. He tilted his head. '*By that villain your friend—*'

'*—so called!—Gentleman; and that bitch Maud Lilly.—*You must make those names stand out.'

The pencil moved on, then stopped. He blushed.

'I won't write that word,' he said.

'What word?'

'That *B*-word.'

'What?'

'Before Miss Lilly.'

I pinched his neck. 'You write it,' I said. 'You hear me? Then you write this, nice and big: *PIGEON MY ARSE! She is WORSE THAN HIM!*'

He hesitated; then bit his lip and wrote.

'That's good. Now this. Put: *Mrs Sucksby, I have escaped and am close at hand. Send me a signal by this boy. He is a friend, he is writing this, his name is Charles. Trust him, and believe me*—oh! if this fails, I'll die!—*believe me as ever as good and as faithful as your own daughter*— There you must leave a space.'

He did. I took the paper from him and wrote, at the bottom, my name.

'Don't look at me!' I said, as I did it; then I kissed where I had written, and folded the paper up.

'Here's what you must do next,' I said then. 'Tonight, when Gentleman—Mr Rivers—leaves the house, you must go over, and knock, and ask to see Mr Ibbs. Say you've got a thing to sell him. You'll know him straight off: he's tall, and trims his whiskers. He'll ask if you've been followed; and you must be sure, when he does, to say you got away clean. Then he'll ask what brought you to him. Say you know Phil. If he asks how you know him you're to say, "Through a pal named George." If he asks which George you must say, "George Joslin, down Collier's Rents." George who, down where?'

'George Joslin, down— Oh, miss! I should rather anything than this!'

'Should you rather the cruel hard men, the unspeakable things, Jamaica?'

He swallowed. 'George Joslin, down Collier's Rents,' he said.

'Good boy. Next you hand him the watch. He will give you a price; but whatever price he gives you—if it be, a hundred pounds, or a thousand—you must say it ain't enough. Say the watch is a good one, with Geneva works. Say—I don't know—say your dad done watches, and you know them. Make him look a bit harder. Any luck, he'll take the back off—that will give you the chance to look about. Here's who you're looking for: a lady, rather old, with hair of silver—she'll be sitting in a rocking-chair, perhaps with a baby in her lap. That's Mrs Sucksby, that brought me up. She'll do anything for me. You find a way to reach her side, and pass this letter to her. You do it, Charles, and we're saved. But listen here. If there's a dark-faced, mean-looking boy about, keep clear of him, he's against us. Same goes for a red-headed girl. And if that viper Miss Maud Lilly is anywhere near, you hide your face. Understand me? If she sees you—more even than the boy—then we are done for.'

He swallowed again. He put the note on the bed, and sat and looked fearfully at it. He practised his piece. I stood at the window, and watched, and waited. First came twilight, then came dark; and with the dark came Gentleman, slipping from Mr Ibbs's door with his hat at an angle and that scarlet cloth at his throat. I saw him go; gave it another half-an-hour, to be sure; then looked at Charles.

'Put your coat on,' I said. 'It's time.'

He grew pale. I gave him his cap and his scarf, and turned up his collar.

'Have you got the letter? Very good. Be brave, now. No funny stuff. I'll be watching, don't forget.'

He did not speak. He went, and after a moment I saw him cross the street and stand before Mr Ibbs's. He walked like a man on his way to the rope. He pulled his scarf a little higher about his face, then he looked round, to where he knew I stood behind the shutter.—'*Don't look round, you fool!*' I thought, when he did that. Then he plucked at his scarf again; and then he knocked. I wondered if he might run from the step. He looked as though he would like to. But before he could, the door was opened, by Dainty. They spoke, and she left him waiting while she went in to Mr Ibbs; then she came back. She glanced up and down the street. Like a fool, he glanced with her, as if to see what she looked for. Then she nodded, and stepped back. He went in, and the door was closed. I imagined her turning the latch with her neat white hand.

Then I waited.

Say five minutes passed. Say ten.

What did I suppose would happen? Perhaps, that the door would open, Mrs Sucksby come flying out, with Mr Ibbs behind her; perhaps only that she'd go to her room—show a light, make a sign—I don't know. But the house stayed quiet, and when at last the door did open, there came only Charles again, with Dainty still behind him; and then again, the door was shut. Charles stood, and quivered. I was used by now to his quivers, and think I knew from the look of this one that things were bad. I saw him look up at our window and think about running.—'*Don't you run, you fuckster!*' I said, and hit the glass; and perhaps he heard it, for he put down his head and came back across the street and up the stairs. By the time he reached the room his face was crimson, and slick with tears and snot.

'God help me, I didn't mean to do it!' he said, bursting in. 'God help me, she found me out and made me!'

'Made you what?' I said. 'What happened? What happened, you little tick?'

I got hold of him and shook him. He put his hands before his face.

'She got the letter off me and read it!' he said.

'Who did?'

'Miss Maud! Miss Maud!'

I looked at him in horror. 'She saw me,' he said, 'and she knew me. I did it all, just as you said. I gave the watch, and the tall man took it and opened its back. He thought my scarf was queer, and asked if I'd the toothache. I said I did. He showed me a pair of nippers, that he said were good for drawing teeth. I think he was teasing. The dark boy was there, burning paper. He called me a—a pigeon. The red-headed girl didn't give me a look. But the lady, your ma, was sleeping; and I tried to reach her side, but Miss Maud saw the letter in my hand. Then she looked at me, and knew me. She said, "Come here, boy, you've hurt your hand," and she got hold of me before the others could see. She had been playing cards at a table, and she held the letter under the table and read it, and she twisted my fingers so hard—'

His words began to dissolve, like salt in the water of his tears.

'Stop crying!' I said. 'Stop crying for once in your life, or I swear, I'll hit you! Tell me now, what did she do?'

He took a breath, and put his hand to his pocket, and brought something out.

'She did nothing,' he said. 'But she gave me this. She took it from the table where she sat. She gave it to me, as if it might be a secret; and then the tall man closed the watch up and she pushed me away. He gave me a pound, and I took it, and the red-headed girl let me out. Miss Maud watched me go, and her eyes were like eyes on fire; but she never said a word. She only gave me this, and I think she must have meant it for you but, oh, miss! you can call me a fool, but God help me if I know what it's for!'

He handed it over. She had made it very small, and it took me a moment to unfold it and know what it was. When I did, I held it, and turned it, then turned it again; then I stood gazing stupidly at it.

'Just this?' I said. Charles nodded.

It was a playing card. It was one of the playing cards from her old French deck at Briar. It was the Two of Hearts. It had got greasy, and was marked by the folds she had put in it; but it still had that crease, in the shape of her heel, across one of its painted red pips.

I held it, and remembered sitting with her in her parlour, springing the pack to tell her fortune. She had worn her blue gown. She had put her hand before her mouth. *Now you are frightening me!* she had said.

How she must have laughed about it, later!

'She's making game of me,' I said, my voice not perfectly steady. 'She has sent me this—you're sure there's no message on it, no mark or sign?—she has sent me this, to tease me. Why else?'

'Miss, I don't know. She took it from the table-top. She took it quick, and there was a—a wildness, about her eye.'

'What sort of a wildness?'

'I can't say. She looked, not like herself. She wore no gloves. Her hair was curled and queer. There was a glass beside her place—I don't like to say—I think it had gin in it.'

'*Gin?*'

We looked at each other.

'What shall we do?' he asked me.

I did not know.

'I must think,' I said, beginning to walk about. 'I must think what *she*'ll do. She'll tell Gentleman—won't she?—and show him our letter. Then he'll move, very quick, to find us. They didn't see you come back here? Someone else might've, though. We can't be sure. We've had luck on our side, so far; now our luck's turning. Oh, if only I'd never taken that woman's wedding-gown!—I knew it would make a bad fortune. Luck's like the tide: it turns, then gets faster and can't be stopped.'

'Don't say it!' cried Charles. He was wringing his hands. 'Send the lady her gown back, can't you?'

'You can't cheat luck like that. The best you can do is, try and outface it.'

'Outface it?'

I went to the window again, and gazed at the house.

'Mrs Sucksby is in there now,' I said. 'Won't one word from me do it? When did I ever let myself be frightened by John Vroom? Dainty I think won't harm me; nor Mr Ibbs. And Maud sounds muddled by gin. Charles, I've been a fool to wait at all. Give me my knife. We are going over.'

He stood, open-mouthed, and did nothing. I got the knife myself, then took him by his wrist and led him from the room, down the slippery staircase. A man and a girl stood at the bottom, quarrelling; but their voices faded and they turned their heads to watch us as we went by. Perhaps they saw my knife. I had nowhere to hide it. The street was blowing about with gusts of grit and paper, the night still hot. My head was bare. Anyone who saw me now would know me for Susan Trinder; but it was too late to care. I ran with Charles to Mr Ibbs's door, knocked on it, then left him on the step while I stood aside with my back to the wall. The door was opened after a minute, just an inch.

'You've come too late.' It was Dainty's voice. 'Mr Ibbs says— Oh! It's you again. What now? Changed your mind?'

The door was opened a little further. Charles stood, and licked his mouth, his eyes on Dainty's. Then he looked at me; and when she saw him do that, she put out her head and also looked. Then she screamed.

'Mrs Sucksby!' I cried. I made a charge at the door, and Dainty went flying. I caught Charles's arm and pulled him into the shop. 'Mrs Sucksby!' I shouted again. I ran to the hanging baize curtain and knocked it back. The passage beyond was dark, and I stumbled, and Charles stumbled with me. Then I reached the door at the end, and threw it open. There came heat, and smoke, and light, that made me wink. I saw Mr Ibbs first. He had come half-way to the door, hearing all the shouting. When he saw me he stopped, and flung up his hands. Behind him was John Vroom, in his dog-skin coat; behind John Vroom—I saw her, and could have cried like a girl—was Mrs Sucksby. At the table, in Mrs Sucksby's great chair, was Maud.

Beneath the chair was Charley Wag. He had begun to bark at the commotion. Now, seeing me, he barked more wildly and beat his tail, then came and rose up before me to give me his paws. The row was awful. Mr Ibbs reached forward and seized his collar and quickly jerked it back. He jerked so hard, Charley was almost throttled. I flinched away and lifted my arms. The others all watched me. If they had not seen my knife before, they saw it now. Mrs Sucksby opened her mouth. She said,

'Sue, I— Sue—'

Then Dainty came running in behind me, from Mr Ibbs's shop.

'Where is she?' she cried. She had made her hands into fists. She pushed Charles aside, saw me, and stamped. 'You've got some cheek, coming back here. You bitch! You have just about broke Mrs Sucksby's heart!'

'Keep off me,' I said, waving my knife. She looked at it in astonishment, then fell back. I wished she hadn't; for there was something awful about it. She was only Dainty, after all. The knife began to shake.

'Mrs Sucksby,' I said, turning to her. 'They have told you lies. I never— They had me—him and her—locked up! And it has taken me all this time—all this time, since May!—to get back to you.'

Mrs Sucksby had her hand at her heart. She looked so surprised and afraid, it might have been her I was pointing the knife at. She looked at Mr Ibbs, and then she looked at Maud. Then she seemed to come to herself. She took two or three nimble steps across the kitchen and put her arms about me, tight.

'Dear girl,' she said.

She pressed my face against her bosom. Something hard struck my cheek. It was Maud's diamond brooch.

'Oh!' I cried, when I felt it. And I struggled away. 'She has taken you from me, with jewels! With jewels and lies!'

'Dear girl,' said Mrs Sucksby again.

But I looked at Maud. She had not flinched, or started, at sight of me, as the others all had; she had only—just like Mrs Sucksby— lifted her hand to her heart. She was dressed like a girl of the Borough, but her face was put back from the light, her eyes in shadow—she looked handsome and proud. Her hand was trembling, though.

'That's right,' I said, when I saw that. 'You shake.'

She swallowed. 'You had much better not have come here, Sue,' she said. 'You had much better have stayed away.'

'You can say so!' I cried. Her voice was clear, and sweet. I remembered hearing it, now, in my dreams at the madhouse. 'You can say so, you cheat, you snake, you viper!'

'Girl-fight!' cried John, with a clap of his hands.

'Hey! hey!' said Mr Ibbs. He had taken out a handkerchief and was wiping his brow. He looked at Mrs Sucksby. She still had her arms about me, and I could not see her face. But I felt her grip grow slack as she reached to take the knife from my hands. 'Why, he's a sharp one, ain't he?' she said, with a nervous laugh. She put the knife gently on the table. I leaned and snatched it up again.

'Don't leave it,' I said, 'where *she* might get it! Oh, Mrs Sucksby, you don't know what a devil she is!'

'Sue, listen to me,' said Maud.

'Dear girl,' said Mrs Sucksby again, over her words. 'This is so astonishingly queer. This is so— Only look at you! Like a regular— ha, ha!—soldier.' She wiped her mouth. 'What say you sit down, now, and be nice? What say we send Miss Lilly upstairs, if looking at her upsets you? Eh? And there's John and Dainty: let's ask them, shall we?'—she jerked her head—'to slip upstairs, too?'

'Don't let them go!' I cried, as Dainty began to move. 'Not her, not them!' I waved the knife. 'You, John Vroom, stay,' I said. And then, to Mrs Sucksby and Mr Ibbs: 'They'll go for Gentleman! Don't trust them!'

'She's lost her mind,' said John, rising from his chair. I made a swipe at the sleeve of his coat.

'I said, stay!' I cried.

He looked at Mrs Sucksby. She looked at Mr Ibbs.

'Sit down, son,' Mr Ibbs said quietly. John sat. I nodded to Charles.

'Charles, stand behind me, by the door to the shop. Keep them from running to it, should they try.'

He had taken off his cap, and was biting the band of it. He went to the door, his face so pale, in the shadows, it seemed to glow.

John looked at him and laughed.

'You leave him alone,' I said at once. 'He has been a friend to me, more ever than you were. Mrs Sucksby, I should never have got back to you, without him. I should never have got free of—of the mad-house.'

She put her fingers to her cheek. 'Helped you so far as that, did he?' she said, with her eyes on Charles. She smiled. 'Then he's a dear boy; and we shall be sure to pay him out. Shan't we, Mr Ibbs?'

Mr Ibbs said nothing. Maud leaned from her chair.

'You must go, Charles,' she said, in her clear, low voice. 'You must go from here.' She looked at me. The look was strange. 'You must both go, before Gentleman comes back.'

I curled my lip at her. '*Gentleman*,' I said. '*Gentleman*. You have learned Borough habits very quick.'

The blood rose in her cheek. 'I am changed,' she murmured. 'I am not what I was.'

'You are not,' I said.

She lowered her eyes. She looked at her hands. And then, as if seeing that they were bare—and as if one could cover the bareness of the other—she put them awkwardly together. There came the faint jingle of metal: she had, upon her wrist, two or three thin silver bangles, of a kind I had used to like to wear. She held them, to make them be still; then lifted her head again and caught my gaze. I said, in a hard, steady voice:

'Was being a lady not enough for you, that you must come to the Borough and take the things that were ours?'

She did not answer.

'Well?' I said.

She began to try to draw free the bangles. 'Take them,' she said. 'I don't want them!'

'You think *I* want them?'

Mrs Sucksby stepped forward, her own hands darting towards Maud's.

'Let them stay!' she cried.

Her voice was hoarse. She looked at me, then gave an awkward sort of laugh. 'Dear girl,' she said, moving back, 'what's silver, in this house? What's silver, compared with the joy of seeing your face?' She put one hand to her throat, and leaned with the other upon the back of a chair. She leaned heavily, and the chair-legs grated on the floor. 'Dainty,' she said, 'fetch me out a tumbler of brandy, will you? This turn of things've quite undone me.'

Like Mr Ibbs, she took out a handkerchief and passed it over her face. Dainty gave her her drink, and she sipped it, and sat.

'Come beside me,' she said to me. 'Put down that old knife, won't you?' And then, when I hesitated: 'What, afraid of Miss Lilly? With me and Mr Ibbs—and your own pal Charles—to mind you? Come, sit.'

I looked again at Maud. I had thought her a viper, but, in the bringing and pouring of the brandy the lamp had got moved about, and I saw in the light of it how slight and pale and tired she was. At Mrs Sucksby's cry, she had fallen still; her hands still shook, however, and she rested her head against the high back of her chair, as if the weight of it hurt her. Her face was damp. A few strands of hair clung to it. Her eyes were darker than they ought to have been, and seemed to glitter.

I sat, and put the knife before me. Mrs Sucksby took my hand. I said,

'I have been done very wrong, Mrs Sucksby.'

Mrs Sucksby slowly shook her head. 'My dear, I begin to see it,' she said.

'God knows what lies they've told you! The truth is, she was in it with him from the start. They set me up, between them, to take her place; and they put me in the madhouse, where everyone supposed me to be her—'

John whistled. 'Double-cross,' he said. 'Nice work but—oh!' He laughed. 'You pigeon!'

Which is what I had known, all along, he would say; though now, it did not seem to matter. Mrs Sucksby looked, not at me, but at our joined hands. She was smoothing her thumb upon mine. I thought the news had stunned her.

'A bad business,' she said quietly.

'Worse than that!' I cried. 'Oh, much, much worse! A madhouse, Mrs Sucksby! With nurses, that hurt and starved me! I was hit one time, so hard—! I was dropped—I was dropped in a bath—!'

She drew free her hand and raised it before her face.

'No more, dear girl! No more. I can't bear to hear it.'

'Did they torture you, with tongs?' asked John. 'Did they put you in a strait-coat?'

'They put me in a tartan gown, and boots of—'

'Of iron?'

I hesitated, then glanced at Charles.

'Boots without laces,' I said. 'They thought that, if they gave me laces, I should hang myself. And my hair—'

'Did they cut it?' said Dainty, sitting, putting a hand before her mouth. Her mouth had a fading bruise beside it—from John, I suppose. 'Did they shave it off?'

I hesitated again, then said, 'They sewed it to my head.'

Her eyes filled with tears. 'Oh, Sue!' she said. 'I swear, I never meant it when I called you a bitch just now!'

'That's all right,' I said. 'You weren't to know.' I turned again to Mrs Sucksby, and touched the skirt of my dress. 'This gown I stole,' I said. 'And these shoes. And I walked, nearly all the way to London. My only thought was to get back here to you. For worse than all the cruel things that were done to me in the madhouse was the thought of the lies that Gentleman must have told you, about where I had gone. I supposed at first, he would have said that I had died.'

She took my hand again. 'He might,' she said, 'have thought of it.'

'But I knew you would ask for my body.'

'Wouldn't I! Straight off!'

'Then I guessed what he would say. He would say I had cut with
the money, and cheated you all.'

'He did,' said John. He sucked his tooth. 'I always said that you
hadn't the nerve.'

I looked into Mrs Sucksby's face. 'But I knew you wouldn't
believe it,' I said, 'of your own daughter.' Her grip on my hand grew
tight. 'I knew you would look for me, until you found me.'

'Dear girl, I— Oh, I should have got you, too, in another month
more!—only, you know, I kept my searching quiet from John and
Dainty.'

'Did you, Mrs Sucksby?' said Dainty.

'My dear, I did. I sent out a man, confidentially.'

She wiped her lips. She looked at Maud. But Maud had her eyes
upon me. I suppose the lamp that lit her face also lit mine, for she
said, softly and suddenly,

'You look ill, Sue.'

It was the third time she had spoken my name. I heard it and—
despite myself—I thought of the other times she had said it, so
softly as that, and felt myself colour.

'You do look done up,' said Dainty. 'You look like you ain't slept
in a week.'

'I haven't,' I said.

'Then why,' said Mrs Sucksby, making to rise, 'won't you go
upstairs now, and put your head down? And then tomorrow, me and
Dainty will come and fix you up in one of your old gowns, and
dress your hair—'

'Don't go to sleep here, Sue!' said Maud, leaning from her chair
and putting her hand towards me. 'There's danger here.'

I took up my knife again, and she drew her hand back. I said,

'You think I don't know danger? You think that, in looking at
you, I'm not seeing danger with a face—a false face, with an actress
mouth—with lying blushes, and two brown treacherous eyes?'

The words were like clinker on my tongue: they were awful, but
I must spit them out or swallow them and choke. She held my gaze,
and her eyes did not seem treacherous, at all. I turned the knife. The

blade took up the light of the lamp and sent it darting across her cheek.

'I came here to kill you,' I said.

Mrs Sucksby shifted in her seat. Maud kept her glittering gaze on mine.

'You came to Briar,' she said, 'to do that . . .'

Then I looked away and let the knife fall. I felt suddenly tired, and sick. I felt all the walking I had done, and all the careful watching. Now nothing was as I had thought it would be. I turned to Mrs Sucksby.

'Can you sit,' I said, 'and hear her tease me? Can you know the wicked trick she played me, and have her here, and not want to throttle her?' I meant it; and yet it sounded like bluster, too. I looked around the room. 'Mr Ibbs, can you?' I said. 'Dainty, shouldn't you like to shake her to pieces, in my behalf?'

'Shouldn't I!' said Dainty. She showed her fist. 'Cheat my best pal, would you?' she said to Maud. 'Lock her up in a madhouse and sew up her hair?' Maud said nothing, but slightly turned her head. Dainty shook her fist again, then let it sink. She caught my eye. 'Seems an awful shame, though, Sue. Miss Lilly turning out to be such a sport, and all. And brave? I done her ears last week, and she never cried once. And then, she has took to taking stitches out, that natural—'

'All right, Dainty,' said Mrs Sucksby quickly.

I looked again at Maud—at her neat ear which, I now saw, had a crystal drop falling from it on a wire of gold; and at the curls in her fair hair; and at her dark eye-brows. They had been tweezered into two fine arches. Above her chair—I had not seen this before, either, but it seemed all of a piece with the drops, the curls and arches, the bangles on her wrist—above her chair there was hanging, from a beam, a little cage of wicker with a yellow bird in it.

I felt tears rise into my throat.

'You have taken everything that was mine,' I said. 'You have taken it, and made it better.'

'I took it,' she answered, '*because* it was yours. Because I must!'

'Why must you? Why?'

She opened her mouth to speak. Then she looked at Mrs Sucksby and her face changed.

'For villainy's sake,' she said flatly. 'For villainy's sake. Because you were right, before: my face is a false one, my mouth is an actress mouth, my blushes tell lies, my eyes— My eyes—' She looked away. Her voice had begun to rise. She made it flat again. 'Richard found that, after all, we must wait for our money, longer than we thought.'

She took up her glass in both her hands, and swallowed what was left in it.

'You haven't got the money?'

She put the glass back down. 'Not yet.'

'That's something, then,' I said. 'I shall want a share of that. I shall want half of it. Mrs Sucksby, do you hear? They shall give me half their fortune, at least. Not a stinking three thousand, but a half. Think what we shall do, with that!'

But I did not want the money; and when I spoke, my voice sounded hateful to me. Mrs Sucksby said nothing. Maud said,

'You shall have what you like. I will give you anything, anything at all—if you will only go from here, now, before Richard comes back.'

'Go from here? Because you tell me to? This is my home! Mrs Sucksby— Mrs Sucksby, will you tell her?'

Mrs Sucksby again passed a hand across her mouth.

'There again, Susie,' she said slowly, 'Miss Lilly might be right. If there is the money to be thought of, you might do well, for now, to keep out of Gentleman's way. Let me speak with him, first. I'll give him a taste of my temper, though!'

She said it in a queer, half-hearted way, with a try at a smile—as she might have said it, I thought, if she had just found out that Gentleman had swindled her out of two or three shillings at cards. I guessed she was thinking about Maud's fortune, and how it might be cut. I couldn't help but wish that, after all, the money was nothing to her. I said,

'Will you make me go?' The words came out like a whisper. I looked away from her, about the kitchen—at the old Dutch clock on the shelf, and the pictures on the walls. On the floor by the door to the stairs was the white china chamber-pot, with the dark eye in it, from my own room, that must have been brought down to be washed and then forgotten. I would not have forgotten it. On the table beneath my hand was a heart: I had scratched it into the wood, the summer before. I had been like a child still, then. I had been like an infant— I looked about me again. Why were there no babies? The kitchen was still. Everyone was still, and watching me.

'Will you make me go,' I said again to Mrs Sucksby, 'and let her stay?' Now my voice was broken as a boy's. 'Will you trust them, not to send Dr Christie to me? Will you— Will you take her gowns, will you take the pins from her head, will you kiss her, will you let her sleep beside you in my old place, while I lie in a bed with—with red hairs in it?'

'Sleep beside me?' said Mrs Sucksby quickly. 'Who told you that?'

'Red hairs?' said John.

But Maud had lifted her head, her gaze grown sharp. 'You have watched us!' she said. And then, when she had thought it through: 'At the shutter!'

'I've watched you,' I answered, more strongly. 'I've watched you, you spider! taking everything of mine. You would rather do that— God damn you!—than sleep with your own husband!'

'Sleep with—with Richard?' She looked astounded. 'You don't suppose—?'

'Susie,' said Mrs Sucksby, putting her hand upon me.

'Sue,' said Maud at the same time, leaning across the table and also reaching for me. 'You don't suppose him anything to me? You don't think him a husband to me, in anything but name? Don't you know I hate him? Don't you know I hated him, at Briar?'

'Will you make out now,' I said, in a kind of trembling scorn, 'that you only did what you did because he made you?'

'He did make me!—But, not in the way you mean.'

I said, 'Will you pretend, that you aren't a swindling cheat?'

She said, 'Will you?'

And again, she held my gaze; and again, I was almost shamed by it, and looked away. Then after a moment I said, more quietly,

'I hated it. I didn't smile, with him, when your back was turned.'

'You think I did?'

'Why not? You are an actress. You are acting now!'

'Am I?'

She said it, still with her eyes on my face, still with her hand reaching for mine but falling short of taking it. The light was all upon us, the rest of the kitchen almost dark. I looked at her fingers. They were marked with dirt, or bruised. I said,

'If you hated him, why did you do it?'

'There was no other way,' she said. 'You saw my life. I needed you, to be me.'

'So you might come here, and be me!' She did not answer. I said, 'We might have cheated him. If you had told me. We might have—'

'What?'

'Anything. Something. I don't know what . . .'

She shook her head. 'How much,' she asked quietly, 'would you have given up?'

Her gaze was so dark, yet so steady and true; but I grew aware, all at once, of Mrs Sucksby—of John and Dainty, Mr Ibbs—all of them, watching, silent and curious, thinking, *What's this . . .?* And in that moment, I saw into my own cowardly heart and knew that I would have given up nothing for her, nothing at all; and that, sooner than be shamed by her now, I would die.

She reached again. Her fingers brushed my wrist. I took up the knife and jabbed at her hand.

'Don't touch me!' I said, as I did it. I got to my feet. 'Don't any of you touch me!' My voice was wild. 'Not any of you! Do you hear me? I came back here, thinking this my home; now you want to cast me out again. I hate you all! I wish I had stayed in the country!'

I looked from face to face. Dainty had begun to cry. John sat, open-mouthed and astonished. Mr Ibbs had his hand at his cheek. Maud nursed her bleeding fingers. Charles shook. Mrs Sucksby said,

'Sue, put down the knife. Cast you out? The idea! I—'

Then she stopped. Charley Wag had lifted his head. From Mr

Ibbs's shop there came the sound of a key, turning in a lock. Then came the kicking of boots; then whistling.

'Gentleman!' she said. She looked at Maud, at Mr Ibbs, at me. She got up, and leaned to catch at my arm. 'Sue,' she said, as she did it. She spoke in a voice that was almost a whisper. 'Susie, sweetheart, will you come upstairs . . .?'

But I did not answer, only gripped the knife more firmly. Charley Wag gave a feeble bark, and Gentleman heard him, and barked in reply. Then he whistled again, a lazy waltz tune, and we heard him stumbling along the passage and watched as he pushed at the door. I think he was drunk. His hat was crooked, his cheek quite pink, his mouth a perfect O. He stood, and slightly swayed, and looked about the room, squinting into the shadows. The whistle died. His lips grew straight, and he licked them.

'Hallo,' he said, 'here's Charles.' He winked. Then he looked at me, and at my knife. 'Hallo, here's Sue.' He took off his hat and began to unwind the scarlet cloth from his throat. 'I supposed you might come. Had you left it another day, I should have been ready. I have just now collected a letter, from that fool Christie. He certainly dragged his heels, in letting me know of your escape! I think he planned to recapture you before he should have to. Bad publicity, when one's lady lunatics run.'

He put the scarlet cloth inside the hat and let them drop. He took out a cigarette.

'You're fucking cool,' I said. I was shaking. 'Here's Mrs Sucksby and Mr Ibbs, know everything.'

He laughed. 'I should say they do.'

'Gentleman!' said Mrs Sucksby. 'Listen to me. Sue has told us terrible things. I want you to go.'

'Don't let him leave!' I said. 'He'll send for Dr Christie!' I waved my knife. 'Charles, stop him!'

Gentleman had lit his cigarette, but apart from that had not moved. He turned to look at Charles, who had taken a couple of doubtful steps towards him. He put his hand to Charles's hair.

'So, Charley,' he said.

'Please, sir,' said Charles.

'You have found me out a villain.'

Charles's lip began to tremble. 'Honest to God, Mr Rivers, I never meant to!'

'There, there,' said Gentleman. He stroked Charles's cheek. Mr Ibbs made a puffing sound with his lips. John got to his feet, then looked about him as if he did not know why he had done it. He blushed.

'Sit down, John,' said Mrs Sucksby.

He folded his arms. 'I shall stand if I like.'

'Sit down, or I'll hit you.'

'Hit me?' His voice was hoarse. 'Hit them two, there!' He pointed to Gentleman and Charles. Mrs Sucksby took two quick steps, and struck him. She struck him hard. He put both his arms to his head and gazed at her from between his elbows.

'You old cow!' he said. 'You been down on me since the day I was born. You touch me again, you'll know it!'

His eyes blazed as he said it; but then, they filled with tears and he began to snivel. He walked to the wall, and kicked it. Charles shuddered and wept harder. Gentleman looked from one to the other, then gazed at Maud in pretend amazement.

'Is it down to me,' he said, 'that small boys weep?'

'Fuck you, I ain't small!' said John.

'Will you be quiet?' said Maud, in her low, clear voice. 'Charles, that's enough.'

Charles wiped his nose. 'Yes, miss.'

Gentleman leaned against the post of the door, still smoking. 'So, Suky,' he said. 'You know all now.'

'I know you're a filthy swindler,' I said. 'But I knew that, six months ago. I was a fool, that's all, to trust you.'

'Dear girl,' said Mrs Sucksby quickly, with her eyes on Gentleman's face. 'Dear girl, the fools were me and Mr Ibbs, to let you.'

Gentleman had taken his cigarette from his mouth to blow against its tip. Now, hearing Mrs Sucksby and meeting her gaze, he stood quite still for a second with it held before his lips. Then he looked away and laughed—a disbelieving sort of laugh—and shook his head.

'Sweet Christ,' he said quietly.

I thought she had shamed him.

'All right,' she said. 'All right.' She lifted her hands. She stood, like a man on a raft—like she was afraid to make too sharp a move for fear of sinking. 'Now, no more wildness. John, no more sulks. Sue, put that knife down, please, I beg you. No-one is to be harmed. Mr Ibbs. Miss Lilly. Dainty. Charles—Sue's pal, dear boy—sit down. Gentleman. Gentleman.'

'Mrs Sucksby,' he said.

'No-one to be harmed. All right?'

He glanced at me. 'Tell it to Sue,' he said. 'She is looking at me with murder in her eyes. Under the circumstances, I don't quite care for that.'

'Circumstances?' I said. 'You mean, your having locked me up in a madhouse and left me to die? I should cut your bloody head off!'

He narrowed his eyes, made a face. 'Do you know,' he said, 'you have a very whining tone to your voice at times? Has no-one told you that?'

I made a lunge at him with the knife; but the truth was, I was still bewildered, and sick, and tired, and the lunge was a feeble one. He watched, not flinching, as I stood with the point of the blade before his heart. Then I grew afraid that the knife would shake and he would see it. I put it down. I put it down on the table—at the edge of the table, just beyond the circle of light that the lamp threw there.

'Now, ain't that nicer?' said Mrs Sucksby.

John's tears had dried, but his face was dark—darker on one cheek than on the other, where Mrs Sucksby had hit him. He looked at Gentleman, but nodded to me.

'She went for Miss Lilly just now,' he said. 'Said she'd come to kill her.'

Gentleman gazed at Maud, who had bound up her bleeding fingers in a handkerchief. He said, 'I should like to have seen it.'

John nodded. 'She wants a half of your fortune.'

'Does she?' said Gentleman, slowly.

'John, shut up,' said Mrs Sucksby. 'Gentleman, don't mind him.

He is only making trouble. Sue said a half, but that was her passion talking. She ain't in her right mind. She ain't—' She put a hand to her brow, and looked a little queerly about the room—at me, and at Maud. She pressed her fingers against her eyes. 'If I might only,' she said, 'have a moment, for thinking in!'

'Think away,' said Gentleman easily, sourly. 'I am longing to know what you will come up with.'

'So am I,' said Mr Ibbs. He said it quietly. Gentleman caught his eye, and raised a brow.

'Sticky, wouldn't you say, sir?'

'Too sticky,' said Mr Ibbs.

'You think so?'

Mr Ibbs gave a nod. Gentleman said,

'You think perhaps I should go, make it simpler?'

'Are you mad?' I said. 'Can't you see, he'll still do anything for his money? Don't let him go! He'll send for Dr Christie.'

'Don't let him go,' said Maud, to Mrs Sucksby.

'Don't you think of going anywhere,' said Mrs Sucksby, to Gentleman.

He shrugged, his colour rising. 'You wanted me to leave, two minutes ago!'

'I have changed my mind.'

She looked at Mr Ibbs; who looked away.

Gentleman took off his coat. 'Fuck me,' he said, as he did it; and he laughed, not nicely. 'It's too warm for work like this.'

'Fuck you,' I said. 'You fucking villain. You do what Mrs Sucksby says, all right?'

'Like you,' he answered, hanging his coat on a chair.

'Yes.'

He snorted. 'You poor little bitch.'

'*Richard*,' said Maud. She had got to her feet and was leaning upon the table. She said, 'Listen to me. Think of all the filthy deeds you've ever done. This will be the worst, and will gain you nothing.'

'What will?' said John.

But Gentleman snorted again. 'Tell me,' he said to Maud, 'when you first started learning to be kind. What's it to you, what Sue knows?—Dear me, how you blush! Not *that* thing, still? And do you look at Mrs Sucksby? Don't say you care what *she* thinks! Why, you're as bad as Sue. Look how you quake! Be bolder, Maud. Think of your mother.'

She had raised her hand to her heart. Now she jumped as if he had pinched her. He saw it, and laughed again. Then he looked at Mrs Sucksby. She had also given a kind of start at his words; and she stood, with her hand, like Maud's, at her bosom, beneath that diamond brooch. Then she felt him looking, glanced quickly at Maud, and let her hand fall.

Gentleman's laughter died. He stood very still.

'What's this?' he said.

'What's what?' said John.

'Now then,' said Mrs Sucksby, moving. 'Dainty—'

'Oh!' said Gentleman. 'Oh!' He watched her as she stepped about the table. Then he looked from her to Maud, in an excited sort of way, his colour rising higher. He put his hand to his hair and tugged it back from his brow.

'Now I see it,' he said. He laughed; then the laugh broke off. 'Oh, now I see it!'

'You see nothing,' said Maud, taking a step towards him, but glancing at me. 'Richard, you see nothing.'

He shook his head at her. 'What a fool I've been, not to have guessed it sooner! Oh, this is marvellous! How long have you known? No wonder you've kicked and cursed! No wonder you've sulked! No wonder she's let you! I always marvelled at that. Poor Maud!' He laughed, properly. 'And, oh, Mrs Sucksby, poor you!'

'That's enough!' said Mrs Sucksby. 'You hear me? I won't have it spoke of!'

She also took a step towards him.

'Poor you,' he said again, still laughing. Then he called: 'Mr Ibbs, sir, did you know of this, too?'

Mr Ibbs did not answer.

'Know what?' asked John, his eyes like two dark points. He looked at me. 'Know what?'

'I don't know,' I said.

'Know nothing,' said Maud. 'Know nothing, nothing!'

She was still moving slowly forward, her eyes—that seemed almost black, now, and glittered worse than ever—all the time on Gentleman's face. I saw her put her hand upon the dark edge of the table, as if to guide herself about it. Mrs Sucksby saw it too, I think. Perhaps she also saw something else. For she started, and then spoke quickly.

'Susie,' she said, 'I want you to go. Take your pal and go.'

'I'm not going anywhere,' I said.

'No Susie, you stay,' said Gentleman, in a rich sort of voice. 'Don't mind Mrs Sucksby's wishes. You have minded them too long. What are they to you, after all?'

'Richard,' said Maud, almost pleading.

'Gentleman,' said Mrs Sucksby, her eyes still on Maud. 'Dear boy. Be silent, will you? I am afraid.'

'Afraid?' he answered. 'You? I should say you never knew fear, in all your life. I should say your hard old leathery heart is beating perfectly quietly now, behind your hard old leathery breast.'

At his words, Mrs Sucksby's face gave a twitch. She raised a hand to the bodice of her dress.

'Feel it!' she said, moving her fingers. 'Feel the motion here, then tell me I ain't afraid!'

'Feel that?' he said, with a glance at her bosom. 'I don't think so.' Then he smiled. 'You may get your daughter to do it, however. She's had practice.'

I cannot say for certain what came next. I know that, hearing his words, I took a step towards him, meaning to strike him or make him be silent. I know that Maud and Mrs Sucksby reached him first. I do not know if Mrs Sucksby, when she darted, darted at him, or only—seeing Maud fly—at her. I know there was the gleam of something bright, the scuffle of shoes, the swish of taffeta and silk, the rushing of someone's breath. I think a chair was scraped or knocked upon the floor. I know Mr Ibbs called out. 'Grace! Grace!' he called: and even in the middle of all the confusion, I thought it a queer thing to call; until I realised it was Mrs Sucksby's first name, that we never heard used.

And so, it was Mr Ibbs I was watching, when it happened. I didn't see it when Gentleman began to stagger. But I heard him groan. It was a soft sort of groan.

'Have you hit me?' he said. His voice was strange.

Then I looked.

He supposed he had only been punched. I think I supposed it, too. He had his hands at his stomach and was leaning forward, as if nursing the pain of the blow. Maud stood a little before him, but now moved away; and as she did I heard something fall, though whether it fell from her hand, or from his—or from Mrs Sucksby's—I cannot tell you. Mrs Sucksby was the closer to him. She was certainly the closer. She put her arm about him, and as he sagged she braced herself against his weight, and held him. 'Have you hit me?' he said again.

'I don't know,' she said.

I don't think anyone knew. His clothes were dark, and Mrs Sucksby's gown was black, and they stood in the shadows, it was hard to see. But at last he took a hand away from his waistcoat and held it before his face; and then we saw the white of his palm made dark with blood.

'My God!' he said then.

Dainty shrieked.

'Bring a light!' said Mrs Sucksby. 'Bring a light!'

John caught up the lamp and held it, shaking. The dark blood turned suddenly crimson. Gentleman's waistcoat and trousers were soaked with it, and Mrs Sucksby's taffeta gown was red and running where she had held him.

I had never seen blood run so freely. I had talked, an hour before, of murdering Maud. I had sharpened the knife. I had left the knife upon the table. It was not there now. I had never seen blood run, like this. I grew sick.

'No,' I said. 'No, no!'

Mrs Sucksby gripped Gentleman's arm. 'Take your hand away,' she said. He still clutched his stomach.

'I can't.'

'Take your hand away!'

She wanted to see how deep the wound went. He grimaced, then drew off his fingers. There came, from a gash in his waistcoat, a bubble—like a bubble of soap, but swirling red—and then a spurt of blood, that fell and struck the floor with a splash—an ordinary splash, like water or soup would make.

Dainty shrieked again. The light wobbled. '*Fuck! Fuck!*' said John.

'Set him down in a chair,' said Mrs Sucksby. 'Fetch a cloth, for the cut. Fetch something to catch this blood. Fetch something, any-thing—'

'Help me,' said Gentleman. 'Help me. Oh, Christ!'

They moved him, awkwardly, with grunts and sighs. They sat him on a hard-backed chair. I stood and looked on, while they did it—held still, I suppose, by horror; though I am ashamed now, that I did nothing. Mr Ibbs plucked a towel from a hook on the wall and Mrs Sucksby knelt at Gentleman's side and held it against the wound. Each time he moved or took his hand from his stomach, the blood spurted. 'Fetch a bucket or a pot,' she said again; and finally Dainty ran to the door, caught up the chamber-pot that had been left there, and brought it and set it down beside the chair. The sound of the blood striking the china—and the sight of the red of it, against the white, and against that great dark eye—was worse than anything. Gentleman heard it and grew frightened.

'Oh, Christ!' he said again. 'Oh, Christ, I'm dying!' In between the words, he moaned—a shuddering, chattering moan, that he could not help or stop. 'Oh, Jesus, save me!'

'There now,' said Mrs Sucksby, touching his face. 'There now. Be brave. I've seen women lose blood like this, from a baby; and live to tell of it.'

'Not like this!' he said. 'Not like this! I'm cut. How badly am I cut? Oh, Christ! I need a surgeon. Do I?'

'Bring him liquor,' said Mrs Sucksby, to Dainty; but he shook his head.

'No liquor. A smoke, though. In my pocket, here.'

He dipped his chin to his waistcoat, and John fished in the folds and brought out a packet of cigarettes, and another of matches.

Half of the cigarettes were soaked with blood, but he found one that was dry, lit it at his own mouth, then put it in Gentleman's.

'Good boy,' said Gentleman, coughing. But he winced, and the cigarette fell. John caught it up in trembling fingers and set it back between his lips. He coughed again. More blood oozed up between his hands. Mrs Sucksby took the towel away and wrung it—wrung it, as if it were filled with water. Gentleman began to shake.

'How did this happen?' he said. I looked at Maud. She had not moved since stepping from him as he began to fall. She had kept still as me, her eyes upon his face. 'How can this be?' He looked wildly about him—at John, at Mr Ibbs, at me. 'Why do you stand and watch me? Bring a doctor. Bring a surgeon!'

I think Dainty took a step. Mr Ibbs caught her arm.

'No surgeons here,' he said firmly. 'No men like that, to this house.'

'No men like that?' cried Gentleman. The cigarette fell. 'What are you saying? Look at me! Christ! Don't you know a crooked man? Look at me! I'm dying! Mrs Sucksby, you love me. Bring a man, I beg you.'

'Dear boy, be still,' she said, still pressing the towel to the cut. He cried out in pain and fear.

'Damn you!' he said. 'You bitches! John—'

John put down the lamp and raised his hand to his eyes. He was weeping and trying to hide it.

'John, go for a surgeon! Johnny! I'll pay you! *Fuck!*' The blood spurted again. Now his face was white, his whiskers black but matted, here and there, with red, his cheek gleaming like lard.

John shook his head. 'I can't! Don't ask me!'

Gentleman turned to me. 'Suky!' he said. 'Suky, they've killed me—'

'No surgeons,' said Mr Ibbs again, when I looked at him. 'Bring a man like that, and we're done for.'

'Take him to the street,' I said. 'Can't you? Call a doctor to the street.'

'He is cut too bad. Look at him. It would bring them here. There is too much blood.'

There was. It now almost filled the china pot. Gentleman's moans had begun to grow fainter.

'Damn you!' he said softly. He had begun to cry. 'Who is there who'll help me? I've money, I swear it. Who is there? Maud?'

Her cheek was almost as pale as his, her lip quite white.

'Maud? Maud?' he said.

She shook her head. Then she said, in a whisper: 'I am sorry. I am sorry.'

'God damn you! Help me! *Oh!*' He coughed. There came, in the spittle at his mouth, a thread of crimson; and then, a moment later, a gush of blood. He raised a feeble hand to it—saw the fresh red upon his fingers—and his look grew wild. He reached, out of the circle of lamp-light, and began to struggle, as if to raise himself from the chair. He reached for Charles. 'Charley?' he said, the blood bubbling and bursting about the word. He clutched at Charles's coat and made to draw him closer. But Charles would not come. He had stood all this time in the shadows, a look of fixed and awful terror on his face. Now he saw the bubbles at Gentleman's lips and whiskers, Gentleman's red and slippery hand gripping the coarse blue collar of his jacket, and he twitched like a hare. He turned and ran. He ran, the way I had brought him—along the passage to Mr Ibbs's shop. And before we could call to him or go to him to make him stop, we heard him tear open the door then shriek, like a girl, into Lant Street:

'Murder! Help! Help! Murder!'

At that we all, save Mrs Sucksby and Maud, sprang back. John made for the shop.—'Too late!' said Mr Ibbs. 'Too late.' He held up his hand. John stood and listened. There had come a swirl of hot wind from the open shop-door and it carried with it what I thought at first was the echo of Charles's cry; then the sound grew stronger, and I understood it was an answering shout, perhaps from the window of a house nearby. In a second it was joined by another. Then it was joined by this—the worst sound of all, to us—the sound of a rattle, rising and falling on the gusting wind; and drawing nearer.

'The blues!' said John. He turned, and came to Dainty. 'Dainty, run!' he said. She stood for a second, then went—the back way—tearing the bolts from their cradles.—'Go on!' he said, when she looked back. But he did not go with her. Instead, he went to Gentleman's side.

'We might take him,' he said to Mrs Sucksby. He looked at me, and then at Maud. 'We might take him between us, if we are quick.'

Mrs Sucksby shook her head. Gentleman's own head hung low upon his breast. The blood still bubbled at his lip; burst, and bubbled again.

'Save yourself,' she said to John. 'Take Sue.'

But he did not go; and I knew—and know, still—that I wouldn't have followed, if he had. I was held there, as if by a charm. I looked at Mr Ibbs. He had run to the wall beside his brazier and, as I watched, he drew out one of the bricks. I only found out later that he kept money there, privately, in an old cigarette box. He put the box inside his waistcoat. Then he began to look about him, at the china, the knives and forks, the ornaments on the shelves: he was looking to see what there might be, that he could be done for. He did not look at Gentleman or Mrs Sucksby. He did not look at me—once he came near me, and thrust me aside, to reach past me for a porcelain cup; and when he had got it he dashed it to the floor. When Charley Wag rose up and gave a strangled sort of bark, he kicked him.

Meanwhile, the sound of shouts and rattles grew close. Gentleman lifted his head. There was blood on his beard, on his cheek, at the corner of his eye.

'Do you hear that?' he said weakly.

'Dear boy, I do,' said Mrs Sucksby. She still knelt at his side.

'What sound is it?'

She put her red hands over his. 'The sound of Fortune,' she said. She looked at me, and then at Maud. 'You might run.'

I said nothing. Maud shook her head. 'Not from this,' she answered. 'Not now.'

'You know what follows?'

She nodded. Mrs Sucksby glanced again at me, and then again at Maud, then closed her eyes. She sighed, as if weary.

'To have lost you once, dear girl,' she said. 'And now, to lose you again—'

'You shall not lose me!' I cried; and her eyes flew open, and she held my gaze for a second, as if not understanding. Then she looked at John. He had tilted his head.

'Here they come!' he said.

Mr Ibbs heard him, and ran; but he got no further than that dark little court at the back of the house before a policeman picked him up and brought him back again; and by then, two more police-men had made their way into the kitchen by the shop. They looked at Gentleman, and at the chamber-pot of blood, and—what we had not thought to look for or to hide—at the knife, which had got kicked into the shadows and had blood upon it; and they shook their heads.—As policeman tend to do when they see things like that, in the Borough.

'This is nasty work, ain't it?' they said. 'This is very bad. Let's see how bad.'

They took hold of Gentleman's hair and drew back his head, and felt for the pulse at his neck; and then they said,

'This is filthy murder. Now, who done it?'

Maud moved, or took a step. But John moved quicker.

'She done it,' he said, without a hesitation. His cheek was darker than ever, where he had been struck before. He lifted his arm and pointed. 'She done it. I saw her.'

He pointed at Mrs Sucksby.

I saw him, and heard him, but could not act. I only said, 'What—?' and Maud, I think, also cried out, 'What—?' or 'Wait—!'

But Mrs Sucksby rose from Gentleman's side. Her taffeta dress was soaked in his blood, the brooch of diamonds at her bosom turned to a brooch of rubies. Her hands were crimson, from fin-gertip to wrist. She looked like the picture of a murderess from one of the penny papers.

'I done it,' she said. 'Lord knows, I'm sorry for it now; but I done it. And these girls here are innocent girls, and know nothing at all about it; and have harmed no-one.'

Chapter Seventeen

*M*y name, in those days, was Susan Trinder. Now those days all came to an end.

The police took every one of us, save Dainty. They took us, and kept us in gaol while they tore up the Lant Street kitchen, looking for clues, for stashes of money and poke. They kept us in separate cells, and every day they came and asked the same set of questions.

'What was the murdered man, to you?'

I said he was a friend of Mrs Sucksby's.

'Been long, at Lant Street?'

I said I was born there.

'What did you see, on the night of the crime?'

Here, however, I always stumbled. Sometimes it seemed to me that I had seen Maud take up the knife; sometimes I even seemed to remember seeing her use it. I know I saw her touch the table-top, I know I saw the glitter of the blade. I know she stepped away as Gentleman started to stagger. But Mrs Sucksby had been there, too, she had moved as quick as anyone; and sometimes I thought it was *her* hand I remembered seeing dart and flash . . . At last I told the simple truth: that I did not know what I had seen. It didn't matter, anyway. They had John Vroom's word, and Mrs Sucksby's own confession. They didn't need me. On the fourth day after they took us, they let me go.

The others they kept longer.

Mr Ibbs was brought before the magistrate first. His trial lasted half-an-hour. He was done, after all, not on account of the poke left lying about the kitchen—he was too good at taking the seals and stampings off, for that—but for the sake of some of the notes in his cigarette box. They were marked ones. The police, it turned out, had been watching the business at Mr Ibbs's shop, for more than a month; and in the end they had got Phil—who, you might remember, had sworn he'd never do another term in gaol, at any cost—to plant the marked notes on him. Mr Ibbs was found to have handled stolen goods: he was sent to Pentonville. Of course, he knew many of the men in there, and might be supposed to have had an easy time among them—except that, here was a funny thing: the fingersmiths and cracksmen who had been so grateful to get an extra shilling from him on the outside, now quite turned against him; and I think his time was very miserable. I went to visit him, a week after he went in. He saw me, and put his hands before his face, and was in general so changed and so brought down, and looked at me so queerly, I could not bear it. I didn't go again.

His sister, poor thing, was found by the police in her bed at Lant Street, while they were going through the house. We had all forgotten her. She was put on the ward of a parish hospital. The move, however, was too great a shock for her; and she died.

John Vroom could not be pinned to any crime, save—through his coat—to that old one of dog-stealing. He was let off with six nights in Tothill Fields, and a flogging. They say he was so disliked in his gaol, the keepers played cards for who should be the one to flog him; that they flung in one or two extras above his twelve, for fun; and that after, he cried like a baby. Dainty met him at the prison gate, and he punched her and blacked her eye. It was thanks to him, though, that she had got clean off from Lant Street.

I never spoke to him again. He took a room for him and Dainty in another house, and kept out of my way. I saw him, only once; and that was in the court-room, at Mrs Sucksby's trial.

The trial came up very quick. I spent the nights before it at Lant Street, lying awake in my old bed; sometimes Dainty came back, to sleep beside me and keep me company. She was the only one, out of all my old pals, who would: for of course, everyone else supposed— from the story having been put about, before—that I was a cheat. It came out that I had taken that room, in the house across from Mr Ibbs's; and had lived there, in what seemed a sneaking sort of way, for almost a week. Why had I done that? Then someone said they saw me running, on the night of the murder, with a look of wildness in my eye. They talked about my mother, and the bad blood that flowed in me. They didn't say I was brave, now; they said I was bold. They said they wouldn't have been surprised if it was me that had put the knife in, after all; and Mrs Sucksby—who still loved me like a daughter, though I had turned out bad—who had stepped forward and taken the blame . . .

When I walked out in the Borough, people cursed me. Once, a girl threw a stone at me.

At any other time it would have broken my heart. Now, I did not care. I had only one thought, and that was to see Mrs Sucksby as often as I could. They had her in the Horsemonger Lane Gaol: I spent all my days there—sitting on the step outside the gate, when it was too early to be let in; talking with her keepers, or with the man who was to plead her case in court. Some pal of Mr Ibbs's had found him for us; he was said to have regularly saved the worst sort of villains from the rope. But he told me, honestly, that our case was a bad one. 'The most we can hope,' he said, 'is that the judge show mercy, for the sake of her age.'

More than once I said, 'Suppose it could be proved she never did it?'

He'd shake his head. 'Where is the evidence?' he'd say. 'Besides, she has admitted to it. Why should she do that?'

I did not know, and could not answer. He would leave me then, at the gate of the gaol—going quickly off, stepping into the street and calling out for a cab-man; and I'd watch him go with my hands at my head, for his shout, and the rattle of hooves and wheels, the movement of people, the very stones beneath my feet, would seem harsh to me. Everything seemed harsh, and loud, and harder and faster than it ought to have been, just then. Many times I would stop, and remember Gentleman, gripping the wound in his stomach, looking disbelievingly at our own disbelieving faces. 'How did this happen?' he had said. I wanted to say it, now, to everyone I saw: *How did this happen? How can this be? Why do you only stand and watch me . . .?*

I would have written letters; if I had known how to write, and who to send them to. I would have gone to the house of the man who was to be judge; if I had known how to find it. But I did nothing like that. What little comfort I got, I got at Mrs Sucksby's side; and the gaol, though it was so grim—so dark, and bleak—at least was also quiet. I got to spend more time there than I ought to have, through the kindness of the keepers: I think they thought me younger and less of a sharper than I was. 'Here's your daughter,' they'd say, unlocking the gate to Mrs Sucksby's cell; and every time, she would quickly lift her head and study my face, or glance beyond my shoulder, with a troubled look—as if, I thought, not quite believing they had let me come again and meant to let me stay.

Then she'd blink, and try at a smile. 'Dear girl. Quite alone?'

'Quite alone,' I'd answer.

'That's good,' she'd say after a moment, taking my hand. 'Ain't it? Just you and me. That's good.'

She liked to sit with my hand in hers. She did not like to talk. When at first I'd weep, and curse, and beg her to take back her story, my words would so upset her I feared she'd grow ill.

'No more,' she'd say, very pale in the face and set about the mouth. 'I done it, that's all. I don't want to hear no more about it.'

So then I'd remember that dander of hers, and keep silent, and only smooth her fingers in mine. They seemed to grow thinner, every time I saw her. The keepers said she left her dinners quite untouched. The sight of the dwindling of those great hands upset me, more than I can say: it seemed to me that everything, that was so wrong, would be put right if only Mrs Sucksby's hands could be made to be handsome again. I had spent what money there was in the house at Lant Street, on finding a lawyer; but all that I could make now through borrowing or pawning I put on little dishes to try and tempt her—on shrimps, and saveloys, and suet-puddings. Once I took her a sugar mouse, thinking she might remember the time she had put me in her bed and told me about Nancy from *Oliver Twist*. I don't think she did, however; she only took it and set it distractedly aside, saying she would try it later, like she did with everything else. In the end her keepers told me to save my money. She had been passing the dishes to them.

Many times she held my face in her hands. Many times she kissed me. Once or twice she gripped me hard, and seemed about to speak on some awful matter; but always, at the last, she would turn the matter aside and it would be lost. If there were things I might have asked her—if I was troubled by queer ideas, and doubts—I kept quiet as she did. That time was bad enough; why make it worse? We talked instead of me—of how I should do now and in the future.

'You'll keep up the old place, at Lant Street?' she'd say.

'Won't I!' I'd answer.

'You won't think of leaving?'

'Leaving? Why, I mean to keep it ready, against the day they let you out . . .'

I did not tell her how very changed the house was, now that she and Mr Ibbs, and Mr Ibbs's sister, had gone. I did not tell her that neighbours had left off calling; that a girl threw a stone at me; that people—strangers—would come and stand, for hours at a time, at the doors and windows, hoping for a glimpse of the place where Gentleman had died. I did not say how hard I had worked, with Dainty, to take the blood-stain from the floor; how we had washed and washed; how many buckets of water we had carried off, crimson; how at last we had had to give it up, because the constant scrubbing began to lift the surface of the boards and turn the pale

wood underneath a horrible pink. I didn't tell her of all the places—
the doors, the ceiling—and all the things—the pictures on the walls,
the ornaments upon the mantel, the dinner-plates, the knives and
forks—that we found marked with streaks and splashes of
Gentleman's blood.

And I did not say how, as I swept and scrubbed the kitchen, I
chanced on a thousand little reminders of my old life—dog-hairs,
and chips of broken cups, bad farthings, playing cards, the cuts on
the door-frame made by Mr Ibbs's knife to mark my height as I
grew up; nor how I covered my face and wept, at every one.

At night, if I slept, I dreamed of murder. I dreamed I killed a man,
and had to walk the streets of London with his body in a bag too
small to hold it. I dreamed of Gentleman. I dreamed I met him
among the graves at the little red chapel at Briar and he showed me
the tomb of his mother. The tomb had a lock upon it, and I had a
blank and file and must cut the key to fit; and every night I would
set to work, knowing I must work quickly, quickly; and every time,
just as the job was almost done, some queer disaster would
happen—the key would shrink or grow too large, the file would
soften in my fingers; there would be a cut—the final cut—I could
not make, never make in time . . .

Too late, Gentleman would say.

One time the voice was Maud's.

Too late.

I looked, but could not see her.

I had not seen her, since the night that Gentleman died. I didn't
know where she was. I knew the police had kept her longer than
they kept me—for she gave them her name, and it got into the
newspapers; and, of course, Dr Christie saw it. I heard it, from the
keepers at the gaol. It had all come out, how she was Gentleman's
wife, and had supposedly been in a madhouse and had escaped; and
how the police didn't know what to do with her—whether to let her
go, or lock her up as a lunatic, or what. Dr Christie said only he
could decide; so they called him in to examine her. I nearly had a fit

when I heard that. I still couldn't go near bath-tubs. But what happened, was this: he took one look at her, was seen to stagger and grow white; then declared himself only overcome with emotion, to find her so perfectly cured. He said this showed how good his methods were. He had the papers give details of his house. He got lots of new lady patients out of it, I think, and quite made his fortune.

Maud herself was set at liberty, then; and after that, she seemed to vanish. I guessed she had gone back home to Briar. I know she never came to Lant Street. I supposed her too afraid!—for of course, I would have throttled her if she had.

I did wonder if she might, however. I wondered it, every day. 'Perhaps today,' I would think each morning, 'will be the day she'll come.' And then, each night: 'Perhaps tomorrow . . .'

But, as I have said, she never did. What came instead, was the day of the trial. It came in the middle of August. The sun had kept on blazing all through that awful summer, and the court—being packed with watchers—was close: every hour a man was called to throw water on the floor to try and cool it. I sat with Dainty. I'd hoped I might sit in the box with Mrs Sucksby, and hold her hand; but the policemen laughed in my face when I asked it. They made her sit alone, and when they took her in and out of the room, they put cuffs on her. She wore a grey prison gown that made her face seem almost yellow, but her silver hair shone very bright against the dark wood walls of the court. She flinched when she first came up, and saw the crowd of strangers that had come to see her tried. Then she found out my face among them and grew, I thought, more easy. Her eye came back to mine, after that, as the day went on—though I saw her looking, too, about the court, as if in search of another. At the last, however, her gaze would always fall.

When she spoke, her voice was weak. She said she had stabbed Gentleman in a moment of anger, in a quarrel over money he owed for the renting of her room.

She earned her money from the letting of rooms? asked the prosecuting lawyer.

'Yes,' she said.

And not from the handling of stolen goods, or the unlicensed nursing—commonly known as farming—of orphaned infants?

'No.'

Then they brought in men to say they had seen her, at different times, with different bits of poke; and—what was worse—found women who swore they had given her babies that had very soon afterwards died . . .

Then John Vroom spoke. They had put him in a suit like a clerk's, and combed and shined his hair; he looked more like an infant than ever. He said he had seen everything that took place in the Lant Street kitchen, on the fatal night. He had seen Mrs Sucksby put in the knife. She had cried, 'You blackguard, take that!' And he had seen her with the knife in her hand, for at least a minute, before she did.

'At least a minute?' the lawyer said. 'You are quite sure? You know how long a minute is? Look at that clock, there. Watch the movement of the hand . . .'

We all watched it sweep. The court fell still, to do it. I never knew a minute so long. The lawyer looked back at John.

'As long as that?' he said.

John began to cry. 'Yes, sir,' he said, through his tears.

Then they brought the knife out, for him to say it was the one. The crowd broke out in murmurs when they saw it; and when John wiped his eyes and looked, and nodded, a lady swooned. The knife was shown to all the men of the jury then, one by one, and the lawyer said they must be sure to note how the blade was sharpened, more than it naturally would have been for a knife of that kind— that it was the sharpening of it that made Gentleman's wound so bad. He said that broke in pieces Mrs Sucksby's story about the quarrel, by showing evidence of forethought—

I nearly started out of my seat, when I heard that. Then I caught Mrs Sucksby's eye. She shook her head, and looked so pleadingly at me to be silent, I fell back; and it never came out that the knife was sharp not because she had sharpened it, but because I had. They never called me to the stand. Mrs Sucksby would not let them. They did call Charles; but he wept so hard, and shook so badly, the judge declared him unfit. He was sent back to his aunty's.

No-one was told about me, and Maud. No-one mentioned Briar or old Mr Lilly. No-one came forward to say that Gentleman was a villain—that he had tried to rob heiresses—that he had ruined people through the selling of counterfeit stock. They made out that he was a decent young man with a promising future; they said that Mrs Sucksby had robbed him of it through simple greed. They even found out his family, and brought his parents to the trial—and you'll never believe it, but it turned out that all his tales of being a gentleman's son were so much puff. His father and mother ran a small kind of draper's shop, in a street off the Holloway Road. His sister taught piano. His real name was not Richard Rivers or even Richard Wells; it was Frederick Bunt.

They drew his picture in the papers. Girls all over England were said to have cut it out and worn it next to their hearts.

But when I looked at that picture—and when I heard people talk of the awful murder of Mr Bunt, and of vices, and sordid trades—it seemed to me as though they must be talking of something else, something else entirely, not of Gentleman, being hurt, by mistake, in my own kitchen, with my own people all about. Even when the judge sent off the jury, and we waited, and watched the newspaper-men getting ready to run with the verdict as soon as it came; even when the jury, after an hour, returned, and one of them stood and gave back their answer in a single word; even when the judge covered up his horse-hair wig with a cloth of black, and hoped that God would have mercy on Mrs Sucksby's soul—even then, I did not really feel it as you would suppose I might, did not believe, I think, that so many dark and sober gentlemen speaking so many grave and monotonous words could pinch out the spirit and the heat and the colour from the lives of people like me and Mrs Sucksby.

Then I looked at her face; and saw the spirit and heat and colour half-gone from it, already. She was looking dully about her, at the murmuring crowd—looking for me, I thought, and I rose, and lifted my hand. But she caught my eye, and her gaze, as it had before, moved on: I watched it roam about the room, as if looking for

someone or something else—finally it settled and seemed to clear,
and I followed it and picked out, at the back of the rows of watchers, a girl dressed all in black, with a veil, that she was just putting
down— It was Maud. I saw her, not expecting to see her: and I'll
tell you this, my heart flew open; then I remembered everything,
and my heart flew shut. She looked miserable—that was something, I thought. She was sitting alone. She made no sort of sign—to
me, I mean; and none to Mrs Sucksby.

Then our lawyer called me to him, to shake my hand and say he
was sorry. Dainty was weeping and needed my arm to help her
walk. When I looked at Mrs Sucksby again, her head was sunk
upon her breast; and when I looked for Maud, she had gone.

The week that passed after that I remember, now, as not a week at
all, but as a single great endless day. It was a day without sleep—for
how could I sleep, when sleep might take away thoughts of Mrs
Sucksby, who was so soon to die? It was a day, almost, without
darkness—for they kept lights in her cell, that burned all through
the night; and in the hours I could not be with her, I kept lights
burning at Lant Street—every light I could find in the house, and
every light I could borrow. I sat alone, with blazing eyes. I sat and
watched, as though she might be ill at my side. I hardly ate. I hardly
changed my clothes. When I walked, it was to walk quickly to
Horsemonger Lane, to be with her; or to walk slowly back, having
left her there.

They had her now, of course, in the condemned cell, and one or
other of a pair of matrons was always with her. They were kind
enough, I suppose; but they were great stout women, like the nurses
at Dr Christie's, and they wore similar canvas aprons, and carried
keys: I would catch their eyes and flinch, and all my old bruises
would seem to start up aching. Then again, I could never quite find
it in my heart to like them, on their own accounts—for surely, if
they were truly worth liking, they would open the door and let Mrs
Sucksby go? Instead they were keeping her there, for men to come
and hang her.

I tried not to think of that, however—or rather, like before, I found I *could* not think of it, could not believe it. How much Mrs Sucksby brooded upon it, I can't say. I know they sent the prison chaplain to her and she spent some hours with him; but she never told me what he said to her, or if it brought her any comfort. Now more than ever, she seemed to like not to speak at all, only to feel the gentle holding of my hand in hers; though now more than ever, too, her gaze as she looked at me would seem sometimes to grow cloudy, and she would colour, and struggle as if with the awful burden of things unsaid . . .

But she said only one thing to me, that she meant for me to remember; and that was on the day before her last—the final time I ever saw her. I went to her, with my heart almost breaking, and thought I should find her pacing her cell or plucking at the bars on her window—in fact, she was calm. It was me who wept, and she sat in her prison chair and let me kneel with my head in her lap, and she put her fingers to my hair—taking the pins from it and letting it fall, until it lay across her knee. I had not had the heart to curl it. It seemed to me that I should never have heart enough, ever again.

'How shall I do, Mrs Sucksby, without you?' I said.

I felt some tremor pass through her. Then: 'Better, dear girl,' she whispered, 'than with me.'

'No!'

She nodded. 'Better, by far.'

'How can you say it? When, if I had stayed with you—if I had never gone with Gentleman to Briar— Oh, I should never have left your side!'

I hid my face in the folds of her skirt, and wept again.

'Hush, now,' she said. She stroked my head. 'Hush, now . . .' Her gown was rough upon my cheek, the prison chair hard against my side. But I sat and let her soothe me, as though I might be a child; and at last we both fell silent. There was a little window, high in the wall of her cell, that let in two or three strips of sunlight: we watched them creep across the stone flags of the floor. I never knew light could creep like that. It crept, like fingers. And when it had crept almost from one wall to another, I heard a step, then felt the matron lean to lay her hand upon my shoulder.—'It's time,' she murmured. 'Say your good-byes, now. All right?'

We stood. I looked at Mrs Sucksby. Her gaze was clear still, but her cheek, in a moment, had changed—was grey, and damp, like clay. She began to tremble.

'Dear Sue,' she said, 'you have been good to me—' She drew me to her, and put her mouth against my ear. It was cold as the mouth on a corpse, already; but twitched, like it might have been palsied. 'Dear girl—' she began, in a broken whisper. I almost drew back. *Don't say it!* I thought.—Though I do not know if I could have said what it was I wished she would not say; I only knew I was suddenly afraid. *Don't say it!* She gripped me tighter. 'Dear girl—' Then the whisper grew fierce. 'Watch me, tomorrow,' she said. 'Watch me. Don't cover your eyes. And then, if you should ever hear hard things of me when I am gone, think back—'

'I will!' I said. I said it, half in terror, half in relief. 'I will!'—Those were my last words to her. Then the matron I suppose must have touched me again; must have led me, stumbling, into the passage beyond the gate.—I don't recall. What I remember next is passing through the prison yard, feeling the sun come upon my face—and giving a cry, turning away—thinking, how queer and wrong and awful it was, that the sun should shine, still shine, even now, even there . . .

There came a keeper's voice. I heard the rumble of it, but not the words. He was asking something of the matron at my side. She nodded.

'One of 'em,' she said, with a glance at me. 'The other came this morning . . .'

I only wondered later what she meant. For now, I was too dazed and miserable to wonder anything. I walked, in a sort of trance, back to Lant Street—only keeping, as much as I could, to the shadows, out of the blazing sun. At the door to Mr Ibbs's shop I found boys, chalking nooses on the step—they saw me come and ran off, shrieking. I was used to that, however, and let them run; but kicked the nooses away. Inside, I stood a minute to get my breath, and to look about me—at the locksmith's counter, streaked with dust; and the tools and key-blanks, that had lost their shine; and the hanging baize curtain, that had got torn from its loops and was drooping. When I walked through to the kitchen, my footsteps crunched: for sometime—I couldn't say when—the brazier had been knocked from its stand, and coals and cinders still lay scattered on the floor. It seemed too ordinary a thing to do, to sweep them up, set the brazier right; and anyway, the floor was ruined—broken and gaping, from where the police had torn up boards. Underneath it seemed dark, till you brought a light: then you could see earth, two feet below—damp earth, with bones and oyster shells in it, and beetles and wriggling worms.

The table had been pushed to the corner of the room. I went and sat at it, in Mrs Sucksby's old chair. Charley Wag lay beneath it—poor Charley Wag, he had not barked since Mr Ibbs had jerked so hard on his collar: he saw me now, and beat his tail, and came and let me tug his ears; but then he slunk away and lay with his head on his paws.

I sat, as still and quiet as him, for almost an hour; then Dainty came. She had brought us a supper. I didn't want it, and neither did she; but she had stolen a purse to buy it, and so I got out bowls and spoons and we ate it slowly, in silence, looking all the time, as we did, at the clock—the old Dutch clock on the mantel—that we knew was steadily ticking, ticking away the last few hours of Mrs Sucksby's life . . . I meant to feel them, if I could. I meant to feel each minute, each second. 'Won't you let me stay?' said Dainty, when it came time for her to go. 'It don't seem right, you being here all on your own.' But I said that that was how I wanted it; and finally she kissed my cheek and went; and then it was just me and Charley Wag again, and the house, growing dark about us. I lit more lights. I thought of Mrs Sucksby, in her bright cell. I thought of her, in all the ways I had seen her, not there, but here, in her own kitchen: dosing babies, sipping tea, lifting up her face so I might kiss it. I thought of her carving meat, wiping her mouth, and yawning . . . The clock ticked on—quicker, and louder, it seemed to me, than it had ever ticked before. I put my head upon the table, upon my arms. How tired I was! I closed my eyes. I could not help it. I meant to keep awake; but I closed my eyes, and slept.

I slept, for once, without dreaming; and I was woken by a curious sound: the tramping and scuffing of feet, and the rising and falling of voices, in the street outside. I thought, in my half-sleep: 'It must be a holiday today, there must be a fair. What day is it?'—Then I opened my eyes. The candles I had lit had burned to puddles of wax, and their flames were like so many ghosts; but the sight of them made me remember where I was. It was seven o'clock in the morning. Mrs Sucksby was going to be hanged in three hours' time. The people I could hear were on their way to Horsemonger Lane, to get their places for watching. They had come down Lant Street first, for a look at the house.

There came more of them, as the morning went on. 'Was it here?' I could hear them say. And then: 'Here's the very identical spot. They say the blood ran so fast and so hard, the walls were painted in it.'—'They say the murdered chap called out against heaven.'—'They say the woman stifled babies.'—'They say he'd bilked her of rent.'—'Puts you into a creep, don't it?'— 'Serves him right.'—'They say—'

They would come, and stop a minute, and then pass on; some found their way to the back of the house and rattled the kitchen door, stood at the window and tried to see through the chinks in the shutters; but I kept everything locked and fast. I don't know if they knew I was inside. Now and then a boy would call: 'Let us in! A shilling, if you'll show us the room!' and, 'Hoo! hoo! I'm the ghost of the feller as was stabbed, come back to haunt you!'—but I think they did it to tease their friends, not to tease me. I hated to hear them, though; and Charley Wag, poor thing, kept close at my side, and shivered and started and tried to bark, with every call and rattle.—At last I took him upstairs, where the sounds were fainter.

But then, after a while the sounds grew fainter still; and that was worse, for it meant that the people had all passed on, found their spots for watching from, and it was almost time. I left Charley then, and climbed the next set of stairs alone—climbed them slowly, like a girl with limbs of lead; then stood at the attic door, afraid to go in. There was the bed I had been born in. There was the wash-stand, the bit of oil-cloth tacked to the wall. The last time I had come here,

Gentleman had been alive and drunk and dancing with Dainty and John, downstairs. I had stood at the window, put my thumb to the glass, made the frost turn to dirty water. Mrs Sucksby had come and stroked my hair . . . I went to the window, now. I went, and looked, and almost swooned away, for the streets of the Borough, that had been dark and empty then, were bright, and filled with people—so many people!—people standing in the road, stopping the traffic; and besides them, people on walls, on sills, clinging to posts and trees and chimneys. Some were holding children up, some were craning for a better view. Most had their hands across their eyes, to keep the sun off. All had their faces turned one way.

They were looking at the roof of the gate of the gaol. The scaffold was up, the rope already on it. A man was walking about, examining the drop.

I saw him do it, feeling almost calm, feeling almost sick. I remembered what Mrs Sucksby had asked, with her last words to me: that I should watch her. I had said I would. I had thought I should bear it. It seemed such a little thing *to* bear, compared with what *she* must suffer . . . Now the man had taken the rope in his hands and was testing the length of it. The people in the crowd stretched their necks further, so they might see. I began to be afraid. Still I thought, however, that I would watch, to the end. Still I said to myself, 'I *will*. I *will*. She did it for my own mother; I'll do it for her. What else can I do for her now, except *this*?'

But I said it; and then came the slow, steady striking of ten o'clock. The man at the rope stood down, the door to the prison steps was thrown open, the chaplain showed himself upon the roof, and then the first of the keepers.—I couldn't do it. I put my back to the window and covered my face with my hands.

I knew what followed, then, from the sounds that rose up from the streets. The people had fallen silent at the striking of the clock, the coming of the chaplain; now I heard them all start up with hisses and with hoots—that, I knew, was for the hangman. I heard the very spreading of the sound about the crowd, like oil on water. When the hoots grew louder, I knew the hangman had made some sign or bow. Then, in an instant, the sound turned again, moved faster, like a shiver, like a thrill, through the streets: the cry was sent out: 'Hats off!', and was mixed with bursts of dreadful laughter. Mrs Sucksby must have come. They were trying to see her. I grew sicker than ever, imagining all those strangers' eyes straining out of their sockets to see what figure she would make, yet not being able to look, myself; but I could not, I could not. I could not turn, or tear the sweating hands from before my face. I could only listen. I heard the laughter change to murmurs and calls for hush: that meant the chaplain was saying prayers. The hush went on, and on. My own heartbeats seemed to fill it. Then the Amen was said; and even while the word was still travelling about the streets, other parts of the crowd—the parts that were nearest the gaol and could see best— broke out in an uneasy sort of murmur. The murmur grew louder, got taken up by every throat—then turned, to something more like a moan, or groan . . . And I knew that meant that they had led her up to the scaffold; that they were tying her hands, and covering up her face, and putting, about her neck, the noose . . .

And then, and then, there came a moment—just a single moment, less time than it takes to say it—of perfect, awful stillness: of the stopping of babies' cries, the holding of breaths, the clapping of hands to hearts and open mouths, the slowing of blood, the shrinking back of thought: This *cannot* be, this *will* not be, they *won't*, they *can't*— And, next, too soon, too quick, the rattle of the drop, the shrieks, as it fell—the groaning gasp, when the rope found its length, as if the crowd had a single stomach and a giant hand had punched it.

Now I did open my eyes, just for a second. I opened them, and turned, and saw—not Mrs Sucksby, not Mrs Sucksby at all, but what might have been a dangling tailor's figure, done up to look like a woman, in a corset and a gown, but with lifeless arms, and a drooping head like a bag of canvas stuffed with straw—

I moved away. I did not weep. I went to the bed and lay upon it. The sounds changed again, as people found their breaths and voices—unstopped their mouths, unloosed their babies, shuffled and danced about. There came more hoots, more cries, more dreadful laughter; and finally, cheers. I think I had used to cheer myself, at other hangings. I never thought what the cheering meant. Now I listened as those *hurrahs* went up, and it seemed to me, even in my grief, that I understood. *She's dead*, they might as well have been calling. The thought was rising, quicker than blood, in every heart. *She's dead—and we're alive.*

Dainty came again that night, to bring me another supper. We didn't eat any of it. We only wept together, and talked of what we had seen. She had watched with Phil and some other of Mr Ibbs's nephews, from a spot close to the gaol. John had said only pigeons watched from there. He knew a man with a roof, he said; and went off to climb it. I wondered if he had watched at all; but didn't say that to Dainty. She herself had seen everything, except the final drop. Phil, who had seen even that, said the fall was a clean one. He thought it was true, after all, what people said, about how the hangman put the knot, when it came to dropping women. Everyone agreed, anyway, that Mrs Sucksby had held herself very boldly, and died very game.

I remembered that dangling tailor's figure, gripped tight in its corset and gown; and I wondered how, if she had shuddered and kicked, we ever should have known it.

But that was something not to be thought on. There were other things to see to, now. I had become an orphan again; and as orphans everywhere must, I began, in the two or three weeks that followed, to look about me, with a sinking heart; to understand that the world was hard and dark, and I must make my own way through it, quite alone. I had no money. The rent on the shop and house had fallen due in August: a man had come and banged on the door, and only gone because Dainty bared her arms and said she would hit him. He had left us alone since then. I think the house had got known as a murder-house, and no-one wanted to take it. But I knew they would, in time. I knew the man would come back one day, with other men, and break in the door. Where would I live, then? How should I do, on my own? I might, I supposed, take a regular job, at a dairy, a dyer's, a furrier's— The very thought of it, however, made me want to be sick. Everybody in my world knew that regular work was only another name for being robbed and dying of boredom. I should rather stay crooked. Dainty said she knew three girls who worked, in a gang, as street-thieves, Woolwich-way, and wanted a fourth . . . But she said it, not quite catching my eye; for we both knew that street-thieving was a pretty poor lay, compared to what I was used to.

But it was all I had; and I thought it might as well do. I hadn't the heart for finding out anything better. I hadn't the heart or the spirit for anything at all. Bit by bit, everything that was left at Lant Street had gone—been pawned, or sold. I still wore the pale print dress I had robbed from the woman in the country!—and now it looked worse on me than ever, for I had grown thin at Dr Christie's, and then thinner still. Dainty said I had got so sharp, if you could have found a way of threading me with cotton, you could have sewn with me.

And so, when I packed the bits of stuff I wanted to take with me to Woolwich, there was almost nothing. And when I thought of the people I ought to call on, to say good-bye to, I could not think of anyone. There was only one thing I knew I must do, before I went; and that was the picking up of Mrs Sucksby's things, from Horsemonger Lane.

I took Dainty with me. I did not think that I could bear it all alone. We went, one day in September—more than a month after the trial. London had changed, since then. The season had turned, and the days grown cooler at last. The streets were filled with dust and straw, and curling leaves. The gaol seemed darker and bleaker than ever. But the porter there knew me, and let me through. He looked at me, I thought, in pity. So did the matrons. They had Mrs Sucksby's things made ready for me, in a wax-paper parcel tied with strings. '*Released, to Daughter,*' they said, as they wrote in a book; and they made me put my name there, underneath.—I could write my name quick as anyone now, since my time at Dr Christie's . . . Then they led me back, across the yards, through the grey prison ground where I knew Mrs Sucksby was buried, with no stone upon her grave, so no-one could come and mourn her; and they took me out under the gate, with its low, flat roof, where I had last seen the scaffold raised. They passed under that roof every day of their lives, it was nothing to them. When they came to say good-bye, they made to take my hand. I could not give it.

The parcel was light. I carried it home, however, in a sort of dread; and the dread seemed to make it heavy. By the time I reached Lant Street, I was almost staggering: I went quickly with it to the kitchen table, and set it down, and caught my breath and rubbed my arms. What I was dreading was having to open it and look at all her things. I thought of what must be inside: her shoes; her stockings, perhaps still in the shape of her toes and heels; her petticoats; her comb, perhaps with some of her hair in it— *Don't do it!* I thought. *Leave it! Hide it! Open it some other time, not today, not now—!*

I sat, and looked at Dainty.

'Dainty,' I said, 'I don't think I can.'

She put her hand over mine.

'I think you ought to,' she said. 'For me and my sister was the same, when we got our mother's bits back from the morgue. And we left that packet in a drawer, and wouldn't look at it for nearly a year; and when Judy opened it up the gown was rotted through, and the shoes and bonnet perished almost to nothing, from having gone so long with river-water on them. And then, we had nothing to remember Mother by, at all; save a little chain she always wore.— Which Pa pawned, in the end, for gin-money . . .'

I saw her lip begin to quiver. I could not face her tears.

'All right,' I said. 'All right. I'll do it.'

My hands were still shaking though, and when I drew the parcel to me and tried to undo its strings, I found the matrons had tied them too tight. So then Dainty tried. She couldn't undo them either. 'We need a knife,' I said, 'or a pair of scissors . . .' But there was a time, after Gentleman died, when I hadn't been able to look at any kind of blade, without wincing; and I had made Dainty take them all away, there wasn't a single sharp thing—except me—in the whole of the house. I tugged and picked at the knots again, but now I was more nervous than ever, and my hands had got damp. At last,

I lifted the parcel to my mouth and took hold of the knots with my teeth: and finally the strings unravelled and the paper sprang out of its folds. I started back. Mrs Sucksby's shoes, her petticoats and comb came tumbling out upon the table-top, looking just as I had feared. And across them, dark and spreading, like tar, came her old black taffeta gown.

I had not thought of that. Why hadn't I? It was the very worst thing of all. It looked like Mrs Sucksby herself was lying there, in some sort of swoon. The gown still had Maud's brooch pinned to its breast. Someone had prised the diamonds out—I didn't care about that—but the silver claws that were left had blood in them, brown blood, so dried it was almost powder. The taffeta itself was stiff. The blood had made it rusty. The rust was traced about with lines of white: the lawyers had shown the gown in court, and had drawn around each stain with chalk.

They seemed to me like marks on Mrs Sucksby's own body.

'Oh, Dainty,' I said, 'I can't bear it! Fetch me a cloth, and water, will you? Oh! How horrible it looks—!' I began to rub. Dainty rubbed, too. We rubbed in the same grim, shuddering way that we had scrubbed the kitchen floor. The cloths grew muddy. Our breaths came quick. We worked first at the skirt. Then I caught up the collar, drew the bodice to me and began to work on that.

And, as I did, the gown made a curious sound—a creaking, or rustling, sound.

Dainty put down her cloth. 'What's that?' she said. I did not know. I drew the dress closer, and the sound came again.

'Is it a moth?' said Dainty. 'Is it flapping about, inside?'

I shook my head. 'I don't think so. It sounds like a paper. Perhaps the matrons have put something there . . .'

But when I lifted the dress and shook it, and looked inside, there was nothing, nothing at all. The rustling came again, however, as I laid the gown back down. It seemed to me that it came from part of the bodice—from that part of the front of the bodice that would have lain just below Mrs Sucksby's heart. I put my hand to it, and felt about. The taffeta there was stiff—stiff not just from the staining of Gentleman's blood, but from something else, something that had got stuck, or been put, behind it, between it and the satin lining of the gown. What was it? I could not tell, from feeling. So then I turned the bodice inside-out, and looked at the seam. The seam was open: the satin was loose, but had been hemmed so as not to fray. It made a sort of pocket, in the gown. I looked at Dainty; then put in my hand. It rustled again, and she drew back.

'Are you sure it ain't a moth? Or a bat?'

But what it was, was a letter. Mrs Sucksby had had it hidden there—how long? I could not guess. I thought at first that she must have put it there for me—that she had written it, in gaol—that it was a message for me to find, after they had hanged her.—The thought made me nervous. But then, the letter was marked with Gentleman's blood; and so must have lain inside the gown since the night he died, at least. Then again, it seemed to me that it must have lain there a good deal longer than that: for as I looked more closely at it I saw how old it was. The creases were soft. The ink was faded. The paper was curved, from where Mrs Sucksby's taffeta bodice had held it, tight, against her stays. The seal—

I looked at Dainty. The seal was unbroken. 'Unbroken!' I said. 'How is that? Why should she have carried a letter, so close, so carefully, so long—and yet not read it?' I turned it in my hands. I gazed again at the direction. 'Whose name is there?' I said. 'Can you see?'

Dainty looked, then shook her head. 'Can't you?' she said. But I could not. Hand-writing was harder even upon my eye, than print; and this hand was small, and sloped, and—as I have said—was partly smeared and spotted with awful stains. I went to the lamp, and held the letter close to the wick. I screwed up my eyes. I looked and looked . . . And it seemed to me at last that if any name was written there, upon the folded paper, it was *my own*.—I was sure I could make out an S, and then the u that followed it; and then, again, an s—

I grew nervous again. 'What is it?' said Dainty, seeing my face.

'I don't know. I think the letter's for me.'

She put her hand to her mouth. And then: 'From your own mother!' she said.

'My mother?'

'Who else? Oh, Sue, you got to open it.'

'I don't know.'

'But say it tells you— Say it tells you where treasure is! Say it's a map!'

I didn't think it was a map. I felt my stomach growing sour with fear. I looked again at the letter, at the *S*, and the *u*— 'You open it,' I said. Dainty licked her lips, then took it, slowly turned it, and slowly broke the seal. The room was so quiet, I think I heard the tumbling of the slivers of wax from the paper to the floor. She unfolded the page; then frowned.

'Just words,' she said.

I went to her side. I saw lines of ink—close, small, baffling. The harder I gazed, the more baffling they grew. And though I had got so nervous and afraid—so sure that the letter was meant for me, yet held the key to some awful, secret thing I should far rather never know—still, to have it open before me, not being able to understand what it said, was worse than anything.

'Come on,' I said to Dainty. I got her her bonnet, and found mine. 'Come out to the street, and we'll find someone to read it for us.'

We went the back way. I would not ask anyone I knew—anyone who had cursed me. I wanted a stranger. So we went north—went fast, towards the breweries up by the river. There was a man there on a corner. He had a tray on a string about his neck, full of nutmeg-graters and thimbles. But he wore eye-glasses and had—I don't know what—an intelligent look.

I said, 'He'll do.'

He saw us coming and gave us a nod. 'Want a grater, girls?'

I shook my head. 'Listen here,' I said—or tried to say, for the walk and my own feeling and fear had taken the breath quite from me. I put my hand to my heart. 'Do you read?' I asked him at last.

He said, 'Read?'

'Letters, in ladies' hands? Not books, I mean.'

Then he saw the paper I held, pushed the glasses further up his nose, and tilted his head.

'*To be opened,*' he read, '*on the eighteenth birthday—*' I shook right through when I heard that. He did not notice. Instead, he straightened his head, and sniffed. 'Not in my line,' he said. 'Not worth my while to stand here and read out letters. That ain't a-going to make the thimbles fly, is it . . .?'

Some people will charge you for taking a punch. I put my shaking hand in my pocket and brought out all it held. Dainty did the same.

'Sevenpence,' I said, when I had put the coins together.

He turned them over. 'Are they good?'

'Good enough,' I said.

He sniffed again. 'All right.' He took them, and hid them. Then he unhooked his glasses from about his ears, and gave them a rub. 'Now then, let's see,' he said. 'You hold it up, though. Looks legal, this does. I been stung by the law, before. I might not want it to come out later, as how I touched it . . .' He put his glasses back on, and got ready to read.

'All the words that are there,' I said, as he did. 'Every one. Do you hear?'

He nodded, and began. '*To be opened on the eighteenth birthday of my daughter, Susan Lilly—*'

I put the paper down. 'Susan Trinder,' I said. 'Susan Trinder, you mean. You are reading it wrong.'

'*Susan Lilly*, it says,' he answered. 'Hold it up, now, and turn it.'

'What's the point,' I said, 'if you ain't going to read what's there . . .?'

But my voice had got thin. There seemed to have come, about my heart, a snake: it was coiling, tight.

'Come on,' he said. His look had changed. 'This is interesting, this is. What is it? A will, is it, or a testament? *The last statement—* there you are—*of Marianne Lilly, made at Lant Street, Southwark, on this day 18th of September 1844, in the presence of Mrs Grace Sucksby, of—*' He stopped. His face had changed again. 'Grace Sucksby?' he said, in a shocked sort of voice. 'What, the murderess? This is stiff stuff, ain't it?'

I did not answer. He looked again at the paper—at the stains.

Perhaps he had supposed them ink, before, or paint. Now he said, 'I don't know as I should . . .' Then he must have seen my face. 'All right, all right,' he said. 'Let's see. What's here?' He drew it closer. '*I, Marianne Lilly, of*—what is it? Bear House? Briar House?—*of Briar House, Buckinghamshire*— *I, Marianne Lilly, being sound in mind though feeble in body, hereby commit my own infant daughter SUSAN*— Now, will you shake it about? That's better—*hereby commit*—hmm, hmm—*to the guardianship of Mrs Grace Sucksby; and desire that she be raised by her in ignorance of her true birth. Which birth is to be made known to her on the day of her eighteenth birthday, 3rd August 1862; on which day I do also desire that there be made over to her one half of my private fortune.*

'*In exchange for which, Grace Sucksby commits into my care her own dear daughter MAUD*— Bless me, if you ain't doing it again! Hold it nice, can't you?—*dear daughter MAUD, and does desire that she be raised similarly ignorant of her name and birth, until the aforementioned date; on which date it is my desire that there be made over to her the remainder of my fortune.*

'*This paper to be a true and legally binding statement of my wishes; a contract between myself and Grace Sucksby, in defiance of my father and brother; which is to be recognised in Law.*

'*Susan Lilly to know nothing of her unhappy mother, but that she strove to keep her from care.*

'*Maud Sucksby to be raised a gentlewoman; and to know that her mother loved her, more than her own life.*—Well!' He straightened up. 'Now tell me that wasn't worth sevenpence. Papers get hold of it, mind, I should say it would be worth a lot more.—Why, how queer you look! Ain't going to faint, are you?'

I had swayed and clutched at his tray. His graters went sliding. 'Now take care, do!' he said, in a peevish way. 'Here's all my stock, look, going to tumble and get mashed—'

Dainty came and caught me. 'I am sorry,' I said. 'I am sorry.'

'All right?' he said, as he put the graters straight.

'Yes.'

'Come as a shock, has it?'

I shook my head—or perhaps I nodded, I don't remember—and

gripped the letter, and stumbled from him. 'Dainty,' I said. 'Dainty—'

She sat me down, against a wall. 'What is it?' she said. 'Oh, Sue, what did it mean?'

The man still looked. 'I should get her water,' he called.

But I didn't want water, and I wouldn't let Dainty go. I clutched her to me and put my face against her sleeve. I began to shake. I began to shake as a rusted lock must shake, when the tumblers lift against their groaning springs, and the bolt is forced loose and flies. 'My mother—' I said. I could not finish. It was too much to say— too much, even, to know! *My mother, Maud's mother!* I could not believe it. I thought of the picture of the handsome lady I had seen in the box at Briar. I thought of the grave that Maud had used to rub and trim. I thought of Maud, and Mrs Sucksby; and then, of Gentleman. *Oh, now I see it!* he had said. Now I saw it, too. Now I knew what Mrs Sucksby had longed but been afraid to tell me, at the gaol. *If you should hear hard things of me—* Why had she kept the secret so long? Why had she lied about my mother? My mother was not a murderess, she was a lady. She was a lady with a fortune, that she meant to be split . . .

If you should hear hard things of me, think back—

I thought, and thought; and began to grow sick. I put the letter before my face and groaned. The thimble man still stood a little way off, and watched me; soon other people gathered and stood watching, too. 'Drunk, is she?' I heard someone say. And, 'Got the horrors?' 'Fallen in a fit, has she? Her pal should put a spoon in her mouth, she'll swallow her tongue.' I could not bear the sound of their voices, the feel of their eyes. I reached for Dainty and got to my feet; she put her arm about me and helped me stagger home. She gave me brandy to drink. She sat me at the table. Mrs Sucksby's dress still lay upon it: I took it up and held it in my two fists, and hid my face in its folds; then I gave a cry like a beast, and cast it to the floor. I spread out the letter, and looked again at the lines of ink. *SUSAN LILLY* . . . I groaned again. Then I got to my feet and began to walk.

'Dainty,' I said in a sort of pant, as I did. 'Dainty, she must have

known. She must have known it, all along. She must have sent me
there, at Gentleman's side, knowing he meant at last to— Oh!' My
voice grew hoarse. 'She sent me there, so he would leave me in that
place and bring her Maud. It was only ever Maud she wanted. She
kept me safe, and gave me up, so Maud, so Maud—'

But then, I grew still. I was thinking of Maud, starting up with
the knife. I was thinking of Maud, letting me hate her. I was thinking of Maud, making me think she'd hurt me, to save me knowing
who had hurt me most . . .

I put my hand across my mouth and burst out weeping. Dainty
began to weep, too.

'What is it?' she said. 'Oh, Sue, you look so queer! What *is* it?'

'The worst thing of all,' I said, through my tears. 'The worst
thing of all!'

I saw it, sharp and clear as a line of lightning in a sky of black.
Maud had tried to save me, and I had not known. I had wanted to
kill her, when all the time—

'And I let her go!' I said, getting up and walking about. 'Where
is she, now?'

'Where's *who*?' said Dainty, almost shrieking.

'Maud!' I said. 'Oh, Maud!'

'Miss Lilly?'

'Miss Sucksby, call her! Oh! I shall go mad! To think I thought
she was a spider that had got you all in her web. To think there was
once a time when I stood, pinning up her hair! If I had said— If she
had turned— If I had known— I would have kissed her—'

'Kissed her?' said Dainty.

'Kissed her!' I said. 'Oh, Dainty, you would have kissed her, too!
Anyone would! She was a pearl, a pearl!—and now, and now I've
lost her, I've thrown her away—!'

So I went on. Dainty tried to calm me, and could not. I would
only walk and wring my hands, tear my own hair; or else I would
sink to the floor and lie groaning. At last, I sank and would not rise.
Dainty wept and pleaded—took up water and threw it in my face—
ran down the street to a neighbour's house, for a bottle of salts; but
I lay, as if dead. I had got sick. I had got sick in a moment, like that.

She carried me up to my old room and put me to sleep in my own bed; when I opened my eyes again she says I looked at her and did not know her, says I fought her, when she tried to take my gown, says I talked like a madwoman, of tartan, and india-rubber boots, and—most especially—of something I said she had taken, that I should die without. 'Where is it?' she says I cried. 'Where is it? Oh!'—She says I cried it so often, so pitifully, she brought me all my things and held them up before me, one by one; and that finally she found, in the pocket of my gown, an old kid glove, quite creased and black and bitten; and that when she held that up I took it from her and wept and wept over it as if my heart would break.

I don't remember. I kept in a fever for nearly a week, and was after that so feeble I might as well have been in a fever still. Dainty nursed me, all that time—feeding me tea and soups and gruels, lifting me so I might use the chamber-pot, wiping off the horrible sweat from my face. I still wept, and cursed and twisted, when I thought of Mrs Sucksby and how she had tricked me; but I wept more, when I thought of Maud. For all this time I had had as it were a sort of dam about my heart, keeping out my love: now the walls had burst, my heart was flooded, I thought I should drown . . . My love grew level, though, as I grew well again. It grew level, and calm—it seemed to me at last that I had never been so calm in all my life. 'I've lost her,' I'd say again to Dainty; I'd say it, over and over. But I'd say it steadily—in a whisper, at first; then, as the days passed by and I got back my strength, in a murmur; finally, in my own voice. 'I've lost her,' I'd say, 'but I mean to find her. I don't care if it takes me all my life. I'll find her out, and tell her what I know. She might have gone away. She might be on the other side of the world. She might be married! I don't care. I'll find her, and tell her everything . . .'

It was all I thought of. I was only waiting, to be well enough to start. And at last I thought I had waited enough. I rose from my bed, and the room—that had used to seem to tilt and turn, whenever I lifted my head—stayed still. I washed, and dressed, got the bag of things I had planned to take with me to Woolwich. I took up the letter, and tucked it into my gown. I think Dainty thought I must have fallen back into my fever. Then I kissed her cheek, and my face was cool. 'Keep Charley Wag for me,' I said. She saw how grave and earnest I was, and began to cry.

'How will you do it?' she said. I said I meant to start my search at Briar. 'But how shall you get there? How shall you pay?' I said: 'I'll walk.' When she heard that, she dried her eyes and bit her lip. 'Wait here,' she said. She ran from the house. She was gone for twenty minutes. When she came back, she was clutching a pound. It was the pound she had put, so long ago, in the wall of the starch-works, that she had said we must use to bury her when she had died. She made me take it. I kissed her again. 'Shall you ever come back?' she said. I said I did not know . . .

And so I left the Borough a second time, and made the journey down to Briar, over again. There were no fogs, this time. The train ran smooth. At Marlow, the same guard who had laughed at me when I'd asked for a cab, now came to help me from the coach. He didn't remember me. He wouldn't have known me if he had. I was so thin, I think he thought I was an invalid girl. 'Come down from London to take the air, have you?' he said kindly. He looked at the little bag I held. 'Shall you manage it?' And then, as he had last time: 'Is no-one come to meet you?'

I said I would walk. I did walk, for a mile or two. Then I stopped to rest on a stile, and a man and a girl went by, with a horse and cart, and they looked at me and must have thought I was an invalid, too: for they pulled their horse up and gave me a ride. They let me sit on the seat. The man put his coat about my shoulders.

'Going far?' he said.

I said I was going to Briar, they could drop me anywhere near Briar—

'To Briar!' they said, when they heard that. 'But, why ever are you going there? There's nobody there, since the old man died. Didn't you know?'

Nobody there! I shook my head. I said I knew Mr Lilly had been ill. That he had lost the use of his hands and voice, and had to be fed off a spoon. They nodded. Poor gentleman! they said. He

had lingered on in a very miserable sort of way, all summer long—
in all that terrible heat. 'They say he stank, in the end,' they said,
dropping their voices. 'But though his niece—the scandalous girl,
that run off with a gentleman—did you know about that?'—I didn't
answer—'though she come back to nurse him, he died, a month
ago; and since then, the house've been quite shut up.'

So Maud had come, and gone! If I had only known . . . I turned
my head. When I spoke, my voice had a catch. I hoped they would
put it down to the jolting of the cart. I said,

'And the niece, Miss Lilly? What happened— What happened to
her?'

But they only shrugged. They did not know. Some people said
she'd gone back to her husband. Some people said she had gone to
France . . .

'Planning on visiting one of the servants, were you?' they said,
looking at my print dress. 'The servants've all gone, too.—All gone
but one, who stays to keep thieves out. Shouldn't like *his* job. They
say the place is haunted, now.'

Here was a blow, all right. But I had expected blows, and was
ready to suffer them. When they asked, Should they drive me back
to Marlow? I said no, I would go on. I thought the servant must be
Mr Way. I thought, 'I'll find him. He'll know me. And oh! he's seen
Maud. He'll tell me where she's gone . . .'

So they put me down where the wall to the Briar park started;
and from there, I walked again. The sound of the horse's hooves
grew faint. The road was lonely, the day was bleak. It was only two
or three o'clock but the dusk seemed gathered in the shadows
already, waiting to creep and rise. The wall seemed longer than
when I had ridden past it in William Inker's trap: I walked for what
felt like an hour, before I saw the arch that marked the gate, and the
roof of the lodge behind it. I quickened my step—but then, my
heart quite sank. The lodge was all shut up and dark. The gates
were fastened with a chain and lock, and piled about with leaves.
Where the wind struck the iron bars it made a low sort of moaning
sound. And when I stepped to the gates and pushed them, they
creaked and creaked.

'Mr Way!' I called. 'Mr Way! Anyone!'

My voice made a dozen black birds start out of the bushes and fly off, cawing. The noise was awful. I thought, 'Surely that will bring someone.' But it didn't: the birds went cawing on, the wind moaned louder through the bars, I called another time; and no-one came. So then I looked at the chain and lock. The chain was a long one. It was only there, I think, to keep out cows, and boys. I was thinner than a boy, however, now. I thought, 'It's not against the law. I used to work here. I might work here, still . . .' I pushed the gates again, as far as they would go: and they made a gap just wide enough for me to wriggle my way through.

They fell together, at my back, with a dreadful clash. The birds started up again. Still no-one came, though.

I gave it a minute, then began to walk.

It seemed quieter inside the walls, than it had been before—quieter, and queer. I kept to the road. The wind made the trees seem to whisper and sigh. The branches were bare. Their leaves lay thick upon the ground: they had got wet, and clung to my skirt. Here and there were puddles of muddy water. Here and there were bushes, overgrown. The grass in the park was overgrown too, and parched from the summer, but beaten about with rain. It was turning to slime at its tips, and smelt peculiar. I think there were mice in it. Perhaps there were rats. I heard them scurrying as I walked.

I began to go quicker. The road ran down, then began to climb. I remembered driving along it with William Inker, in the dark. I knew what was coming: I knew where it turned, and what I would see when it did . . . I knew it; but it still made me start, to come so suddenly upon the house again—to see it seem to rise out of the earth, so grey and grim. I stopped, on the edge of the walk of gravel. I was almost afraid. It was all so perfectly quiet and dark. The windows were shuttered. There were more black birds upon the roof. The ivy on the walls had lost its hold and was waving like hair. The great front door—that was always swollen, from the rain—bulged worse than ever. The porch was filled with more wet leaves. It seemed like a house not meant for people but for ghosts.

I remembered, suddenly, what the man and the girl had said, about it being haunted . . .

That made me shiver. I looked about me—back, the way I had come; and then, across the lawns. They ran into dark and tangled woods. The paths I had used to take with Maud, had disappeared. I put back my head. The sky was grey and spitting rain. The wind still whispered and sighed in the trees. I shivered again. The house seemed to watch me. I thought, 'If I can only find Mr Way! Where can he be?'—and I began to walk, around to the back of the house, to the stables and yards. I went carefully, for my steps sounded loud. But here, it was just as quiet and empty as everywhere else. No dogs started barking. The stable doors were open, the horses gone. The great white clock was there, but the hands—this shocked me, more than anything—the hands were stuck, the hour was wrong. The clock had not chimed, all the time I had walked: it was that, I think, that had made the silence so strange. 'Mr Way!' I called—but I called it softly. It seemed wrong to call out, here. 'Mr Way! Mr Way!'

Then I saw, rising up from one of the chimneys, a single thread of smoke. That gave me heart. I went to the kitchen door, and tapped. No answer. I tried the handle. Locked. Then I went to the garden door—the door that I had run from, that night, with Maud. That was also locked. So then I went around to the front again. I went to a window, drew back a shutter, and looked inside. I could not see. I put my hands and my face to the glass; and the window, as I pressed, seemed to give against its bolt . . . I hesitated for almost a minute; then the rain came, hard as hail. I gave a shove. The bolt flew from its screws and the window swung inwards. I lifted myself up on to the sill, and jumped inside.

Then I stood, quite still. The sound of the breaking bolt must have been awful. What if Mr Way had heard it and came with a gun, supposing me a burglar? I felt like a burglar, now. I thought of my mother— My mother was never a thief, however. My mother was a lady. My mother was the lady of this great house . . . I shook my head. I should never believe it. I began to walk softly about. The room was dark—the dining-room, I thought. I had never been in here before. But I had used to try and imagine Maud, as she sat, with her uncle, at her supper; I had used to imagine the little bites she would take at her meat . . . I stepped to the table. It was still set, with candlesticks, a knife and a fork, a plate of apples; but it was covered all over with dust and cobwebs, and the apples had rotted. The air was thick. Upon the floor was a broken glass—a crystal glass, with gold at the rim.

The door was closed: I do not think it had been opened in many weeks. But still, when I turned the handle and pushed it, it moved perfectly silently. All the doors moved silently, in that house. The floor had a dusty carpet, that smothered my steps.

So when I went, I made no sound, and might have glided—as if *I* were a ghost. The thought was queer. Across from me was another door: the door to the drawing-room. I had never been there, either; so now I crossed to it and looked inside. That room was also dark and hung with cobwebs. There was ash spilling out from the grate. There were chairs, by the hearth, where I thought that Mr Lilly and Gentleman must once have sat, to listen while Maud read books. There was a hard little sofa, with a lamp beside it, that I imagined had been hers. I imagined her sitting there, now. I remembered her soft voice.

I forgot to think about Mr Way, remembering that. I forgot to think of my mother. What was she, to me? It was Maud I thought of. I had meant to go down to the kitchen. Instead I went slowly about the hall, by the swollen front door. I climbed the stairs. I wanted to go to her old rooms. I wanted to stand, where she had stood—at the window, at the glass. I wanted to lie upon her bed. I wanted to think how I had kissed her and lost her . . .

I walked, as I have said, as a ghost might walk; and when I wept, I wept as a ghost would: silently, not minding the tears as they came falling—as though I knew I had tears enough for a hundred years, and in time would weep them all. I reached the gallery. The door to the library was there, standing part-way open. The creature's head still hung beside it, with its one glass eye and pointed teeth. I thought of how I had put my fingers to it, the first time I came for Maud. I had waited outside the door, I had heard her reading.— Again, I thought of her voice. I thought so fiercely of it, it seemed to me at last that I could almost hear it. I could hear it as a whisper, as a murmur, in the stillness of the house.

I caught my breath. The murmur stopped, then started again. It was not in my own head, I *could* hear it—it came, from the library . . . I began to shake. Perhaps the house was haunted after all. Or perhaps, perhaps— I moved to the door and put a trembling hand to it, and pushed it open. Then I stood, and blinked. The room was changed. The paint had all been scraped from the windows, the finger of brass prised from the floor. The shelves were almost bare of books. A little fire burned in the grate. I pushed the door further. There was Mr Lilly's old desk. Its lamp was lit.

And in the glow of it, was Maud.

She was sitting, writing. She had an elbow on the desk, a cheek upon her upturned hand, her fingers half-curled over her eyes. I saw her clearly, because of the light. Her brows were drawn into a frown. Her hands were bare, her sleeves put back, her fingers dark with smudges of ink. I stood and watched her write a line. The page was thick with lines already. Then she lifted the pen, and turned and turned it, as if not sure what to put next. Again she murmured, beneath her breath. She bit her mouth.

Then she wrote again; and then she moved to dip her pen in a jar of ink. And as she did that, she drew her fingers from her eyes, her face came up; and she saw me watching.

She did not start. She grew perfectly still. She did not cry out. She did not say anything, at first. She only sat with her eyes on mine, a look of astonishment on her face. Then I took a step; and as I did, she got to her feet, letting the pen with the ink upon it roll across the papers and desk and drop to the floor. Her cheek had grown white. She gripped the back of her chair, as if to take her hand from it might mean to fall, or swoon. When I took another step, she gripped it harder.

'Have you come,' she said, 'to kill me?'

She said it, in a sort of awful whisper; and I heard her, and saw that her face was white, not just from astonishment, but also from fear. The thought was terrible. I turned away, and hid my own face

in my hands. It was still wet, from my falling tears. Now other tears
came and made it wetter. 'Oh, Maud!' I said. 'Oh, Maud!'

I had never spoken her name to her before like that, I had only
ever said *miss*; and even now, even here, after everything, I felt the
strangeness of it. I pressed my fingers hard into my eyes. I had been
thinking, a moment ago, of how I loved her. I'd supposed her lost.
I had meant to find her out, through years of searching. To come
upon her now—so warm, so real—when I had ached and ached for
her— It was too much.

'I don't—' I said. 'I can't—' She did not come. She only stood,
still white, still gripping the back of the chair. So then I wiped my
face upon my sleeve, and spoke more steadily. 'There was a paper,'
I said. 'I found a paper, hidden in Mrs Sucksby's gown . . .'

I felt the letter, stiff, in my own gown, as I spoke; but she didn't
answer, and I guessed from that—and saw, by the look upon her
face—that she knew what paper it was I meant, and what it said.
Despite myself, I had a moment of hating her then—just a single
moment; and when it passed, it left me weak. I went to the window,
so I might sit upon the sill. I said, 'I paid someone to read it to me.
And then, I got sick.'

'I am sorry,' she said. 'Sue, I am sorry.'

She still did not come to me, though. I wiped my face again.

I said, 'I got a lift with a man and a girl. They said your uncle
died. They said there was nobody here, save Mr Way—'

'Mr Way?' She frowned. 'Mr Way is gone.'

'A servant, they said.'

'William Inker, they must have meant. He stays with me. And
his wife cooks my meals. That's all.'

'Only them, and you? In this great house.' I looked about me,
and shivered. 'Don't you grow frightened?'

She shrugged, gazed down at her hands. Her look grew dark.
'What have I,' she said, 'to be frightened of, now?'

There was so much to the words, and to the way she said them,
I did not answer at first. When I spoke again, I spoke more quietly.

'When did you know?' I said. 'When did you know everything,
about us, about— Did you know, at the start?'

She shook her head. She spoke quietly, too. 'Not then,' she said. 'Not until Richard took me to London. Then she—' She coloured, but lifted her head. 'Then I was told.'

'Not before?' I said.

'Not before.'

'They tricked you, too, then.'

I should have been glad to think it, once. Now it was all of a piece with every bleak and terrible thing I had suffered and seen and learned, in the past nine months. For a minute, we said nothing. I let myself sink against the window and put my cheek against the glass. The glass was cold. The rain fell hard, still. It struck the gravel before the house and made it churn. The lawn seemed bruised. Through the bare wet branches of the tangled wood I could just make out the shape of yews, and the pointed roof of the little red chapel.

'My mother is buried there,' I said. 'I used to look at her grave, thinking nothing. I thought my mother was a murderess.'

'I thought my mother was mad,' she said. 'Instead—'

She could not say it. Neither could I. Not yet. But I turned to look at her again, and swallowed, and said,

'You went to see her, at the gaol.' I had remembered the matron's words.

She nodded. 'She spoke of you,' she said.

'Of me? What did she say?'

'That she hoped you never knew. That she wished they might hang her, ten times over, before you should. That she and your mother had been wrong. That they meant to make you a commonplace girl. That that was like taking a jewel, and hiding it in dust. That dust falls away . . .'

I closed my eyes. When I looked again, she had at last come closer.

'Sue,' she said. 'This house is yours.'

'I don't want it,' I said.

'The money is yours. Half of your mother's money. All of it, if you wish. I have claimed none of it. You shall be rich.'

'I don't want to be rich. I never wanted to be rich. I only want—'

But I hesitated. My heart was too full. Her gaze was too close, too clear. I thought how I had seen her, last—not at the trial, but on the night that Gentleman died. Her eyes had glittered. They did not glitter now. Her hair had been curled. Now it was smooth, unpinned, she had put it back and tied it with a simple ribbon. Her hands did not tremble. They were bare, and marked, as I have said, with spots and smudges of ink. Her brow had ink upon it, too, from where she had pressed it. Her dress was dark, and long, yet fell not quite to the floor. It was silk, but fastened at the front. The highest hook was left undone. I saw the beating of her throat behind it. I looked away.

Then I looked back, into her eyes.

'I only want you,' I said.

The blood spread across her face. She unjoined her hands, took another step to me and almost, almost reached. But then she turned and lowered her gaze. She stood at the desk. She put her hand to the paper and pen.

'You do not know me,' she said, in a queer, flat voice. 'You never did. There were things—'

She drew in her breath and would not go on. 'What things?' I said. She didn't answer. I rose, and went closer to her. 'What things?'

'My uncle—' she said, looking up fearfully. 'My uncle's books— You thought me good. Didn't you? I was never that. I was—' She seemed, for a moment, almost to struggle with herself. Then she moved again, went to the shelves behind the desk, and took up a book. She held it, tight to her breast; then turned and brought it to me. She opened it up in her hands. Her hands, I think, were shaking. 'Here,' she said, as she looked across the page. 'Or, here.' I saw her gaze settle. And then, in the same flat voice she had spoken in before, she began to read.

'*How delicious,*' she read, '*was the glow upon her beauteous neck and bare ivory shoulders, as I forced her on her back on the couch. How luxuriously did her snowy hillocks rise against my bosom in wild confusion—*'

'What?' I said.

She did not answer, did not look up; but turned that page and read from another.

'*I scarcely knew what I was about; everything now was in active exertion—tongues, lips, bellies, arms, thighs, legs, bottoms, every part in voluptuous motion.*'

Now my own cheek coloured. '*What?*' I said, in a whisper.

She turned more pages, read again.

'*Quickly my daring hand seized her most secret treasure, regardless of her soft complaints, which my burning kisses reduced to mere murmurs, while my fingers penetrated into the covered way of love—*'

She stopped. Her heart was beating harder, though she had kept her voice so flat. My own heart was also beating rather hard. I said—still not quite understanding:

'Your uncle's books?'

She nodded.

'All, like this?'

She nodded again.

'Every one of them, like this? Are you sure?'

'Quite sure.'

I took the book from her and looked at the print on the pages. It looked like any book would, to me. So I put it down, and went to the shelves and picked up another. That looked the same. Then I took up another; and that had pictures. You never saw any pictures like them. One was of two bare girls. I looked at Maud, and my heart seemed to shrink.

'You knew it all,' I said. That's the first thing I thought. 'You said that you knew nothing, when all the time—'

'I did know nothing,' she said.

'You knew it all! You made me kiss you. You made me want to kiss you again! When all the time, you had been coming here and—'

My voice broke off. She watched my face. I thought of the times I had come to the library door, heard the smothered rising and falling of her voice. I thought of her reading to gentlemen—to Gentleman—while I sat, eating tarts and custards with Mrs Stiles and Mr Way. I put my hand to my heart. It had shrunk so small and tight, it hurt me.

'Oh, Maud,' I said. 'If I had only known! To think, of you—' I
began to cry. 'To think of your uncle— Oh!' My hand flew to my
mouth. '*My* uncle!' That thought was queerer than anything. 'Oh!'
I still held the book. Now I looked at it and let it drop as if it
burned me. 'Oh!'

It was all I could say. Maud stood very still, her hand upon the
desk. I wiped my eyes. Then I looked again at the smears of ink on
her fingers.

'How can you bear it?'

She did not answer.

'To think of him,' I said, 'that *sod*! Oh, stinking was too good for
him!' I wrung my hands. 'And now, to look at you and see you here,
still here, with his books about you—!'

I gazed across the shelves; and wanted to smash them. I went to
her, and reached to draw her close. But she held me off. She moved
her head, in a way that at any other time I should have called
proud.

'Don't pity me,' she said, 'because of *him*. He's dead. But I am
still what he made me. I shall always be that. Half of the books are
spoiled, or sold. But I am here. And look. You must know everything. Look how I get my living.'

She picked up a paper from the desk—the paper that I had seen
her write on. The ink was still damp. 'I asked a friend of my uncle's,
once,' she said, 'if I might write for him. He sent me to a home for
distressed gentlewomen.' She smiled, unhappily. 'They say that
ladies don't write such things. But, I am not a lady . . .'

I looked at her, not understanding. I looked at the paper in her
hand. Then my heart missed its beat.

'You are writing books, like his!' I said. She nodded, not speaking.
Her face was grave. I don't know how my face seemed. I think it was
burning. 'Books, like that!' I said. 'I can't believe it. Of all the ways
I thought I'd find you— And then, to find you here, all on your own
in this great house—'

'I am not alone,' she said. 'I have told you: I have William Inker
and his wife to care for me.'

'To find you here, all on your own, writing *books like that*—!'

Again, she looked almost proud. 'Why shouldn't I?' she said.

I did not know. 'It just don't seem right,' I said. 'A girl, like you—'

'Like me? There are no girls like me.'

I did not answer for a moment. I looked again at the paper in her hand. Then I said quietly,

'Is there money in it?'

She blushed. 'A little,' she said. 'Enough, if I write swiftly.'

'And you— You like it?'

She blushed still harder. 'I find I am good at it . . .' She bit her lip. She was still watching my face. 'Do you hate me for it?' she said.

'Hate you!' I said. 'When I have fifty proper reasons for hating you, already; and only—'

Only love you, I wanted to say. I didn't say it, though. What can I tell you? If she could still be proud, then so, for now, could I . . . I didn't need to say it, anyway: she could read the words in my face. Her colour changed, her gaze grew clearer. She put a hand across her eyes. Her fingers left more smudges of black there. I still couldn't bear it. I quickly reached and stopped her wrist; then wet my thumb and began to rub at the flesh of her brow. I did it, thinking only of the ink, and her white skin; but she felt my hand and grew very still. My thumb moved slower. It moved to her cheek. Then I found I had cupped her face in my hand. She closed her eyes. Her cheek was smooth—not like a pearl, warmer than pearls. She turned her head and put her mouth against my palm. Her lips were soft. The smudge stayed black upon her brow; and after all, I thought, was only ink.

When I kissed her, she shook. I remembered what it was, then, to make her shake by kissing her; and began to shake, too. I had been ill. I thought I might faint! We moved apart. She put her hand against her heart. She had still held the paper. Now it fluttered to the floor. I stooped and caught it up and smoothed the creases from it.

'What does it say?' I said, when I had.

She said, 'It is filled with all the words for how I want you . . . Look.'

She took up the lamp. The room had got darker, the rain still beat against the glass. But she led me to the fire and made me sit, and sat beside me. Her silk skirts rose in a rush, then sank. She put the lamp upon the floor, spread the paper flat; and began to show me the words she had written, one by one.

Notes

Many books provided historical detail and inspiration. I'm particularly indebted to V.A.C. Gatrell's *The Hanging Tree: Execution and the English People, 1770-1868* (Oxford, 1994) and Marcia Hamilcar's *Legally Dead: Experiences During Seven Weeks' Detention in a Private Asylum* (London, 1910).

The index upon which Christopher Lilly is at work is based on the three annotated bibliographies published by Henry Spencer Ashbee under the pseudonym Pisanus Fraxi: *Index Librorum Prohibitorum: being Notes Bio- Biblio- Icono- graphical and Critical, on Curious and Uncommon Books* (London, 1877); *Centuria Librorum Absconditorum: being Notes Bio- Biblio- Icono- graphical and Critical, on Curious and Uncommon Books* (London, 1879); and *Catena Librorum Tacendorum: being Notes Bio- Biblio- Icono- graphical and critical, on Curious and Uncommon Books* (London, 1885). Mr Lilly's statements on book-collecting echo those of Ashbee, but in all other respects he is entirely fictitious.

All of the texts cited by Maud are real. They include: *The Festival of the Passions, Memoirs of a Woman of Pleasure, The Curtain Drawn Up, The Bagnio Miscellany, The Birchen Bouquet*, and *The Lustful Turk*. For publishing details of these see Ashbee, above.

TIPPING THE VELVET

Sarah Waters

Nan is captivated by the music hall phenomenon that is Kitty Butler, a male impersonator extraordinaire treading the boards in Canterbury. Through a friend at the box office, Nan manages to visit all her shows and finally meet her heroine. Soon after, she becomes Kitty's dresser and the two head for the bright lights of Leicester Square where they start an all-singing and dancing double act. At the same time, behind closed doors, they admit their attraction to each other and their affair begins.

'This could be the most important début of its kind since that of Jeanette Winterson' – *Daily Telegraph*

'An unstoppable read, a sexy and picaresque romp through the lesbian and queer demi-monde of the roaring Nineties. Could this be a new genre? The bawdy lesbian picaresque novel?' – *Independent on Sunday*

£6.99 paperback

AFFINITY

Sarah Waters

Set in and around the women's prison at Milbank in the 1870s, *Affinity* is an eerie and utterly compelling ghost story, a complex and intriguing literary mystery and a poignant love story with an unexpected twist in the tale. Following the death of her father, Margaret Prior has decided to pursue some 'good work' with the lady criminals of one of London's most notorious gaols. Surrounded by prisoners, murderers and common thieves, Margaret feels herself drawn to one of the prison's more unlikely inmates – the imprisoned spiritualist – Selina Dawes. Sympathetic to the plight of this innocent-seeming girl, Margaret sees herself dispensing guidance and perhaps friendship on her visits, little expecting to find herself dabbling in a twilight world of seances, shadows, unruly spirits and unseemly passions.

'Sexy, spooky, stylish – *Affinity* is a wonderful book' – *Guardian*

'Spooky, spellbinding, exquisitely written . . . I do believe
Waters is on the way to becoming a major
literary star' – *Val Hennessy*

£6.99 paperback

Now you can order directly from Virago

	Title	Author	Price
☐	Tipping the Velvet	Sarah Waters	£6.99
☐	Affinity	Sarah Waters	£6.99
☐	Sweet Desserts	Lucy Ellmann	£6.99
☐	Lesbianism Made Easy	Helen Eisenbach	£6.99
☐	Going Down	Jennifer Belle	£6.99
☐	In Search of an Impotent Man	Gaby Hauptmann	£6.99
☐	Like Being Killed	Ellen Miller	£6.99
☐	What Girls Learn	Karin Cook	£6.99
☐	Omnivores	Lydia Millett	£6.99
☐	Needles	Andie Dominick	£6.99
☐	Tongue First	Emily Jenkins	£6.99

The prices shown above are correct at time of going to press. However, the publishers reserve the right to increase prices on covers from those previously advertised, without further notice.

Virago

Please allow for postage and packing: **Free UK delivery.**
Europe: add 25% of retail price; Rest of World: 45% of retail price.

To order any of the above or any other Virago titles, please call our credit card orderline or fill in this coupon and send/fax it to:

Virago, PO Box 121, Kettering, Northants NN14 4ZQ
Fax: 01832 737526   Tel: 01832 733076
Email: aspenhouse@FSBDial.co.uk

☐ I enclose a UK bank cheque made payable to Virago for £ . . . .
☐ Please charge £ . . . . . . to my Visa/Access/Mastercard/Eurocard

Expiry Date | | | | | Switch Issue No. | | |

NAME (BLOCK LETTERS please) . . . .

ADDRESS . . . .

. . . .

. . . .

Postcode . . . . Telephone . . . .

Signature . . . .

Please allow 28 days for delivery within the UK. Offer subject to price and availability.
Please do not send any further mailings from companies carefully selected by Virago ☐